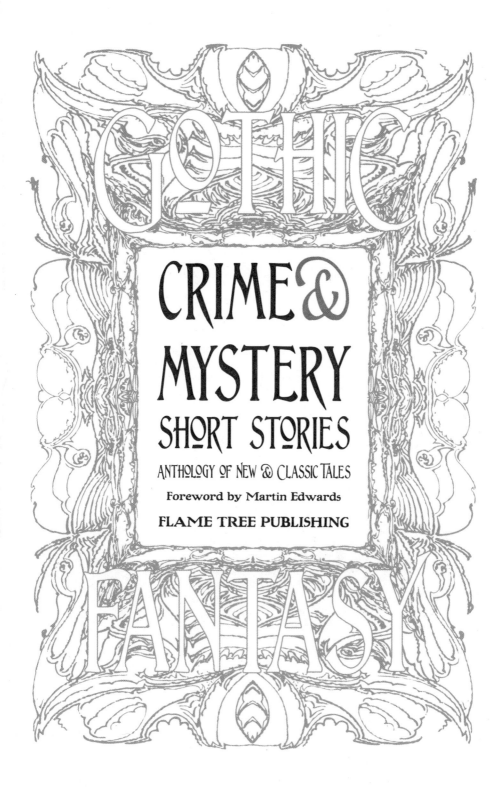

GOTHIC

CRIME &
MYSTERY
SHORT STORIES

ANTHOLOGY OF NEW & CLASSIC TALES

Foreword by Martin Edwards

FLAME TREE PUBLISHING

FANTASY

Publisher & Creative Director: Nick Wells
Project Editor: Laura Bulbeck
Editorial Board: Frances Bodiam, Josie Mitchell, Gillian Whitaker

With special thanks to Amanda Crook, Kaiti Porter

FLAME TREE PUBLISHING
6 Melbray Mews, Fulham,
London SW6 3NS,
United Kingdom

First published 2015

The cover image is created by Flame Tree Studio
based on artwork by Slava Gerj and Gabor Ruszkai.

ISBN: 978-1-78361-988-7
Special ISBN: 978-1-78664-070-3

1 3 5 7 9 10 8 6 4 2

Manufactured in Turkey

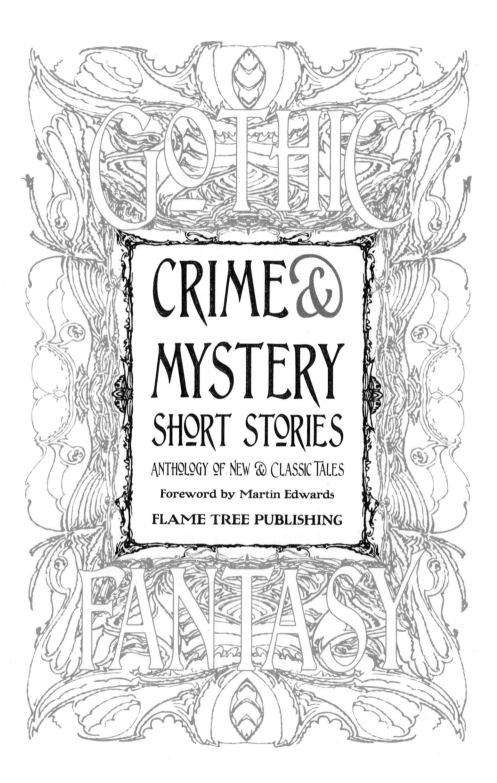

GOTHIC

CRIME & MYSTERY

SHORT STORIES

ANTHOLOGY OF NEW & CLASSIC TALES

Foreword by Martin Edwards

FLAME TREE PUBLISHING

FANTASY

Contents

Foreword: Crime & Mystery

CRIME & MYSTERY, an eclectic collection of stories, is an anthology with a difference. Flame Tree Publishing have had the interesting idea of blending classics of the genre with brand new work. This gives readers a chance to compare and contrast the literary styles and storytelling techniques of writers old and new, famous and (in some cases) hitherto little-known.

Many notable authors of nineteenth century fiction are represented here, including Edgar Allan Poe; 'The Murders in the Rue Morgue' is widely regarded as the first detective story, and is also famous as an example of the 'locked room mystery'. Among other gems, there are stories by Charles Dickens and his good friend Wilkie Collins, as well as a highly regarded novella by the American journalist Richard Harding Davis, 'In the Fog'.

If Poe, by creating Chevalier C. Auguste Dupin, introduced the concept of the Great Detective whose sleuthing exploits leave the official police looking hopelessly inadequate, Arthur Conan Doyle refined and improved upon it with Sherlock Holmes. Holmes is not only the most popular detective character of all time, he is also, arguably, the most popular character in *any* form of fiction. He is seen at his best in the two superb stories included here, 'The Red-Headed League' and 'The Speckled Band'. Another Great Detective, 'The Thinking Machine', appears in 'The Problem of Cell 13' whose author's premature death when the *Titanic* sank robbed classic crime fiction of one of its greatest talents.

G.K. Chesterton's Father Brown is very different from the legendary consulting detective of 221b Baker Street, and from Futrelle's Professor Van Dusen, but he too has an enduring popular appeal, as witnessed by the success of the recent television series starring Mark Williams. Rather less well-known today than the little priest is Dr. John Thordyke, created by Richard Austin Freeman, yet for the first half of the twentieth century Thorndyke was renowned as the leading exponent of scientific detection.

Turning to the new stories, Flame Tree put out a call for submissions through social media, as well as pursuing direct contacts with groups of crime writers. An in-house editorial board read all submissions, judging them by two distinct criteria. The first question was whether the story was of sufficiently high quality and entertainment value. The second was how the overall mix of stories, old and new, would work, so as to make sure that themes and storylines were suitably varied.

The results were interesting, with contributors ranging from promising newcomers to distinguished authors such as Josh Pachter, whose first crime short story appeared in *Ellery Queen's Mystery Magazine* as long ago as 1968, when he was a mere 16 years old.

Diversity is the hallmark of this collection, as it is of most good anthologies. The juxtaposition of legendary authors and detectives with writers who are almost wholly unfamiliar to most readers is bold yet intriguing. Above all, *Crime and Mystery* reflects the enduring appeal – to writers as well as to readers – of the most popular of all literary genres.

Martin Edwards
www.martinedwardsbooks.com

Publisher's Note

LAST YEAR we were thrilled to publish the first in our new collections of short story anthologies, and 2016 brings two fantastic new titles, *Crime & Mystery* and *Murder Mayhem*. Still offering up the potent mix of classic tales and new fiction, we explore the roots of the genre, from golden age detective tales and whodunnits featuring Sherlock Holmes and Father Brown to more chilling, gory tales by the likes of William Hope Hodgson or Ambrose Bierce. We have tried to mix some tales and authors that were seminal to the development of the genre, such as Edgar Allan Poe's 'Murders in the Rue Morgue', with authors who have since been much forgotten, but whose stories are entertaining in their own right, and deserve to be brought back to light.

Our 2016 call for new submissions was met with a fantastic response, and as ever the final selection was extremely tough, but made to provide a wide range of tales we hope any lover of mystery, murder and intrigue will enjoy. Our editorial board read each entry carefully, and it was difficult to turn down so many good stories, but inevitably those which made the final cut were deemed to be the best for our purpose, and we're delighted to publish them here.

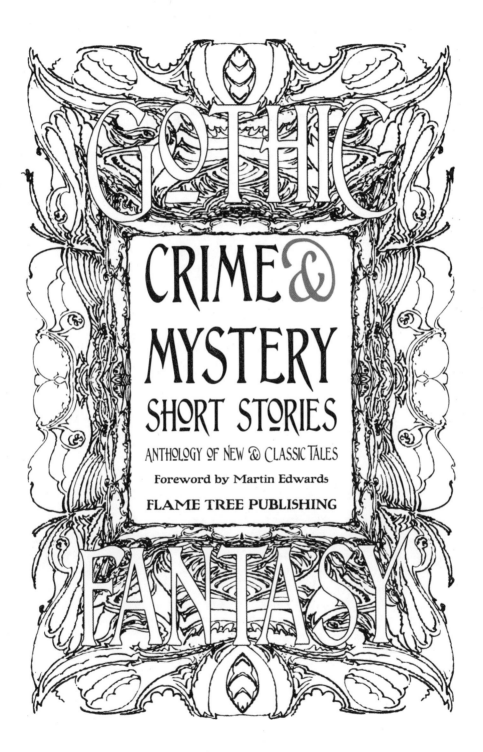

GOTHIC

CRIME & MYSTERY
SHORT STORIES

ANTHOLOGY OF NEW & CLASSIC TALES

Foreword by Martin Edwards

FLAME TREE PUBLISHING

FANTASY

The Coin of Dionysius

Ernest Bramah

IT WAS EIGHT O'CLOCK at night and raining, scarcely a time when a business so limited in its clientele as that of a coin dealer could hope to attract any customer, but a light was still showing in the small shop that bore over its window the name of Baxter, and in the even smaller office at the back the proprietor himself sat reading the latest *Pall Mall*. His enterprise seemed to be justified, for presently the door bell gave its announcement, and throwing down his paper Mr. Baxter went forward.

As a matter of fact the dealer had been expecting someone and his manner as he passed into the shop was unmistakably suggestive of a caller of importance. But at the first glance towards his visitor the excess of deference melted out of his bearing, leaving the urbane, self-possessed shopman in the presence of the casual customer.

"Mr. Baxter, I think?" said the latter. He had laid aside his dripping umbrella and was unbuttoning overcoat and coat to reach an inner pocket. "You hardly remember me, I suppose? Mr. Carlyle – two years ago I took up a case for you –"

"To be sure. Mr. Carlyle, the private detective –"

"Inquiry agent," corrected Mr. Carlyle precisely.

"Well," smiled Mr. Baxter, "for that matter I am a coin dealer and not an antiquarian or a numismatist. Is there anything in that way that I can do for you?"

"Yes," replied his visitor; "it is my turn to consult you." He had taken a small wash-leather bag from the inner pocket and now turned something carefully out upon the counter. "What can you tell me about that?"

The dealer gave the coin a moment's scrutiny.

"There is no question about this," he replied. "It is a Sicilian tetradrachm of Dionysius."

"Yes, I know that – I have it on the label out of the cabinet. I can tell you further that it's supposed to be one that Lord Seastoke gave two hundred and fifty pounds for at the Brice sale in '94."

"It seems to me that you can tell me more about it than I can tell you," remarked Mr. Baxter. "What is it that you really want to know?"

"I want to know," replied Mr. Carlyle, "whether it is genuine or not."

"Has any doubt been cast upon it?"

"Certain circumstances raised a suspicion – that is all."

The dealer took another look at the tetradrachm through his magnifying glass, holding it by the edge with the careful touch of an expert. Then he shook his head slowly in a confession of ignorance.

"Of course I could make a guess –"

"No, don't," interrupted Mr. Carlyle hastily. "An arrest hangs on it and nothing short of certainty is any good to me."

"Is that so, Mr. Carlyle?" said Mr. Baxter, with increased interest. "Well, to be quite candid, the thing is out of my line. Now if it was a rare Saxon penny or a doubtful noble I'd stake my reputation on my opinion, but I do very little in the classical series."

Mr. Carlyle did not attempt to conceal his disappointment as he returned the coin to the bag and replaced the bag in the inner pocket.

"I had been relying on you," he grumbled reproachfully. "Where on earth am I to go now?"

"There is always the British Museum."

"Ah, to be sure, thanks. But will anyone who can tell me be there now?"

"Now? No fear!" replied Mr. Baxter. "Go round in the morning –"

"But I must know tonight," explained the visitor, reduced to despair again. "Tomorrow will be too late for the purpose."

Mr. Baxter did not hold out much encouragement in the circumstances.

"You can scarcely expect to find anyone at business now," he remarked. "I should have been gone these two hours myself only I happened to have an appointment with an American millionaire who fixed his own time." Something indistinguishable from a wink slid off Mr. Baxter's right eye. "Offmunson he's called, and a bright young pedigree-hunter has traced his descent from Offa, King of Mercia. So he – quite naturally – wants a set of Offas as a sort of collateral proof."

"Very interesting," murmured Mr. Carlyle, fidgeting with his watch. "I should love an hour's chat with you about your millionaire customers – some other time. Just now – look here, Baxter, can't you give me a line of introduction to some dealer in this sort of thing who happens to live in town? You must know dozens of experts."

"Why, bless my soul, Mr. Carlyle, I don't know a man of them away from his business," said Mr. Baxter, staring. "They may live in Park Lane or they may live in Petticoat Lane for all I know. Besides, there aren't so many experts as you seem to imagine. And the two best will very likely quarrel over it. You've had to do with 'expert witnesses', I suppose?"

"I don't want a witness; there will be no need to give evidence. All I want is an absolutely authoritative pronouncement that I can act on. Is there no one who can really say whether the thing is genuine or not?"

Mr. Baxter's meaning silence became cynical in its implication as he continued to look at his visitor across the counter. Then he relaxed.

"Stay a bit; there is a man – an amateur – I remember hearing wonderful things about some time ago. They say he really does know."

"There you are," explained Mr. Carlyle, much relieved. "There always is someone. Who is he?"

"Funny name," replied Baxter. "Something Wynn or Wynn something." He craned his neck to catch sight of an important motor-car that was drawing to the kerb before his window. "Wynn Carrados! You'll excuse me now, Mr. Carlyle, won't you? This looks like Mr. Offmunson."

Mr. Carlyle hastily scribbled the name down on his cuff.

"Wynn Carrados, right. Where does he live?"

"Haven't the remotest idea," replied Baxter, referring the arrangement of his tie to the judgment of the wall mirror. "I have never seen the man myself. Now, Mr. Carlyle, I'm sorry I can't do any more for you. You won't mind, will you?"

Mr. Carlyle could not pretend to misunderstand. He enjoyed the distinction of holding open the door for the transatlantic representative of the line of Offa as he went out, and then made his way through the muddy streets back to his office. There was only one way of tracing a private individual at such short notice – through the pages of the directories, and the gentleman did not flatter himself by a very high estimate of his chances.

Fortune favoured him, however. He very soon discovered a Wynn Carrados living at Richmond, and, better still, further search failed to unearth another. There was, apparently, only one householder at all events of that name in the neighbourhood of London. He jotted down the address and set out for Richmond.

The house was some distance from the station, Mr. Carlyle learned. He took a taxicab and drove, dismissing the vehicle at the gate. He prided himself on his power of observation and the accuracy of his deductions which resulted from it – a detail of his business. "It's nothing more than using one's eyes and putting two and two together," he would modestly declare, when he wished to be deprecatory rather than impressive. By the time he had reached the front door of 'The Turrets' he had formed some opinion of the position and tastes of the people who lived there.

A man-servant admitted Mr. Carlyle and took his card – his private card, with the bare request for an interview that would not detain Mr. Carrados for ten minutes. Luck still favoured him; Mr. Carrados was at home and would see him at once. The servant, the hall through which they passed, and the room into which he was shown, all contributed something to the deductions which the quietly observant gentleman was half unconsciously recording.

"Mr. Carlyle," announced the servant.

The room was a library or study. The only occupant, a man of about Carlyle's own age, had been using a typewriter up to the moment of his visitor's entrance. He now turned and stood up with an expression of formal courtesy.

"It's very good of you to see me at this hour," apologised Mr. Carlyle.

The conventional expression of Mr. Carrados's face changed a little.

"Surely my man has got your name wrong?" he explained. "Isn't it Louis Calling?"

Mr. Carlyle stopped short and his agreeable smile gave place to a sudden flash of anger or annoyance.

"No sir," he replied stiffly. "My name is on the card which you have before you."

"I beg your pardon," said Mr. Carrados, with perfect good-humour. "I hadn't seen it. But I used to know a Calling some years ago – at St. Michael's."

"St. Michael's!" Mr. Carlyle's features underwent another change, no less instant and sweeping than before. "St. Michael's! Wynn Carrados? Good heavens! It isn't Max Wynn – old 'Winning' Wynn"?

"A little older and a little fatter – yes," replied Carrados. "I have changed my name you see."

"Extraordinary thing meeting like this," said his visitor, dropping into a chair and staring hard at Mr. Carrados. "I have changed more than my name. How did you recognize me?"

"The voice," replied Carrados. "It took me back to that little smoke-dried attic den of yours where we –"

"My God!" exclaimed Carlyle bitterly, "don't remind me of what we were going to do in those days." He looked round the well-furnished, handsome room and recalled the other signs of wealth that he had noticed. "At all events, you seem fairly comfortable, Wynn."

"I am alternately envied and pitied," replied Carrados, with a placid tolerance of circumstance that seemed characteristic of him. "Still, as you say, I am fairly comfortable."

"Envied, I can understand. But why are you pitied?"

"Because I am blind," was the tranquil reply.

"Blind!" exclaimed Mr. Carlyle, using his own eyes superlatively. "Do you mean – literally blind?"

"Literally.... I was riding along a bridle-path through a wood about a dozen years ago with a friend. He was in front. At one point a twig sprang back – you know how easily a thing like that happens. It just flicked my eye – nothing to think twice about."

"And that blinded you?"

"Yes, ultimately. It's called amaurosis."

"I can scarcely believe it. You seem so sure and self-reliant. Your eyes are full of expression – only a little quieter than they used to be. I believe you were typing when I came.... Aren't you having me?"

"You miss the dog and the stick?" smiled Carrados. "No; it's a fact."

"What an awful affliction for you, Max. You were always such an impulsive, reckless sort of fellow – never quiet. You must miss such a fearful lot."

"Has anyone else recognized you?" asked Carrados quietly.

"Ah, that was the voice, you said," replied Carlyle.

"Yes; but other people heard the voice as well. Only I had no blundering, self-confident eyes to be hoodwinked."

"That's a rum way of putting it," said Carlyle. "Are your ears never hoodwinked, may I ask?"

"Not now. Nor my fingers. Nor any of my other senses that have to look out for themselves."

"Well, well," murmured Mr. Carlyle, cut short in his sympathetic emotions. "I'm glad you take it so well. Of course, if you find it an advantage to be blind, old man –" He stopped and reddened. "I beg your pardon," he concluded stiffly.

"Not an advantage perhaps," replied the other thoughtfully. "Still it has compensations that one might not think of. A new world to explore, new experiences, new powers awakening; strange new perceptions; life in the fourth dimension. But why do you beg my pardon, Louis?"

"I am an ex-solicitor, struck off in connexion with the falsifying of a trust account, Mr. Carrados," replied Carlyle, rising.

"Sit down, Louis," said Carrados suavely. His face, even his incredibly living eyes, beamed placid good-nature. "The chair on which you will sit, the roof above you, all the comfortable surroundings to which you have so amiably alluded, are the direct result of falsifying a trust account. But do I call you 'Mr. Carlyle' in consequence? Certainly not, Louis."

"I did not falsify the account," cried Carlyle hotly. He sat down however, and added more quietly: "But why do I tell you all this? I have never spoken of it before."

"Blindness invites confidence," replied Carrados. "We are out of the running – human rivalry ceases to exist. Besides, why shouldn't you? In my case the account *was* falsified."

"Of course that's all bunkum, Max" commented Carlyle. "Still, I appreciate your motive."

"Practically everything I possess was left to me by an American cousin, on the condition that I took the name of Carrados. He made his fortune by an ingenious conspiracy of doctoring the crop reports and unloading favourably in consequence. And I need hardly remind you that the receiver is equally guilty with the thief."

"But twice as safe. I know something of that, Max ... Have you any idea what my business is?"

"You shall tell me," replied Carrados.

"I run a private inquiry agency. When I lost my profession I had to do something for a living. This occurred. I dropped my name, changed my appearance and opened an office. I knew the legal side down to the ground and I got a retired Scotland Yard man to organize the outside work."

"Excellent!" cried Carrados. "Do you unearth many murders?"

"No," admitted Mr. Carlyle; "our business lies mostly on the conventional lines among divorce and defalcation."

"That's a pity," remarked Carrados. "Do you know, Louis, I always had a secret ambition to be a detective myself. I have even thought lately that I might still be able to do something at it if the chance came my way. That makes you smile?"

"Well, certainly, the idea –"

"Yes, the idea of a blind detective – the blind tracking the alert –"

"Of course, as you say, certain facilities are no doubt quickened," Mr. Carlyle hastened to add considerately, "but, seriously, with the exception of an artist, I don't suppose there is any man who is more utterly dependent on his eyes."

Whatever opinion Carrados might have held privately, his genial exterior did not betray a shadow of dissent. For a full minute he continued to smoke as though he derived an actual visual enjoyment from the blue sprays that travelled and dispersed across the room. He had already placed before his visitor a box containing cigars of a brand which that gentleman keenly appreciated but generally regarded as unattainable, and the matter-of-fact ease and certainty with which the blind man had brought the box and put it before him had sent a questioning flicker through Carlyle's mind.

"You used to be rather fond of art yourself, Louis," he remarked presently. "Give me your opinion of my latest purchase – the bronze lion on the cabinet there." Then, as Carlyle's gaze went about the room, he added quickly: "No, not that cabinet – the one on your left."

Carlyle shot a sharp glance at his host as he got up, but Carrados's expression was merely benignly complacent. Then he strolled across to the figure.

"Very nice," he admitted. "Late Flemish, isn't it?"

"No, it is a copy of Vidal's 'Roaring Lion.' "

"Vidal?"

"A French artist." The voice became indescribably flat. "He, also, had the misfortune to be blind, by the way."

"You old humbug, Max!" shrieked Carlyle, "You've been thinking that out for the last five minutes." Then the unfortunate man bit his lip and turned his back towards his host.

"Do you remember how we used to pile it up on that obtuse ass Sanders, and then roast him?" asked Carrados, ignoring the half-smothered exclamation with which the other man had recalled himself.

"Yes," replied Carlyle quietly. "This is very good," he continued, addressing himself to the bronze again. "How ever did he do it?"

"With his hands."

"Naturally. But, I mean, how did he study his model?"

"Also with his hands. He called it 'seeing near.' "

"Even with a lion – handled it?"

"In such cases he required the services of a keeper, who brought the animal to bay while Vidal exercised his own particular gifts ... You don't feel inclined to put me on the track of a mystery, Louis?"

Unable to regard this request as anything but one of old Max's unquenchable pleasantries, Mr. Carlyle was on the point of making a suitable reply when a sudden thought caused him to smile knowingly. Up to that point, he had, indeed, completely forgotten the object of his visit. Now that he remembered the doubtful Dionysius and Baxter's recommendation he immediately assumed that some mistake had been made. Either Max was not the Wynn Carrados he had been seeking or else the dealer had been misinformed; for although his host was wonderfully expert in the face of his misfortune, it was inconceivable that he could decide the genuineness of a coin without seeing it. The opportunity seemed a good one of getting even with Carrados by taking him at his word.

"Yes," he accordingly replied, with crisp deliberation, as he re-crossed the room; "yes, I will, Max. Here is the clue to what seems to be a rather remarkable fraud." He put the tetradrachm into his host's hand. "What do you make of it?"

For a few seconds Carrados handled the piece with the delicate manipulation of his finger-tips while Carlyle looked on with a self-appreciative grin. Then with equal gravity the blind man weighed the coin in the balance of his hand. Finally he touched it with his tongue.

"Well?" demanded the other.

"Of course I have not much to go on, and if I was more fully in your confidence I might come to another conclusion –"

"Yes, yes," interposed Carlyle, with amused encouragement.

"Then I should advise you to arrest the parlourmaid, Nina Brun, communicate with the police authorities of Padua for particulars of the career of Helene Brunesi, and suggest to Lord Seastoke that he should return to London to see what further depredations have been made in his cabinet."

Mr. Carlyle's groping hand sought and found a chair, on to which he dropped blankly. His eyes were unable to detach themselves for a single moment from the very ordinary spectacle of Mr. Carrados's mildly benevolent face, while the sterilized ghost of his now forgotten amusement still lingered about his features.

"Good heavens!" he managed to articulate, "How do you know?"

"Isn't that what you wanted of me?" asked Carrados suavely.

"Don't humbug, Max," said Carlyle severely. "This is no joke." An undefined mistrust of his own powers suddenly possessed him in the presence of this mystery. "How do you come to know of Nina Brun and Lord Seastoke?"

"You are a detective, Louis," replied Carrados. "How does one know these things? By using one's eyes and putting two and two together."

Carlyle groaned and flung out an arm petulantly.

"Is it all bunkum, Max? Do you really see all the time – though that doesn't go very far towards explaining it."

"Like Vidal, I see very well – at close quarters," replied Carrados, lightly running a forefinger along the inscription on the tetradrachm. "For longer range I keep another pair of eyes. Would you like to test them?"

Mr. Carlyle's assent was not very gracious; it was, in fact, faintly sulky. He was suffering the annoyance of feeling distinctly unimpressive in his own department; but he was also curious.

"The bell is just behind you, if you don't mind," said his host. "Parkinson will appear. You might take note of him while he is in."

The man who had admitted Mr. Carlyle proved to be Parkinson.

"This gentleman is Mr. Carlyle, Parkinson," explained Carrados the moment the man entered. "You will remember him for the future?"

Parkinson's apologetic eye swept the visitor from head to foot, but so lightly and swiftly that it conveyed to that gentleman the comparison of being very deftly dusted.

"I will endeavour to do so, sir," replied Parkinson, turning again to his master.

"I shall be at home to Mr. Carlyle whenever he calls. That is all."

"Very well, sir."

"Now, Louis," remarked Mr. Carrados briskly, when the door had closed again, "you have had a good opportunity of studying Parkinson. What is he like?"

"In what way?"

"I mean as a matter of description. I am a blind man – I haven't seen my servant for twelve years – what idea can you give me of him? I asked you to notice."

"I know you did, but your Parkinson is the sort of man who has very little about him to describe. He is the embodiment of the ordinary. His height is about average –"

"Five feet nine," murmured Carrados. "Slightly above the mean."

"Scarcely noticeably so. Clean-shaven. Medium brown hair. No particularly marked features. Dark eyes. Good teeth."

"False," interposed Carrados. "The teeth – not the statement."

"Possibly," admitted Mr. Carlyle. "I am not a dental expert and I had no opportunity of examining Mr. Parkinson's mouth in detail. But what is the drift of all this?"

"His clothes?"

"Oh, just the ordinary evening dress of a valet. There is not much room for variety in that."

"You noticed, in fact, nothing special by which Parkinson could be identified?"

"Well, he wore an unusually broad gold ring on the little finger of the left hand."

"But that is removable. And yet Parkinson has an ineradicable mole – a small one, I admit – on his chin. And you a human sleuth-hound. Oh, Louis!"

"At all events," retorted Carlyle, writhing a little under this good-humoured satire, although it was easy enough to see in it Carrados's affectionate intention – "at all events, I dare say I can give as good a description of Parkinson as he can give of me."

"That is what we are going to test. Ring the bell again."

"Seriously?"

"Quite. I am trying my eyes against yours. If I can't give you fifty out of a hundred I'll renounce my private detectorial ambition for ever."

"It isn't quite the same," objected Carlyle, but he rang the bell.

"Come in and close the door, Parkinson," said Carrados when the man appeared. "Don't look at Mr. Carlyle again – in fact, you had better stand with your back towards him, he won't mind. Now describe to me his appearance as you observed it."

Parkinson tendered his respectful apologies to Mr. Carlyle for the liberty he was compelled to take, by the deferential quality of his voice.

"Mr. Carlyle, sir, wears patent leather boots of about size seven and very little used. There are five buttons, but on the left boot one button – the third up – is missing, leaving loose threads and not the more usual metal fastener. Mr. Carlyle's trousers, sir, are of a dark material, a dark grey line of about a quarter of an inch width on a darker ground. The bottoms are turned permanently up and are, just now, a little muddy, if I may say so."

"Very muddy," interposed Mr. Carlyle generously. "It is a wet night, Parkinson."

"Yes, sir; very unpleasant weather. If you will allow me, sir, I will brush you in the hall. The mud is dry now, I notice. Then, sir," continued Parkinson, reverting to the business in hand, "there are dark green cashmere hose. A curb-pattern key-chain passes into the left-hand trouser pocket."

From the visitor's nether garments the photographic-eyed Parkinson proceeded to higher ground, and with increasing wonder Mr. Carlyle listened to the faithful catalogue of his possessions. His fetter-and-link albert of gold and platinum was minutely described. His spotted blue ascot, with its gentlemanly pearl scarfpin, was set forth, and the fact that the buttonhole in the left lapel of his morning coat showed signs of use was duly noted. What Parkinson saw he recorded, but he made no deductions. A handkerchief carried in the cuff of the right sleeve was simply that to him and not an indication that Mr. Carlyle was, indeed, left-handed.

But a more delicate part of Parkinson's undertaking remained. He approached it with a double cough.

"As regards Mr. Carlyle's personal appearance, sir –"

"No, enough!" cried the gentleman concerned hastily. "I am more than satisfied. You are a keen observer, Parkinson."

"I have trained myself to suit my master's requirements, sir," replied the man. He looked towards Mr. Carrados, received a nod and withdrew.

Mr. Carlyle was the first to speak.

"That man of yours would be worth five pounds a week to me, Max," he remarked thoughtfully. "But, of course –"

"I don't think that he would take it," replied Carrados, in a voice of equally detached speculation. "He suits me very well. But you have the chance of using his services – indirectly."

"You still mean that – seriously?"

"I notice in you a chronic disinclination to take me seriously, Louis. It is really – to an Englishman – almost painful. Is there something inherently comic about me or the atmosphere of The Turrets?"

"No, my friend," replied Mr. Carlyle, "but there is something essentially prosperous. That is what points to the improbable. Now what is it?"

"It might be merely a whim, but it is more than that," replied Carrados. "It is, well, partly vanity, partly ennui, partly" – certainly there was something more nearly tragic in his voice than comic now – "partly hope."

Mr. Carlyle was too tactful to pursue the subject.

"Those are three tolerable motives," he acquiesced. "I'll do anything you want, Max, on one condition."

"Agreed. And it is?"

"That you tell me how you knew so much of this affair." He tapped the silver coin which lay on the table near them. "I am not easily flabbergasted," he added.

"You won't believe that there is nothing to explain – that it was purely second-sight?"

"No," replied Carlyle tersely: "I won't."

"You are quite right. And yet the thing is very simple."

"They always are – when you know," soliloquised the other. "That's what makes them so confoundedly difficult when you don't."

"Here is this one then. In Padua, which seems to be regaining its old reputation as the birthplace of spurious antiques, by the way, there lives an ingenious craftsman named Pietro Stelli. This simple soul, who possesses a talent not inferior to that of Cavino at his best, has for many years turned his hand to the not unprofitable occupation of forging rare Greek and Roman coins. As a collector and student of certain Greek colonials and a specialist in forgeries I have been familiar with Stelli's workmanship for years. Latterly he seems to have come under the influence of an international crook called – at the moment – Dompierre, who soon saw a way of utilizing Stelli's genius on a royal scale. Helene Brunesi, who in private life is – and really is, I believe – Madame Dompierre, readily lent her services to the enterprise."

"Quite so," nodded Mr. Carlyle, as his host paused.

"You see the whole sequence, of course?"

"Not exactly – not in detail," confessed Mr. Carlyle.

"Dompierre's idea was to gain access to some of the most celebrated cabinets of Europe and substitute Stelli's fabrications for the genuine coins. The princely collection of rarities that he would thus amass might be difficult to dispose of safely, but I have no doubt that he had matured his plans. Helene, in the person of Nina Brun, an Anglicised French parlourmaid – a part which she fills to perfection – was to obtain wax impressions of the most valuable pieces and to make the exchange when the counterfeits reached her. In this way it was obviously hoped that the fraud would not come to light until long after the real coins had been sold, and I gather that she has already done her work successfully in general houses. Then, impressed by her excellent references and capable manner, my housekeeper engaged her, and for a few weeks she went about her duties here. It was fatal to this detail of the scheme, however, that I have the misfortune to be blind. I am told that Helene has so innocently angelic a face as to disarm suspicion, but I was incapable of being impressed and that good material was thrown away. But one morning my material fingers – which, of course, knew nothing of Helene's angelic face – discovered an unfamiliar touch about the surface of my favourite Euclideas, and, although there was doubtless nothing to be seen, my critical sense of smell reported that wax had been recently pressed against it. I began to make discreet inquiries and in the meantime my cabinets went to the local bank for safety. Helene countered by receiving a telegram from Angiers, calling her to the death-bed of her aged mother. The aged mother succumbed; duty compelled Helene to remain at the side of her stricken patriarchal father, and doubtless The Turrets was written off the syndicate's operations as a bad debt."

"Very interesting," admitted Mr. Carlyle; "but at the risk of seeming obtuse" – his manner had become delicately chastened – "I must say that I fail to trace the inevitable connexion between Nina Brun and this particular forgery – assuming that it is a forgery."

"Set your mind at rest about that, Louis," replied Carrados. "It is a forgery, and it is a forgery that none but Pietro Stelli could have achieved. That is the essential connexion. Of course, there are accessories. A private detective coming urgently to see me with a notable tetradrachm in his pocket, which he announces to be the clue to a remarkable fraud – well, really, Louis, one scarcely needs to be blind to see through that."

"And Lord Seastoke? I suppose you happened to discover that Nina Brun had gone there?"

"No, I cannot claim to have discovered that, or I should certainly have warned him at once when I found out – only recently – about the gang. As a matter of fact, the last information I had of Lord Seastoke was a line in yesterday's *Morning Post* to the effect that he was still at Cairo. But many of these pieces –" He brushed his finger almost lovingly across the vivid chariot race that embellished the reverse of the coin, and broke off to remark: "You really ought to take up the subject, Louis. You have no idea how useful it might prove to you some day."

"I really think I must," replied Carlyle grimly. "Two hundred and fifty pounds the original of this cost, I believe."

"Cheap, too; it would make five hundred pounds in New York today. As I was saying, many are literally unique. This gem by Kimon is – here is his signature, you see; Peter is particularly good at lettering – and as I handled the genuine tetradrachm about two years ago, when Lord Seastoke exhibited it at a meeting of our society in Albemarle Street, there is nothing at all wonderful in my being able to fix the locale of your mystery. Indeed, I feel that I ought to apologize for it all being so simple."

"I think," remarked Mr. Carlyle, critically examining the loose threads on his left boot, "that the apology on that head would be more appropriate from me."

The Cost of Security

Tara Campbell

A LIGHT SNOW was falling as Charlie Reardon left the diner and made his way down Madison Street. The wind blew in icy gusts, sending flakes swirling before they hit the ground. Charlie plodded steadily down the block as people scurried around him to duck under awnings and bus shelters.

He'd nursed his coffee as long as he could before leaving the diner. He didn't dare drink another cup; his leg had been jumping up and down as it was. It was dinnertime, so he should have ordered something to eat; but he couldn't have actually choked anything down, which would have looked even more suspicious than not ordering anything at all.

A blast of wind caught him full in the face as he rounded the corner onto Fremont. He turned up his collar and leaned into the wind, stuffing his hands into his pockets until the squall passed. Looking at his watch, he calculated how slowly he had to walk to give Harry's guy enough time to do the job.

The job. He'd left the house that morning knowing today was the day: he would never see his wife Alice alive again.

As long as he'd planned for this day, he still wasn't ready for it. He'd gone through the whole week in a fog, knowing it was coming. In six days, in five days, in four days... He slowed down at the door of the next bar.

No, gotta get home. Gotta go through with the plan.

Snowflakes wheeled around Charlie as he trudged toward the subway. He wasn't missing the irony of the situation: suddenly, the one thing he'd wanted for years, to go home to a life without Alice, was the last thing he wanted to face right now.

Except she *would* be there. He was supposed to find her body in the bedroom, the result of a robbery gone tragically awry.

Over the past 20 years his hatred of Alice had bubbled up from a simmer to a roiling boil. Time had not been kind to her. Her sultry, smoky voice had turned harsh and raspy; her ripe, ample figure had sagged. But he could handle all that. It was the laugh that got to him. It had once tinkled with optimism and pride. Pride in him. But over the years – well, things can go wrong. A man makes mistakes. The restaurant, the jazz bar, the hotel in the Poconos: his businesses hadn't taken off. But you learn from mistakes, right? Though all she learned to do was laugh, and now every time he had an idea, a new way to spread his wings and be his own boss, that disdainful laugh of hers needled into his ears and drew blood.

A man couldn't grow with a woman like that hanging from his neck. Sealing the deal with Harry Munson had been an unreal moment of elation. He could almost touch it, he could feel that freedom! But over the past week the fever had leached out of him a little each day, and now he just felt numb. Worse than numb, like jelly.

Charlie stopped. His shoulders drooped and his eyes focused on the pavement, then on nothing. He reached a hand out to the wall and leaned against it. His brain was a giant cotton ball, and all his thoughts were getting snagged on the clingy strands inside his head. He ran his other hand over his face and pinched the space between his eyes.

Oh god.

Reminding himself he was in public, he pushed up off the wall and continued the route to his subway stop. There was nothing to do but go home.

* * *

Harry Munson had originally come to bid on the security contract for the house. Charlie's discussions with him about how to protect the house had turned into an analysis of the vulnerabilities of various security systems, which in turn became a conversation about how to best exploit said vulnerabilities to reach other ends. Turned out, Harry was no stranger to this series of conversations – the wealthy often had more to hide than their valuables – and he said he knew a guy who could help with this other project Charlie wanted done.

But it would be bad for business, Harry explained, if it looked like one of his own clients had gotten robbed and his wife killed on his company's watch. To solve this problem, he and Charlie staged a series of arguments over the price of the security system. Charlie acted like he didn't want to deal with Harry, which left Harry having to speak to Alice – all the better to get to know her habits and weaknesses. Once Harry had gotten all the information he needed, Charlie called the security contract negotiations off.

And at that point, the other contract had begun.

* * *

Charlie sat in the subway, trying to keep his leg from bobbing up and down. He looked around to see if anyone else looked as hot as he felt. His wool coat hung on him like a suit of armor, pinning him to his seat, and he barely registered his stop in time to get out.

Driving home from the parking garage, he fought the urge to turn around and go the other way. But where would he go anyhow?

It was snowing harder out here than in the city. It was dark now, but the roads were still relatively clear. Charlie gripped the wheel as the wipers batted away thickening flakes. *Slow and careful,* he told himself. Now was not the time to slip up.

It's the only way, he kept reminding himself. This was the only way he could see to get out without losing everything. He'd put up with Alice for 20 years – although it hadn't always been bad. Their passion-filled honeymoon in the Poconos (there was a reason he'd wanted to go back), her pride in her work (when she used to work). She mixed a mean martini. And those eyes. After all those years, their vivid green sparkle could still set his stomach aflutter.

But those same eyes were the sucker punch when she laughed at him, which happened way too often now. She and her father, that elitist asshole who never thought Charlie was good enough for his daughter. Old goat. Despite whatever business failures he'd had, Charlie had worked hard to make sure he could give Alice whatever she wanted. And she wanted, and wanted. It was never enough.

Well, the one thing he wasn't going to give her was a divorce. He wasn't about to just hand over everything he'd worked for. And she'd never agree to let him keep the house, a gift from her father. But both their names were on it, husband and wife; and after all the grief that old goat had given him, didn't Charlie deserve to keep something?

Without even realizing it, he'd already pulled up into the driveway alongside his house, and parked next to Alice's car. He was home.

The moon glinted off a thin coat of snow on his wife's Volvo – another gift from her father. The lights inside the house were off. Harry's guy must have turned them off when he was done. He would have to talk to Harry about this – would a robber-turned-killer really go around the house and turn off all the lights while fleeing the scene of a crime? Didn't that look suspicious?

Charlie's anxiety spiked as he stepped out of his car. *Did the guy even come at all? Maybe it didn't happen; maybe she just went to bed early. Maybe she's still alive.* He felt a flicker of relief at the thought. Then he saw that the side door was slightly ajar. A line of footprints from the front door to the back yard dimpled the moonlit snow. Harry's guy had been there.

He thought one more time through the scenarios they'd discussed. One option had been to immediately call the police; another was to go to the neighbors and ask if they'd seen Alice. But they'd settled on his rushing in to "save" her because it would give him time to 'discover' the body and make sure she was really dead before getting the police involved. After all, it wouldn't do for the victim to make a miraculous recovery and live to identify the killer. Once that happened, the whole plot would unravel.

Charlie entered the darkened house. He left the lights off and crossed through the living room to the back hallway. Their bedroom loomed at the end of the hall. The door was cracked open. He pushed his hand against it and walked inside.

He heard a rustle of sheets.

Alice?

"Honey, you're home," she said, switching on the bedside lamp.

As Charlie blinked against the sudden light, a man in dark clothing and a ski mask stepped out from the corner of the room. "Sorry, baby," murmured the man. He slapped Alice in the face and she fell back onto the bed.

The man pulled out a large knife and lunged at Charlie. Charlie's face contorted in shock and pain as the blade twisted in his gut. The man stepped back and let Charlie fall to the floor.

* * *

Alice dragged herself out of the bed, her breathing ragged. She watched in silence as Charlie writhed and wheezed. After a few minutes he stopped moving, and she stooped down to check his pulse – because they all knew what would happen if the victim were to make a miraculous recovery.

"Go on, Harry," she said, "get out of here."

The man in black wiped the knife off on his pants and slipped it back into its sheath. He stepped toward her.

"Later," she commanded, raising a hand to stop him.

He glanced down at Charlie, then rushed out of the room.

Alice gave Harry a minute to run. His footsteps shushed through the snow, fading, fading. Every step he put between the two of them brought them one step closer to the jackpot. Fading, fading, gone.

Alice thought about the weeks and months to come, about playing the grieving widow who felt unsafe in her own home. Of course she would rehire the security firm her late husband had deemed too expensive, and naturally she would spend long days and nights with Harry, her personal guard. A widow needs her security.

But she also needs to calm her nerves, so after a decent interval – measured in months, not weeks – they would fly to Barbados together on Charlie's life insurance payout. By that point, they figured, it would be safe for them to fall publicly in love.

Time was up. She had to start screaming for the neighbors to hear. She had to call the police and get everything started. Alice lifted her head and opened her mouth, trying to keep any hint of joy from creeping into her widow's wail.

The Blue Cross

G.K. Chesterton

BETWEEN THE SILVER ribbon of morning and the green glittering ribbon of sea, the boat touched Harwich and let loose a swarm of folk like flies, among whom the man we must follow was by no means conspicuous – nor wished to be. There was nothing notable about him, except a slight contrast between the holiday gaiety of his clothes and the official gravity of his face. His clothes included a slight, pale grey jacket, a white waistcoat, and a silver straw hat with a grey-blue ribbon. His lean face was dark by contrast, and ended in a curt black beard that looked Spanish and suggested an Elizabethan ruff. He was smoking a cigarette with the seriousness of an idler. There was nothing about him to indicate the fact that the grey jacket covered a loaded revolver, that the white waistcoat covered a police card, or that the straw hat covered one of the most powerful intellects in Europe. For this was Valentin himself, the head of the Paris police and the most famous investigator of the world; and he was coming from Brussels to London to make the greatest arrest of the century.

Flambeau was in England. The police of three countries had tracked the great criminal at last from Ghent to Brussels, from Brussels to the Hook of Holland; and it was conjectured that he would take some advantage of the unfamiliarity and confusion of the Eucharistic Congress, then taking place in London. Probably he would travel as some minor clerk or secretary connected with it; but, of course, Valentin could not be certain; nobody could be certain about Flambeau.

It is many years now since this colossus of crime suddenly ceased keeping the world in a turmoil; and when he ceased, as they said after the death of Roland, there was a great quiet upon the earth. But in his best days (I mean, of course, his worst) Flambeau was a figure as statuesque and international as the Kaiser. Almost every morning the daily paper announced that he had escaped the consequences of one extraordinary crime by committing another. He was a Gascon of gigantic stature and bodily daring; and the wildest tales were told of his outbursts of athletic humour; how he turned the juge d'instruction upside down and stood him on his head, 'to clear his mind'; how he ran down the Rue de Rivoli with a policeman under each arm. It is due to him to say that his fantastic physical strength was generally employed in such bloodless though undignified scenes; his real crimes were chiefly those of ingenious and wholesale robbery. But each of his thefts was almost a new sin, and would make a story by itself. It was he who ran the great Tyrolean Dairy Company in London, with no dairies, no cows, no carts, no milk, but with some thousand subscribers. These he served by the simple operation of moving the little milk cans outside people's doors to the doors of his own customers. It was he who had kept up an unaccountable and close correspondence with a young lady whose whole letter-bag was intercepted, by the extraordinary trick of photographing his messages infinitesimally small upon the slides of a microscope. A sweeping simplicity, however, marked many of his experiments. It is said that he once repainted all the numbers in a street in the dead of night merely to divert one traveller into a trap. It is quite certain that he invented a portable pillar-box, which he put up at corners in quiet suburbs on the chance of strangers dropping postal orders into it. Lastly, he was known to be a startling acrobat; despite his huge figure, he could leap like a grasshopper and melt into the tree-tops like a monkey. Hence the great Valentin, when he set out to find Flambeau, was perfectly aware that his adventures would not end when he had found him.

But how was he to find him? On this the great Valentin's ideas were still in process of settlement.

There was one thing which Flambeau, with all his dexterity of disguise, could not cover, and that was his singular height. If Valentin's quick eye had caught a tall apple-woman, a tall grenadier, or even a tolerably tall duchess, he might have arrested them on the spot. But all along his train there was nobody that could be a disguised Flambeau, any more than a cat could be a disguised giraffe. About the people on the boat he had already satisfied himself; and the people picked up at Harwich or on the journey limited themselves with certainty to six. There was a short railway official travelling up to the terminus, three fairly short market gardeners picked up two stations afterwards, one very short widow lady going up from a small Essex town, and a very short Roman Catholic priest going up from a small Essex village. When it came to the last case, Valentin gave it up and almost laughed. The little priest was so much the essence of those Eastern flats; he had a face as round and dull as a Norfolk dumpling; he had eyes as empty as the North Sea; he had several brown paper parcels, which he was quite incapable of collecting. The Eucharistic Congress had doubtless sucked out of their local stagnation many such creatures, blind and helpless, like moles disinterred. Valentin was a sceptic in the severe style of France, and could have no love for priests. But he could have pity for them, and this one might have provoked pity in anybody. He had a large, shabby umbrella, which constantly fell on the floor. He did not seem to know which was the right end of his return ticket. He explained with a moon-calf simplicity to everybody in the carriage that he had to be careful, because he had something made of real silver 'with blue stones' in one of his brown-paper parcels. His quaint blending of Essex flatness with saintly simplicity continuously amused the Frenchman till the priest arrived (somehow) at Tottenham with all his parcels, and came back for his umbrella. When he did the last, Valentin even had the good nature to warn him not to take care of the silver by telling everybody about it. But to whomever he talked, Valentin kept his eye open for someone else; he looked out steadily for anyone, rich or poor, male or female, who was well up to six feet; for Flambeau was four inches above it.

He alighted at Liverpool Street, however, quite conscientiously secure that he had not missed the criminal so far. He then went to Scotland Yard to regularise his position and arrange for help in case of need; he then lit another cigarette and went for a long stroll in the streets of London. As he was walking in the streets and squares beyond Victoria, he paused suddenly and stood. It was a quaint, quiet square, very typical of London, full of an accidental stillness. The tall, flat houses round looked at once prosperous and uninhabited; the square of shrubbery in the centre looked as deserted as a green Pacific islet. One of the four sides was much higher than the rest, like a dais; and the line of this side was broken by one of London's admirable accidents – a restaurant that looked as if it had strayed from Soho. It was an unreasonably attractive object, with dwarf plants in pots and long, striped blinds of lemon yellow and white. It stood specially high above the street, and in the usual patchwork way of London, a flight of steps from the street ran up to meet the front door almost as a fire-escape might run up to a first-floor window. Valentin stood and smoked in front of the yellow-white blinds and considered them long.

The most incredible thing about miracles is that they happen. A few clouds in heaven do come together into the staring shape of one human eye. A tree does stand up in the landscape of a doubtful journey in the exact and elaborate shape of a note of interrogation. I have seen both these things myself within the last few days. Nelson does die in the instant of victory; and a man named Williams does quite accidentally murder a man named Williamson; it sounds like a sort of infanticide. In short, there is in life an element of elfin coincidence which people reckoning on the prosaic may perpetually miss. As it has been well expressed in the paradox of Poe, wisdom should reckon on the unforeseen.

Aristide Valentin was unfathomably French; and the French intelligence is intelligence specially and solely. He was not 'a thinking machine'; for that is a brainless phrase of modern fatalism and materialism. A machine only is a machine because it cannot think. But he was a thinking man, and a plain man at the same time. All his wonderful successes, that looked like conjuring, had been gained by plodding logic, by clear and commonplace French thought. The French electrify the world not by starting any paradox, they electrify it by carrying out a truism. They carry a truism so far – as in the French Revolution. But exactly because Valentin understood reason, he understood the limits of reason. Only a man who knows nothing of motors talks of motoring without petrol; only a man who knows nothing of reason talks of reasoning without strong, undisputed first principles. Here he had no strong first principles. Flambeau had been missed at Harwich; and if he was in London at all, he might be anything from a tall tramp on Wimbledon Common to a tall toast-master at the Hotel Metropole. In such a naked state of nescience, Valentin had a view and a method of his own.

In such cases he reckoned on the unforeseen. In such cases, when he could not follow the train of the reasonable, he coldly and carefully followed the train of the unreasonable. Instead of going to the right places – banks, police stations, rendezvous – he systematically went to the wrong places; knocked at every empty house, turned down every cul de sac, went up every lane blocked with rubbish, went round every crescent that led him uselessly out of the way. He defended this crazy course quite logically. He said that if one had a clue this was the worst way; but if one had no clue at all it was the best, because there was just the chance that any oddity that caught the eye of the pursuer might be the same that had caught the eye of the pursued. Somewhere a man must begin, and it had better be just where another man might stop. Something about that flight of steps up to the shop, something about the quietude and quaintness of the restaurant, roused all the detective's rare romantic fancy and made him resolve to strike at random. He went up the steps, and sitting down at a table by the window, asked for a cup of black coffee.

It was half-way through the morning, and he had not breakfasted; the slight litter of other breakfasts stood about on the table to remind him of his hunger; and adding a poached egg to his order, he proceeded musingly to shake some white sugar into his coffee, thinking all the time about Flambeau. He remembered how Flambeau had escaped, once by a pair of nail scissors, and once by a house on fire; once by having to pay for an unstamped letter, and once by getting people to look through a telescope at a comet that might destroy the world. He thought his detective brain as good as the criminal's, which was true. But he fully realised the disadvantage. "The criminal is the creative artist; the detective only the critic," he said with a sour smile, and lifted his coffee cup to his lips slowly, and put it down very quickly. He had put salt in it.

He looked at the vessel from which the silvery powder had come; it was certainly a sugar-basin; as unmistakably meant for sugar as a champagne-bottle for champagne. He wondered why they should keep salt in it. He looked to see if there were any more orthodox vessels. Yes; there were two salt-cellars quite full. Perhaps there was some speciality in the condiment in the salt-cellars. He tasted it; it was sugar. Then he looked round at the restaurant with a refreshed air of interest, to see if there were any other traces of that singular artistic taste which puts the sugar in the salt-cellars and the salt in the sugar-basin. Except for an odd splash of some dark fluid on one of the white-papered walls, the whole place appeared neat, cheerful and ordinary. He rang the bell for the waiter.

When that official hurried up, fuzzy-haired and somewhat blear-eyed at that early hour, the detective (who was not without an appreciation of the simpler forms of humour) asked him to taste the sugar and see if it was up to the high reputation of the hotel. The result was that the waiter yawned suddenly and woke up.

"Do you play this delicate joke on your customers every morning?" inquired Valentin. "Does changing the salt and sugar never pall on you as a jest?"

The waiter, when this irony grew clearer, stammeringly assured him that the establishment had certainly no such intention; it must be a most curious mistake. He picked up the sugar-basin and looked at it; he picked up the salt-cellar and looked at that, his face growing more and more bewildered. At last he abruptly excused himself, and hurrying away, returned in a few seconds with the proprietor. The proprietor also examined the sugar-basin and then the salt-cellar; the proprietor also looked bewildered.

Suddenly the waiter seemed to grow inarticulate with a rush of words.

"I zink," he stuttered eagerly, "I zink it is those two clergy-men."

"What two clergymen?"

"The two clergymen," said the waiter, "that threw soup at the wall."

"Threw soup at the wall?" repeated Valentin, feeling sure this must be some singular Italian metaphor.

"Yes, yes," said the attendant excitedly, and pointed at the dark splash on the white paper; "threw it over there on the wall."

Valentin looked his query at the proprietor, who came to his rescue with fuller reports.

"Yes, sir," he said, "it's quite true, though I don't suppose it has anything to do with the sugar and salt. Two clergymen came in and drank soup here very early, as soon as the shutters were taken down. They were both very quiet, respectable people; one of them paid the bill and went out; the other, who seemed a slower coach altogether, was some minutes longer getting his things together. But he went at last. Only, the instant before he stepped into the street he deliberately picked up his cup, which he had only half emptied, and threw the soup slap on the wall. I was in the back room myself, and so was the waiter; so I could only rush out in time to find the wall splashed and the shop empty. It don't do any particular damage, but it was confounded cheek; and I tried to catch the men in the street. They were too far off though; I only noticed they went round the next corner into Carstairs Street."

The detective was on his feet, hat settled and stick in hand. He had already decided that in the universal darkness of his mind he could only follow the first odd finger that pointed; and this finger was odd enough. Paying his bill and clashing the glass doors behind him, he was soon swinging round into the other street.

It was fortunate that even in such fevered moments his eye was cool and quick. Something in a shop-front went by him like a mere flash; yet he went back to look at it. The shop was a popular greengrocer and fruiterer's, an array of goods set out in the open air and plainly ticketed with their names and prices. In the two most prominent compartments were two heaps, of oranges and of nuts respectively. On the heap of nuts lay a scrap of cardboard, on which was written in bold, blue chalk, 'Best tangerine oranges, two a penny.' On the oranges was the equally clear and exact description, 'Finest Brazil nuts, 4d. a lb.' M. Valentin looked at these two placards and fancied he had met this highly subtle form of humour before, and that somewhat recently. He drew the attention of the red-faced fruiterer, who was looking rather sullenly up and down the street, to this inaccuracy in his advertisements. The fruiterer said nothing, but sharply put each card into its proper place. The detective, leaning elegantly on his walking-cane, continued to scrutinise the shop. At last he said, "Pray excuse my apparent irrelevance, my good sir, but I should like to ask you a question in experimental psychology and the association of ideas."

The red-faced shopman regarded him with an eye of menace; but he continued gaily, swinging his cane, "Why," he pursued, "why are two tickets wrongly placed in a greengrocer's shop like a shovel hat that has come to London for a holiday? Or, in case I do not make myself clear, what is the mystical association which connects the idea of nuts marked as oranges with the idea of two clergymen, one tall and the other short?"

The eyes of the tradesman stood out of his head like a snail's; he really seemed for an instant likely to fling himself upon the stranger. At last he stammered angrily: "I don't know what you 'ave to do with it, but if you're one of their friends, you can tell 'em from me that I'll knock their silly 'eads off, parsons or no parsons, if they upset my apples again."

"Indeed?" asked the detective, with great sympathy. "Did they upset your apples?"

"One of 'em did," said the heated shopman; "rolled 'em all over the street. I'd 'ave caught the fool but for havin' to pick 'em up."

"Which way did these parsons go?" asked Valentin.

"Up that second road on the left-hand side, and then across the square," said the other promptly.

"Thanks," replied Valentin, and vanished like a fairy. On the other side of the second square he found a policeman, and said: "This is urgent, constable; have you seen two clergymen in shovel hats?"

The policeman began to chuckle heavily. "I 'ave, sir; and if you arst me, one of 'em was drunk. He stood in the middle of the road that bewildered that —"

"Which way did they go?" snapped Valentin.

"They took one of them yellow buses over there," answered the man; "them that go to Hampstead."

Valentin produced his official card and said very rapidly: "Call up two of your men to come with me in pursuit," and crossed the road with such contagious energy that the ponderous policeman was moved to almost agile obedience. In a minute and a half the French detective was joined on the opposite pavement by an inspector and a man in plain clothes.

"Well, sir," began the former, with smiling importance, "and what may —?"

Valentin pointed suddenly with his cane. "I'll tell you on the top of that omnibus," he said, and was darting and dodging across the tangle of the traffic. When all three sank panting on the top seats of the yellow vehicle, the inspector said: "We could go four times as quick in a taxi."

"Quite true," replied their leader placidly, "if we only had an idea of where we were going."

"Well, where are you going?" asked the other, staring.

Valentin smoked frowningly for a few seconds; then, removing his cigarette, he said: "If you know what a man's doing, get in front of him; but if you want to guess what he's doing, keep behind him. Stray when he strays; stop when he stops; travel as slowly as he. Then you may see what he saw and may act as he acted. All we can do is to keep our eyes skinned for a queer thing."

"What sort of queer thing do you mean?" asked the inspector.

"Any sort of queer thing," answered Valentin, and relapsed into obstinate silence.

The yellow omnibus crawled up the northern roads for what seemed like hours on end; the great detective would not explain further, and perhaps his assistants felt a silent and growing doubt of his errand. Perhaps, also, they felt a silent and growing desire for lunch, for the hours crept long past the normal luncheon hour, and the long roads of the North London suburbs seemed to shoot out into length after length like an infernal telescope. It was one of those journeys on which a man perpetually feels that now at last he must have come to the end of the universe, and then finds he has only come to the beginning of Tufnell Park. London died away in draggled taverns and dreary scrubs, and then was unaccountably born again in blazing high streets and blatant hotels. It was like passing through thirteen separate vulgar cities all just touching each other. But though the winter twilight was already threatening the road ahead of them, the Parisian detective still sat silent and watchful, eyeing the frontage of the streets that slid by on either side. By the time they had left Camden Town behind, the policemen were nearly asleep; at least, they gave something like a jump as Valentin leapt erect, struck a hand on each man's shoulder, and shouted to the driver to stop.

They tumbled down the steps into the road without realising why they had been dislodged; when they looked round for enlightenment they found Valentin triumphantly pointing his finger towards a window on the left side of the road. It was a large window, forming part of the long facade of a gilt and palatial public-house; it was the part reserved for respectable dining, and labelled 'Restaurant.' This window, like all the rest along the frontage of the hotel, was of frosted and figured glass; but in the middle of it was a big, black smash, like a star in the ice.

"Our cue at last," cried Valentin, waving his stick; "the place with the broken window."

"What window? What cue?" asked his principal assistant. "Why, what proof is there that this has anything to do with them?"

Valentin almost broke his bamboo stick with rage.

"Proof!" he cried. "Good God! The man is looking for proof! Why, of course, the chances are twenty to one that it has nothing to do with them. But what else can we do? Don't you see we must either follow one wild possibility or else go home to bed?" He banged his way into the restaurant, followed by his companions, and they were soon seated at a late luncheon at a little table, and looked at the star of smashed glass from the inside. Not that it was very informative to them even then.

"Got your window broken, I see," said Valentin to the waiter as he paid the bill.

"Yes, sir," answered the attendant, bending busily over the change, to which Valentin silently added an enormous tip. The waiter straightened himself with mild but unmistakable animation.

"Ah, yes, sir," he said. "Very odd thing, that, sir."

"Indeed?" Tell us about it," said the detective with careless curiosity.

"Well, two gents in black came in," said the waiter; "two of those foreign parsons that are running about. They had a cheap and quiet little lunch, and one of them paid for it and went out. The other was just going out to join him when I looked at my change again and found he'd paid me more than three times too much. 'Here,' I says to the chap who was nearly out of the door, 'you've paid too much.' 'Oh,' he says, very cool, 'have we?' 'Yes,' I says, and picks up the bill to show him. Well, that was a knock-out."

"What do you mean?" asked his interlocutor.

"Well, I'd have sworn on seven Bibles that I'd put 4s on that bill. But now I saw I'd put 14s, as plain as paint."

"Well?" cried Valentin, moving slowly, but with burning eyes, "And then?"

"The parson at the door he says all serene, 'Sorry to confuse your accounts, but it'll pay for the window.' 'What window?' I says. 'The one I'm going to break,' he says, and smashed that blessed pane with his umbrella."

All three inquirers made an exclamation; and the inspector said under his breath, "Are we after escaped lunatics?" The waiter went on with some relish for the ridiculous story:

"I was so knocked silly for a second, I couldn't do anything. The man marched out of the place and joined his friend just round the corner. Then they went so quick up Bullock Street that I couldn't catch them, though I ran round the bars to do it."

"Bullock Street," said the detective, and shot up that thoroughfare as quickly as the strange couple he pursued.

Their journey now took them through bare brick ways like tunnels; streets with few lights and even with few windows; streets that seemed built out of the blank backs of everything and everywhere. Dusk was deepening, and it was not easy even for the London policemen to guess in what exact direction they were treading. The inspector, however, was pretty certain that they would eventually strike some part of Hampstead Heath. Abruptly one bulging gas-lit window broke the blue twilight like a bull's-eye lantern; and Valentin stopped an instant before a little garish sweetstuff shop. After an instant's hesitation he went in; he stood amid the gaudy colours of the confectionery with entire gravity and bought thirteen chocolate cigars with a certain care. He was clearly preparing an opening; but he did not need one.

An angular, elderly young woman in the shop had regarded his elegant appearance with a merely automatic inquiry; but when she saw the door behind him blocked with the blue uniform of the inspector, her eyes seemed to wake up.

"Oh," she said, "if you've come about that parcel, I've sent it off already."

"Parcel?" repeated Valentin; and it was his turn to look inquiring.

"I mean the parcel the gentleman left – the clergyman gentleman."

"For goodness' sake," said Valentin, leaning forward with his first real confession of eagerness, "for Heaven's sake tell us what happened exactly."

"Well," said the woman a little doubtfully, "the clergymen came in about half an hour ago and bought some peppermints and talked a bit, and then went off towards the Heath. But a second after, one of them runs back into the shop and says, 'Have I left a parcel!' Well, I looked everywhere and couldn't see one; so he says, 'Never mind; but if it should turn up, please post it to this address,' and he left me the address and a shilling for my trouble. And sure enough, though I thought I'd looked everywhere, I found he'd left a brown paper parcel, so I posted it to the place he said. I can't remember the address now; it was somewhere in Westminster. But as the thing seemed so important, I thought perhaps the police had come about it."

"So they have," said Valentin shortly. "Is Hampstead Heath near here?"

"Straight on for fifteen minutes," said the woman, "and you'll come right out on the open." Valentin sprang out of the shop and began to run. The other detectives followed him at a reluctant trot.

The street they threaded was so narrow and shut in by shadows that when they came out unexpectedly into the void common and vast sky they were startled to find the evening still so light and clear. A perfect dome of peacock-green sank into gold amid the blackening trees and the dark violet distances. The glowing green tint was just deep enough to pick out in points of crystal one or two stars. All that was left of the daylight lay in a golden glitter across the edge of Hampstead and that popular hollow which is called the Vale of Health. The holiday makers who roam this region had not wholly dispersed; a few couples sat shapelessly on benches; and here and there a distant girl still shrieked in one of the swings. The glory of heaven deepened and darkened around the sublime vulgarity of man; and standing on the slope and looking across the valley, Valentin beheld the thing which he sought.

Among the black and breaking groups in that distance was one especially black which did not break – a group of two figures clerically clad. Though they seemed as small as insects, Valentin could see that one of them was much smaller than the other. Though the other had a student's stoop and an inconspicuous manner, he could see that the man was well over six feet high. He shut his teeth and went forward, whirling his stick impatiently. By the time he had substantially diminished the distance and magnified the two black figures as in a vast microscope, he had perceived something else; something which startled him, and yet which he had somehow expected. Whoever was the tall priest, there could be no doubt about the identity of the short one. It was his friend of the Harwich train, the stumpy little cure of Essex whom he had warned about his brown paper parcels.

Now, so far as this went, everything fitted in finally and rationally enough. Valentin had learned by his inquiries that morning that a Father Brown from Essex was bringing up a silver cross with sapphires, a relic of considerable value, to show some of the foreign priests at the congress. This undoubtedly was the 'silver with blue stones'; and Father Brown undoubtedly was the little greenhorn in the train. Now there was nothing wonderful about the fact that what Valentin had found out Flambeau had also found out; Flambeau found out everything. Also there was nothing wonderful in the fact that when Flambeau heard of a sapphire cross he should try to steal it; that was the most natural thing in all natural history. And most certainly there was nothing wonderful about the fact that Flambeau should have it all his own way with such a silly sheep as the man with the umbrella and the parcels. He was the sort of man whom anybody could lead on a string to the North Pole; it was not surprising that an actor like Flambeau, dressed as another priest, could lead him to Hampstead Heath. So far the crime seemed clear enough; and while the detective pitied the priest for his helplessness, he almost despised Flambeau for condescending to so gullible a victim. But when Valentin thought of all that had happened in between, of all that had led him to his triumph, he racked his brains for the smallest rhyme or reason in it. What had the stealing of a blue-and-silver cross from a priest from Essex to do with chucking soup at wall paper? What had it to do with calling nuts oranges, or with paying for windows first and breaking them afterwards? He had come to the end of his chase; yet somehow he had missed the middle of it. When he failed (which was seldom), he had usually grasped the clue, but nevertheless missed the criminal. Here he had grasped the criminal, but still he could not grasp the clue.

The two figures that they followed were crawling like black flies across the huge green contour of a hill. They were evidently sunk in conversation, and perhaps did not notice where they were going; but they were certainly going to the wilder and more silent heights of the Heath. As their pursuers gained on them, the latter had to use the undignified attitudes of the deer-stalker, to crouch behind clumps of trees and even to crawl prostrate in deep grass. By these ungainly ingenuities the hunters even came close enough to the quarry to hear the murmur of the discussion, but no word could be distinguished except the word 'reason' recurring frequently in a high and almost childish voice. Once over an abrupt dip of land and a dense tangle of thickets, the detectives actually lost the two figures they were following. They did not find the trail again for an agonising ten minutes, and then it led round the brow of a great dome of hill overlooking an amphitheatre of rich and desolate sunset scenery. Under a tree in this commanding yet neglected spot was an old ramshackle wooden seat. On this seat sat the two priests still in serious speech together. The gorgeous green and gold still clung to the darkening horizon; but the dome above was turning slowly from peacock-green to peacock-blue, and the stars detached themselves more and more like solid jewels. Mutely motioning to his followers, Valentin contrived to creep up behind the big branching tree, and, standing there in deathly silence, heard the words of the strange priests for the first time.

After he had listened for a minute and a half, he was gripped by a devilish doubt. Perhaps he had dragged the two English policemen to the wastes of a nocturnal heath on an errand no saner than seeking figs on its thistles. For the two priests were talking exactly like priests, piously, with learning and leisure, about the most aerial enigmas of theology. The little Essex priest spoke the more simply, with his round face turned to the strengthening stars; the other talked with his head bowed, as if he were not even worthy to look at them. But no more innocently clerical conversation could have been heard in any white Italian cloister or black Spanish cathedral.

The first he heard was the tail of one of Father Brown's sentences, which ended: "... what they really meant in the Middle Ages by the heavens being incorruptible."

The taller priest nodded his bowed head and said:

"Ah, yes, these modern infidels appeal to their reason; but who can look at those millions of worlds and not feel that there may well be wonderful universes above us where reason is utterly unreasonable?"

"No," said the other priest; "reason is always reasonable, even in the last limbo, in the lost borderland of things. I know that people charge the Church with lowering reason, but it is just the other way. Alone on earth, the Church makes reason really supreme. Alone on earth, the Church affirms that God himself is bound by reason."

The other priest raised his austere face to the spangled sky and said:

"Yet who knows if in that infinite universe – ?"

"Only infinite physically," said the little priest, turning sharply in his seat, "not infinite in the sense of escaping from the laws of truth."

Valentin behind his tree was tearing his fingernails with silent fury. He seemed almost to hear the sniggers of the English detectives whom he had brought so far on a fantastic guess only to listen to the metaphysical gossip of two mild old parsons. In his impatience he lost the equally elaborate answer of the tall cleric, and when he listened again it was again Father Brown who was speaking:

"Reason and justice grip the remotest and the loneliest star. Look at those stars. Don't they look as if they were single diamonds and sapphires? Well, you can imagine any mad botany or geology you please. Think of forests of adamant with leaves of brilliants. Think the moon is a blue moon, a single elephantine sapphire. But don't fancy that all that frantic astronomy would make the smallest difference to the reason and justice of conduct. On plains of opal, under cliffs cut out of pearl, you would still find a notice-board, 'Thou shalt not steal.' "

Valentin was just in the act of rising from his rigid and crouching attitude and creeping away as softly as might be, felled by the one great folly of his life. But something in the very silence of the tall priest made him stop until the latter spoke. When at last he did speak, he said simply, his head bowed and his hands on his knees:

"Well, I think that other worlds may perhaps rise higher than our reason. The mystery of heaven is unfathomable, and I for one can only bow my head."

Then, with brow yet bent and without changing by the faintest shade his attitude or voice, he added:

"Just hand over that sapphire cross of yours, will you? We're all alone here, and I could pull you to pieces like a straw doll."

The utterly unaltered voice and attitude added a strange violence to that shocking change of speech. But the guarder of the relic only seemed to turn his head by the smallest section of the compass. He seemed still to have a somewhat foolish face turned to the stars. Perhaps he had not understood. Or, perhaps, he had understood and sat rigid with terror.

"Yes," said the tall priest, in the same low voice and in the same still posture, "yes, I am Flambeau."

Then, after a pause, he said:

"Come, will you give me that cross?"

"No," said the other, and the monosyllable had an odd sound.

Flambeau suddenly flung off all his pontifical pretensions. The great robber leaned back in his seat and laughed low but long.

"No," he cried, "you won't give it me, you proud prelate. You won't give it me, you little celibate simpleton. Shall I tell you why you won't give it me? Because I've got it already in my own breast-pocket."

The small man from Essex turned what seemed to be a dazed face in the dusk, and said, with the timid eagerness of 'The Private Secretary':

"Are – are you sure?"

Flambeau yelled with delight.

"Really, you're as good as a three-act farce," he cried. "Yes, you turnip, I am quite sure. I had the sense to make a duplicate of the right parcel, and now, my friend, you've got the duplicate and I've got the jewels. An old dodge, Father Brown – a very old dodge."

"Yes," said Father Brown, and passed his hand through his hair with the same strange vagueness of manner. "Yes, I've heard of it before."

The colossus of crime leaned over to the little rustic priest with a sort of sudden interest.

"You have heard of it?" he asked. "Where have you heard of it?"

"Well, I mustn't tell you his name, of course," said the little man simply. "He was a penitent, you know. He had lived prosperously for about twenty years entirely on duplicate brown paper parcels. And so, you see, when I began to suspect you, I thought of this poor chap's way of doing it at once."

"Began to suspect me?" repeated the outlaw with increased intensity. "Did you really have the gumption to suspect me just because I brought you up to this bare part of the heath?"

"No, no," said Brown with an air of apology. "You see, I suspected you when we first met. It's that little bulge up the sleeve where you people have the spiked bracelet."

"How in Tartarus," cried Flambeau, "did you ever hear of the spiked bracelet?"

"Oh, one's little flock, you know!" said Father Brown, arching his eyebrows rather blankly. "When I was a curate in Hartlepool, there were three of them with spiked bracelets. So, as I suspected you from the first, don't you see, I made sure that the cross should go safe, anyhow. I'm afraid I watched you, you know. So at last I saw you change the parcels. Then, don't you see, I changed them back again. And then I left the right one behind."

"Left it behind?" repeated Flambeau, and for the first time there was another note in his voice beside his triumph.

"Well, it was like this," said the little priest, speaking in the same unaffected way. "I went back to that sweet-shop and asked if I'd left a parcel, and gave them a particular address if it turned up. Well, I knew I hadn't; but when I went away again I did. So, instead of running after me with that valuable parcel, they have sent it flying to a friend of mine in Westminster." Then he added rather sadly: "I learnt that, too, from a poor fellow in Hartlepool. He used to do it with handbags he stole at railway stations, but he's in a monastery now. Oh, one gets to know, you know," he added, rubbing his head again with the same sort of desperate apology. "We can't help being priests. People come and tell us these things."

Flambeau tore a brown-paper parcel out of his inner pocket and rent it in pieces. There was nothing but paper and sticks of lead inside it. He sprang to his feet with a gigantic gesture, and cried:

"I don't believe you. I don't believe a bumpkin like you could manage all that. I believe you've still got the stuff on you, and if you don't give it up – why, we're all alone, and I'll take it by force!"

"No," said Father Brown simply, and stood up also, "you won't take it by force. First, because I really haven't still got it. And, second, because we are not alone."

Flambeau stopped in his stride forward.

"Behind that tree," said Father Brown, pointing, "are two strong policemen and the greatest detective alive. How did they come here, do you ask? Why, I brought them, of course! How did I do it? Why, I'll tell you if you like! Lord bless you, we have to know twenty such things when we work among the criminal classes! Well, I wasn't sure you were a thief, and it would never do to make a scandal against one of our own clergy. So I just tested you to see if anything would make you show yourself. A man generally makes a small scene if he finds salt in his coffee; if he doesn't, he has some reason for keeping quiet. I changed the salt and sugar, and you kept quiet. A man generally objects if his bill is three times too big. If he pays it, he has some motive for passing unnoticed. I altered your bill, and you paid it."

The world seemed waiting for Flambeau to leap like a tiger. But he was held back as by a spell; he was stunned with the utmost curiosity.

"Well," went on Father Brown, with lumbering lucidity, "as you wouldn't leave any tracks for the police, of course somebody had to. At every place we went to, I took care to do something that would get us talked about for the rest of the day. I didn't do much harm – a splashed wall, spilt apples, a broken window; but I saved the cross, as the cross will always be saved. It is at Westminster by now. I rather wonder you didn't stop it with the Donkey's Whistle."

"With the what?" asked Flambeau.

"I'm glad you've never heard of it," said the priest, making a face. "It's a foul thing. I'm sure you're too good a man for a Whistler. I couldn't have countered it even with the Spots myself; I'm not strong enough in the legs."

"What on earth are you talking about?" asked the other.

"Well, I did think you'd know the Spots," said Father Brown, agreeably surprised. "Oh, you can't have gone so very wrong yet!"

"How in blazes do you know all these horrors?" cried Flambeau.

The shadow of a smile crossed the round, simple face of his clerical opponent.

"Oh, by being a celibate simpleton, I suppose," he said. "Has it never struck you that a man who does next to nothing but hear men's real sins is not likely to be wholly unaware of human evil? But, as a matter of fact, another part of my trade, too, made me sure you weren't a priest."

"What?" asked the thief, almost gaping.

"You attacked reason," said Father Brown. "It's bad theology."

And even as he turned away to collect his property, the three policemen came out from under the twilight trees. Flambeau was an artist and a sportsman. He stepped back and swept Valentin a great bow.

"Do not bow to me, *mon ami*," said Valentin with silver clearness. "Let us both bow to our master."

And they both stood an instant uncovered while the little Essex priest blinked about for his umbrella.

Brother Griffith's Story
of the Biter Bit

Wilkie Collins

EXTRACTED FROM *the Correspondence of the London Police.*

FROM CHIEF INSPECTOR THEAKSTONE, OF THE DETECTIVE POLICE, TO SERGEANT BULMER, OF THE SAME FORCE.

London, 4th July, 18– .

SERGEANT BULMER,

This is to inform you that you are wanted to assist in looking up a case of importance, which will require all the attention of an experienced member of the force. The matter of the robbery on which you are now engaged you will please to shift over to the young man who brings you this letter. You will tell him all the circumstances of the case, just as they stand; you will put him up to the progress you have made (if any) toward detecting the person or persons by whom the money has been stolen; and you will leave him to make the best he can of the matter now in your hands. He is to have the whole responsibility of the case, and the whole credit of his success if he brings it to a proper issue.

So much for the orders that I am desired to communicate to you.

A word in your ear, next, about this new man who is to take your place. His name is Matthew Sharpin, and he is to have the chance given him of dashing into our office at one jump – supposing he turns out strong enough to take it. You will naturally ask me how he comes by this privilege. I can only tell you that he has some uncommonly strong interest to back him in certain high quarters, which you and I had better not mention except under our breaths. He has been a lawyer's clerk, and he is wonderfully conceited in his opinion of himself, as well as mean and underhand, to look at. According to his own account, he leaves his old trade and joins ours of his own free will and preference. You will no more believe that than I do. My notion is, that he has managed to ferret out some private information in connection with the affairs of one of his master's clients, which makes him rather an awkward customer to keep in the office for the future, and which, at the same time, gives him hold enough over his employer to make it dangerous to drive him into a corner by turning him away. I think the giving him this unheard-of chance among us is, in plain words, pretty much like giving him hush money to keep him quiet. However that may be, Mr. Matthew Sharpin is to have the case now in your hands, and if he succeeds with it he pokes his ugly nose into our office as sure as fate. I put you up to this, sergeant, so that you may not stand in your own light by giving the new man any cause to complain of you at headquarters, and remain yours,

FRANCIS THEAKSTONE.

FROM MR. MATTHEW SHARPIN TO CHIEF INSPECTOR THEAKSTONE.

London, 5th July, 18–.

DEAR SIR,

Having now been favoured with the necessary instructions from Sergeant Bulmer, I beg to remind you of certain directions which I have received relating to the report of my future proceedings which I am to prepare for examination at headquarters.

The object of my writing, and of your examining what I have written before you send it to the higher authorities, is, I am informed, to give me, as an untried hand, the benefit of your advice in case I want it (which I venture to think I shall not) at any stage of my proceedings. As the extraordinary circumstances of the case on which I am now engaged make it impossible for me to absent myself from the place where the robbery was committed until I have made some progress toward discovering the thief, I am necessarily precluded from consulting you personally. Hence the necessity of my writing down the various details, which might perhaps be better communicated by word of mouth. This, if I am not mistaken, is the position in which we are now placed. I state my own impressions on the subject in writing, in order that we may clearly understand each other at the outset; and have the honor to remain your obedient servant,

MATTHEW SHARPIN.

FROM CHIEF INSPECTOR THEAKSTONE TO MR. MATTHEW SHARPIN.

London, 5th July, 18–.

SIR,

You have begun by wasting time, ink, and paper. We both of us perfectly well knew the position we stood in toward each other when I sent you with my letter to Sergeant Bulmer. There was not the least need to repeat it in writing. Be so good as to employ your pen in future on the business actually in hand.

You have now three separate matters on which to write me. First, you have to draw up a statement of your instructions received from Sergeant Bulmer, in order to show us that nothing has escaped your memory, and that you are thoroughly acquainted with all the circumstances of the case which has been entrusted to you. Secondly, you are to inform me what it is you propose to do. Thirdly, you are to report every inch of your progress (if you make any) from day to day, and, if need be, from hour to hour as well. This is *your* duty. As to what *my* duty may be, when I want you to remind me of it, I will write and tell you so. In the meantime, I remain yours,

FRANCIS THEAKSTONE.

FROM MR. MATTHEW SHARPIN TO CHIEF INSPECTOR THEAKSTONE.

London, 6th July, 18–.

SIR,

You are rather an elderly person, and as such, naturally inclined to be a little jealous of men like me, who are in the prime of their lives and their faculties. Under these circumstances, it is my duty to be considerate toward you, and not to bear too hardly on your small failings. I decline, therefore, altogether to take offense at the tone of your letter; I give you the full benefit of the natural generosity of my nature; I sponge the very existence of your surly communication out of my memory – in short, Chief Inspector Theakstone, I forgive you, and proceed to business.

My first duty is to draw up a full statement of the instructions I have received from Sergeant Bulmer. Here they are at your service, according to my version of them.

At Number Thirteen Rutherford Street, Soho, there is a stationer's shop. It is kept by one Mr. Yatman. He is a married man, but has no family. Besides Mr. and Mrs. Yatman, the other inmates in the house are a lodger, a young single man named Jay, who occupies the front room on the second floor – a shopman, who sleeps in one of the attics, and a servant-of-all-work, whose bed is in the back kitchen. Once a week a charwoman comes to help this servant. These are all the persons who, on ordinary occasions, have means of access to the interior of the house, placed, as a matter of course, at their disposal. Mr. Yatman has been in business for many years, carrying on his affairs prosperously enough to realize a handsome independence for a person in his position. Unfortunately for himself, he endeavored to increase the amount of his property by speculating. He ventured boldly in his investments; luck went against him; and rather less than two years ago he found himself a poor man again. All that was saved out of the wreck of his property was the sum of two hundred pounds.

Although Mr. Yatman did his best to meet his altered circumstances, by giving up many of the luxuries and comforts to which he and his wife had been accustomed, he found it impossible to retrench so far as to allow of putting by any money from the income produced by his shop. The business has been declining of late years, the cheap advertising stationers having done it injury with the public. Consequently, up to the last week, the only surplus property possessed by Mr. Yatman consisted of the two hundred pounds which had been recovered from the wreck of his fortune. This sum was placed as a deposit in a joint-stock bank of the highest possible character.

Eight days ago Mr. Yatman and his lodger, Mr. Jay, held a conversation on the subject of the commercial difficulties which are hampering trade in all directions at the present time. Mr. Jay (who lives by supplying the newspapers with short paragraphs relating to accidents, offences, and brief records of remarkable occurrences in general – who is, in short, what they call a penny-a-liner) told his landlord that he had been in the city that day and heard unfavorable rumours on the subject of the joint-stock banks. The rumours to which he alluded had already reached the ears of Mr. Yatman from other quarters, and the confirmation of them by his lodger had such an effect on his mind – predisposed as it was to alarm by the experience of his former losses – that he resolved to go at once to the bank and withdraw his deposit. It was then getting on toward the end of the afternoon, and he arrived just in time to receive his money before the bank closed.

He received the deposit in bank notes of the following amounts: one fifty-pound note, three twenty-pound notes, six ten-pound notes, and six five-pound notes. His object in drawing the money in this form was to have it ready to lay out immediately in trifling loans, on good security, among the small tradespeople of his district, some of whom are sorely pressed for the very means of existence at the present time. Investments of this kind seemed to Mr. Yatman to be the most safe and the most profitable on which he could now venture.

He brought the money back in an envelope placed in his breast pocket, and asked his shopman, on getting home, to look for a small, flat, tin cash-box, which had not been used for years, and which, as Mr. Yatman remembered it, was exactly of the right size to hold the bank notes. For some time the cash-box was searched for in vain. Mr. Yatman called to his wife to know if she had any idea where it was. The question was overheard by the servant-of-all-work, who was taking up the tea-tray at the time, and by Mr. Jay, who was coming downstairs on his way out to the theater. Ultimately the cash-box was found by the shopman. Mr. Yatman placed the bank notes in it, secured them by a padlock, and put the box in his coat pocket. It stuck out of the coat pocket a very little, but enough to be seen. Mr. Yatman remained at home, upstairs, all that evening. No visitors called. At eleven o'clock he went to bed, and put the cash-box under his pillow.

When he and his wife woke the next morning the box was gone. Payment of the notes was immediately stopped at the Bank of England, but no news of the money has been heard of since that time.

So far the circumstances of the case are perfectly clear. They point unmistakably to the conclusion that the robbery must have been committed by some person living in the house. Suspicion falls, therefore, upon the servant-of-all-work, upon the shopman, and upon Mr. Jay. The two first knew that the cash-box was being inquired for by their master, but did not know what it was he wanted to put into it. They would assume, of course, that it was money. They both had opportunities (the servant when she took away the tea, and the shopman when he came, after shutting up, to give the keys of the till to his master) of seeing the cash-box in Mr. Yatman's pocket, and of inferring naturally, from its position there, that he intended to take it into his bedroom with him at night.

Mr. Jay, on the other hand, had been told, during the afternoon's conversation on the subject of joint-stock banks, that his landlord had a deposit of two hundred pounds in one of them. He also knew that Mr. Yatman left him with the intention of drawing that money out; and he heard the inquiry for the cash-box afterward, when he was coming downstairs. He must, therefore, have inferred that the money was in the house, and that the cash-box was the receptacle intended to contain it. That he could have had any idea, however, of the place in which Mr. Yatman intended to keep it for the night is impossible, seeing that he went out before the box was found, and did not return till his landlord was in bed. Consequently, if he committed the robbery, he must have gone into the bedroom purely on speculation.

Speaking of the bedroom reminds me of the necessity of noticing the situation of it in the house, and the means that exist of gaining easy access to it at any hour of the night.

The room in question is the back room on the first floor. In consequence of Mrs. Yatman's constitutional nervousness on the subject of fire, which makes her apprehend being burned alive in her room, in case of accident, by the hampering of the lock if the key is turned in it, her husband has never been accustomed to lock the bedroom door. Both he and his wife are, by their own admission, heavy sleepers; consequently, the risk to be run by any evil-disposed persons wishing to plunder the bedroom was of the most trifling kind. They could enter the room by merely turning the handle of the door; and, if they moved with ordinary caution, there was no fear of their waking the sleepers inside. This fact is of importance. It strengthens our conviction that the money must have been taken by one of the inmates of the house, because it tends to show that the robbery, in this case, might have been committed by persons not possessed of the superior vigilance and cunning of the experienced thief.

Such are the circumstances, as they were related to Sergeant Bulmer, when he was first called in to discover the guilty parties, and, if possible, to recover the lost bank notes. The strictest inquiry which he could institute failed of producing the smallest fragment of evidence against any of the persons on whom suspicion naturally fell. Their language and behavior on being informed of the robbery was perfectly consistent with the language and behavior of innocent people. Sergeant Bulmer felt from the first that this was a case for private inquiry and secret observation. He began by recommending Mr. and Mrs. Yatman to affect a feeling of perfect confidence in the innocence of the persons living under their roof, and he then opened the campaign by employing himself in following the goings and comings, and in discovering the friends, the habits, and the secrets of the maid-of-all-work.

Three days and nights of exertion on his own part, and on that of others who were competent to assist his investigations, were enough to satisfy him that there was no sound cause for suspicion against the girl.

He next practised the same precaution in relation to the shopman. There was more difficulty and uncertainty in privately clearing up this person's character without his knowledge, but the obstacles were at last smoothed away with tolerable success; and, though there is not the same amount of certainty in this case which there was in the case of the girl, there is still fair reason for supposing that the shopman has had nothing to do with the robbery of the cash-box.

As a necessary consequence of these proceedings, the range of suspicion now becomes limited to the lodger, Mr. Jay.

When I presented your letter of introduction to Sergeant Bulmer, he had already made some inquiries on the subject of this young man. The result, so far, has not been at all favorable. Mr. Jay's habits are irregular; he frequents public houses, and seems to be familiarly acquainted with a great many dissolute characters; he is in debt to most of the tradespeople whom he employs; he has not paid his rent to Mr. Yatman for the last month; yesterday evening he came home excited by liquor, and last week he was seen talking to a prize-fighter; in short, though Mr. Jay does call himself a journalist, in virtue of his penny-a-line contributions to the newspapers, he is a young man of low tastes, vulgar manners, and bad habits. Nothing has yet been discovered in relation to him which redounds to his credit in the smallest degree.

I have now reported, down to the very last details, all the particulars communicated to me by Sergeant Bulmer. I believe you will not find an omission anywhere; and I think you will admit, though you are prejudiced against me, that a clearer statement of facts was never laid before you than the statement I have now made. My next duty is to tell you what I propose to do now that the case is confided to my hands.

In the first place, it is clearly my business to take up the case at the point where Sergeant Bulmer has left it. On his authority, I am justified in assuming that I have no need to trouble myself about the maid-of-all-work and the shopman. Their characters are now to be considered as cleared up. What remains to be privately investigated is the question of the guilt or innocence of Mr. Jay. Before we give up the notes for lost, we must make sure, if we can, that he knows nothing about them.

This is the plan that I have adopted, with the full approval of Mr. and Mrs. Yatman, for discovering whether Mr. Jay is or is not the person who has stolen the cash-box:

I propose today to present myself at the house in the character of a young man who is looking for lodgings. The back room on the second floor will be shown to me as the room to let, and I shall establish myself there tonight as a person from the country who has come to London to look for a situation in a respectable shop or office.

By this means I shall be living next to the room occupied by Mr. Jay. The partition between us is mere lath and plaster. I shall make a small hole in it, near the cornice, through which I can see what Mr. Jay does in his room, and hear every word that is said when any friend happens to call on him. Whenever he is at home, I shall be at my post of observation; whenever he goes out, I shall be after him. By employing these means of watching him, I believe I may look forward to the discovery of his secret – if he knows anything about the lost bank notes – as to a dead certainty.

What you may think of my plan of observation I cannot undertake to say. It appears to me to unite the invaluable merits of boldness and simplicity. Fortified by this conviction, I close the present communication with feelings of the most sanguine description in regard to the future, and remain your obedient servant,

MATTHEW SHARPIN.

FROM THE SAME TO THE SAME.

7th July.

SIR,

As you have not honoured me with any answer to my last communication, I assume that, in spite of your prejudices against me, it has produced the favourable impression on your mind which I ventured to anticipate. Gratified and encouraged beyond measure by the token of approval which your eloquent silence conveys to me, I proceed to report the progress that has been made in the course of the last twenty-four hours.

I am now comfortably established next door to Mr. Jay, and I am delighted to say that I have two holes in the partition instead of one. My natural sense of humor has led me into the pardonable extravagance of giving them both appropriate names. One I call my peep-hole, and the other my pipe-hole. The name of the first explains itself; the name of the second refers to a small tin pipe or tube inserted in the hole, and twisted so that the mouth of it comes close to my ear while I am standing at my post of observation. Thus, while I am looking at Mr. Jay through my peep-hole, I can hear every word that may be spoken in his room through my pipe-hole.

Perfect candour – a virtue which I have possessed from my childhood – compels me to acknowledge, before I go any further, that the ingenious notion of adding a pipe-hole to my proposed peep-hole originated with Mrs. Yatman. This lady – a most intelligent and accomplished person, simple, and yet distinguished in her manners, has entered into all my little plans with an enthusiasm and intelligence which I cannot too highly praise. Mr. Yatman is so cast down by his loss that he is quite incapable of affording me any assistance. Mrs. Yatman, who is evidently most tenderly attached to him, feels her husband's sad condition of mind even more acutely than she feels the loss of the money, and is mainly stimulated to exertion by her desire to assist in raising him from the miserable state of prostration into which he has now fallen.

"The money, Mr. Sharpin," she said to me yesterday evening, with tears in her eyes, "the money may be regained by rigid economy and strict attention to business. It is my husband's wretched state of mind that makes me so anxious for the discovery of the thief. I may be wrong, but I felt hopeful of success as soon as you entered the house; and I believe that, if the wretch who robbed us is to be found, you are the man to discover him." I accepted this gratifying compliment in the spirit in which it was offered, firmly believing that I shall be found, sooner or later, to have thoroughly deserved it.

Let me now return to business – that is to say, to my peep-hole and my pipe-hole.

I have enjoyed some hours of calm observation of Mr. Jay. Though rarely at home, as I understand from Mrs. Yatman, on ordinary occasions, he has been indoors the whole of this day. That is suspicious, to begin with. I have to report, further, that he rose at a late hour this morning (always a bad sign in a young man), and that he lost a great deal of time, after he was up, in yawning and complaining to himself of headache. Like other debauched characters, he ate little or nothing for breakfast. His next proceeding was to smoke a pipe – a dirty clay pipe, which a gentleman would have been ashamed to put between his lips. When he had done smoking he took out pen, ink and paper, and sat down to write with a groan – whether of remorse for having taken the bank notes, or of disgust at the task before him, I am unable to say. After writing a few lines (too far away from my peep-hole to give me a chance of reading over his shoulder), he leaned back in his chair, and amused himself by humming the tunes of popular songs. I recognized 'My Mary Anne,' 'Bobbin' Around,' and 'Old Dog Tray,' among other melodies. Whether these do or do not represent secret signals by which he communicates with his accomplices remains to be seen. After he had amused himself for some time by humming, he got up and began to walk about the room, occasionally stopping to add a sentence to the paper on his desk. Before long he went to a locked cupboard and opened it. I strained my eyes eagerly, in expectation of making a discovery. I saw him take something carefully out of the cupboard – he turned round – and it was only a pint bottle of brandy! Having drunk some of the liquor, this extremely indolent reprobate lay down on his bed again, and in five minutes was fast asleep.

After hearing him snoring for at least two hours, I was recalled to my peep-hole by a knock at his door. He jumped up and opened it with suspicious activity.

A very small boy, with a very dirty face, walked in, said: "Please, sir, they're waiting for you," sat down on a chair with his legs a long way from the ground, and instantly fell asleep! Mr. Jay swore an oath, tied a wet towel round his head, and, going back to his paper, began to cover it with writing as fast as his fingers could move the pen. Occasionally getting up to dip the towel in water and tie it on again, he continued at this employment for nearly three hours; then folded up the leaves of writing, woke the boy, and gave them to him, with this remarkable expression: "Now, then, young sleepy-head, quick march! If you see the governor, tell him to have the money ready for me when I call for it." The boy grinned and disappeared. I was sorely tempted to follow 'sleepy-head,' but, on reflection, considered it safest still to keep my eye on the proceedings of Mr. Jay.

In half an hour's time he put on his hat and walked out. Of course I put on my hat and walked out also. As I went downstairs I passed Mrs. Yatman going up. The lady has been kind enough to undertake, by previous arrangement between us, to search Mr. Jay's room while he is out of the way, and while I am necessarily engaged in the pleasing duty of following him wherever he goes. On the occasion to which I now refer, he walked straight to the nearest tavern and ordered a couple of mutton-chops for his dinner. I placed myself in the next box to him, and ordered a couple of mutton-chops for my dinner. Before I had been in the room a minute, a young man of highly suspicious manners and appearance, sitting at a table opposite, took his glass of porter in his hand and joined Mr. Jay. I pretended to be reading the newspaper, and listened, as in duty bound, with all my might.

"Jack has been here inquiring after you," says the young man.

"Did he leave any message?" asks Mr. Jay.

"Yes," says the other. "He told me, if I met with you, to say that he wished very particularly to see you tonight, and that he would give you a look in at Rutherford Street at seven o'clock."

"All right," says Mr. Jay. "I'll get back in time to see him."

Upon this, the suspicious-looking young man finished his porter, and saying that he was rather in a hurry, took leave of his friend (perhaps I should not be wrong if I said his accomplice?), and left the room.

At twenty-five minutes and a half past six – in these serious cases it is important to be particular about time – Mr. Jay finished his chops and paid his bill. At twenty-six minutes and three-quarters I finished my chops and paid mine. In ten minutes more I was inside the house in Rutherford Street, and was received by Mrs. Yatman in the passage. That charming woman's face exhibited an expression of melancholy and disappointment which it quite grieved me to see.

"I am afraid, ma'am," says I, "that you have not hit on any little criminating discovery in the lodger's room?"

She shook her head and sighed. It was a soft, languid, fluttering sigh – and, upon my life, it quite upset me. For the moment I forgot business, and burned with envy of Mr. Yatman.

"Don't despair, ma'am," I said, with an insinuating mildness which seemed to touch her. "I have heard a mysterious conversation – I know of a guilty appointment – and I expect great things from my peep-hole and my pipe-hole tonight. Pray don't be alarmed, but I think we are on the brink of a discovery."

Here my enthusiastic devotion to business got the better part of my tender feelings. I looked – winked – nodded – left her.

When I got back to my observatory, I found Mr. Jay digesting his mutton-chops in an armchair, with his pipe in his mouth. On his table were two tumblers, a jug of water, and the pint bottle of brandy. It was then close upon seven o'clock. As the hour struck the person described as 'Jack' walked in.

He looked agitated – I am happy to say he looked violently agitated. The cheerful glow of anticipated success diffused itself (to use a strong expression) all over me, from head to foot. With breathless interest I looked through my peep-hole, and saw the visitor – the 'Jack' of this delightful case – sit down, facing me, at the opposite side of the table to Mr. Jay. Making allowance for the difference in expression which their countenances just now happened to exhibit, these two abandoned villains were so much alike in other respects as to lead at once to the conclusion that they were brothers. Jack was the cleaner man and the better dressed of the two. I admit that, at the outset. It is, perhaps, one of my failings to push justice and impartiality to their utmost limits. I am no Pharisee; and where Vice has its redeeming point, I say, let Vice have its due – yes, yes, by all manner of means, let Vice have its due.

"What's the matter now, Jack?" says Mr. Jay.

"Can't you see it in my face?" says Jack. "My dear fellow, delays are dangerous. Let us have done with suspense, and risk it, the day after tomorrow."

"So soon as that?" cries Mr. Jay, looking very much astonished. "Well, I'm ready, if you are. But, I say, Jack, is somebody else ready, too? Are you quite sure of that?"

He smiled as he spoke – a frightful smile – and laid a very strong emphasis on those two words, "Somebody else." There is evidently a third ruffian, a nameless desperado, concerned in the business.

"Meet us tomorrow," says Jack, "and judge for yourself. Be in the Regent's Park at eleven in the morning, and look out for us at the turning that leads to the Avenue Road."

"I'll be there," says Mr. Jay. "Have a drop of brandy-and-water? What are you getting up for? You're not going already?"

"Yes, I am," says Jack. "The fact is, I'm so excited and agitated that I can't sit still anywhere for five minutes together. Ridiculous as it may appear to you, I'm in a perpetual state of nervous flutter. I can't, for the life of me, help fearing that we shall be found out. I fancy that every man who looks twice at me in the street is a spy –"

At these words I thought my legs would have given way under me. Nothing but strength of mind kept me at my peep-hole – nothing else, I give you my word of honour.

"Stuff and nonsense!" cries Mr. Jay, with all the effrontery of a veteran in crime. "We have kept the secret up to this time, and we will manage cleverly to the end. Have a drop of brandy-and-water, and you will feel as certain about it as I do."

Jack steadily refused the brandy-and-water, and steadily persisted in taking his leave.

"I must try if I can't walk it off," he said. "Remember tomorrow morning – eleven o'clock, Avenue Road, side of the Regent's Park."

With those words he went out. His hardened relative laughed desperately and resumed the dirty clay pipe.

I sat down on the side of my bed, actually quivering with excitement.

It is clear to me that no attempt has yet been made to change the stolen bank notes, and I may add that Sergeant Bulmer was of that opinion also when he left the case in my hands. What is the natural conclusion to draw from the conversation which I have just set down? Evidently that the confederates meet tomorrow to take their respective shares in the stolen money, and to decide on the safest means of getting the notes changed the day after. Mr. Jay is, beyond a doubt, the leading criminal in this business, and he will probably run the chief risk – that of changing the fifty-pound note. I shall, therefore, still make it my business to follow him – attending at the Regent's Park tomorrow, and doing my best to hear what is said there. If another appointment is made for the day after, I shall, of course, go to it. In the meantime, I shall want the immediate assistance of two competent persons (supposing the rascals separate after their meeting) to follow the two minor criminals. It is only fair to add that, if the rogues all retire together, I shall probably keep my subordinates in reserve. Being naturally ambitious, I desire, if possible, to have the whole credit of discovering this robbery to myself.

8th July.

I have to acknowledge, with thanks, the speedy arrival of my two subordinates – men of very average abilities, I am afraid; but, fortunately, I shall always be on the spot to direct them.

My first business this morning was necessarily to prevent possible mistakes by accounting to Mr. and Mrs. Yatman for the presence of two strangers on the scene. Mr. Yatman (between ourselves, a poor, feeble man) only shook his head and groaned. Mrs. Yatman (that superior woman) favoured me with a charming look of intelligence.

"Oh, Mr. Sharpin!" she said, "I am so sorry to see those two men! Your sending for their assistance looks as if you were beginning to be doubtful of success."

I privately winked at her (she is very good in allowing me to do so without taking offence), and told her, in my facetious way, that she laboured under a slight mistake.

"It is because I am sure of success, ma'am, that I send for them. I am determined to recover the money, not for my own sake only, but for Mr. Yatman's sake – and for yours."

I laid a considerable amount of stress on those last three words. She said: "Oh, Mr. Sharpin!" again, and blushed of a heavenly red, and looked down at her work. I could go to the world's end with that woman if Mr. Yatman would only die.

I sent off the two subordinates to wait until I wanted them at the Avenue Road gate of the Regent's Park. Half an hour afterwards I was following the same direction myself at the heels of Mr. Jay.

The two confederates were punctual to the appointed time. I blush to record it, but it is nevertheless necessary to state that the third rogue – the nameless desperado of my report, or, if you prefer it, the mysterious 'somebody else' of the conversation between the two brothers – is – a woman! And, what is worse, a young woman! And, what is more lamentable still, a nice-looking woman! I have long resisted a growing conviction that, wherever there is mischief in this world, an individual of the fair sex is inevitably certain to be mixed up in it. After the experience of this morning, I can struggle against that sad conclusion no longer. I give up the sex – excepting Mrs. Yatman, I give up the sex.

The man named 'Jack' offered the woman his arm. Mr. Jay placed himself on the other side of her. The three then walked away slowly among the trees. I followed them at a respectful distance. My two subordinates, at a respectful distance, also, followed me.

It was, I deeply regret to say, impossible to get near enough to them to overhear their conversation without running too great a risk of being discovered. I could only infer from their gestures and actions that they were all three talking with extraordinary earnestness on some subject which deeply interested them. After having been engaged in this way a full quarter of an hour, they suddenly turned round to retrace their steps. My presence of mind did not forsake me in this emergency. I signed to the two subordinates to walk on carelessly and pass them, while I myself slipped dexterously behind a tree. As they came by me, I heard 'Jack' address these words to Mr. Jay:

"Let us say half-past ten tomorrow morning. And mind you come in a cab. We had better not risk taking one in this neighbourhood."

Mr. Jay made some brief reply which I could not overhear. They walked back to the place at which they had met, shaking hands there with an audacious cordiality which it quite sickened me to see. They then separated. I followed Mr. Jay. My subordinates paid the same delicate attention to the other two.

Instead of taking me back to Rutherford Street, Mr. Jay led me to the Strand. He stopped at a dingy, disreputable-looking house, which, according to the inscription over the door, was a newspaper office, but which, in my judgment, had all the external appearance of a place devoted to the reception of stolen goods.

After remaining inside for a few minutes, he came out whistling, with his finger and thumb in his waistcoat pocket. Some men would now have arrested him on the spot. I remembered the necessity of catching the two confederates, and the importance of not interfering with the appointment that had been made for the next morning. Such coolness as this, under trying circumstances, is rarely to be found, I should imagine, in a young beginner, whose reputation as a detective policeman is still to make.

From the house of suspicious appearance Mr. Jay betook himself to a cigar-divan, and read the magazines over a cheroot. From the divan he strolled to the tavern and had his chops. I strolled to the tavern and had my chops. When he had done he went back to his lodging. When I had done I went back to mine. He was overcome with drowsiness early in the evening, and went to bed. As soon as I heard him snoring, I was overcome with drowsiness and went to bed also.

Early in the morning my two subordinates came to make their report.

They had seen the man named 'Jack' leave the woman at the gate of an apparently respectable villa residence not far from the Regent's Park. Left to himself, he took a turning to the right, which led to a sort of suburban street, principally inhabited by shopkeepers. He stopped at the private door of one of the houses, and let himself in with his own key – looking about him as he opened the door, and staring suspiciously at my men as they lounged along on the opposite side of the way. These were all the particulars which the subordinates had to communicate. I kept them in my room to attend on me, if needful, and mounted to my peep-hole to have a look at Mr. Jay.

He was occupied in dressing himself, and was taking extraordinary pains to destroy all traces of the natural slovenliness of his appearance. This was precisely what I expected. A vagabond like Mr. Jay knows the importance of giving himself a respectable look when he is going to run the risk of changing a stolen bank note. At five minutes past ten o'clock he had given the last brush to his shabby hat and the last scouring with bread-crumb to his dirty gloves. At ten minutes past ten he was in the street, on his way to the nearest cab-stand, and I and my subordinates were close on his heels.

He took a cab and we took a cab. I had not overheard them appoint a place of meeting when following them in the Park on the previous day, but I soon found that we were proceeding in the old direction of the Avenue Road gate. The cab in which Mr. Jay was riding turned into the Park slowly. We stopped outside, to avoid exciting suspicion. I got out to follow the cab on foot. Just as I did so, I saw it stop, and detected the two confederates approaching it from among the trees. They got in, and the cab was turned about directly. I ran back to my own cab and told the driver to let them pass him, and then to follow as before.

The man obeyed my directions, but so clumsily as to excite their suspicions. We had been driving after them about three minutes (returning along the road by which we had advanced) when I looked out of the window to see how far they might be ahead of us. As I did this, I saw two hats popped out of the windows of their cab, and two faces looking back at me. I sank into my place in a cold sweat; the expression is coarse, but no other form of words can describe my condition at that trying moment.

"We are found out!" I said, faintly, to my two subordinates. They stared at me in astonishment. My feelings changed instantly from the depth of despair to the height of indignation.

"It is the cabman's fault. Get out, one of you," I said, with dignity – "get out, and punch his head."

Instead of following my directions (I should wish this act of disobedience to be reported at headquarters) they both looked out of the window. Before I could pull them back they both sat down again. Before I could express my just indignation, they both grinned, and said to me: "Please to look out, sir!"

I did look out. Their cab had stopped.

Where?

At a church door!

What effect this discovery might have had upon the ordinary run of men I don't know. Being of a strong religious turn myself, it filled me with horror. I have often read of the unprincipled cunning of criminal persons, but I never before heard of three thieves attempting to double on their pursuers by entering a church! The sacrilegious audacity of that proceeding is, I should think, unparalleled in the annals of crime.

I checked my grinning subordinates by a frown. It was easy to see what was passing in their superficial minds. If I had not been able to look below the surface, I might, on observing two nicely dressed men and one nicely dressed woman enter a church before eleven in the morning on a week day, have come to the same hasty conclusion at which my inferiors had evidently arrived. As it was, appearances had no power to impose on *me*. I got out, and, followed by one of my men, entered the church. The other man I sent round to watch the vestry door. You may catch a weasel asleep, but not your humble servant, Matthew Sharpin!

We stole up the gallery stairs, diverged to the organ-loft, and peered through the curtains in front. There they were, all three, sitting in a pew below – yes, incredible as it may appear, sitting in a pew below!

Before I could determine what to do, a clergyman made his appearance in full canonicals from the vestry door, followed by a clerk. My brain whirled and my eyesight grew dim. Dark remembrances of robberies committed in vestries floated through my mind. I trembled for the excellent man in full canonicals – I even trembled for the clerk.

The clergyman placed himself inside the altar rails. The three desperadoes approached him. He opened his book and began to read. What? you will ask.

I answer, without the slightest hesitation, the first lines of the Marriage Service.

My subordinate had the audacity to look at me, and then to stuff his pocket-handkerchief into his mouth. I scorned to pay any attention to him. After I had discovered that the man "Jack" was the bridegroom, and that the man Jay acted the part of father, and gave away the bride, I left the church, followed by my men, and joined the other subordinate outside the vestry door. Some people in my position would now have felt rather crestfallen, and would have begun to think that they had made a very foolish mistake. Not the faintest misgiving of any kind troubled me. I did not feel in the slightest degree depreciated in my own estimation. And even now, after a lapse of three hours, my mind remains, I am happy to say, in the same calm and hopeful condition.

As soon as I and my subordinates were assembled together outside the church, I intimated my intention of still following the other cab in spite of what had occurred. My reason for deciding on this course will appear presently. The two subordinates appeared to be astonished at my resolution. One of them had the impertinence to say to me:

"If you please, sir, who is it that we are after? A man who has stolen money, or a man who has stolen a wife?"

The other low person encouraged him by laughing. Both have deserved an official reprimand, and both, I sincerely trust, will be sure to get it.

When the marriage ceremony was over, the three got into their cab and once more our vehicle (neatly hidden round the corner of the church, so that they could not suspect it to be near them) started to follow theirs.

We traced them to the terminus of the Southwestern Railway. The newly-married couple took tickets for Richmond, paying their fare with a half sovereign, and so depriving me of the pleasure of arresting them, which I should certainly have done if they had offered a bank note. They parted from Mr. Jay, saying: "Remember the address – 14 Babylon Terrace. You dine with us tomorrow week." Mr. Jay accepted the invitation, and added, jocosely, that he was going home at once to get off his clean clothes, and to be comfortable and dirty again for the rest of the day. I have to report that I saw him home safely, and that he is comfortable and dirty again (to use his own disgraceful language) at the present moment.

Here the affair rests, having by this time reached what I may call its first stage.

I know very well what persons of hasty judgment will be inclined to say of my proceedings thus far. They will assert that I have been deceiving myself all through in the most absurd way; they will declare that the suspicious conversations which I have reported referred solely to the difficulties and dangers of successfully carrying out a runaway match; and they will appeal to the scene in the church as offering undeniable proof of the correctness of their assertions. So let it be. I dispute nothing up to this point. But I ask a question, out of the depths of my own sagacity as a man of the world, which the bitterest of my enemies will not, I think, find it particularly easy to answer.

Granted the fact of the marriage, what proof does it afford me of the innocence of the three persons concerned in that clandestine transaction? It gives me none. On the contrary, it strengthens my suspicions against Mr. Jay and his confederates, because it suggests a distinct motive for their stealing the money. A gentleman who is going to spend his honeymoon at Richmond wants money; and a gentleman who is in debt to all his tradespeople wants money. Is this an unjustifiable imputation of bad motives? In the name of outraged Morality, I deny it. These men have combined together, and have stolen a woman. Why should they not combine together and steal a cash-box? I take my stand on the logic of rigid Virtue, and I defy all the sophistry of Vice to move me an inch out of my position.

Speaking of virtue, I may add that I have put this view of the case to Mr. and Mrs. Yatman. That accomplished and charming woman found it difficult at first to follow the close chain of my reasoning. I am free to confess that she shook her head, and shed tears, and joined her husband in premature lamentation over the loss of the two hundred pounds. But a little careful explanation on my part, and a little attentive listening on hers, ultimately changed her opinion. She now agrees with me that there is nothing in this unexpected circumstance of the clandestine marriage which absolutely tends to divert suspicion from Mr. Jay, or Mr. 'Jack,' or the runaway lady. 'Audacious hussy' was the term my fair friend used in speaking of her; but let that pass. It is more to the purpose to record that Mrs. Yatman has not lost confidence in me, and that Mr. Yatman promises to follow her example, and do his best to look hopefully for future results.

I have now, in the new turn that circumstances have taken, to await advice from your office. I pause for fresh orders with all the composure of a man who has got two strings to his bow. When I traced the three confederates from the church door to the railway terminus, I had two motives for doing so. First, I followed them as a matter of official business, believing them still to have been guilty of the robbery. Secondly, I followed them as a matter of private speculation, with a view of discovering the place of refuge to which the runaway couple intended to retreat, and of making my information a marketable commodity to offer to the young lady's family and friends. Thus, whatever happens, I may congratulate myself beforehand on not having wasted my time. If the office approves of my conduct, I have my plan ready for further proceedings. If the office blames me, I shall take myself off, with my marketable information, to the genteel villa residence in the neighborhood of the Regent's Park. Anyway, the affair puts money into my pocket, and does credit to my penetration as an uncommonly sharp man.

I have only one word more to add, and it is this: If any individual ventures to assert that Mr. Jay and his confederates are innocent of all share in the stealing of the cash-box, I, in return, defy that individual – though he may even be Chief Inspector Theakstone himself – to tell me who has committed the robbery at Rutherford Street, Soho.

Strong in that conviction, I have the honour to be your very obedient servant,
MATTHEW SHARPIN.

FROM CHIEF INSPECTOR THEAKSTONE TO SERGEANT BULMER.

Birmingham, July 9th.

SERGEANT BULMER,

That empty-headed puppy, Mr. Matthew Sharpin, has made a mess of the case at Rutherford Street, exactly as I expected he would. Business keeps me in this town, so I write to you to set the matter straight. I enclose with this the pages of feeble scribble-scrabble which the creature Sharpin calls a report. Look them over; and when you have made your way through all the gabble, I think you will agree with me that the conceited booby has looked for the thief in every direction but the right one. You can lay your hand on the guilty person in five minutes, now. Settle the case at once; forward your report to me at this place, and tell Mr. Sharpin that he is suspended till further notice.

Yours,
FRANCIS THEAKSTONE.

FROM SERGEANT BULMER TO CHIEF INSPECTOR THEAKSTONE.

London, July 10th.

INSPECTOR THEAKSTONE

Your letter and enclosure came safe to hand. Wise men, they say, may always learn something even from a fool. By the time I had got through Sharpin's maundering report of his own folly, I saw my way clear enough to the end of the Rutherford Street case, just as you thought I should. In half an hour's time I was at the house. The first person I saw there was Mr. Sharpin himself.

"Have you come to help me?" says he.

"Not exactly," says I. "I've come to tell you that you are suspended till further notice."

"Very good," says he, not taken down by so much as a single peg in his own estimation. "I thought you would be jealous of me. It's very natural and I don't blame you. Walk in, pray, and make yourself at home. I'm off to do a little detective business on my own account, in the neighborhood of the Regent's Park. Ta – ta, sergeant, ta – ta!"

With those words he took himself out of the way, which was exactly what I wanted him to do.

As soon as the maid-servant had shut the door, I told her to inform her master that I wanted to say a word to him in private. She showed me into the parlour behind the shop, and there was Mr. Yatman all alone, reading the newspaper.

"About this matter of the robbery, sir," says I.

He cut me short, peevishly enough, being naturally a poor, weak, womanish sort of man.

"Yes, yes, I know," says he. "You have come to tell me that your wonderfully clever man, who has bored holes in my second floor partition, has made a mistake, and is off the scent of the scoundrel who has stolen my money."

"Yes, sir," says I. "That *is* one of the things I came to tell you. But I have got something else to say besides that."

"Can you tell me who the thief is?" says he, more pettish than ever.

"Yes, sir," says I, "I think I can."

He put down the newspaper, and began to look rather anxious and frightened.

"Not my shopman?" says he. "I hope, for the man's own sake, it's not my shopman."

"Guess again, sir," says I.

"That idle slut, the maid?" says he.

"She is idle, sir," says I, "and she is also a slut; my first inquiries about her proved as much as that. But she's not the thief."

"Then, in the name of Heaven, who is?" says he.

"Will you please to prepare yourself for a very disagreeable surprise, sir?" says I. "And, in case you lose your temper, will you excuse my remarking that I am the stronger man of the two, and that if you allow yourself to lay hands on me, I may unintentionally hurt you, in pure self-defence."

He turned as pale as ashes, and pushed his chair two or three feet away from me.

"You have asked me to tell you, sir, who has taken your money," I went on. "If you insist on my giving you an answer –"

"I do insist," he said, faintly. "Who has taken it?"

"Your wife has taken it," I said, very quietly, and very positively at the same time.

He jumped out of the chair as if I had put a knife into him, and struck his fist on the table so heavily that the wood cracked again.

"Steady, sir," says I. "Flying into a passion won't help you to the truth."

"It's a lie!" says he, with another smack of his fist on the table – "a base, vile, infamous lie! How dare you –"

He stopped, and fell back into the chair again, looked about him in a bewildered way, and ended by bursting out crying.

"When your better sense comes back to you, sir," says I, "I am sure you will be gentleman enough to make an apology for the language you have just used. In the meantime, please to listen, if you can, to a word of explanation. Mr. Sharpin has sent in a report to our inspector of the most irregular and ridiculous kind, setting down not only all his own foolish doings and sayings, but the doings and sayings of Mrs. Yatman as well. In most cases, such a document would have been fit only for the waste-paper basket; but in this particular case it so happens that Mr. Sharpin's budget of nonsense leads to a certain conclusion, which the simpleton of a writer has been quite innocent of suspecting from the beginning to the end. Of that conclusion I am so sure that I will forfeit my place if it does not turn out that Mrs. Yatman has been practising upon the folly and conceit of this young man, and that she has tried to shield herself from discovery by purposely encouraging him to suspect the wrong persons. I tell you that confidently; and I will even go further. I will undertake to give a decided opinion as to why Mrs. Yatman took the money, and what she has done with it, or with a part of it. Nobody can look at that lady, sir, without being struck by the great taste and beauty of her dress –"

As I said those last words, the poor man seemed to find his powers of speech again. He cut me short directly as haughtily as if he had been a duke instead of a stationer.

"Try some other means of justifying your vile calumny against my wife," says he. "Her milliner's bill for the past year is on my file of receipted accounts at this moment."

"Excuse me, sir," says I, "but that proves nothing. Milliners, I must tell you, have a certain rascally custom which comes within the daily experience of our office. A married lady who wishes it can keep two accounts at her dressmaker's; one is the account which her husband sees and pays; the other is the private account, which contains all the extravagant items, and which the wife pays secretly, by instalments, whenever she can. According to our usual experience, these instalments are mostly squeezed out of the housekeeping money. In your case, I suspect, no instalments have been paid; proceedings have been threatened; Mrs. Yatman, knowing your altered circumstances, has felt herself driven into a corner, and she has paid her private account out of your cash-box."

"I won't believe it," says he. "Every word you speak is an abominable insult to me and to my wife."

"Are you man enough, sir," says I, taking him up short, in order to save time and words, "to get that receipted bill you spoke of just now off the file, and come with me at once to the milliner's shop where Mrs. Yatman deals?"

He turned red in the face at that, got the bill directly, and put on his hat. I took out of my pocket-book the list containing the numbers of the lost notes, and we left the house together immediately.

Arrived at the milliner's (one of the expensive West-End houses, as I expected), I asked for a private interview, on important business, with the mistress of the concern. It was not the first time that she and I had met over the same delicate investigation. The moment she set eyes on me she sent for her husband. I mentioned who Mr. Yatman was, and what we wanted.

"This is strictly private?" inquires the husband. I nodded my head.

"And confidential?" says the wife. I nodded again.

"Do you see any objection, dear, to obliging the sergeant with a sight of the books?" says the husband.

"None in the world, love, if you approve of it," says the wife.

All this while poor Mr. Yatman sat looking the picture of astonishment and distress, quite out of place at our polite conference. The books were brought, and one minute's look at the pages in which Mrs. Yatman's name figured was enough, and more than enough, to prove the truth of every word that I had spoken.

There, in one book, was the husband's account which Mr. Yatman had settled; and there, in the other, was the private account, crossed off also, the date of settlement being the very day after the loss of the cash-box. This said private account amounted to the sum of a hundred and seventy-five pounds, odd shillings, and it extended over a period of three years. Not a single instalment had been paid on it. Under the last line was an entry to this effect: 'Written to for the third time, June 23rd.' I pointed to it, and asked the milliner if that meant 'last June.' Yes, it did mean last June; and she now deeply regretted to say that it had been accompanied by a threat of legal proceedings.

"I thought you gave good customers more than three years' credit?" says I.

The milliner looks at Mr. Yatman, and whispers to me, "Not when a lady's husband gets into difficulties."

She pointed to the account as she spoke. The entries after the time when Mr. Yatman's circumstances became involved were just as extravagant, for a person in his wife's situation, as the entries for the year before that period. If the lady had economized in other things, she had certainly not economized in the matter of dress.

There was nothing left now but to examine the cash-book, for form's sake. The money had been paid in notes, the amounts and numbers of which exactly tallied with the figures set down in my list.

After that, I thought it best to get Mr. Yatman out of the house immediately. He was in such a pitiable condition that I called a cab and accompanied him home in it. At first he cried and raved like a child; but I soon quieted him; and I must add, to his credit, that he made me a most handsome apology for his language as the cab drew up at his house door. In return, I tried to give him some advice about how to set matters right for the future with his wife. He paid very little attention to me, and went upstairs muttering to himself about a separation. Whether Mrs. Yatman will come cleverly out of the scrape or not seems doubtful. I should say myself that she would go into screeching hysterics, and so frighten the poor man into forgiving her. But this is no business of ours. So far as we are concerned, the case is now at an end, and the present report may come to a conclusion along with it.

I remain, accordingly, yours to command,

THOMAS BULMER.

P.S. – I have to add that, on leaving Rutherford Street, I met Mr. Matthew Sharpin coming to pack up his things.

"Only think!" says he, rubbing his hands in great spirits, "I've been to the genteel villa residence, and the moment I mentioned my business they kicked me out directly. There were two witnesses of the assault, and it's worth a hundred pounds to me if it's worth a farthing."

"I wish you joy of your luck," says I.

"Thank you," says he. "When may I pay you the same compliment on finding the thief?"

"Whenever you like," says I, "for the thief is found."

"Just what I expected," says he. "I've done all the work, and now you cut in and claim all the credit – Mr. Jay, of course."

"No," says I.

"Who is it then?" says he.

"Ask Mrs. Yatman," says I. "She's waiting to tell you."

"All right! I'd much rather hear it from that charming woman than from you," says he, and goes into the house in a mighty hurry.

What do you think of that, Inspector Theakstone? Would you like to stand in Mr. Sharpin's shoes? I shouldn't, I can promise you.

FROM CHIEF INSPECTOR THEAKSTONE TO MR. MATTHEW SHARPIN.

July 12th.

SIR,

Sergeant Bulmer has already told you to consider yourself suspended until further notice. I have now authority to add that your services as a member of the Detective Police are positively declined. You will please to take this letter as notifying officially your dismissal from the force.

I may inform you, privately, that your rejection is not intended to cast any reflections on your character. It merely implies that you are not quite sharp enough for our purposes. If we *are* to have a new recruit among us, we should infinitely prefer Mrs. Yatman.

Your obedient servant,

FRANCIS THEAKSTONE.

NOTE ON THE PRECEDING CORRESPONDENCE, ADDED BY MR. THEAKSTONE.

The inspector is not in a position to append any explanations of importance to the last of the letters. It has been discovered that Mr. Matthew Sharpin left the house in Rutherford Street five minutes after his interview outside of it with Sergeant Bulmer, his manner expressing the liveliest emotions of terror and astonishment, and his left cheek displaying a bright patch of red, which looked as if it might have been the result of what is popularly termed a smart box on the ear. He was also heard by the shopman at Rutherford Street to use a very shocking expression in reference to Mrs. Yatman, and was seen to clinch his fist vindictively as he ran round the corner of the street. Nothing more has been heard of him; and it is conjectured that he has left London with the intention of offering his valuable services to the provincial police.

On the interesting domestic subject of Mr. and Mrs. Yatman still less is known. It has, however, been positively ascertained that the medical attendant of the family was sent for in a great hurry on the day when Mr. Yatman returned from the milliner's shop. The neighbouring chemist received, soon afterward, a prescription of a soothing nature to make up for Mrs. Yatman. The day after, Mr. Yatman purchased some smelling-salts at the shop, and afterward appeared at the circulating library to ask for a novel descriptive of high life that would amuse an invalid lady. It has been inferred from these circumstances that he has not thought it desirable to carry out his threat of separating from his wife, at least in the present (presumed) condition of that lady's sensitive nervous system.

In the Fog

Richard Harding Davis

Chapter I

THE GRILL is the club most difficult of access in the world. To be placed on its rolls distinguishes the new member as greatly as though he had received a vacant Garter or had been caricatured in *Vanity Fair*.

Men who belong to the Grill Club never mention that fact. If you were to ask one of them which clubs he frequents, he will name all save that particular one. He is afraid if he told you he belonged to the Grill, that it would sound like boasting.

The Grill Club dates back to the days when Shakespeare's Theatre stood on the present site of the *Times* office. It has a golden Grill which Charles the Second presented to the Club, and the original manuscript of 'Tom and Jerry in London,' which was bequeathed to it by Pierce Egan himself. The members, when they write letters at the Club, still use sand to blot the ink.

The Grill enjoys the distinction of having blackballed, without political prejudice, a Prime Minister of each party. At the same sitting at which one of these fell, it elected, on account of his brogue and his bulls, Quiller, Q. C., who was then a penniless barrister.

When Paul Preval, the French artist who came to London by royal command to paint a portrait of the Prince of Wales, was made an honorary member – only foreigners may be honorary members – he said, as he signed his first wine card, "I would rather see my name on that, than on a picture in the Louvre."

At which Quiller remarked, "That is a devil of a compliment, because the only men who can read their names in the Louvre today have been dead fifty years."

On the night after the great fog of 1897 there were five members in the Club, four of them busy with supper and one reading in front of the fireplace. There is only one room to the Club, and one long table. At the far end of the room the fire of the grill glows red, and, when the fat falls, blazes into flame, and at the other there is a broad bow window of diamond panes, which looks down upon the street. The four men at the table were strangers to each other, but as they picked at the grilled bones, and sipped their Scotch and soda, they conversed with such charming animation that a visitor to the Club, which does not tolerate visitors, would have counted them as friends of long acquaintance, certainly not as Englishmen who had met for the first time, and without the form of an introduction. But it is the etiquette and tradition of the Grill, that whoever enters it must speak with whomever he finds there. It is to enforce this rule that there is but one long table, and whether there are twenty men at it or two, the waiters, supporting the rule, will place them side-by-side.

For this reason the four strangers at supper were seated together, with the candles grouped about them, and the long length of the table cutting a white path through the outer gloom.

"I repeat," said the gentleman with the black pearl stud, "that the days for romantic adventure and deeds of foolish daring have passed, and that the fault lies with ourselves. Voyages to the pole I do not catalogue as adventures. That African explorer, young Chetney, who turned up yesterday after he was supposed to have died in Uganda, did nothing adventurous. He made maps and explored the sources of rivers. He was in constant danger, but the presence of danger does not constitute adventure. Were that so, the chemist who studies high explosives, or who investigates deadly poisons, passes through adventures daily. No, 'adventures are for the adventurous.' But one no longer ventures. The spirit of it has died of inertia. We are grown too practical, too just, above all, too sensible. In this room, for instance, members of this Club have, at the sword's point, disputed the proper scanning of one of Pope's couplets. Over so weighty a matter as spilled Burgundy on a gentleman's cuff, ten men fought across this table, each with his rapier in one hand and a candle in the other. All ten were wounded. The question of the spilled Burgundy concerned but two of them. The eight others engaged because they were men of 'spirit.' They were, indeed, the first gentlemen of the day. Tonight, were you to spill Burgundy on my cuff, were you even to insult me grossly, these gentlemen would not consider it incumbent upon them to kill each other. They would separate us, and tomorrow morning appear as witnesses against us at Bow Street. We have here tonight, in the persons of Sir Andrew and myself, an illustration of how the ways have changed."

The men around the table turned and glanced toward the gentleman in front of the fireplace. He was an elderly and somewhat portly person, with a kindly, wrinkled countenance, which wore continually a smile of almost childish confidence and good-nature. It was a face which the illustrated prints had made intimately familiar. He held a book from him at arm's-length, as if to adjust his eyesight, and his brows were knit with interest.

"Now, were this the eighteenth century," continued the gentleman with the black pearl, "when Sir Andrew left the Club tonight I would have him bound and gagged and thrown into a sedan chair. The watch would not interfere, the passers-by would take to their heels, my hired bullies and ruffians would convey him to some lonely spot where we would guard him until morning. Nothing would come of it, except added reputation to myself as a gentleman of adventurous spirit, and possibly an essay in the *Tatler*, with stars for names, entitled, let us say, 'The Budget and the Baronet.' '

"But to what end, sir?" inquired the youngest of the members. "And why Sir Andrew, of all persons – why should you select him for this adventure?"

The gentleman with the black pearl shrugged his shoulders.

"It would prevent him speaking in the House tonight. The Navy Increase Bill," he added gloomily. "It is a Government measure, and Sir Andrew speaks for it. And so great is his influence and so large his following that if he does" – the gentleman laughed ruefully – "if he does, it will go through. Now, had I the spirit of our ancestors," he exclaimed, "I would bring chloroform from the nearest chemist's and drug him in that chair. I would tumble his unconscious form into a hansom cab, and hold him prisoner until daylight. If I did, I would save the British taxpayer the cost of five more battleships, many millions of pounds."

The gentlemen again turned, and surveyed the baronet with freshened interest. The honorary member of the Grill, whose accent already had betrayed him as an American, laughed softly.

"To look at him now," he said, "one would not guess he was deeply concerned with the affairs of state."

The others nodded silently.

"He has not lifted his eyes from that book since we first entered," added the youngest member. "He surely cannot mean to speak tonight."

"Oh, yes, he will speak," muttered the one with the black pearl moodily. "During these last hours of the session the House sits late, but when the Navy bill comes up on its third reading he will be in his place – and he will pass it."

The fourth member, a stout and florid gentleman of a somewhat sporting appearance, in a short smoking-jacket and black tie, sighed enviously.

"Fancy one of us being as cool as that, if he knew he had to stand up within an hour and rattle off a speech in Parliament. I'd be in a devil of a funk myself. And yet he is as keen over that book he's reading as though he had nothing before him until bedtime."

"Yes, see how eager he is," whispered the youngest member. "He does not lift his eyes even now when he cuts the pages. It is probably an Admiralty Report, or some other weighty work of statistics which bears upon his speech."

The gentleman with the black pearl laughed morosely.

"The weighty work in which the eminent statesman is so deeply engrossed," he said, "is called 'The Great Rand Robbery.' It is a detective novel, for sale at all bookstalls."

The American raised his eyebrows in disbelief.

" 'The Great Rand Robbery'?" he repeated incredulously. "What an odd taste!"

"It is not a taste, it is his vice," returned the gentleman with the pearl stud. "It is his one dissipation. He is noted for it. You, as a stranger, could hardly be expected to know of this idiosyncrasy. Mr. Gladstone sought relaxation in the Greek poets, Sir Andrew finds his in Gaboriau. Since I have been a Member of Parliament I have never seen him in the library without a shilling shocker in his hands. He brings them even into the sacred precincts of the House, and from the Government benches reads them concealed inside his hat. Once started on a tale of murder, robbery, and sudden death, nothing can tear him from it, not even the call of the division bell, nor of hunger, nor the prayers of the party Whip. He gave up his country house because when he journeyed to it in the train he would become so absorbed in his detective stories that he was invariably carried past his station." The Member of Parliament twisted his pearl stud nervously, and bit at the edge of his mustache. "If it only were the first pages of 'The Rand Robbery' that he were reading," he murmured bitterly, "instead of the last! With such another book as that, I swear I could hold him here until morning. There would be no need of chloroform to keep him from the House."

The eyes of all were fastened upon Sir Andrew, and each saw with fascination that with his forefinger he was now separating the last two pages of the book. The Member of Parliament struck the table softly with his open palm.

"I would give a hundred pounds," he whispered, "if I could place in his hands at this moment a new story of Sherlock Holmes – a thousand pounds," he added wildly – "five thousand pounds!"

The American observed the speaker sharply, as though the words bore to him some special application, and then at an idea which apparently had but just come to him, smiled in great embarrassment.

Sir Andrew ceased reading, but, as though still under the influence of the book, sat looking blankly into the open fire. For a brief space no one moved until the baronet withdrew his eyes and, with a sudden start of recollection, felt anxiously for his watch. He scanned its face eagerly, and scrambled to his feet.

The voice of the American instantly broke the silence in a high, nervous accent.

"And yet Sherlock Holmes himself," he cried, "could not decipher the mystery which tonight baffles the police of London."

At these unexpected words, which carried in them something of the tone of a challenge, the gentlemen about the table started as suddenly as though the American had fired a pistol in the air, and Sir Andrew halted abruptly and stood observing him with grave surprise.

The gentleman with the black pearl was the first to recover.

"Yes, yes," he said eagerly, throwing himself across the table. "A mystery that baffles the police of London."

"I have heard nothing of it. Tell us at once, pray do – tell us at once."

The American flushed uncomfortably, and picked uneasily at the tablecloth.

"No one but the police has heard of it," he murmured, "and they only through me. It is a remarkable crime, to, which, unfortunately, I am the only person who can bear witness. Because I am the only witness, I am, in spite of my immunity as a diplomat, detained in London by the authorities of Scotland Yard. My name," he said, inclining his head politely, "is Sears, Lieutenant Ripley Sears of the United States Navy, at present Naval Attaché to the Court of Russia. Had I not been detained today by the police I would have started this morning for Petersburg."

The gentleman with the black pearl interrupted with so pronounced an exclamation of excitement and delight that the American stammered and ceased speaking.

"Do you hear, Sir Andrew!" cried the Member of Parliament jubilantly. "An American diplomat halted by our police because he is the only witness of a most remarkable crime – *the* most remarkable crime, I believe you said, sir," he added, bending eagerly toward the naval officer, "which has occurred in London in many years."

The American moved his head in assent and glanced at the two other members. They were looking doubtfully at him, and the face of each showed that he was greatly perplexed.

Sir Andrew advanced to within the light of the candles and drew a chair toward him.

"The crime must be exceptional indeed," he said, "to justify the police in interfering with a representative of a friendly power. If I were not forced to leave at once, I should take the liberty of asking you to tell us the details."

The gentleman with the pearl pushed the chair toward Sir Andrew, and motioned him to be seated.

"You cannot leave us now," he exclaimed. "Mr. Sears is just about to tell us of this remarkable crime."

He nodded vigorously at the naval officer and the American, after first glancing doubtfully toward the servants at the far end of the room, leaned forward across the table. The others drew their chairs nearer and bent toward him. The baronet glanced irresolutely at his watch, and with an exclamation of annoyance snapped down the lid. "They can wait," he muttered. He seated himself quickly and nodded at Lieutenant Sears.

"If you will be so kind as to begin, sir," he said impatiently.

"Of course," said the American, "you understand that I understand that I am speaking to gentlemen. The confidences of this Club are inviolate. Until the police give the facts to the public press, I must consider you my confederates. You have heard nothing, you know no one connected with this mystery. Even I must remain anonymous."

The gentlemen seated around him nodded gravely.

"Of course," the baronet assented with eagerness, "of course."

"We will refer to it," said the gentleman with the black pearl, "as 'The Story of the Naval Attaché.' "

"I arrived in London two days ago," said the American, "and I engaged a room at the Bath Hotel. I know very few people in London, and even the members of our embassy were strangers to me. But in Hong Kong I had become great pals with an officer in your navy, who has since retired, and who is now living in a small house in Rutland Gardens opposite the Knightsbridge barracks. I telegraphed him that I was in London, and yesterday morning I received a most hearty invitation to dine with him the same evening at his house. He is a bachelor, so we dined alone and talked over all our old days on the Asiatic Station, and of the changes which had come to us since we had last met there. As I was leaving the next morning for my post at Petersburg, and had many letters to write, I told him, about ten o'clock, that I must get back to the hotel, and he sent out his servant to call a hansom.

"For the next quarter of an hour, as we sat talking, we could hear the cab whistle sounding violently from the doorstep, but apparently with no result.

" 'It cannot be that the cabmen are on strike,' my friend said, as he rose and walked to the window.

"He pulled back the curtains and at once called to me.

" 'You have never seen a London fog, have you?' he asked. 'Well, come here. This is one of the best, or, rather, one of the worst, of them.' I joined him at the window, but I could see nothing. Had I not known that the house looked out upon the street I would have believed that I was facing a dead wall. I raised the sash and stretched out my head, but still I could see nothing. Even the light of the street lamps opposite, and in the upper windows of the barracks, had been smothered in the yellow mist. The lights of the room in which I stood penetrated the fog only to the distance of a few inches from my eyes.

"Below me the servant was still sounding his whistle, but I could afford to wait no longer, and told my friend that I would try and find the way to my hotel on foot. He objected, but the letters I had to write were for the Navy Department, and, besides, I had always heard that to be out in a London fog was the most wonderful experience, and I was curious to investigate one for myself.

"My friend went with me to his front door, and laid down a course for me to follow. I was first to walk straight across the street to the brick wall of the Knightsbridge Barracks. I was then to feel my way along the wall until I came to a row of houses set back from the sidewalk. They would bring me to a cross street. On the other side of this street was a row of shops which I was to follow until they joined the iron railings of Hyde Park. I was to keep to the railings until I reached the gates at Hyde Park Corner, where I was to lay a diagonal course across Piccadilly, and tack in toward the railings of Green Park. At the end of these railings, going east, I would find the Walsingham, and my own hotel.

"To a sailor the course did not seem difficult, so I bade my friend goodnight and walked forward until my feet touched the paving. I continued upon it until I reached the curbing of the sidewalk. A few steps further, and my hands struck the wall of the barracks. I turned in the direction from which I had just come, and saw a square of faint light cut in the yellow fog. I shouted 'All right,' and the voice of my friend answered, 'Good luck to you.' The light from his open door disappeared with a bang, and I was left alone in a dripping, yellow darkness. I have been in the Navy for ten years, but I have never known such a fog as that of last night, not even among the icebergs of Behring Sea. There one at least could see the light of the binnacle, but last night I could not even distinguish the hand by which I guided myself along the barrack wall. At sea a fog is a natural phenomenon. It is as familiar as the rainbow which follows a storm, it is as proper that a fog should spread upon the waters as that steam shall rise from a kettle. But a fog which springs from the paved streets, that rolls between solid house-fronts, that forces cabs to move at half speed, that drowns policemen and extinguishes the electric lights of the music hall, that to me is incomprehensible. It is as out of place as a tidal wave on Broadway.

"As I felt my way along the wall, I encountered other men who were coming from the opposite direction, and each time when we hailed each other I stepped away from the wall to make room for them to pass. But the third time I did this, when I reached out my hand, the wall had disappeared, and the further I moved to find it the further I seemed to be sinking into space. I had the unpleasant conviction that at any moment I might step over a precipice. Since I had set out I had heard no traffic in the street, and now, although I listened some minutes, I could only distinguish the occasional footfalls of pedestrians. Several times I called aloud, and once a jocular gentleman answered me, but only to ask me where I thought he was, and then even he was swallowed up in the silence. Just above me I could make out a jet of gas which I guessed came from a street lamp, and I moved over to that, and, while I tried to recover my bearings, kept my hand on the iron post. Except for this flicker of gas, no larger than the tip of my finger, I could distinguish nothing about me. For the rest, the mist hung between me and the world like a damp and heavy blanket.

"I could hear voices, but I could not tell from whence they came, and the scrape of a foot moving cautiously, or a muffled cry as some one stumbled, were the only sounds that reached me.

"I decided that until some one took me in tow I had best remain where I was, and it must have been for ten minutes that I waited by the lamp, straining my ears and hailing distant footfalls. In a house near me some people were dancing to the music of a Hungarian band. I even fancied I could hear the windows shake to the rhythm of their feet, but I could not make out from which part of the compass the sounds came. And sometimes, as the music rose, it seemed close at my hand, and again, to be floating high in the air above my head. Although I was surrounded by thousands of householders – 13 – I was as completely lost as though I had been set down by night in the Sahara Desert. There seemed to be no reason in waiting longer for an escort, so I again set out, and at once bumped against a low iron fence. At first I believed this to be an area railing, but on following it I found that it stretched for a long distance, and that it was pierced at regular intervals with gates. I was standing uncertainly with my hand on one of these when a square of light suddenly opened in the night, and in it I saw, as you see a picture thrown by a biograph in a darkened theatre, a young gentleman in evening dress, and back of him the lights of a hall. I guessed from its elevation and distance from the side-walk that this light must come from the door of a house set back from the street, and I determined to approach it and ask the young man to tell me where I was. But in fumbling with the lock of the gate I instinctively bent my head, and when I raised it again the door had partly closed, leaving only a narrow shaft of light. Whether the young man had re-entered the house, or had left it I could not tell, but I hastened to open the gate, and as I stepped forward I found myself upon an asphalt walk. At the same instant there was the sound of quick steps upon the path, and some one rushed past me. I called to him, but he made no reply, and I heard the gate click and the footsteps hurrying away upon the sidewalk.

"Under other circumstances the young man's rudeness, and his recklessness in dashing so hurriedly through the mist, would have struck me as peculiar, but everything was so distorted by the fog that at the moment I did not consider it. The door was still as he had left it, partly open. I went up the path, and, after much fumbling, found the knob of the door-bell and gave it a sharp pull. The bell answered me from a great depth and distance, but no movement followed from inside the house, and although I pulled the bell again and again I could hear nothing save the dripping of the mist about me. I was anxious to be on my way, but unless I knew where I was going there was little chance of my making any speed, and I was determined that until I learned my bearings I would not venture back into the fog. So I pushed the door open and stepped into the house.

"I found myself in a long and narrow hall, upon which doors opened from either side. At the end of the hall was a staircase with a balustrade which ended in a sweeping curve. The balustrade was covered with heavy Persian rugs, and the walls of the hall were also hung with them. The door on my left was closed, but the one nearer me on the right was open, and as I stepped opposite to it I saw that it was a sort of reception or waiting-room, and that it was empty. The door below it was also open, and with the idea that I would surely find some one there, I walked on up the hall. I was in evening dress, and I felt I did not look like a burglar, so I had no great fear that, should I encounter one of the inmates of the house, he would shoot me on sight. The second door in the hall opened into a dining-room. This was also empty. One person had been dining at the table, but the cloth had not been cleared away, and a nickering candle showed half-filled wineglasses and the ashes of cigarettes. The greater part of the room was in complete darkness.

"By this time I had grown conscious of the fact that I was wandering about in a strange house, and that, apparently, I was alone in it. The silence of the place began to try my nerves, and in a sudden, unexplainable panic I started for the open street. But as I turned, I saw a man sitting on a bench, which the curve of the balustrade had hidden from me. His eyes were shut, and he was sleeping soundly.

"The moment before I had been bewildered because I could see no one, but at sight of this man I was much more bewildered.

"He was a very large man, a giant in height, with long yellow hair which hung below his shoulders. He was dressed in a red silk shirt that was belted at the waist and hung outside black velvet trousers which, in turn, were stuffed into high black boots. I recognized the costume at once as that of a Russian servant, but what a Russian servant in his native livery could be doing in a private house in Knightsbridge was incomprehensible.

"I advanced and touched the man on the shoulder, and after an effort he awoke, and, on seeing me, sprang to his feet and began bowing rapidly and making deprecatory gestures. I had picked up enough Russian in Petersburg to make out that the man was apologizing for having fallen asleep, and I also was able to explain to him that I desired to see his master.

"He nodded vigorously, and said, 'Will the Excellency come this way? The Princess is here.'

"I distinctly made out the word 'princess,' and I was a good deal embarrassed. I had thought it would be easy enough to explain my intrusion to a man, but how a woman would look at it was another matter, and as I followed him down the hall I was somewhat puzzled.

"As we advanced, he noticed that the front door was standing open, and with an exclamation of surprise, hastened toward it and closed it. Then he rapped twice on the door of what was apparently the drawing-room. There was no reply to his knock, and he tapped again, and then timidly, and cringing subserviently, opened the door and stepped inside. He withdrew himself at once and stared stupidly at me, shaking his head.

" 'She is not there,' he said. He stood for a moment gazing blankly through the open door, and then hastened toward the dining-room. The solitary candle which still burned there seemed to assure him that the room also was empty. He came back and bowed me toward the drawing-room. 'She is above,' he said; 'I will inform the Princess of the Excellency's presence.'

"Before I could stop him he had turned and was running up the staircase, leaving me alone at the open door of the drawing-room. I decided that the adventure had gone quite far enough, and if I had been able to explain to the Russian that I had lost my way in the fog, and only wanted to get back into the street again, I would have left the house on the instant.

"Of course, when I first rang the bell of the house I had no other expectation than that it would be answered by a parlor-maid who would direct me on my way. I certainly could not then foresee that I would disturb a Russian princess in her boudoir, or that I might be thrown out by her athletic bodyguard. Still, I thought I ought not now to leave the house without making some apology, and, if the worst should come, I could show my card. They could hardly believe that a member of an Embassy had any designs upon the hat-rack.

"The room in which I stood was dimly lighted, but I could see that, like the hall, it was hung with heavy Persian rugs. The corners were filled with palms, and there was the unmistakable odor in the air of Russian cigarettes, and strange, dry scents that carried me back to the bazaars of Vladivostock. Near the front windows was a grand piano, and at the other end of the room a heavily carved screen of some black wood, picked out with ivory. The screen was overhung with a canopy of silken draperies, and formed a sort of alcove. In front of the alcove was spread the white skin of a polar bear, and set on that was one of those low Turkish coffee tables. It held a lighted spirit-lamp and two gold coffee cups. I had heard no movement from above stairs, and it must have been fully three minutes that I stood waiting, noting these details of the room and wondering at the delay, and at the strange silence.

"And then, suddenly, as my eye grew more used to the half-light, I saw, projecting from behind the screen as though it were stretched along the back of a divan, the hand of a man and the lower part of his arm. I was as startled as though I had come across a footprint on a deserted island. Evidently the man had been sitting there since I had come into the room, even since I had entered the house, and he had heard the servant knocking upon the door. Why he had not declared himself I could not understand, but I supposed that possibly he was a guest, with no reason to interest himself in the Princess's other visitors, or perhaps, for some reason, he did not wish to be observed. I could see nothing of him except his hand, but I had an unpleasant feeling that he had been peering at me through the carving in the screen, and that he still was doing so. I moved my feet noisily on the floor and said tentatively, 'I beg your pardon.'

"There was no reply, and the hand did not stir. Apparently the man was bent upon ignoring me, but as all I wished was to apologize for my intrusion and to leave the house, I walked up to the alcove and peered around it. Inside the screen was a divan piled with cushions, and on the end of it nearer me the man was sitting. He was a young Englishman with light yellow hair and a deeply bronzed face.

"He was seated with his arms stretched out along the back of the divan, and with his head resting against a cushion. His attitude was one of complete ease. But his mouth had fallen open, and his eyes were set with an expression of utter horror. At the first glance I saw that he was quite dead.

"For a flash of time I was too startled to act, but in the same flash I was convinced that the man had met his death from no accident, that he had not died through any ordinary failure of the laws of nature. The expression on his face was much too terrible to be misinterpreted. It spoke as eloquently as words. It told me that before the end had come he had watched his death approach and threaten him.

"I was so sure he had been murdered that I instinctively looked on the floor for the weapon, and, at the same moment, out of concern for my own safety, quickly behind me; but the silence of the house continued unbroken.

"I have seen a great number of dead men; I was on the Asiatic Station during the Japanese-Chinese war. I was in Port Arthur after the massacre. So a dead man, for the single reason that he is dead, does not repel me, and, though I knew that there was no hope that this man was alive, still for decency's sake, I felt his pulse, and while I kept my ears alert for any sound from the floors above me, I pulled open his shirt and placed my hand upon his heart. My fingers instantly touched upon the opening of a wound, and as I withdrew them I found them wet with blood. He was in evening dress, and in the wide bosom of his shirt I found a narrow slit, so narrow that in the dim light it was scarcely discernable. The wound was no wider than the smallest blade of a pocket-knife, but when I stripped the shirt away from the chest and left it bare, I found that the weapon, narrow as it was, had been long enough to reach his heart. There is no need to tell you how I felt as I stood by the body of this boy, for he was hardly older than a boy, or of the thoughts that came into my head. I was bitterly sorry for this stranger, bitterly indignant at his murderer, and, at the same time, selfishly concerned for my own safety and for the notoriety which I saw was sure to follow. My instinct was to leave the body where it lay, and to hide myself in the fog, but I also felt that since a succession of accidents had made me the only witness to a crime, my duty was to make myself a good witness and to assist to establish the facts of this murder.

"That it might possibly be a suicide, and not a murder, did not disturb me for a moment. The fact that the weapon had disappeared, and the expression on the boy's face were enough to convince, at least me, that he had had no hand in his own death. I judged it, therefore, of the first importance to discover who was in the house, or, if they had escaped from it, who had been in the house before I entered it. I had seen one man leave it; but all I could tell of him was that he was a young man, that he was in evening dress, and that he had fled in such haste that he had not stopped to close the door behind him.

"The Russian servant I had found apparently asleep, and, unless he acted a part with supreme skill, he was a stupid and ignorant boor, and as innocent of the murder as myself. There was still the Russian princess whom he had expected to find, or had pretended to expect to find, in the same room with the murdered man. I judged that she must now be either upstairs with the servant, or that she had, without his knowledge, already fled from the house. When I recalled his apparently genuine surprise at not finding her in the drawing-room, this latter supposition seemed the more probable. Nevertheless, I decided that it was my duty to make a search, and after a second hurried look for the weapon among the cushions of the divan, and upon the floor, I cautiously crossed the hall and entered the dining-room.

"The single candle was still flickering in the draught, and showed only the white cloth. The rest of the room was draped in shadows. I picked up the candle, and, lifting it high above my head, moved around the corner of the table. Either my nerves were on such a stretch that no shock could strain them further, or my mind was inoculated to horrors, for I did not cry out at what I saw nor retreat from it. Immediately at my feet was the body of a beautiful woman, lying at full length upon the floor, her arms flung out on either side of her, and her white face and shoulders gleaming dully in the unsteady light of the candle. Around her throat was a great chain of diamonds, and the light played upon these and made them flash and blaze in tiny flames. But the woman who wore them was dead, and I was so certain as to how she had died that without an instant's hesitation I dropped on my knees beside her and placed my hands above her heart. My fingers again touched the thin slit of a wound. I had no doubt in my mind but that this was the Russian princess, and when I lowered the candle to her face I was assured that this was so. Her features showed the finest lines of both the Slav and the Jewess; the eyes were black, the hair blue-black and wonderfully heavy, and her skin, even in death, was rich in color. She was a surpassingly beautiful woman.

"I rose and tried to light another candle with the one I held, but I found that my hand was so unsteady that I could not keep the wicks together. It was my intention to again search for this strange dagger which had been used to kill both the English boy and the beautiful princess, but before I could light the second candle I heard footsteps descending the stairs, and the Russian servant appeared in the doorway.

"My face was in darkness, or I am sure that at the sight of it he would have taken alarm, for at that moment I was not sure but that this man himself was the murderer. His own face was plainly visible to me in the light from the hall, and I could see that it wore an expression of dull bewilderment. I stepped quickly toward him and took a firm hold upon his wrist.

" 'She is not there,' he said. 'The Princess has gone. They have all gone.'

" 'Who have gone?' I demanded. 'Who else has been here?'

" 'The two Englishmen,' he said.

" 'What two Englishmen?' I demanded. 'What are their names?'

"The man now saw by my manner that some question of great moment hung upon his answer, and he began to protest that he did not know the names of the visitors and that until that evening he had never seen them.

"I guessed that it was my tone which frightened him, so I took my hand off his wrist and spoke less eagerly.

" 'How long have they been here?' I asked, 'and when did they go?'

"He pointed behind him toward the drawing-room.

" 'One sat there with the Princess,' he said; 'the other came after I had placed the coffee in the drawing-room. The two Englishmen talked together and the Princess returned here to the table. She sat there in that chair, and I brought her cognac and cigarettes. Then I sat outside upon the bench. It was a feast day, and I had been drinking. Pardon, Excellency, but I fell asleep. When I woke, your Excellency was standing by me, but the Princess and the two Englishmen had gone. That is all I know.'

"I believed that the man was telling me the truth. His fright had passed, and he was now apparently puzzled, but not alarmed.

" 'You must remember the names of the Englishmen,' I urged. 'Try to think. When you announced them to the Princess what name did you give?'

"At this question he exclaimed with pleasure, and, beckoning to me, ran hurriedly down the hall and into the drawing-room. In the corner furthest from the screen was the piano, and on it was a silver tray. He picked this up and, smiling with pride at his own intelligence, pointed at two cards that lay upon it. I took them up and read the names engraved upon them."

The American paused abruptly, and glanced at the faces about him. "I read the names," he repeated. He spoke with great reluctance.

"Continue!" cried the Baronet, sharply.

"I read the names," said the American with evident distaste, "and the family name of each was the same. They were the names of two brothers. One is well known to you. It is that of the African explorer of whom this gentleman was just speaking. I mean the Earl of Chetney. The other was the name of his brother, Lord Arthur Chetney."

The men at the table fell back as though a trapdoor had fallen open at their feet.

"Lord Chetney!" they exclaimed in chorus. They glanced at each other and back to the American with every expression of concern and disbelief.

"It is impossible!" cried the Baronet. "Why, my dear sir, young Chetney only arrived from Africa yesterday. It was so stated in the evening papers."

The jaw of the American set in a resolute square, and he pressed his lips together.

"You are perfectly right, sir," he said, "Lord Chetney did arrive in London yesterday morning, and yesterday night I found his dead body."

The youngest member present was the first to recover. He seemed much less concerned over the identity of the murdered man than at the interruption of the narrative.

"Oh, please let him go on!" he cried. "What happened then? You say you found two visiting cards. How do you know which card was that of the murdered man?"

The American, before he answered, waited until the chorus of exclamations had ceased. Then he continued as though he had not been interrupted.

"The instant I read the names upon the cards," he said, "I ran to the screen and, kneeling beside the dead man, began a search through his pockets. My hand at once fell upon a card-case, and I found on all the cards it contained the title of the Earl of Chetney. His watch and cigarette-case also bore his name. These evidences, and the fact of his bronzed skin, and that his cheekbones were worn with fever, convinced me that the dead man was the African explorer, and the boy who had fled past me in the night was Arthur, his younger brother.

"I was so intent upon my search that I had forgotten the servant, and I was still on my knees when I heard a cry behind me. I turned, and saw the man gazing down at the body in abject horror.

"Before I could rise, he gave another cry of terror, and, flinging himself into the hall, raced toward the door to the street. I leaped after him, shouting to him to halt, but before I could reach the hall he had torn open the door, and I saw him spring out into the yellow fog. I cleared the steps in a jump and ran down the garden walk but just as the gate clicked in front of me. I had it open on the instant, and, following the sound of the man's footsteps, I raced after him across the open street. He, also, could hear me, and he instantly stopped running, and there was absolute silence. He was so near that I almost fancied I could hear him panting, and I held my own breath to listen. But I could distinguish nothing but the dripping of the mist about us, and from far off the music of the Hungarian band, which I had heard when I first lost myself.

"All I could see was the square of light from the door I had left open behind me, and a lamp in the hall beyond it flickering in the draught. But even as I watched it, the flame of the lamp was blown violently to and fro, and the door, caught in the same current of air, closed slowly. I knew if it shut I could not again enter the house, and I rushed madly toward it. I believe I even shouted out, as though it were something human which I could compel to obey me, and then I caught my foot against the curb and smashed into the sidewalk. When I rose to my feet I was dizzy and half stunned, and though I thought then that I was moving toward the door, I know now that I probably turned directly from it; for, as I groped about in the night, calling frantically for the police, my fingers touched nothing but the dripping fog, and the iron railings for which I sought seemed to have melted away. For many minutes I beat the mist with my arms like one at blind man's buff, turning sharply in circles, cursing aloud at my stupidity and crying continually for help. At last a voice answered me from the fog, and I found myself held in the circle of a policeman's lantern.

"That is the end of my adventure. What I have to tell you now is what I learned from the police.

"At the station-house to which the man guided me I related what you have just heard. I told them that the house they must at once find was one set back from the street within a radius of two hundred yards from the Knightsbridge Barracks, that within fifty yards of it some one was giving a dance to the music of a Hungarian band, and that the railings before it were as high as a man's waist and filed to a point. With that to work upon, twenty men were at once ordered out into the fog to search for the house, and Inspector Lyle himself was despatched to the home of Lord Edam, Chetney's father, with a warrant for Lord Arthur's arrest. I was thanked and dismissed on my own recognizance.

"This morning, Inspector Lyle called on me, and from him I learned the police theory of the scene I have just described.

"Apparently I had wandered very far in the fog, for up to noon today the house had not been found, nor had they been able to arrest Lord Arthur. He did not return to his father's house last night, and there is no trace of him; but from what the police knew of the past lives of the people I found in that lost house, they have evolved a theory, and their theory is that the murders were committed by Lord Arthur.

"The infatuation of his elder brother, Lord Chetney, for a Russian princess, so Inspector Lyle tells me, is well known to every one. About two years ago the Princess Zichy, as she calls herself, and he were constantly together, and Chetney informed his friends that they were about to be married. The woman was notorious in two continents, and when Lord Edam heard of his son's infatuation he appealed to the police for her record.

"It is through his having applied to them that they know so much concerning her and her relations with the Chetneys. From the police Lord Edam learned that Madame Zichy had once been a spy in the employ of the Russian Third Section, but that lately she had been repudiated by her own government and was living by her wits, by blackmail, and by her beauty. Lord Edam laid this record before his son, but Chetney either knew it already or the woman persuaded him not to believe in it, and the father and son parted in great anger. Two days later the marquis altered his will, leaving all of his money to the younger brother, Arthur.

"The title and some of the landed property he could not keep from Chetney, but he swore if his son saw the woman again that the will should stand as it was, and he would be left without a penny.

"This was about eighteen months ago, when apparently Chetney tired of the Princess, and suddenly went off to shoot and explore in Central Africa. No word came from him, except that twice he was reported as having died of fever in the jungle, and finally two traders reached the coast who said they had seen his body. This was accepted by all as conclusive, and young Arthur was recognized as the heir to the Edam millions. On the strength of this supposition he at once began to borrow enormous sums from the money lenders. This is of great importance, as the police believe it was these debts which drove him to the murder of his brother. Yesterday, as you know, Lord Chetney suddenly returned from the grave, and it was the fact that for two years he had been considered as dead which lent such importance to his return and which gave rise to those columns of detail concerning him which appeared in all the afternoon papers. But, obviously, during his absence he had not tired of the Princess Zichy, for we know that a few hours after he reached London he sought her out. His brother, who had also learned of his reappearance through the papers, probably suspected which would be the house he would first visit, and followed him there, arriving, so the Russian servant tells us, while the two were at coffee in the drawing-room. The Princess, then, we also learn from the servant, withdrew to the dining-room, leaving the brothers together. What happened one can only guess.

"Lord Arthur knew now that when it was discovered he was no longer the heir, the money-lenders would come down upon him. The police believe that he at once sought out his brother to beg for money to cover the post-obits, but that, considering the sum he needed was several hundreds of thousands of pounds, Chetney refused to give it him. No one knew that Arthur had gone to seek out his brother. They were alone. It is possible, then, that in a passion of disappointment, and crazed with the disgrace which he saw before him, young Arthur made himself the heir beyond further question. The death of his brother would have availed nothing if the woman remained alive. It is then possible that he crossed the hall, and with the same weapon which made him Lord Edam's heir destroyed the solitary witness to the murder. The only other person who could have seen it was sleeping in a drunken stupor, to which fact undoubtedly he owed his life. And yet," concluded the Naval Attaché, leaning forward and marking each word with his finger, "Lord Arthur blundered fatally. In his haste he left the door of the house open, so giving access to the first passer-by, and he forgot that when he entered it he had handed his card to the servant. That piece of paper may yet send him to the gallows. In the mean time he has disappeared completely, and somewhere, in one of the millions of streets of this great capital, in a locked and empty house, lies the body of his brother, and of the woman his brother loved, undiscovered, unburied, and with their murder unavenged."

In the discussion which followed the conclusion of the story of the Naval Attaché the gentleman with the pearl took no part. Instead, he arose, and, beckoning a servant to a far corner of the room, whispered earnestly to him until a sudden movement on the part of Sir Andrew caused him to return hurriedly to the table.

"There are several points in Mr. Sears's story I want explained," he cried. "Be seated, Sir Andrew," he begged. "Let us have the opinion of an expert. I do not care what the police think, I want to know what you think."

But Sir Henry rose reluctantly from his chair.

"I should like nothing better than to discuss this," he said. "But it is most important that I proceed to the House. I should have been there some time ago." He turned toward the servant and directed him to call a hansom.

The gentleman with the pearl stud looked appealingly at the Naval Attaché. "There are surely many details that you have not told us," he urged. "Some you have forgotten."

The Baronet interrupted quickly.

"I trust not," he said, "for I could not possibly stop to hear them."

"The story is finished," declared the Naval Attaché; "until Lord Arthur is arrested or the bodies are found there is nothing more to tell of either Chetney or the Princess Zichy."

"Of Lord Chetney perhaps not," interrupted the sporting-looking gentleman with the black tie, "but there'll always be something to tell of the Princess Zichy. I know enough stories about her to fill a book. She was a most remarkable woman." The speaker dropped the end of his cigar into his coffee cup and, taking his case from his pocket, selected a fresh one. As he did so he laughed and held up the case that the others might see it. It was an ordinary cigar-case of well-worn pig-skin, with a silver clasp.

"The only time I ever met her," he said, "she tried to rob me of this."

The Baronet regarded him closely.

"She tried to rob you?" he repeated.

"Tried to rob me of this," continued the gentleman in the black tie, "and of the Czarina's diamonds." His tone was one of mingled admiration and injury.

"The Czarina's diamonds!" exclaimed the Baronet. He glanced quickly and suspiciously at the speaker, and then at the others about the table. But their faces gave evidence of no other emotion than that of ordinary interest.

"Yes, the Czarina's diamonds," repeated the man with the black tie. "It was a necklace of diamonds. I was told to take them to the Russian Ambassador in Paris who was to deliver them at Moscow. I am a Queen's Messenger," he added.

"Oh, I see," exclaimed Sir Andrew in a tone of relief. "And you say that this same Princess Zichy, one of the victims of this double murder, endeavored to rob you of – of – that cigar-case."

"And the Czarina's diamonds," answered the Queen's Messenger imperturbably. "It's not much of a story, but it gives you an idea of the woman's character. The robbery took place between Paris and Marseilles."

The Baronet interrupted him with an abrupt movement. "No, no," he cried, shaking his head in protest. "Do not tempt me. I really cannot listen. I must be at the House in ten minutes."

"I am sorry," said the Queen's Messenger. He turned to those seated about him. "I wonder if the other gentlemen –" he inquired tentatively. There was a chorus of polite murmurs, and the Queen's Messenger, bowing his head in acknowledgment, took a preparatory sip from his glass. At the same moment the servant to whom the man with the black pearl had spoken, slipped a piece of paper into his hand. He glanced at it, frowned, and threw it under the table.

The servant bowed to the Baronet.

"Your hansom is waiting, Sir Andrew," he said.

"The necklace was worth twenty thousand pounds," began the Queen's Messenger. "It was a present from the Queen of England to celebrate –" The Baronet gave an exclamation of angry annoyance.

"Upon my word, this is most provoking," he interrupted. "I really ought not to stay. But I certainly mean to hear this." He turned irritably to the servant. "Tell the hansom to wait," he commanded, and, with an air of a boy who is playing truant, slipped guiltily into his chair.

The gentleman with the black pearl smiled blandly, and rapped upon the table.

"Order, gentlemen," he said. "Order for the story of the Queen's Messenger and the Czarina's diamonds."

Chapter II

"THE NECKLACE was a present from the Queen of England to the Czarina of Russia," began the Queen's Messenger. "It was to celebrate the occasion of the Czar's coronation. Our Foreign Office knew that the Russian Ambassador in Paris was to proceed to Moscow for that ceremony, and I was directed to go to Paris and turn over the necklace to him. But when I reached Paris I found he had not expected me for a week later and was taking a few days' vacation at Nice. His people asked me to leave the necklace with them at the Embassy, but I had been charged to get a receipt for it from the Ambassador himself, so I started at once for Nice The fact that Monte Carlo is not two thousand miles from Nice may have had something to do with making me carry out my instructions so carefully. Now, how the Princess Zichy came to find out about the necklace I don't know, but I can guess. As you have just heard, she was at one time a spy in the service of the Russian government. And after they dismissed her she kept up her acquaintance with many of the Russian agents in London. It is probable that through one of them she learned that the necklace was to be sent to Moscow, and which one of the Queen's Messengers had been detailed to take it there. Still, I doubt if even that knowledge would have helped her if she had not also known something which I supposed no one else in the world knew but myself and one other man. And, curiously enough, the other man was a Queen's Messenger too, and a friend of mine. You must know that up to the time of this robbery I had always concealed my despatches in a manner peculiarly my own. I got the idea from that play called 'A Scrap of Paper.' In it a man wants to hide a certain compromising document. He knows that all his rooms will be secretly searched for it, so he puts it in a torn envelope and sticks it up where any one can see it on his mantel shelf. The result is that the woman who is ransacking the house to find it looks in all the unlikely places, but passes over the scrap of paper that is just under her nose. Sometimes the papers and packages they give us to carry about Europe are of very great value, and sometimes they are special makes of cigarettes, and orders to court dressmakers. Sometimes we know what we are carrying and sometimes we do not. If it is a large sum of money or a treaty, they generally tell us. But, as a rule, we have no knowledge of what the package contains; so, to be on the safe side, we naturally take just as great care of it as though we knew it held the terms of an ultimatum or the crown jewels. As a rule, my confreres carry the official packages in a despatch-box, which is just as obvious as a lady's jewel bag in the hands of her maid. Every one knows they are carrying something of value. They put a premium on dishonesty. Well, after I saw the 'Scrap of Paper' play, I determined to put the government valuables in the most unlikely place that any one would look for them. So I used to hide the documents they gave me inside my riding-boots, and small articles, such as money or jewels, I carried in an old cigar-case. After I took to using my case for that purpose I bought a new one, exactly like it, for my cigars. But to avoid mistakes, I had my initials placed on both sides of the new one, and the moment I touched the case, even in the dark, I could tell which it was by the raised initials.

"No one knew of this except the Queen's Messenger of whom I spoke. We once left Paris together on the Orient Express. I was going to Constantinople and he was to stop off at Vienna. On the journey I told him of my peculiar way of hiding things and showed him my cigar-case. If I recollect rightly, on that trip it held the grand cross of St. Michael and St. George, which the Queen was sending to our Ambassador. The Messenger was very much entertained at my scheme, and some months later when he met the Princess he told her about it as an amusing story. Of course, he had no idea she was a Russian spy. He didn't know anything at all about her, except that she was a very attractive woman.

"It was indiscreet, but he could not possibly have guessed that she could ever make any use of what he told her.

"Later, after the robbery, I remembered that I had informed this young chap of my secret hiding-place, and when I saw him again I questioned him about it. He was greatly distressed, and said he had never seen the importance of the secret. He remembered he had told several people of it, and among others the Princess Zichy. In that way I found out that it was she who had robbed me, and I know that from the moment I left London she was following me and that she knew then that the diamonds were concealed in my cigar-case.

"My train for Nice left Paris at ten in the morning. When I travel at night I generally tell the *chef de gare* that I am a Queen's Messenger, and he gives me a compartment to myself, but in the daytime I take whatever offers. On this morning I had found an empty compartment, and I had tipped the guard to keep every one else out, not from any fear of losing the diamonds, but because I wanted to smoke. He had locked the door, and as the last bell had rung I supposed I was to travel alone, so I began to arrange my traps and make myself comfortable. The diamonds in the cigar-case were in the inside pocket of my waistcoat, and as they made a bulky package, I took them out, intending to put them in my handbag. It is a small satchel like a bookmaker's, or those handbags that couriers carry. I wear it slung from a strap across my shoulder, and, no matter whether I am sitting or walking, it never leaves me.

"I took the cigar-case which held the necklace from my inside pocket and the case which held the cigars out of the satchel, and while I was searching through it for a box of matches I laid the two cases beside me on the seat.

"At that moment the train started, but at the same instant there was a rattle at the lock of the compartment, and a couple of porters lifted and shoved a woman through the door, and hurled her rugs and umbrellas in after her.

"Instinctively I reached for the diamonds. I shoved them quickly into the satchel and, pushing them far down to the bottom of the bag, snapped the spring lock. Then I put the cigars in the pocket of my coat, but with the thought that now that I had a woman as a travelling companion I would probably not be allowed to enjoy them.

"One of her pieces of luggage had fallen at my feet, and a roll of rugs had landed at my side. I thought if I hid the fact that the lady was not welcome, and at once endeavored to be civil, she might permit me to smoke. So I picked her handbag off the floor and asked her where I might place it.

"As I spoke I looked at her for the first time, and saw that she was a most remarkably handsome woman.

"She smiled charmingly and begged me not to disturb myself. Then she arranged her own things about her, and, opening her dressing-bag, took out a gold cigarette case.

" 'Do you object to smoke?' she asked.

"I laughed and assured her I had been in great terror lest she might object to it herself.

" 'If you like cigarettes,' she said, 'will you try some of these? They are rolled especially for my husband in Russia, and they are supposed to be very good.'

"I thanked her, and took one from her case, and I found it so much better than my own that I continued to smoke her cigarettes throughout the rest of the journey. I must say that we got on very well. I judged from the coronet on her cigarette-case, and from her manner, which was quite as well bred as that of any woman I ever met, that she was some one of importance, and though she seemed almost too good looking to be respectable, I determined that she was some *grande dame* who was so assured of her position that she could afford to be unconventional. At first she read her novel, and then she made some comment on the scenery, and finally we began to discuss the current politics of the Continent. She talked of all the cities in Europe, and seemed to know every one worth knowing. But she volunteered nothing about herself except that she frequently made use of the expression, 'When my husband was stationed at Vienna,' or 'When my husband was promoted to Rome.' Once she said to me, 'I have often seen you at Monte Carlo. I saw you when you won the pigeon championship.' I told her that I was not a pigeon shot, and she gave a little start of surprise. 'Oh, I beg your pardon,' she said; 'I thought you were Morton Hamilton, the English champion.' As a matter of fact, I do look like Hamilton, but I know now that her object was to make me think that she had no idea as to who I really was. She needn't have acted at all, for I certainly had no suspicions of her, and was only too pleased to have so charming a companion.

"The one thing that should have made me suspicious was the fact that at every station she made some trivial excuse to get me out of the compartment. She pretended that her maid was travelling back of us in one of the second-class carriages, and kept saying she could not imagine why the woman did not come to look after her, and if the maid did not turn up at the next stop, would I be so very kind as to get out and bring her whatever it was she pretended she wanted.

"I had taken my dressing-case from the rack to get out a novel, and had left it on the seat opposite to mine, and at the end of the compartment farthest from her. And once when I came back from buying her a cup of chocolate, or from some other fool errand, I found her standing at my end of the compartment with both hands on the dressing-bag. She looked at me without so much as winking an eye, and shoved the case carefully into a corner. 'Your bag slipped off on the floor,' she said. 'If you've got any bottles in it, you had better look and see that they're not broken.'

"And I give you my word, I was such an ass that I did open the case and looked all through it. She must have thought I was a Juggins. I get hot all over whenever I remember it. But in spite of my dullness, and her cleverness, she couldn't gain anything by sending me away, because what she wanted was in the handbag and every time she sent me away the handbag went with me.

"After the incident of the dressing-case her manner changed. Either in my absence she had had time to look through it, or, when I was examining it for broken bottles, she had seen everything it held.

"From that moment she must have been certain that the cigar-case, in which she knew I carried the diamonds, was in the bag that was fastened to my body, and from that time on she probably was plotting how to get it from me. Her anxiety became most apparent. She dropped the great lady manner, and her charming condescension went with it. She ceased talking, and, when I spoke, answered me irritably, or at random. No doubt her mind was entirely occupied with her plan. The end of our journey was drawing rapidly nearer, and her time for action was being cut down with the speed of the express train. Even I, unsuspicious as I was, noticed that something was very wrong with her. I really believe that before we reached Marseilles if I had not, through my own stupidity, given her the chance she wanted, she might have stuck a knife in me and rolled me out on the rails. But as it was, I only thought that the long journey had tired her. I suggested that it was a very trying trip, and asked her if she would allow me to offer her some of my cognac.

"She thanked me and said, 'No,' and then suddenly her eyes lighted, and she exclaimed, 'Yes, thank you, if you will be so kind.'

"My flask was in the handbag, and I placed it on my lap and with my thumb slipped back the catch. As I keep my tickets and railroad guide in the bag, I am so constantly opening it that I never bother to lock it, and the fact that it is strapped to me has always been sufficient protection. But I can appreciate now what a satisfaction, and what a torment too, it must have been to that woman when she saw that the bag opened without a key.

"While we were crossing the mountains I had felt rather chilly and had been wearing a light racing coat. But after the lamps were lighted the compartment became very hot and stuffy, and I found the coat uncomfortable. So I stood up, and, after first slipping the strap of the bag over my head, I placed the bag in the seat next me and pulled off the racing coat. I don't blame myself for being careless; the bag was still within reach of my hand, and nothing would have happened if at that exact moment the train had not stopped at Arles. It was the combination of my removing the bag and our entering the station at the same instant which gave the Princess Zichy the chance she wanted to rob me.

"I needn't say that she was clever enough to take it. The train ran into the station at full speed and came to a sudden stop. I had just thrown my coat into the rack, and had reached out my hand for the bag. In another instant I would have had the strap around my shoulder. But at that moment the Princess threw open the door of the compartment and beckoned wildly at the people on the platform. 'Natalie!' she called, 'Natalie! here I am. Come here! This way!' She turned upon me in the greatest excitement. 'My maid!' she cried. 'She is looking for me. She passed the window without seeing me. Go, please, and bring her back.' She continued pointing out of the door and beckoning me with her other hand.

There certainly was something about that woman's tone which made one jump. When she was giving orders you had no chance to think of anything else. So I rushed out on my errand of mercy, and then rushed back again to ask what the maid looked like.

" 'In black,' she answered, rising and blocking the door of the compartment. 'All in black, with a bonnet!'

"The train waited three minutes at Aries, and in that time I suppose I must have rushed up to over twenty women and asked, 'Are you Natalie?' The only reason I wasn't punched with an umbrella or handed over to the police was that they probably thought I was crazy.

"When I jumped back into the compartment the Princess was seated where I had left her, but her eyes were burning with happiness. She placed her hand on my arm almost affectionately, and said in a hysterical way, 'You are very kind to me. I am so sorry to have troubled you.'

"I protested that every woman on the platform was dressed in black.

" 'Indeed I am so sorry,' she said, laughing; and she continued to laugh until she began to breathe so quickly that I thought she was going to faint.

"I can see now that the last part of that journey must have been a terrible half hour for her. She had the cigar-case safe enough, but she knew that she herself was not safe. She understood if I were to open my bag, even at the last minute, and miss the case, I would know positively that she had taken it. I had placed the diamonds in the bag at the very moment she entered the compartment, and no one but our two selves had occupied it since. She knew that when we reached Marseilles she would either be twenty thousand pounds richer than when she left Paris, or that she would go to jail. That was the situation as she must have read it, and I don't envy her her state of mind during that last half hour. It must have been hell.

"I saw that something was wrong, and in my innocence I even wondered if possibly my cognac had not been a little too strong. For she suddenly developed into a most brilliant conversationalist, and applauded and laughed at everything I said, and fired off questions at me like a machine gun, so that I had no time to think of anything but of what she was saying. Whenever I stirred she stopped her chattering and leaned toward me, and watched me like a cat over a mouse-hole. I wondered how I could have considered her an agreeable travelling companion. I thought I would have preferred to be locked in with a lunatic. I don't like to think how she would have acted if I had made a move to examine the bag, but as I had it safely strapped around me again, I did not open it, and I reached Marseilles alive. As we drew into the station she shook hands with me and grinned at me like a Cheshire cat.

" 'I cannot tell you,' she said, 'how much I have to thank you for.' What do you think of that for impudence!

"I offered to put her in a carriage, but she said she must find Natalie, and that she hoped we would meet again at the hotel. So I drove off by myself, wondering who she was, and whether Natalie was not her keeper.

"I had to wait several hours for the train to Nice, and as I wanted to stroll around the city I thought I had better put the diamonds in the safe of the hotel. As soon as I reached my room I locked the door, placed the handbag on the table and opened it. I felt among the things at the top of it, but failed to touch the cigar-case. I shoved my hand in deeper, and stirred the things about, but still I did not reach it. A cold wave swept down my spine, and a sort of emptiness came to the pit of my stomach. Then I turned red-hot, and the sweat sprung out all over me. I wet my lips with my tongue, and said to myself, 'Don't be an ass. Pull yourself together, pull yourself together. Take the things out, one at a time. It's there, of course it's there. Don't be an ass.'

"So I put a brake on my nerves and began very carefully to pick out the things one by one, but after another second I could not stand it, and I rushed across the room and threw out everything on the bed. But the diamonds were not among them. I pulled the things about and tore them open and shuffled and rearranged and sorted them, but it was no use. The cigar-case was gone. I threw everything in the dressing-case out on the floor, although I knew it was useless to look for it there. I knew that I had put it in the bag. I sat down and tried to think. I remembered I had put it in the satchel at Paris just as that woman had entered the compartment, and I had been alone with her ever since, so it was she who had robbed me. But how? It had never left my shoulder. And then I remembered that it had – that I had taken it off when I had changed my coat and for the few moments that I was searching for Natalie. I remembered that the woman had sent me on that goose chase, and that at every other station she had tried to get rid of me on some fool errand.

"I gave a roar like a mad bull, and I jumped down the stairs six steps at a time.

"I demanded at the office if a distinguished lady of title, possibly a Russian, had just entered the hotel.

"As I expected, she had not. I sprang into a cab and inquired at two other hotels, and then I saw the folly of trying to catch her without outside help, and I ordered the fellow to gallop to the office of the Chief of Police. I told my story, and the ass in charge asked me to calm myself, and wanted to take notes. I told him this was no time for taking notes, but for doing something. He got wrathy at that, and I demanded to be taken at once to his Chief. The Chief, he said, was very busy, and could not see me. So I showed him my silver greyhound. In eleven years I had never used it but once before. I stated in pretty vigorous language that I was a Queen's Messenger, and that if the Chief of Police did not see me instantly he would lose his official head. At that the fellow jumped off his high horse and ran with me to his Chief, – a smart young chap, a colonel in the army, and a very intelligent man.

"I explained that I had been robbed in a French railway carriage of a diamond necklace belonging to the Queen of England, which her Majesty was sending as a present to the Czarina of Russia. I pointed out to him that if he succeeded in capturing the thief he would be made for life, and would receive the gratitude of three great powers.

"He wasn't the sort that thinks second thoughts are best. He saw Russian and French decorations sprouting all over his chest, and he hit a bell, and pressed buttons, and yelled out orders like the captain of a penny steamer in a fog. He sent her description to all the city gates, and ordered all cabmen and railway porters to search all trains leaving Marseilles. He ordered all passengers on outgoing vessels to be examined, and telegraphed the proprietors of every hotel and pension to send him a complete list of their guests within the hour. While I was standing there he must have given at least a hundred orders, and sent out enough commissaires, sergeants de ville, gendarmes, bicycle police, and plain-clothes Johnnies to have captured the entire German army. When they had gone he assured me that the woman was as good as arrested already. Indeed, officially, she was arrested; for she had no more chance of escape from Marseilles than from the Chateau D'If.

"He told me to return to my hotel and possess my soul in peace. Within an hour he assured me he would acquaint me with her arrest.

"I thanked him, and complimented him on his energy, and left him. But I didn't share in his confidence. I felt that she was a very clever woman, and a match for any and all of us. It was all very well for him to be jubilant. He had not lost the diamonds, and had everything to gain if he found them; while I, even if I did recover the necklace, would only be where I was before I lost them, and if he did not recover it I was a ruined man. It was an awful facer for me.

I had always prided myself on my record. In eleven years I had never mislaid an envelope, nor missed taking the first train. And now I had failed in the most important mission that had ever been intrusted to me. And it wasn't a thing that could be hushed up, either. It was too conspicuous, too spectacular. It was sure to invite the widest notoriety. I saw myself ridiculed all over the Continent, and perhaps dismissed, even suspected of having taken the thing myself.

"I was walking in front of a lighted cafe, and I felt so sick and miserable that I stopped for a pick-me-up. Then I considered that if I took one drink I would probably, in my present state of mind, not want to stop under twenty, and I decided I had better leave it alone. But my nerves were jumping like a frightened rabbit, and I felt I must have something to quiet them, or I would go crazy. I reached for my cigarette-case, but a cigarette seemed hardly adequate, so I put it back again and took out this cigar-case, in which I keep only the strongest and blackest cigars. I opened it and stuck in my fingers, but instead of a cigar they touched on a thin leather envelope. My heart stood perfectly still. I did not dare to look, but I dug my fingernails into the leather and I felt layers of thin paper, then a layer of cotton, and then they scratched on the facets of the Czarina's diamonds!

"I stumbled as though I had been hit in the face, and fell back into one of the chairs on the sidewalk. I tore off the wrappings and spread out the diamonds on the cafe table; I could not believe they were real. I twisted the necklace between my fingers and crushed it between my palms and tossed it up in the air. I believe I almost kissed it. The women in the cafe stood tip on the chairs to see better, and laughed and screamed, and the people crowded so close around me that the waiters had to form a bodyguard. The proprietor thought there was a fight, and called for the police. I was so happy I didn't care. I laughed, too, and gave the proprietor a five-pound note, and told him to stand every one a drink. Then I tumbled into a fiacre and galloped off to my friend the Chief of Police. I felt very sorry for him. He had been so happy at the chance I gave him, and he was sure to be disappointed when he learned I had sent him off on a false alarm.

"But now that I had found the necklace, I did not want him to find the woman. Indeed, I was most anxious that she should get clear away, for if she were caught the truth would come out, and I was likely to get a sharp reprimand, and sure to be laughed at.

"I could see now how it had happened. In my haste to hide the diamonds when the woman was hustled into the carriage, I had shoved the cigars into the satchel, and the diamonds into the pocket of my coat. Now that I had the diamonds safe again, it seemed a very natural mistake. But I doubted if the Foreign Office would think so. I was afraid it might not appreciate the beautiful simplicity of my secret hiding-place. So, when I reached the police station, and found that the woman was still at large, I was more than relieved.

"As I expected, the Chief was extremely chagrined when he learned of my mistake, and that there was nothing for him to do. But I was feeling so happy myself that I hated to have any one else miserable, so I suggested that this attempt to steal the Czarina's necklace might be only the first of a series of such attempts by an unscrupulous gang, and that I might still be in danger.

"I winked at the Chief and the Chief smiled at me, and we went to Nice together in a saloon car with a guard of twelve carabineers and twelve plain-clothes men, and the Chief and I drank champagne all the way. We marched together up to the hotel where the Russian Ambassador was stopping, closely surrounded by our escort of carabineers, and delivered the necklace with the most profound ceremony. The old Ambassador was immensely impressed, and when we hinted that already I had been made the object of an attack by robbers, he assured us that his Imperial Majesty would not prove ungrateful.

"I wrote a swinging personal letter about the invaluable services of the Chief to the French Minister of Foreign Affairs, and they gave him enough Russian and French medals to satisfy even a French soldier. So, though he never caught the woman, he received his just reward."

The Queen's Messenger paused and surveyed the faces of those about him in some embarrassment.

"But the worst of it is," he added, "that the story must have got about; for, while the Princess obtained nothing from me but a cigar-case and five excellent cigars, a few weeks after the coronation the Czar sent me a gold cigar-case with his monogram in diamonds. And I don't know yet whether that was a coincidence, or whether the Czar wanted me to know that he knew that I had been carrying the Czarina's diamonds in my pigskin cigar-case. What do you fellows think?"

Chapter III

SIR ANDREW rose with disapproval written in every lineament.

"I thought your story would bear upon the murder," he said. "Had I imagined it would have nothing whatsoever to do with it I would not have remained." He pushed back his chair and bowed stiffly. "I wish you good night," he said.

There was a chorus of remonstrance, and under cover of this and the Baronet's answering protests a servant for the second time slipped a piece of paper into the hand of the gentleman with the pearl stud. He read the lines written upon it and tore it into tiny fragments.

The youngest member, who had remained an interested but silent listener to the tale of the Queen's Messenger, raised his hand commandingly.

"Sir Andrew," he cried, "in justice to Lord Arthur Chetney I must ask you to be seated. He has been accused in our hearing of a most serious crime, and I insist that you remain until you have heard me clear his character."

"You!" cried the Baronet.

"Yes," answered the young man briskly. "I would have spoken sooner," he explained, "but that I thought this gentleman" – he inclined his head toward the Queen's Messenger – "was about to contribute some facts of which I was ignorant. He, however, has told us nothing, and so I will take up the tale at the point where Lieutenant Sears laid it down and give you those details of which Lieutenant Sears is ignorant. It seems strange to you that I should be able to add the sequel to this story. But the coincidence is easily explained. I am the junior member of the law firm of Chudleigh & Chudleigh. We have been solicitors for the Chetneys for the last two hundred years. Nothing, no matter how unimportant, which concerns Lord Edam and his two sons is unknown to us, and naturally we are acquainted with every detail of the terrible catastrophe of last night."

The Baronet, bewildered but eager, sank back into his chair.

"Will you be long, sir!" he demanded.

"I shall endeavor to be brief," said the young solicitor; "and," he added, in a tone which gave his words almost the weight of a threat, "I promise to be interesting."

"There is no need to promise that," said Sir Andrew, "I find it much too interesting as it is." He glanced ruefully at the clock and turned his eyes quickly from it.

"Tell the driver of that hansom," he called to the servant, "that I take him by the hour."

"For the last three days," began young Mr. Chudleigh, "as you have probably read in the daily papers, the Marquis of Edam has been at the point of death, and his physicians have never left his house. Every hour he seemed to grow weaker; but although his bodily strength is apparently leaving him forever, his mind has remained clear and active. Late yesterday evening word was received at our office that he wished my father to come at once to Chetney House and to bring with him certain papers. What these papers were is not essential; I mention them only to explain how it was that last night I happened to be at Lord Edam's bed-side. I accompanied my father to Chetney House, but at the time we reached there Lord Edam was sleeping, and his physicians refused to have him awakened. My father urged that he should be allowed to receive Lord Edam's instructions concerning the documents, but the physicians would not disturb him, and we all gathered in the library to wait until he should awake of his own accord. It was about one o'clock in the morning, while we were still there, that Inspector Lyle and the officers from Scotland Yard came to arrest Lord Arthur on the charge of murdering his brother. You can imagine our dismay and distress. Like every one else, I had learned from the afternoon papers that Lord Chetney was not dead, but that he had returned to England, and on arriving at Chetney House I had been told that Lord Arthur had gone to the Bath Hotel to look for his brother and to inform him that if he wished to see their father alive he must come to him at once. Although it was now past one o'clock, Arthur had not returned. None of us knew where Madame Zichy lived, so we could not go to recover Lord Chetney's body. We spent a most miserable night, hastening to the window whenever a cab came into the square, in the hope that it was Arthur returning, and endeavoring to explain away the facts that pointed to him as the murderer. I am a friend of Arthur's, I was with him at Harrow and at Oxford, and I refused to believe for an instant that he was capable of such a crime; but as a lawyer I could not help but see that the circumstantial evidence was strongly against him.

"Toward early morning Lord Edam awoke, and in so much better a state of health that he refused to make the changes in the papers which he had intended, declaring that he was no nearer death than ourselves. Under other circumstances, this happy change in him would have relieved us greatly, but none of us could think of anything save the death of his elder son and of the charge which hung over Arthur.

"As long as Inspector Lyle remained in the house my father decided that I, as one of the legal advisers of the family, should also remain there. But there was little for either of us to do. Arthur did not return, and nothing occurred until late this morning, when Lyle received word that the Russian servant had been arrested. He at once drove to Scotland Yard to question him. He came back to us in an hour, and informed me that the servant had refused to tell anything of what had happened the night before, or of himself, or of the Princess Zichy. He would not even give them the address of her house.

" 'He is in abject terror,' Lyle said. 'I assured him that he was not suspected of the crime, but he would tell me nothing.'

"There were no other developments until two o'clock this afternoon, when word was brought to us that Arthur had been found, and that he was lying in the accident ward of St. George's Hospital. Lyle and I drove there together, and found him propped up in bed with his head bound in a bandage. He had been brought to the hospital the night before by the driver of a hansom that had run over him in the fog. The cab-horse had kicked him on the head, and he had been carried in unconscious. There was nothing on him to tell who he was, and it was not until he came to his senses this afternoon that the hospital authorities had been able to send word to his people. Lyle at once informed him that he was under arrest, and with what he was charged, and though the inspector warned him to say nothing which might be used against him, I, as his solicitor, instructed him to speak freely and to tell us all he knew of the occurrences of last night. It was evident to any one that the fact of his brother's death was of much greater concern to him, than that he was accused of his murder.

" 'That,' Arthur said contemptuously, 'that is damned nonsense. It is monstrous and cruel. We parted better friends than we have been in years. I will tell you all that happened – not to clear myself, but to help you to find out the truth.' His story is as follows: Yesterday afternoon, owing to his constant attendance on his father, he did not look at the evening papers, and it was not until after dinner, when the butler brought him one and told him of its contents, that he learned that his brother was alive and at the Bath Hotel. He drove there at once, but was told that about eight o'clock his brother had gone out, but without giving any clew to his destination. As Chetney had not at once come to see his father, Arthur decided that he was still angry with him, and his mind, turning naturally to the cause of their quarrel, determined him to look for Chetney at the home of the Princess Zichy.

"Her house had been pointed out to him, and though he had never visited it, he had passed it many times and knew its exact location. He accordingly drove in that direction, as far as the fog would permit the hansom to go, and walked the rest of the way, reaching the house about nine o'clock. He rang, and was admitted by the Russian servant. The man took his card into the drawing-room, and at once his brother ran out and welcomed him. He was followed by the Princess Zichy, who also received Arthur most cordially.

" 'You brothers will have much to talk about,' she said. 'I am going to the dining-room. When you have finished, let me know.'

"As soon as she had left them, Arthur told his brother that their father was not expected to outlive the night, and that he must come to him at once.

" 'This is not the moment to remember your quarrel,' Arthur said to him; 'you have come back from the dead only in time to make your peace with him before he dies.'

"Arthur says that at this Chetney was greatly moved.

" 'You entirely misunderstand me, Arthur,' he returned. 'I did not know the governor was ill, or I would have gone to him the instant I arrived. My only reason for not doing so was because I thought he was still angry with me. I shall return with you immediately, as soon as I have said goodbye to the Princess. It is a final good-bye. After tonight, I shall never see her again.'

" 'Do you mean that?' Arthur cried.

" 'Yes,' Chetney answered. 'When I returned to London I had no intention of seeking her again, and I am here only through a mistake.' He then told Arthur that he had separated from the Princess even before he went to Central Africa, and that, moreover, while at Cairo on his way south, he had learned certain facts concerning her life there during the previous season, which made it impossible for him to ever wish to see her again. Their separation was final and complete.

" 'She deceived me cruelly,' he said; 'I cannot tell you how cruelly. During the two years when I was trying to obtain my father's consent to our marriage she was in love with a Russian diplomat. During all that time he was secretly visiting her here in London, and her trip to Cairo was only an excuse to meet him there.'

" 'Yet you are here with her tonight,' Arthur protested, 'only a few hours after your return.'

" 'That is easily explained,' Chetney answered. 'As I finished dinner tonight at the hotel, I received a note from her from this address. In it she said she had but just learned of my arrival, and begged me to come to her at once. She wrote that she was in great and present trouble, dying of an incurable illness, and without friends or money. She begged me, for the sake of old times, to come to her assistance. During the last two years in the jungle all my former feeling for Ziehy has utterly passed away, but no one could have dismissed the appeal she made in that letter. So I came here, and found her, as you have seen her, quite as beautiful as she ever was, in very good health, and, from the look of the house, in no need of money.

" 'I asked her what she meant by writing me that she was dying in a garret, and she laughed, and said she had done so because she was afraid, unless I thought she needed help, I would not try to see her. That was where we were when you arrived. And now,' Chetney added, 'I will say goodbye to her, and you had better return home. No, you can trust me, I shall follow you at once. She has no influence over me now, but I believe, in spite of the way she has used me, that she is, after her queer fashion, still fond of me, and when she learns that this goodbye is final there may be a scene, and it is not fair to her that you should be here. So, go home at once, and tell the governor that I am following you in ten minutes.'

" 'That,' said Arthur, 'is the way we parted. I never left him on more friendly terms. I was happy to see him alive again, I was happy to think he had returned in time to make up his quarrel with my father, and I was happy that at last he was shut of that woman. I was never better pleased with him in my life.' He turned to Inspector Lyle, who was sitting at the foot of the bed taking notes of all he told us.

" 'Why in the name of common sense,' he cried, 'should I have chosen that moment of all others to send my brother back to the grave!' For a moment the Inspector did not answer him. I do not know if any of you gentlemen are acquainted with Inspector Lyle, but if you are not, I can assure you that he is a very remarkable man. Our firm often applies to him for aid, and he has never failed us; my father has the greatest possible respect for him. Where he has the advantage over the ordinary police official is in the fact that he possesses imagination. He imagines himself to be the criminal, imagines how he would act under the same circumstances, and he imagines to such purpose that he generally finds the man he wants. I have often told Lyle that if he had not been a detective he would have made a great success as a poet, or a playwright.

"When Arthur turned on him Lyle hesitated for a moment, and then told him exactly what was the case against him.

" 'Ever since your brother was reported as having died in Africa,' he said, 'your Lordship has been collecting money on post obits. Lord Chetney's arrival last night turned them into waste paper. You were suddenly in debt for thousands of pounds – for much more than you could ever possibly pay. No one knew that you and your brother had met at Madame Zichy's. But you knew that your father was not expected to outlive the night, and that if your brother were dead also, you would be saved from complete ruin, and that you would become the Marquis of Edam.'

" 'Oh, that is how you have worked it out, is it?' Arthur cried. 'And for me to become Lord Edam was it necessary that the woman should die, too!'

" 'They will say,' Lyle answered, 'that she was a witness to the murder – that she would have told.'

" 'Then why did I not kill the servant as well!' Arthur said.

" 'He was asleep, and saw nothing.'

" 'And you believe *that*?' Arthur demanded.

" 'It is not a question of what I believe,' Lyle said gravely. 'It is a question for your peers.'

" 'The man is insolent!' Arthur cried. 'The thing is monstrous! Horrible!'

"Before we could stop him he sprang out of his cot and began pulling on his clothes. When the nurses tried to hold him down, he fought with them.

" 'Do you think you can keep me here,' he shouted, 'when they are plotting to hang me? I am going with you to that house!' he cried at Lyle. 'When you find those bodies I shall be beside you. It is my right. He is my brother. He has been murdered, and I can tell you who murdered him. That woman murdered him. She first ruined his life, and now she has killed him. For the last five years she has been plotting to make herself his wife, and last night, when he told her he had discovered the truth about the Russian, and that she would never see him again, she flew into a passion and stabbed him, and then, in terror of the gallows, killed herself. She murdered him, I tell you, and I promise you that we will find the knife she used near her – perhaps still in her hand. What will you say to that?'

"Lyle turned his head away and stared down at the floor. 'I might say,' he answered, 'that you placed it there.'

"Arthur gave a cry of anger and sprang at him, and then pitched forward into his arms. The blood was running from the cut under the bandage, and he had fainted. Lyle carried him back to the bed again, and we left him with the police and the doctors, and drove at once to the address he had given us. We found the house not three minutes' walk from St. George's Hospital. It stands in Trevor Terrace, that little row of houses set back from Knightsbridge, with one end in Hill Street.

"As we left the hospital Lyle had said to me, 'You must not blame me for treating him as I did. All is fair in this work, and if by angering that boy I could have made him commit himself I was right in trying to do so; though, I assure you, no one would be better pleased than myself if I could prove his theory to be correct. But we cannot tell. Everything depends upon what we see for ourselves within the next few minutes.'

"When we reached the house, Lyle broke open the fastenings of one of the windows on the ground floor, and, hidden by the trees in the garden, we scrambled in. We found ourselves in the reception-room, which was the first room on the right of the hall. The gas was still burning behind the colored glass and red silk shades, and when the daylight streamed in after us it gave the hall a hideously dissipated look, like the foyer of a theatre at a matinee, or the entrance to an all-day gambling hell. The house was oppressively silent, and because we knew why it was so silent we spoke in whispers. When Lyle turned the handle of the drawing-room door, I felt as though some one had put his hand upon my throat. But I followed close at his shoulder, and saw, in the subdued light of many-tinted lamps, the body of Chetney at the foot of the divan, just as Lieutenant Sears had described it. In the drawing-room we found the body of the Princess Zichy, her arms thrown out, and the blood from her heart frozen in a tiny line across her bare shoulder. But neither of us, although we searched the floor on our hands and knees, could find the weapon which had killed her.

" 'For Arthur's sake,' I said, 'I would have given a thousand pounds if we had found the knife in her hand, as he said we would.'

" 'That we have not found it there,' Lyle answered, 'is to my mind the strongest proof that he is telling the truth, that he left the house before the murder took place. He is not a fool, and had he stabbed his brother and this woman, he would have seen that by placing the knife near her he could help to make it appear as if she had killed Chetney and then committed suicide. Besides, Lord Arthur insisted that the evidence in his behalf would be our finding the knife here. He would not have urged that if he knew we would not find it, if he knew he himself had carried it away. This is no suicide. A suicide does not rise and hide the weapon with which he kills himself, and then lie down again. No, this has been a double murder, and we must look outside of the house for the murderer.'

"While he was speaking Lyle and I had been searching every corner, studying the details of each room. I was so afraid that, without telling me, he would make some deductions prejudicial to Arthur, that I never left his side. I was determined to see everything that he saw, and, if possible, to prevent his interpreting it in the wrong way. He finally finished his examination, and we sat down together in the drawing-room, and he took out his notebook and read aloud all that Mr. Sears had told him of the murder and what we had just learned from Arthur. We compared the two accounts word for word, and weighed statement with statement, but I could not determine from anything Lyle said which of the two versions he had decided to believe.

" 'We are trying to build a house of blocks,' he exclaimed, 'with half of the blocks missing. We have been considering two theories,' he went on: 'one that Lord Arthur is responsible for both murders, and the other that the dead woman in there is responsible for one of them, and has committed suicide; but, until the Russian servant is ready to talk, I shall refuse to believe in the guilt of either.'

" 'What can you prove by him!' I asked. 'He was drunk and asleep. He saw nothing.'

"Lyle hesitated, and then, as though he had made up his mind to be quite frank with me, spoke freely.

" 'I do not know that he was either drunk or asleep,' he answered. 'Lieutenant Sears describes him as a stupid boor. I am not satisfied that he is not a clever actor. What was his position in this house! What was his real duty here? Suppose it was not to guard this woman, but to watch her. Let us imagine that it was not the woman he served, but a master, and see where that leads us. For this house has a master, a mysterious, absentee landlord, who lives in St. Petersburg, the unknown Russian who came between Chetney and Zichy, and because of whom Chetney left her. He is the man who bought this house for Madame Zichy, who sent these rugs and curtains from St. Petersburg to furnish it for her after his own tastes, and, I believe, it was he also who placed the Russian servant here, ostensibly to serve the Princess, but in reality to spy upon her. At Scotland Yard we do not know who this gentleman is; the Russian police confess to equal ignorance concerning him. When Lord Chetney went to Africa, Madame Zichy lived in St. Petersburg; but there her receptions and dinners were so crowded with members of the nobility and of the army and diplomats, that among so many visitors the police could not learn which was the one for whom she most greatly cared.'

"Lyle pointed at the modern French paintings and the heavy silk rugs which hung upon the walls.

" 'The unknown is a man of taste and of some fortune,' he said, 'not the sort of man to send a stupid peasant to guard the woman he loves. So I am not content to believe, with Mr. Sears, that the servant is a boor. I believe him instead to be a very clever ruffian. I believe him to be the protector of his master's honor, or, let us say, of his master's property, whether that property be silver plate or the woman his master loves. Last night, after Lord Arthur had gone away, the servant was left alone in this house with Lord Chetney and Madame Zichy. From where he sat in the hall he could hear Lord Chetney bidding her farewell; for, if my idea of him is correct, he understands English quite as well as you or I. Let us imagine that he heard her entreating Chetney not to leave her, reminding him of his former wish to marry her, and let us suppose that he hears Chetney denounce her, and tell her that at Cairo he has learned of this Russian admirer – the servant's master. He hears the woman declare that she has had no admirer but himself, that this unknown Russian was, and is, nothing to her, that there is no man she loves but him, and that she cannot live, knowing that he is alive, without his love. Suppose Chetney believed her, suppose his former infatuation for her returned, and that in a moment of weakness he forgave her and took her in his arms. That is the moment the Russian master has feared. It is to guard against it that he has placed his watchdog over the Princess, and how do we know but that, when the moment came, the watchdog served his master, as he saw his duty, and killed them both? What do you think?' Lyle demanded. 'Would not that explain both murders?'

"I was only too willing to hear any theory which pointed to any one else as the criminal than Arthur, but Lyle's explanation was too utterly fantastic. I told him that he certainly showed imagination, but that he could not hang a man for what he imagined he had done.

" 'No,' Lyle answered, 'but I can frighten him by telling him what I think he has done, and now when I again question the Russian servant I will make it quite clear to him that I believe he is the murderer. I think that will open his mouth. A man will at least talk to defend himself. Come,' he said, 'we must return at once to Scotland Yard and see him. There is nothing more to do here.'

"He arose, and I followed him into the hall, and in another minute we would have been on our way to Scotland Yard. But just as he opened the street door a postman halted at the gate of the garden, and began fumbling with the latch.

"Lyle stopped, with an exclamation of chagrin.

" 'How stupid of me!' he exclaimed. He turned quickly and pointed to a narrow slit cut in the brass plate of the front door. 'The house has a private letter-box,' he said, 'and I had not thought to look in it! If we had gone out as we came in, by the window, I would never have seen it. The moment I entered the house I should have thought of securing the letters which came this morning. I have been grossly careless.' He stepped back into the hall and pulled at the lid of the letterbox, which hung on the inside of the door, but it was tightly locked. At the same moment the postman came up the steps holding a letter. Without a word Lyle took it from his hand and began to examine it. It was addressed to the Princess Zichy, and on the back of the envelope was the name of a West End dressmaker.

" 'That is of no use to me,' Lyle said. He took out his card and showed it to the postman. 'I am Inspector Lyle from Scotland Yard,' he said. 'The people in this house are under arrest. Everything it contains is now in my keeping. Did you deliver any other letters here this morning?'

"The man looked frightened, but answered promptly that he was now upon his third round. He had made one postal delivery at seven that morning and another at eleven.

" 'How many letters did you leave here!' Lyle asked.

" 'About six altogether,' the man answered.

" 'Did you put them through the door into the letter-box!'

"The postman said, 'Yes, I always slip them into the box, and ring and go away. The servants collect them from the inside.'

" 'Have you noticed if any of the letters you leave here bear a Russian postage stamp!' Lyle asked.

"The man answered, 'Oh, yes, sir, a great many.'

" 'From the same person, would you say!'

" 'The writing seems to be the same,' the man answered. 'They come regularly about once a week – one of those I delivered this morning had a Russian postmark.'

" 'That will do,' said Lyle eagerly. 'Thank you, thank you very much.'

"He ran back into the hall, and, pulling out his penknife, began to pick at the lock of the letter-box.

" 'I have been supremely careless,' he said in great excitement. 'Twice before when people I wanted had flown from a house I have been able to follow them by putting a guard over their mail-box. These letters, which arrive regularly every week from Russia in the same handwriting, they can come but from one person. At least, we shall now know the name of the master of this house. Undoubtedly it is one of his letters that the man placed here this morning. We may make a most important discovery.'

"As he was talking he was picking at the lock with his knife, but he was so impatient to reach the letters that he pressed too heavily on the blade and it broke in his hand. I took a step backward and drove my heel into the lock, and burst it open. The lid flew back, and we pressed forward, and each ran his hand down into the letterbox. For a moment we were both too startled to move. The box was empty.

"I do not know how long we stood staring stupidly at each other, but it was Lyle who was the first to recover. He seized me by the arm and pointed excitedly into the empty box.

" 'Do you appreciate what that means?' he cried. 'It means that some one has been here ahead of us. Some one has entered this house not three hours before we came, since eleven o'clock this morning.'

" 'It was the Russian servant!' I exclaimed.

" 'The Russian servant has been under arrest at Scotland Yard,' Lyle cried. 'He could not have taken the letters. Lord Arthur has been in his cot at the hospital. That is his alibi. There is some one else, some one we do not suspect, and that some one is the murderer. He came back here either to obtain those letters because he knew they would convict him, or to remove something he had left here at the time of the murder, something incriminating, – the weapon, perhaps, or some personal article; a cigarette-case, a handkerchief with his name upon it, or a pair of gloves. Whatever it was it must have been damning evidence against him to have made him take so desperate a chance.'

" 'How do we know,' I whispered, 'that he is not hidden here now?'

" 'No, I'll swear he is not,' Lyle answered. 'I may have bungled in some things, but I have searched this house thoroughly. Nevertheless,' he added, 'we must go over it again, from the cellar to the roof. We have the real clew now, and we must forget the others and work only it.' As he spoke he began again to search the drawing-room, turning over even the books on the tables and the music on the piano.

" 'Whoever the man is,' he said over his shoulder, 'we know that he has a key to the front door and a key to the letter-box. That shows us he is either an inmate of the house or that he comes here when he wishes. The Russian says that he was the only servant in the house. Certainly we have found no evidence to show that any other servant slept here. There could be but one other person who would possess a key to the house and the letter-box – and he lives in St. Petersburg. At the time of the murder he was two thousand miles away.' Lyle interrupted himself suddenly with a sharp cry and turned upon me with his eyes flashing. 'But was he?' he cried. 'Was he? How do we know that last night he was not in London, in this very house when Zichy and Chetney met?'

"He stood staring at me without seeing me, muttering, and arguing with himself.

" 'Don't speak to me,' he cried, as I ventured to interrupt him. 'I can see it now. It is all plain. It was not the servant, but his master, the Russian himself, and it was he who came back for the letters! He came back for them because he knew they would convict him. We must find them. We must have those letters. If we find the one with the Russian postmark, we shall have found the murderer.' He spoke like a madman, and as he spoke he ran around the room with one hand held out in front of him as you have seen a mind-reader at a theatre seeking for something hidden in the stalls. He pulled the old letters from the writing-desk, and ran them over as swiftly as a gambler deals out cards; he dropped on his knees before the fireplace and dragged out the dead coals with his bare fingers, and then with a low, worried cry, like a hound on a scent, he ran back to the waste-paper basket and, lifting the papers from it, shook them out upon the floor. Instantly he gave a shout of triumph, and, separating a number of torn pieces from the others, held them up before me.

" 'Look!' he cried. 'Do you see? Here are five letters, torn across in two places. The Russian did not stop to read them, for, as you see, he has left them still sealed. I have been wrong.

He did not return for the letters. He could not have known their value. He must have returned for some other reason, and, as he was leaving, saw the letter-box, and taking out the letters, held them together – so – and tore them twice across, and then, as the fire had gone out, tossed them into this basket. Look!' he cried, 'here in the upper corner of this piece is a Russian stamp. This is his own letter – unopened!'

"We examined the Russian stamp and found it had been cancelled in St. Petersburg four days ago. The back of the envelope bore the postmark of the branch station in upper Sloane Street, and was dated this morning. The envelope was of official blue paper and we had no difficulty in finding the two other parts of it. We drew the torn pieces of the letter from them and joined them together side by side. There were but two lines of writing, and this was the message: 'I leave Petersburg on the night train, and I shall see you at Trevor Terrace after dinner Monday evening.'

" 'That was last night!' Lyle cried. 'He arrived twelve hours ahead of his letter – but it came in time – it came in time to hang him!' "

The Baronet struck the table with his hand.

"The name!" he demanded. "How was it signed? What was the man's name!"

The young Solicitor rose to his feet and, leaning forward, stretched out his arm. "There was no name," he cried. "The letter was signed with only two initials. But engraved at the top of the sheet was the man's address. That address was 'The American Embassy, St. Petersburg, Bureau or The Naval Attaché,' and the initials," he shouted, his voice rising into an exultant and bitter cry, "were those of the gentleman who sits opposite who told us that he was the first to find the murdered bodies, the Naval Attaché to Russia, Lieutenant Sears!"

A strained and awful hush followed the Solicitor's words, which seemed to vibrate like a twanging bowstring that had just hurled its bolt. Sir Andrew, pale and staring, drew away with an exclamation of repulsion. His eyes were fastened upon the Naval Attaché with fascinated horror. But the American emitted a sigh of great content, and sank comfortably into the arms of his chair. He clapped his hands softly together.

"Capital!" he murmured. "I give you my word I never guessed what you were driving at. You fooled me, I'll be hanged if you didn't – you certainly fooled me."

The man with the pearl stud leaned forward with a nervous gesture. "Hush! Be careful!" he whispered. But at that instant, for the third time, a servant, hastening through the room, handed him a piece of paper which he scanned eagerly. The message on the paper read,

'The light over the Commons is out. The House has risen.'

The man with the black pearl gave a mighty shout, and tossed the paper from him upon the table.

"Hurrah!" he cried. "The House is up! We've won!" He caught up his glass, and slapped the Naval Attaché violently upon the shoulder. He nodded joyously at him, at the Solicitor, and at the Queen's Messenger. "Gentlemen, to you!" he cried; "my thanks and my congratulations!" He drank deep from the glass, and breathed forth a long sigh of satisfaction and relief.

"But I say," protested the Queen's Messenger, shaking his finger violently at the Solicitor, "that story won't do. You didn't play fair – and – and you talked so fast I couldn't make out what it was all about. I'll bet you that evidence wouldn't hold in a court of law – you couldn't hang a cat on such evidence. Your story is condemned tommy-rot. Now my story might have happened, my story bore the mark –"

In the joy of creation the story-tellers had forgotten their audience, until a sudden exclamation from Sir Andrew caused them to turn guiltily toward him. His face was knit with lines of anger, doubt, and amazement.

"What does this mean!" he cried. "Is this a jest, or are you mad? If you know this man is a murderer, why is he at large? Is this a game you have been playing? Explain yourselves at once. What does it mean?"

The American, with first a glance at the others, rose and bowed courteously.

"I am not a murderer, Sir Andrew, believe me," he said; "you need not be alarmed. As a matter of fact, at this moment I am much more afraid of you than you could possibly be of me. I beg you please to be indulgent. I assure you, we meant no disrespect. We have been matching stories, that is all, pretending that we are people we are not, endeavoring to entertain you with better detective tales than, for instance, the last one you read, 'The Great Rand Robbery.' "

The Baronet brushed his hand nervously across his forehead.

"Do you mean to tell me," he exclaimed, "that none of this has happened? That Lord Chetney is not dead, that his Solicitor did not find a letter of yours written from your post in Petersburg, and that just now, when he charged you with murder, he was in jest?"

"I am really very sorry," said the American, "but you see, sir, he could not have found a letter written by me in St. Petersburg because I have never been in Petersburg. Until this week, I have never been outside of my own country. I am not a naval officer. I am a writer of short stories. And tonight, when this gentleman told me that you were fond of detective stories, I thought it would be amusing to tell you one of my own – one I had just mapped out this afternoon."

"But Lord Chetney is a real person," interrupted the Baronet, "and he did go to Africa two years ago, and he was supposed to have died there, and his brother, Lord Arthur, has been the heir. And yesterday Chetney did return. I read it in the papers."

"So did I," assented the American soothingly; "and it struck me as being a very good plot for a story. I mean his unexpected return from the dead, and the probable disappointment of the younger brother. So I decided that the younger brother had better murder the older one. The Princess Zichy I invented out of a clear sky. The fog I did not have to invent. Since last night I know all that there is to know about a London fog. I was lost in one for three hours."

The Baronet turned grimly upon the Queen's Messenger.

"But this gentleman," he protested, "he is not a writer of short stories; he is a member of the Foreign Office. I have often seen him in Whitehall, and, according to him, the Princess Zichy is not an invention. He says she is very well known, that she tried to rob him."

The servant of the Foreign Office looked unhappily at the Cabinet Minister, and puffed nervously on his cigar.

"It's true, Sir Andrew, that I am a Queen's Messenger," he said appealingly, "and a Russian woman once did try to rob a Queen's Messenger in a railway carriage – only it did not happen to me, but to a pal of mine. The only Russian princess I ever knew called herself Zabrisky. You may have seen her. She used to do a dive from the roof of the Aquarium."

Sir Andrew, with a snort of indignation, fronted the young Solicitor.

"And I suppose yours was a cock-and-bull story, too," he said. "Of course, it must have been, since Lord Chetney is not dead. But don't tell me," he protested, "that you are not Chudleigh's son either."

"I'm sorry," said the youngest member, smiling in some embarrassment, "but my name is not Chudleigh. I assure you, though, that I know the family very well, and that I am on very good terms with them."

"You should be!" exclaimed the Baronet; "and, judging from the liberties you take with the Chetneys, you had better be on very good terms with them, too."

The young man leaned back and glanced toward the servants at the far end of the room.

"It has been so long since I have been in the Club," he said, "that I doubt if even the waiters remember me. Perhaps Joseph may," he added. "Joseph!" he called, and at the word a servant stepped briskly forward.

The young man pointed to the stuffed head of a great lion which was suspended above the fireplace.

"Joseph," he said, "I want you to tell these gentlemen who shot that lion. Who presented it to the Grill?"

Joseph, unused to acting as master of ceremonies to members of the Club, shifted nervously from one foot to the other.

"Why, you – you did," he stammered.

"Of course I did!" exclaimed the young man. "I mean, what is the name of the man who shot it! Tell the gentlemen who I am. They wouldn't believe me."

"Who you are, my lord?" said Joseph. "You are Lord Edam's son, the Earl of Chetney."

"You must admit," said Lord Chetney, when the noise had died away, "that I couldn't remain dead while my little brother was accused of murder. I had to do something. Family pride demanded it. Now, Arthur, as the younger brother, can't afford to be squeamish, but personally I should hate to have a brother of mine hanged for murder."

"You certainly showed no scruples against hanging me," said the American, "but in the face of your evidence I admit my guilt, and I sentence myself to pay the full penalty of the law as we are made to pay it in my own country. The order of this court is," he announced, "that Joseph shall bring me a wine-card, and that I sign it for five bottles of the Club's best champagne."

"Oh, no!" protested the man with the pearl stud, "It is not for you to sign it. In my opinion it is Sir Andrew who should pay the costs. It is time you knew," he said, turning to that gentleman, "that unconsciously you have been the victim of what I may call a patriotic conspiracy. These stories have had a more serious purpose than merely to amuse. They have been told with the worthy object of detaining you from the House of Commons. I must explain to you, that all through this evening I have had a servant waiting in Trafalgar Square with instructions to bring me word as soon as the light over the House of Commons had ceased to burn. The light is now out, and the object for which we plotted is attained."

The Baronet glanced keenly at the man with the black pearl, and then quickly at his watch. The smile disappeared from his lips, and his face was set in stern and forbidding lines.

"And may I know," he asked icily, "what was the object of your plot!"

"A most worthy one," the other retorted. "Our object was to keep you from advocating the expenditure of many millions of the people's money upon more battleships. In a word, we have been working together to prevent you from passing the Navy Increase Bill."

Sir Andrew's face bloomed with brilliant color. His body shook with suppressed emotion.

"My dear sir!" he cried, "You should spend more time at the House and less at your Club. The Navy Bill was brought up on its third reading at eight o'clock this evening. I spoke for three hours in its favor. My only reason for wishing to return again to the House tonight was to sup on the terrace with my old friend, Admiral Simons; for my work at the House was completed five hours ago, when the Navy Increase Bill was passed by an overwhelming majority."

The Baronet rose and bowed. "I have to thank you, sir," he said, "for a most interesting evening."

The American shoved the wine-card which Joseph had given him toward the gentleman with the black pearl.

"You sign it," he said.

Hunted Down

Charles Dickens

I

MOST OF US see some romances in life. In my capacity as Chief Manager of a Life Assurance Office, I think I have within the last thirty years seen more romances than the generality of men, however unpromising the opportunity may, at first sight, seem.

As I have retired, and live at my ease, I possess the means that I used to want, of considering what I have seen, at leisure. My experiences have a more remarkable aspect, so reviewed, than they had when they were in progress. I have come home from the Play now, and can recall the scenes of the Drama upon which the curtain has fallen, free from the glare, bewilderment, and bustle of the Theatre.

Let me recall one of these Romances of the real world.

There is nothing truer than physiognomy, taken in connection with manner. The art of reading that book of which Eternal Wisdom obliges every human creature to present his or her own page with the individual character written on it, is a difficult one, perhaps, and is little studied. It may require some natural aptitude, and it must require (for everything does) some patience and some pains. That these are not usually given to it, – that numbers of people accept a few stock commonplace expressions of the face as the whole list of characteristics, and neither seek nor know the refinements that are truest, – that You, for instance, give a great deal of time and attention to the reading of music, Greek, Latin, French, Italian, Hebrew, if you please, and do not qualify yourself to read the face of the master or mistress looking over your shoulder teaching it to you, – I assume to be five hundred times more probable than improbable. Perhaps a little self-sufficiency may be at the bottom of this; facial expression requires no study from you, you think; it comes by nature to you to know enough about it, and you are not to be taken in.

I confess, for my part, that I *have* been taken in, over and over again. I have been taken in by acquaintances, and I have been taken in (of course) by friends; far oftener by friends than by any other class of persons. How came I to be so deceived? Had I quite misread their faces?

No. Believe me, my first impression of those people, founded on face and manner alone, was invariably true. My mistake was in suffering them to come nearer to me and explain themselves away.

II

THE PARTITION which separated my own office from our general outer office in the City was of thick plate-glass. I could see through it what passed in the outer office, without hearing a word. I had it put up in place of a wall that had been there for years, – ever since the house was built. It is no matter whether I did or did not make the change in order that I might derive my first impression of strangers, who came to us on business, from their faces alone, without being influenced by anything they said. Enough to mention that I turned my glass partition to that account, and that a Life Assurance Office is at all times exposed to be practised upon by the most crafty and cruel of the human race.

It was through my glass partition that I first saw the gentleman whose story I am going to tell.

He had come in without my observing it, and had put his hat and umbrella on the broad counter, and was bending over it to take some papers from one of the clerks. He was about forty or so, dark, exceedingly well dressed in black, – being in mourning, – and the hand he extended with a polite air, had a particularly well-fitting black-kid glove upon it. His hair, which was elaborately brushed and oiled, was parted straight up the middle; and he presented this parting to the clerk, exactly (to my thinking) as if he had said, in so many words: "You must take me, if you please, my friend, just as I show myself. Come straight up here, follow the gravel path, keep off the grass, I allow no trespassing."

I conceived a very great aversion to that man the moment I thus saw him.

He had asked for some of our printed forms, and the clerk was giving them to him and explaining them. An obliged and agreeable smile was on his face, and his eyes met those of the clerk with a sprightly look. (I have known a vast quantity of nonsense talked about bad men not looking you in the face. Don't trust that conventional idea. Dishonesty will stare honesty out of countenance, any day in the week, if there is anything to be got by it.)

I saw, in the corner of his eyelash, that he became aware of my looking at him. Immediately he turned the parting in his hair toward the glass partition, as if he said to me with a sweet smile, "Straight up here, if you please. Off the grass!"

In a few moments he had put on his hat and taken up his umbrella, and was gone.

I beckoned the clerk into my room, and asked, "Who was that?"

He had the gentleman's card in his hand. "Mr. Julius Slinkton, Middle Temple."

"A barrister, Mr. Adams?"

"I think not, sir."

"I should have thought him a clergyman, but for his having no Reverend here," said I.

"Probably, from his appearance," Mr. Adams replied, "he is reading for orders."

I should mention that he wore a dainty white cravat, and dainty linen altogether.

"What did he want, Mr. Adams?"

"Merely a form of proposal, sir, and form of reference."

"Recommended here? Did he say?"

"Yes, he said he was recommended here by a friend of yours. He noticed you, but said that as he had not the pleasure of your personal acquaintance he would not trouble you."

"Did he know my name?"

"O yes, sir! He said, 'There *is* Mr. Sampson, I see!' "

"A well-spoken gentleman, apparently?"

"Remarkably so, sir."

"Insinuating manners, apparently?"

"Very much so, indeed, sir."

"Hah!" said I. "I want nothing at present, Mr. Adams."

Within a fortnight of that day I went to dine with a friend of mine, a merchant, a man of taste, who buys pictures and books, and the first man I saw among the company was Mr. Julius Slinkton. There he was, standing before the fire, with good large eyes and an open expression of face; but still (I thought) requiring everybody to come at him by the prepared way he offered, and by no other.

I noticed him ask my friend to introduce him to Mr. Sampson, and my friend did so. Mr. Slinkton was very happy to see me. Not too happy; there was no over-doing of the matter; happy in a thoroughly well-bred, perfectly unmeaning way.

"I thought you had met," our host observed.

"No," said Mr. Slinkton. "I did look in at Mr. Sampson's office, on your recommendation; but I really did not feel justified in troubling Mr. Sampson himself, on a point in the everyday routine of an ordinary clerk."

I said I should have been glad to show him any attention on our friend's introduction.

"I am sure of that," said he, "and am much obliged. At another time, perhaps, I may be less delicate. Only, however, if I have real business; for I know, Mr. Sampson, how precious business time is, and what a vast number of impertinent people there are in the world."

I acknowledged his consideration with a slight bow. "You were thinking," said I, "of effecting a policy on your life."

"O dear no! I am afraid I am not so prudent as you pay me the compliment of supposing me to be, Mr. Sampson. I merely inquired for a friend. But you know what friends are in such matters. Nothing may ever come of it. I have the greatest reluctance to trouble men of business with inquiries for friends, knowing the probabilities to be a thousand to one that the friends will never follow them up. People are so fickle, so selfish, so inconsiderate. Don't you, in your business, find them so every day, Mr. Sampson?"

I was going to give a qualified answer; but he turned his smooth, white parting on me with its "Straight up here, if you please!" and I answered "Yes."

"I hear, Mr. Sampson," he resumed presently, for our friend had a new cook, and dinner was not so punctual as usual, "that your profession has recently suffered a great loss."

"In money?" said I.

He laughed at my ready association of loss with money, and replied, "No, in talent and vigour."

Not at once following out his allusion, I considered for a moment. "*Has* it sustained a loss of that kind?" said I. "I was not aware of it."

"Understand me, Mr. Sampson. I don't imagine that you have retired. It is not so bad as that. But Mr. Meltham –"

"O, to be sure!" said I. "Yes! Mr. Meltham, the young actuary of the 'Inestimable.' "

"Just so," he returned in a consoling way.

"He is a great loss. He was at once the most profound, the most original, and the most energetic man I have ever known connected with Life Assurance."

I spoke strongly; for I had a high esteem and admiration for Meltham; and my gentleman had indefinitely conveyed to me some suspicion that he wanted to sneer at him. He recalled me to my guard by presenting that trim pathway up his head, with its internal "Not on the grass, if you please – the gravel."

"You knew him, Mr. Slinkton."

"Only by reputation. To have known him as an acquaintance or as a friend, is an honour I should have sought if he had remained in society, though I might never have had the good fortune to attain it, being a man of far inferior mark. He was scarcely above thirty, I suppose?"

"About thirty."

"Ah!" he sighed in his former consoling way. "What creatures we are! To break up, Mr. Sampson, and become incapable of business at that time of life! – Any reason assigned for the melancholy fact?"

("Humph!" thought I, as I looked at him. "But I *won't* go up the track, and I *will* go on the grass.")

"What reason have you heard assigned, Mr. Slinkton?" I asked, point-blank.

"Most likely a false one. You know what Rumour is, Mr. Sampson. I never repeat what I hear; it is the only way of paring the nails and shaving the head of Rumour. But when *you* ask me what reason I have heard assigned for Mr. Meltham's passing away from among men, it is another thing. I am not gratifying idle gossip then. I was told, Mr. Sampson, that Mr. Meltham had relinquished all his avocations and all his prospects, because he was, in fact, broken-hearted. A disappointed attachment I heard, – though it hardly seems probable, in the case of a man so distinguished and so attractive."

"Attractions and distinctions are no armour against death," said I.

"O, she died? Pray pardon me. I did not hear that. That, indeed, makes it very, very sad. Poor Mr. Meltham! She died? Ah, dear me! Lamentable, lamentable!"

I still thought his pity was not quite genuine, and I still suspected an unaccountable sneer under all this, until he said, as we were parted, like the other knots of talkers, by the announcement of dinner:

"Mr. Sampson, you are surprised to see me so moved on behalf of a man whom I have never known. I am not so disinterested as you may suppose. I have suffered, and recently too, from death myself. I have lost one of two charming nieces, who were my constant companions. She died young – barely three-and-twenty; and even her remaining sister is far from strong. The world is a grave!"

He said this with deep feeling, and I felt reproached for the coldness of my manner. Coldness and distrust had been engendered in me, I knew, by my bad experiences; they were not natural to me; and I often thought how much I had lost in life, losing trustfulness, and how little I had gained, gaining hard caution. This state of mind being habitual to me, I troubled myself more about this conversation than I might have troubled myself about a greater matter. I listened to his talk at dinner, and observed how readily other men responded to it, and with what a graceful instinct he adapted his subjects to the knowledge and habits of those he talked with. As, in talking with me, he had easily started the subject I might be supposed to understand best, and to be the most interested in, so, in talking with others, he guided himself by the same rule. The company was of a varied character; but he was not at fault, that I could discover, with any member of it. He knew just as much of each man's pursuit as made him agreeable to that man in reference to it, and just as little as made it natural in him to seek modestly for information when the theme was broached.

As he talked and talked – but really not too much, for the rest of us seemed to force it upon him – I became quite angry with myself. I took his face to pieces in my mind, like a watch, and examined it in detail. I could not say much against any of his features separately; I could say even less against them when they were put together. "Then is it not monstrous," I asked myself, "that because a man happens to part his hair straight up the middle of his head, I should permit myself to suspect, and even to detest him?"

(I may stop to remark that this was no proof of my sense. An observer of men who finds himself steadily repelled by some apparently trifling thing in a stranger is right to give it great weight. It may be the clue to the whole mystery. A hair or two will show where a lion is hidden. A very little key will open a very heavy door.)

I took my part in the conversation with him after a time, and we got on remarkably well. In the drawing-room I asked the host how long he had known Mr. Slinkton. He answered, not many months; he had met him at the house of a celebrated painter then present, who had known him well when he was travelling with his nieces in Italy for their health. His plans in life being broken by the death of one of them, he was reading with the intention of going back to college as a matter of form, taking his degree, and going into orders. I could not but argue with myself that here was the true explanation of his interest in poor Meltham, and that I had been almost brutal in my distrust on that simple head.

III

ON THE VERY next day but one I was sitting behind my glass partition, as before, when he came into the outer office, as before. The moment I saw him again without hearing him, I hated him worse than ever.

It was only for a moment that I had this opportunity; for he waved his tight-fitting black glove the instant I looked at him, and came straight in.

"Mr. Sampson, good-day! I presume, you see, upon your kind permission to intrude upon you. I don't keep my word in being justified by business, for my business here – if I may so abuse the word – is of the slightest nature."

I asked, was it anything I could assist him in?

"I thank you, no. I merely called to inquire outside whether my dilatory friend had been so false to himself as to be practical and sensible. But, of course, he has done nothing. I gave him your papers with my own hand, and he was hot upon the intention, but of course he has done nothing. Apart from the general human disinclination to do anything that ought to be done, I dare say there is a specialty about assuring one's life. You find it like will-making. People are so superstitious, and take it for granted they will die soon afterwards."

"Up here, if you please; straight up here, Mr. Sampson. Neither to the right nor to the left." I almost fancied I could hear him breathe the words as he sat smiling at me, with that intolerable parting exactly opposite the bridge of my nose.

"There is such a feeling sometimes, no doubt," I replied; "but I don't think it obtains to any great extent."

"Well," said he, with a shrug and a smile, "I wish some good angel would influence my friend in the right direction. I rashly promised his mother and sister in Norfolk to see it done, and he promised them that he would do it. But I suppose he never will."

He spoke for a minute or two on indifferent topics, and went away.

I had scarcely unlocked the drawers of my writing-table next morning, when he reappeared. I noticed that he came straight to the door in the glass partition, and did not pause a single moment outside.

"Can you spare me two minutes, my dear Mr. Sampson?"

"By all means."

"Much obliged," laying his hat and umbrella on the table; "I came early, not to interrupt you. The fact is, I am taken by surprise in reference to this proposal my friend has made."

"Has he made one?" said I.

"Ye-es," he answered, deliberately looking at me; and then a bright idea seemed to strike him – "or he only tells me he has. Perhaps that may be a new way of evading the matter. By Jupiter, I never thought of that!"

Mr. Adams was opening the morning's letters in the outer office. "What is the name, Mr. Slinkton?" I asked.

"Beckwith."

I looked out at the door and requested Mr. Adams, if there were a proposal in that name, to bring it in. He had already laid it out of his hand on the counter. It was easily selected from the rest, and he gave it me. Alfred Beckwith. Proposal to effect a policy with us for two thousand pounds. Dated yesterday.

"From the Middle Temple, I see, Mr. Slinkton."

"Yes. He lives on the same staircase with me; his door is opposite. I never thought he would make me his reference though."

"It seems natural enough that he should."

"Quite so, Mr. Sampson; but I never thought of it. Let me see." He took the printed paper from his pocket. "How am I to answer all these questions?"

"According to the truth, of course," said I.

"O, of course!" he answered, looking up from the paper with a smile; "I meant they were so many. But you do right to be particular. It stands to reason that you must be particular. Will you allow me to use your pen and ink?"

"Certainly."

"And your desk?"

"Certainly."

He had been hovering about between his hat and his umbrella for a place to write on. He now sat down in my chair, at my blotting-paper and inkstand, with the long walk up his head in accurate perspective before me, as I stood with my back to the fire.

Before answering each question he ran over it aloud, and discussed it. How long had he known Mr. Alfred Beckwith? That he had to calculate by years upon his fingers. What were his habits? No difficulty about them; temperate in the last degree, and took a little too much exercise, if anything. All the answers were satisfactory. When he had written them all, he looked them over, and finally signed them in a very pretty hand. He supposed he had now done with the business. I told him he was not likely to be troubled any farther. Should he leave the papers there? If he pleased. Much obliged. Good-morning.

I had had one other visitor before him; not at the office, but at my own house. That visitor had come to my bedside when it was not yet daylight, and had been seen by no one else but by my faithful confidential servant.

A second reference paper (for we required always two) was sent down into Norfolk, and was duly received back by post. This, likewise, was satisfactorily answered in every respect. Our forms were all complied with; we accepted the proposal, and the premium for one year was paid.

IV

FOR SIX or seven months I saw no more of Mr. Slinkton. He called once at my house, but I was not at home; and he once asked me to dine with him in the Temple, but I was engaged. His friend's assurance was effected in March. Late in September or early in October I was down at Scarborough for a breath of sea-air, where I met him on the beach. It was a hot evening; he came toward me with his hat in his hand; and there was the walk I had felt so strongly disinclined to take in perfect order again, exactly in front of the bridge of my nose.

He was not alone, but had a young lady on his arm.

She was dressed in mourning, and I looked at her with great interest. She had the appearance of being extremely delicate, and her face was remarkably pale and melancholy; but she was very pretty. He introduced her as his niece, Miss Niner.

"Are you strolling, Mr. Sampson? Is it possible you can be idle?"

It *was* possible, and I *was* strolling.

"Shall we stroll together?"

"With pleasure."

The young lady walked between us, and we walked on the cool sea sand, in the direction of Filey.

"There have been wheels here," said Mr. Slinkton. "And now I look again, the wheels of a hand-carriage! Margaret, my love, your shadow without doubt!"

"Miss Niner's shadow?" I repeated, looking down at it on the sand.

"Not that one," Mr. Slinkton returned, laughing. "Margaret, my dear, tell Mr. Sampson."

"Indeed," said the young lady, turning to me, "there is nothing to tell – except that I constantly see the same invalid old gentleman at all times, wherever I go. I have mentioned it to my uncle, and he calls the gentleman my shadow."

"Does he live in Scarborough?" I asked.

"He is staying here."

"Do you live in Scarborough?"

"No, I am staying here. My uncle has placed me with a family here, for my health."

"And your shadow?" said I, smiling.

"My shadow," she answered, smiling too, "is – like myself – not very robust, I fear; for I lose my shadow sometimes, as my shadow loses me at other times. We both seem liable to confinement to the house. I have not seen my shadow for days and days; but it does oddly happen, occasionally, that wherever I go, for many days together, this gentleman goes. We have come together in the most unfrequented nooks on this shore."

"Is this he?" said I, pointing before us.

The wheels had swept down to the water's edge, and described a great loop on the sand in turning. Bringing the loop back towards us, and spinning it out as it came, was a hand-carriage, drawn by a man.

"Yes," said Miss Niner, "this really is my shadow, uncle."

As the carriage approached us and we approached the carriage, I saw within it an old man, whose head was sunk on his breast, and who was enveloped in a variety of wrappers. He was drawn by a very quiet but very keen-looking man, with iron-gray hair, who was slightly lame. They had passed us, when the carriage stopped, and the old gentleman within, putting out his arm, called to me by my name. I went back, and was absent from Mr. Slinkton and his niece for about five minutes.

When I rejoined them, Mr. Slinkton was the first to speak. Indeed, he said to me in a raised voice before I came up with him:

"It is well you have not been longer, or my niece might have died of curiosity to know who her shadow is, Mr. Sampson."

"An old East India Director," said I. "An intimate friend of our friend's, at whose house I first had the pleasure of meeting you. A certain Major Banks. You have heard of him?"

"Never."

"Very rich, Miss Niner; but very old, and very crippled. An amiable man, sensible – much interested in you. He has just been expatiating on the affection that he has observed to exist between you and your uncle."

Mr. Slinkton was holding his hat again, and he passed his hand up the straight walk, as if he himself went up it serenely, after me.

"Mr. Sampson," he said, tenderly pressing his niece's arm in his, "our affection was always a strong one, for we have had but few near ties. We have still fewer now. We have associations to bring us together, that are not of this world, Margaret."

"Dear uncle!" murmured the young lady, and turned her face aside to hide her tears.

"My niece and I have such remembrances and regrets in common, Mr. Sampson," he feelingly pursued, "that it would be strange indeed if the relations between us were cold or indifferent. If I remember a conversation we once had together, you will understand the reference I make. Cheer up, dear Margaret. Don't droop, don't droop. My Margaret! I cannot bear to see you droop!"

The poor young lady was very much affected, but controlled herself. His feelings, too, were very acute. In a word, he found himself under such great need of a restorative, that he presently went away, to take a bath of sea-water, leaving the young lady and me sitting by a point of rock, and probably presuming – but that you will say was a pardonable indulgence in a luxury – that she would praise him with all her heart.

She did, poor thing! With all her confiding heart, she praised him to me, for his care of her dead sister, and for his untiring devotion in her last illness. The sister had wasted away very slowly, and wild and terrible fantasies had come over her toward the end, but he had never been impatient with her, or at a loss; had always been gentle, watchful, and self-possessed. The sister had known him, as she had known him, to be the best of men, the kindest of men, and yet a man of such admirable strength of character, as to be a very tower for the support of their weak natures while their poor lives endured.

"I shall leave him, Mr. Sampson, very soon," said the young lady; "I know my life is drawing to an end; and when I am gone, I hope he will marry and be happy. I am sure he has lived single so long, only for my sake, and for my poor, poor sister's."

The little hand-carriage had made another great loop on the damp sand, and was coming back again, gradually spinning out a slim figure of eight, half a mile long.

"Young lady," said I, looking around, laying my hand upon her arm, and speaking in a low voice, "time presses. You hear the gentle murmur of that sea?"

She looked at me with the utmost wonder and alarm, saying, "Yes!"

"And you know what a voice is in it when the storm comes?"

"Yes!"

"You see how quiet and peaceful it lies before us, and you know what an awful sight of power without pity it might be, this very night!"

"Yes!"

"But if you had never heard or seen it, or heard of it in its cruelty, could you believe that it beats every inanimate thing in its way to pieces, without mercy, and destroys life without remorse?"

"You terrify me, sir, by these questions!"

"To save you, young lady, to save you! For God's sake, collect your strength and collect your firmness! If you were here alone, and hemmed in by the rising tide on the flow to fifty feet above your head, you could not be in greater danger than the danger you are now to be saved from."

The figure on the sand was spun out, and straggled off into a crooked little jerk that ended at the cliff very near us.

"As I am, before Heaven and the Judge of all mankind, your friend, and your dead sister's friend, I solemnly entreat you, Miss Niner, without one moment's loss of time, to come to this gentleman with me!"

If the little carriage had been less near to us, I doubt if I could have got her away; but it was so near that we were there before she had recovered the hurry of being urged from the rock. I did not remain there with her two minutes. Certainly within five, I had the inexpressible satisfaction of seeing her – from the point we had sat on, and to which I had returned – half supported and half carried up some rude steps notched in the cliff, by the figure of an active man. With that figure beside her, I knew she was safe anywhere.

I sat alone on the rock, awaiting Mr. Slinkton's return. The twilight was deepening and the shadows were heavy, when he came round the point, with his hat hanging at his button-hole, smoothing his wet hair with one of his hands, and picking out the old path with the other and a pocket-comb.

"My niece not here, Mr. Sampson?" he said, looking about.

"Miss Niner seemed to feel a chill in the air after the sun was down, and has gone home."

He looked surprised, as though she were not accustomed to do anything without him; even to originate so slight a proceeding.

"I persuaded Miss Niner," I explained.

"Ah!" said he. "She is easily persuaded – for her good. Thank you, Mr. Sampson; she is better within doors. The bathing-place was farther than I thought, to say the truth."

"Miss Niner is very delicate," I observed.

He shook his head and drew a deep sigh. "Very, very, very. You may recollect my saying so. The time that has since intervened has not strengthened her. The gloomy shadow that fell upon her sister so early in life seems, in my anxious eyes, to gather over her, ever darker, ever darker. Dear Margaret, dear Margaret! But we must hope."

The hand-carriage was spinning away before us at a most indecorous pace for an invalid vehicle, and was making most irregular curves upon the sand. Mr. Slinkton, noticing it after he had put his handkerchief to his eyes, said:

"If I may judge from appearances, your friend will be upset, Mr. Sampson."

"It looks probable, certainly," said I.

"The servant must be drunk."

"The servants of old gentlemen will get drunk sometimes," said I.

"The major draws very light, Mr. Sampson."

"The major does draw light," said I.

By this time the carriage, much to my relief, was lost in the darkness. We walked on for a little, side by side over the sand, in silence. After a short while he said, in a voice still affected by the emotion that his niece's state of health had awakened in him,

"Do you stay here long, Mr. Sampson?"

"Why, no. I am going away tonight."

"So soon? But business always holds you in request. Men like Mr. Sampson are too important to others, to be spared to their own need of relaxation and enjoyment."

"I don't know about that," said I. "However, I am going back."

"To London?"

"To London."

"I shall be there too, soon after you."

I knew that as well as he did. But I did not tell him so. Any more than I told him what defensive weapon my right hand rested on in my pocket, as I walked by his side. Any more than I told him why I did not walk on the sea side of him with the night closing in.

We left the beach, and our ways diverged. We exchanged good-night, and had parted indeed, when he said, returning,

"Mr. Sampson, *may* I ask? Poor Meltham, whom we spoke of, – dead yet?"

"Not when I last heard of him; but too broken a man to live long, and hopelessly lost to his old calling."

"Dear, dear, dear!" said he, with great feeling. "Sad, sad, sad! The world is a grave!" And so went his way.

It was not his fault if the world were not a grave; but I did not call that observation after him, any more than I had mentioned those other things just now enumerated. He went his way, and I went mine with all expedition. This happened, as I have said, either at the end of September or beginning of October. The next time I saw him, and the last time, was late in November.

V

I HAD a very particular engagement to breakfast in the Temple. It was a bitter north-easterly morning, and the sleet and slush lay inches deep in the streets. I could get no conveyance, and was soon wet to the knees; but I should have been true to that appointment, though I had to wade to it up to my neck in the same impediments.

The appointment took me to some chambers in the Temple. They were at the top of a lonely corner house overlooking the river. The name, Mr. Alfred Beckwith, was painted on the outer door. On the door opposite, on the same landing, the name Mr. Julius Slinkton. The doors of both sets of chambers stood open, so that anything said aloud in one set could be heard in the other.

I had never been in those chambers before. They were dismal, close, unwholesome, and oppressive; the furniture, originally good, and not yet old, was faded and dirty, – the rooms were in great disorder; there was a strong prevailing smell of opium, brandy, and tobacco; the grate and fire-irons were splashed all over with unsightly blotches of rust; and on a sofa by the fire, in the room where breakfast had been prepared, lay the host, Mr. Beckwith, a man with all the appearances of the worst kind of drunkard, very far advanced upon his shameful way to death.

"Slinkton is not come yet," said this creature, staggering up when I went in; "I'll call him. – Halloa! Julius Cæsar! Come and drink!" As he hoarsely roared this out, he beat the poker and tongs together in a mad way, as if that were his usual manner of summoning his associate.

The voice of Mr. Slinkton was heard through the clatter from the opposite side of the staircase, and he came in. He had not expected the pleasure of meeting me. I have seen several artful men brought to a stand, but I never saw a man so aghast as he was when his eyes rested on mine.

"Julius Cæsar," cried Beckwith, staggering between us, "Mist' Sampson! Mist' Sampson, Julius Cæsar! Julius, Mist' Sampson, is the friend of my soul. Julius keeps me plied with liquor, morning, noon, and night. Julius is a real benefactor. Julius threw the tea and coffee out of window when I used to have any. Julius empties all the water-jugs of their contents, and fills 'em with spirits. Julius winds me up and keeps me going. – Boil the brandy, Julius!"

There was a rusty and furred saucepan in the ashes, – the ashes looked like the accumulation of weeks, – and Beckwith, rolling and staggering between us as if he were going to plunge headlong into the fire, got the saucepan out, and tried to force it into Slinkton's hand.

"Boil the brandy, Julius Cæsar! Come! Do your usual office. Boil the brandy!"

He became so fierce in his gesticulations with the saucepan, that I expected to see him lay open Slinkton's head with it. I therefore put out my hand to check him. He reeled back to the sofa, and sat there panting, shaking, and red-eyed, in his rags of dressing-gown, looking at us both. I noticed then that there was nothing to drink on the table but brandy, and nothing to eat but salted herrings, and a hot, sickly, highly-peppered stew.

"At all events, Mr. Sampson," said Slinkton, offering me the smooth gravel path for the last time, "I thank you for interfering between me and this unfortunate man's violence. However you came here, Mr. Sampson, or with whatever motive you came here, at least I thank you for that."

"Boil the brandy," muttered Beckwith.

Without gratifying his desire to know how I came there, I said, quietly, "How is your niece, Mr. Slinkton?"

He looked hard at me, and I looked hard at him.

"I am sorry to say, Mr. Sampson, that my niece has proved treacherous and ungrateful to her best friend. She left me without a word of notice or explanation. She was misled, no doubt, by some designing rascal. Perhaps you may have heard of it."

"I did hear that she was misled by a designing rascal. In fact, I have proof of it."

"Are you sure of that?" said he.

"Quite."

"Boil the brandy," muttered Beckwith. "Company to breakfast, Julius Cæsar. Do your usual office, – provide the usual breakfast, dinner, tea, and supper. Boil the brandy!"

The eyes of Slinkton looked from him to me, and he said, after a moment's consideration, "Mr. Sampson, you are a man of the world, and so am I. I will be plain with you."

"O no, you won't," said I, shaking my head.

"I tell you, sir, I will be plain with you."

"And I tell you you will not," said I. "I know all about you. *You* plain with any one? Nonsense, nonsense!"

"I plainly tell you, Mr. Sampson," he went on, with a manner almost composed, "that I understand your object. You want to save your funds, and escape from your liabilities; these are old tricks of trade with you Office-gentlemen. But you will not do it, sir; you will not succeed. You have not an easy adversary to play against, when you play against me. We shall have to inquire, in due time, when and how Mr. Beckwith fell into his present habits. With that remark, sir, I put this poor creature, and his incoherent wanderings of speech, aside, and wish you a good morning and a better case next time."

While he was saying this, Beckwith had filled a half-pint glass with brandy. At this moment, he threw the brandy at his face, and threw the glass after it. Slinkton put his hands up, half blinded with the spirit, and cut with the glass across the forehead. At the sound of the breakage, a fourth person came into the room, closed the door, and stood at it; he was a very quiet but very keen-looking man, with iron-gray hair, and slightly lame.

Slinkton pulled out his handkerchief, assuaged the pain in his smarting eyes, and dabbled the blood on his forehead. He was a long time about it, and I saw that in the doing of it, a tremendous change came over him, occasioned by the change in Beckwith, – who ceased to pant and tremble, sat upright, and never took his eyes off him. I never in my life saw a face in which abhorrence and determination were so forcibly painted as in Beckwith's then.

"Look at me, you villain," said Beckwith, "and see me as I really am. I took these rooms, to make them a trap for you. I came into them as a drunkard, to bait the trap for you. You fell into the trap, and you will never leave it alive. On the morning when you last went to Mr. Sampson's office, I had seen him first. Your plot has been known to both of us, all along, and you have been counter-plotted all along. What? Having been cajoled into putting that prize of two thousand pounds in your power, I was to be done to death with brandy, and, brandy not proving quick enough, with something quicker? Have I never seen you, when you thought my senses gone, pouring from your little bottle into my glass? Why, you Murderer and Forger, alone here with you in the dead of night, as I have so often been, I have had my hand upon the trigger of a pistol, twenty times, to blow your brains out!"

This sudden starting up of the thing that he had supposed to be his imbecile victim into a determined man, with a settled resolution to hunt him down and be the death of him, mercilessly expressed from head to foot, was, in the first shock, too much for him. Without any figure of speech, he staggered under it. But there is no greater mistake than to suppose that a man who is a calculating criminal, is, in any phase of his guilt, otherwise than true to himself, and perfectly consistent with his whole character. Such a man commits murder, and murder is the natural culmination of his course; such a man has to outface murder, and will do it with hardihood and effrontery. It is a sort of fashion to express surprise that any notorious criminal, having such crime upon his conscience, can so brave it out. Do you think that if he had it on his conscience at all, or had a conscience to have it upon, he would ever have committed the crime?

Perfectly consistent with himself, as I believe all such monsters to be, this Slinkton recovered himself, and showed a defiance that was sufficiently cold and quiet. He was white, he was haggard, he was changed; but only as a sharper who had played for a great stake and had been outwitted and had lost the game.

"Listen to me, you villain," said Beckwith, "and let every word you hear me say be a stab in your wicked heart. When I took these rooms, to throw myself in your way and lead you on to the scheme that I knew my appearance and supposed character and habits would suggest to such a devil, how did I know that? Because you were no stranger to me. I knew you well. And I knew you to be the cruel wretch who, for so much money, had killed one innocent girl while she trusted him implicitly, and who was by inches killing another."

Slinkton took out a snuff-box, took a pinch of snuff, and laughed.

"But see here," said Beckwith, never looking away, never raising his voice, never relaxing his face, never unclenching his hand. "See what a dull wolf you have been, after all! The infatuated drunkard who never drank a fiftieth part of the liquor you plied him with, but poured it away, here, there, everywhere – almost before your eyes; who bought over the fellow you set to watch him and to ply him, by outbidding you in his bribe, before he had been at his work three days – with whom you have observed no caution, yet who was so bent on ridding the earth of you as a wild beast, that he would have defeated you if you had been ever so prudent – that drunkard whom you have, many a time, left on the floor of this room, and who has even let you go out of it, alive and undeceived, when you have turned him over with your foot – has, almost as often, on the same night, within an hour, within a few minutes, watched you awake, had his hand at your pillow when you were asleep, turned over your papers, taken samples from your bottles and packets of powder, changed their contents, rifled every secret of your life!"

He had had another pinch of snuff in his hand, but had gradually let it drop from between his fingers to the floor; where he now smoothed it out with his foot, looking down at it the while.

"That drunkard," said Beckwith, "who had free access to your rooms at all times, that he might drink the strong drinks that you left in his way and be the sooner ended, holding no more terms with you than he would hold with a tiger, has had his master-key for all your locks, his test for all your poisons, his clue to your cipher-writing. He can tell you, as well as you can tell him, how long it took to complete that deed, what doses there were, what intervals, what signs of gradual decay upon mind and body; what distempered fancies were produced, what observable changes, what physical pain. He can tell you, as well as you can tell him, that all this was recorded day by day, as a lesson of experience for future service. He can tell you, better than you can tell him, where that journal is at this moment."

Slinkton stopped the action of his foot, and looked at Beckwith.

"No," said the latter, as if answering a question from him. "Not in the drawer of the writing-desk that opens with a spring; it is not there, and it never will be there again."

"Then you are a thief!" said Slinkton.

Without any change whatever in the inflexible purpose, which it was quite terrific even to me to contemplate, and from the power of which I had always felt convinced it was impossible for this wretch to escape, Beckwith returned, "And I am your niece's shadow, too."

With an imprecation Slinkton put his hand to his head, tore out some hair, and flung it to the ground. It was the end of the smooth walk; he destroyed it in the action, and it will soon be seen that his use for it was past.

Beckwith went on: "Whenever you left here, I left here. Although I understood that you found it necessary to pause in the completion of that purpose, to avert suspicion, still I watched you close, with the poor confiding girl. When I had the diary, and could read it word by word, – it was only about the night before your last visit to Scarborough, – you remember the night? you slept with a small flat vial tied to your wrist, – I sent to Mr. Sampson, who was kept out of view. This is Mr. Sampson's trusty servant standing by the door. We three saved your niece among us."

Slinkton looked at us all, took an uncertain step or two from the place where he had stood, returned to it, and glanced about him in a very curious way, – as one of the meaner reptiles might, looking for a hole to hide in. I noticed at the same time, that a singular change took place in the figure of the man, – as if it collapsed within his clothes, and they consequently became ill-shapen and ill-fitting.

"You shall know," said Beckwith, "for I hope the knowledge will be bitter and terrible to you, why you have been pursued by one man, and why, when the whole interest that Mr. Sampson represents would have expended any money in hunting you down, you have been tracked to death at a single individual's charge. I hear you have had the name of Meltham on your lips sometimes?"

I saw, in addition to those other changes, a sudden stoppage come upon his breathing.

"When you sent the sweet girl whom you murdered (you know with what artfully made-out surroundings and probabilities you sent her) to Meltham's office, before taking her abroad to originate the transaction that doomed her to the grave, it fell to Meltham's lot to see her and to speak with her. It did not fall to his lot to save her, though I know he would freely give his own life to have done it. He admired her; – I would say he loved her deeply, if I thought it possible that you could understand the word. When she was sacrificed, he was thoroughly assured of your guilt. Having lost her, he had but one object left in life, and that was to avenge her and destroy you."

I saw the villain's nostrils rise and fall convulsively; but I saw no moving at his mouth.

"That man Meltham," Beckwith steadily pursued, "was as absolutely certain that you could never elude him in this world, if he devoted himself to your destruction with his utmost fidelity and earnestness, and if he divided the sacred duty with no other duty in life, as he was certain that in achieving it he would be a poor instrument in the hands of Providence, and would do well before Heaven in striking you out from among living men. I am that man, and I thank God that I have done my work!"

If Slinkton had been running for his life from swift-footed savages, a dozen miles, he could not have shown more emphatic signs of being oppressed at heart and labouring for breath, than he showed now, when he looked at the pursuer who had so relentlessly hunted him down.

"You never saw me under my right name before; you see me under my right name now. You shall see me once again in the body, when you are tried for your life. You shall see me once again in the spirit, when the cord is round your neck, and the crowd are crying against you!"

When Meltham had spoken these last words, the miscreant suddenly turned away his face, and seemed to strike his mouth with his open hand. At the same instant, the room was filled with a new and powerful odour, and, almost at the same instant, he broke into a crooked run, leap, start, – I have no name for the spasm, – and fell, with a dull weight that shook the heavy old doors and windows in their frames.

That was the fitting end of him.

When we saw that he was dead, we drew away from the room, and Meltham, giving me his hand, said, with a weary air,

"I have no more work on earth, my friend. But I shall see her again elsewhere."

It was in vain that I tried to rally him. He might have saved her, he said; he had not saved her, and he reproached himself; he had lost her, and he was broken-hearted.

"The purpose that sustained me is over, Sampson, and there is nothing now to hold me to life. I am not fit for life; I am weak and spiritless; I have no hope and no object; my day is done."

In truth, I could hardly have believed that the broken man who then spoke to me was the man who had so strongly and so differently impressed me when his purpose was before him. I used such entreaties with him, as I could; but he still said, and always said, in a patient, undemonstrative way, – nothing could avail him, – he was broken-hearted.

He died early in the next spring. He was buried by the side of the poor young lady for whom he had cherished those tender and unhappy regrets; and he left all he had to her sister. She lived to be a happy wife and mother; she married my sister's son, who succeeded poor Meltham; she is living now, and her children ride about the garden on my walking-stick when I go to see her.

Skitter and Click

Jennifer Dornan-Fish

THE PHONE RANG just after Katie Swanson took a half-frozen bite from the TV dinner balanced on her knees. She picked up expecting her ex. She'd let Cole keep the goddamned house, what else could he want from her?

"Jake never did understand why you didn't come save him."

Katie blinked at the phone. It took her a moment to understand what the synthesized electronic voice said. Five years after her son was murdered and sickos still took the time to taunt her with crank calls. Unbelievable.

She slammed down the phone, took another bite and let the slushy gravy roll on her tongue while her heart pounded in her ears. She looked around at her new apartment. Towering boxes stood sentry along bare white walls. Faded yellow linoleum floor. Used furniture in shades of grey and brown.

The soulless space was a relief after so many years living with Jake's ghost, fading crayon marks on the walls and scooter marks on the wood floors. How could Cole stand to live there?

The phone rang again and she picked up, ready to lash out.

"At least poor Jake had Skitter as he died."

Katie's heart stopped beating. Who knew the name of Jake's stuffed tiger? They hadn't even told the cops. It had hurt too much to repeat the name that Jake said so often with his little lisp. The night that Jake's body was found, Katie couldn't stop wondering where Skitter was with his tattered ears and love-worn tail. Had the killer kept Jake's object of comfort as a trophy?

Laughter echoed in her ear and then he hung up.

Click.

Katie slammed the phone to the ground then vomited half-frozen Salisbury steak onto the cracked linoleum floor.

* * *

"I'm sorry Mr. and Mrs. Swanson, the calls can't be traced." The detective from Jake's case sat across from them, calm hands in his lap.

Katie remembered every detail of Detective Franklin. She could picture him five years ago as he sat in the exact same spot on their sofa and explained how their son's broken body was found. How the detective's cracked lips moved as he described the horrors that had been done to Jake. The way the shadow cut across his puffy blue eyes as he reassured them that the killer would be found.

Now Detective Franklin had a few wrinkles and gray peppered his temples but he had the same calm hands.

"They came from what we call a burner phone, pay as you go, no records to track."

"It was him. No one else could have known about Skitter." Katie fought tears, furious that they would rise just when she wanted to be taken seriously.

Cole put his hand over hers, a gesture of habit. "Katie, it's just another crank call. Anyone could have found out what he called that stuffed tiger."

"How? How could they know?" The tears pushed out of her eyes and she turned, ready to scream into Cole's impassive face.

Detective Franklin interrupted the impending fight. "I'll let myself out. We will definitely follow up on this, don't worry Mrs. Swanson. The crew will come out to your apartment later today and set up a trace on your phone."

As the detective left, Katie pulled her hand from under Cole's.

* * *

The next call came that night.

"Jake never gave up on you. He never stopped calling out for his mommy."

Katie's chest heaved with emotion but she remained silent.

"I told him you didn't care any more."

The words shattered Katie into a thousand pieces. Her worst fear... that Jake had died scared, alone, convinced that his mommy had abandoned him.

"But don't worry. He at least had Skitter."

Click.

Katie let out the guttural sound that welled from her mouth.

* * *

Then the next night.

"I'm calling to help you."

"You're calling to torture me," Katie answered. Detective Franklin said she should try to engage him in conversation.

"No, really." the electronic voice said, "I'll answer your question if you let me."

"What question?" Katie whispered, not really wanting to know.

"After they found Jake, you asked how someone could do that to your son. How someone could murder an innocent child. I'm going to answer your question."

Click.

* * *

"It's been over five weeks Mrs. Swanson." Detective Franklin's cheeks sagged with defeat. "We've done all we can. Can't trace the calls. Nothing on the audio. Our language expert says he isn't talking enough to give them anything to go on."

For once, the detective's calm hands fidgeted. "I hate to say it, but we've run out of resources for such an old case, especially since we aren't a hundred percent sure this is even the killer calling you."

"It's him. I know it is," Katie insisted. Tears flooded her eyes again.

"Katie, let the detective leave. I'm sure he has a lot of new cases he should be working on. Thank you so much for all your help Detective Franklin."

She heard the men shaking hands at the door.

Cole came back frowning, "Kathryn, you've just got to stop taking those calls. He's just hurting you all over again which is clearly what this guy wants. It won't bring Jake back."

Katie let herself out without responding.

* * *

By the sixth week of calls, she was numb to the familiar electronic voice. She knew it was sick, but talking to the disembodied voice made her feel closer to Jake, her last connection to her son.

"Jake was strong. It took him a long time to die."

She listened with resignation, her penance for letting Jake ride his scooter alone in the front yard.

"He t-t-t-tried to stop the bleeding. Poor Jake wanted to see you again."

Click.

The stutter snapped Katie to full attention. A stutter... a stutter. Something rang deep in her memory.

Who involved in Jake's case had a stutter? She frantically called Detective Franklin who tried to sound enthusiastic.

"Sounds interesting Mrs. Swanson, I'll take a look back through my notes when I have time. Maybe next week."

Click.

She called Cole.

"Dammit Katie, let this go. Who the fuck cares if the caller stuttered. I don't even think it's the killer calling you, just some sick asshole. I think it's time for you to just stop calling me at all."

Click.

Katie stared at the gunmetal filing cabinet in the corner of her apartment. Inside sat The File – everything she had collected about Jake's murder – the newspaper clippings, case files, and general ephemera that accumulated around any public tragedy.

She rescued The File from Cole only a few weeks before. He'd been about to throw it away. Apparently it was creeping out his new girlfriend. Katie briefly imagined Cole's girlfriend walking over the scuffs left on the floor left by Jake's scooter. Her bare feet sliding over the gouges. Did that creep her out too?

With that thought rolling around her brain, Katie sat on the threadbare sofa with a beer, then another, and another, until the anger outweighed her fear. With booze flaming the wild animal in her gut, she pulled open the drawer. On top a magazine cover screamed *Child Murder!* The cover photo was of Katie alone, kneeling on the ground, head buried in her hands.

"My life achievement... the cover model for a story on child murder," she slurred.

Katie yanked out the pile of clipped articles and threw them on the table where they smacked down with a puff of dust. *Missing Boy Found Tortured! Suburban Neighborhood Shattered! How Could Someone Do This Cries Mother!* The media frenzy had been intense.

With more care she moved onto the case files. After pestering him for months, Detective Franklin broke every rule in the book and shared almost everything with her, including the suspect list he had diligently worked through. He had really cared. Katie remembered watched his failure eat him just like it ate her. She ran her finger along the old photocopy of the suspect list until she came to the name Zachary Taylor.

A door in her memory unlocked as she pictured Zach, the neighborhood boy with the stutter. Closing her eyes, Katie only had one true memory of him; willowy, thin lipped, he rode by on his skateboard. Jake ran after him hoping the older boy would stop and let him have a ride. Instead, Zach scowled back at Jake and kept on going. It was a trifling image that suddenly felt very important.

Hands shaking, Katie flipped through the case file until she found his name. Zach Taylor, then thirteen, had been questioned after being seen alone behind the mall where Jake's body was recovered. Zach claimed he was hanging out alone in the arcade at the time of Jake's disappearance. *Alibi corroborated.* That's all the case file said. Corroborated by what?

Katie dialed the detective.

Franklin answered with a sleep-thick voice. "Yeah, I remember that kid. He felt weaselly but his alibi checked out so it couldn't have been him, Mrs. Swanson."

"How did it check out?"

Detective Franklin sighed. "Listen, I promise you we didn't miss anything. I can't remember that kid's alibi, but we checked it. It will be there in the file."

"But, the caller stuttered. On the phone..." Katie trailed off.

"I'm going to have to go Mrs. Swanson. Send me the tape and I'll take a listen when I can."

Click.

* * *

She combed the files and found nothing about Zachary Taylor's alibi. She went through it again. After the third read, Katie swigged the warm remnants of beer and stared down at the photo of her collapsed in grief on the front of the old magazine.

Victim's Mother.

Poor Katie Swanson.

Mother of a murdered child, full of nothing but impotent grief. That was how she had spent the last five years of her life: swallowed by a fog of sorrow.

"No." Katie said it softly at first but the sound of her own voice knocked something loose at the center of her chest.

"No," she said again, louder.

She stood up. "No! I won't let it go. I won't walk away."

On her ancient computer, she searched for Zachary Taylor and found him, now eighteen, still living at home with his parents just two blocks away from her old home.

Katie Swanson strode out the front door.

* * *

She sat in her car and watched the suburban house where Zach Taylor lived. The unkept lawn and rusting junker in the driveway suggested that the Taylors weren't exactly keeping up with the Joneses.

The house remained quiet and dark as the sun set. Katie played the stuttering phone call over and over in her mind. She pictured the thin-lipped boy glancing back at Jake with hatred in his eyes.

The moon rose and cicadas began their raucous serenade. Dancing fireflies lit the tall grass. Things Jake would never get to enjoy.

Katie felt slightly shaky with a dull headache working on her optic nerves. Buzz fading she knew her liquid courage was almost gone.

"Now or never Katie."

She decided she would just sneak into the house. Look around. Get a feel for Zack Taylor at eighteen. Was he a man now? Did he have a girlfriend? Did he plan to go to college? Did he steal those possible futures from her own son?

* * *

The back door swung open, unlocked.

Katie stood in the doorway listening for any sign of life.

Nothing.

On cat feet she crept into the kitchen and along the darkened hallway.

Behind her a light clicked on and she spun, panting with adrenaline.

Silence.

She approached the lamp and found it plugged into a vacation timer. In the hall, bills and catalogues piled on the floor in front of the mail slot.

The Taylors were out of town.

Wiping paste from the corner of her mouth, Katie continued her circuit of the house, more boldly now.

A single photo on the mantle showed a narrow shouldered young man smiling in a green cap and gown. His lips were still thin but his eyes sparkled with joy. Shouldn't his eyes seem cold?

Upstairs, Katie found Zach's room. It smelled of musty sweat and lemon cleaner. In the moonlight she could make out skate posters, a rumpled bed, dirty socks on the floor.

She clicked on the light in his closet. Swept her arm under the bed. Rifled through his drawers.

Nothing but a well-worn copy of playboy stuffed under his mattress.

"What did you expect to find? You idiot," Katie chastised herself.

Making sure she left everything undisturbed, she was about to retreat to her car when she noticed the basement door. A bright new padlock hung open on the latch. Body crackling with anticipation, she lifted the padlock, opened the heavy metal door, and descended into the darkness.

Her hand skipped along the wall until it found a light switch.

Katie flipped the switch and yellow light temporarily blinded her.

Disappointment settled in as she stared at a well-used workshop. Scarred workbench covered by sawdust, a power saw, two hammers, a case of wrenches, everything a handyman would need.

But then Katie noticed the small stuffed animal nestled high on a shelf between a toolbox and pair of clunky work gloves.

Katie felt like she was floating above the floor as she moved toward it.

They found Jakes clothes, his little bike helmet and white sneakers, his electric green scooter, even his good luck coin. The only thing missing from his body was Skitter.

Not daring to breathe, she gently lifted the stuffed animal and turned it over like a baby bird. The little tiger's head flopped to the side, tattered ears and love-worn tail exactly as she remembered.

Chest aching from holding her breath she lifted the silky tag to her face. In her own handwriting the scrawled ink said Jake Swanson.

Katie dropped Skitter and stumbled back.

As she did, a sound echoed from above.

Heavy footfalls and a reedy voice, "Mom? Dad? D-d-d-did you guys come back early?"

Katie stared at Skitter. Images flooded her. Jake crying, alone and scared in this very basement. The hammer and drill suddenly instruments of torture. The drain at the center of the cement floor running with Jake's blood. Then a jolt as she imagined Jake's lopsided grin as he figured out how to button his own jacket. Jake slowly bleeding out, confused by the pain. Jake's peels of laughter as Cole chased him around the house. The little being she had loved more than her own heart, gone. Her breath came in small gasps. A moaning animal welled from her chest, tearing its way out of her body.

More heavy footfalls from above.

"Mom? Is that you? Are y-y-you okay down there?" The door at the top of the stairs swung open.

Katie's entire body shuddered. The world faded to roaring static as she reached for something. Her fingers closed on metal and she turned just as Zach Taylor stepped into the basement, squinting in the bright light.

Groaning a sound that had lived trapped inside of her since the afternoon Jake went missing, Katie swung the hammer down into his face.

Zachary Taylor collapsed to the floor, dead before Katie could swing at him again.

* * *

Katie had no memory of her vague attempt to clean up nor her trip home.

She knew she as going to jail, but she had done it! She didn't care if she died tomorrow. She had found and destroyed Jake's killer.

Giggling with manic joy, Katie stumbled into her apartment as the phone began to ring.

She answered hoping it was Cole so she could tell him what she'd done.

"Hello Katie," said the flat electronic voice.

"But... what?" was all she managed to say, heart fluttering.

"I've answered your question."

"I... I don't understand." Katie's head spun. Had she gone crazy? How could Zach Taylor be calling her now?

"A little stutter here. A planted Skitter there. It was easy to frame p-p-poor Zach. I told you to let these calls go, Kathryn."

The electronic voice chuckled.

Katie stared down at a streak of blood drying on her shaking hand still clenching Skitter.

"But... why..."

"That hatred you felt. The rage that let you do such a terrible thing. That is how I feel every day. That is how you kill an innocent person... which is exactly what you just did."

Click.

Paperboxing Art

James Dorr

RED. The color of fire.

Of pain.

The color of flames that tear through my head, destroying soft gray synapses beneath them.

The color of drugs – except I don't use drugs.

But also, the color of pretty paper.

* * *

I woke in a paper white room long ago to a smell of perfume, cool and antiseptic. A woman's face hovered just above mine, surrounded with cloud-pale yellow hair. A memory behind it, a darker haired woman.

But then a voice that cut through all thinking, softer than birdsong. Sweeter than water.

"I'm Dr. Rhodes." That's all the voice said then. Later it added, "Call me Cecilia," and, later still, taught me how to make boxes.

* * *

Dr. Cecilia Rhodes was my therapist and she taught me to make paper boxes. She taught me what happened, guiding my memory. She led me by hand through the red-pain haze of a trip on bad drugs to the more cheerful scarlet of China-smooth sizing.

She taught me selection – you first choose your paper for beauty, for strength. She taught me dimension, the eight-times scale between unformed sheet and the finished object. She taught me the folds, first crease, second crease, both to the center for all four sides. The cutting, the gluing. The gluing is optional, yet adds permanence to one's creation.

She taught me surfaces. Taught me my name.

"Anton," she said. I was called Anton Wyckoff, before I came here. "Anton," she said, "you once were a sculptor. A good one too. You were on television once – I remember. In New York harbor."

"I covered a statue," I said, remembering. "A statue that carried a torch in its hand."

The red of its flame – no a cool, green copper. The orange of plastic.

"You covered it with a plastic cone," she said. "A rocket shaped cone that stayed up for a week. There were some people who didn't like it, but it was a tribute you'd built to honor America's spacemen."

"Yes." I remembered. My first large commission. I'd called it *Ad Astra* and built it to show the soaring of dreams.

"That's why I chose this therapy for you," Cecilia continued. "Making boxes to help you remember being an artist. The calmness of shaping things with your hands, before you were famous. Before life drove you..."

She left it unfinished. Before life drove me to drugs, she would say – I'd heard her speak to the other doctors – and landed me here.

But I never used drugs.

* * *

In my second month of recovery I caught a glimpse of a dark haired woman with ivory-carved cheekbones and sapphire eyes. The one I'd remembered when I saw Cecilia the morning I woke in the white-flooded room. By now I could roam the hospital grounds – it was really more of a sanitarium, out in the country – and spotted her coming through the trees of the northwest quarter.

I turned and ran.

* * *

The next time I saw her, she and a man I halfway remembered were walking again, this time with Cecilia. When my time for therapy came, I asked about her.

"Are you sure you don't know her?" Cecilia asked.

I shook my head slowly, but then I *did* know her.

"Mara," I said. "She's my wife, isn't she?"

Cecilia nodded, then handed me a poorly wrapped package, done up in brown with badly creased corners. Not neat, like my boxes.

"She gave you this, Anton," Cecilia said. "She asked how you were doing here. How you were coming along with your therapy. Then she said she'd picked this out specially, so you'd have something to read if you wanted."

I unwrapped the package. Inside was a book on the history and manufacture of paper.

* * *

Making Boxes: The Basic Box.

After the paper is selected, it must be cut to be perfectly square. At first Cecilia helped me with this, but now I can do it without supervision. Then the ruling – two lines are drawn from corner to corner, making an 'X' through the paper's center – and then the first creases, corner to middle, to form a diamond within the square.

The squareness, the ruling – both teach proportion. Proportion in beauty as well as in life. And then the first fold, from square to diamond, followed by the second creases – all four new sides bent on themselves till they touch the center – to form a new diamond half again as small as the old one. The folds teach eye-hand coordination. They teach the mind calmness.

And then the *un*folding – a network of diamonds within the square, the centermost of which will be the box's bottom. This brings revelation. It brings the mind focus. I know who the man is who walked with Mara.

I know that he smokes strong black cigars and his name is Tom Peters. He wears pinstriped suits and he worked for me once, before I came here, as my business manager.

I don't remember whether I liked him – Mara hired him – but he got me exhibitions and helped me make money.

That's what Cecilia said when I asked her. "Money," she added, "is what pays your fees here. Mr. Peters invested part of it in a trust for you. It lets us bend the rules when he brings your wife here to visit" – she looked a little sad when she said this – "about his smoking. It buys you your paper."

The paper unfolded, a network of diamonds. Along the lines that form the diamonds, two pairs of cuts are made toward the center. On opposite sides the paper is lifted, folded again and again on itself to form two 'U' shapes standing at right angles to the bottom.

This is for the basic box – a box with no lid. The remaining sides are lifted and pressed, along the creases, over the upright sides of the 'U'. Four drops of contact cement at the bottom – the optional gluing – and then the four sides all fold together, as if they were *meant* to.

As if, like the form of a statue in granite, a stabile in metal, the box-form always existed within the flat sheet of paper.

* * *

"Perhaps, Cecilia," I said one day, "Mr. Peters could arrange an exhibition of some of my boxes." I no longer made just basic boxes, but different shaped boxes and different sized boxes, some with their own lids, some still open-topped, some of them even equipped with secret side-lifting panels.

"Perhaps he can, Anton," Cecilia replied. "Perhaps in a month or so more you'll be ready." She nodded back toward the catalog we'd been going over to make selections for my next project.

The catalog, yes. I'd advanced by now to insisting on different kinds of papers for different projects – I'd read the history book Mara had given me. Different papers from different lands, like Egyptian papyrus or Chinese rice paper; American coated, calendared paper or hand made rag.

Each had its own properties, each its uses, just like, to a stoneworker, one kind of statue might only be carved from Italian marble while a second might scream out for limestone.

I told this to Mara. On visiting days we would walk together, sometimes with Peters and his ever-present cigar, sometimes as a twosome. We'd walk in the woods in the northwest quarter of the sanitarium grounds, where, after my third month of recovery, Cecilia had arranged for an unused gardener's cabin to be renovated into a studio. For my box-sculptures.

I'd talk to Mara about kinds of paper – how each had its uses. How paper was even used for windows in pioneer homes, because it turns clear when it's treated with oil. I'd tell her about the strength of paper: The famous bet about whether a prizefighter could escape from a paper bag and how – even though paper will easily tear when your hands can grip it – its smooth surfaced inside absorbed his best punches. I'd tell her about the making of paper, explaining the difference between the Bel Baie 'twin-wire' process and the more common Fourdriner machine, and Mara would nod with a patient smile. A smile I remembered once filled me with passion.

A long time ago.

And yet she would smile again and say, "I'm glad you're getting better, Anton. When will you be home?"

"I don't know," I'd tell her. "I'll ask."

I'd ask Cecilia.

* * *

An exhibition. Cecilia said she had talked to Peters about inviting people to my studio cabin and showing some of my latest boxes. Peters had said he thought he could arrange it, possibly by the end of the month. Mara had said she approved the idea too. And then Cecilia had added the news that, if the showing went off without trouble, perhaps I could be released to go home.

Cecilia told me this after I asked her, yet, instead of seeming happy, she looked down at the latest catalog we had been going over together. Her voice sounded worried – possibly sad.

"Anton," she said, "it will be a big moment. A dangerous moment. If anything goes wrong, it could cause a relapse. Therefore, you must be very careful in selecting the works you will show."

"I understand," I said. "And yet, perhaps I should start off with some simpler works. Some basic boxes. Let them greet visitors at the door, stark and white. Maybe some red colored. Let them build in complexity – perhaps, on one side, different shapes, on the other multi-papered boxes with different textures combined within them. Different designs."

Cecilia nodded. "And in the center? Between the shaped and the textured boxes?"

"In the center, a sort of aisle. But there must be a focus. A masterwork box – something big that they'll see from the door, yet won't see entirely. Something to give the show a message. To draw people in."

"To draw people in, yes," Cecilia said. I looked at her, her head still bowed to the catalog pages, her pale blonde hair floating as if in a halo. I thought of her and the contrast with Mara – Mara glamorous, Cecilia just pretty, but in a sweeter, more basic way.

I thought of Mara – walking with Peters. Flame rushed through my head.

I thought of the Statue of Liberty project, the tribute to science and America's spacemen. The first big commission that Peters had gotten me.

"Are you all right, Anton?"

Peters liked science – he'd once been a chemist. Mara had told me. A long time ago.

"I'm sorry, Cecilia." I nodded and smiled, saw she'd raised her head. I looked into her eyes. "I have an idea. For the centerpiece box. But I'll need special paper. Other things too."

Cecilia smiled back. "All of your projects seem to need some kind of special paper..."

"Yes," I agreed. "But this will be big. A forty, forty-five foot square of paper. Tough, but flexible. Not too heavy. A raw, smooth paper without any coating."

"Forty-five feet, though – are you sure, Anton? Where would you get it?" Cecilia was laughing, feeling, through me, the excitement of a new act of creation.

"Maybe down south. One of the old mills – one that still uses the cylinder process. Call around for me, will you, Cecilia?"

Cecilia nodded.

* * *

Chemistry. Science. Flame and re-entry. I'd found a new project – not a whole rocket, as the cone in New York harbor had represented – but just the capsule. The Astronaut Box.

I kept to myself, was barely civil when Mara and Peters came on their visits. Like in the old days when I was creating – I meant no harm by it.

I scarcely even saw Cecilia except to order new papers for overlays. Black for the top. The jet black extension of the night sky – with star-shaped transparencies. Special oils would be needed to be painted onto the paper. Then, white for the near side, the one facing visitors as they came in, and a different, more volatile oil for a crescent-shaped pilot's window. Black and white. And blue – the royal blue of Earth's oceans. For bottom and back.

Papers and chemicals. Glue for permanence. Everything ordered. Lacquer – re-entry red flame splashed and dappled, as if it shone through the moon-crescent window, reflecting inside.

I had to bar Peters, with his cigar, from my studio cabin. For fear of *real* flame.

I thought to bar Mara.

But then, when the work was almost completed, I found myself weak from the chemical smell. The work was on schedule – the box lay open, nearly completed, only awaiting the final folds to bring it together. The final gluing to seal it tight.

The final painting – the crescent-shaped window.

I needed fresh air.

I left the cabin and went to the woods. I was well on schedule. I saw – I wondered – in the bushes behind the cabin a five gallon can. I shrugged and continued along the path that led into the trees when I smelled another, more acrid smell. The smell of cigar smoke.

And then, like a final folding together, the memory came back of the night before I'd come to the hospital. The night I'd been told that I'd taken bad drugs.

Except... I don't use drugs.

I do drink coffee. Rich, black coffee, even at night. Rich, bitter coffee, like the coffee Mara had served me, ex-chemist Tom Peters standing behind her.

The night that ended with my waking here.

I smelled cigar smoke coming closer, heard Mara giggle. I hid and waited and heard their voices.

"Are you sure the gasoline you've gotten will be enough, Tom?" Mara asked. "Remember we have to burn the whole thing. But it's got to look as though those stupid paints and things he's got in there caused it."

"Yeah," Peters answered. "Enough to burn the whole cabin down. But why do you insist that he be inside when I do it?"

She kissed his cheek. "You know why. He's getting better. Even if he has a relapse – whatever it is that Dr. Rhodes said could happen if his exhibit's a failure – he could still get better *again*. That's something we hadn't counted on, Tom – as long as he lives, he could be a threat to us."

* * *

I waited, silently, until they'd left, then returned to my cabin. The exhibition would be next Monday, two days from now. The fire would be Sunday, late at night – when help would come slowly. Just like my 'accident' with drugs so long before.

Mara's next visit would be Sunday evening – technically a violation of rules, like Peters' smoking on hospital grounds – to help me get ready. Peters, technically, wouldn't be with her.

He'd come on his own.

I slept in the main hospital that night. Cecilia slept in the room next to mine. But I didn't tell her.

I thought of the months since I'd made my first box. About how I'd been happy – happier, possibly, than I had ever been before.

I thought about art and about exhibitions. The joy of creation, but then the intrusion of having to sell. The press of the public. The posing. The fawning. The need for people who smoked cigars, and wore pinstriped suits, to take care of the business.

I could have almost forgiven Mara, who'd brought me happiness in her own way. Mara and Peters – except that it didn't bother them that they'd destroy my art when they killed me.

I thought of my boxes. The Astronaut Box. About how, if I escaped Sunday's fire, I'd continue creating.

I knew what the Astronaut Box was missing.

* * *

"Mara," I said when she came to my cabin, "I need you to model the Astronaut Box."

"I beg your pardon?"

"For only a moment." I sniffed her perfume as she came through the door, barely masking the smell of cigar smoke. I watched as she stopped, her mouth half open, and gazed at the box where it lay, nearly five-and-a-half feet long, its top still open.

"Anton, it's beautiful," she said. "The stars – it's like night. The blue, the white, the depth of the sky..."

"Yes," I said. "And the red of re-entry. See. Look inside."

"I see," she said. "But what do you mean, you want me to model?"

"I want you to climb inside, just for a moment. To look through the transparent stars of the sky."

She shook her head, slowly, then shrugged her shoulders and stepped, gingerly, over the lip.

"Do you want me to lie down, Anton? I think it's going to be too short to fit me."

"Here, take your shoes off" – she handed them to me. "Now lie on your side, face to me. That's right. Don't bring your knees up, just scrunch yourself smaller. Think like an astronaut."

"I'll try," she said.

I helped her fit her shoulders in, her arms at her sides. I kissed her forehead.

"Now just lie still – just for a moment. Think how you'll see the moon and the stars." I made the final crease in the top, put four spots of contact cement on its lip.

I folded it down, till it touched the back, the jet of its star field blending with blue.

The final sealing.

"Anton?"

I barely heard her voice, muffled in paper, as I opened the oil for the crescent window.

"Anton? Get me out of here, Anton."

I saw the top of the box bulge outward, as she attempted to force it open. The glued lid held. And the inside of the box was smooth, like a prizefighter's paper bag, with no projections to grip for tearing.

I started to paint – a wild, splashing moon shape. The front, where I painted, became transparent.

I saw her start screaming.

"Have a pleasant voyage," I whispered. I couldn't resist it. I watched her lips form a four-letter word as I backed to the cabin's single entrance, trailing the rest of the oil in a ribbon along the floor. I let the oil puddle along the threshold and breathed in its smell – a perfume more subtle than that of gasoline, yet just as deadly.

"Peters," I called as I stepped outside. "Tom – are you there?"

I heard something rustle, far in the distance.

"Tom," I called again, "can you hear me? Mara's in trouble!"

The rustling was nearer.

I ran, crouching, into the woods, trying my best to make as little noise as I could. I hid behind the first large tree I came to.

I watched as a glow – a red cigar glow – went rushing past me. Saw Peters' silhouette suddenly framed by the cabin door.

"Mara – Jesus!"

Watched him stumble. Launch himself inside.

The color of fire...

* * *

Red – the color of fire and pain. The flames of destruction.

And white. The paper white walls of a room.

The smell of perfume, cool and antiseptic. Cecilia's perfume. The sight of her hair.

"I'm sorry, Anton," she said as I woke, her face just above mine. "We found you wandering, alone, in the woods. We got there too late to help the others."

"The others?" I asked.

"Your wife and your friend." She shook her head slowly. "Don't you remember?"

I tried to think, but her voice was distracting – sweeter than birdsong and softer than water. I shook my head too.

The only things that I could remember, other than her, were paper boxes.

The Red-Headed League

Arthur Conan Doyle

I HAD called upon my friend, Mr. Sherlock Holmes, one day in the autumn of last year and found him in deep conversation with a very stout, florid-faced, elderly gentleman with fiery red hair. With an apology for my intrusion, I was about to withdraw when Holmes pulled me abruptly into the room and closed the door behind me.

"You could not possibly have come at a better time, my dear Watson," he said cordially.

"I was afraid that you were engaged."

"So I am. Very much so."

"Then I can wait in the next room."

"Not at all. This gentleman, Mr. Wilson, has been my partner and helper in many of my most successful cases, and I have no doubt that he will be of the utmost use to me in yours also."

The stout gentleman half rose from his chair and gave a bob of greeting, with a quick little questioning glance from his small fat-encircled eyes.

"Try the settee," said Holmes, relapsing into his armchair and putting his fingertips together, as was his custom when in judicial moods. "I know, my dear Watson, that you share my love of all that is bizarre and outside the conventions and humdrum routine of everyday life. You have shown your relish for it by the enthusiasm which has prompted you to chronicle, and, if you will excuse my saying so, somewhat to embellish so many of my own little adventures."

"Your cases have indeed been of the greatest interest to me," I observed.

"You will remember that I remarked the other day, just before we went into the very simple problem presented by Miss Mary Sutherland, that for strange effects and extraordinary combinations we must go to life itself, which is always far more daring than any effort of the imagination."

"A proposition which I took the liberty of doubting."

"You did, Doctor, but none the less you must come round to my view, for otherwise I shall keep on piling fact upon fact on you until your reason breaks down under them and acknowledges me to be right. Now, Mr. Jabez Wilson here has been good enough to call upon me this morning, and to begin a narrative which promises to be one of the most singular which I have listened to for some time. You have heard me remark that the strangest and most unique things are very often connected not with the larger but with the smaller crimes, and occasionally, indeed, where there is room for doubt whether any positive crime has been committed. As far as I have heard, it is impossible for me to say whether the present case is an instance of crime or not, but the course of events is certainly among the most singular that I have ever listened to. Perhaps, Mr. Wilson, you would have the great kindness to recommence your narrative. I ask you not merely because my friend Dr. Watson has not heard the opening part but also because the peculiar nature of the story makes me anxious to have every possible detail from your lips. As a rule, when I have heard some slight indication of the course of events, I am able to guide myself by the thousands of other similar cases which occur to my memory. In the present instance I am forced to admit that the facts are, to the best of my belief, unique."

The portly client puffed out his chest with an appearance of some little pride and pulled a dirty and wrinkled newspaper from the inside pocket of his greatcoat. As he glanced down the advertisement column, with his head thrust forward and the paper flattened out upon his knee, I took a good look at the man and endeavoured, after the fashion of my companion, to read the indications which might be presented by his dress or appearance.

I did not gain very much, however, by my inspection. Our visitor bore every mark of being an average commonplace British tradesman, obese, pompous, and slow. He wore rather baggy grey shepherd's check trousers, a not over-clean black frock-coat, unbuttoned in the front, and a drab waistcoat with a heavy brassy Albert chain, and a square pierced bit of metal dangling down as an ornament. A frayed top-hat and a faded brown overcoat with a wrinkled velvet collar lay upon a chair beside him. Altogether, look as I would, there was nothing remarkable about the man save his blazing red head, and the expression of extreme chagrin and discontent upon his features.

Sherlock Holmes' quick eye took in my occupation, and he shook his head with a smile as he noticed my questioning glances. "Beyond the obvious facts that he has at some time done manual labour, that he takes snuff, that he is a Freemason, that he has been in China, and that he has done a considerable amount of writing lately, I can deduce nothing else."

Mr. Jabez Wilson started up in his chair, with his forefinger upon the paper, but his eyes upon my companion.

"How, in the name of good-fortune, did you know all that, Mr. Holmes?" he asked. "How did you know, for example, that I did manual labour. It's as true as gospel, for I began as a ship's carpenter."

"Your hands, my dear sir. Your right hand is quite a size larger than your left. You have worked with it, and the muscles are more developed."

"Well, the snuff, then, and the Freemasonry?"

"I won't insult your intelligence by telling you how I read that, especially as, rather against the strict rules of your order, you use an arc-and-compass breastpin."

"Ah, of course, I forgot that. But the writing?"

"What else can be indicated by that right cuff so very shiny for five inches, and the left one with the smooth patch near the elbow where you rest it upon the desk?"

"Well, but China?"

"The fish that you have tattooed immediately above your right wrist could only have been done in China. I have made a small study of tattoo marks and have even contributed to the literature of the subject. That trick of staining the fishes' scales of a delicate pink is quite peculiar to China. When, in addition, I see a Chinese coin hanging from your watch-chain, the matter becomes even more simple."

Mr. Jabez Wilson laughed heavily. "Well, I never!" said he. "I thought at first that you had done something clever, but I see that there was nothing in it after all."

"I begin to think, Watson," said Holmes, "that I make a mistake in explaining. '*Omne ignotum pro magnifico*,' you know, and my poor little reputation, such as it is, will suffer shipwreck if I am so candid. Can you not find the advertisement, Mr. Wilson?"

"Yes, I have got it now," he answered with his thick red finger planted halfway down the column. "Here it is. This is what began it all. You just read it for yourself, sir."

I took the paper from him and read as follows:

"*TO THE RED-HEADED LEAGUE:*
On account of the bequest of the late Ezekiah Hopkins, of Lebanon,
Pennsylvania, U. S. A., there is now another vacancy open which entitles a member
of the League to a salary of £4 a week for purely nominal services. All red-headed
men who are sound in body and mind and above the age of twenty-one years, are
eligible. Apply in person on Monday, at eleven o'clock, to Duncan Ross, at the offices
of the League, 7 Pope's Court, Fleet Street."

"What on earth does this mean?" I ejaculated after I had twice read over the extraordinary announcement.

Holmes chuckled and wriggled in his chair, as was his habit when in high spirits. "It is a little off the beaten track, isn't it?" said he. "And now, Mr. Wilson, off you go at scratch and tell us all about yourself, your household, and the effect which this advertisement had upon your fortunes. You will first make a note, Doctor, of the paper and the date."

"It is *The Morning Chronicle* of April 27, 1890. Just two months ago."

"Very good. Now, Mr. Wilson?"

"Well, it is just as I have been telling you, Mr. Sherlock Holmes," said Jabez Wilson, mopping his forehead; "I have a small pawnbroker's business at Coburg Square, near the City. It's not a very large affair, and of late years it has not done more than just give me a living. I used to be able to keep two assistants, but now I only keep one; and I would have a job to pay him but that he is willing to come for half wages so as to learn the business."

"What is the name of this obliging youth?" asked Sherlock Holmes.

"His name is Vincent Spaulding, and he's not such a youth, either. It's hard to say his age. I should not wish a smarter assistant, Mr. Holmes; and I know very well that he could better himself and earn twice what I am able to give him. But, after all, if he is satisfied, why should I put ideas in his head?"

"Why, indeed? You seem most fortunate in having an employee who comes under the full market price. It is not a common experience among employers in this age. I don't know that your assistant is not as remarkable as your advertisement."

"Oh, he has his faults, too," said Mr. Wilson. "Never was such a fellow for photography. Snapping away with a camera when he ought to be improving his mind, and then diving down into the cellar like a rabbit into its hole to develop his pictures. That is his main fault, but on the whole he's a good worker. There's no vice in him."

"He is still with you, I presume?"

"Yes, sir. He and a girl of fourteen, who does a bit of simple cooking and keeps the place clean – that's all I have in the house, for I am a widower and never had any family. We live very quietly, sir, the three of us; and we keep a roof over our heads and pay our debts, if we do nothing more.

"The first thing that put us out was that advertisement. Spaulding, he came down into the office just this day eight weeks, with this very paper in his hand, and he says:

" 'I wish to the Lord, Mr. Wilson, that I was a red-headed man.'

" 'Why that?' I asks.

" 'Why,' says he, 'here's another vacancy on the League of the Red-headed Men. It's worth quite a little fortune to any man who gets it, and I understand that there are more vacancies than there are men, so that the trustees are at their wits' end what to do with the money. If my hair would only change colour, here's a nice little crib all ready for me to step into.'

" 'Why, what is it, then?' I asked. You see, Mr. Holmes, I am a very stay-at-home man, and as my business came to me instead of my having to go to it, I was often weeks on end without putting my foot over the doormat. In that way I didn't know much of what was going on outside, and I was always glad of a bit of news.

" 'Have you never heard of the League of the Red-headed Men?' he asked with his eyes open.

" 'Never.'

" 'Why, I wonder at that, for you are eligible yourself for one of the vacancies.'

" 'And what are they worth?' I asked.

" 'Oh, merely a couple of hundred a year, but the work is slight, and it need not interfere very much with one's other occupations.'

"Well, you can easily think that that made me prick up my ears, for the business has not been over good for some years, and an extra couple of hundred would have been very handy.

" 'Tell me all about it,' said I.

" 'Well,' said he, showing me the advertisement, 'you can see for yourself that the League has a vacancy, and there is the address where you should apply for particulars. As far as I can make out, the League was founded by an American millionaire, Ezekiah Hopkins, who was very peculiar in his ways. He was himself red-headed, and he had a great sympathy for all red-headed men; so, when he died, it was found that he had left his enormous fortune in the hands of trustees, with instructions to apply the interest to the providing of easy berths to men whose hair is of that colour. From all I hear it is splendid pay and very little to do.'

" 'But,' said I, 'there would be millions of red-headed men who would apply.'

" 'Not so many as you might think,' he answered. 'You see it is really confined to Londoners, and to grown men. This American had started from London when he was young, and he wanted to do the old town a good turn. Then, again, I have heard it is no use your applying if your hair is light red, or dark red, or anything but real bright, blazing, fiery red. Now, if you cared to apply, Mr. Wilson, you would just walk in; but perhaps it would hardly be worth your while to put yourself out of the way for the sake of a few hundred pounds.'

"Now, it is a fact, gentlemen, as you may see for yourselves, that my hair is of a very full and rich tint, so that it seemed to me that if there was to be any competition in the matter I stood as good a chance as any man that I had ever met. Vincent Spaulding seemed to know so much about it that I thought he might prove useful, so I just ordered him to put up the shutters for the day and to come right away with me. He was very willing to have a holiday, so we shut the business up and started off for the address that was given us in the advertisement.

"I never hope to see such a sight as that again, Mr. Holmes. From north, south, east, and west every man who had a shade of red in his hair had tramped into the city to answer the advertisement. Fleet Street was choked with red-headed folk, and Pope's Court looked like a coster's orange barrow. I should not have thought there were so many in the whole country as were brought together by that single advertisement. Every shade of colour they were – straw, lemon, orange, brick, Irish-setter, liver, clay; but, as Spaulding said, there were not many who had the real vivid flame-coloured tint. When I saw how many were waiting, I would have given it up in despair; but Spaulding would not hear of it. How he did it I could not imagine, but he pushed and pulled and butted until he got me through the crowd, and right up to the steps which led to the office. There was a double stream upon the stair, some going up in hope, and some coming back dejected; but we wedged in as well as we could and soon found ourselves in the office."

"Your experience has been a most entertaining one," remarked Holmes as his client paused and refreshed his memory with a huge pinch of snuff. "Pray continue your very interesting statement."

"There was nothing in the office but a couple of wooden chairs and a deal table, behind which sat a small man with a head that was even redder than mine. He said a few words to each candidate as he came up, and then he always managed to find some fault in them which would disqualify them. Getting a vacancy did not seem to be such a very easy matter, after all. However, when our turn came the little man was much more favourable to me than to any of the others, and he closed the door as we entered, so that he might have a private word with us.

" 'This is Mr. Jabez Wilson,' said my assistant, 'and he is willing to fill a vacancy in the League.'

" 'And he is admirably suited for it,' the other answered. 'He has every requirement. I cannot recall when I have seen anything so fine.' He took a step backward, cocked his head on one side, and gazed at my hair until I felt quite bashful. Then suddenly he plunged forward, wrung my hand, and congratulated me warmly on my success.

" 'It would be injustice to hesitate,' said he. 'You will, however, I am sure, excuse me for taking an obvious precaution.' With that he seized my hair in both his hands, and tugged until I yelled with the pain. 'There is water in your eyes,' said he as he released me. 'I perceive that all is as it should be. But we have to be careful, for we have twice been deceived by wigs and once by paint. I could tell you tales of cobbler's wax which would disgust you with human nature.' He stepped over to the window and shouted through it at the top of his voice that the vacancy was filled. A groan of disappointment came up from below, and the folk all trooped away in different directions until there was not a red-head to be seen except my own and that of the manager.

" 'My name,' said he, 'is Mr. Duncan Ross, and I am myself one of the pensioners upon the fund left by our noble benefactor. Are you a married man, Mr. Wilson? Have you a family?'

"I answered that I had not.

"His face fell immediately.

" 'Dear me!' he said gravely, 'That is very serious indeed! I am sorry to hear you say that. The fund was, of course, for the propagation and spread of the red-heads as well as for their maintenance. It is exceedingly unfortunate that you should be a bachelor.'

"My face lengthened at this, Mr. Holmes, for I thought that I was not to have the vacancy after all; but after thinking it over for a few minutes he said that it would be all right.

" 'In the case of another,' said he, 'the objection might be fatal, but we must stretch a point in favour of a man with such a head of hair as yours. When shall you be able to enter upon your new duties?'

" 'Well, it is a little awkward, for I have a business already,' said I.

" 'Oh, never mind about that, Mr. Wilson!' said Vincent Spaulding. 'I should be able to look after that for you.'

" 'What would be the hours?' I asked.

" 'Ten to two.'

"Now a pawnbroker's business is mostly done of an evening, Mr. Holmes, especially Thursday and Friday evening, which is just before pay-day; so it would suit me very well to earn a little in the mornings. Besides, I knew that my assistant was a good man, and that he would see to anything that turned up.

" 'That would suit me very well,' said I. 'And the pay?'

" 'Is £4 a week.'

" 'And the work?'

" 'Is purely nominal.'

" 'What do you call purely nominal?'

" 'Well, you have to be in the office, or at least in the building, the whole time. If you leave, you forfeit your whole position forever. The will is very clear upon that point. You don't comply with the conditions if you budge from the office during that time.'

" 'It's only four hours a day, and I should not think of leaving,' said I.

" 'No excuse will avail,' said Mr. Duncan Ross; 'neither sickness nor business nor anything else. There you must stay, or you lose your billet.'

" 'And the work?'

" 'Is to copy out the *Encyclopaedia Britannica*. There is the first volume of it in that press. You must find your own ink, pens, and blotting-paper, but we provide this table and chair. Will you be ready tomorrow?'

" 'Certainly,' I answered.

" 'Then, goodbye, Mr. Jabez Wilson, and let me congratulate you once more on the important position which you have been fortunate enough to gain.' He bowed me out of the room and I went home with my assistant, hardly knowing what to say or do, I was so pleased at my own good fortune.

"Well, I thought over the matter all day, and by evening I was in low spirits again; for I had quite persuaded myself that the whole affair must be some great hoax or fraud, though what its object might be I could not imagine. It seemed altogether past belief that anyone could make such a will, or that they would pay such a sum for doing anything so simple as copying out the *Encyclopaedia Britannica*. Vincent Spaulding did what he could to cheer me up, but by bedtime I had reasoned myself out of the whole thing. However, in the morning I determined to have a look at it anyhow, so I bought a penny bottle of ink, and with a quill-pen, and seven sheets of foolscap paper, I started off for Pope's Court.

"Well, to my surprise and delight, everything was as right as possible. The table was set out ready for me, and Mr. Duncan Ross was there to see that I got fairly to work. He started me off upon the letter A, and then he left me; but he would drop in from time to time to see that all was right with me. At two o'clock he bade me good day, complimented me upon the amount that I had written, and locked the door of the office after me.

"This went on day after day, Mr. Holmes, and on Saturday the manager came in and planked down four golden sovereigns for my week's work. It was the same next week, and the same the week after. Every morning I was there at ten, and every afternoon I left at two. By degrees Mr. Duncan Ross took to coming in only once of a morning, and then, after a time, he did not come in at all. Still, of course, I never dared to leave the room for an instant, for I was not sure when he might come, and the billet was such a good one, and suited me so well, that I would not risk the loss of it.

"Eight weeks passed away like this, and I had written about Abbots and Archery and Armour and Architecture and Attica, and hoped with diligence that I might get on to the B's before very long. It cost me something in foolscap, and I had pretty nearly filled a shelf with my writings. And then suddenly the whole business came to an end."

"To an end?"

"Yes, sir. And no later than this morning. I went to my work as usual at ten o'clock, but the door was shut and locked, with a little square of cardboard hammered on to the middle of the panel with a tack. Here it is, and you can read for yourself."

He held up a piece of white cardboard about the size of a sheet of note-paper. It read in this fashion:

> THE RED-HEADED LEAGUE
> IS
> DISSOLVED.
> October 9, 1890.

Sherlock Holmes and I surveyed this curt announcement and the rueful face behind it, until the comical side of the affair so completely overtopped every other consideration that we both burst out into a roar of laughter.

"I cannot see that there is anything very funny," cried our client, flushing up to the roots of his flaming head. "If you can do nothing better than laugh at me, I can go elsewhere."

"No, no," cried Holmes, shoving him back into the chair from which he had half risen. "I really wouldn't miss your case for the world. It is most refreshingly unusual. But there is, if you will excuse my saying so, something just a little funny about it. Pray what steps did you take when you found the card upon the door?"

"I was staggered, sir. I did not know what to do. Then I called at the offices round, but none of them seemed to know anything about it. Finally, I went to the landlord, who is an accountant living on the ground floor, and I asked him if he could tell me what had become of the Red-headed League. He said that he had never heard of any such body. Then I asked him who Mr. Duncan Ross was. He answered that the name was new to him.

" 'Well,' said I, 'the gentleman at No. 4.'

" 'What, the red-headed man?'

" 'Yes.'

" 'Oh,' said he, 'his name was William Morris. He was a solicitor and was using my room as a temporary convenience until his new premises were ready. He moved out yesterday.'

" 'Where could I find him?'

" 'Oh, at his new offices. He did tell me the address. Yes, 17 King Edward Street, near St. Paul's.'

"I started off, Mr. Holmes, but when I got to that address it was a manufactory of artificial knee-caps, and no one in it had ever heard of either Mr. William Morris or Mr. Duncan Ross."

"And what did you do then?" asked Holmes.

"I went home to Saxe-Coburg Square, and I took the advice of my assistant. But he could not help me in any way. He could only say that if I waited I should hear by post. But that was not quite good enough, Mr. Holmes. I did not wish to lose such a place without a struggle, so, as I had heard that you were good enough to give advice to poor folk who were in need of it, I came right away to you."

"And you did very wisely," said Holmes. "Your case is an exceedingly remarkable one, and I shall be happy to look into it. From what you have told me I think that it is possible that graver issues hang from it than might at first sight appear."

"Grave enough!" said Mr. Jabez Wilson. "Why, I have lost four pound a week."

"As far as you are personally concerned," remarked Holmes, "I do not see that you have any grievance against this extraordinary league. On the contrary, you are, as I understand, richer by some £30, to say nothing of the minute knowledge which you have gained on every subject which comes under the letter A. You have lost nothing by them."

"No, sir. But I want to find out about them, and who they are, and what their object was in playing this prank – if it was a prank – upon me. It was a pretty expensive joke for them, for it cost them two and thirty pounds."

"We shall endeavour to clear up these points for you. And, first, one or two questions, Mr. Wilson. This assistant of yours who first called your attention to the advertisement – how long had he been with you?"

"About a month then."

"How did he come?"

"In answer to an advertisement."

"Was he the only applicant?"

"No, I had a dozen."

"Why did you pick him?"

"Because he was handy and would come cheap."

"At half wages, in fact."

"Yes."

"What is he like, this Vincent Spaulding?"

"Small, stout-built, very quick in his ways, no hair on his face, though he's not short of thirty. Has a white splash of acid upon his forehead."

Holmes sat up in his chair in considerable excitement. "I thought as much," said he. "Have you ever observed that his ears are pierced for earrings?"

"Yes, sir. He told me that a gipsy had done it for him when he was a lad."

"Hum!" said Holmes, sinking back in deep thought. "He is still with you?"

"Oh, yes, sir; I have only just left him."

"And has your business been attended to in your absence?"

"Nothing to complain of, sir. There's never very much to do of a morning."

"That will do, Mr. Wilson. I shall be happy to give you an opinion upon the subject in the course of a day or two. Today is Saturday, and I hope that by Monday we may come to a conclusion."

"Well, Watson," said Holmes when our visitor had left us, "what do you make of it all?"

"I make nothing of it," I answered frankly. "It is a most mysterious business."

"As a rule," said Holmes, "the more bizarre a thing is the less mysterious it proves to be. It is your commonplace, featureless crimes which are really puzzling, just as a commonplace face is the most difficult to identify. But I must be prompt over this matter."

"What are you going to do, then?" I asked.

"To smoke," he answered. "It is quite a three pipe problem, and I beg that you won't speak to me for fifty minutes." He curled himself up in his chair, with his thin knees drawn up to his hawk-like nose, and there he sat with his eyes closed and his black clay pipe thrusting out like the bill of some strange bird. I had come to the conclusion that he had dropped asleep, and indeed was nodding myself, when he suddenly sprang out of his chair with the gesture of a man who has made up his mind and put his pipe down upon the mantelpiece.

"Sarasate plays at the St. James's Hall this afternoon," he remarked. "What do you think, Watson? Could your patients spare you for a few hours?"

"I have nothing to do today. My practice is never very absorbing."

"Then put on your hat and come. I am going through the City first, and we can have some lunch on the way. I observe that there is a good deal of German music on the programme, which is rather more to my taste than Italian or French. It is introspective, and I want to introspect. Come along!"

We travelled by the Underground as far as Aldersgate; and a short walk took us to Saxe-Coburg Square, the scene of the singular story which we had listened to in the morning. It was a poky, little, shabby-genteel place, where four lines of dingy two-storied brick houses looked out into a small railed-in enclosure, where a lawn of weedy grass and a few clumps of faded laurel bushes made a hard fight against a smoke-laden and uncongenial atmosphere. Three gilt balls and a brown board with 'JABEZ WILSON' in white letters, upon a corner house, announced the place where our red-headed client carried on his business. Sherlock Holmes stopped in front of it with his head on one side and looked it all over, with his eyes shining brightly between puckered lids. Then he walked slowly up the street, and then down again to the corner, still looking keenly at the houses. Finally he returned to the pawnbroker's, and, having thumped vigorously upon the pavement with his stick two or three times, he went up to the door and knocked. It was instantly opened by a bright-looking, clean-shaven young fellow, who asked him to step in.

"Thank you," said Holmes, "I only wished to ask you how you would go from here to the Strand."

"Third right, fourth left," answered the assistant promptly, closing the door.

"Smart fellow, that," observed Holmes as we walked away. "He is, in my judgment, the fourth smartest man in London, and for daring I am not sure that he has not a claim to be third. I have known something of him before."

"Evidently," said I, "Mr. Wilson's assistant counts for a good deal in this mystery of the Red-headed League. I am sure that you inquired your way merely in order that you might see him."

"Not him."

"What then?"

"The knees of his trousers."

"And what did you see?"

"What I expected to see."

"Why did you beat the pavement?"

"My dear doctor, this is a time for observation, not for talk. We are spies in an enemy's country. We know something of Saxe-Coburg Square. Let us now explore the parts which lie behind it."

The road in which we found ourselves as we turned round the corner from the retired Saxe-Coburg Square presented as great a contrast to it as the front of a picture does to the back. It was one of the main arteries which conveyed the traffic of the City to the north and west. The roadway was blocked with the immense stream of commerce flowing in a double tide inward and outward, while the footpaths were black with the hurrying swarm of pedestrians. It was difficult to realise as we looked at the line of fine shops and stately business premises that they really abutted on the other side upon the faded and stagnant square which we had just quitted.

"Let me see," said Holmes, standing at the corner and glancing along the line, "I should like just to remember the order of the houses here. It is a hobby of mine to have an exact knowledge of London. There is Mortimer's, the tobacconist, the little newspaper shop, the Coburg branch of the City and Suburban Bank, the Vegetarian Restaurant, and McFarlane's carriage-building depot. That carries us right on to the other block. And now, Doctor, we've done our work, so it's time we had some play. A sandwich and a cup of coffee, and then off to violin-land, where all is sweetness and delicacy and harmony, and there are no red-headed clients to vex us with their conundrums."

My friend was an enthusiastic musician, being himself not only a very capable performer but a composer of no ordinary merit. All the afternoon he sat in the stalls wrapped in the most perfect happiness, gently waving his long, thin fingers in time to the music, while his gently smiling face and his languid, dreamy eyes were as unlike those of Holmes the sleuth-hound, Holmes the relentless, keen-witted, ready-handed criminal agent, as it was possible to conceive. In his singular character the dual nature alternately asserted itself, and his extreme exactness and astuteness represented, as I have often thought, the reaction against the poetic and contemplative mood which occasionally predominated in him. The swing of his nature took him from extreme languor to devouring energy; and, as I knew well, he was never so truly formidable as when, for days on end, he had been lounging in his armchair amid his improvisations and his black-letter editions. Then it was that the lust of the chase would suddenly come upon him, and that his brilliant reasoning power would rise to the level of intuition, until those who were unacquainted with his methods would look askance at him as on a man whose knowledge was not that of other mortals. When I saw him that afternoon so enwrapped in the music at St. James's Hall I felt that an evil time might be coming upon those whom he had set himself to hunt down.

"You want to go home, no doubt, Doctor," he remarked as we emerged.

"Yes, it would be as well."

"And I have some business to do which will take some hours. This business at Coburg Square is serious."

"Why serious?"

"A considerable crime is in contemplation. I have every reason to believe that we shall be in time to stop it. But today being Saturday rather complicates matters. I shall want your help tonight."

"At what time?"

"Ten will be early enough."

"I shall be at Baker Street at ten."

"Very well. And, I say, Doctor, there may be some little danger, so kindly put your army revolver in your pocket." He waved his hand, turned on his heel, and disappeared in an instant among the crowd.

I trust that I am not more dense than my neighbours, but I was always oppressed with a sense of my own stupidity in my dealings with Sherlock Holmes. Here I had heard what he had heard, I had seen what he had seen, and yet from his words it was evident that he saw clearly not only what had happened but what was about to happen, while to me the whole business was still confused and grotesque. As I drove home to my house in Kensington I thought over it all, from the extraordinary story of the red-headed copier of the *Encyclopaedia* down to the visit to Saxe-Coburg Square, and the ominous words with which he had parted from me. What was this nocturnal expedition, and why should I go armed? Where were we going, and what were we to do? I had the hint from Holmes that this smooth-faced pawnbroker's assistant was a formidable man – a man who might play a deep game. I tried to puzzle it out, but gave it up in despair and set the matter aside until night should bring an explanation.

It was a quarter-past nine when I started from home and made my way across the Park, and so through Oxford Street to Baker Street. Two hansoms were standing at the door, and as I entered the passage I heard the sound of voices from above. On entering his room, I found Holmes in animated conversation with two men, one of whom I recognised as Peter Jones, the official police agent, while the other was a long, thin, sad-faced man, with a very shiny hat and oppressively respectable frock-coat.

"Ha! Our party is complete," said Holmes, buttoning up his pea-jacket and taking his heavy hunting crop from the rack. "Watson, I think you know Mr. Jones, of Scotland Yard? Let me introduce you to Mr. Merryweather, who is to be our companion in tonight's adventure."

"We're hunting in couples again, Doctor, you see," said Jones in his consequential way. "Our friend here is a wonderful man for starting a chase. All he wants is an old dog to help him to do the running down."

"I hope a wild goose may not prove to be the end of our chase," observed Mr. Merryweather gloomily.

"You may place considerable confidence in Mr. Holmes, sir," said the police agent loftily. "He has his own little methods, which are, if he won't mind my saying so, just a little too theoretical and fantastic, but he has the makings of a detective in him. It is not too much to say that once or twice, as in that business of the Sholto murder and the Agra treasure, he has been more nearly correct than the official force."

"Oh, if you say so, Mr. Jones, it is all right," said the stranger with deference. "Still, I confess that I miss my rubber. It is the first Saturday night for seven-and-twenty years that I have not had my rubber."

"I think you will find," said Sherlock Holmes, "that you will play for a higher stake tonight than you have ever done yet, and that the play will be more exciting. For you, Mr. Merryweather, the stake will be some £30,000; and for you, Jones, it will be the man upon whom you wish to lay your hands."

"John Clay, the murderer, thief, smasher, and forger. He's a young man, Mr. Merryweather, but he is at the head of his profession, and I would rather have my bracelets on him than on any criminal in London. He's a remarkable man, is young John Clay. His grandfather was a royal duke, and he himself has been to Eton and Oxford. His brain is as cunning as his fingers, and though we meet signs of him at every turn, we never know where to find the man himself. He'll crack a crib in Scotland one week, and be raising money to build an orphanage in Cornwall the next. I've been on his track for years and have never set eyes on him yet."

"I hope that I may have the pleasure of introducing you tonight. I've had one or two little turns also with Mr. John Clay, and I agree with you that he is at the head of his profession. It is past ten, however, and quite time that we started. If you two will take the first hansom, Watson and I will follow in the second."

Sherlock Holmes was not very communicative during the long drive and lay back in the cab humming the tunes which he had heard in the afternoon. We rattled through an endless labyrinth of gas-lit streets until we emerged into Farrington Street.

"We are close there now," my friend remarked. "This fellow Merryweather is a bank director, and personally interested in the matter. I thought it as well to have Jones with us also. He is not a bad fellow, though an absolute imbecile in his profession. He has one positive virtue. He is as brave as a bulldog and as tenacious as a lobster if he gets his claws upon anyone. Here we are, and they are waiting for us."

We had reached the same crowded thoroughfare in which we had found ourselves in the morning. Our cabs were dismissed, and, following the guidance of Mr. Merryweather, we passed down a narrow passage and through a side door, which he opened for us. Within there was a small corridor, which ended in a very massive iron gate. This also was opened, and led down a flight of winding stone steps, which terminated at another formidable gate. Mr. Merryweather stopped to light a lantern, and then conducted us down a dark, earth-smelling passage, and so, after opening a third door, into a huge vault or cellar, which was piled all round with crates and massive boxes.

"You are not very vulnerable from above," Holmes remarked as he held up the lantern and gazed about him.

"Nor from below," said Mr. Merryweather, striking his stick upon the flags which lined the floor. "Why, dear me, it sounds quite hollow!" he remarked, looking up in surprise.

"I must really ask you to be a little more quiet!" said Holmes severely. "You have already imperilled the whole success of our expedition. Might I beg that you would have the goodness to sit down upon one of those boxes, and not to interfere?"

The solemn Mr. Merryweather perched himself upon a crate, with a very injured expression upon his face, while Holmes fell upon his knees upon the floor and, with the lantern and a magnifying lens, began to examine minutely the cracks between the stones. A few seconds sufficed to satisfy him, for he sprang to his feet again and put his glass in his pocket.

"We have at least an hour before us," he remarked, "for they can hardly take any steps until the good pawnbroker is safely in bed. Then they will not lose a minute, for the sooner they do their work the longer time they will have for their escape. We are at present, Doctor – as no doubt you have divined – in the cellar of the City branch of one of the principal London banks. Mr. Merryweather is the chairman of directors, and he will explain to you that there are reasons why the more daring criminals of London should take a considerable interest in this cellar at present."

"It is our French gold," whispered the director. "We have had several warnings that an attempt might be made upon it."

"Your French gold?"

"Yes. We had occasion some months ago to strengthen our resources and borrowed for that purpose 30,000 napoleons from the Bank of France. It has become known that we have never had occasion to unpack the money, and that it is still lying in our cellar. The crate upon which I sit contains 2,000 napoleons packed between layers of lead foil. Our reserve of bullion is much larger at present than is usually kept in a single branch office, and the directors have had misgivings upon the subject."

"Which were very well justified," observed Holmes. "And now it is time that we arranged our little plans. I expect that within an hour matters will come to a head. In the meantime Mr. Merryweather, we must put the screen over that dark lantern."

"And sit in the dark?"

"I am afraid so. I had brought a pack of cards in my pocket, and I thought that, as we were a *partie carrée*, you might have your rubber after all. But I see that the enemy's preparations have gone so far that we cannot risk the presence of a light. And, first of all, we must choose our positions. These are daring men, and though we shall take them at a disadvantage, they may do us some harm unless we are careful. I shall stand behind this crate, and do you conceal yourselves behind those. Then, when I flash a light upon them, close in swiftly. If they fire, Watson, have no compunction about shooting them down."

I placed my revolver, cocked, upon the top of the wooden case behind which I crouched. Holmes shot the slide across the front of his lantern and left us in pitch darkness – such an absolute darkness as I have never before experienced. The smell of hot metal remained to assure us that the light was still there, ready to flash out at a moment's notice. To me, with my nerves worked up to a pitch of expectancy, there was something depressing and subduing in the sudden gloom, and in the cold dank air of the vault.

"They have but one retreat," whispered Holmes. "That is back through the house into Saxe-Coburg Square. I hope that you have done what I asked you, Jones?"

"I have an inspector and two officers waiting at the front door."

"Then we have stopped all the holes. And now we must be silent and wait."

What a time it seemed! From comparing notes afterwards it was but an hour and a quarter, yet it appeared to me that the night must have almost gone, and the dawn be breaking above us. My limbs were weary and stiff, for I feared to change my position; yet my nerves were worked up to the highest pitch of tension, and my hearing was so acute that I could not only hear the gentle breathing of my companions, but I could distinguish the deeper, heavier in-breath of the bulky Jones from the thin, sighing note of the bank director. From my position I could look over the case in the direction of the floor. Suddenly my eyes caught the glint of a light.

At first it was but a lurid spark upon the stone pavement. Then it lengthened out until it became a yellow line, and then, without any warning or sound, a gash seemed to open and a hand appeared, a white, almost womanly hand, which felt about in the centre of the little area of light. For a minute or more the hand, with its writhing fingers, protruded out of the floor. Then it was withdrawn as suddenly as it appeared, and all was dark again save the single lurid spark which marked a chink between the stones.

Its disappearance, however, was but momentary. With a rending, tearing sound, one of the broad, white stones turned over upon its side and left a square, gaping hole, through which streamed the light of a lantern. Over the edge there peeped a clean-cut, boyish face, which looked keenly about it, and then, with a hand on either side of the aperture, drew itself shoulder-high and waist-high, until one knee rested upon the edge. In another instant he stood at the side of the hole and was hauling after him a companion, lithe and small like himself, with a pale face and a shock of very red hair.

"It's all clear," he whispered. "Have you the chisel and the bags? Great Scott! Jump, Archie, jump, and I'll swing for it!"

Sherlock Holmes had sprung out and seized the intruder by the collar. The other dived down the hole, and I heard the sound of rending cloth as Jones clutched at his skirts. The light flashed upon the barrel of a revolver, but Holmes' hunting crop came down on the man's wrist, and the pistol clinked upon the stone floor.

"It's no use, John Clay," said Holmes blandly. "You have no chance at all."

"So I see," the other answered with the utmost coolness. "I fancy that my pal is all right, though I see you have got his coat-tails."

"There are three men waiting for him at the door," said Holmes.

"Oh, indeed! You seem to have done the thing very completely. I must compliment you."

"And I you," Holmes answered. "Your red-headed idea was very new and effective."

"You'll see your pal again presently," said Jones. "He's quicker at climbing down holes than I am. Just hold out while I fix the derbies."

"I beg that you will not touch me with your filthy hands," remarked our prisoner as the handcuffs clattered upon his wrists. "You may not be aware that I have royal blood in my veins. Have the goodness, also, when you address me always to say 'sir' and 'please.' "

"All right," said Jones with a stare and a snigger. "Well, would you please, sir, march upstairs, where we can get a cab to carry your Highness to the police-station?"

"That is better," said John Clay serenely. He made a sweeping bow to the three of us and walked quietly off in the custody of the detective.

"Really, Mr. Holmes," said Mr. Merryweather as we followed them from the cellar, "I do not know how the bank can thank you or repay you. There is no doubt that you have detected and defeated in the most complete manner one of the most determined attempts at bank robbery that have ever come within my experience."

"I have had one or two little scores of my own to settle with Mr. John Clay," said Holmes. "I have been at some small expense over this matter, which I shall expect the bank to refund, but beyond that I am amply repaid by having had an experience which is in many ways unique, and by hearing the very remarkable narrative of the Red-headed League."

"You see, Watson," he explained in the early hours of the morning as we sat over a glass of whisky and soda in Baker Street, "it was perfectly obvious from the first that the only possible object of this rather fantastic business of the advertisement of the League, and the copying of the *Encyclopaedia*, must be to get this not over-bright pawnbroker out of the way for a number of hours every day. It was a curious way of managing it, but, really, it would be difficult to suggest a better. The method was no doubt suggested to Clay's ingenious mind by the colour of his accomplice's hair. The £4 a week was a lure which must draw him, and what was it to them, who were playing for thousands? They put in the advertisement, one rogue has the temporary office, the other rogue incites the man to apply for it, and together they manage to secure his absence every morning in the week. From the time that I heard of the assistant having come for half wages, it was obvious to me that he had some strong motive for securing the situation."

"But how could you guess what the motive was?"

"Had there been women in the house, I should have suspected a mere vulgar intrigue. That, however, was out of the question. The man's business was a small one, and there was nothing in his house which could account for such elaborate preparations, and such an expenditure as they were at. It must, then, be something out of the house. What could it be? I thought of the assistant's fondness for photography, and his trick of vanishing into the cellar. The cellar! There was the end of this tangled clue. Then I made inquiries as to this mysterious assistant and found that I had to deal with one of the coolest and most daring criminals in London. He was doing something in the cellar – something which took many hours a day for months on end. What could it be, once more? I could think of nothing save that he was running a tunnel to some other building.

"So far I had got when we went to visit the scene of action. I surprised you by beating upon the pavement with my stick. I was ascertaining whether the cellar stretched out in front or behind. It was not in front. Then I rang the bell, and, as I hoped, the assistant answered it. We have had some skirmishes, but we had never set eyes upon each other before. I hardly looked at his face. His knees were what I wished to see. You must yourself have remarked how worn, wrinkled, and stained they were. They spoke of those hours of burrowing. The only remaining point was what they were burrowing for. I walked round the corner, saw the City and Suburban Bank abutted on our friend's premises, and felt that I had solved my problem. When you drove home after the concert I called upon Scotland Yard and upon the chairman of the bank directors, with the result that you have seen."

"And how could you tell that they would make their attempt tonight?" I asked.

"Well, when they closed their League offices that was a sign that they cared no longer about Mr. Jabez Wilson's presence – in other words, that they had completed their tunnel. But it was essential that they should use it soon, as it might be discovered, or the bullion might be removed. Saturday would suit them better than any other day, as it would give them two days for their escape. For all these reasons I expected them to come tonight."

"You reasoned it out beautifully," I exclaimed in unfeigned admiration. "It is so long a chain, and yet every link rings true."

"It saved me from ennui," he answered, yawning. "Alas! I already feel it closing in upon me. My life is spent in one long effort to escape from the commonplaces of existence. These little problems help me to do so."

"And you are a benefactor of the race," said I.

He shrugged his shoulders. "Well, perhaps, after all, it is of some little use," he remarked. " '*L'homme c'est rien – l'oeuvre c'est tout*,' as Gustave Flaubert wrote to George Sand."

The Adventure of the Speckled Band

Arthur Conan Doyle

ON GLANCING OVER my notes of the seventy odd cases in which I have during the last eight years studied the methods of my friend Sherlock Holmes, I find many tragic, some comic, a large number merely strange, but none commonplace; for, working as he did rather for the love of his art than for the acquirement of wealth, he refused to associate himself with any investigation which did not tend towards the unusual, and even the fantastic. Of all these varied cases, however, I cannot recall any which presented more singular features than that which was associated with the well-known Surrey family of the Roylotts of Stoke Moran. The events in question occurred in the early days of my association with Holmes, when we were sharing rooms as bachelors in Baker Street. It is possible that I might have placed them upon record before, but a promise of secrecy was made at the time, from which I have only been freed during the last month by the untimely death of the lady to whom the pledge was given. It is perhaps as well that the facts should now come to light, for I have reasons to know that there are widespread rumours as to the death of Dr. Grimesby Roylott which tend to make the matter even more terrible than the truth.

It was early in April in the year '83 that I woke one morning to find Sherlock Holmes standing, fully dressed, by the side of my bed. He was a late riser, as a rule, and as the clock on the mantelpiece showed me that it was only a quarter-past seven, I blinked up at him in some surprise, and perhaps just a little resentment, for I was myself regular in my habits.

"Very sorry to knock you up, Watson," said he, "but it's the common lot this morning. Mrs. Hudson has been knocked up, she retorted upon me, and I on you."

"What is it, then – a fire?"

"No; a client. It seems that a young lady has arrived in a considerable state of excitement, who insists upon seeing me. She is waiting now in the sitting-room. Now, when young ladies wander about the metropolis at this hour of the morning, and knock sleepy people up out of their beds, I presume that it is something very pressing which they have to communicate. Should it prove to be an interesting case, you would, I am sure, wish to follow it from the outset. I thought, at any rate, that I should call you and give you the chance."

"My dear fellow, I would not miss it for anything."

I had no keener pleasure than in following Holmes in his professional investigations, and in admiring the rapid deductions, as swift as intuitions, and yet always founded on a logical basis with which he unravelled the problems which were submitted to him. I rapidly threw on my clothes and was ready in a few minutes to accompany my friend down to the sitting-room. A lady dressed in black and heavily veiled, who had been sitting in the window, rose as we entered.

"Good morning, madam," said Holmes cheerily. "My name is Sherlock Holmes. This is my intimate friend and associate, Dr. Watson, before whom you can speak as freely as before myself.

Ha! I am glad to see that Mrs. Hudson has had the good sense to light the fire. Pray draw up to it, and I shall order you a cup of hot coffee, for I observe that you are shivering."

"It is not cold which makes me shiver," said the woman in a low voice, changing her seat as requested.

"What, then?"

"It is fear, Mr. Holmes. It is terror." She raised her veil as she spoke, and we could see that she was indeed in a pitiable state of agitation, her face all drawn and grey, with restless frightened eyes, like those of some hunted animal. Her features and figure were those of a woman of thirty, but her hair was shot with premature grey, and her expression was weary and haggard. Sherlock Holmes ran her over with one of his quick, all-comprehensive glances.

"You must not fear," said he soothingly, bending forward and patting her forearm. "We shall soon set matters right, I have no doubt. You have come in by train this morning, I see."

"You know me, then?"

"No, but I observe the second half of a return ticket in the palm of your left glove. You must have started early, and yet you had a good drive in a dog-cart, along heavy roads, before you reached the station."

The lady gave a violent start and stared in bewilderment at my companion.

"There is no mystery, my dear madam," said he, smiling. "The left arm of your jacket is spattered with mud in no less than seven places. The marks are perfectly fresh. There is no vehicle save a dog-cart which throws up mud in that way, and then only when you sit on the left-hand side of the driver."

"Whatever your reasons may be, you are perfectly correct," said she. "I started from home before six, reached Leatherhead at twenty past, and came in by the first train to Waterloo. Sir, I can stand this strain no longer; I shall go mad if it continues. I have no one to turn to – none, save only one, who cares for me, and he, poor fellow, can be of little aid. I have heard of you, Mr. Holmes; I have heard of you from Mrs. Farintosh, whom you helped in the hour of her sore need. It was from her that I had your address. Oh, sir, do you not think that you could help me, too, and at least throw a little light through the dense darkness which surrounds me? At present it is out of my power to reward you for your services, but in a month or six weeks I shall be married, with the control of my own income, and then at least you shall not find me ungrateful."

Holmes turned to his desk and, unlocking it, drew out a small case-book, which he consulted.

"Farintosh," said he. "Ah yes, I recall the case; it was concerned with an opal tiara. I think it was before your time, Watson. I can only say, madam, that I shall be happy to devote the same care to your case as I did to that of your friend. As to reward, my profession is its own reward; but you are at liberty to defray whatever expenses I may be put to, at the time which suits you best. And now I beg that you will lay before us everything that may help us in forming an opinion upon the matter."

"Alas!" replied our visitor, "the very horror of my situation lies in the fact that my fears are so vague, and my suspicions depend so entirely upon small points, which might seem trivial to another, that even he to whom of all others I have a right to look for help and advice looks upon all that I tell him about it as the fancies of a nervous woman. He does not say so, but I can read it from his soothing answers and averted eyes. But I have heard, Mr. Holmes, that you can see deeply into the manifold wickedness of the human heart. You may advise me how to walk amid the dangers which encompass me."

"I am all attention, madam."

"My name is Helen Stoner, and I am living with my stepfather, who is the last survivor of one of the oldest Saxon families in England, the Roylotts of Stoke Moran, on the western border of Surrey."

Holmes nodded his head. "The name is familiar to me," said he.

"The family was at one time among the richest in England, and the estates extended over the borders into Berkshire in the north, and Hampshire in the west. In the last century, however, four successive heirs were of a dissolute and wasteful disposition, and the family ruin was eventually completed by a gambler in the days of the Regency. Nothing was left save a few acres of ground, and the two-hundred-year-old house, which is itself crushed under a heavy mortgage. The last squire dragged out his existence there, living the horrible life of an aristocratic pauper; but his only son, my stepfather, seeing that he must adapt himself to the new conditions, obtained an advance from a relative, which enabled him to take a medical degree and went out to Calcutta, where, by his professional skill and his force of character, he established a large practice. In a fit of anger, however, caused by some robberies which had been perpetrated in the house, he beat his native butler to death and narrowly escaped a capital sentence. As it was, he suffered a long term of imprisonment and afterwards returned to England a morose and disappointed man.

"When Dr. Roylott was in India he married my mother, Mrs. Stoner, the young widow of Major-General Stoner, of the Bengal Artillery. My sister Julia and I were twins, and we were only two years old at the time of my mother's remarriage. She had a considerable sum of money – not less than £1000 a year – and this she bequeathed to Dr. Roylott entirely while we resided with him, with a provision that a certain annual sum should be allowed to each of us in the event of our marriage. Shortly after our return to England my mother died – she was killed eight years ago in a railway accident near Crewe. Dr. Roylott then abandoned his attempts to establish himself in practice in London and took us to live with him in the old ancestral house at Stoke Moran. The money which my mother had left was enough for all our wants, and there seemed to be no obstacle to our happiness.

"But a terrible change came over our stepfather about this time. Instead of making friends and exchanging visits with our neighbours, who had at first been overjoyed to see a Roylott of Stoke Moran back in the old family seat, he shut himself up in his house and seldom came out save to indulge in ferocious quarrels with whoever might cross his path. Violence of temper approaching to mania has been hereditary in the men of the family, and in my stepfather's case it had, I believe, been intensified by his long residence in the tropics. A series of disgraceful brawls took place, two of which ended in the police-court, until at last he became the terror of the village, and the folks would fly at his approach, for he is a man of immense strength, and absolutely uncontrollable in his anger.

"Last week he hurled the local blacksmith over a parapet into a stream, and it was only by paying over all the money which I could gather together that I was able to avert another public exposure. He had no friends at all save the wandering gipsies, and he would give these vagabonds leave to encamp upon the few acres of bramble-covered land which represent the family estate, and would accept in return the hospitality of their tents, wandering away with them sometimes for weeks on end. He has a passion also for Indian animals, which are sent over to him by a correspondent, and he has at this moment a cheetah and a baboon, which wander freely over his grounds and are feared by the villagers almost as much as their master.

"You can imagine from what I say that my poor sister Julia and I had no great pleasure in our lives. No servant would stay with us, and for a long time we did all the work of the house. She was but thirty at the time of her death, and yet her hair had already begun to whiten, even as mine has."

"Your sister is dead, then?"

"She died just two years ago, and it is of her death that I wish to speak to you. You can understand that, living the life which I have described, we were little likely to see anyone of our own age and position. We had, however, an aunt, my mother's maiden sister, Miss Honoria Westphail, who lives near Harrow, and we were occasionally allowed to pay short visits at this lady's house. Julia went there at Christmas two years ago, and met there a half-pay major of marines, to whom she became engaged. My stepfather learned of the engagement when my sister returned and offered no objection to the marriage; but within a fortnight of the day which had been fixed for the wedding, the terrible event occurred which has deprived me of my only companion."

Sherlock Holmes had been leaning back in his chair with his eyes closed and his head sunk in a cushion, but he half opened his lids now and glanced across at his visitor.

"Pray be precise as to details," said he.

"It is easy for me to be so, for every event of that dreadful time is seared into my memory. The manor-house is, as I have already said, very old, and only one wing is now inhabited. The bedrooms in this wing are on the ground floor, the sitting-rooms being in the central block of the buildings. Of these bedrooms the first is Dr. Roylott's, the second my sister's, and the third my own. There is no communication between them, but they all open out into the same corridor. Do I make myself plain?"

"Perfectly so."

"The windows of the three rooms open out upon the lawn. That fatal night Dr. Roylott had gone to his room early, though we knew that he had not retired to rest, for my sister was troubled by the smell of the strong Indian cigars which it was his custom to smoke. She left her room, therefore, and came into mine, where she sat for some time, chatting about her approaching wedding. At eleven o'clock she rose to leave me, but she paused at the door and looked back.

" 'Tell me, Helen,' said she, 'have you ever heard anyone whistle in the dead of the night?'

" 'Never,' said I.

" 'I suppose that you could not possibly whistle, yourself, in your sleep?'

" 'Certainly not. But why?'

" 'Because during the last few nights I have always, about three in the morning, heard a low, clear whistle. I am a light sleeper, and it has awakened me. I cannot tell where it came from – perhaps from the next room, perhaps from the lawn. I thought that I would just ask you whether you had heard it.'

" 'No, I have not. It must be those wretched gipsies in the plantation.'

" 'Very likely. And yet if it were on the lawn, I wonder that you did not hear it also.'

" 'Ah, but I sleep more heavily than you.'

" 'Well, it is of no great consequence, at any rate.' She smiled back at me, closed my door, and a few moments later I heard her key turn in the lock."

"Indeed," said Holmes. "Was it your custom always to lock yourselves in at night?"

"Always."

"And why?"

"I think that I mentioned to you that the doctor kept a cheetah and a baboon. We had no feeling of security unless our doors were locked."

"Quite so. Pray proceed with your statement."

"I could not sleep that night. A vague feeling of impending misfortune impressed me. My sister and I, you will recollect, were twins, and you know how subtle are the links which bind two souls which are so closely allied. It was a wild night. The wind was howling outside, and the rain was beating and splashing against the windows. Suddenly, amid all the hubbub of the gale, there burst forth the wild scream of a terrified woman. I knew that it was my sister's voice.

I sprang from my bed, wrapped a shawl round me, and rushed into the corridor. As I opened my door I seemed to hear a low whistle, such as my sister described, and a few moments later a clanging sound, as if a mass of metal had fallen. As I ran down the passage, my sister's door was unlocked, and revolved slowly upon its hinges. I stared at it horror-stricken, not knowing what was about to issue from it. By the light of the corridor-lamp I saw my sister appear at the opening, her face blanched with terror, her hands groping for help, her whole figure swaying to and fro like that of a drunkard. I ran to her and threw my arms round her, but at that moment her knees seemed to give way and she fell to the ground. She writhed as one who is in terrible pain, and her limbs were dreadfully convulsed. At first I thought that she had not recognised me, but as I bent over her she suddenly shrieked out in a voice which I shall never forget, 'Oh, my God! Helen! It was the band! The speckled band!' There was something else which she would fain have said, and she stabbed with her finger into the air in the direction of the doctor's room, but a fresh convulsion seized her and choked her words. I rushed out, calling loudly for my stepfather, and I met him hastening from his room in his dressing-gown. When he reached my sister's side she was unconscious, and though he poured brandy down her throat and sent for medical aid from the village, all efforts were in vain, for she slowly sank and died without having recovered her consciousness. Such was the dreadful end of my beloved sister."

"One moment," said Holmes, "are you sure about this whistle and metallic sound? Could you swear to it?"

"That was what the county coroner asked me at the inquiry. It is my strong impression that I heard it, and yet, among the crash of the gale and the creaking of an old house, I may possibly have been deceived."

"Was your sister dressed?"

"No, she was in her night-dress. In her right hand was found the charred stump of a match, and in her left a match-box."

"Showing that she had struck a light and looked about her when the alarm took place. That is important. And what conclusions did the coroner come to?"

"He investigated the case with great care, for Dr. Roylott's conduct had long been notorious in the county, but he was unable to find any satisfactory cause of death. My evidence showed that the door had been fastened upon the inner side, and the windows were blocked by old-fashioned shutters with broad iron bars, which were secured every night. The walls were carefully sounded, and were shown to be quite solid all round, and the flooring was also thoroughly examined, with the same result. The chimney is wide, but is barred up by four large staples. It is certain, therefore, that my sister was quite alone when she met her end. Besides, there were no marks of any violence upon her."

"How about poison?"

"The doctors examined her for it, but without success."

"What do you think that this unfortunate lady died of, then?"

"It is my belief that she died of pure fear and nervous shock, though what it was that frightened her I cannot imagine."

"Were there gipsies in the plantation at the time?"

"Yes, there are nearly always some there."

"Ah, and what did you gather from this allusion to a band – a speckled band?"

"Sometimes I have thought that it was merely the wild talk of delirium, sometimes that it may have referred to some band of people, perhaps to these very gipsies in the plantation. I do not know whether the spotted handkerchiefs which so many of them wear over their heads might have suggested the strange adjective which she used."

Holmes shook his head like a man who is far from being satisfied.

"These are very deep waters," said he; "pray go on with your narrative."

"Two years have passed since then, and my life has been until lately lonelier than ever. A month ago, however, a dear friend, whom I have known for many years, has done me the honour to ask my hand in marriage. His name is Armitage – Percy Armitage – the second son of Mr. Armitage, of Crane Water, near Reading. My stepfather has offered no opposition to the match, and we are to be married in the course of the spring. Two days ago some repairs were started in the west wing of the building, and my bedroom wall has been pierced, so that I have had to move into the chamber in which my sister died, and to sleep in the very bed in which she slept. Imagine, then, my thrill of terror when last night, as I lay awake, thinking over her terrible fate, I suddenly heard in the silence of the night the low whistle which had been the herald of her own death. I sprang up and lit the lamp, but nothing was to be seen in the room. I was too shaken to go to bed again, however, so I dressed, and as soon as it was daylight I slipped down, got a dog-cart at the Crown Inn, which is opposite, and drove to Leatherhead, from whence I have come on this morning with the one object of seeing you and asking your advice."

"You have done wisely," said my friend. "But have you told me all?"

"Yes, all."

"Miss Roylott, you have not. You are screening your stepfather."

"Why, what do you mean?"

For answer Holmes pushed back the frill of black lace which fringed the hand that lay upon our visitor's knee. Five little livid spots, the marks of four fingers and a thumb, were printed upon the white wrist.

"You have been cruelly used," said Holmes.

The lady coloured deeply and covered over her injured wrist. "He is a hard man," she said, "and perhaps he hardly knows his own strength."

There was a long silence, during which Holmes leaned his chin upon his hands and stared into the crackling fire.

"This is a very deep business," he said at last. "There are a thousand details which I should desire to know before I decide upon our course of action. Yet we have not a moment to lose. If we were to come to Stoke Moran today, would it be possible for us to see over these rooms without the knowledge of your stepfather?"

"As it happens, he spoke of coming into town today upon some most important business. It is probable that he will be away all day, and that there would be nothing to disturb you. We have a housekeeper now, but she is old and foolish, and I could easily get her out of the way."

"Excellent. You are not averse to this trip, Watson?"

"By no means."

"Then we shall both come. What are you going to do yourself?"

"I have one or two things which I would wish to do now that I am in town. But I shall return by the twelve o'clock train, so as to be there in time for your coming."

"And you may expect us early in the afternoon. I have myself some small business matters to attend to. Will you not wait and breakfast?"

"No, I must go. My heart is lightened already since I have confided my trouble to you. I shall look forward to seeing you again this afternoon." She dropped her thick black veil over her face and glided from the room.

"And what do you think of it all, Watson?" asked Sherlock Holmes, leaning back in his chair.

"It seems to me to be a most dark and sinister business."

"Dark enough and sinister enough."

"Yet if the lady is correct in saying that the flooring and walls are sound, and that the door, window, and chimney are impassable, then her sister must have been undoubtedly alone when she met her mysterious end."

"What becomes, then, of these nocturnal whistles, and what of the very peculiar words of the dying woman?"

"I cannot think."

"When you combine the ideas of whistles at night, the presence of a band of gipsies who are on intimate terms with this old doctor, the fact that we have every reason to believe that the doctor has an interest in preventing his stepdaughter's marriage, the dying allusion to a band, and, finally, the fact that Miss Helen Stoner heard a metallic clang, which might have been caused by one of those metal bars that secured the shutters falling back into its place, I think that there is good ground to think that the mystery may be cleared along those lines."

"But what, then, did the gipsies do?"

"I cannot imagine."

"I see many objections to any such theory."

"And so do I. It is precisely for that reason that we are going to Stoke Moran this day. I want to see whether the objections are fatal, or if they may be explained away. But what in the name of the devil!"

The ejaculation had been drawn from my companion by the fact that our door had been suddenly dashed open, and that a huge man had framed himself in the aperture. His costume was a peculiar mixture of the professional and of the agricultural, having a black top-hat, a long frock-coat, and a pair of high gaiters, with a hunting-crop swinging in his hand. So tall was he that his hat actually brushed the cross bar of the doorway, and his breadth seemed to span it across from side to side. A large face, seared with a thousand wrinkles, burned yellow with the sun, and marked with every evil passion, was turned from one to the other of us, while his deep-set, bile-shot eyes, and his high, thin, fleshless nose, gave him somewhat the resemblance to a fierce old bird of prey.

"Which of you is Holmes?" asked this apparition.

"My name, sir; but you have the advantage of me," said my companion quietly.

"I am Dr. Grimesby Roylott, of Stoke Moran."

"Indeed, Doctor," said Holmes blandly. "Pray take a seat."

"I will do nothing of the kind. My stepdaughter has been here. I have traced her. What has she been saying to you?"

"It is a little cold for the time of the year," said Holmes.

"What has she been saying to you?" screamed the old man furiously.

"But I have heard that the crocuses promise well," continued my companion imperturbably.

"Ha! You put me off, do you?" said our new visitor, taking a step forward and shaking his hunting-crop. "I know you, you scoundrel! I have heard of you before. You are Holmes, the meddler."

My friend smiled.

"Holmes, the busybody!"

His smile broadened.

"Holmes, the Scotland Yard Jack-in-office!"

Holmes chuckled heartily. "Your conversation is most entertaining," said he. "When you go out close the door, for there is a decided draught."

"I will go when I have said my say. Don't you dare to meddle with my affairs. I know that Miss Stoner has been here. I traced her! I am a dangerous man to fall foul of! See here." He stepped swiftly forward, seized the poker, and bent it into a curve with his huge brown hands.

"See that you keep yourself out of my grip," he snarled, and hurling the twisted poker into the fireplace he strode out of the room.

"He seems a very amiable person," said Holmes, laughing. "I am not quite so bulky, but if he had remained I might have shown him that my grip was not much more feeble than his own." As he spoke he picked up the steel poker and, with a sudden effort, straightened it out again.

"Fancy his having the insolence to confound me with the official detective force! This incident gives zest to our investigation, however, and I only trust that our little friend will not suffer from her imprudence in allowing this brute to trace her. And now, Watson, we shall order breakfast, and afterwards I shall walk down to Doctors' Commons, where I hope to get some data which may help us in this matter."

It was nearly one o'clock when Sherlock Holmes returned from his excursion. He held in his hand a sheet of blue paper, scrawled over with notes and figures.

"I have seen the will of the deceased wife," said he. "To determine its exact meaning I have been obliged to work out the present prices of the investments with which it is concerned. The total income, which at the time of the wife's death was little short of £1100, is now, through the fall in agricultural prices, not more than £750. Each daughter can claim an income of £250, in case of marriage. It is evident, therefore, that if both girls had married, this beauty would have had a mere pittance, while even one of them would cripple him to a very serious extent. My morning's work has not been wasted, since it has proved that he has the very strongest motives for standing in the way of anything of the sort. And now, Watson, this is too serious for dawdling, especially as the old man is aware that we are interesting ourselves in his affairs; so if you are ready, we shall call a cab and drive to Waterloo. I should be very much obliged if you would slip your revolver into your pocket. An Eley's No. 2 is an excellent argument with gentlemen who can twist steel pokers into knots. That and a toothbrush are, I think, all that we need."

At Waterloo we were fortunate in catching a train for Leatherhead, where we hired a trap at the station inn and drove for four or five miles through the lovely Surrey lanes. It was a perfect day, with a bright sun and a few fleecy clouds in the heavens. The trees and wayside hedges were just throwing out their first green shoots, and the air was full of the pleasant smell of the moist earth. To me at least there was a strange contrast between the sweet promise of the spring and this sinister quest upon which we were engaged. My companion sat in the front of the trap, his arms folded, his hat pulled down over his eyes, and his chin sunk upon his breast, buried in the deepest thought. Suddenly, however, he started, tapped me on the shoulder, and pointed over the meadows.

"Look there!" said he.

A heavily timbered park stretched up in a gentle slope, thickening into a grove at the highest point. From amid the branches there jutted out the grey gables and high roof-tree of a very old mansion.

"Stoke Moran?" said he.

"Yes, sir, that be the house of Dr. Grimesby Roylott," remarked the driver.

"There is some building going on there," said Holmes; "that is where we are going."

"There's the village," said the driver, pointing to a cluster of roofs some distance to the left; "but if you want to get to the house, you'll find it shorter to get over this stile, and so by the foot-path over the fields. There it is, where the lady is walking."

"And the lady, I fancy, is Miss Stoner," observed Holmes, shading his eyes. "Yes, I think we had better do as you suggest."

We got off, paid our fare, and the trap rattled back on its way to Leatherhead.

"I thought it as well," said Holmes as we climbed the stile, "that this fellow should think we had come here as architects, or on some definite business. It may stop his gossip. Good afternoon, Miss Stoner. You see that we have been as good as our word."

Our client of the morning had hurried forward to meet us with a face which spoke her joy. "I have been waiting so eagerly for you," she cried, shaking hands with us warmly. "All has turned out splendidly. Dr. Roylott has gone to town, and it is unlikely that he will be back before evening."

"We have had the pleasure of making the doctor's acquaintance," said Holmes, and in a few words he sketched out what had occurred. Miss Stoner turned white to the lips as she listened.

"Good heavens!" she cried, "he has followed me, then."

"So it appears."

"He is so cunning that I never know when I am safe from him. What will he say when he returns?"

"He must guard himself, for he may find that there is someone more cunning than himself upon his track. You must lock yourself up from him tonight. If he is violent, we shall take you away to your aunt's at Harrow. Now, we must make the best use of our time, so kindly take us at once to the rooms which we are to examine."

The building was of grey, lichen-blotched stone, with a high central portion and two curving wings, like the claws of a crab, thrown out on each side. In one of these wings the windows were broken and blocked with wooden boards, while the roof was partly caved in, a picture of ruin. The central portion was in little better repair, but the right-hand block was comparatively modern, and the blinds in the windows, with the blue smoke curling up from the chimneys, showed that this was where the family resided. Some scaffolding had been erected against the end wall, and the stone-work had been broken into, but there were no signs of any workmen at the moment of our visit. Holmes walked slowly up and down the ill-trimmed lawn and examined with deep attention the outsides of the windows.

"This, I take it, belongs to the room in which you used to sleep, the centre one to your sister's, and the one next to the main building to Dr. Roylott's chamber?"

"Exactly so. But I am now sleeping in the middle one."

"Pending the alterations, as I understand. By the way, there does not seem to be any very pressing need for repairs at that end wall."

"There were none. I believe that it was an excuse to move me from my room."

"Ah! That is suggestive. Now, on the other side of this narrow wing runs the corridor from which these three rooms open. There are windows in it, of course?"

"Yes, but very small ones. Too narrow for anyone to pass through."

"As you both locked your doors at night, your rooms were unapproachable from that side. Now, would you have the kindness to go into your room and bar your shutters?"

Miss Stoner did so, and Holmes, after a careful examination through the open window, endeavoured in every way to force the shutter open, but without success. There was no slit through which a knife could be passed to raise the bar. Then with his lens he tested the hinges, but they were of solid iron, built firmly into the massive masonry. "Hum!" said he, scratching his chin in some perplexity, "my theory certainly presents some difficulties. No one could pass these shutters if they were bolted. Well, we shall see if the inside throws any light upon the matter."

A small side door led into the whitewashed corridor from which the three bedrooms opened. Holmes refused to examine the third chamber, so we passed at once to the second, that in which Miss Stoner was now sleeping, and in which her sister had met with her fate.

It was a homely little room, with a low ceiling and a gaping fireplace, after the fashion of old country-houses. A brown chest of drawers stood in one corner, a narrow white-counterpaned bed in another, and a dressing-table on the left-hand side of the window. These articles, with two small wicker-work chairs, made up all the furniture in the room save for a square of Wilton carpet in the centre. The boards round and the panelling of the walls were of brown, worm-eaten oak, so old and discoloured that it may have dated from the original building of the house. Holmes drew one of the chairs into a corner and sat silent, while his eyes travelled round and round and up and down, taking in every detail of the apartment.

"Where does that bell communicate with?" he asked at last pointing to a thick bell-rope which hung down beside the bed, the tassel actually lying upon the pillow.

"It goes to the housekeeper's room."

"It looks newer than the other things?"

"Yes, it was only put there a couple of years ago."

"Your sister asked for it, I suppose?"

"No, I never heard of her using it. We used always to get what we wanted for ourselves."

"Indeed, it seemed unnecessary to put so nice a bell-pull there. You will excuse me for a few minutes while I satisfy myself as to this floor." He threw himself down upon his face with his lens in his hand and crawled swiftly backward and forward, examining minutely the cracks between the boards. Then he did the same with the wood-work with which the chamber was panelled. Finally he walked over to the bed and spent some time in staring at it and in running his eye up and down the wall. Finally he took the bell-rope in his hand and gave it a brisk tug.

"Why, it's a dummy," said he.

"Won't it ring?"

"No, it is not even attached to a wire. This is very interesting. You can see now that it is fastened to a hook just above where the little opening for the ventilator is."

"How very absurd! I never noticed that before."

"Very strange!" muttered Holmes, pulling at the rope. "There are one or two very singular points about this room. For example, what a fool a builder must be to open a ventilator into another room, when, with the same trouble, he might have communicated with the outside air!"

"That is also quite modern," said the lady.

"Done about the same time as the bell-rope?" remarked Holmes.

"Yes, there were several little changes carried out about that time."

"They seem to have been of a most interesting character – dummy bell-ropes, and ventilators which do not ventilate. With your permission, Miss Stoner, we shall now carry our researches into the inner apartment."

Dr. Grimesby Roylott's chamber was larger than that of his step-daughter, but was as plainly furnished. A camp-bed, a small wooden shelf full of books, mostly of a technical character, an armchair beside the bed, a plain wooden chair against the wall, a round table, and a large iron safe were the principal things which met the eye. Holmes walked slowly round and examined each and all of them with the keenest interest.

"What's in here?" he asked, tapping the safe.

"My stepfather's business papers."

"Oh! You have seen inside, then?"

"Only once, some years ago. I remember that it was full of papers."

"There isn't a cat in it, for example?"

"No. What a strange idea!"

"Well, look at this!" He took up a small saucer of milk which stood on the top of it.

"No; we don't keep a cat. But there is a cheetah and a baboon."

"Ah, yes, of course! Well, a cheetah is just a big cat, and yet a saucer of milk does not go very far in satisfying its wants, I daresay. There is one point which I should wish to determine." He squatted down in front of the wooden chair and examined the seat of it with the greatest attention.

"Thank you. That is quite settled," said he, rising and putting his lens in his pocket. "Hullo! Here is something interesting!"

The object which had caught his eye was a small dog lash hung on one corner of the bed. The lash, however, was curled upon itself and tied so as to make a loop of whipcord.

"What do you make of that, Watson?"

"It's a common enough lash. But I don't know why it should be tied."

"That is not quite so common, is it? Ah, me! It's a wicked world, and when a clever man turns his brains to crime it is the worst of all. I think that I have seen enough now, Miss Stoner, and with your permission we shall walk out upon the lawn."

I had never seen my friend's face so grim or his brow so dark as it was when we turned from the scene of this investigation. We had walked several times up and down the lawn, neither Miss Stoner nor myself liking to break in upon his thoughts before he roused himself from his reverie.

"It is very essential, Miss Stoner," said he, "that you should absolutely follow my advice in every respect."

"I shall most certainly do so."

"The matter is too serious for any hesitation. Your life may depend upon your compliance."

"I assure you that I am in your hands."

"In the first place, both my friend and I must spend the night in your room."

Both Miss Stoner and I gazed at him in astonishment.

"Yes, it must be so. Let me explain. I believe that that is the village inn over there?"

"Yes, that is the Crown."

"Very good. Your windows would be visible from there?"

"Certainly."

"You must confine yourself to your room, on pretence of a headache, when your stepfather comes back. Then when you hear him retire for the night, you must open the shutters of your window, undo the hasp, put your lamp there as a signal to us, and then withdraw quietly with everything which you are likely to want into the room which you used to occupy. I have no doubt that, in spite of the repairs, you could manage there for one night."

"Oh, yes, easily."

"The rest you will leave in our hands."

"But what will you do?"

"We shall spend the night in your room, and we shall investigate the cause of this noise which has disturbed you."

"I believe, Mr. Holmes, that you have already made up your mind," said Miss Stoner, laying her hand upon my companion's sleeve.

"Perhaps I have."

"Then, for pity's sake, tell me what was the cause of my sister's death."

"I should prefer to have clearer proofs before I speak."

"You can at least tell me whether my own thought is correct, and if she died from some sudden fright."

"No, I do not think so. I think that there was probably some more tangible cause. And now, Miss Stoner, we must leave you for if Dr. Roylott returned and saw us our journey would be in vain. Goodbye, and be brave, for if you will do what I have told you, you may rest assured that we shall soon drive away the dangers that threaten you."

Sherlock Holmes and I had no difficulty in engaging a bedroom and sitting-room at the Crown Inn. They were on the upper floor, and from our window we could command a view of the avenue gate, and of the inhabited wing of Stoke Moran Manor House. At dusk we saw Dr. Grimesby Roylott drive past, his huge form looming up beside the little figure of the lad who drove him. The boy had some slight difficulty in undoing the heavy iron gates, and we heard the hoarse roar of the doctor's voice and saw the fury with which he shook his clinched fists at him. The trap drove on, and a few minutes later we saw a sudden light spring up among the trees as the lamp was lit in one of the sitting-rooms.

"Do you know, Watson," said Holmes as we sat together in the gathering darkness, "I have really some scruples as to taking you tonight. There is a distinct element of danger."

"Can I be of assistance?"

"Your presence might be invaluable."

"Then I shall certainly come."

"It is very kind of you."

"You speak of danger. You have evidently seen more in these rooms than was visible to me."

"No, but I fancy that I may have deduced a little more. I imagine that you saw all that I did."

"I saw nothing remarkable save the bell-rope, and what purpose that could answer I confess is more than I can imagine."

"You saw the ventilator, too?"

"Yes, but I do not think that it is such a very unusual thing to have a small opening between two rooms. It was so small that a rat could hardly pass through."

"I knew that we should find a ventilator before ever we came to Stoke Moran."

"My dear Holmes!"

"Oh, yes, I did. You remember in her statement she said that her sister could smell Dr. Roylott's cigar. Now, of course that suggested at once that there must be a communication between the two rooms. It could only be a small one, or it would have been remarked upon at the coroner's inquiry. I deduced a ventilator."

"But what harm can there be in that?"

"Well, there is at least a curious coincidence of dates. A ventilator is made, a cord is hung, and a lady who sleeps in the bed dies. Does not that strike you?"

"I cannot as yet see any connection."

"Did you observe anything very peculiar about that bed?"

"No."

"It was clamped to the floor. Did you ever see a bed fastened like that before?"

"I cannot say that I have."

"The lady could not move her bed. It must always be in the same relative position to the ventilator and to the rope – or so we may call it, since it was clearly never meant for a bell-pull."

"Holmes," I cried, "I seem to see dimly what you are hinting at. We are only just in time to prevent some subtle and horrible crime."

"Subtle enough and horrible enough. When a doctor does go wrong he is the first of criminals. He has nerve and he has knowledge. Palmer and Pritchard were among the heads of their profession. This man strikes even deeper, but I think, Watson, that we shall be able to strike deeper still. But we shall have horrors enough before the night is over; for goodness' sake let us have a quiet pipe and turn our minds for a few hours to something more cheerful."

About nine o'clock the light among the trees was extinguished, and all was dark in the direction of the Manor House. Two hours passed slowly away, and then, suddenly, just at the stroke of eleven, a single bright light shone out right in front of us.

"That is our signal," said Holmes, springing to his feet; "it comes from the middle window."

As we passed out he exchanged a few words with the landlord, explaining that we were going on a late visit to an acquaintance, and that it was possible that we might spend the night there. A moment later we were out on the dark road, a chill wind blowing in our faces, and one yellow light twinkling in front of us through the gloom to guide us on our sombre errand.

There was little difficulty in entering the grounds, for unrepaired breaches gaped in the old park wall. Making our way among the trees, we reached the lawn, crossed it, and were about to enter through the window when out from a clump of laurel bushes there darted what seemed to be a hideous and distorted child, who threw itself upon the grass with writhing limbs and then ran swiftly across the lawn into the darkness.

"My God!" I whispered; "did you see it?"

Holmes was for the moment as startled as I. His hand closed like a vice upon my wrist in his agitation. Then he broke into a low laugh and put his lips to my ear.

"It is a nice household," he murmured. "That is the baboon."

I had forgotten the strange pets which the doctor affected. There was a cheetah, too; perhaps we might find it upon our shoulders at any moment. I confess that I felt easier in my mind when, after following Holmes' example and slipping off my shoes, I found myself inside the bedroom. My companion noiselessly closed the shutters, moved the lamp onto the table, and cast his eyes round the room. All was as we had seen it in the daytime. Then creeping up to me and making a trumpet of his hand, he whispered into my ear again so gently that it was all that I could do to distinguish the words:

"The least sound would be fatal to our plans."

I nodded to show that I had heard.

"We must sit without light. He would see it through the ventilator."

I nodded again.

"Do not go asleep; your very life may depend upon it. Have your pistol ready in case we should need it. I will sit on the side of the bed, and you in that chair."

I took out my revolver and laid it on the corner of the table.

Holmes had brought up a long thin cane, and this he placed upon the bed beside him. By it he laid the box of matches and the stump of a candle. Then he turned down the lamp, and we were left in darkness.

How shall I ever forget that dreadful vigil? I could not hear a sound, not even the drawing of a breath, and yet I knew that my companion sat open-eyed, within a few feet of me, in the same state of nervous tension in which I was myself. The shutters cut off the least ray of light, and we waited in absolute darkness.

From outside came the occasional cry of a night-bird, and once at our very window a long drawn catlike whine, which told us that the cheetah was indeed at liberty. Far away we could hear the deep tones of the parish clock, which boomed out every quarter of an hour. How long they seemed, those quarters! Twelve struck, and one and two and three, and still we sat waiting silently for whatever might befall.

Suddenly there was the momentary gleam of a light up in the direction of the ventilator, which vanished immediately, but was succeeded by a strong smell of burning oil and heated metal.

Someone in the next room had lit a dark-lantern. I heard a gentle sound of movement, and then all was silent once more, though the smell grew stronger. For half an hour I sat with straining ears. Then suddenly another sound became audible – a very gentle, soothing sound, like that of a small jet of steam escaping continually from a kettle. The instant that we heard it, Holmes sprang from the bed, struck a match, and lashed furiously with his cane at the bell-pull.

"You see it, Watson?" he yelled. "You see it?"

But I saw nothing. At the moment when Holmes struck the light I heard a low, clear whistle, but the sudden glare flashing into my weary eyes made it impossible for me to tell what it was at which my friend lashed so savagely. I could, however, see that his face was deadly pale and filled with horror and loathing. He had ceased to strike and was gazing up at the ventilator when suddenly there broke from the silence of the night the most horrible cry to which I have ever listened. It swelled up louder and louder, a hoarse yell of pain and fear and anger all mingled in the one dreadful shriek. They say that away down in the village, and even in the distant parsonage, that cry raised the sleepers from their beds. It struck cold to our hearts, and I stood gazing at Holmes, and he at me, until the last echoes of it had died away into the silence from which it rose.

"What can it mean?" I gasped.

"It means that it is all over," Holmes answered. "And perhaps, after all, it is for the best. Take your pistol, and we will enter Dr. Roylott's room."

With a grave face he lit the lamp and led the way down the corridor. Twice he struck at the chamber door without any reply from within. Then he turned the handle and entered, I at his heels, with the cocked pistol in my hand.

It was a singular sight which met our eyes. On the table stood a dark-lantern with the shutter half open, throwing a brilliant beam of light upon the iron safe, the door of which was ajar. Beside this table, on the wooden chair, sat Dr. Grimesby Roylott clad in a long grey dressing-gown, his bare ankles protruding beneath, and his feet thrust into red heelless Turkish slippers. Across his lap lay the short stock with the long lash which we had noticed during the day. His chin was cocked upward and his eyes were fixed in a dreadful, rigid stare at the corner of the ceiling. Round his brow he had a peculiar yellow band, with brownish speckles, which seemed to be bound tightly round his head. As we entered he made neither sound nor motion.

"The band! The speckled band!" whispered Holmes.

I took a step forward. In an instant his strange headgear began to move, and there reared itself from among his hair the squat diamond-shaped head and puffed neck of a loathsome serpent.

"It is a swamp adder!" cried Holmes; "the deadliest snake in India. He has died within ten seconds of being bitten. Violence does, in truth, recoil upon the violent, and the schemer falls into the pit which he digs for another. Let us thrust this creature back into its den, and we can then remove Miss Stoner to some place of shelter and let the county police know what has happened."

As he spoke he drew the dog-whip swiftly from the dead man's lap, and throwing the noose round the reptile's neck he drew it from its horrid perch and, carrying it at arm's length, threw it into the iron safe, which he closed upon it.

Such are the true facts of the death of Dr. Grimesby Roylott, of Stoke Moran. It is not necessary that I should prolong a narrative which has already run to too great a length by telling how we broke the sad news to the terrified girl, how we conveyed her by the morning train to the care of her good aunt at Harrow, of how the slow process of official inquiry came to the conclusion that the doctor met his fate while indiscreetly playing with a dangerous pet. The little which I had yet to learn of the case was told me by Sherlock Holmes as we travelled back next day.

"I had," said he, "come to an entirely erroneous conclusion which shows, my dear Watson, how dangerous it always is to reason from insufficient data. The presence of the gipsies, and the use of the word 'band,' which was used by the poor girl, no doubt, to explain the appearance which she had caught a hurried glimpse of by the light of her match, were sufficient to put me upon an entirely wrong scent. I can only claim the merit that I instantly reconsidered my position when, however, it became clear to me that whatever danger threatened an occupant of the room could not come either from the window or the door. My attention was speedily drawn, as I have already remarked to you, to this ventilator, and to the bell-rope which hung down to the bed. The discovery that this was a dummy, and that the bed was clamped to the floor, instantly gave rise to the suspicion that the rope was there as a bridge for something passing through the hole and coming to the bed. The idea of a snake instantly occurred to me, and when I coupled it with my knowledge that the doctor was furnished with a supply of creatures from India, I felt that I was probably on the right track. The idea of using a form of poison which could not possibly be discovered by any chemical test was just such a one as would occur to a clever and ruthless man who had had an Eastern training. The rapidity with which such a poison would take effect would also, from his point of view, be an advantage. It would be a sharp-eyed coroner, indeed, who could distinguish the two little dark punctures which would show where the poison fangs had done their work. Then I thought of the whistle. Of course he must recall the snake before the morning light revealed it to the victim. He had trained it, probably by the use of the milk which we saw, to return to him when summoned. He would put it through this ventilator at the hour that he thought best, with the certainty that it would crawl down the rope and land on the bed. It might or might not bite the occupant, perhaps she might escape every night for a week, but sooner or later she must fall a victim.

"I had come to these conclusions before ever I had entered his room. An inspection of his chair showed me that he had been in the habit of standing on it, which of course would be necessary in order that he should reach the ventilator. The sight of the safe, the saucer of milk, and the loop of whipcord were enough to finally dispel any doubts which may have remained. The metallic clang heard by Miss Stoner was obviously caused by her stepfather hastily closing the door of his safe upon its terrible occupant. Having once made up my mind, you know the steps which I took in order to put the matter to the proof. I heard the creature hiss as I have no doubt that you did also, and I instantly lit the light and attacked it."

"With the result of driving it through the ventilator."

"And also with the result of causing it to turn upon its master at the other side. Some of the blows of my cane came home and roused its snakish temper, so that it flew upon the first person it saw. In this way I am no doubt indirectly responsible for Dr. Grimesby Roylott's death, and I cannot say that it is likely to weigh very heavily upon my conscience."

Home Run

Marcelle Dubé

THE DAY the monster tracked them down in Mendenhall, Cooper was too busy playing baseball with the rest of the kids at the Prairie Dog Summer Day Camp to notice right away.

Standing at home plate, wooden bat in hand, Cooper ignored the catcalls from the other team and the cheering from the parents on the stands. He adjusted his cap to keep the beating sun out of eyes that already felt like dried up raisins. Sweat made the inside of his baseball cap slick and sticky, even while the breeze ruffled the hairs on his bare arms. All around the baseball diamond, sunflowers turned their dark hearts to follow the sun – whole fields of them nodding in the breeze, sunlight sparking off their petals like shards of light.

It was always windy here. Mom didn't like the wind but he did – it carried the rich smell of earth and fishy water from the Red River. And underneath it all, it brought the sound of grasshoppers singing a warning in the heat.

At least fifty people sat in the bleachers or stood around watching the game. Even policemen stood by, watching. Cooper had gotten used to seeing them around. They dropped by at least once a day to watch the practices. Sometimes even the chief of police came by.

He spotted Mom sitting at the top of the bleachers. She waved at him and he almost waved back, but he was ten now, too old for that kind of stuff. He nodded instead.

The baseball field was off Henrietta Blum Elementary School, where he'd be going in another two weeks. This time wasn't nearly so bad as all the other times he and Mom had moved to a new place. Mom had put him in summer camp as soon as they got here and he made friends with some of the kids who were going to be in his Grade 5 class. For the first time, he was actually looking forward to school.

"Hey, batta batta!" cried someone from the sidelines. Cooper ignored it.

They'd been practicing all summer and today was the exhibition game, the day they got to show their parents how good they'd gotten.

He shifted his hips the way he'd seen the Blue Jays' Dave Price do it on television and tried to stare down the pitcher, a girl called Samantha but that everyone called Sam.

She grinned at him.

"Nervous, Coop?"

He grinned back. "You wish."

Sam wound her arm back and when it whipped forward, she released the ball. Cooper felt his shoulders relax as he tracked the ball's approach. He was good at this game. As long as the pitch was true, he rarely missed.

He swung and the loud smack of the ball connecting with the bat was just about lost under the wild cheering and clapping from the stands. The ball had gone sailing off into the sunflower field. His hands tingling from the impact of the ball against the bat, he looked around to find his mom standing and cheering.

"Cooper, run!" cried Mr. Stuart, their coach.

Cooper flung the bat to the side and took off at a run toward first base.

He landed on the base with both feet, earning a disgusted look from Jase, the first baseman. Then a movement caught his eye and he looked to his right, where the sunflowers grew closest to the baseball diamond. A dark figure disappeared into the field, the tall stalks closing behind like a curtain.

All the joy rushed out of him. The monster had found them. Again.

* * *

"Are you excited about school starting?" Mom flipped the hamburgers on the barbecue, her back to him. The late afternoon sun shone on the top of her blonde hair, turning it yellow like the sunflowers.

They had rented a big old farmhouse just at the edge of Mendenhall. A bunch of trees – oaks and spruce – surrounded the house. Mom said it was for a windbreak. When the wind blew, which was pretty much always, the trees made a noise like someone sighing.

Beyond the trees, fields of canola and potatoes filled the horizon. The canola grew taller than him but the potato plants only came up to his knees. He liked watching the grasshoppers jump away when he walked through the potato field.

They had neighbors, but the closest one was old Mr. Jacobs and he was almost deaf. His house was just over the rise. Cooper could see Mr. Jacob's house from Mom's bedroom on the second floor. His bedroom was across the hall and looked onto the back yard with its shed and small garden. The next closest house belonged to the Sigurdsen family. They had a boy close to Cooper's age, Eric, and a little girl. Cooper sometimes stayed with them if Mom had to work late at the dentist's office.

He liked the farmhouse, with its creaky floors and wood stove. It was big and had lots of rooms and hidden spaces – like the attic, which still had a lot of cool stuff stored in it.

He didn't like that there weren't many people around. He knew why Mom had picked the farmhouse, though. The last place they'd lived, in Toronto, had been on the top floor of a row house. The monster had found them and set the apartment on fire. They'd barely escaped and a lot of people could have gotten hurt.

If something happened at the farmhouse, at least they wouldn't be putting anyone else in danger.

He didn't like to think about it.

"You already know a lot of kids," continued Mom, adding cheese to the burgers. She opened two buns and placed them on the top shelf where they would toast. The picnic table was already set with their plates and a couple of napkins tucked under them. Cooper placed another plate on top of the potato salad bowl to keep the bugs out. The plastic containers with the tomatoes and dill pickles were there and so was the most important ingredient for the perfect hamburger: ketchup. He still had to bring the lemonade and the glasses out, but he'd wait until the hamburgers were cooked.

The sun warmed the top of his head and reflected off the kitchen windows, and the breeze blew the smell of sizzling burgers toward him. It should have been driving him crazy, but he'd lost his appetite.

It was as if the monster wanted Cooper to see him.

In Toronto, Cooper had spotted the monster on their street the day before the fire broke out. The time before that, in Montreal, he had seen him the day before the monster tried to snatch him from the schoolyard. If not for his teacher, the monster would have gotten him.

He didn't have much time. Should he warn Mom?

She had put her curly blonde hair up in a bun and was wearing a white, sleeveless shirt that buttoned down the front and a pair of blue shorts. She looked great. He could see where the mosquitoes had bitten her bare arms but there were no bruises or bandages. Not for three years.

Three years ago, the monster would have been the one cooking the burgers. And drinking beer. And later, there would have been screams.

Cooper swallowed hard. He remembered the time before he and Mom ran, remembered how the monster had hurt Mom. Had hurt him.

He studied his mom. She smiled a lot now, ever since they had moved here. She thought they had escaped the monster, but Cooper knew better.

"Coop? Everything okay?" Mom turned to look at him, concern in her eyes. She was the prettiest mom he had ever seen. The best mom a kid could ask for. He couldn't let the monster get to her.

"Yep." He forced a grin. "Everything's fine."

* * *

Before Mom went to bed, she always made sure the doors and windows were locked. But she seemed so happy lately, so relaxed, that Cooper worried she wasn't being careful. That night, when she went to bed, he snuck out of his bedroom and double-checked that everything in the old farmhouse was locked up tight. He kept the lights off and looked out of every window. The moon was half full and it gleamed on the grass that needed mowing in the front yard. That was his job on the weekend, while Mom tended to the flowers in the front and the vegetable garden in the back.

He went from living room to bathroom to laundry room to kitchen, avoiding all the creaky spots in the oak floor. The floor around the front door felt cold to his bare feet and his toes curled up as he thought of winter. The kitchen still smelled of the coffee Mom drank. The clock by the fridge ticked loudly in the silence.

All the windows were latched.

He was just about to turn away from the window over the kitchen sink when he caught a glimpse of a figure at the edge of the cornfield, where it met the back garden.

As the spruce tree swayed in the moonlight, Cooper's heart thudded like the one of the bird he had found a few weeks ago, stunned by flying into the window.

The monster knew where they lived.

* * *

Rain moved in overnight and by the time Mom dropped him off at the school gym, where everyone in the day camp met in the morning, the whole world was soaked and gray.

Mom had taken one look at his face and decided she would stay home and let him sleep, as he seemed to be coming down with something. It took all of Cooper's persuasion to convince her he was fine.

Derek, one of the camp counsellors, stood at the front door to usher the kids inside and waved at Mom as she drove off. Cooper glanced around outside but saw nothing out of the ordinary. He'd stayed up all night, sitting on the leather couch in his pajamas and holding his baseball bat across his lap, but the monster hadn't tried anything.

Maybe he should have told Mom, but she would just pack them up and move again. And he was so tired of moving. In the last three years, they had moved seven times. He liked it here. And he was sick of being afraid, for himself and for Mom.

He couldn't call the cops. He'd tried that, twice. They hadn't believed him. And they hadn't believed that the monster had set the fire, either.

He was ten, almost eleven. He would take care of the monster.

"Hey, buddy." Derek held the door open for him. "You look beat. Bad night?"

Cooper shrugged.

"Should you be here?" asked Derek with a frown.

Cooper nodded and stepped inside the school. "Totally."

* * *

When they got home that night, Cooper could tell the monster had been in the house. It wasn't much. Nothing was out of place and Mom didn't notice anything, but Cooper could tell. It was like there was a wire connecting him to the monster and every move the monster made vibrated down the wire to Cooper.

While Mom made supper, Cooper snooped around the house, watching where he put his feet on the creaky boards so as not to alarm Mom. He finally found what he was looking for in the laundry room. The window over the clothes dryer was unlocked. Mom only ever opened it when she used the dryer and she'd been using the clothes line all summer. Last night the window had been locked. He'd checked it himself.

That was where the monster planned to come in.

"Cooper, supper's ready!" called Mom from the kitchen.

"Coming!" He turned away from the window, feeling like the monster was already in the room. But he had time. The monster would wait until night. Until they were asleep.

* * *

For the second night in a row, Cooper stayed up to keep watch over his mother. And to kill a monster.

He leaned against the wall between the small bathroom and the laundry room. The wall felt cool through his cotton t-shirt and pajama bottoms and he struggled to keep from shivering. If he started, he wouldn't be able to stop. He didn't dare sit down because he was afraid he'd fall asleep. His eyes burned and he couldn't stop yawning.

He held the baseball bat loosely, so as not to cramp his hands. He liked the weight of it in his hands. He figured it was about two in the morning. So far, nothing. The laundry room smelled of the flowery detergent Mom used, and shampoo from the bathroom. It was so quiet he could hear his heart thudding in his chest.

A sudden creaking sent his heart slamming against his rib cage. It sounded again and he finally recognized it as the springs from mom's bed. He waited to see if she was getting up. After a while, he relaxed. She'd just been turning around.

Wood slid against wood in the laundry room and Cooper stopped breathing.

A soft grunt was the only other warning until the grunt turned into a curse as the monster slid on the oil-covered dryer and scrambled for traction. Then a loud yell as the monster fell off the slick dryer and landed on the tacks Cooper had carefully spread over the laundry room floor.

As if he was playing baseball, Cooper's shoulders relaxed and he stepped into the laundry room, his heavy-duty hiking boots protecting his feet from the tacks. In the darkness, the monster was only a darker, moving shadow flailing and cursing.

Cooper stepped forward and swung with all his strength. The hard bat connected with a thunk and the monster yelled in pain. Cooper swung again, this time hitting something soft, and the monster grunted. Cooper swung again and again. A big hand grabbed his ankle and tried to unbalance him but Cooper swung down with all his might and heard a sickening sound, like a branch cracking in winter. The monster screamed.

Suddenly, light flooded the laundry room.

"Cooper! Cooper, stop!" cried Mom, her face contorted by fear.

Cooper blinked at her, not understanding her. He had to kill the monster.

He turned away and raised the baseball bat, only then realizing that it was splattered with blood.

"Please, sweetheart." Mom's voice was softer now. "You need to stop."

He blinked down at his father, writhing on the floor of the laundry room, holding his broken arm, his plaid shirt covered in pinpricks of blood from the tacks. Cooper hadn't had a good look since they'd escaped him, three years ago, and now he found himself surprised at the change in him. He'd always been tall and lean, but now he looked skinny. A short beard covered his hollow cheeks and his lips were chapped. His blonde hair was always short, but now it was almost shaved. Even his eyes looked different, as if he had a fever. He laid on the floor, cursing softly, blood streaming down his face from a cut on his head.

Cooper took a deep breath and lowered the bat to rest against the floor.

Mom gathered him in her arms. She didn't even look at his father. "I've called the police, James."

Cooper rested his forehead against her chest. He was trembling.

"We should kill him," he said softly. "He'll never stop until we do."

"Shh, sweetheart," she said. "You can't kill your father. There's no going back from that."

Without warning, Mom wrenched away from him, spinning him back, and he looked up to see his father, face livid, wrapping his good hand around Mom's neck.

"You stupid bitch!" he said, spittle flying from his mouth. "Did you really think I wouldn't find you?"

Cooper didn't dare swing the bat now for fear of hitting Mom, so he launched himself at his father's back. He wrapped his legs around his father's skinny waist and clawed at his eyes.

"Let her go!"

His father roared and slammed Cooper against the wall. Head ringing, Cooper tightened his hold.

"Let her go!" he screamed.

Something suddenly crashed against the kitchen wall and a chair scraped against the linoleum floor. Then heavy boots pounded on the wood floor of the living room. Men ran into the laundry room, yelling. They pulled Cooper off and pried his father's hand from Mom's throat.

Cooper reeled and looked around for the bat. Then he saw the police uniforms and sagged with relief.

* * *

The ambulance had come and gone, taking Cooper's dad with it, followed by one of the cop cars. Someone had shined a light in Cooper's eyes and said he was fine but Mom should take him to the doctor's in the morning.

Mom had put him to bed and tucked him in, like he was a little kid, and she'd kissed his forehead, then turned the light off, but not before speaking in a hoarse whisper into his ear.

"Thank you, sweetheart."

He wasn't sure what she was thanking him for. He hadn't killed the monster. His whole body trembled and he thought he might be sick, but he took a deep breath to calm himself. He wished he still had his bat, but someone had taken it away.

Once he was sure Mom was downstairs, he tiptoed to the door and opened it a crack to hear what the cops had to say.

"... knew about your troubles," said a woman's voice. That had to be the chief of police. She'd arrived minutes after the first two cops got here. "We've been keeping an eye on the place. That's why the patrol car was so close."

"Thank God," said Mom and even from the bedroom, he could hear the shakiness in her voice. "What'll happen now?"

"He's going to jail for a long time," said the chief. "You can finally stop looking over your shoulder."

Cooper closed the door softly and retreated to his bed. Tomorrow, he would talk to Mom about getting a new baseball bat.

The monster was going to jail for a long time, but not for ever. But by the time he got out, Cooper would be older and stronger.

He would deal with him then.

The Aluminium Dagger

R. Austin Freeman

THE 'URGENT CALL' – the instant, peremptory summons to professional duty – is an experience that appertains to the medical rather than the legal practitioner, and I had supposed, when I abandoned the clinical side of my profession in favour of the forensic, that henceforth I should know it no more; that the interrupted meal, the broken leisure, and the jangle of the night-bell, were things of the past; but in practice it was otherwise. The medical jurist is, so to speak, on the borderland of the two professions, and exposed to the vicissitudes of each calling, and so it happened from time to time that the professional services of my colleague or myself were demanded at a moment's notice. And thus it was in the case that I am about to relate.

The sacred rite of the 'tub' had been duly performed, and the freshly-dried person of the present narrator was about to be insinuated into the first instalment of clothing, when a hurried step was heard upon the stair, and the voice of our laboratory assistant, Polton, arose at my colleague's door.

"There's a gentleman downstairs, sir, who says he must see you instantly on most urgent business. He seems to be in a rare twitter, sir –"

Polton was proceeding to descriptive particulars, when a second and more hurried step became audible, and a strange voice addressed Thorndyke.

"I have come to beg your immediate assistance, sir; a most dreadful thing has happened. A horrible murder has been committed. Can you come with me now?"

"I will be with you almost immediately," said Thorndyke. "Is the victim quite dead?"

"Quite. Cold and stiff. The police think –"

"Do the police know that you have come for me?" interrupted Thorndyke.

"Yes. Nothing is to be done until you arrive."

"Very well. I will be ready in a few minutes."

"And if you would wait downstairs, sir," Polton added persuasively, "I could help the doctor to get ready."

With this crafty appeal, he lured the intruder back to the sitting-room, and shortly after stole softly up the stairs with a small breakfast tray, the contents of which he deposited firmly in our respective rooms, with a few timely words on the folly of "undertaking murders on an empty stomach." Thorndyke and I had meanwhile clothed ourselves with a celerity known only to medical practitioners and quick-change artists, and in a few minutes descended the stairs together, calling in at the laboratory for a few appliances that Thorndyke usually took with him on a visit of investigation.

As we entered the sitting-room, our visitor, who was feverishly pacing up and down, seized his hat with a gasp of relief. "You are ready to come?" he asked. "My carriage is at the door;" and, without waiting for an answer, he hurried out, and rapidly preceded us down the stairs.

The carriage was a roomy brougham, which fortunately accommodated the three of us, and as soon as we had entered and shut the door, the coachman whipped up his horse and drove off at a smart trot.

"I had better give you some account of the circumstances, as we go," said our agitated friend. "In the first place, my name is Curtis, Henry Curtis; here is my card. Ah! And here is another card, which I should have given you before. My solicitor, Mr. Marchmont, was with me when I made this dreadful discovery, and he sent me to you. He remained in the rooms to see that nothing is disturbed until you arrive."

"That was wise of him," said Thorndyke. "But now tell us exactly what has occurred."

"I will," said Mr. Curtis. "The murdered man was my brother-in-law, Alfred Hartridge, and I am sorry to say he was – well, he was a bad man. It grieves me to speak of him thus – *de mortuis*, you know – but, still, we must deal with the facts, even though they be painful."

"Undoubtedly," agreed Thorndyke.

"I have had a great deal of very unpleasant correspondence with him – Marchmont will tell you about that – and yesterday I left a note for him, asking for an interview, to settle the business, naming eight o'clock this morning as the hour, because I had to leave town before noon. He replied, in a very singular letter, that he would see me at that hour, and Mr. Marchmont very kindly consented to accompany me. Accordingly, we went to his chambers together this morning, arriving punctually at eight o'clock. We rang the bell several times, and knocked loudly at the door, but as there was no response, we went down and spoke to the hall-porter. This man, it seems, had already noticed, from the courtyard, that the electric lights were full on in Mr. Hartridge's sitting-room, as they had been all night, according to the statement of the night-porter; so now, suspecting that something was wrong, he came up with us, and rang the bell and battered at the door. Then, as there was still no sign of life within, he inserted his duplicate key and tried to open the door – unsuccessfully, however, as it proved to be bolted on the inside. Thereupon the porter fetched a constable, and, after a consultation, we decided that we were justified in breaking open the door; the porter produced a crowbar, and by our unified efforts the door was eventually burst open. We entered, and – my God! Dr. Thorndyke, what a terrible sight it was that met our eyes! My brother-in-law was lying dead on the floor of the sitting-room. He had been stabbed – stabbed to death; and the dagger had not even been withdrawn. It was still sticking out of his back."

He mopped his face with his handkerchief, and was about to continue his account of the catastrophe when the carriage entered a quiet side-street between Westminster and Victoria, and drew up before a block of tall, new, red-brick buildings. A flurried hall-porter ran out to open the door, and we alighted opposite the main entrance.

"My brother-in-law's chambers are on the second-floor," said Mr. Curtis. "We can go up in the lift."

The porter had hurried before us, and already stood with his hand upon the rope. We entered the lift, and in a few seconds were discharged on to the second floor, the porter, with furtive curiosity, following us down the corridor. At the end of the passage was a half-open door, considerably battered and bruised. Above the door, painted in white lettering, was the inscription, 'Mr. Hartridge'; and through the doorway protruded the rather foxy countenance of Inspector Badger.

"I am glad you have come, sir," said he, as he recognized my colleague. "Mr. Marchmont is sitting inside like a watch-dog, and he growls if any of us even walks across the room."

The words formed a complaint, but there was a certain geniality in the speaker's manner which made me suspect that Inspector Badger was already navigating his craft on a lee shore.

CRIME & MYSTERY SHORT STORIES

We entered a small lobby or hall, and from thence passed into the sitting-room, where we found Mr. Marchmont keeping his vigil, in company with a constable and a uniformed inspector. The three rose softly as we entered, and greeted us in a whisper; and then, with one accord, we all looked towards the other end of the room, and so remained for a time without speaking.

There was, in the entire aspect of the room, something very grim and dreadful. An atmosphere of tragic mystery enveloped the most commonplace objects; and sinister suggestions lurked in the most familiar appearances. Especially impressive was the air of suspense – of ordinary, every-day life suddenly arrested – cut short in the twinkling of an eye. The electric lamps, still burning dim and red, though the summer sunshine streamed in through the windows; the half-emptied tumbler and open book by the empty chair, had each its whispered message of swift and sudden disaster, as had the hushed voices and stealthy movements of the waiting men, and, above all, an awesome shape that was but a few hours since a living man, and that now sprawled, prone and motionless, on the floor.

"This is a mysterious affair," observed Inspector Badger, breaking the silence at length, "though it is clear enough up to a certain point. The body tells its own story."

We stepped across and looked down at the corpse. It was that of a somewhat elderly man, and lay, on an open space of floor before the fireplace, face downwards, with the arms extended. The slender hilt of a dagger projected from the back below the left shoulder, and, with the exception of a trace of blood upon the lips, this was the only indication of the mode of death. A little way from the body a clock-key lay on the carpet, and, glancing up at the clock on the mantelpiece, I perceived that the glass front was open.

"You see," pursued the inspector, noting my glance, "he was standing in front of the fireplace, winding the clock. Then the murderer stole up behind him – the noise of the turning key must have covered his movements – and stabbed him. And you see, from the position of the dagger on the left side of the back, that the murderer must have been left-handed. That is all clear enough. What is not clear is how he got in, and how he got out again."

"The body has not been moved, I suppose," said Thorndyke.

"No. We sent for Dr. Egerton, the police-surgeon, and he certified that the man was dead. He will be back presently to see you and arrange about the post-mortem."

"Then," said Thorndyke, "we will not disturb the body till he comes, except to take the temperature and dust the dagger-hilt."

He took from his bag a long, registering chemical thermometer and an insufflator or powder-blower. The former he introduced under the dead man's clothing against the abdomen, and with the latter blew a stream of fine yellow powder on to the black leather handle of the dagger. Inspector Badger stooped eagerly to examine the handle, as Thorndyke blew away the powder that had settled evenly on the surface.

"No fingerprints," said he, in a disappointed tone. "He must have worn gloves. But that inscription gives a pretty broad hint."

He pointed, as he spoke, to the metal guard of the dagger, on which was engraved, in clumsy lettering, the single word, '*TRADITORE.*'

"That's the Italian for 'traitor,' " continued the inspector, "and I got some information from the porter that fits in with that suggestion. We'll have him in presently, and you shall hear."

"Meanwhile," said Thorndyke, "as the position of the body may be of importance in the inquiry, I will take one or two photographs and make a rough plan to scale. Nothing has been moved, you say? Who opened the windows?"

"They were open when we came in," said Mr. Marchmont. "Last night was very hot, you remember. Nothing whatever has been moved."

Thorndyke produced from his bag a small folding camera, a telescopic tripod, a surveyor's measuring-tape, a boxwood scale, and a sketch-block. He set up the camera in a corner, and exposed a plate, taking a general view of the room, and including the corpse. Then he moved to the door and made a second exposure.

"Will you stand in front of the clock, Jervis," he said, "and raise your hand as if winding it? Thanks; keep like that while I expose a plate."

I remained thus, in the position that the dead man was assumed to have occupied at the moment of the murder, while the plate was exposed, and then, before I moved, Thorndyke marked the position of my feet with a blackboard chalk. He next set up the tripod over the chalk marks, and took two photographs from that position, and finally photographed the body itself.

The photographic operations being concluded, he next proceeded, with remarkable skill and rapidity, to lay out on the sketch-block a ground-plan of the room, showing the exact position of the various objects, on a scale of a quarter of an inch to the foot – a process that the inspector was inclined to view with some impatience.

"You don't spare trouble, Doctor," he remarked; "nor time either," he added, with a significant glance at his watch.

"No," answered Thorndyke, as he detached the finished sketch from the block; "I try to collect all the facts that may bear on a case. They may prove worthless, or they may turn out of vital importance; one never knows beforehand, so I collect them all. But here, I think, is Dr. Egerton."

The police-surgeon greeted Thorndyke with respectful cordiality, and we proceeded at once to the examination of the body. Drawing out the thermometer, my colleague noted the reading, and passed the instrument to Dr. Egerton.

"Dead about ten hours," remarked the latter, after a glance at it. "This was a very determined and mysterious murder."

"Very," said Thorndyke. "Feel that dagger, Jervis."

I touched the hilt, and felt the characteristic grating of bone.

"It is through the edge of a rib!" I exclaimed.

"Yes; it must have been used with extraordinary force. And you notice that the clothing is screwed up slightly, as if the blade had been rotated as it was driven in. That is a very peculiar feature, especially when taken together with the violence of the blow."

"It is singular, certainly," said Dr. Egerton, "though I don't know that it helps us much. Shall we withdraw the dagger before moving the body?"

"Certainly," replied Thorndyke, "or the movement may produce fresh injuries. But wait." He took a piece of string from his pocket, and, having drawn the dagger out a couple of inches, stretched the string in a line parallel to the flat of the blade. Then, giving me the ends to hold, he drew the weapon out completely. As the blade emerged, the twist in the clothing disappeared. "Observe," said he, "that the string gives the direction of the wound, and that the cut in the clothing no longer coincides with it. There is quite a considerable angle, which is the measure of the rotation of the blade."

"Yes, it is odd," said Dr. Egerton, "though, as I said, I doubt that it helps us."

"At present," Thorndyke rejoined dryly, "we are noting the facts."

"Quite so," agreed the other, reddening slightly; "and perhaps we had better move the body to the bedroom, and make a preliminary inspection of the wound."

We carried the corpse into the bedroom, and, having examined the wound without eliciting anything new, covered the remains with a sheet, and returned to the sitting-room.

"Well, gentlemen," said the inspector, "you have examined the body and the wound, and you have measured the floor and the furniture, and taken photographs, and made a plan, but we don't seem much more forward. Here's a man murdered in his rooms. There is only one entrance to the flat, and that was bolted on the inside at the time of the murder. The windows are some forty feet from the ground; there is no rain-pipe near any of them; they are set flush in the wall, and there isn't a foothold for a fly on any part of that wall. The grates are modern, and there isn't room for a good-sized cat to crawl up any of the chimneys. Now, the question is, How did the murderer get in, and how did he get out again?"

"Still," said Mr. Marchmont, "the fact is that he did get in, and that he is not here now; and therefore he must have got out; and therefore it must have been possible for him to get out. And, further, it must be possible to discover how he got out."

The inspector smiled sourly, but made no reply.

"The circumstances," said Thorndyke, "appear to have been these: The deceased seems to have been alone; there is no trace of a second occupant of the room, and only one half-emptied tumbler on the table. He was sitting reading when apparently he noticed that the clock had stopped – at ten minutes to twelve; he laid his book, face downwards, on the table, and rose to wind the clock, and as he was winding it he met his death."

"By a stab dealt by a left-handed man, who crept up behind him on tiptoe," added the inspector.

Thorndyke nodded. "That would seem to be so," he said. "But now let us call in the porter, and hear what he has to tell us."

The custodian was not difficult to find, being, in fact, engaged at that moment in a survey of the premises through the slit of the letter-box.

"Do you know what persons visited these rooms last night?" Thorndyke asked him, when he entered looking somewhat sheepish.

"A good many were in and out of the building," was the answer, "but I can't say if any of them came to this flat. I saw Miss Curtis pass in about nine."

"My daughter!" exclaimed Mr. Curtis, with a start. "I didn't know that."

"She left about nine-thirty," the porter added.

"Do you know what she came about?" asked the inspector.

"I can guess," replied Mr. Curtis.

"Then don't say," interrupted Mr. Marchmont. "Answer no questions."

"You're very close, Mr. Marchmont," said the inspector; "we are not suspecting the young lady. We don't ask, for instance, if she is left-handed."

He glanced craftily at Mr. Curtis as he made this remark, and I noticed that our client suddenly turned deathly pale, whereupon the inspector looked away again quickly, as though he had not observed the change.

"Tell us about those Italians again," he said, addressing the porter. "When did the first of them come here?"

"About a week ago," was the reply. "He was a common-looking man – looked like an organ-grinder – and he brought a note to my lodge. It was in a dirty envelope, and was addressed 'Mr. Hartridge, Esq., Brackenhurst Mansions,' in a very bad handwriting. The man gave me the note and asked me to give it to Mr. Hartridge; then he went away, and I took the note up and dropped it into the letter-box."

"What happened next?"

"Why, the very next day an old hag of an Italian woman – one of them fortune-telling swines with a cage of birds on a stand – came and set up just by the main doorway. I soon sent her packing, but, bless you! She was back again in ten minutes, birds and all. I sent her off again – I kept on sending her off, and she kept on coming back, until I was reg'lar wore to a thread."

"You seem to have picked up a bit since then," remarked the inspector with a grin and a glance at the sufferer's very pronounced bow-window.

"Perhaps I have," the custodian replied haughtily. "Well, the next day there was a ice-cream man – a reg'lar waster, *he* was. Stuck outside as if he was froze to the pavement. Kept giving the errand-boys tasters, and when I tried to move him on, he told me not to obstruct his business. Business, indeed! Well, there them boys stuck, one after the other, wiping their tongues round the bottoms of them glasses, until I was fit to bust with aggravation. And *he* kept me going all day.

"Then, the day after that there was a barrel-organ, with a mangy-looking monkey on it. He was the worst of all. Profane, too, *he* was. Kept mixing up sacred tunes and comic songs: 'Rock of Ages,' 'Bill Bailey,' 'Cujus Animal,' and 'Over the Garden Wall.' And when I tried to move him on, that little blighter of a monkey made a run at my leg; and then the man grinned and started playing, 'Wait till the Clouds roll by.' I tell you, it was fair sickening."

He wiped his brow at the recollection, and the inspector smiled appreciatively.

"And that was the last of them?" said the latter; and as the porter nodded sulkily, he asked: "Should you recognize the note that the Italian gave you?"

"I should," answered the porter with frosty dignity.

The inspector bustled out of the room, and returned a minute later with a letter-case in his hand.

"This was in his breast-pocket," said he, laying the bulging case on the table, and drawing up a chair. "Now, here are three letters tied together. Ah! This will be the one." He untied the tape, and held out a dirty envelope addressed in a sprawling, illiterate hand to 'Mr. Hartridge, Esq.' "Is that the note the Italian gave you?"

The porter examined it critically. "Yes," said he; "that is the one."

The inspector drew the letter out of the envelope, and, as he opened it, his eyebrows went up.

"What do you make of that, Doctor?" he said, handing the sheet to Thorndyke.

Thorndyke regarded it for a while in silence, with deep attention. Then he carried it to the window, and, taking his lens from his pocket, examined the paper closely, first with the low power, and then with the highly magnifying Coddington attachment.

"I should have thought you could see that with the naked eye," said the inspector, with a sly grin at me. "It's a pretty bold design."

"Yes," replied Thorndyke; "a very interesting production. What do you say, Mr. Marchmont?"

The solicitor took the note, and I looked over his shoulder. It was certainly a curious production. Written in red ink, on the commonest notepaper, and in the same sprawling hand as the address, was the following message:

You are given six days to do what is just. By the sign above, know what to expect if you fail.

The sign referred to was a skull and crossbones, very neatly, but rather unskilfully, drawn at the top of the paper.

"This," said Mr. Marchmont, handing the document to Mr. Curtis, "explains the singular letter that he wrote yesterday. You have it with you, I think?"

"Yes," replied Mr. Curtis; "here it is."

He produced a letter from his pocket, and read aloud:

"Yes: come if you like, though it is an ungodly hour. Your threatening letters have caused me great amusement. They are worthy of Sadler's Wells in its prime.
ALFRED HARTRIDGE."

"Was Mr. Hartridge ever in Italy?" asked Inspector Badger.

"Oh yes," replied Mr. Curtis. "He stayed at Capri nearly the whole of last year."

"Why, then, that gives us our clue. Look here. Here are these two other letters; E.C. postmark – Saffron Hill is E.C. And just look at that!"

He spread out the last of the mysterious letters, and we saw that, besides the *memento mori*, it contained only three words:

Beware! Remember Capri!

"If you have finished, Doctor, I'll be off and have a look round Little Italy. Those four Italians oughtn't to be difficult to find, and we've got the porter here to identify them."

"Before you go," said Thorndyke, "there are two little matters that I should like to settle. One is the dagger: it is in your pocket, I think. May I have a look at it?"

The inspector rather reluctantly produced the dagger and handed it to my colleague.

"A very singular weapon, this," said Thorndyke, regarding the dagger thoughtfully, and turning it about to view its different parts. "Singular both in shape and material. I have never seen an aluminium hilt before, and bookbinder's morocco is a little unusual."

"The aluminium was for lightness," explained the inspector, "and it was made narrow to carry up the sleeve, I expect."

"Perhaps so," said Thorndyke.

He continued his examination, and presently, to the inspector's delight, brought forth his pocket lens.

"I never saw such a man!" exclaimed the jocose detective. "His motto ought to be, 'We magnify thee.' I suppose he'll measure it next."

The inspector was not mistaken. Having made a rough sketch of the weapon on his block, Thorndyke produced from his bag a folding rule and a delicate calliper-gauge. With these instruments he proceeded, with extraordinary care and precision, to take the dimensions of the various parts of the dagger, entering each measurement in its place on the sketch, with a few brief, descriptive details.

"The other matter," said he at length, handing the dagger back to the inspector, "refers to the houses opposite."

He walked to the window, and looked out at the backs of a row of tall buildings similar to the one we were in. They were about thirty yards distant, and were separated from us by a piece of ground, planted with shrubs and intersected by gravel paths.

"If any of those rooms were occupied last night," continued Thorndyke, "we might obtain an actual eyewitness of the crime. This room was brilliantly lighted, and all the blinds were up, so that an observer at any of those windows could see right into the room, and very distinctly, too. It might be worth inquiring into."

"Yes, that's true," said the inspector; "though I expect, if any of them have seen anything, they will come forward quick enough when they read the report in the papers. But I must be off now, and I shall have to lock you out of the rooms."

As we went down the stairs, Mr. Marchmont announced his intention of calling on us in the evening, "unless," he added, "you want any information from me now."

"I do," said Thorndyke. "I want to know who is interested in this man's death."

"That," replied Marchmont, "is rather a queer story. Let us take a turn in that garden that we saw from the window. We shall be quite private there."

He beckoned to Mr. Curtis, and, when the inspector had departed with the police-surgeon, we induced the porter to let us into the garden.

"The question that you asked," Mr. Marchmont began, looking up curiously at the tall houses opposite, "is very simply answered. The only person immediately interested in the death of Alfred Hartridge is his executor and sole legatee, a man named Leonard Wolfe. He is no relation of the deceased, merely a friend, but he inherits the entire estate – about twenty thousand pounds. The circumstances are these: Alfred Hartridge was the elder of two brothers, of whom the younger, Charles, died before his father, leaving a widow and three children. Fifteen years ago the father died, leaving the whole of his property to Alfred, with the understanding that he should support his brother's family and make the children his heirs."

"Was there no will?" asked Thorndyke.

"Under great pressure from the friends of his son's widow, the old man made a will shortly before he died; but he was then very old and rather childish, so the will was contested by Alfred, on the grounds of undue influence, and was ultimately set aside. Since then Alfred Hartridge has not paid a penny towards the support of his brother's family. If it had not been for my client, Mr. Curtis, they might have starved; the whole burden of the support of the widow and the education of the children has fallen upon him.

"Well, just lately the matter has assumed an acute form, for two reasons. The first is that Charles's eldest son, Edmund, has come of age. Mr. Curtis had him articled to a solicitor, and, as he is now fully qualified, and a most advantageous proposal for a partnership has been made, we have been putting pressure on Alfred to supply the necessary capital in accordance with his father's wishes. This he had refused to do, and it was with reference to this matter that we were calling on him this morning. The second reason involves a curious and disgraceful story. There is a certain Leonard Wolfe, who has been an intimate friend of the deceased. He is, I may say, a man of bad character, and their association has been of a kind creditable to neither. There is also a certain woman named Hester Greene, who had certain claims upon the deceased, which we need not go into at present. Now, Leonard Wolfe and the deceased, Alfred Hartridge, entered into an agreement, the terms of which were these: (1) Wolfe was to marry Hester Greene, and in consideration of this service (2) Alfred Hartridge was to assign to Wolfe the whole of his property, absolutely, the actual transfer to take place on the death of Hartridge."

"And has this transaction been completed?" asked Thorndyke.

"Yes, it has, unfortunately. But we wished to see if anything could be done for the widow and the children during Hartridge's lifetime. No doubt, my client's daughter, Miss Curtis, called last night on a similar mission – very indiscreetly, since the matter was in our hands; but, you know, she is engaged to Edmund Hartridge – and I expect the interview was a pretty stormy one."

Thorndyke remained silent for a while, pacing slowly along the gravel path, with his eyes bent on the ground: not abstractedly, however, but with a searching, attentive glance that roved amongst the shrubs and bushes, as though he were looking for something.

"What sort of man," he asked presently, "is this Leonard Wolfe? Obviously he is a low scoundrel, but what is he like in other respects? Is he a fool, for instance?"

"Not at all, I should say," said Mr. Curtis. "He was formerly an engineer, and, I believe, a very capable mechanician. Latterly he has lived on some property that came to him, and has spent both his time and his money in gambling and dissipation. Consequently, I expect he is pretty short of funds at present."

"And in appearance?"

"I only saw him once," replied Mr. Curtis, "and all I can remember of him is that he is rather short, fair, thin, and clean-shaven, and that he has lost the middle finger of his left hand."

"And he lives at?"

"Eltham, in Kent. Morton Grange, Eltham," said Mr. Marchmont. "And now, if you have all the information that you require, I must really be off, and so must Mr. Curtis."

The two men shook our hands and hurried away, leaving Thorndyke gazing meditatively at the dingy flower-beds.

"A strange and interesting case, this, Jervis," said he, stooping to peer under a laurel-bush. "The inspector is on a hot scent – a most palpable red herring on a most obvious string; but that is his business. Ah, here comes the porter, intent, no doubt, on pumping us, whereas –" He smiled genially at the approaching custodian, and asked: "Where did you say those houses fronted?"

"Cotman Street, sir," answered the porter. "They are nearly all offices."

"And the numbers? That open second-floor window, for instance?"

"That is number six; but the house opposite Mr. Hartridge's rooms is number eight."

"Thank you."

Thorndyke was moving away, but suddenly turned again to the porter.

"By the way," said he, "I dropped something out of the window just now – a small flat piece of metal, like this." He made on the back of his visiting card a neat sketch of a circular disc, with a hexagonal hole through it, and handed the card to the porter. "I can't say where it fell," he continued; "these flat things scale about so; but you might ask the gardener to look for it. I will give him a sovereign if he brings it to my chambers, for, although it is of no value to anyone else, it is of considerable value to me."

The porter touched his hat briskly, and as we turned out at the gate, I looked back and saw him already wading among the shrubs.

The object of the porter's quest gave me considerable mental occupation. I had not seen Thorndyke drop any thing, and it was not his way to finger carelessly any object of value. I was about to question him on the subject, when, turning sharply round into Cotman Street, he drew up at the doorway of number six, and began attentively to read the names of the occupants.

" 'Third-floor,' " he read out, " 'Mr. Thomas Barlow, Commission Agent.' Hum! I think we will look in on Mr. Barlow."

He stepped quickly up the stone stairs, and I followed, until we arrived, somewhat out of breath, on the third-floor. Outside the Commission Agent's door he paused for a moment, and we both listened curiously to an irregular sound of shuffling feet from within. Then he softly opened the door and looked into the room. After remaining thus for nearly a minute, he looked round at me with a broad smile, and noiselessly set the door wide open. Inside, a lanky youth of fourteen was practising, with no mean skill, the manipulation of an appliance known by the appropriate name of diabolo; and so absorbed was he in his occupation that we entered and shut the door without being observed. At length the shuttle missed the string and flew into a large waste-paper basket; the boy turned and confronted us, and was instantly covered with confusion.

"Allow me," said Thorndyke, rooting rather unnecessarily in the waste-paper basket, and handing the toy to its owner. "I need not ask if Mr. Barlow is in," he added, "nor if he is likely to return shortly."

"He won't be back today," said the boy, perspiring with embarrassment; "he left before I came. I was rather late."

"I see," said Thorndyke. "The early bird catches the worm, but the late bird catches the diabolo. How did you know he would not be back?"

"He left a note. Here it is."

He exhibited the document, which was neatly written in red ink. Thorndyke examined it attentively, and then asked:

"Did you break the inkstand yesterday?"

The boy stared at him in amazement. "Yes, I did," he answered. "How did you know?"

"I didn't, or I should not have asked. But I see that he has used his stylo to write this note."

The boy regarded Thorndyke distrustfully, as he continued:

"I really called to see if your Mr. Barlow was a gentleman whom I used to know; but I expect you can tell me. My friend was tall and thin, dark, and clean-shaved."

"This ain't him, then," said the boy. "He's thin, but he ain't tall or dark. He's got a sandy beard, and he wears spectacles and a wig. I know a wig when I see one," he added cunningly, " 'cause my father wears one. He puts it on a peg to comb it, and he swears at me when I larf."

"My friend had injured his left hand," pursued Thorndyke.

"I dunno about that," said the youth. "Mr. Barlow nearly always wears gloves; he always wears one on his left hand, anyhow."

"Ah well! I'll just write him a note on the chance, if you will give me a piece of notepaper. Have you any ink?"

"There's some in the bottle. I'll dip the pen in for you."

He produced, from the cupboard, an opened packet of cheap notepaper and a packet of similar envelopes, and, having dipped the pen to the bottom of the ink-bottle, handed it to Thorndyke, who sat down and hastily scribbled a short note. He had folded the paper, and was about to address the envelope, when he appeared suddenly to alter his mind.

"I don't think I will leave it, after all," he said, slipping the folded paper into his pocket. "No. Tell him I called – Mr. Horace Budge – and say I will look in again in a day or two."

The youth watched our exit with an air of perplexity, and he even came out on to the landing, the better to observe us over the balusters; until, unexpectedly catching Thorndyke's eye, he withdrew his head with remarkable suddenness, and retired in disorder.

To tell the truth, I was now little less perplexed than the office-boy by Thorndyke's proceedings; in which I could discover no relevancy to the investigation that I presumed he was engaged upon: and the last straw was laid upon the burden of my curiosity when he stopped at a staircase window, drew the note out of his pocket, examined it with his lens, held it up to the light, and chuckled aloud.

"Luck," he observed, "though no substitute for care and intelligence, is a very pleasant addition. Really, my learned brother, we are doing uncommonly well."

When we reached the hall, Thorndyke stopped at the housekeeper's box, and looked in with a genial nod.

"I have just been up to see Mr. Barlow," said he. "He seems to have left quite early."

"Yes, sir," the man replied. "He went away about half-past eight."

"That was very early; and presumably he came earlier still?"

"I suppose so," the man assented, with a grin; "but I had only just come on when he left."

"Had he any luggage with him?"

"Yes, sir. There was two cases, a square one and a long, narrow one, about five foot long. I helped him to carry them down to the cab."

"Which was a four-wheeler, I suppose?"

"Yes, sir."

"Mr. Barlow hasn't been here very long, has he?" Thorndyke inquired.

"No. He only came in last quarter-day – about six weeks ago."

"Ah well! I must call another day. Good morning;" and Thorndyke strode out of the building, and made directly for the cab-rank in the adjoining street. Here he stopped for a minute or two to parley with the driver of a four-wheeled cab, whom he finally commissioned to convey us to a shop in New Oxford Street. Having dismissed the cabman with his blessing and a half-sovereign, he vanished into the shop, leaving me to gaze at the lathes, drills, and bars of metal displayed in the window. Presently he emerged with a small parcel, and explained, in answer to my inquiring look: "A strip of tool steel and a block of metal for Polton."

His next purchase was rather more eccentric. We were proceeding along Holborn when his attention was suddenly arrested by the window of a furniture shop, in which was displayed a collection of obsolete French small-arms – relics of the tragedy of 1870 – which were being sold for decorative purposes. After a brief inspection, he entered the shop, and shortly reappeared carrying a long sword-bayonet and an old Chassepôt rifle.

"What may be the meaning of this martial display?" I asked, as we turned down Fetter Lane.

"House protection," he replied promptly. "You will agree that a discharge of musketry, followed by a bayonet charge, would disconcert the boldest of burglars."

I laughed at the absurd picture thus drawn of the strenuous house-protector, but nevertheless continued to speculate on the meaning of my friend's eccentric proceedings, which I felt sure were in some way related to the murder in Brackenhurst Chambers, though I could not trace the connection.

After a late lunch, I hurried out to transact such of my business as had been interrupted by the stirring events of the morning, leaving Thorndyke busy with a drawing-board, squares, scale, and compasses, making accurate, scaled drawings from his rough sketches; while Polton, with the brown-paper parcel in his hand, looked on at him with an air of anxious expectation.

As I was returning homeward in the evening by way of Mitre Court, I overtook Mr. Marchmont, who was also bound for our chambers, and we walked on together.

"I had a note from Thorndyke," he explained, "asking for a specimen of handwriting, so I thought I would bring it along myself, and hear if he has any news."

When we entered the chambers, we found Thorndyke in earnest consultation with Polton, and on the table before them I observed, to my great surprise, the dagger with which the murder had been committed.

"I have got you the specimen that you asked for," said Marchmont. "I didn't think I should be able to, but, by a lucky chance, Curtis kept the only letter he ever received from the party in question."

He drew the letter from his wallet, and handed it to Thorndyke, who looked at it attentively and with evident satisfaction.

"By the way," said Marchmont, taking up the dagger, "I thought the inspector took this away with him."

"He took the original," replied Thorndyke. "This is a duplicate, which Polton has made, for experimental purposes, from my drawings."

"Really!" exclaimed Marchmont, with a glance of respectful admiration at Polton; "it is a perfect replica – and you have made it so quickly, too."

"It was quite easy to make," said Polton, "to a man accustomed to work in metal."

"Which," added Thorndyke, "is a fact of some evidential value."

At this moment a hansom drew up outside. A moment later flying footsteps were heard on the stairs. There was a furious battering at the door, and, as Polton threw it open, Mr. Curtis burst wildly into the room.

"Here is a frightful thing, Marchmont!" he gasped. "Edith – my daughter – arrested for the murder. Inspector Badger came to our house and took her. My God! I shall go mad!"

Thorndyke laid his hand on the excited man's shoulder. "Don't distress yourself, Mr. Curtis," said he. "There is no occasion, I assure you. I suppose," he added, "your daughter is left-handed?"

"Yes, she is, by a most disastrous coincidence. But what are we to do? Good God! Dr. Thorndyke, they have taken her to prison – to prison – think of it! My poor Edith!"

"We'll soon have her out," said Thorndyke. "But listen; there is someone at the door."

A brisk rat-tat confirmed his statement; and when I rose to open the door, I found myself confronted by Inspector Badger. There was a moment of extreme awkwardness, and then both the detective and Mr. Curtis proposed to retire in favour of the other.

"Don't go, inspector," said Thorndyke; "I want to have a word with you. Perhaps Mr. Curtis would look in again, say, in an hour. Will you? We shall have news for you by then, I hope."

Mr. Curtis agreed hastily, and dashed out of the room with his characteristic impetuosity. When he had gone, Thorndyke turned to the detective, and remarked dryly:

"You seem to have been busy, inspector?"

"Yes," replied Badger; "I haven't let the grass grow under my feet; and I've got a pretty strong case against Miss Curtis already. You see, she was the last person seen in the company of the deceased; she had a grievance against him; she is left-handed, and you remember that the murder was committed by a left-handed person."

"Anything else?"

"Yes. I have seen those Italians, and the whole thing was a put-up job. A woman, in a widow's dress and veil, paid them to go and play the fool outside the building, and she gave them the letter that was left with the porter. They haven't identified her yet, but she seems to agree in size with Miss Curtis."

"And how did she get out of the chambers, with the door bolted on the inside?"

"Ah, there you are! That's a mystery at present – unless you can give us an explanation." The inspector made this qualification with a faint grin, and added: "As there was no one in the place when we broke into it, the murderer must have got out somehow. You can't deny that."

"I do deny it, nevertheless," said Thorndyke. "You look surprised," he continued (which was undoubtedly true), "but yet the whole thing is exceedingly obvious. The explanation struck me directly I looked at the body. There was evidently no practicable exit from the flat, and there was certainly no one in it when you entered. Clearly, then, *the murderer had never been in the place at all*."

"I don't follow you in the least," said the inspector.

"Well," said Thorndyke, "as I have finished with the case, and am handing it over to you, I will put the evidence before you *seriatim*. Now, I think we are agreed that, at the moment when the blow was struck, the deceased was standing before the fireplace, winding the clock. The dagger entered obliquely from the left, and, if you recall its position, you will remember that its hilt pointed directly towards an open window."

"Which was forty feet from the ground."

"Yes. And now we will consider the very peculiar character of the weapon with which the crime was committed."

He had placed his hand upon the knob of a drawer, when we were interrupted by a knock at the door. I sprang up, and, opening it, admitted no less a person than the porter of

Brackenhurst Chambers. The man looked somewhat surprised on recognizing our visitors, but advanced to Thorndyke, drawing a folded paper from his pocket.

"I've found the article you were looking for, sir," said he, "and a rare hunt I had for it. It had stuck in the leaves of one of them shrubs."

Thorndyke opened the packet, and, having glanced inside, laid it on the table.

"Thank you," said he, pushing a sovereign across to the gratified official. "The inspector has your name, I think?"

"He have, sir," replied the porter; and, pocketing his fee, he departed, beaming.

"To return to the dagger," said Thorndyke, opening the drawer. "It was a very peculiar one, as I have said, and as you will see from this model, which is an exact duplicate." Here he exhibited Polton's production to the astonished detective. "You see that it is extraordinarily slender, and free from projections, and of unusual materials. You also see that it was obviously not made by an ordinary dagger-maker; that, in spite of the Italian word scrawled on it, there is plainly written all over it 'British mechanic.' The blade is made from a strip of common three-quarter-inch tool steel; the hilt is turned from an aluminium rod; and there is not a line of engraving on it that could not be produced in a lathe by any engineer's apprentice. Even the boss at the top is mechanical, for it is just like an ordinary hexagon nut. Then, notice the dimensions, as shown on my drawing. The parts A and B, which just project beyond the blade, are exactly similar in diameter – and such exactness could hardly be accidental. They are each parts of a circle having a diameter of 10.9 millimetres – a dimension which happens, by a singular coincidence, to be exactly the calibre of the old Chassepôt rifle, specimens of which are now on sale at several shops in London. Here is one, for instance."

He fetched the rifle that he had bought, from the corner in which it was standing, and, lifting the dagger by its point, slipped the hilt into the muzzle. When he let go, the dagger slid quietly down the barrel, until its hilt appeared in the open breech.

"Good God!" exclaimed Marchmont. "You don't suggest that the dagger was shot from a gun?"

"I do, indeed; and you now see the reason for the aluminium hilt – to diminish the weight of the already heavy projectile – and also for this hexagonal boss on the end?"

"No, I do not," said the inspector; "but I say that you are suggesting an impossibility."

"Then," replied Thorndyke, "I must explain and demonstrate. To begin with, this projectile had to travel point foremost; therefore it had to be made to spin – and it certainly was spinning when it entered the body, as the clothing and the wound showed us. Now, to make it spin, it had to be fired from a rifled barrel; but as the hilt would not engage in the rifling, it had to be fitted with something that would. That something was evidently a soft metal washer, which fitted on to this hexagon, and which would be pressed into the grooves of the rifling, and so spin the dagger, but would drop off as soon as the weapon left the barrel. Here is such a washer, which Polton has made for us."

He laid on the table a metal disc, with a hexagonal hole through it.

"This is all very ingenious," said the inspector, "but I say it is impossible and fantastic."

"It certainly sounds rather improbable," Marchmont agreed.

"We will see," said Thorndyke. "Here is a makeshift cartridge of Polton's manufacture, containing an eighth charge of smokeless powder for a 20-bore gun."

He fitted the washer on to the boss of the dagger in the open breech of the rifle, pushed it into the barrel, inserted the cartridge, and closed the breech. Then, opening the office-door, he displayed a target of padded strawboard against the wall.

"The length of the two rooms," said he, "gives us a distance of thirty-two feet. Will you shut the windows, Jervis?"

I complied, and he then pointed the rifle at the target. There was a dull report – much less loud than I had expected – and when we looked at the target, we saw the dagger driven in up to its hilt at the margin of the bull's-eye.

"You see," said Thorndyke, laying down the rifle, "that the thing is practicable. Now for the evidence as to the actual occurrence. First, on the original dagger there are linear scratches which exactly correspond with the grooves of the rifling. Then there is the fact that the dagger was certainly spinning from left to right – in the direction of the rifling, that is – when it entered the body. And then there is this, which, as you heard, the porter found in the garden."

He opened the paper packet. In it lay a metal disc, perforated by a hexagonal hole. Stepping into the office, he picked up from the floor the washer that he had put on the dagger, and laid it on the paper beside the other. The two discs were identical in size, and the margin of each was indented with identical markings, corresponding to the rifling of the barrel.

The inspector gazed at the two discs in silence for a while; then, looking up at Thorndyke, he said:

"I give in, Doctor. You're right, beyond all doubt; but how you came to think of it beats me into fits. The only question now is, who fired the gun, and why wasn't the report heard?"

"As to the latter," said Thorndyke, "it is probable that he used a compressed-air attachment, not only to diminish the noise, but also to prevent any traces of the explosive from being left on the dagger. As to the former, I think I can give you the murderer's name; but we had better take the evidence in order. You may remember," he continued, "that when Dr. Jervis stood as if winding the clock, I chalked a mark on the floor where he stood. Now, standing on that marked spot, and looking out of the open window, I could see two of the windows of a house nearly opposite. They were the second- and third-floor windows of No. 6, Cotman Street. The second-floor is occupied by a firm of architects; the third-floor by a commission agent named Thomas Barlow. I called on Mr. Barlow, but before describing my visit, I will refer to another matter. You haven't those threatening letters about you, I suppose?"

"Yes, I have," said the inspector; and he drew forth a wallet from his breast-pocket.

"Let us take the first one, then," said Thorndyke. "You see that the paper and envelope are of the very commonest, and the writing illiterate. But the ink does not agree with this. Illiterate people usually buy their ink in penny bottles. Now, this envelope is addressed with Draper's dichroic ink – a superior office ink, sold only in large bottles – and the red ink in which the note is written is an unfixed, scarlet ink, such as is used by draughtsmen, and has been used, as you can see, in a stylographic pen. But the most interesting thing about this letter is the design drawn at the top. In an artistic sense, the man could not draw, and the anatomical details of the skull are ridiculous. Yet the drawing is very neat. It has the clean, wiry line of a machine drawing, and is done with a steady, practised hand. It is also perfectly symmetrical; the skull, for instance, is exactly in the centre, and, when we examine it through a lens, we see why it is so, for we discover traces of a pencilled centre-line and ruled cross-lines. Moreover, the lens reveals a tiny particle of draughtsman's soft, red, rubber, with which the pencil lines were taken out; and all these facts, taken together, suggest that the drawing was made by someone accustomed to making accurate mechanical drawings. And now we will return to Mr. Barlow. He was out when I called, but I took the liberty of glancing round the office, and this is what I saw. On the mantelshelf was a twelve-inch flat boxwood rule, such as engineers use, a piece of soft, red rubber, and a stone bottle of Draper's dichroic ink. I obtained, by a simple ruse, a specimen of the office notepaper and the ink. We will examine it presently. I found that Mr. Barlow is a new tenant, that he is rather short, wears a wig and spectacles, and always wears a glove on his left hand. He left the office at 8.30 this morning, and no one saw him arrive. He had with him a square case, and a narrow, oblong one about five feet in length; and he took a cab to Victoria, and apparently caught the 8.51 train to Chatham."

"Ah!" exclaimed the inspector.

"But," continued Thorndyke, "now examine those three letters, and compare them with this note that I wrote in Mr. Barlow's office. You see that the paper is of the same make, with the same water-mark, but that is of no great significance. What is of crucial importance is this: You see, in each of these letters, two tiny indentations near the bottom corner. Somebody has used compasses or drawing-pins over the packet of notepaper, and the points have made little indentations, which have marked several of the sheets. Now, notepaper is cut to its size after it is folded, and if you stick a pin into the top sheet of a section, the indentations on all the underlying sheets will be at exactly similar distances from the edges and corners of the sheet. But you see that these little dents are all at the same distance from the edges and the corner." He demonstrated the fact with a pair of compasses. "And now look at this sheet, which I obtained at Mr. Barlow's office. There are two little indentations – rather faint, but quite visible – near the bottom corner, and when we measure them with the compasses, we find that they are exactly the same distance apart as the others, and the same distance from the edges and the bottom corner. The irresistible conclusion is that these four sheets came from the same packet."

The inspector started up from his chair, and faced Thorndyke. "Who is this Mr. Barlow?" he asked.

"That," replied Thorndyke, "is for you to determine; but I can give you a useful hint. There is only one person who benefits by the death of Alfred Hartridge, but he benefits to the extent of twenty thousand pounds. His name is Leonard Wolfe, and I learn from Mr. Marchmont that he is a man of indifferent character – a gambler and a spendthrift. By profession he is an engineer, and he is a capable mechanician. In appearance he is thin, short, fair, and clean-shaven, and he has lost the middle finger of his left hand. Mr. Barlow is also short, thin, and fair, but wears a wig, a beard, and spectacles, and always wears a glove on his left hand. I have seen the handwriting of both these gentlemen, and should say that it would be difficult to distinguish one from the other."

"That's good enough for me," said the inspector. "Give me his address, and I'll have Miss Curtis released at once."

* * *

The same night Leonard Wolfe was arrested at Eltham, in the very act of burying in his garden a large and powerful compressed-air rifle. He was never brought to trial, however, for he had in his pocket a more portable weapon – a large-bore Derringer pistol – with which he managed to terminate an exceedingly ill-spent life.

"And, after all," was Thorndyke's comment, when he heard of the event, "he had his uses. He has relieved society of two very bad men, and he has given us a most instructive case. He has shown us how a clever and ingenious criminal may take endless pains to mislead and delude the police, and yet, by inattention to trivial details, may scatter clues broadcast. We can only say to the criminal class generally, in both respects, 'Go thou and do likewise.' "

Suggestive Thoughts

H.L. Fullerton

"TERRIBLE WHAT HAPPENED to Lottie, isn't it?" Mrs. Yeminski says as we wait outside our apartments for the elevator. One of her toy poodles rushes about her ankles. She always takes the dogs out one at a time – claims she's too frail to handle all three at once. I believe it's so she can waylay more tenants with her nasty gossip. I've heard things she's said about me. At least, I think I have.

I don't answer her gambit. It's best not to. Mrs. Yeminski's yapping can make me forget where I'm headed. Sometimes I fear her treble-like voice will induce a seizure.

"Hannah? Don't you think it's terrible? Such a beautiful girl. And so young. That poor man." She sighs heavily, flutters her hand against her bosom.

Already I am swimming in her words. Who is Lottie? Do I know her? Is she one of Mrs. Yeminski's poodles? What poor man? "Yes," I say. "Terrible." The elevator is still not here. "What happened?" I shouldn't encourage her, but the name is ringing in my brain like a bell. Lottie, Lottie, Lottie.

"Didn't you hear?"

"Er, no."

"She fell down the elevator shaft."

"Oh. Here? In our building?" This elevator shaft?

Mrs. Yeminski looks annoyed with me. "Of course here. There were ambulances and fire trucks and everything. Yesterday. Around three. Honest, Hannah, you think you would have heard."

"Is she ok?"

"She's dead! She fell down an elevator shaft!"

My face flushes. I mumble, "I thought maybe she broke a leg. It's only five floors."

"I'd like to see you after you fell five floors down an elevator shaft." Her eyes burn me.

"Did she live on this floor?"

"Did she live on this floor! She's your next-door neighbor. Jamison's quite broken up about it. He was..."

Jamison's girlfriend. My heart triples its beat. "*Charlotte?*"

"Everyone called her Lottie."

Everyone but me and I feel small the way Mrs. Y intended. The way Charlotte intended when Jamison introduced us and she said, "You must call me Charlotte." That doesn't matter now. I have bigger issues to sort through. Where was I yesterday at three? Did I push her? My mind is blank. I start to sweat.

Sometimes I forget things. Not ordinary things like where's my credit card, did I turn the oven off, is this pile of clothes clean or dirty. I forget my mother's given name, where I went to high school or how I like my lattes. (I don't drink coffee. Only sometimes I think I do.)

It's because of the epilepsy. I take medication to ward off the seizures. Nothing can be done about the memory quirks. My brain is like a sponge; except, when it gets squeezed, memories, instead of water, rush out. Usually they come back, but I can't help thinking that waterlogged recollections aren't as good as the originals.

Mrs. Y says, "Jamison was with her. Saw the whole thing. Can you imagine?"

I can. Too clearly. I blurt out, "Did he push her?" Because if he did, I can stop worrying about transient epileptic amnesia, blackouts, fugue states and leaky memories.

"Of course not. He loved her. Anyone with eyes could see that." The elevator arrives. I let Mrs. Y get on first. When it holds her weight, I join her. Her eyes narrow as if she knows why I hesitated. "A waste," she mutters. I'm unsure whether she's referring to Charlotte's death or me.

At work, I cling to the fact that Jamison was there because if I'd pushed her, he would have told someone and I'd be in jail. So I didn't do it. I know I didn't do it, but still I feel responsible. Like I made it happen. If anyone knew how many times I imagined Charlotte sliding over a cliff in Great Falls Park or getting hit by a delivery truck (usually FedEx but sometimes UPS). Or stepping into an elevator that wasn't there.

The elevator one was my favorite. Because what if, instead of plunging nicely into the Potomac, she got caught on a branch or rock ledge? Jamison might try to rescue her and hurt himself. Nor did I want the FedEx driver to face criminal charges. But with the elevator, no one got hurt but Charlotte. It also made her look stupid. Too dumb to see if the cab was there before she stepped in. Sometimes I imagined my hand on her back sending her into the darkened shaft. Not an accidental bump, but a good hearty shove into the abyss. Bye bye, Charlotte.

And yesterday at three o'clock it happened. Just the way I pictured it. I'd feel less anxious if I remembered where I'd been.

"Are you going to eat that thing?" a coworker asks, interrupting my self-flagellation. I take the pen out of my mouth and look at it. All mangled and twisted. Like a body at the bottom of an elevator shaft.

* * *

I sit next to Mrs. Y at the funeral because the only other person I recognize is Jamison, and he is orbited by a throng of sad-eyed faces who look like Charlotte. Her father clasps Jamison's shoulder and I think, "I hate it when he does that." Which is silly. I don't know the man, don't think I've ever seen her family before. And better the father than the pretty little sister with the weepy calculating eyes. Charlotte snatched Jamison before I could make a play. Hooked him well and good with her classy chic and smart ambition. First time I saw her, I knew death was the only thing that'd free him from her claws. Well now she's in a box by the altar and I won't let this opportunity slide by. I am not in Charlotte's league, but Jamison is grief-struck. The girl across the hall, me, is exactly what he needs. Someone comforting and uncomplicated. Someone who will adore him.

I smooth my skirt. I'm wearing my somber and compassionate outfit: black pencil skirt and royal blue oxford with black pinstripes. Black and blue. Bruises and tears. What man could resist such a combination?

I imagine me and Jamison, in his apartment, maybe mine. Definitely mine. I offer him something cool to drink. He cries. I console him. We have sex on my sofa.

Mrs. Y leans in and whispers, "You look very professional today. Are you going to work after?"

I'm not. I say I am.

"It's a blessing," she says after the Mass. "If he'd been standing next to her, he might have fallen, too."

"What? I thought he was there. Right there, you said." Blood pounds in my brain. He didn't see? If he didn't see – No, I couldn't have.

"No, no. He was locking up. Heard her scream and ran over."

"Was anyone else around?" Me? Did anyone see me? Although why am I asking her? She was already wrong once. Obviously she can't be trusted.

Mrs. Y hoists her handbag. "Ghoul," she says and pushes past me. I trip on the kneeler. A hand steadies me. Charlotte's father. I jerk free and sprawl back onto the pew.

"Dizzy spell," I murmur. "I'm good. You can go." He moves off and I rub my shoulder, stunned. I do hate when he does that.

* * *

I found a ticket stub in my coat pocket this morning. Two o'clock showing for the day Lottie died. I don't recall the plot or any of the characters, but that is not uncommon for me. Point is, I was somewhere else.

Silly to think I had anything to do with her death. No way I could've forgotten a murder.

* * *

Happy day. Jamison and I are alone in the elevator. All the way down to the parking garage, I feel his eyes on me. I pretend not to notice, pray very hard that he will ask me out.

"Thank you," he says, voice tight.

"What?" I say.

"Thanks. For coming to the service."

"Sure." What service? What is he talking about? Did we go somewhere?

"Lottie would've appreciated you being there."

Three years rush back into my head like an avalanche. Charlotte. His dead girlfriend. The one I didn't kill. Her. I'd forgotten she existed. Stupid, leaky brain.

"I didn't know her well." I pick my way carefully over the words, landmines abound. "But I thought you could use a friendly face." I offer a small smile as I brush past him on my way off. Nothing too suggestive, mind you, just the casual touch of clothing. His shirtsleeve brushes my coat. The friction is unbearably exciting.

While waiting for the red line, my right hand caresses the spot where our sleeves met.

* * *

Now that Charlotte, *Lottie's* gone, I can't stop imagining Jamison and I having sex. Not Funereal Jamison, but the Jamison who carried boxes up to my new apartment. The one who always held the elevator for me. That Jamison. With crinkly blue eyes the color of sky on an October afternoon and close-cropped brown hair the shade of drying corn stalks. Neatly dressed, not wrinkly or in need of a haircut and three days sleep. Sexy Jamison. Pre-Lottie.

I picture him: standing in my blue and yellow kitchen with hungry eyes, he moves towards me quickly and says something like, "I've waited so long for this, please don't make me wait any longer." Then he lifts me onto my oaken kitchen table and ravishes me. I thread my fingers through his hair; it feels like corn silk not the dried husks it resembles. I call him Jami; he whispers urgent words into my skin. It's messy and sweaty and wonderful. Afterwards, I make us something to eat. Sometimes these images are so real, I can taste him on my tongue, not to mention the damp underwear.

* * *

"Hannah? Hannah?" The woman's voice seems far away, like a dream upon waking. Not a dream. I recognize this feeling. Oh, no. Not again.

She's talking to me. I'm Hannah. Except I don't feel like Hannah. Not yet. My head is too crowded: swamped and matted. I unstick my tongue from the roof of my mouth. "I'm fine," I lie.

"The report," some woman, my boss – memory of her locks into place – Lorna asks.

Report? Brain is still foggy. When memories come rushing back like this, when I black out completely, it takes them time to settle. "I'll send it to you," seems a safe answer. On its heels, anger roils in, stirring up the muck in my head. *Stupid prick,* I think. *Thinks because he's boss, I have to jump. He should jump. Hate him, hate him. Hope he dies.* But the pronouns are all wrong and I don't hate Lorna. The emotion feels off, too. My anger is usually like a bird's wings beating against glass, its tiny heart fluttering madly. This anger is deep enough to sink ships; powerful, directed. My hands clench into fists. What is happening?

"You already sent it. I wanted to thank you. For finishing so quickly."

"Oh," I say, trying to concentrate on the moment instead of the jumble in my head. "I forgot. Busy, you know."

"Are you okay?" She leans close; her eyes delve into mine.

No, I am not. They say nature abhors a vacuum and I am riddled with empty spaces. I'm worried my spongy brain was squeezed too tight, that this time when my memories were wrung out like water, other memories were sopped up with my waterlogged ones.

"Headache," I say and it isn't a lie, not completely.

* * *

I find it difficult to concentrate on the numbers in front of me; my hand keeps twitching. I shake it, try to get it to stop. What is its problem? I scratch, but this itch can't be scratched with fingernails or woolen pants. All that anger, the anger that's not mine, seems to have settled in my hand, making it dance.

What if – No. No. But –

What if this isn't the first time this anger filled me up? What if it happened once before? Maybe I pushed Charlotte. Maybe I just don't remember.

My fingers tap themselves across the mousepad, onto the desk. As if my hand doesn't know what to do now that Charlotte's dead.

* * *

I picture: Jamison and me in my bed. In his bed. The shower. Me going down on him in his Audi. My favorite is still the kitchen one. He can't help himself. He has to have me. I let him. Images of tables and teapots and kitchen ceilings fill my brain. My eyes roll into the back of my head. A co-worker asks if I'm okay, am I having a seizure?

"No," I tell him. "No seizure." He doesn't quite believe me, but I convince him to put down my phone without dialing 911.

It's raining when I leave work. People are huddled under umbrellas, swathed in raincoats, hidden in plain sight. I avoid puddles as I make my way to the Metro. The platform is crowded, people press against each other. The smells of damp wool and office sweat mingle unpleasantly in my nose. I shuffle my feet to make room for myself and get an elbow in the chest. My eyes water and my itchy hand dances up and hovers over the lower back of some unsuspecting stranger. It wants to shove. I yank it back to my side. Bad hand. Bad.

The next few weeks, my hand, although restless, behaves itself. I sign up for a kickboxing class hoping the punching will tire it. It relieves some of the itching, but I can feel the sensation creeping up my arm. I know it's waiting. I just don't know what for.

On Thursday, I find out.

* * *

I switch trains at Metro Center to catch a blue Franconia-Springfield train. I'm supposed to meet friends in Old Town for dinner. The platform is packed. Orange-line commuters push their way through the throng onto a waiting train. Doors try vainly to close. The driver threatens to take the train out of service if people don't stand clear.

My train will never make the platform if this one doesn't leave. I peer down the tunnel to see the color of the next train. To my left, I catch sight of someone I know, but when I edge closer to say hi, I realize he's a stranger. I blush, glad I didn't call out and take a step behind him to avoid any awkward eye contact.

The orange train manages to shut its doors and pull out. A blue train approaches and I'm jostled towards the yellow demarcation line as people catch sight of it. Suddenly, my right hand shoots out and shoves at the quasi-stranger in front of me. Presses itself against his raincoat – I feel his belt cross my palm – and propels him forward. The crowd surges around us, jockeying for position. My hand keeps pushing, his shoes skid on the rain-slicked floor. He crosses the bumpy warning strip. His arms pinwheel to regain his balance. My hand continues its arc and comes up to tuck a strand of hair behind my ear.

The man falls onto the tracks and the train pulls through. There is a sound, then silence. A woman screams. The crowd stops pushing against me. I glance around to see if anyone points in my direction, accuses me of murder. No one does. People murmur, "What happened? What happened?"

WMATA personnel force us back, clearing the platform, asking if anyone saw the accident. A portly man says, "He was standing on the yellow line. He slipped." Heads shake in disapproval. People complain that they'll never get home now.

I drift up the escalators amongst a thinning crowd, afraid accusations will be hurled at me. I wait for a Shady Grove, take it one stop, then walk home. I call and cancel dinner, tell my friends there was a problem with the blue line. Again. We laugh about it. Then I sit at my kitchen table, tracing whorls in the grain and think, "What did I do?"

I'd been so worried I'd killed Charlotte and forgotten it, then I go and shove a stranger in front of a Franconia-Springfield. In front of fifty or so witnesses.

Figures. The only perfect thing I've ever done and it's murder.

* * *

When I arrive home the following evening, two policemen are standing near Jamison's door. Are they here for me? Did someone see? *Was I taped?*

I make myself walk past them to my apartment. Hear them ask Jamison if they can come in, they have a few questions. They're here about the elevator thing, not me. I breathe easier knowing. If they told him I was a murder suspect, he'd never date me.

I purposely run into Mrs. Yeminski at the elevator the next morning. She tells me Jamison's supervisor was hit by a Metro train. She says it was the red line, but I know better. I act uninterested and she can't help blurting that the police questioned Jamison because he joked with a co-worker about nudging the boss under a train.

I ask her, "Did he? Did he push him?" I hear my echo asking, *Did he push her?*

"Of course not. I vouched for him myself. Saw with my own two eyes: him walking into the building same time that man killed himself."

"So it was a suicide?" I press.

She sniffs and looks at the elevator, pretends I'm not next to her. If the doors open and the elevator isn't there, I'm sending her over the edge.

It's there. I feel cheated the whole day.

* * *

On Saturdays, I lounge in my fluffy, white robe and drink tea and eat toast and forget to worry about buttery crumbs ruining my clothes.

I finish my pot of oolong and begin clearing the table. I get some butter on my fingers. The teapot was too close and the stick has softened. It will firm up in the refrigerator, but it upsets me. Makes me think of someone's fingers poking my soft brain. I picture it mushed like warm butter. Then I picture a mashed stranger under a train. Maybe I should call my doctor and make an appointment to have my brain scanned.

A knock on the apartment door interrupts my morbid thoughts. I tighten the belt on my robe, check that I am not gaping and go peer through the peephole. Jamison. He looks agitated. A little gaping wouldn't hurt, I think, and tug on the neckline to expose more skin.

"Jamison. Come in." I step back and he steps into me, catching the door on his shoe, but getting it closed. He is all over me. Hands, tongue, teeth. I stumble backwards. Into the kitchen.

"Hannah, oh God, Hannah," he says, then his mouth is moving over mine again. Oh *God* yes. We bump into walls, doorways, a chair screeches across the floor, tumbles and falls. Something digs into the back of my legs. I have time to think, *the table*, before I'm lifted onto it. I hear my teacup hit the floor.

"I can't, oh God, I can't wait." He unzips and pushes his jeans towards his ankles.

"It's okay, it's okay." My breathing hitches. He is moving too fast for me to catch up, but I don't care. Jamison Lang is naked in my kitchen. All the times I've imagined this and now it's happening, actually happening.

Then, as things are getting interesting, he comes and collapses. Past him, I see the mess of broken china and scattered silverware on the floor. "Good thing you kept your shoes on or you'd have cut yourself."

"I don't know what's wrong with me."

"It's all right. I don't mind." Much. I didn't get my moment; it wasn't exactly how I pictured it. My breathing slows, then the look in his eyes makes air rush out of my lungs. "What?"

"Your turn." He smiles and I think, *Yes.*

* * *

"I think I'm going crazy. Honestly, Hannah, I don't know what's happening to me," he says. It's later. We are sitting on my couch, dressed. I am humming and smiling and humming, I can't help it. A dream come true. "I'm not usually like this."

My smile falters. "Like what?" Like interested in me? I should've been more specific in picturing my happy-after.

"Can I trust you, Hannah?"

"Of course. What is it, Jami?"

He looks away, out my window at the ugly apartment building across the street. I take his hand.

"I pushed her," he says. "I pushed Lottie. I don't know why. I loved her. I didn't want her dead, but those doors opened and I saw those metal cables and then she was gasping and falling and my hand... My hand."

I remember my hand itching and searching out backs on train platforms. I don't say anything.

"I never meant to... I'd never hurt her but then I... and everyone assumed it was an accident and I let them."

I squeeze his hand. "No wonder you looked so tortured."

"Then my boss, and him I hated, but I was nowhere near. Do you know? About the train and – ?" *Hate him, hate him. Hope he jumps.* I nod and he continues. "Everyone thought I did it, but I didn't. I almost said I did because... *Lottie.*" He stops. Puts his head in his hand. Lowers his voice to a whisper. I have to bend my ear close to his mouth to hear. "I wished the train on him. Pictured it so many times in my head – him slipping in front of the train – he always stood too close and I wished one day... but never thought...

"And with you. I'm not normally like that. I'm not, Hannah, but I couldn't get you out of my mind. All the time... seeing you, me, together. The table... the kitchen. God, I've never seen your apartment before, but it looks exactly like I thought it would and am I? Crazy?"

I clutch his hand. "No," I say, but my mind turns over and over, a regular rollercoaster ride. I wanted Lottie dead, pictured it, and he did it. He loved her and killed her anyway. He wanted his boss dead, pictured it, and I did it. What if it'd been the wrong raincoat, wrong bald head? And then... the kitchen table. I pictured it, over and over *and he saw it.* Saw and did it. Did me. I hold him close. My brain starts to fuzz.

What other thoughts, terrible thoughts might spill out? Who might hear?

Picture this...

The Problem of Cell 13

Jacques Futrelle

PRACTICALLY ALL those letters remaining in the alphabet after Augustus S.F.X. Van Dusen was named were afterward acquired by that gentleman in the course of a brilliant scientific career, and, being honorably acquired, were tacked on to the other end. His name, therefore, taken with all that belonged it, was a wonderfully imposing structure. He was a Ph.D., an LL.D., an F.R.S., an M.D., and an M.D.S. He was also some other things – just what he himself couldn't say – through recognition of his ability by various foreign educational and scientific institutions.

In appearance he was no less striking than in nomenclature. He was slender with the droop of the student in his thin shoulders and the pallor of a close, sedentary life on his clean-shaven face. His eyes wore a perceptual, forbidding squint – the squint of a man who studies little things – and when they could be seen at all through his thick spectacles, were mere slits of watery blue. But above his eyes was his most striking feature. This was a tall, broad brow, almost abnormal in height and width, crowned by a heavy shock of bushy, yellow hair. All these things conspired to give him a peculiar, almost grotesque, personality.

Professor Van Dusen was remotely German. For generations his ancestors had been noted in the sciences; he was the logical result, the mastermind. First and above all he was a logician. At least thirty-five years of the half century or so of his existence had been devoted exclusively to providing that two and two always equal four, except in unusual cases, where they equalled three or five, as the case may be. He stood broadly on the general propositions that all things that start must go somewhere, and was able to bring the concentrated mental force of his forefathers to bear on a given problem. Incidentally it may be remarked that Professor Van Dusen wore a No. 8 hat.

The world at large had heard vaguely of Professor Van Dusen as The Thinking Machine. It was a newspaper catchphrase applied to him at the time of a remarkable exhibition at chess; he had demonstrated then that a stranger to the game might, by the force of inevitable logic, defeat a champion who had devoted a lifetime to its study. The Thinking Machine! Perhaps that more nearly described him than all his honorary initials, for he had spent week after week, month after month, in the seclusion of his small laboratory from which had gone forth thoughts that staggered scientific associates and deeply stirred the world at large.

It was only occasionally that The Thinking Machine had visitors, and these were usually men who, themselves high in the sciences, dropped in to argue a point and perhaps convince themselves. Two of these men, Dr. Charles Ransome and Alfred Fielding, called one evening to discuss some theory which is not of consequence here.

"Such a thing is impossible," declared Dr. Ransome emphatically, in the course of the conversation.

"Nothing is impossible," declared The Thinking Machine with equal emphasis. He always spoke petulantly. "The mind is master of all things. When science fully recognizes that fact a great advance will have been made."

"How about the airship?" asked Dr. Ransome.

"That's not impossible at all," asserted The Thinking Machine "it will be invented some time. I'd do it myself, but I'm busy."

Dr. Ransome laughed tolerantly.

"I've heard you say such things before," he said. "But they mean nothing. Mind may be master of matter, but it hasn't yet found a way to apply itself. There are some things that can't be thought out of existence, or rather which would not yield to any amount of thinking."

"What, for instance?" demanded The Thinking Machine.

Dr. Ransome was thoughtful for a moment as he smoked.

"Well, say prison walls," he replied. "No man can think himself out of a cell. If he could, there would be no prisoners."

"A man can so apply his brain and ingenuity that he can leave a cell, which is the same thing," snapped The Thinking Machine.

Dr. Ransome was slightly amused.

"Let's suppose a case," he said, after a moment. "Take a cell where prisoners under sentence of death are confined – men who are desperate and, maddened by fear, would take any chance to escape – suppose you were locked in such a cell. Could you escape?"

"Certainly," declared The Thinking Machine.

"Of course," said Mr. Fielding, who entered the conversation for the first time, "you might wreck the cell with an explosive – but inside, a prisoner, you couldn't have that."

"There would be nothing of that kind," said The Thinking Machine. "You might treat me precisely as you treated prisoners under sentence of death, and I would leave the cell."

"Not unless you entered it with tools prepared to get out," said Dr. Ransome.

The Thinking Machine was visibly annoyed and his blue eyes snapped.

"Lock me in any cell in any prison anywhere at any time, wearing only what is necessary, and I'll escape in a week," he declared, sharply. Dr. Ransome sat up straight in his chair, interested. Mr. Fielding lighted a new cigar.

"You mean you could actually think yourself out?" asked Dr. Ransome.

"I would get out," was the response.

"Are you serious?"

"Certainly I am serious."

Dr. Ransome and Mr. Fielding were silent for a long time.

"Would you be willing to try it?" asked Mr. Fielding, finally.

"Certainly," said Professor Van Dusen, and there was a trace of irony in his voice. "I have done more asinine things than that to convince other men of less important truths."

The tone was offensive and there was an undercurrent strongly resembling anger on both sides. Of course it was an absurd thing, but Professor Van Dusen reiterated his willingness to undertake the escape and it was decided on.

"To begin now," added Dr. Ransome.

"I'd prefer that it begin tomorrow," said The Thinking Machine, "because –"

"No, now," said Mr. Fielding, flatly. "You are arrested, figuratively speaking, of course, without any warning locked in a cell with no chance to communicate with friends, and left there with identically the same care and attention that would be given to a man under sentence of death. Are you willing?"

"All right, now, then," said The Thinking Machine, and he arose.

"Say, the death cell in Chisholm Prison."

"The death cell in Chisholm Prison."

"And what will you wear?"

"As little as possible," said The Thinking Machine. "Shoes, stockings, trousers and a shirt."

"You will permit yourself to be searched, of course?"

"I am to be treated precisely as all prisoners are treated," said The Thinking Machine. "No more attention and no less."

There were some preliminaries to be arranged in the matter of obtaining permission for the test, but all these were influential men and everything was done satisfactorily by telephone, albeit the prison commissioners, to whom the experiment was explained on purely scientific grounds, were sadly bewildered. Professor Van Dusen would be the most distinguished prisoner they had ever entertained.

When The Thinking Machine had donned those things which he was to wear during his incarceration, he called the little old woman who was his housekeeper, cook and maidservant all in one.

"Martha," he said, "it is now twenty-seven minutes past nine o'clock. I am going away. One week from tonight, at half past nine, these gentlemen and one, possibly two, others will take supper with me here. Remember Dr. Ransome is very fond of artichokes."

The three men were driven to Chisholm Prison, where the warden was awaiting them, having been informed of the matter by telephone. He understood merely that the eminent Professor Van Dusen was to be his prisoner, if he could keep him, for one week; that he had committed no crime, but that he was to be treated as all other prisoners were treated.

"Search him," instructed Dr. Ransome.

The Thinking Machine was searched. Nothing was found on him; the pockets of the trousers were empty; the white, stiff-bosomed shirt had no pocket. The shoes and stockings were removed, examined, then replaced. As he watched all these preliminaries, and noted the pitiful, childlike physical weakness of the man – the colourless face, and the thin, white hands – Dr. Ransome almost regretted his part in the affair.

"Are you sure you want to do this?" he asked.

"Would you be convinced if I did not?" inquired The Thinking Machine in turn.

"No."

"All right. I'll do it."

What sympathy Dr. Ransome had was dissipated by the tone. It nettled him, and he resolved to see the experiment to the end; it would be a stinging reproof to egotism.

"It will be impossible for him to communicate with anyone outside?" he asked.

"Absolutely impossible," replied the warden. "He will not be permitted writing materials of any sort."

"And your jailers, would they deliver a message from him?"

"Not one word, directly or indirectly," said the warden. "You may rest assured of that. They will report anything he might say or turn over to me, anything he might give them."

"That seems entirely satisfactory," said Mr. Fielding, who was frankly interested in the problem.

"Of course, in the event he fails," said Dr. Ransome, "and asks for his liberty, you understand you are to set him free?"

"I understand," replied the warden.

The Thinking Machine stood listening, but had nothing to say until all this was ended, then:

"I should like to make three small requests. You may grant them or not, as you wish."

"No special favours, now," warned Mr. Fielding.

"I am asking none," was the stiff response. "I should like to have some tooth powder – buy it yourself to see that it is tooth powder – and I should like to have one five-dollar and two ten-dollar bills."

Dr. Ransome, Mr. Fielding and the warden exchanged astonished glances. They were not surprised at the request for tooth powder, but were at the request for money.

"Is there any man with whom our friend would come in contact that he could bribe with twenty-five dollars?"

"Not for twenty-five hundred dollars," was the positive reply.

"And what is the third request?" asked Dr. Ransome.

"I should like to have my shoes polished."

Again the astonished glances were exchanged. This last request was the height of absurdity, so they agreed to it. These things all being attended to, The Thinking Machine was led back into the prison from which he had undertaken to escape.

"Here is Cell 13," said the warden, stopping three doors down the steel corridor. "This is where we keep condemned murderers. No one can leave it without my permission; and no one in it can communicate with the outside. I'll stake my reputation on that. It's only three doors back of my office and I can readily hear any unusual noise."

"Will this cell do, gentleman?" asked The Thinking Machine. There was a touch of irony in his voice.

"Admirably," was the reply.

The heavy steel door was thrown open, there was a great scurrying and scampering of tiny feet, and The Thinking Machine passed into the gloom of the cell. Then the door was closed and double locked by the warden.

"What is that noise in there?" asked Dr. Ransome, through the bars.

"Rats – dozens of them," replied The Thinking Machine, tersely.

The three men, with final good nights, were turning away when The Thinking Machine called:

"What time is it exactly, Warden?"

"Eleven-seventeen," replied the warden.

"Thanks. I will join you gentlemen in your office at half past eight o'clock one week from tonight," said The Thinking Machine.

"And if you do not?"

"There is no 'if' about it."

Chisholm Prison was a great, spreading structure of granite, four stories in all, which stood in the centre of acres of open space. It was surrounded by a wall of solid masonry eighteen feet high, and so smoothly finished inside and out as to offer no foothold to a climber, no matter how expert. Atop of this fence, as a further precaution, was a five-foot fence of steel rods, each terminating in a keen point. This fence in itself marked an absolute deadline between freedom and imprisonment, for, even if a man escaped from his cell, it would seem impossible for him to pass the wall.

The yard, which on all sides of the prison building was twenty-five feet wide, that being the distance from the building to the wall, was by day an exercises ground for those prisoners to whom was granted the boon of occasional semi-liberty. But that was not for those in Cell 13. At all times of the day there were armed guards in the yard, four of them, one patrolling each side of the prison building.

By night the yard was almost as brilliantly lighted as by day. On each of the four sides was a great arc light which rose above the prison wall and gave to the guards a clear sight. The lights, too, brightly illuminated the spiked top of the wall. The wires which fed the arc lights ran up the side of the prison building on insulators and from the top story led out to the poles supporting the arc lights. All these things were seen and comprehended by The Thinking Machine, who was only enabled to see out his closely barred cell window by standing on his bed. This was on the morning following his incarceration. He gathered, too, that the river lay over there beyond the wall somewhere, because he heard faintly the pulsation of a motor boat and high up in the air he saw a river bird. From that same direction came the shouts of boys at play and the occasional crack of a batted ball. He knew then that between the prison wall and the river was an open space, a playground.

Chisholm Prison was regarded as absolutely safe. No man had ever escaped from it. The Thinking Machine, from his perch on the bed, seeing what he saw, could readily understand why. The wall of the cell, though built he judged twenty years before, were perfectly solid, and the window bars of new iron had not a shadow of rust on them. The window itself, even with the bars out, would be a difficult mode of egress because it was small.

Yet, seeing these things, The Thinking Machine was not discouraged. Instead, he thoughtfully squinted at the great arc light – there was bright sunlight now – and traced with his eyes the wire which led from it to the building. That electric wire, he reasoned, must come down the side of the building not a great distance from his cell. That might be worth knowing.

Cell 13 was on the same floor with the offices of the prison – that is, not in the basement, nor yet upstairs. There were only four steps up to the office floor, therefore the level of the floor must be only three or four feet above the ground. He couldn't see the ground directly beneath his window, but he could see it further out toward the wall. It would be an easy drop from the window. Well and good.

Then The Thinking Machine fell to remembering how he had come to the cell. First, there was the outside guards booth, a part of the wall. There were two heavily barred gates there, both of steel. At this gate was one man always on guard. He admitted persons to the prison after much clanking of keys and locks, and let them out when ordered to do so. The warden's office was in the prison building, and in order to reach that official from the prison yard one had to pass a gate of solid steel with only a peephole in it. Then coming from that inner office to Cell 13, where he was now, one must pass a heavy wooden door and two steel doors into the corridors of the prison; and always there was the double-locked door of Cell 13 to reckon with.

There were then, The Thinking Machine recalled, seven doors to be overcome before one could pass from Cell 13 into the outer world, a free man. But against this was the fact that he was rarely interrupted. A jailer appeared at his cell door at six in the morning with a breakfast of prison fare; he would come again at noon, and again at six in the afternoon. At nine o'clock at night would come the inspection tour. That would be all.

"It's admirably arranged, this prison system," was the mental tribute paid by The Thinking Machine. "I'll have to study it a little when I get out. I had no idea there was such great care exercised in the prisons."

There was nothing, positively nothing, in his cell, except his iron bed, so firmly put together that no man could tear it to pieces save with sledges or a file. He had neither of these. There was not even a chair, or a small table, or a bit of crockery. Nothing! The jailer stood by when he ate, then took away the wooden spoon and bowl which he had used.

One by one these things sank into the brain of The Thinking Machine. When the last possibility had been considered he began an examination of his cell. From the roof, down the walls on all sides, he examined the stones and the cement between them. He stamped over the floor carefully time after time, but it was cement, perfectly solid. After the examination he sat on the edge of the iron bed and was lost in thought for a long time. For Professor Augustus S.F.X. Van Dusen, The Thinking Machine, had something to think about.

He was disturbed by a rat, which ran across his foot, then scampered away into a dark corner of the cell, frightened at its own daring. After a while The Thinking Machine, squinting steadily into the darkness of the corner where the rat had gone, was able to make out in the gloom many little beady eyes staring at him. He counted six pair, and there were perhaps others; he didn't see very well.

Then The Thinking Machine, from his seat on the bed, noticed for the first time the bottom of his cell door. There was an opening there of two inches between the steel bar and the floor. Still looking steadily at the opening, The Thinking Machine backed suddenly into the corner where he had seen the beady eyes. There was a great scampering of tiny feet, several squeaks of frightened rodents, and then silence.

None of the rats had gone out the door, yet there were none in the cell. Therefore there must be another way out of the cell, however small. The Thinking Machine, on hands and knees, started a search for the spot, feeling in the darkness with his long, slender fingers.

At last his search was rewarded. He came upon a small opening in the floor, level with the cement. It was perfectly round and somewhat larger than a silver dollar. This was the way the rats had gone. He put his fingers deep into the opening; it seemed to be a disused drainage pipe and was dry and dusty.

Having satisfied himself on this point, he sat on the bed again for an hour, then made another inspection of his surroundings through the small cell window. One of the outside guards stood directly opposite, beside the wall, and happened to be looking at the window of Cell 13 when the head of The Thinking Machine appeared. But the scientist didn't notice the guard.

Noon came and the jailer appeared with the prison dinner of repulsively plain food. At home The Thinking Machine merely ate to live; here he took what was offered without comment. Occasionally he spoke to the jailer who stood outside the door watching him.

"Any improvements made here in the last few years?" he asked.

"Nothing particularly," replied the jailer. "New wall was built four years ago."

"Anything done to the prison proper?"

"Painted the woodwork outside, and I believe about seven years ago a new system of plumbing was put in."

"Ah!" said the prisoner. "How far is the river over there?"

"About three hundred feet. The boys have a baseball ground between the wall and the river."

The Thinking Machine had nothing further to say just then, but when the jailer was ready to go he asked for some water.

"I get very thirsty here," he explained. "Would it be possible for you to leave a little water in a bowl for me?"

"I'll ask the warden," replied the jailer, and he went away.

Half an hour later he returned with water in a small earthen bowl.

"The warden says you may keep this bowl," he informed the prisoner. "But you must show it to me when I ask for it. If it is broken, it will be the last."

"Thank you," said The Thinking Machine. "I shan't break it."

The jailer went on about his duties. For just the fraction of a second it seemed that The Thinking Machine wanted to ask a question, but he didn't.

Two hours later this same jailer, in passing the door of Cell No. 13, heard a noise inside and stopped. The Thinking Machine was down on his hands and knees in a corner of the cell, and from that same corner came several frightened squeaks. The jailer looked on interestedly.

"Ah, I've got you," he heard the prisoner say.

"Got what?" he asked, sharply.

"One of these rats," was the reply. "See?" And between the scientist's long fingers the jailer saw a small gray rat struggling. The prisoner brought it over to the light and looked at it closely.

"It's a water rat," he said.

"Ain't you got anything better to do than catch rats?" asked the jailer.

"It's disgraceful that they should be here at all," was the irritated reply. "Take this one away and kill it. There are dozens more where it came from."

The jailer took the wriggling, squirmy rodent and flung it down on the floor violently. It gave one squeak and lay still. Later he reported the incident to the warden, who only smiled.

Still later that afternoon the outside armed guard on the Cell 13 side of the prison looked up again at the window and saw the prisoner looking out. He saw a hand raised to the barred window and then something white fluttered to the ground, directly under the window of Cell 13. It was a little roll of linen, evidently of white shirting material, and tied around it was a five-dollar bill. The guard looked up at the window again, but the face had disappeared.

With a grim smile he took the little linen roll and the five-dollar bill to the warden's office. There together they deciphered something which was written on it in a queer sort of ink, frequently blurred. On the outside was this:

"Finder of this please deliver to Dr. Charles Ransome."

"Ah," said the warden, with a chuckle, "plan of escape number one has gone wrong." Then, as an afterthought: "But why did he address it to Dr. Ransome?"

"And where did he get the pen and ink to write with?" asked the guard.

The warden looked at the guard and the guard looked at the warden. There was no apparent solution of that mystery. The warden studied the writing carefully, then shook his head.

"Well, let's see what he was going to say to Dr. Ransome," he said at length, still puzzled, and he unrolled the inner piece of linen.

"Well, if that – what – what do you think of that?" he asked dazed.

The guard took the bit of linen and read this:

"Epa cseot d'net niiy awe htto n'si sih. T."

The warden spent an hour wondering what sort of cipher it was, and half an hour wondering why his prisoner should attempt to communicate with Dr. Ransome, who was the cause of his being there. After this the warden devoted some thought to the question of where the prisoner got writing materials, and what sort of writing materials he had. With the idea of illuminating this point, he examined the linen again. It was a torn part of a white shirt and had ragged edges.

Now it was possible to account for the linen, but what the prisoner had used to write with was another matter. The warden knew it would have been impossible for him to have either pen or pencil, and, besides, neither pen nor pencil had been used in this writing. What then? The warden decided to investigate personally. The Thinking Machine was his prisoner; he had orders to hold his prisoners; if this one sought to escape by sending cipher messages to persons outside, he would stop it, as he would have stopped it in the case of any other prisoner.

The warden went back to Cell 13 and found The Thinking Machine on his hands and knees on the floor, engaged in nothing more alarming than catching rats. The prisoner heard the warden's step and turned to him quickly.

"It's disgraceful," he snapped, "these rats. There are scores of them."

"Other men have been able to stand them," said the warden. "Here is another shirt for you – let me have the one you have on."

"Why?" demanded The Thinking Machine, quickly. His tone was hardly natural, his manner suggested actual perturbation.

"You have attempted to communicate with Dr. Ransome," said the warden severely. "As my prisoner, it is my duty to put a stop to it."

The Thinking Machine was silent for a moment.

"All right," he said, finally. "Do your duty."

The warden smiled grimly. The prisoner arose from the floor and removed the white shirt, putting on instead a striped convict shirt the warden had bought. The warden took the white shirt eagerly, and then and there compared the pieces of linen on which was written the cipher with certain torn places in the shirt. The Thinking Machine looked on curiously.

"The guard brought you those, then?" he asked.

"He certainly did," relied the warden triumphantly. "And that ends your first attempt to escape."

The Thinking Machine watched the warden as he, by comparison, established to his own satisfaction that only two pieces of linen had been torn from the white shirt.

"What did you write this with?' demanded the warden.

"I should think it part of your duty to find out," said The Thinking Machine, irritably.

The warden started to say some harsh things, then restrained himself and made a minute search of the cell and of the prisoner instead. He found absolutely nothing; not even a match or toothpick which might have been used for a pen. The same mystery surrounded the fluid with which the cipher had been written. Although the warden left Cell 13 visibly annoyed, he took the torn shirt in triumph.

"Well, writing notes on a shirt won't get him out, that's certain," he told himself with some complacency. He put the linen scraps into his desk to await developments. "If that man escapes from that cell I'll – hang it – I'll resign."

On the third day of his incarceration The Thinking Machine openly attempted to bribe his way out. The jailer had brought his dinner and was leaning against the barred door, waiting, when The Thinking Machine began the conversation.

"The drainage pipes of the prison lead to the river, don't they?" he asked.

"Yes," said the jailer.

"I suppose they are very small."

"Too small to crawl through, if that's what you're thinking about," was the grinning response.

There was a silence until The Thinking Machine finished his meal. Then: "You know I'm not a criminal, don't you?"

"Yes."

"And that I've a perfect right to be freed if I demand it?"

"Yes."

"Well, I came here believing I could make my escape," said the prisoner, and his squint eyes studied the face of the jailer. "Would you consider a financial reward for aiding me to escape?"

The jailer, who happened to be an honest man, looked at the slender, weak figure of the prisoner, at the large head with its mass of yellow hair, and was almost sorry.

"I guess prisons like these were not built for the likes of you to get out of," he said at last.

"But would you consider a proposition to help me get out?" the prisoner insisted, almost beseechingly.

"No," said the jailer, shortly.

"Five hundred dollars," urged The Thinking Machine. "I am not a criminal."

"No," said the jailer.

"A thousand?"

"No," again said the jailer, and he started away hurriedly to escape further temptation. Then he turned back. "If you should give me ten thousand dollars I couldn't get you out. You'd have to pass through seven doors, and I only have the keys to two."

Then he told the warden all about it.

"Plan number two fails," said the warden, smiling grimly. "First a cipher, then bribery."

When the jailer was on his way to Cell 13 at six o'clock, again bearing food to The Thinking Machine, he paused, startled by the unmistakable scrape, scrape of steel versus steel. It stopped at the sound of his steps, then craftily the jailer, who was beyond the prisoner's range of vision, resumed his trampling, the sound being apparently that of a man going away from Cell 13. As a matter of fact he was in the same spot.

After a moment there came again the steady scrape, scrape, and the jailer crept cautiously on tiptoes to the door and peered between the bars. The Thinking Machine was standing in the iron bed working at the bars of the little window. He was using a file, judging from the backward and forward swing of his arms.

Cautiously the jailer crept back to the office, summoned the warden in person, and they returned to Cell 13 on tiptoes. The steady scrape was still audible. The warden listened to satisfy himself and then suddenly appeared at the door.

"Well?" he demanded, and there was a smile on his face.

The Thinking Machine glanced back from his perch on the bed and leaped suddenly to the floor, making frantic efforts to hide something. The warden went in, with hand extended.

"Give it up," he said.

"No," said the prisoner, sharply.

"Come, give it up," urged the warden. "I don't want to have to search you again."

"No," repeated the prisoner.

"What was it – a file?" asked the warden.

The Thinking Machine was silent and stood squinting at the warden with something very nearly approaching disappointment on his face – nearly, but not quite. The warden was almost sympathetic.

"Plan number three fails, eh?" he asked, good-naturedly. "Too bad, isn't it?"

The prisoner didn't say.

"Search him." instructed the warden.

The jailer searched the prisoner carefully. At last, artfully concealed in the waistband of the trousers, he found a piece of steel about two inches long, with one side curved like a half moon.

"Ah!" said the warden, as he received it from the jailer. "From your shoe heel," and he smiled pleasantly.

The jailer continued his search and on the other side of the trousers waistband found another piece of steel identical with the first. The edges showed where they had been worn against the bars of the window.

"You couldn't saw through those bars with these," said the warden.

"I could have," said The Thinking Machine firmly.

"In six months, perhaps," said the warden, good-naturedly.

The warden shook his head slowly as he gazed into the slightly flushed face of his prisoner.

"Ready to give up?" he asked.

"I haven't started yet," was the prompt reply.

Then came another exhaustive search of the cell. Carefully the two men went over it, finally turning out the bed and searching that. Nothing. The warden in person climbed upon the bed and examined the bars of the window where the prisoner had been sawing. When he looked he was amused.

"Just made it a little bright by hard rubbing," he said to the prisoner, who stood looking on with a somewhat crestfallen air. The warden grasped the iron bars in his strong hands and tried to shake them. They were immovable, set firmly in the solid granite. He examined each in turn and found them all satisfactory. Finally he climbed down from the bed.

"Give it up, Professor," he advised.

The Thinking Machine shook his head and the warden and jailer passed on again. As they disappeared down the corridor The Thinking Machine sat on the edge of the bed with his head in his hands.

"He's crazy to try and get out of that cell," commented the jailer.

"Of course he can't get out," said the warden. "But he's clever. I would like to know what he wrote that cipher with."

It was four o'clock next morning when an awful, heartracking shriek of terror resounded through the great prison. It came from a cell, somewhere about the centre, and its tone told a tale of horror, agony, terrible fear. The warden heard and with three of his men rushed into the long corridor leading to Cell 13.

As they ran there came again that awful cry. It died away in a sort of a wail. The white faces of prisoners appeared at cell doors upstairs and down, staring out wonderingly, frightened.

"It's that fool in Cell 13," grumbled the warden.

He stopped and stared in as one of the jailers flashed a lantern. "That fool in Cell 13" lay comfortably on his cot, flat on his back with his mouth open, snoring. Even as they looked there came again the piercing cry, from somewhere above. The warden's face blanched a little as he started up the stairs. There on the top floor he found a man in Cell 43, directly above Cell 13, but two floors higher, cowering in the corner of his cell.

"What's the matter?" demanded the warden.

"Thank God you've come," exclaimed the prisoner, and he cast himself against the bars of his cell.

"What is it?" demanded the warden again.

He threw open the door and went in. The prisoner dropped on his knees and clasped the warden about the body. His face was white with terror, his eyes were widely distended, and he was shuddering. His hands, icy cold, clutched at the warden's.

"Take me out of this cell, please take me out," he pleaded.

"What's the matter with you, anyhow?" insisted the warden, impatiently.

"I've heard something – something," said the prisoner, and his eyes roved nervously around the cell.

"What did you hear?"

"I – I can't tell you," stammered the prisoner. Then in a sudden burst of terror: "Take me out of this cell – put me anywhere – but take me out of here."

The warden and the three jailers exchanged glances.

"Who is this fellow? What's he accused of?" asked the warden.

"Joseph Ballard," said one of the jailers. "He's accused of throwing acid in a woman's face. She died from it."

"But they can't prove it," gasped the prisoner. "They can't prove it. Please put me in some other cell."

He was still clinging to the warden, and that official threw his arms off roughly. Then for a time he stood looking at the cowering wretch, who seemed possessed of all the wild, unreasoning terror of a child.

"Look here, Ballard," said the warden, finally, "if you heard anything, I want to know what it was. Now tell me."

"I can't, I can't," was the reply. He was sobbing.

"Where did it come from?"

"I don't know. Everywhere – nowhere. I just heard it."

"What was it – a voice?"

"Please don't make me answer," pleaded the prisoner.

"You must answer," said the warden, sharply.

"It was a voice – but – but it wasn't human," was the sobbing reply.

"Voice, but not human?" repeated the warden, puzzled.

"It sounded muffled and – and far away – and ghostly," explained the man.

"Did it come from inside or outside the prison?"

"It didn't seem to come from anywhere – it was just here, here, everywhere. I heard it. I heard it."

For an hour the warden tried to get the story, but Ballard had become suddenly obstinate and would say nothing – only pleaded to be placed in another cell, or to have one of the jailers remain near him until daylight. These requests were gruffly refused.

"And see here," said the warden, in conclusion, "if there's any more of this screaming I'll put you in a padded cell."

Then the warden went his way, a sadly puzzled man. Ballard sat at his cell door until daylight, his face, drawn and white with terror, pressed against the bars, and looked out into the prison with wide, staring eyes.

That day, the fourth since the incarceration of The Thinking Machine, was enlivened considerably by the volunteer prisoner, who spent most of his time at the little window of his cell. He began proceedings by throwing another piece of linen down to the guard, who picked it up dutifully and took it to the warden. On it was written:

Only three days more.

The warden was in no way surprised at what he read; he understood that The Thinking Machine meant only three days more of his imprisonment, and he regarded the note as a boast. But how was the thing written? Where had The Thinking Machine found the new piece of linen? Where? How? He carefully examined the linen. It was white, of fine texture, shirting material. He took the shirt which he had taken and carefully fitted the two original pieces of the linen to the torn places. The third piece was entirely superfluous; it didn't fit anywhere, and yet it was unmistakably the same goods.

"And where – where does he get anything to write with?" demanded the warden of the world at large.

Still later on the fourth day The Thinking Machine, through the window of his cell, spoke to the armed guard outside.

"What day of the month is it?" he asked.

"The fifteenth," was the answer.

The Thinking Machine made a mental astronomical calculation and satisfied himself that the moon would not rise until after nine o'clock that night. Then he asked another question: "Who attends to those arc lights?"

"Man from the company."

"You have no electricians in the building?"

"No."

"I should think you could save money if you had your own man."

"None of my business," replied the guard.

The guard noticed The Thinking Machine at the cell window frequently during that day, but always the face seemed listless and there was a certain wistfulness in the squint eyes behind the glasses. After a while he accepted the presence of the leonine head as a matter of course. He had seen other prisoners do the same thing; it was the longing for the outside world.

That afternoon, just before the day guard was relieved, the head appeared at the window again, and The Thinking Machine's hand held something out between the bars. It fluttered to the ground and the guard picked it up. It was five-dollar bill.

"That's for you," called the prisoner.

As usual, the guard took it to the warden. The gentleman looked at it suspiciously; he looked at everything that came from Cell 13 with suspicion.

"He said it was for me," explained the guard.

"It's a sort of tip, I suppose," said the warden. "I see no particular reason why you shouldn't accept –"

Suddenly he stopped. He had remembered that The Thinking Machine had gone into Cell 13 with one five-dollar bill and two ten-dollar bills; twenty-five dollars in all. Now a five-dollar bill had been tied around the first pieces of linen that came from the cell. The warden still had it, and to convince himself he took it out and looked at it. It was five dollars; yet here was another five dollars, and The Thinking Machine had only had ten-dollar bills.

"Perhaps somebody changed one of the bills for him," he thought at last, with a sigh of relief.

But then and there he made up his mind. He would search Cell 13 as a cell was never searched in this world. When a man could write at will, and change money, and do other wholly inexplicable things, there was something radically wrong with his prison. He planned to enter the cell at night – three o'clock would be an excellent time. The Thinking Machine must do all the weird things he did sometime. Night seemed the most reasonable.

Thus it happened that the warden stealthily descended upon Cell 13 that night at three o'clock. He paused at the door and listened. There was no sound save the steady, regular breathing of the prisoner. The keys unfastened the double locks with scarcely a clank, and the warden entered, locking the door behind him. Suddenly he flashed his dark lantern in the face of the recumbent figure.

If the warden had planned to startle The Thinking Machine he was mistaken, for that individual merely opened his eyes quietly, reached for his glasses and inquired, in a most matter-of-fact tone: "Who is it?"

It would be useless to describe the search that the warden made. It was minute. Not one inch of the cell or the bed was overlooked. He found the round hole in the floor, and with a flash of inspiration thrust his fingers into it. After a moment of fumbling there he drew up something and looked at it in the light of his lantern.

"Ugh!" he exclaimed.

The thing he had taken out was a rat – a dead rat. His inspiration fled as a mist before the sun. But he continued the search. The Thinking Machine, without a word, arose and kicked the rat out of the cell into the corridor.

The warden climbed on the bed and tried the steel bars in the tiny window. They were perfectly rigid; every bar of the door was the same.

Then the warden searched the prisoner's clothing, beginning at the shoes. Nothing hidden in them! Then the trousers waistband. Still nothing! Then the pockets of the trousers. From one side he drew out some paper money and examined it.

"Five one-dollar bills," he gasped.

"That's right," said the prisoner.

"But the – you had two tens and a five – what the – how do you do it?"

"That's my business," said The Thinking Machine.

"Did any of my men change this money for you – on your word of honour?"

The Thinking Machine paused just a fraction of a second.

"No," he said.

"Well, do you make it?" asked the warden. He was prepared to believe anything.

"That's my business," again said the prisoner.

The warden glared at the eminent scientist fiercely. He felt – he knew – that this man was making a fool out of him, yet he didn't know how. If he were a real prisoner he would get the truth – but, then, perhaps, these inexplicable things which had happened would not have been brought before him so sharply. Neither of the men spoke for a long time, then suddenly the warden turned fiercely and left the cell, slamming the door behind him. He didn't dare speak then.

He glanced at the clock. It was ten minutes to four. He had hardly settled himself in bed when again came the heart-breaking shriek through the prison. With a few muttered words, which, while not elegant, were highly expressive, he relighted his lantern and rushed through the prison again to the cell on the upper floor.

Again Ballard was crushing himself against the steel door, shrieking, shrieking at the top of his voice. He stopped only when the warden flashed his lamp in the cell.

"Take me out, take me out," he screamed. "I did it, I did it, I killed her. Take it away."

"Take what away?" asked the warden.

"I threw the acid in her face – I did it – I confess. Take me out of here."

Ballard's condition was pitiable; it was only an act of mercy to let him out into the corridor. There he crouched in a corner, like an animal at bay, and clasped his hands to his ears. It took half an hour to calm him sufficiently to speak. Then he told incoherently what had happened. On the night before at four o'clock he had heard a voice – a sepulchral voice, muffled and wailing in tone.

"What did it say?" asked the warden, curiously.

"Acid – acid – acid!" gasped the prisoner. "It accused me. Acid! I threw the acid, and the woman died. Oh!" It was a long, shuddering wail of terror.

"Acid?" echoed the warden, puzzled. The case was beyond him.

"Acid. That's all I heard – that one word, repeated several times. There were other things too, but I didn't hear them."

"That was last night, eh?" asked the warden. "What happened tonight – what frightened you just now?"

"It was the same thing," gasped the prisoner. "Acid – acid – acid!" He covered his face with his hands and sat shivering. "It was acid I used on her, but I didn't mean to kill her. I just heard the words. It was something accusing me – accusing me." He mumbled, and was silent.

"Did you hear anything else?"

"Yes – but I could understand – only a little bit – just a word or two."

"Well, what was it?"

"I heard 'acid' three times, then I heard a long, moaning sound, then – then – I heard 'No. 8 hat.' I heard that twice."

"No. 8 hat," repeated the warden. "What the devil – No. 8 hat? Accusing voices of conscience have never talked about No. 8 hats, so far as I ever heard."

"He's insane," said one of the jailers, with an air of finality.

"I believe you," said the warden. "He must be. He probably heard something and got frightened. He's trembling now. No. 8 hat! What the –"

When the fifth day of The Thinking Machine's imprisonment rolled around the warden was wearing a hunted look. He was anxious for the end of the thing. He could not help but feel that his distinguished prisoner had been amusing himself. And if this were so, The Thinking Machine had lost none of his sense of humour. For on this fifth day he flung down another linen note to the outside guard, bearing the words:

Only two days more.

Also he flung down half a dollar.

Now the warden knew – he knew – that the man in Cell 13 didn't have any half dollars – he couldn't have any half dollars, no more than he could have pen and ink and linen, and yet he did have them. It was a condition, not a theory; that is one reason why the warden was wearing a hunted look.

That ghastly, uncanny thing, too, about 'Acid' and 'No. 8 hat' clung to him tenaciously. They didn't mean anything, of course, merely the ravings of an insane murderer who had been driven by fear to confess his crime, still there were so many things that 'didn't mean anything' happening in the prison now since The Thinking Machine was there.

On the sixth day the warden received a card stating that Dr. Ransome and Mr. Fielding would be at Chisholm Prison on the following evening, Thursday, and in the event that Professor Van Dusen had not yet escaped – and they presumed he had not because they had not heard from him – they would meet him there.

"In the event he had not yet escaped!" The warden smiled grimly. Escaped!

The Thinking Machine enlivened this day for the warden with three notes. They were on the usual linen and bore generally on the appointment at half past eight o'clock Thursday night, which appointment the scientist had made at the time of his imprisonment.

On the afternoon of the seventh day the warden passed Cell 13 and glanced in. The Thinking Machine was lying on the iron bed, apparently sleeping lightly. The cell appeared precisely as it always did from a casual glance. The warden would swear that no man was going to leave it between that hour – it was then four o'clock – and half past eight o'clock that evening.

On his way back past the cell the warden heard the steady breathing again, and coming close to the door looked in. He wouldn't have done so if The Thinking Machine had been looking, but now – well, it was different.

A ray of light came through the high window and fell on the face of the sleeping man. It occurred to the warden for the first time that his prisoner appeared haggard and weary. Just then The Thinking Machine stirred slightly and the warden hurried on up the corridor guiltily. That evening after six o'clock he saw the jailer.

"Everything all right in Cell 13?" he asked.

"Yes sir," replied the jailer. "He didn't eat much, though."

It was with a feeling of having done his duty that the warden received Dr. Ransome and Mr. Fielding shortly after seven o'clock. He intended to show them the linen notes and lay before them the full story of his woes, which was a long one. But before this came to pass the guard from the river side of the prison yard entered the office.

"The arc light in my side of the yard won't light," he informed the warden.

"Confound it, that man's a hoodoo," thundered the official. "everything has happened since he's been here."

The guard went back to his post in the darkness, and the warden phoned to the electric light company.

"This is Chisholm Prison," he said through the phone. "Send three or four men down here quick, to fix an arc light."

The reply was evidently satisfactory, for the warden hung up the receiver and passed out into the yard. While Dr. Ransome and Mr. Fielding sat waiting, the guard at the outer gate came in with a special-delivery letter. Dr. Ransome happened to notice the address, and, when the guard went out, looked at the letter more closely.

"By George!" he exclaimed.

"What is it?" asked Mr. Fielding.

Silently the doctor offered the letter. Mr. Fielding examined it closely.

"Coincidence," he said. "It must be."

It was nearly eight o'clock when the warden returned to his office. The electricians had arrived in a wagon, and were now at work. The warden pressed the buzz-button communicating with the man at the outer gate in the wall.

"How many electricians came in?" he asked, over the short phone. "Four? Three workmen in jumpers and overalls and the manager? Frock coat and silk hat? All right. Be certain that only four go out. That's all."

He turned to Dr. Ransome and Mr. Fielding.

"We have to be careful here – particularly," and there was broad sarcasm in his tone, "since we have scientists locked up."

The warden picked up the special delivery letter carelessly, and then began to open it.

"When I read this I want to tell you gentlemen something about how – Great Caesar!" he ended, suddenly, as he glanced at the letter. He sat with mouth open, motionless, from astonishment.

"What is it?" asked Mr. Fielding.

"A special delivery letter from Cell 13," gasped the warden. "An invitation to supper."

"What?" and the two others arose, unanimously.

The warden sat dazed, staring at the letter for a moment, then called sharply to a guard outside the corridor.

"Run down to Cell 13 and see if that man's in there."

The guard went as directed, while Dr. Ransome and Mr. Fielding examined the letter.

"It's Van Dusen's handwriting; there's no question of that," said Dr. Ransome. "I've seen too much of it."

Just then the buzz on the telephone from the outer gate sounded, and the warden, in a semi-trance, picked up the receiver.

"Hello! Two reporters, eh? Let 'em come in." He turned suddenly to the doctor and Mr. Fielding. "Why; the man can't be out. He must be in his cell."

Just at that moment the guard returned.

"He's still in his cell, sir," he reported, "I saw him. He's lying down."

"There, I told you so," said the warden, and he breathed freely again. "But how did he mail that letter?"

There was a rap on the steel door which led from the jail yard into the warden's office.

"It's the reporters," said the warden. "Let them in," he instructed the guard; then to the other two gentlemen: "Don't say anything about this before them, because I'd never hear the last of it."

The door opened, and the two men from the front gate entered.

"Good evening, gentlemen," said one. That was Hutchinson Hatch; the warden knew him well.

"Well?" demanded the other, irritably. "I'm here."

That was The Thinking Machine.

He squinted belligerently at the warden, who sat with mouth agape. For the moment that official had nothing to say. Dr. Ransome and Mr. Fielding were amazed, but they didn't know what the warden knew. They were only amazed; he was paralyzed. Hutchinson Hatch, the reporter, took in the scene with greedy eyes.

"How – how – how did you do it?" gasped the warden, finally.

"Come back to the cell," said The Thinking Machine, in the irritated voice which his scientific associates knew so well.

The warden, still in a condition bordering on trance, led the way.

"Flash your light in there," directed The Thinking Machine.

The warden did so. There was nothing unusual in the appearance of the cell, and there – there on the bed lay the figure of The Thinking Machine. Certainly! There was the yellow hair! Again the warden looked at the man beside him and wondered at the strangeness of his own dreams.

With trembling hands he unlocked the cell door and The Thinking Machine passed inside.

"See here," he said.

He kicked at the steel bars in the bottom of the cell door and three of them were pushed out of place. A fourth broke off and rolled away in the corridor.

"And here, too," directed the erstwhile prisoner as he stood on the bed to reach the small window. He swept his hand across the opening and every bar came out.

"What's this in bed?" demanded the warden, who was slowly recovering.

"A wig," was the reply. "Turn down the cover."

The warden did so. Beneath it lay a large coil of strong rope, thirty feet or more, a dagger, three files, ten feet of electric wire, a thin, powerful pair of steel pliers, a small track hammer with its handle, and – a derringer pistol.

"How did you do it?" demanded the warden.

"You gentlemen have an engagement to supper with me at half past nine o'clock," said The Thinking Machine. "Come on, or we shall be late."

"But how did you do it?" insisted the warden.

"Don't ever think you can hold any man who can use his brain," said The Thinking Machine. "Come on; we shall be late."

It was an impatient supper party in the rooms of Professor Van Dusen and a somewhat silent one. The guests were Dr. Ransome, Alfred Fielding, the warden, and Hutchinson Hatch, reporter. The meal was served to the minute, in accordance with Professor Van Dusen's instructions of one week before; Dr. Ransome found the artichokes delicious. At last supper was finished and The Thinking Machine turned on Dr. Ransome and squinted at him fiercely.

"Do you believe it now?" he demanded.

"I do," replied Dr. Ransome.

"Do you admit that it was a fair test?"

"I do."

With the others, particularly the warden, he was waiting anxiously for the explanation.

"Suppose you tell us how –" began Mr. Fielding.

"Yes, tell us how," said the warden.

The Thinking Machine readjusted his glasses, took a couple of preparatory squints at his audience, and began his story. He told it from the beginning logically; and no man ever talked to more interested listeners.

"My agreement was," he began, "to go into a cell, carrying nothing except what was necessary to wear, and to leave that cell within a week. I had never seen Chisholm Prison. When I went into the cell I asked for tooth powder, two ten – and one five-dollar bills, and also to have my shoes blacked. Even if these requests had been refused it would not have mattered seriously. But you agreed to them.

"I knew there would be nothing in the cell which you thought I might use to advantage. So when the warden locked the door on me I was apparently helpless, unless I could turn three seemingly innocent things to use. They were things which would have been permitted any prisoner under sentence of death, were they not, warden?"

"Tooth powder and polished shoes, yes, but not money," replied the warden.

"Anything is dangerous in the hands of a man who knows how to use it," went on The Thinking Machine. "I did nothing that first night but sleep and chase rats." he glared at the warden. "When the subject was broached I knew I could do nothing that night, so suggested the next day. You gentleman thought I wanted time to arrange an escape with outside assistance, but this was not true. I knew I could communicate with whom I pleased, when I pleased."

The warden stared at him a moment, then went on smoking solemnly.

"I was aroused next morning at six o'clock by the jailer with my breakfast," continued the scientist. "He told me dinner was at twelve and supper at six. Between these times, I gathered, I would be pretty much to myself. So immediately after breakfast I examined my outside surroundings from my cell window. One look told me it would be useless to try to scale the wall, even should I decide to leave my cell by the window, for my purpose was to leave not only the cell, but the prison. Of course, I could have gone over the wall, but it would have taken me longer to lay my plans that way. Therefore, for the moment, I dismissed all idea of that.

"From this first observation I knew the river was on that side of the prison, and that there was also a playground there. Subsequently these surmises were verified by a keeper.

I knew then one important thing – that anyone might approach the prison wall from that side if necessary without attracting any particular attention. That was well to remember. I remembered it.

"But the outside thing which most attracted my attention was the feed wire to the arc light which ran within a few feet – probably three or four – of my cell window. I knew that would be valuable in the event I found it necessary to cut off that arc light."

"Oh, you shut it off tonight, then?" asked the warden.

"Having learned all I could from the window," resumes The Thinking Machine, without heeding the interruption, "I considered the idea of escaping through the prison proper. I recalled just how I had come into the cell, which I knew would be the only way. Seven doors lay between me and the outside. So, also for the time being, I gave up the idea of escaping that way. And I couldn't go through the solid granite walls of the cell."

The Thinking Machine paused for a moment and Dr. Ransome lighted a new cigar. For several minutes there was silence, then the scientific jailbreaker went on:

"While I was thinking about these things a rat ran across my foot. It suggested a new line of thought. There were at least half a dozen rats in the cell – I could see their beady eyes. Yet I had noticed none come under the cell door. I frightened them purposely and watched the cell door to see if they went out that way. They did not, but they were gone. Obviously they went another way. Another way meant another opening.

"I searched for this opening and found it. It was an old drain pipe, long unused and partly choked with dirt and dust. But this was the way the rats had come. They came from somewhere. Where? Drain pipes usually lead outside prison grounds. This one probably led to the river, or near it. The rats must therefore come from that direction. If they came a part of the way, I reasoned they came all the way, because it was extremely unlikely that a solid iron or lead pipe would have any hole in it except at the exit.

"When the jailer came with my luncheon he told me two important things, although he didn't know it. One was that a new system of plumbing had been put in the prison seven years before; another that the river was only three hundred feet away. Then I knew positively that the pipe was a part of the old system; I knew, too, that it slanted generally toward the river. But did the pipe end on the water or on land?

"This was the next question to be decided. I decided it by catching several of the rats in the cell. My jailer was surprised to see me engaged in this work. I examined at least a dozen of them. They were perfectly dry; they had come through the pipe, and, most important of all, they were not house rats, but field rats. The other end of the pipe was on land, then, outside the prison walls. So far, so good.

"Then, I knew that if I worked freely from this point I must attract the warden's attention in another direction. You see, by telling the warden that I had come to escape you made the test more severe, because I had to trick him by false scents."

The warden looked up with a sad expression in his eyes.

"The first thing was to make him think I was trying to communicate with you, Dr. Ransome. So I wrote a note on a piece of linen I tore from my shirt, addressed it to Dr. Ransome, tied a five-dollar bill around it and threw it out the window. I knew the guard would take it to the warden, but I rather hoped the warden would send it as addressed. Have you the first linen note, warden?"

The warden produced the cipher.

"What does it mean, anyhow?" he asked.

"Read it backward, beginning with the 'T' signature and disregard the division into words," instructed The Thinking Machine.

The warden did so. "T-h-i-s, this," he spelled, studied it for a moment, then read it off, grinning:

"This is not the way I intend to escape.

"Well, now what do you think o' that?" he demanded, still grinning.

"I knew that would attract your attention, just as it did," said The Thinking Machine, "and if you really found out what it was it would be a sort of gentle rebuke."

"What did you write it with?" asked Dr. Ransome, after he had examined the linen and passed it to Mr. Fielding.

"This," said the erstwhile prisoner, and he extended his foot. On it was the shoe he had worn in prison, though the polish was gone – scraped off clean. "The shoe blacking, moistened with water, was my ink; the metal tip of the shoe lace made a fairly good pen."

The warden looked up and suddenly burst into a laugh, half of relief, half of amusement.

"You're a wonder," he said, admiringly. "Go on."

"That precipitated a search of my cell by the warden, as I had intended," continued The Thinking Machine. "I was anxious to get the warden in the habit of searching my cell, so that finally, constantly finding nothing, he would get disgusted and quit. This at last happened, practically."

The warden blushed.

"He then took my white shirt away and gave me a prison shirt. He was satisfied that those two pieces of the shirt were all that was missing. But while he was searching my cell I had another pieces of that same shirt, about nine inches square, rolled up into a small ball in my mouth."

"Nine inches of that shirt?" demanded the warden. "Where did it come from?"

"The bosoms of all stiff white shirts are of triple thickness," was the explanation. "I tore out the inside thickness, leaving the bosom only two thicknesses. I knew you wouldn't see it. So much for that."

There was a little pause, and the warden looked from one to another of the men with a sheepish grin.

"Having disposed of the warden for the time being by giving him something else to think about, I took my first serious step toward freedom," said Professor Van Dusen. "I knew, within reason, that the pipe led somewhere to the playground outside; I knew a great many boys played there; I knew the rats came into my cell from out there. Could I communicate with some one outside with these things at hand?

"First was necessary, I saw, a long and fairly reliable thread, so – but here," he pulled up his trousers legs and showed that the tops of both stockings, of fine, strong lisle, were gone. "I unravelled those – after I got them started it wasn't difficult – and I had easily a quarter of a mile of thread that I could depend on.

"Then on half of my remaining linen I wrote, laboriously enough I assure you, a letter explaining my situation to this gentleman here," and he indicated Hutchinson Hatch. "I knew he would assist me – for the value of the newspaper story. I tied firmly to this linen letter a ten-dollar bill – there is no surer way of attracting the eye of anyone – and wrote on the linen:

"Finder of this deliver to Hutchinson Hatch, Daily American, who will give another ten dollars for the information.

"The next thing was to get this note outside on that playground where a boy might find it.

There were two ways, but I chose the best. I took one of the rats – I became adept at catching them – tied the linen and money firmly to one leg, fastened my lisle thread to another, and turned him loose in the drain pipe. I reasoned that the natural fright of the rodent would make him run until he was outside the pipe and then out on earth he would probably stop to gnaw off the linen and money.

"From the moment the rat disappeared into that dusty pipe I became anxious. I was taking so many chances. The rat might gnaw the string, of which I held one end; other rats might gnaw at it; the rat might run out of the pipe and leave the linen and money where they would never be found; a thousand other things might have happened. So began some nervous hours, but the fact that the rat ran on until only a few feet of the string remained in my cell made me think he was outside the pipe. I had carefully instructed Mr. Hatch what to do in case the note reached him. The question was: Would it reach him?

"This done, I could only wait and make other plans in case this one failed. I openly attempted to bribe my jailer, and I learned from him that he held the keys to only two of seven doors between me and freedom. Then I did something else to make the warden nervous. I took the steel supports out of the heels of my shoes and made a pretence of sawing the bars of my cell window. The warden raised a pretty row about that. He developed, too, the habit of shaking the bars of my cell window to see if they were solid. They were – then."

Again the warden grinned. He had ceased being astonished.

"With this one plan I had done all I could and could only wait to see what happened," the scientist went on. "I couldn't know whether my note had been delivered or even found, or whether the mouse had gnawed it up. And I didn't dare to draw back through the pipe the one slender thread which connected me with the outside.

"When I went to bed that night I didn't sleep, for fear there would come the slight signal twitch at the thread which was to tell me that Mr. Hatch had received the note. At half past three o'clock, I judge, I felt this twitch, and no prisoner actually under sentence of death ever welcomed a thing more heartily."

The Thinking Machine stopped and turned to the reporter.

"You'd better explain just what you did," he said.

"The linen note was brought to me by a small boy who had been playing baseball," said Mr. Hatch. "I immediately saw a big story in it, so I gave the boy another ten dollars, and got several spools of silk, some twine, and a roll of light, pliable wire. The Professor's note suggested that I have the finder of the note show me just where it was picked up, and told me to make my search from there, beginning at two o'clock in the morning. If I found the other end of the thread, I was to twitch it gently three times, then a fourth.

"I began the search with a small-bulb electric light. It was an hour and twenty minutes before I found the end of the drain pipe, half hidden in the weeds. The pipe was very large there, say twelve inches across. Then I found the end of the lisle thread, twitched it as directed and immediately I got an answering twitch.

"Then I fastened the silk to this and Professor Van Dusen began to pull it into his cell. I nearly had heart disease for fear the string would break. To the end of the silk I fastened the twine, and when that had been pulled in I tied on the wire. Then that was drawn into the pipe and we had a substantial line, which rats couldn't gnaw, from the mouth of the drain into the cell."

The Thinking Machine raised his hand and Hatch stopped.

"All this was done in absolute silence," said the scientist, "but when the wire reached my hand I could have shouted. Then we tried another experiment, which Mr. Hatch was prepared for.

I tested the pipe as a speaking tube. Neither of us could hear very clearly, but I dared not speak loud for fear of attracting attention in the prison. At last I made him understand what I wanted immediately. He seemed to have great difficulty in understanding when I asked for nitric acid, and I repeated the word 'acid' several times.

"Then I heard a shriek from a cell above me. I knew instantly that someone had overheard, and when I heard you coming, Mr. Warden, I feigned sleep. If you had entered my cell at that moment the whole plan of escape would have ended there. But you passed on. That was the nearest I ever came to being caught.

"Having established this improvised trolley it is easy to see how I got things into the cell and made them disappear at will. I merely dropped them back into the pipe. You, Mr. Warden, could not have reached the connecting wire with your fingers; they are too large. My fingers, you see, are longer and more slender. In addition I guarded the top of that pipe with a rat – you remember how."

"I remember," said the warden, with a grimace.

"I thought that if anyone were tempted to investigate that hole the rat would dampen his ardour. Mr. Hatch could not send me anything useful through the pipe until next night, although he did send me change for ten dollars as a test, so I proceeded with other parts of my plan. Then I evolved the method of escape I finally employed.

"In order to carry this out successfully it was necessary for the guard in the yard to get accustomed to seeing me at the cell window. I arranged this by dropping linen notes to him, boastful in tone, to make the warden believe, if possible, one of his assistants was communicating with the outside for me. I would stand at my window for hours gazing out, so the guard could see me, and occasionally I spoke to him. In that way I learned the prison had no electricians of its own, but was dependent upon the lighting company should anything go wrong.

"That cleared the way to freedom perfectly. Early in the evening of the last day of my imprisonment, when it was dark, I planned to cut the feed wire which was only a few feet from my window, reaching it with an acid tipped wire I had. That would make that side of the prison perfectly dark while the electricians were searching for the break. That would also bring Mr. Hatch into the prison yard."

"There was only one more thing to do before I actually began the work of setting myself free. This was to arrange final details with Mr. Hatch through our speaking tube. I did this within half an hour after the warden left my cell on the fourth night of my imprisonment. Mr. Hatch again had serious difficulty in understanding me, and I repeated the word 'acid' to him several time, and later on the words: 'No. 8 hat' – that's my size – and these were the things which made the prisoner upstairs confess to murder, so one of the jailers told me the next day. The prisoner had heard our voices, confused of course, through the pipe, which also went to his cell. The cell directly over me was not occupied, hence no one else heard.

"Of course the actual work of cutting the steel bars out of the window and door was comparatively easy with nitric acid, which I got through the pipe in tin bottles, but it took time. Hour after hour on the fifth and sixth and seventh days the guard below was looking at me as I worked on the bars of the window with the acid on a piece of wire. I used the tooth powder to prevent the acid spreading. I looked away abstractly as I worked and each minute the acid cut deeper into the metal. I noticed that the jailers always tried the door by shaking the upper part, never the lower bars, therefore I cut the lower bars, leaving them hanging in place by thin strips of metal. But that was a bit of daredevilry. I could not have gone away so easily."

The Thinking Machine sat silent for several minutes.

"I think that makes everything clear," he went on. "Whatever points I have not explained were merely to confuse the warden and jailers. These things in my bed I brought in to please Mr. Hatch, who wanted to improve the story. Of course, the wig was necessary in my plan. The special delivery letter I wrote and directed in my cell with Mr. Hatch's fountain pen, then sent it out to him and he mailed it. That's all, I think."

"But your actually leaving the prison grounds and then coming in through the outer gate to my office?" asked the warden.

"Perfectly simple," said the scientist. "I cut the electric light wire with acid, as I said, when the current was off. Therefore when the current was turned on the arc didn't light. I knew it would take some time to find out what was the matter and make repairs. When the guard went to report to you the yard was dark, I crept out the window – it was a tight fit, too – replaced the bars by standing on a narrow ledge and remained in shadow until the force of electricians arrived. Mr. Hatch was one of them.

"When I saw him I spoke and he handed me a cap, a jumper and overalls, which I put on within ten feet of you, Mr. Warden, while you were in the yard. Later Mr. Hatch called me, presumably as a workman, and together we went out the gate to get something out of the wagon. The gate guard let us pass out readily as two workmen who had just passed in. We changed our clothing and reappeared, asking to see you. We saw you. That's all."

There was a silence for several minutes. Dr. Ransome was first to speak.

"Wonderful!" he exclaimed. "Perfectly amazing."

"How did Mr. Hatch happen to come in with the electricians?" asked Mr. Fielding.

"His father is manager of the company," relied The Thinking Machine.

"But what if there had been no Mr. Hatch outside to help?"

"Every prisoner has one friend outside who would help him escape if he could."

"Suppose – just suppose – there had been no old plumbing system there?" asked the warden, curiously.

"There were two other ways out," said The Thinking Machine, enigmatically.

Ten minutes later the telephone bell rang, it was a request for the warden.

"Light all right, eh?" the warden asked, through the phone. "Good. Wire cut beside Cell 13? Yes, I know. One electrician too many? What's that? Two came out?"

The warden turned to the others with a puzzled expression.

"He only let in four electricians, he has let out two and says there are three left."

"I was the odd one," said The Thinking Machine.

"Oh," said the warden. "I see." Then through the phone: "Let the fifth man go. He's all right."

I Am Nightmare

Jennifer Gifford

SOME CALL ME OPPORTUNITY. Others have called me Fate. In religious circles, I'm the Devil, or the more poetic, Tragedy. The title I hate the most is God's Will. I am not of His creation, and He never wanted anything to do with me. Some even refer to me as the Grim Reaper. Though I admit, I am none of those things. At best, I am a parasite. An invisible symbiotic leach.

Of all the titles, I hate the ones that chalk up my art as 'Gods work.' How foolish, after all these centuries, you humans still like to explain away the bizarre happenstances in life to your religious preferences of choice. None of you has ever stopped to think that when you say, "God is in everything," that the Devil can be too.

While I am an opportunist, I have my own agenda, and I work alone. I prefer it that way. I don't like the notion of sharing credit for anything, and I like the sharing of spoils even less. I do all the work, from the targeting, scoping, and silencing of my target. I am Darkness. I am Nightmare, and I am coming for you.

I'm intangible, though I am given credit for taking many forms. I manifest myself into the foggy crevices of dreams, lurking about in the subconscious waiting for the right moment to plant my seed. Waiting. Watching. The mind is a vast ocean of sensory impulses tied to memories. A mesh-like web of who we really are, and the mind never lies. The beauty of it all is that I'm a true serial killer. The beauty of my unique existence and methodologies means that there will be no long arm of the law coming for me. There is no technology around, past, present, or future that can track me.

My world is a realm of sultry shadows and lurid thoughts tangled together like broken love knots, and bound by emotions far greater than love. It's true that love knows no bounds, but lust knows no ends. Lust is twice as strong, and even sweeter.

Jealously comes in the color of jade. Green is the color that makes the world go round. There are hungers that the simplistic human palate cannot even begin to fathom, and those taboo and forbidden desires are a delicacy that have created an addiction in me that cannot be satiated.

As I said, I am an intangible mist of twisted terrors, like barbed wire around the soul, and I manifest my image into the living nightmare of whoever's mind I am rushing. I infest slowly, creeping and skulking around in the person's subconscious, and I wait until the very moment where I can infest my diseased thoughts into the altered reality of their dreams, where I induce fear, and always death. At their precise moment of death, I get their life essence in its purest form, before the soul vanishes towards the end of its journey. In those few moments, as the soul detaches itself from the human shell, I get an emotional rush of adrenaline-laced fear that is stronger than any man made concoction. But its volume is small, and it rushes through me all too quickly, and I'm left longing for more. Too soon, the fervor is gone, and it takes more of my energy to create a darker realm where I can terrorize them. Thanks to human technology and modernization, my efforts require more of my skills, yet they yield less of what I need. It's a vivacious cycle that is bound to me, and I to reality. I am my own crown of thorns.

When I let the fear rush their mind, it makes the brain scramble all the senses. I can almost smell their sweet divinity preparing to leave them. It attracts me, turns me on like a bee to honey. The look in their eyes as it happens is wickedly delicious. Their greatest fear is my weapon of choice. The destructive beauty of their last breath of life from my handiwork is a euphoria that only those who've touched evil can know.

Every junkie has that vision of their ultimate high, that one idealistic moment that binds them to the destructive repetition, and though I am not tangible, I suffer the same snare. My favorite accomplishment was Amber McCarty. She was all sweetness and light, young and naïve, although because of my immortality, I have a tendency to remember everyone as young. Occupational hazard of the trade.

She was an ordinary girl on a farm in one of the middle states, somewhere in the Midwest, maybe Kansas, or Iowa. Geography means nothing to something like me, who has seen the birth of ancient civilizations crumble while new cultures were born. She was petite, attractive, funny, and everyone seemed to want to be around her. Even me.

I had taken the chance and came in with the fog one cool September morning, and waited. I waited. I watched. She gave the appearance of being a good daughter, good student, and a good sister to her younger brother. The kids in Sunday school liked her, and everyone seemed to relax whenever she was around. I could see why. I was just as attracted to her as they were, but for ultraistic reasons. On my last few kills, I decided to test a theory of mine: would the volume and potency of the life essence would be stronger and sweeter if the original source of life was to?

Her sweetness and purity stirred in me a hunger I hadn't felt in years. I knew when the moment came, and she tasted the fear, and I tasted her divinity. It was the closest thing something like me could ever get to heaven.

I waited, and my opportunity presented itself three days later. A typical Monday morning, but she was running late for school. Today she had to look perfect. It was the day that they would announce the nominations for Homecoming Queen, and Amber had her heart set on being a member of Summersville High School's Royal Court. Her parents were busy. Her dad on a tractor in the west field, and her mother was in the barn with the chickens. Her younger brother was still asleep, and I crept into her bathroom under the guise of the steam from the shower. Of all the forms I can take, vapor is the easiest and most overlooked.

I knew what lurked in the small cubby beneath the sink. I knew what lay hidden there, and I knew what was going to happen. I knew Amber's worst fear. I saw it unfold in a bad dream, saw the panic and shock on her face when it happened. It was then that I knew. My mouth started to salivate at the impending unfortunate certainty that awaited poor Amber.

The minutes ticked by, painfully delicious as I waited. I was giddy with anticipation and could barely contain the rush I felt from the sugary sweet life that pulsed around me, unaware of what was going to happen to her.

She got out of the shower, and checked the time on the clock hanging on the wall. Muttering a soft curse, she quickly dried off. Hearing her swear sent a new shiver of heightened hunger and longing within me. It turned out she was sugar and a little spice.

I watched, transparent like the wind, while she toweled her hair. She let the cheap terrycloth towel fall from around her body to pool at her feet. I watched as she looked at herself in the mirror, moving her body into various positions to observe it from every angle. Somewhere in the distance, a rooster's cry snapped her out of her reverie.

She looked up at the clock again, frantically grabbing her hairbrush. Almost as if in slow motion, I watched her reach under the sink, into the cabinet, and pull out the hairdryer. I watched breathlessly, felt the tingling sensation of adrenaline pulse through me, building to that one twisted and beautiful moment where I watched my art come to life. In that moment, I too was like God. All those days of probing her subconscious, watching her in her day-to-day routine had come to the perfect timing of this moment. I knew her fear.

She flipped on the little radio, the FM station starting to blast the upbeat twang of a local country station. Plugging in the cord to the hairdryer, she grabbed her brush, and flipped the switch of the hairdryer to high.

The heat from the dryer fluffed her hair, spraying the layers of the short auburn bob like wet strings of cotton candy. Her voice was angelic, singing along to the song as it ended and to the one after that.

She flipped her head upside down, shaking it rhythmically as the heat from the dryer started to dry her hair.

I knew what was inside the hairdryer. I knew what the heat from the hairdryer would do.

It didn't take too long before small black specks began to emerge from the tube of the hairdryer, like an eerie foam slowly coating her damp locks. First a few, then a few dozen. Then a hundred. Hundreds of newly hatched, fresh black spiders scrambled out of the safety of their cocoon in the barrel of seldom used hairdryer. Struggling to get away from the heat, they frantically crawled away from the source, their almond shaped bodies and tiny sinewy young legs stampeding with ardent haste into the safety and damp coolness of Amber's wet hair.

The tiny arachnids crawled mercilessly, struggling to get away from the scorching heat; they crawled further, down her hair to the nape of her neck. Then Amber flipped the switch of the hairdryer off, flipping her head back up.

Only the tiny spiders didn't stop moving. They hurriedly crept over her neck, some choosing to move down her spine towards the small of her naked back. But the others moved over her neck, towards her face.

Amber flashed her reflection to the mirror, watching in paralyzed terror as hundreds of little black spiders crept over the smooth honeyed complexion of her neck and face. Then it happened. Her pupils dilated, and her mouth open, barely in time to let out the most gut wrenching terrified scream before frantically trying to swish the spiders off her face and neck.

But the spiders didn't stop crawling. She waved her arms around and around, screaming loudly again until she felt the soft pin pokes of legs creep towards her lips. The needle-like sensations didn't stop; they only ran further up and down her skin, making her flesh crawl with gooselike pimples.

Amber ran, flailing her arms around her, clawing at her face with her hands in a desperate attempt to get the spiders to stop their persistent mechanical-like crawling over her flesh. They rushed up her hands, past her elbows. Their feathery light touch poured over her skin in an unnatural dance macabre. They made their way down her back, over her hips and onto her thighs seeking refuge away from the intense burning heat that awakened them from their sheltered cocoon.

As she ran past me, I could smell the raw fear, boiling and ebbing around her like waves. I inhaled sharply, drawing in the frightened essence of her innocence and purity. Her divinity washed through me, pushing me into a state of sadistic elation. It tasted like sweet peaches and honey. She thrashed around, stumbling out of her open bedroom door, and accidentally slipping over the wooden railing of the staircase landing on the hardwood floor of the farmhouse with a sickening thud. Everyone thought Amber died from the fall, but I know firsthand she died from her fear. I cannot imagine a sweeter way to go.

It was the most exquisite kill I have ever had. It's the one that sets the bar for all the others that have followed.

I lurk in the darkened shadows and wait, searching for a new victim, seeking out that brief moment that will allow me another fix. Whatever others call me, I know that there is nothing else like me. I am immortal. I am Nightmare.

Everyone has a morbid story to tell, and I am no exception. I'm just the precipice of other people's morbid tales. Eventually, I'll be a part of yours as well.

A Mysterious Case

Anna Katharine Green

IT WAS A MYSTERY to me, but not to the other doctors. They took, as was natural, the worst possible view of the matter, and accepted the only solution which the facts seem to warrant. But they are men, and I am a woman; besides, I knew the nurse well, and I could not believe her capable of wilful deceit, much less of the heinous crime which deceit in this case involved. So to me the affair was a mystery.

The facts were these:

My patient, a young typewriter, seemingly without friends or enemies, lay in a small room of a boardinghouse, afflicted with a painful but not dangerous malady. Though she was comparatively helpless, her vital organs were strong, and we never had a moment's uneasiness concerning her, till one morning when we found her in an almost dying condition from having taken, as we quickly discovered, a dose of poison, instead of the soothing mixture which had been left for her with the nurse. Poison! And no one, not even herself or the nurse, could explain how the same got into the room, much less into her medicine. And when I came to study the situation, I found myself as much at loss as they; indeed, more so; for I knew I had made no mistake in preparing the mixture, and that, even if I had, this especial poison could not have found its way into it, owing to the fact that there neither was nor ever had been a drop of it in my possession.

The mixture, then, was pure when it left my hand, and, according to the nurse, whom, as I have said, I implicitly believe, it went into the glass pure. And yet when, two hours later, without her having left the room or anybody coming into it, she found occasion to administer the draught, poison was in the cup, and the patient was only saved from death by the most immediate and energetic measures, not only on her part, but on that of Dr. Holmes, whom in her haste and perturbation she had called in from the adjacent house.

The patient, young, innocent, unfortunate, but of a strangely courageous disposition, betrayed nothing but the utmost surprise at the peril she had so narrowly escaped. When Dr. Holmes intimated that perhaps she had been tired of suffering, and had herself found means of putting the deadly drug into her medicine, she opened her great gray eyes, with such a look of childlike surprise and reproach, that he blushed, and murmured some sort of apology.

"Poison myself?" she cried, "when you promise me that I shall get well? You do not know what a horror I have of dying in debt, or you would never say that."

This was some time after the critical moment had passed, and there were in the room Mrs. Dayton, the landlady, Dr. Holmes, the nurse, and myself. At the utterance of these words we all felt ashamed and cast looks of increased interest at the poor girl.

She was very lovely. Though without means, and to all appearance without friends, she possessed in great degree the charm of winsomeness, and not even her many sufferings, nor the indignation under which she was then laboring, could quite rob her countenance of that tender and confiding expression which so often redeems the plainest face and makes beauty doubly attractive.

"Dr. Holmes does not know you," I hastened to say; "I do, and utterly repel for you any such insinuation. In return, will you tell me if there is any one in the world whom you can call your enemy? Though the chief mystery is how so deadly and unusual a poison could have gotten into a clean glass, without the knowledge of yourself or the nurse, still it might not be amiss to know if there is any one, here or elsewhere, who for any reason might desire your death."

The surprise in the childlike eyes increased rather than diminished.

"I don't know what to say," she murmured. "I am so insignificant and feeble a person that it seems absurd for me to talk of having an enemy. Besides, I have none. On the contrary, every one seems to love me more than I deserve. Haven't you noticed it, Mrs. Dayton?"

The landlady smiled and stroked the sick girl's hand.

"Indeed," she replied, "I have noticed that people love you, but I have never thought that it was more than you deserved. You are a dear little thing, Addie."

And though she knew and I knew that the 'every one' mentioned by the poor girl meant ourselves, and possibly her unknown employer, we were nonetheless touched by her words. The more we studied the mystery, the deeper and less explainable did it become.

And indeed I doubt if we should have ever got to the bottom of it, if there had not presently occurred in my patient a repetition of the same dangerous symptoms, followed by the same discovery, of poison in the glass, and the same failure on the part of herself and nurse to account for it. I was aroused from my bed at midnight to attend her, and as I entered her room and met her beseeching eyes looking upon me from the very shadow of death, I made a vow that I would never cease my efforts till I had penetrated the secret of what certainly looked like a persistent attempt upon this poor girl's life.

I went about the matter deliberately. As soon as I could leave her side, I drew the nurse into a corner and again questioned her. The answers were the same as before. Addie had shown distress as soon as she had swallowed her usual quantity of medicine, and in a few minutes more was in a perilous condition.

"Did you hand the glass yourself to Addie?"

"I did."

"Where did you take it from?"

"From the place where you left it – the little stand on the farther side of the bed."

"And do you mean to say that you had not touched it since I prepared it?"

"I do, ma'am."

"And that no one else has been in the room?"

"No one, ma'am."

I looked at her intently. I trusted her, but the best of us are but mortal.

"Can you assure me that you have not been asleep during this time?"

"Look at this letter I have been writing," she returned. "It is eight pages long, and it was not begun when you left us at 10 o'clock."

I shook my head and fell into a deep revery. How was that matter to be elucidated, and how was my patient to be saved? Another draught of this deadly poison, and no power on earth could resuscitate her. What should I do, and with what weapons should I combat a danger at once so subtle and so deadly? Reflection brought no decision, and I left the room at last, determined upon but one point, and that was the immediate removal of my patient. But before I had left the house I changed my mind even on this point. Removal of the patient meant safety to her, perhaps, but not the explanation of her mysterious poisoning.

I would change the position of her bed, and I would even set a watch over her and the nurse, but I would not take her out of the house – not yet.

And what had produced this change in my plans? The look of a woman whom I met on the stairs. I did not know her, but when I encountered her glance I felt that there was some connection between us, and I was not at all surprised to hear her ask:

"And how is Miss Wilcox today?"

"Miss Wilcox is very low," I returned. "The least neglect, the least shock to her nerves, would be sufficient to make all my efforts useless. Otherwise –"

"She will get well?"

I nodded. I had exaggerated the condition of the sufferer, but some secret instinct compelled me to do so. The look which passed over the woman's face satisfied me that I had done well; and, though I left the house, it was with the intention of speedily returning and making inquiries into the woman's character and position in the household.

I learned little or nothing. That she occupied a good room and paid for it regularly seemed to be sufficient to satisfy Mrs. Dayton. Her name, which proved to be Leroux, showed her to be French, and her promptly paid $10 a week showed her to be respectable – what more could any hard-working landlady require? But I was distrustful. Her face, though handsome, possessed an eager, ferocious look which I could not forget, and the slight gesture with which she had passed me at the close of the short conversation I have given above had a suggestion of triumph in it which seemed to contain whole volumes of secret and mysterious hate. I went into Miss Wilcox's room very thoughtful.

"I am going –"

But here the nurse held up her hand. "Hark," she whispered; she had just set the clock, and was listening to its striking.

I did hark, but not to the clock.

"Whose step is that?" I asked, after she had left the clock, and sat down.

"Oh, someone in the next room. The walls here are very thin – only boards in places."

I did not complete what I had begun to say. If I could hear steps through the partition, then could our neighbors hear us talk, and what I had determined upon must be kept secret from all outsiders. I drew a sheet of paper toward me and wrote:

"I shall stay here tonight. Something tells me that in doing this I shall solve this mystery. But I must appear to go. Take my instructions as usual, and bid me goodnight. Lock the door after me, but with a turn of the key instantly unlock it again. I shall go down stairs, see that my carriage drives away, and quietly return. On my re-entrance I shall expect to find Miss Wilcox on the couch with the screen drawn up around it, you in your big chair, and the light lowered. What I do thereafter need not concern you. Pretend to go to sleep."

The nurse nodded, and immediately entered upon the programme I had planned. I prepared the medicine as usual, placed it in its usual glass, and laid that glass where it had always been set, on a small table at the farther side of the bed. Then I said "Goodnight," and passed hurriedly out.

I was fortunate enough to meet no one, going or coming. I regained the room, pushed open the door, and finding everything in order, proceeded at once to the bed, upon which, after taking off my hat and cloak and carefully concealing them, I lay down and deftly covered myself up.

My idea was this – that by some mesmeric influence of which she was ignorant, the nurse had been forced to either poison the glass herself or open the door for another to do it. If this were so, she or the other person would be obliged to pass around the foot of the bed in order to reach the glass, and I should be sure to see it, for I did not pretend to sleep. By the low light enough could be discerned for safe movement about the room, and not enough to make apparent the change which had been made in the occupant of the bed. I waited with indescribable anxiety, and more than once fancied I heard steps, if not a feverish breathing close to my bed-head; but no one appeared, and the nurse in her big chair did not move.

At last I grew weary, and fearful of losing control over my eyelids, I fixed my gaze upon the glass, as if in so doing I should find a talisman to keep me awake, when, great God! What was it I saw! A hand, a creeping hand coming from nowhere and joined to nothing, closing about that glass and drawing it slowly away till it disappeared entirely from before my eyes!

I gasped – I could not help it – but I did not stir. For now I knew I was asleep and dreaming. But no, I pinch myself under the clothes, and find that I am very wide awake indeed; and then – look! look! the glass is returning; the hand – a woman's hand – is slowly setting it back in its place, and –

With a bound I have that hand in my grasp. It is a living hand, and it is very warm and strong and fierce, and the glass has fallen and lies shattered between us, and a double cry is heard, one from behind the partition, through an opening in which this hand had been thrust, and one from the nurse, who has jumped to her feet and is even now assisting me in holding the struggling member, upon which I have managed to scratch a telltale mark with a piece of the fallen glass. At sight of the iron-like grip which this latter lays upon the intruding member, I at once release my own grasp.

"Hold on," I cried, and leaping from the bed, I hastened first to my patient, whom I carefully reassured, and then into the hall, where I found the landlady running to see what was the matter. "I have found the wretch," I cried, and drawing her after me, hurried about to the other side of the partition, where I found a closet, and in it the woman I had met on the stairs, but glaring now like a tiger in her rage, menace, and fear.

That woman was my humble little patient's bitter but unknown enemy. Enamoured of a man who – unwisely, perhaps – had expressed in her hearing his admiration for the pretty typewriter, she had conceived the idea that he intended to marry the latter, and, vowing vengeance, had taken up her abode in the same house with the innocent girl, where, had it not been for the fortunate circumstance of my meeting her on the stairs, she would certainly have carried out her scheme of vile and secret murder. The poison she had bought in another city, and the hole in the partition she had herself cut. This had been done at first for the purpose of observation, she having detected in passing by Miss Wilcox's open door that a banner of painted silk hung over that portion of the wall in such a way as to hide any aperture which might be made there.

Afterward, when Miss Wilcox fell sick, and she discovered by short glimpses through her loop-hole that the glass of medicine was placed on a table just under this banner, she could not resist the temptation to enlarge the hole to a size sufficient to admit the pushing aside of the banner and the reaching through of her murderous hand. Why she did not put poison enough in the glass to kill Miss Wilcox at once I have never discovered. Probably she feared detection. That by doing as she did she brought about the very event she had endeavored to avert, is the most pleasing part of the tale. When the gentleman of whom I have spoken learned of the wicked attempt which had been made upon Miss Wilcox's life, his heart took pity upon her, and a marriage ensued, which I have every reason to believe is a happy one.

The Rome Express

Arthur Griffiths

Chapter I

THE ROME EXPRESS, the *direttissimo*, or most direct, was approaching Paris one morning in March, when it became known to the occupants of the sleeping-car that there was something amiss, very much amiss, in the car.

The train was travelling the last stage, between Laroche and Paris, a run of a hundred miles without a stop. It had halted at Laroche for early breakfast, and many, if not all the passengers, had turned out. Of those in the sleeping-car, seven in number, six had been seen in the restaurant, or about the platform; the seventh, a lady, had not stirred. All had reentered their berths to sleep or doze when the train went on, but several were on the move as it neared Paris, taking their turn at the lavatory, calling for water, towels, making the usual stir of preparation as the end of a journey was at hand.

There were many calls for the porter, yet no porter appeared. At last the attendant was found – lazy villain! – asleep, snoring loudly, stertorously, in his little bunk at the end of the car. He was roused with difficulty, and set about his work in a dull, unwilling, lethargic way, which promised badly for his tips from those he was supposed to serve.

By degrees all the passengers got dressed, all but two – the lady in 9 and 10, who had made no sign as yet; and the man who occupied alone a double berth next her, numbered 7 and 8.

As it was the porter's duty to call everyone, and as he was anxious, like the rest of his class, to get rid of his travellers as soon as possible after arrival, he rapped at each of the two closed doors behind which people presumably still slept.

The lady cried "All right," but there was no answer from No. 7 and 8.

Again and again the porter knocked and called loudly. Still meeting with no response, he opened the door of the compartment and went in.

It was now broad daylight. No blind was down; indeed, the one narrow window was open, wide; and the whole of the interior of the compartment was plainly visible, all and everything in it.

The occupant lay on his bed motionless. Sound asleep? No, not merely asleep – the twisted unnatural lie of the limbs, the contorted legs, the one arm drooping listlessly but stiffly over the side of the berth, told of a deeper, more eternal sleep.

The man was dead. Dead – and not from natural causes.

One glance at the blood-stained bedclothes, one look at the gaping wound in the breast, at the battered, mangled face, told the terrible story.

It was murder! Murder most foul! The victim had been stabbed to the heart.

With a wild, affrighted, cry the porter rushed out of the compartment, and to the eager questioning of all who crowded round him, he could only mutter in confused and trembling accents:

"There! There! In there!"

Thus the fact of the murder became known to every one by personal inspection, for every one (even the lady had appeared for just a moment) had looked in where the body lay. The compartment was filled for some ten minutes or more by an excited, gesticulating, polyglot mob of half a dozen, all talking at once in French, English, and Italian.

The first attempt to restore order was made by a tall man, middle-aged, but erect in his bearing, with bright eyes and alert manner, who took the porter aside, and said sharply in good French, but with a strong English accent:

"Here! It's your business to do something. No one has any right to be in that compartment now. There may be reasons – traces – things to remove; never mind what. But get them all out. Be sharp about it; and lock the door. Remember you will be held responsible to justice."

The porter shuddered, so did many of the passengers who had overheard the Englishman's last words.

Justice! It is not to be trifled with anywhere, least of all in France, where the uncomfortable superstition prevails that everyone who can be reasonably suspected of a crime is held to be guilty of that crime until his innocence is clearly proved.

All those six passengers and the porter were now brought within the category of the accused. They were all open to suspicion; they, and they alone, for the murdered man had been seen alive at Laroche, and the fell deed must have been done since then, while the train was in transit, that is to say, going at express speed, when no one could leave it except at peril of his life.

"Deuced awkward for us!" said the tall English general, Sir Charles Collingham by name, to his brother the parson, when he had reentered their compartment and shut the door.

"I can't see it. In what way?" asked the Reverend Silas Collingham, a typical English cleric, with a rubicund face and square-cut white whiskers, dressed in a suit of black serge, and wearing the professional white tie.

"Why, we shall be detained, of course; arrested, probably – certainly detained. Examined, cross-examined, bully-ragged – I know something of the French police and their ways."

"If they stop us, I shall write to the Times," cried his brother, by profession a man of peace, but with a choleric eye that told of an angry temperament.

"By all means, my dear Silas, when you get the chance. That won't be just yet, for I tell you we're in a tight place, and may expect a good deal of worry." With that he took out his cigarette-case, and his match-box, lighted his cigarette, and calmly watched the smoke rising with all the coolness of an old campaigner accustomed to encounter and face the ups and downs of life. "I only hope to goodness they'll run straight on to Paris," he added in a fervent tone, not unmixed with apprehension. "No! By jingo, we're slackening speed –"

"Why shouldn't we? It's right the conductor, or chief of the train, or whatever you call him, should know what has happened."

"Why, man, can't you see? While the train is travelling express, everyone must stay on board it; if it slows, it is possible to leave it."

"Who would want to leave it?"

"Oh, I don't know," said the General, rather testily. "Anyway, the thing's done now."

The train had pulled up in obedience to the signal of alarm given by some one in the sleeping-car, but by whom it was impossible to say. Not by the porter, for he seemed greatly surprised as the conductor came up to him.

"How did you know?" he asked.

"Know! Know what? You stopped me."

"I didn't."

"Who rang the bell, then?"

"I did not. But I'm glad you've come. There has been a crime – murder."

"Good Heavens!" cried the conductor, jumping up on to the car, and entering into the situation at once. His business was only to verify the fact, and take all necessary precautions. He was a burly, brusque, peremptory person, the despotic, self-important French official, who knew what to do – as he thought – and did it without hesitation or apology.

"No one must leave the car," he said in a tone not to be misunderstood. "Neither now, nor on arrival at the station."

There was a shout of protest and dismay, which he quickly cut short.

"You will have to arrange it with the authorities in Paris; they can alone decide. My duty is plain: to detain you, place you under surveillance till then. Afterwards, we will see. Enough, gentlemen and madame –"

He bowed with the instinctive gallantry of his nation to the female figure which now appeared at the door of her compartment. She stood for a moment listening, seemingly greatly agitated, and then, without a word, disappeared, retreating hastily into her own private room, where she shut herself in.

Almost immediately, at a signal from the conductor, the train resumed its journey. The distance remaining to be traversed was short; half an hour more, and the Lyons station, at Paris, was reached, where the bulk of the passengers – all, indeed, but the occupants of the sleeper – descended and passed through the barriers. The latter were again desired to keep their places, while a posse of officials came and mounted guard. Presently they were told to leave the car one by one, but to take nothing with them. All their hand-bags, rugs, and belongings were to remain in the berths, just as they lay. One by one they were marched under escort to a large and bare waiting-room, which had, no doubt, been prepared for their reception.

Here they took their seats on chairs placed at wide intervals apart, and were peremptorily forbidden to hold any communication with each other, by word or gesture. This order was enforced by a fierce-looking guard in blue and red uniform, who stood facing them with his arms folded, gnawing his moustache and frowning severely.

Last of all, the porter was brought in and treated like the passengers, but more distinctly as a prisoner. He had a guard all to himself; and it seemed as though he was the object of peculiar suspicion. It had no great effect upon him, for, while the rest of the party were very plainly sad, and a prey to lively apprehension, the porter sat dull and unmoved, with the stolid, sluggish, unconcerned aspect of a man just roused from sound sleep and relapsing into slumber, who takes little notice of what is passing around.

Meanwhile, the sleeping-car, with its contents, especially the corpse of the victim, was shunted into a siding, and sentries were placed on it at both ends. Seals had been affixed upon the entrance doors, so that the interior might be kept inviolate until it could be visited and examined by the Chef de la Sûrêté, or Chief of the Detective Service. Everyone and everything awaited the arrival of this all-important functionary.

Chapter II

M. FLOÇON, the Chief, was an early man, and he paid a first visit to his office about 7 A.M.

He lived just round the corner in the Rue des Arcs, and had not far to go to the Prefecture. But even now, soon after daylight, he was correctly dressed, as became a responsible ministerial officer. He wore a tight frock coat and an immaculate white tie; under his arm he carried the regulation portfolio, or lawyer's bag, stuffed full of reports, dispositions, and documents dealing with cases in hand. He was altogether a very precise and natty little personage, quiet and unpretending in demeanour, with a mild, thoughtful face in which two small ferrety eyes blinked and twinkled behind gold-rimmed glasses. But when things went wrong, when he had to deal with fools, or when scent was keen, or the enemy near, he would become as fierce and eager as any terrier.

He had just taken his place at his table and begun to arrange his papers, which, being a man of method, he kept carefully sorted by lots each in an old copy of the Figaro, when he was called to the telephone. His services were greatly needed, as we know, at the Lyons station and the summons was to the following effect:

"Crime on train No. 45. A man murdered in the sleeper. All the passengers held. Please come at once. Most important."

A fiacre was called instantly, and M. Floçon, accompanied by Galipaud and Block, the two first inspectors for duty, was driven with all possible speed across Paris.

He was met outside the station, just under the wide verandah, by the officials, who gave him a brief outline of the facts, so far as they were known, and as they have already been put before the reader.

"The passengers have been detained?" asked M. Floçon at once.

"Those in the sleeping-car only –"

"Tut, tut! They should have been all kept – at least until you had taken their names and addresses. Who knows what they might not have been able to tell?"

It was suggested that as the crime was committed presumably while the train was in motion, only those in the one car could be implicated.

"We should never jump to conclusions," said the Chief snappishly. "Well, show me the train card – the list of the travellers in the sleeper."

"It cannot be found, sir."

"Impossible! Why, it is the porter's business to deliver it at the end of the journey to his superiors, and under the law – to us. Where is the porter? In custody?"

"Surely, sir, but there is something wrong with him."

"So I should think! Nothing of this kind could well occur without his knowledge. If he was doing his duty – unless, of course, he – but let us avoid hasty conjectures."

"He has also lost the passengers' tickets, which you know he retains till the end of the journey. After the catastrophe, however, he was unable to lay his hand upon his pocket-book. It contained all his papers."

"Worse and worse. There is something behind all this. Take me to him. Stay, can I have a private room close to the other – where the prisoners, those held on suspicion, are? It will be necessary to hold investigations, take their depositions. M. le Juge will be here directly."

M. Floçon was soon installed in a room actually communicating with the waiting-room, and as a preliminary of the first importance, taking precedence even of the examination of the sleeping-car, he ordered the porter to be brought in to answer certain questions.

The man, Ludwig Groote, as he presently gave his name, thirty-two years of age, born at Amsterdam, looked such a sluggish, slouching, blear-eyed creature that M. Floçon began by a sharp rebuke.

"Now. Sharp! Are you always like this?" cried the Chief.

The porter still stared straight before him with lack-lustre eyes, and made no immediate reply.

"Are you drunk? Are you – can it be possible?" he said, and in vague reply to a sudden strong suspicion, he went on:

"What were you doing between Laroche and Paris? Sleeping?"

The man roused himself a little. "I think I slept. I must have slept. I was very drowsy. I had been up two nights; but so it is always, and I am not like this generally. I do not understand."

"Hah!" The Chief thought he understood. "Did you feel this drowsiness before leaving Laroche?"

"No, monsieur, I did not. Certainly not. I was fresh till then – quite fresh."

"Hum; exactly; I see;" and the little Chief jumped to his feet and ran round to where the porter stood sheepishly, and sniffed and smelt at him.

"Yes, yes." Sniff, sniff, sniff, the little man danced round and round him, then took hold of the porter's head with one hand, and with the other turned down his lower eyelid so as to expose the eyeball, sniffed a little more, and then resumed his seat.

"Exactly. And now, where is your train card?"

"Pardon, monsieur, I cannot find it."

"That is absurd. Where do you keep it? Look again – search – I must have it."

The porter shook his head hopelessly.

"It is gone, monsieur, and my pocket-book."

"But your papers, the tickets –"

"Everything was in it, monsieur. I must have dropped it."

Strange, very strange. However – the fact was to be recorded, for the moment. He could of course return to it.

"You can give me the names of the passengers?"

"No, monsieur. Not exactly. I cannot remember, not enough to distinguish between them."

"Fichtre! But this is most devilishly irritating. To think that I have to do with a man so stupid – such an idiot, such an ass! At least you know how the berths were occupied, how many in each, and which persons? Yes? You can tell me that? Well, go on. By and by we will have the passengers in, and you can fix their places, after I have ascertained their names. Now, please! For how many was the car?"

"Sixteen. There were two compartments of four berths each, and four of two berths each."

"Stay, let us make a plan. I will draw it. Here, now, is that right?" and the Chief held up the rough diagram.

"Here we have the six compartments. Now take *a*, with berths 1, 2, 3, and 4. Were they all occupied?"

"No; only two, by Englishmen. I know that they talked English, which I understand a little. One was a soldier; the other, I think, a clergyman, or priest."

"Good! We can verify that directly. Now, *b*, with berths 5 and 6. Who was there?"

"One gentleman. I don't remember his name. But I shall know him by appearance."

"Go on. In *c*, two berths, 7 and 8?"

"Also one gentleman. It was he who – I mean, that is where the crime occurred."

"Ah, indeed, in 7 and 8? Very well. And the next, 9 and 10?"

"A lady. Our only lady. She came from Rome."

"One moment. Where did the rest come from? Did any embark on the road?"

"No, monsieur; all the passengers travelled through from Rome."

"The dead man included? Was he Roman?"

"That I cannot say, but he came on board at Rome."

"Very well. This lady – she was alone?"

"In the compartment, yes. But not altogether."

"I do not understand!"

"She had her servant with her."

"In the car?"

"No, not in the car. As a passenger by second class. But she came to her mistress sometimes, in the car."

"For her service, I presume?"

"Well, yes, monsieur, when I would permit it. But she came a little too often, and I was compelled to protest, to speak to Madame la Comtesse –"

"She was a countess, then?"

"The maid addressed her by that title. That is all I know. I heard her."

"When did you see the lady's maid last?"

"Last night. I think at Amberieux. About 8 P.M."

"Not this morning?"

"No, sir, I am quite sure of that."

"Not at Laroche? She did not come on board to stay, for the last stage, when her mistress would be getting up, dressing, and likely to require her?"

"No; I should not have permitted it."

"And where is the maid now, d'you suppose?"

The porter looked at him with an air of complete imbecility.

"She is surely somewhere near, in or about the station. She would hardly desert her mistress now," he said, stupidly, at last.

"At any rate we can soon settle that." The Chief turned to one of his assistants, both of whom had been standing behind him all the time, and said:

"Step out, Galipaud, and see. No, wait. I am nearly as stupid as this simpleton. Describe this maid."

"Tall and slight, dark-eyed, very black hair. Dressed all in black, plain black bonnet. I cannot remember more."

"Find her, Galipaud – keep your eye on her. We may want her – why, I cannot say, as she seems disconnected with the event, but still she ought to be at hand." Then, turning to the porter, he went on. "Finish, please. You said 9 and 10 was the lady's. Well, 11 and 12?"

"It was vacant all through the run."

"And the last compartment, for four?"

"There were two berths, occupied both by Frenchmen, at least so I judged them. They talked French to each other and to me."

"Then now we have them all. Stand aside, please, and I will make the passengers come in. We will then determine their places and affix their names from their own admissions. Call them in, Block, one by one."

Chapter III

THE QUESTIONS put by M. Floçon were much the same in every case, and were limited in this early stage of the inquiry to the one point of identity.

The first who entered was a Frenchman. He was a jovial, fat-faced, portly man, who answered to the name of Anatole Lafolay, and who described himself as a traveller in precious stones.

The berth he had occupied was No. 13 in compartment *f*. His companion in the berth was a younger man, smaller, slighter, but of much the same stamp. His name was Jules Devaux, and he was a commission agent. His berth had been No. 15 in the same compartment, *f*. Both these Frenchmen gave their addresses with the names of many people to whom they were well known, and established at once a reputation for respectability which was greatly in their favour.

The third to appear was the tall, gray-headed Englishman, who had taken a certain lead at the first discovery of the crime. He called himself General Sir Charles Collingham, an officer of her Majesty's army; and the clergyman who shared the compartment was his brother, the Reverend Silas Collingham, rector of Theakstone-Lammas, in the county of Norfolk. Their berths were numbered 1 and 4 in *a*.

Before the English General was dismissed, he asked whether he was likely to be detained.

"For the present, yes," replied M. Floçon, briefly. He did not care to be asked questions. That, under the circumstances, was his business.

"Because I should like to communicate with the British Embassy."

"You are known there?" asked the detective, not choosing to believe the story at first. It might be a ruse of some sort.

"I know Lord Dufferin personally; I was with him in India. Also Colonel Papillon, the military attaché; we were in the same regiment. If I sent to the Embassy, the latter would, no doubt, come himself."

"How do you propose to send?"

"That is for you to decide. All I wish is that it should be known that my brother and I are detained under suspicion, and incriminated."

"Hardly that, Monsieur le General. But it shall be as you wish. We will telephone from here to the post nearest the Embassy to inform his Excellency –"

"Certainly, Lord Dufferin, and my friend, Colonel Papillon."

"– of what has occurred. And now, if you will permit me to proceed?"

So the single occupant of the compartment *b*, that adjoining the Englishmen, was called in. He was an Italian, by name Natale Ripaldi; a dark-skinned man, with very black hair and a bristling black moustache. He wore a long dark cloak of the Inverness order, and, with the slouch hat he carried in his hand, and his downcast, secretive look, he had the rather conventional aspect of a conspirator.

"If monsieur permits," he volunteered to say after the formal questioning was over, "I can throw some light on this catastrophe."

"And how so, pray? Did you assist? Were you present? If so, why wait to speak till now?" said the detective, receiving the advance rather coldly. It behooved him to be very much on his guard.

"I have had no opportunity till now of addressing anyone in authority. You are in authority, I presume?"

"I am the Chief of the Detective Service."

"Then, monsieur, remember, please, that I can give some useful information when called upon. Now, indeed, if you will receive it."

M. Floçon was so anxious to approach the inquiry without prejudice that he put up his hand.

"We will wait, if you please. When M. le Juge arrives, then, perhaps; at any rate, at a later stage. That will do now, thank you."

The Italian's lip curled with a slight indication of contempt at the French detective's methods, but he bowed without speaking, and went out.

Last of all the lady appeared, in a long sealskin travelling cloak, and closely veiled. She answered M. Floçon's questions in a low, tremulous voice, as though greatly perturbed.

She was the Contessa di Castagneto, she said, an Englishwoman by birth; but her husband had been an Italian, as the name implied, and they resided in Rome. He was dead – she had been a widow for two or three years, and was on her way now to London.

"That will do, madame, thank you," said the detective, politely, "for the present at least."

"Why, are we likely to be detained? I trust not." Her voice became appealing, almost piteous. Her hands, restlessly moving, showed how much she was distressed.

"Indeed, Madame la Comtesse, it must be so. I regret it infinitely; but until we have gone further into this, have elicited some facts, arrived at some conclusions – But there, madame, I need not, must not say more."

"Oh, monsieur, I was so anxious to continue my journey. Friends are awaiting me in London. I do hope – I most earnestly beg and entreat you to spare me. I am not very strong; my health is indifferent. Do, sir, be so good as to release me from –"

As she spoke, she raised her veil, and showed what no woman wishes to hide, least of all when seeking the good-will of one of the opposite sex. She had a handsome face – strikingly so. Not even the long journey, the fatigue, the worries and anxieties which had supervened, could rob her of her marvellous beauty.

She was a brilliant brunette, dark-skinned; but her complexion was of a clear, pale olive, and as soft, as lustrous as pure ivory. Her great eyes, of a deep velvety brown, were saddened by near tears. She had rich red lips, the only colour in her face, and these, habitually slightly apart, showed pearly-white glistening teeth.

It was difficult to look at this charming woman without being affected by her beauty. M. Floçon was a Frenchman, gallant and impressionable; yet he steeled his heart. A detective must beware of sentiment, and he seemed to see something insidious in this appeal, which he resented.

"Madame, it is useless," he answered gruffly. "I do not make the law; I have only to support it. Every good citizen is bound to that."

"I trust I am a good citizen," said the Countess, with a wan smile, but very wearily. "Still, I should wish to be let off now. I have suffered greatly, terribly, by this horrible catastrophe. My nerves are quite shattered. It is too cruel. However, I can say no more, except to ask that you will let my maid come to me."

M. Floçon, still obdurate, would not even consent to that.

"I fear, madame, that for the present at least you cannot be allowed to communicate with anyone, not even with your maid."

"But she is not implicated; she was not in the car. I have not seen her since –"

"Since?" repeated M. Floçon, after a pause.

"Since last night, at Amberieux, about eight o'clock. She helped me to undress, and saw me to bed. I sent her away then, and said I should not need her till we reached Paris. But I want her now, indeed I do."

"She did not come to you at Laroche?"

"No. Have I not said so? The porter," – here she pointed to the man, who stood staring at her from the other side of the table – "he made difficulties about her being in the car, saying that she came too often, stayed too long, that I must pay for her berth, and so on. I did not see why I should do that; so she stayed away."

"Except from time to time?"

"Precisely."

"And the last time was at Amberieux?"

"As I have told you, and he will tell you the same."

"Thank you, madame, that will do." The Chief rose from his chair, plainly intimating that the interview was at an end.

Chapter IV

HE HAD other work to do, and was eager to get at it. So he left Block to show the Countess back to the waiting-room, and, motioning to the porter that he might also go, the Chief hastened to the sleeping-car, the examination of which, too long delayed, claimed his urgent attention.

It is the first duty of a good detective to visit the actual theatre of a crime and overhaul it inch by inch – seeking, searching, investigating, looking for any, even the most insignificant, traces of the murderer's hands.

The sleeping-car, as I have said, had been side-tracked, its doors were sealed, and it was under strict watch and ward. But everything, of course, gave way before the detective, and, breaking through the seals, he walked in, making straight for the little room or compartment where the body of the victim still lay untended and absolutely untouched.

It was a ghastly sight, although not new in M. Floçon's experience. There lay the corpse in the narrow berth, just as it had been stricken. It was partially undressed, wearing only shirt and drawers. The former lay open at the chest, and showed the gaping wound that had, no doubt, caused death, probably instantaneous death. But other blows had been struck; there must have been a struggle, fierce and embittered, as for dear life. The savage truculence of the murderer had triumphed, but not until he had battered in the face, destroying features and rendering recognition almost impossible.

A knife had given the mortal wound; that was at once apparent from the shape of the wound. It was the knife, too, which had gashed and stabbed the face, almost wantonly; for some of these wounds had not bled, and the plain inference was that they had been inflicted after life had sped. M. Floçon examined the body closely, but without disturbing it. The police medical officer would wish to see it as it was found. The exact position, as well as the nature of the wounds, might afford evidence as to the manner of death.

But the Chief looked long, and with absorbed, concentrated interest, at the murdered man, noting all he actually saw, and conjecturing a good deal more.

The features of the mutilated face were all but unrecognizable, but the hair, which was abundant, was long, black, and inclined to curl; the black moustache was thick and drooping. The shirt was of fine linen, the drawers silk. On one finger were two good rings, the hands were clean, the nails well kept, and there was every evidence that the man did not live by manual labour. He was of the easy, cultured class, as distinct from the workman or operative.

This conclusion was borne out by his light baggage, which still lay about the berth – hat-box, rugs, umbrella, brown morocco hand-bag. All were the property of someone well to do, or at least possessed of decent belongings. One or two pieces bore a monogram, 'F.Q.,' the same as on the shirt and under-linen; but on the bag was a luggage label, with the name, 'Francis Quadling, passenger to Paris,' in full. Its owner had apparently no reason to conceal his name. More strangely, those who had done him to death had been at no pains to remove all traces of his identity.

M. Floçon opened the hand-bag, seeking for further evidence; but found nothing of importance – only loose collars, cuffs, a sponge and slippers, two Italian newspapers of an earlier date. No money, valuables, or papers. All these had been removed probably, and presumably, by the perpetrator of the crime.

Having settled the first preliminary but essential points, he next surveyed the whole compartment critically. Now, for the first time, he was struck with the fact that the window was open to its full height. Since when was this? It was a question to be put presently to the porter and any others who had entered the car, but the discovery drew him to examine the window more closely, and with good results.

At the ledge, caught on a projecting point on the far side, partly in, partly out of the car, was a morsel of white lace, a scrap of feminine apparel; although what part, or how it had come there, was not at once obvious to M. Floçon. A long and minute inspection of this bit of lace, which he was careful not to detach as yet from the place in which he found it, showed that it was ragged, and frayed, and fast caught where it hung. It could not have been blown there by any chance air; it must have been torn from the article to which it belonged, whatever that might be – head-dress, nightcap, night-dress, or handkerchief. The lace was of a kind to serve any of these purposes.

Inspecting further, M. Floçon made a second discovery. On the small table under the window was a short length of black jet beading, part of the trimming or ornamentation of a lady's dress.

These two objects of feminine origin – one partly outside the car, the other near it, but quite inside – gave rise to many conjectures. It led, however, to the inevitable conclusion that a woman had been at some time or other in the berth. M. Floçon could not but connect these two finds with the fact of the open window. The latter might, of course, have been the work of the murdered man himself at an earlier hour. Yet it is unusual, as the detective imagined, for a passenger, and especially an Italian, to lie under an open window in a sleeping-berth when travelling by express train before daylight in March.

Who opened that window, then, and why? Perhaps some further facts might be found on the outside of the car. With this idea, M. Floçon left it, and passed on to the line or permanent way.

Here he found himself a good deal below the level of the car. These sleepers have no foot-boards like ordinary carriages; access to them is gained from a platform by the steps at each end. The Chief was short of stature, and he could only approach the window outside by calling one of the guards and ordering him to make the small ladder (*faire la petite echelle*). This meant stooping and giving a back, on which little M. Floçon climbed nimbly, and so was raised to the necessary height.

A close scrutiny revealed nothing unusual. The exterior of the car was encrusted with the mud and dust gathered in the journey, none of which appeared to have been disturbed.

M. Floçon reentered the carriage neither disappointed nor pleased; his mind was in an open state, ready to receive any impressions, and as yet only one that was at all clear and distinct was borne in on him.

This was the presence of the lace and the jet beads in the theatre of the crime. The inference was fair and simple. He came logically and surely to this:

1. That some woman had entered the compartment.

2. That whether or not she had come in before the crime, she was there after the window had been opened, which was not done by the murdered man.

3. That she had leaned out, or partly passed out, of the window at some time or other, as the scrap of lace testified.

4. Why had she leaned out? To seek some means of exit or escape, of course.

But escape from whom? From what? The murderer? Then she must know him, and unless an accomplice (if so, why run from him?), she would give up her knowledge on compulsion, if not voluntarily, as seemed doubtful, seeing she (his suspicions were consolidating) had not done so already.

But there might be another even stronger reason to attempt escape at such imminent risk as leaving an express train at full speed. To escape from her own act and the consequences it must entail – escape from horror first, from detection next, and then from arrest and punishment.

All this would imperiously impel even a weak woman to face the worst peril, to look out, lean out, even try the terrible but impossible feat of climbing out of the car.

So M. Floçon, by fair process of reasoning, reached a point which incriminated one woman, the only woman possible, and that was the titled, high-bred lady who called herself the Contessa di Castagneto.

This conclusion gave a definite direction to further search. Consulting the rough plan which he had constructed to take the place of the missing train card, he entered the compartment which the Countess had occupied, and which was actually next door.

It was in the tumbled, untidy condition of a sleeping-place but just vacated. The sex and quality of its recent occupant were plainly apparent in the goods and chattels lying about, the property and possessions of a delicate, well-bred woman of the world, things still left as she had used them last – rugs still unrolled, a pair of easy-slippers on the floor, the sponge in its waterproof bag on the bed, brushes, bottles, button-hook, hand-glass, many things belonging to the dressing-bag, not yet returned to that receptacle. The maid was no doubt to have attended to all these, but as she had not come, they remained unpacked and strewn about in some disorder.

M. Floçon pounced down upon the contents of the berth, and commenced an immediate search for a lace scarf, or any wrap or cover with lace.

He found nothing, and was hardly disappointed. It told more against the Countess, who, if innocent, would have no reason to conceal or make away with a possibly incriminating possession, the need for which she could not of course understand.

Next, he handled the dressing-bag, and with deft fingers replaced everything.

Everything was forthcoming but one glass bottle, a small one, the absence of which he noted, but thought of little consequence, till, by and by, he came upon it under peculiar circumstances.

Before leaving the car, and after walking through the other compartments, M. Floçon made an especially strict search of the corner where the porter had his own small chair, his only resting-place, indeed, throughout the journey. He had not forgotten the attendant's condition when first examined, and he had even then been nearly satisfied that the man had been hocussed, narcotized, drugged.

Any doubts were entirely removed by his picking up near the porter's seat a small silver-topped bottle and a handkerchief, both marked with coronet and monogram, the last of which, although the letters were much interlaced and involved, were decipherable as S.L.L.C.

It was that of the Countess, and corresponded with the marks on her other belongings. He put it to his nostril, and recognized at once by its smell that it had contained tincture of laudanum, or some preparation of that drug.

Chapter V

M. FLOÇON was an experienced detective, and he knew so well that he ought to be on his guard against the most plausible suggestions, that he did not like to make too much of these discoveries. Still, he was distinctly satisfied, if not exactly exultant, and he went back towards the station with a strong predisposition against the Contessa di Castagneto.

Just outside the waiting-room, however, his assistant, Galipaud, met him with news which rather dashed his hopes, and gave a new direction to his thoughts.

The lady's maid was not to be found.

"Impossible!" cried the Chief, and then at once suspicion followed surprise.

"I have looked, monsieur, inquired everywhere; the maid has not been seen. She certainly is not here."

"Did she go through the barrier with the other passengers?"

"No one knows; no one remembers her; not even the conductor. But she has gone. That is positive."

"Yet it was her duty to be here; to attend to her service. Her mistress would certainly want her – has asked for her! Why should she run away?"

This question presented itself as one of infinite importance, to be pondered over seriously before he went further into the inquiry.

Did the Countess know of this disappearance?

She had asked imploringly for her maid. True, but might that not be a blind? Women are born actresses, and at need can assume any part, convey any impression. Might not the Countess have wished to be dissociated from the maid, and therefore have affected complete ignorance of her flight?

"I will try her further," said M. Floçon to himself.

But then, supposing that the maid had taken herself off of her own accord? Why was it? Why had she done so? Because – because she was afraid of something. If so, of what? No direct accusation could be brought against her on the face of it. She had not been in the sleeping-car at the time of the murder, while the Countess as certainly was; and, according to strong presumption, in the very compartment where the deed was done. If the maid was afraid, why was she afraid?

Only on one possible hypothesis. That she was either in collusion with the Countess, or possessed of some guilty knowledge tending to incriminate the Countess and probably herself. She had run away to avoid any inconvenient questioning tending to get her mistress into trouble, which would react probably on herself.

"We must press the Countess on this point closely; I will put it plainly to M. le Juge," said the detective, as he entered the private room set apart for the police authorities, where he found M. Beaumont le Hardi, the instructing judge, and the Commissary of the Quartier (arrondissement).

A lengthy conference followed among the officials. M. Floçon told all he knew, all he had discovered, gave his views with all the force and fluency of a public prosecutor, and was congratulated warmly on the progress he had made.

"I agree with you, sir," said the instructing judge: "we must have in the Countess first, and pursue the line indicated as regards the missing maid."

"I will fetch her, then. Stay, what can be going on in there?" cried M. Floçon, rising from his seat and running into the outer waiting-room, which, to his surprise and indignation, he found in great confusion.

The guard who was on duty was struggling, in personal conflict almost, with the English General. There was a great hubbub of voices, and the Countess was lying back half-fainting in her chair.

"What's all this? How dare you, sir?"

This to the General, who now had the man by the throat with one hand and with the other was preventing him from drawing his sword. "Desist – forbear! You are opposing legal authority; desist, or I will call in assistance and will have you secured and removed."

The little Chief's blood was up; he spoke warmly, with all the force and dignity of an official who sees the law outraged.

"It is entirely the fault of this ruffian of yours; he has behaved most brutally," replied Sir Charles, still holding him tight.

"Let him go, monsieur; your behaviour is inexcusable. What! You, a military officer of the highest rank, to assault a sentinel! For shame! This is unworthy of you!"

"He deserves to be scragged, the beast!" went on the General, as with one sharp turn of the wrist he threw the guard off, and sent him flying nearly across the room, where, being free at last, the Frenchman drew his sword and brandished it threateningly – from a distance.

But M. Floçon interposed with uplifted hand and insisted upon an explanation.

"It is just this," replied Sir Charles, speaking fast and with much fierceness: "that lady there – poor thing, she is ill, you can see that for yourself, suffering, overwrought; she asked for a glass of water, and this brute, triple brute, as you say in French, refused to bring it."

"I could not leave the room," protested the guard. "My orders were precise."

"So I was going to fetch the water," went on the General angrily, eying the guard as though he would like to make another grab at him, "and this fellow interfered."

"Very properly," added M. Floçon.

"Then why didn't he go himself, or call someone? Upon my word, monsieur, you are not to be complimented upon your people, nor your methods. I used to think that a Frenchman was gallant, courteous, especially to ladies."

The Chief looked a little disconcerted, but remembering what he knew against this particular lady, he stiffened and said severely, "I am responsible for my conduct to my superiors, and not to you. Besides, you appear to forget your position. You are here, detained – all of you" – he spoke to the whole room – "under suspicion. A ghastly crime has been perpetrated – by someone among you –"

"Do not be too sure of that," interposed the irrepressible General.

"Who else could be concerned? The train never stopped after leaving Laroche," said the detective, allowing himself to be betrayed into argument.

"Yes, it did," corrected Sir Charles, with a contemptuous laugh; "shows how much you know."

Again the Chief looked unhappy. He was on dangerous ground, face to face with a new fact affecting all his theories, – if fact it was, not mere assertion, and that he must speedily verify. But nothing was to be gained – much, indeed, might be lost – by prolonging this discussion in the presence of the whole party. It was entirely opposed to the French practice of investigation, which works secretly, taking witnesses separately, one by one, and strictly preventing all intercommunication or collusion among them.

"What I know or do not know is my affair," he said, with an indifference he did not feel. "I shall call upon you, M. le Général, for your statement in due course, and that of the others." He bowed stiffly to the whole room. "Every one must be interrogated. M. le Juge is now here, and he proposes to begin, madame, with you."

The Countess gave a little start, shivered, and turned very pale.

"Can't you see she is not equal to it?" cried the General, hotly. "She has not yet recovered. In the name of – I do not say chivalry, for that would be useless – but of common humanity, spare madame, at least for the present."

"That is impossible, quite impossible. There are reasons why Madame la Comtesse should be examined first. I trust, therefore, she will make an effort."

"I will try, if you wish it." She rose from her chair and walked a few steps rather feebly, then stopped.

"No, no, Countess, do not go," said Sir Charles, hastily, in English, as he moved across to where she stood and gave her his hand. "This is sheer cruelty, sir, and cannot be permitted."

"Stand aside!" shouted M. Floçon; "I forbid you to approach that lady, to address her, or communicate with her. Guard, advance, do your duty."

But the guard, although his sword was still out of its sheath, showed great reluctance to move. He had no desire to try conclusions again with this very masterful person, who was, moreover, a general; as he had seen service, he had a deep respect for generals, even of foreign growth.

Meanwhile the General held his ground and continued his conversation with the Countess, speaking still in English, thus exasperating M. Floçon, who did not understand the language, almost to madness.

"This is not to be borne!" he cried. "Here, Galipaud, Block;" and when his two trusty assistants came rushing in, he pointed furiously to the General. "Seize him, remove him by force if necessary. He shall go to the *violon* – to the nearest lock-up."

The noise attracted also the Judge and the Commissary, and there were now six officials in all, including the guard, all surrounding the General, a sufficiently imposing force to overawe even the most recalcitrant fire-eater.

But now the General seemed to see only the comic side of the situation, and he burst out laughing.

"What, all of you? How many more? Why not bring up cavalry and artillery, horse, foot, and guns?" he asked, derisively. "All to prevent one old man from offering his services to one weak woman! Gentlemen, my regards!"

"Really, Charles, I fear you are going too far," said his brother the clergyman, who, however, had been manifestly enjoying the whole scene.

"Indeed, yes. It is not necessary, I assure you," added the Countess, with tears of gratitude in her big brown eyes. "I am most touched, most thankful. You are a true soldier, a true English gentleman, and I shall never forget your kindness." Then she put her hand in his with a pretty, winning gesture that was reward enough for any man.

Meanwhile, the Judge, the senior official present, had learned exactly what had happened, and he now addressed the General with a calm but stern rebuke.

"Monsieur will not, I trust, oblige us to put in force the full power of the law. I might, if I chose, and as I am fully entitled, commit you at once to Mazas, to keep you in solitary confinement. Your conduct has been deplorable, well calculated to traverse and impede justice. But I am willing to believe that you were led away, not unnaturally, as a gallant gentleman – it is the characteristic of your nation, of your cloth – and that on more mature consideration you will acknowledge and not repeat your error."

M. Beaumont le Hardi was a grave, florid, soft-voiced person, with a bald head and a comfortably-lined white waistcoat; one who sought his ends by persuasion, not force, but who had the instincts of a gentleman, and little sympathy with the peremptory methods of his more inflammable colleague.

"Oh, with all my heart, monsieur," said Sir Charles, cordially. "You saw, or at least know, how this has occurred. I did not begin it, nor was I the most to blame. But I was in the wrong, I admit. What do you wish me to do now?"

"Give me your promise to abide by our rules – they may be irksome, but we think them necessary – and hold no further converse with your companions."

"Certainly, certainly, monsieur – at least after I have said one word more to Madame la Comtesse."

"No, no, I cannot permit even that –"

But Sir Charles, in spite of the warning finger held up by the Judge, insisted upon crying out to her, as she was being led into the other room:

"Courage, dear lady, courage. Don't let them bully you. You have nothing to fear."

Any further defiance of authority was now prevented by her almost forcible removal from the room.

Chapter VI

THE STORMY episode just ended had rather a disturbing effect on M. Floçon, who could scarcely give his full attention to all the points, old and new, that had now arisen in the investigation. But he would have time to go over them at his leisure, while the work of interrogation was undertaken by the Judge.

The latter had taken his seat at a small table, and just opposite was his *greffier*, or clerk, who was to write down question and answer, *verbatim*. A little to one side, with the light full on the face, the witness was seated, bearing the scrutiny of three pairs of eyes – the Judge first, and behind him, those of the Chief Detective and the Commissary of Police.

"I trust, madame, that you are equal to answering a few questions?" began M. le Hardi, blandly.

"Oh, yes, I hope so. Indeed, I have no choice," replied the Countess, bravely resigned.

"They will refer principally to your maid."

"Ah!" said the Countess, quickly and in a troubled voice, yet she bore the gaze of the three officials without flinching.

"I want to know a little more about her, if you please."

"Of course. Anything I know I will tell you." She spoke now with perfect self-possession. "But if I might ask – why this interest?"

"I will tell you frankly. You asked for her, we sent for her, and –"

"Yes?"

"She cannot be found. She is not in the station."

The Countess all but jumped from her chair in her surprise – surprise that seemed too spontaneous to be feigned.

"Impossible! It cannot be. She would not dare to leave me here like this, all alone."

"*Parbleu!* She has dared. Most certainly she is not here."

"But what can have become of her?"

"Ah, madame, what indeed? Can you form any idea? We hoped you might have been able to enlighten us."

"I cannot, monsieur, not in the least."

"Perchance you sent her on to your hotel to warn your friends that you were detained? To fetch them, perhaps, to you in your trouble?"

The trap was neatly contrived, but she was not deceived.

"How could I? I knew of no trouble when I saw her last."

"Oh, indeed? And when was that?"

"Last night, at Amberieux, as I have already told that gentleman." She pointed to M. Floçon, who was obliged to nod his head.

"Well, she has gone away somewhere. It does not much matter, still it is odd, and for your sake we should like to help you to find her, if you do wish to find her?"

Another little trap which failed.

"Indeed I hardly think she is worth keeping after this barefaced desertion."

"No, indeed. And she must be held to strict account for it, must justify it, give her reasons. So we must find her for you–"

"I am not at all anxious, really," the Countess said, quickly, and the remark told against her.

"Well, now, Madame la Comtesse, as to her description. Will you tell us what was her height, figure, colour of eyes, hair, general appearance?"

"She was tall, above the middle height, at least; slight, good figure, black hair and eyes."

"Pretty?"

"That depends upon what you mean by 'pretty.' Some people might think so, in her own class."

"How was she dressed?"

"In plain dark serge, bonnet of black straw and brown ribbons. I do not allow my maid to wear colours."

"Exactly. And her name, age, place of birth?"

"Hortense Petitpré, thirty-two, born, I believe, in Paris."

The Judge, when these particulars had been given, looked over his shoulder towards the detective, but said nothing. It was quite unnecessary, for M. Floçon, who had been writing in his note-book, now rose and left the room. He called Galipaud to him, saying sharply:

"Here is the more detailed description of the lady's maid, and in writing. Have it copied and circulate it at once. Give it to the station-master, and to the agents of police round about here. I have an idea – only an idea – that this woman has not gone far. It may be worth nothing, still there is the chance. People who are wanted often hang about the very place they would *not* stay in if they were wise. Anyhow, set a watch for her and come back here."

Meanwhile, the Judge had continued his questioning.

"And where, madame, did you obtain your maid?"

"In Rome. She was there, out of a place. I heard of her at an agency and registry office, when I was looking for a maid a month or two ago."

"Then she has not been long in your service?"

"No; as I tell you, she came to me in December last."

"Well recommended?"

"Strongly. She had lived with good families, French and English."

"And with you, what was her character?"

"Irreproachable."

"Well, so much for Hortense Petitpré. She is not far off, I dare say. When we want her we shall be able to lay hands on her, I do not doubt, madame may rest assured."

"Pray take no trouble in the matter. I certainly should not keep her."

"Very well, very well. And now, another small matter. I see," he referred to the rough plan of the sleeping-car prepared by M. Floçon – "I see that you occupied the compartment *d*, with berths Nos. 9 and 10?"

"I think 9 was the number of my berth."

"It was. You may be certain of that. Now next door to your compartment – do you know who was next door? I mean in 7 and 8?"

The Countess's lip quivered, and she was a prey to sudden emotion as she answered in a low voice:

"It was where – where –"

"There, there, madame," said the Judge, reassuring her as he would a little child. "You need not say. It is no doubt very distressing to you. Yet, you know?"

She bent her head slowly, but uttered no word.

"Now this man, this poor man, had you noticed him at all? No – no – not afterwards, of course. It would not be likely. But during the journey. Did you speak to him, or he to you?"

"No, no – distinctly no."

"Nor see him?"

"Yes, I saw him, I believe, at Modane with the rest when we dined."

"Ah! Exactly so. He dined at Modane. Was that the only occasion on which you saw him? You had never met him previously in Rome, where you resided?"

"Whom do you mean? The murdered man?"

"Who else?"

"No, not that I am aware of. At least I did not recognize him as a friend."

"I presume, if he was among your friends –"

"Pardon me, that he certainly was not," interrupted the Countess.

"Well, among your acquaintances – he would probably have made himself known to you?"

"I suppose so."

"And he did not do so? He never spoke to you, nor you to him?"

"I never saw him, the occupant of that compartment, except on that one occasion. I kept a good deal in my compartment during the journey."

"Alone? It must have been very dull for you," said the Judge, pleasantly.

"I was not always alone," said the Countess, hesitatingly, and with a slight flush. "I had friends in the car."

"Oh – oh" – the exclamation was long-drawn and rather significant.

"Who were they? You may as well tell us, madame, we should certainly find out."

"I have no wish to withhold the information," she replied, now turning pale, possibly at the imputation conveyed. "Why should I?"

"And these friends were –?"

"Sir Charles Collingham and his brother. They came and sat with me occasionally; sometimes one, sometimes the other."

"During the day?"

"Of course, during the day." Her eyes flashed, as though the question was another offence.

"Have you known them long?"

"The General I met in Roman society last winter. It was he who introduced his brother."

"Very good, so far. The General knew you, took an interest in you. That explains his strange, unjustifiable conduct just now –"

"I do not think it was either strange or unjustifiable," interrupted the Countess, hotly. "*He* is a gentleman."

"Quite a *preux cavalier*, of course. But we will pass on. You are not a good sleeper, I believe, madame?"

"Indeed no, I sleep badly, as a rule."

"Then you would be easily disturbed. Now, last night, did you hear anything strange in the car, more particularly in the adjoining compartment?"

"Nothing."

"No sound of voices raised high, no noise of a conflict, a struggle?"

"No, monsieur."

"That is odd. I cannot understand it. We know, beyond all question, from the appearance of the body – the corpse – that there was a fight, an encounter. Yet you, a wretched sleeper, with only a thin plank of wood between you and the affray, hear nothing, absolutely nothing. It is *most* extraordinary."

"I was asleep. I must have been asleep."

"A light sleeper would certainly be awakened. How can you explain – how can you reconcile that?" The question was blandly put, but the Judge's incredulity verged upon actual insolence.

"Easily: I had taken a soporific. I always do, on a journey. I am obliged to keep something, sulphonal or chloral, by me, on purpose."

"Then this, madame, is yours?" And the Judge, with an air of undisguised triumph, produced the small glass vial which M. Floçon had picked up in the sleeping-car near the conductor's seat.

The Countess, with a quick gesture, put out her hand to take it.

"No, I cannot give it up. Look as near as you like, and say is it yours?"

"Of course it is mine. Where did you get it? Not in my berth?"

"No, madame, not in your berth."

"But where?"

"Pardon me, we shall not tell you – not just now."

"I missed it last night," went on the Countess, slightly confused.

"After you had taken your dose of chloral?"

"No, before."

"And why did you want this? It is laudanum."

"For my nerves. I have a toothache. I – I – really, sir, I need not tell you all my ailments."

"And the maid had removed it?"

"So I presume; she must have taken it out of the bag in the first instance."

"And then kept it?"

"That is what I can only suppose."

"Ah!"

Chapter VII

WHEN THE JUDGE had brought down the interrogation of the Countess to the production of the small glass bottle, he paused, and with a long-drawn "Ah!" of satisfaction, looked round at his colleagues.

Both M. Floçon and the Commissary nodded their heads approvingly, plainly sharing his triumph.

Then they all put their heads together in close, whispered conference.

"Admirable, M. le Juge!" said the detective. "You have been most adroit. It is a clear case."

"No doubt," said the Commissary, who was a blunt, rather coarse person, believing that to take anybody and everybody into custody is always the safest and simplest course. "It looks black against her. I think she ought to be arrested at once."

"We might, indeed we ought to have more evidence, more definite evidence, perhaps?" The Judge was musing over the facts as he knew them. "I should like, before going further, to look at the car," he said, suddenly coming to a conclusion.

M. Floçon readily agreed. "We will go together," he said, adding, "Madame will remain here, please, until we return. It may not be for long."

"And afterwards?" asked the Countess, whose nervousness had if anything increased during the whispered colloquy of the officials.

"Ah, afterwards! Who knows?" was the reply, with a shrug of the shoulders, all most enigmatic and unsatisfactory.

"What have we against her?" said the Judge, as soon as they had gained the absolute privacy of the sleeping-car.

"The bottle of laudanum and the porter's condition. He was undoubtedly drugged," answered the detective; and the discussion which followed took the form of a dialogue between them, for the Commissary took no part in it.

"Yes; but why by the Countess? How do we know that positively?"

"It is her bottle," said M. Floçon.

"Her story may be true – that she missed it, that the maid took it."

"We have nothing whatever against the maid. We know nothing about her."

"No. Except that she has disappeared. But that tells more against her mistress. It is all very vague. I do not see my way quite, as yet."

"But the fragment of lace, the broken beading? Surely, M. le Juge, they are a woman's, and only one woman was in the car –"

"So far as we know."

"But if these could be proved to be hers?"

"Ah! If you could prove that!"

"Easy enough. Have her searched, here at once, in the station. There is a female searcher attached to the detention-room."

"It is a strong measure. She is a lady."

"Ladies who commit crimes must not expect to be handled with kid gloves."

"She is an Englishwoman, or with English connections; titled, too. I hesitate, upon my word. Suppose we are wrong? It may lead to unpleasantness. M. le Prefet is anxious to avoid complications possibly international."

As he spoke, he bent over, and, taking a magnifier from his pocket, examined the lace, which still fluttered where it was caught.

"It is fine lace, I think. What say you, M. Floçon? You may be more experienced in such matters."

"The finest, or nearly so; I believe it is Valenciennes – the trimming of some underclothing, I should think. That surely is sufficient, M. le Juge?"

M. Beaumont le Hardi gave a reluctant consent, and the Chief went back himself to see that the searching was undertaken without loss of time.

The Countess protested, but vainly, against this new indignity. What could she do? A prisoner, practically friendless – for the General was not within reach – to resist was out of the question. Indeed, she was plainly told that force would be employed unless she submitted with a good grace. There was nothing for it but to obey.

Mother Tontaine, as the female searcher called herself, was an evil-visaged, corpulent old creature, with a sickly, soft, insinuating voice, and a greasy, familiar manner that was most offensive. They had given her the scrap of torn lace and the débris of the jet as a guide, with very particular directions to see if they corresponded with any part of the lady's apparel.

She soon showed her quality.

"Aha! Oho! What is this, my pretty princess? How comes so great a lady into the hands of Mother Tontaine? But I will not harm you, my beauty, my pretty, my little one. Oh, no, no, I will not trouble you, dearie. No, trust to me;" and she held out one skinny claw, and looked the other way. The Countess did not or would not understand.

"Madame has money?" went on the old hag in a half-threatening, half-coaxing whisper, as she came up quite close, and fastened on her victim like a bird of prey.

"If you mean that I am to bribe you –"

"Fie, the nasty word! But just a small present, a pretty gift, one or two yellow bits, twenty, thirty, forty francs – you'd better." She shook the soft arm she held roughly, and anything seemed preferable than to be touched by this horrible woman.

"Wait, wait!" cried the Countess, shivering all over, and, feeling hastily for her purse, she took out several napoleons.

"Aha! Oho! One, two, three," said the searcher in a fat, wheedling voice. "Four, yes, four, five;" and she clinked the coins together in her palm, while a covetous light came into her faded eyes at the joyous sound. "Five – make it five at once, d'ye hear me? Or I'll call them in and tell them. That will go against you, my princess. What, try to bribe a poor old woman, Mother Tontaine, honest and incorruptible Tontaine? Five, then, five!"

With trembling haste the Countess emptied the whole contents of her purse in the old hag's hand.

"*Bon aubaine*. Nice pickings. It is a misery what they pay me here. I am, oh, so poor, and I have children, many babies. You will not tell them – the police – you dare not. No, no, no."

Thus muttering to herself, she shambled across the room to a corner, where she stowed the money safely away. Then she came back, showed the bit of lace, and pressed it into the Countess's hands.

"Do you know this, little one? Where it comes from, where there is much more? I was told to look for it, to search for it on you;" and with a quick gesture she lifted the edge of the Countess's skirt, dropping it next moment with a low, chuckling laugh.

"Oho! Aha! You were right, my pretty, to pay me, my pretty – right. And some day, today, tomorrow, whenever I ask you, you will remember Mother Tontaine."

The Countess listened with dismay. What had she done? Put herself into the power of this greedy and unscrupulous old beldame?

"And this, my princess? What have we here, aha?"

Mère Tontaine held up next the broken bit of jet ornament for inspection, and as the Countess leaned forward to examine it more closely, gave it into her hand.

"You recognize it, of course. But be careful, my pretty! Beware! If anyone were looking, it would ruin you. I could not save you then. Sh! Say nothing, only look, and quick, give it me back. I must have it to show."

All this time the Countess was turning the jet over and over in her open palm, with a perplexed, disturbed, but hardly a terrified air.

Yes, she knew it, or thought she knew it. It had been – but how had it come here, into the possession of this base myrmidon of the French police?

"Give it me, quick!" There was a loud knock at the door. "They are coming. Remember!" Mother Tontaine put her long finger to her lip. "Not a word! I have found nothing, of course. Nothing, I can swear to that, and you will not forget Mother Tontaine?"

Now M. Floçon stood at the open door awaiting the searcher's report. He looked much disconcerted when the old woman took him on one side and briefly explained that the search had been altogether fruitless.

There was nothing to justify suspicion, nothing, so far as she could find.

The detective looked from one to the other – from the hag he had employed in this unpleasant quest, to the lady on whom it had been tried. The Countess, to his surprise, did not complain. He had expected further and strong upbraidings. Strange to say, she took it very quietly.

There was no indignation in her face. She was still pale, and her hands trembled, but she said nothing, made no reference, at least, to what she had just gone through.

Again he took counsel with his colleague, while the Countess was kept apart.

"What next, M. Floçon?" asked the Judge. "What shall we do with her?"

"Let her go," answered the detective, briefly.

"What! Do you suggest this, sir," said the Judge, slyly. "After your strong and well-grounded suspicions?"

"They are as strong as ever, stronger: and I feel sure I shall yet justify them. But what I wish now is to let her go at large, under surveillance."

"Ah! You would shadow her?"

"Precisely. By a good agent. Galipaud, for instance. He speaks English, and he can, if necessary, follow her anywhere, even to England."

"She can be extradited," said the Commissary, with his one prominent idea of arrest.

"Do you agree, M. le Juge? Then, if you will permit me, I will give the necessary orders, and perhaps you will inform the lady that she is free to leave the station?"

The Countess now had reason to change her opinion of the French officials. Great politeness now replaced the first severity that had been so cruel. She was told, with many bows and apologies, that her regretted but unavoidable detention was at an end. Not only was she freely allowed to depart, but she was escorted by both M. Floçon and the Commissary outside, to where an omnibus was in waiting, and all her baggage piled on top, even to the dressing-bag, which had been neatly repacked for her.

But the little silver-topped vial had not been restored to her, nor the handkerchief.

In her joy at her deliverance, either she had not given these a second thought, or she did not wish to appear anxious to recover them.

Nor did she notice that, as the bus passed through the gates at the bottom of the large slope that leads from the Lyons Station, it was followed at a discreet distance by a modest fiacre, which pulled up, eventually, outside the Hôtel Madagascar. Its occupant, M. Galipaud, kept the Countess in sight, and, entering the hotel at her heels, waited till she had left the office, when he held a long conference with the proprietor.

Chapter VIII

A FIRST STAGE in the inquiry had now been reached, with results that seemed promising, and were yet contradictory.

No doubt the watch to be set on the Countess might lead to something yet – something to bring first plausible suspicion to a triumphant issue; but the examination of the other occupants of the car should not be allowed to slacken on that account. The Countess might have some confederate among them – this pestilent English General, perhaps, who had made himself so conspicuous in her defence; or someone of them might throw light upon her movements, upon her conduct during the journey.

Then, with a spasm of self-reproach, M. Floçon remembered that two distinct suggestions had been made to him by two of the travellers, and that, so far, he had neglected them. One was the significant hint from the Italian that he could materially help the inquiry. The other was the General's sneering assertion that the train had not continued its journey uninterruptedly between Laroche and Paris.

Consulting the Judge, and laying these facts before him, it was agreed that the Italian's offer seemed the most important, and he was accordingly called in next.

"Who and what are you?" asked the Judge, carelessly, but the answer roused him at once to intense interest, and he could not quite resist a glance of reproach at M. Floçon.

"My name I have given you – Natale Ripaldi. I am a detective officer belonging to the Roman police."

"What!" cried M. Floçon, colouring deeply. "This is unheard of. Why in the name of all the devils have you withheld this most astonishing statement until now?"

"Monsieur surely remembers. I told him half an hour ago I had something important to communicate –"

"Yes, yes, of course. But why were you so reticent. Good Heavens!"

"Monsieur was not so encouraging that I felt disposed to force on him what I knew he would have to hear in due course."

"It is monstrous – quite abominable, and shall not end here. Your superiors shall hear of your conduct," went on the Chief, hotly.

"They will also hear, and, I think, listen to my version of the story – that I offered you fairly, and at the first opportunity, all the information I had, and that you refused to accept it."

"You should have persisted. It was your manifest duty. You are an officer of the law, or you say you are."

"Pray telegraph at once, if you think fit, to Rome, to the police authorities, and you will find that Natale Ripaldi – your humble servant – travelled by the through express with their knowledge and authority. And here are my credentials, my official card, some official letters –"

"And what, in a word, have you to tell us?"

"I can tell you who the murdered man was."

"We know that already."

"Possibly; but only his name, I apprehend. I know his profession, his business, his object in travelling, for I was appointed to watch and follow him. That is why I am here."

"Was he a suspicious character, then? A criminal?"

"At any rate he was absconding from Rome, with valuables."

"A thief, in fact?"

The Italian put out the palms of his hands with a gesture of doubt and deprecation.

"Thief is a hard, ugly word. That which he was removing was, or had been, his own property."

"Tut, tut! Do be more explicit and get on," interrupted the little Chief, testily.

"I ask nothing better; but if questions are put to me –"

The Judge interposed.

"Give us your story. We can interrogate you afterwards."

"The murdered man is Francis A. Quadling, of the firm of Correse & Quadling, bankers, in the Via Condotti, Rome. It was an old house, once of good, of the highest repute, but of late years it has fallen into difficulties. Its financial soundness was doubted in certain circles, and the Government was warned that a great scandal was imminent. So the matter was handed over to the police, and I was directed to make inquiries, and to keep my eye on this Quadling" – he jerked his thumb towards the platform, where the body might be supposed to be.

"This Quadling was the only surviving partner. He was well known and liked in Rome, indeed, many who heard the adverse reports disbelieved them, I myself among the number. But my duty was plain –"

"Naturally," echoed the fiery little detective.

"I made it my business to place the banker under surveillance, to learn his habits, his ways of life, see who were his friends, the houses he visited. I soon knew much that I wanted to know, although not all. But one fact I discovered, and think it right to inform you of it at once. He was on intimate terms with La Castagneto – at least, he frequently called upon her."

"La Castagneto! Do you mean the Countess of that name, who was a passenger in the sleeper?"

"Beyond doubt! It is she I mean." The officials looked at each other eagerly, and M. Beaumont le Hardi quickly turned over the sheets on which the Countess's evidence was recorded.

She had denied acquaintance with this murdered man, Quadling, and here was positive evidence that they were on intimate terms!

"He was at her house on the very day we all left Rome – in the evening, towards dusk. The Countess had an apartment in the Via Margutta, and when he left her he returned to his own place in the Condotti, entered the bank, stayed half an hour, then came out with one hand-bag and rug, called a cab, and was driven straight to the railway station."

"And you followed?"

"Of course. When I saw him walk straight to the sleeping-car, and ask the conductor for 7 and 8, I knew that his plans had been laid, and that he was on the point of leaving Rome secretly. When, presently, La Castagneto also arrived, I concluded that she was in his confidence, and that possibly they were eloping together."

"Why did you not arrest him?"

"I had no authority, even if I had had the time. Although I was ordered to watch the Signor Quadling, I had no warrant for his arrest. But I decided on the spur of the moment what course I should take. It seemed to be the only one, and that was to embark in the same train and stick close to my man."

"You informed your superiors, I suppose?"

"Pardon me, monsieur," said the Italian blandly to the Chief, who asked the question, "but have you any right to inquire into my conduct towards my superiors? In all that affects the murder I am at your orders, but in this other matter it is between me and them."

"Ta, ta, ta! They will tell us if you will not. And you had better be careful, lest you obstruct justice. Speak out, sir, and beware. What did you intend to do?"

"To act according to circumstances. If my suspicions were confirmed –"

"What suspicions?"

"Why – that this banker was carrying off any large sum in cash, notes, securities, as in effect he was."

"Ah! You know that? How?"

"By my own eyes. I looked into his compartment once and saw him in the act of counting them over, a great quantity, in fact –"

Again the officials looked at each other significantly. They had got at last to a motive for the crime.

"And that, of course, would have justified his arrest?"

"Exactly. I proposed, directly we arrived in Paris, to claim the assistance of your police and take him into custody. But his fate interposed."

There was a pause, a long pause, for another important point had been reached in the inquiry: the motive for the murder had been made clear, and with it the presumption against the Countess gained terrible strength.

But there was more, perhaps, to be got out of this dark-visaged Italian detective, who had already proved so useful an ally.

"One or two words more," said the Judge to Ripaldi. "During the journey, now, did you have any conversation with this Quadling?"

"None. He kept very much to himself."

"You saw him, I suppose, at the restaurants?"

"Yes, at Modane and Laroche."

"But did not speak to him?"

"Not a word."

"Had he any suspicion, do you think, as to who you were?"

"Why should he? He did not know me. I had taken pains he should never see me."

"Did he speak to any other passenger?"

"Very little. To the Countess. Yes, once or twice, I think, to her maid."

"Ah! That maid. Did you notice her at all? She has not been seen. It is strange. She seems to have disappeared."

"To have run away, in fact?" suggested Ripaldi, with a queer smile.

"Well, at least she is not here with her mistress. Can you offer any explanation of that?"

"She was perhaps afraid. The Countess and she were very good friends, I think. On better, more familiar terms, than is usual between mistress and maid."

"The maid knew something?"

"Ah, monsieur, it is only an idea. But I give it you for what it is worth."

"Well, well, this maid – what was she like?"

"Tall, dark, good-looking, not too reserved. She made other friends – the porter and the English Colonel. I saw the last speaking to her. I spoke to her myself."

"What can have become of her?" said the Judge.

"Would M. le Juge like me to go in search of her? That is, if you have no more questions to ask, no wish to detain me further?"

"We will consider that, and let you know in a moment, if you will wait outside."

And then, when alone, the officials deliberated.

It was a good offer, the man knew her appearance, he was in possession of all the facts, he could be trusted –

"Ah, but can he, though?" queried the detective. "How do we know he has told us truth? What guarantee have we of his loyalty, his good faith? What if he is also concerned in the crime – has some guilty knowledge? What if he killed Quadling himself, or was an accomplice before or after the fact?"

"All these are possibilities, of course, but – pardon me, dear colleague – a little far-fetched, eh?" said the Judge. "Why not utilize this man? If he betrays us – serves us ill – if we had reason to lay hands on him again, he could hardly escape us."

"Let him go, and send someone with him," said the Commissary, the first practical suggestion he had yet made.

"Excellent!" cried the Judge. "You have another man here, Chief; let him go with this Italian."

They called in Ripaldi and told him, "We will accept your services, monsieur, and you can begin your search at once. In what direction do you propose to begin?"

"Where has her mistress gone?"

"How do you know she has gone?"

"At least, she is no longer with us out there. Have you arrested her – or what?"

"No, she is still at large, but we have our eye upon her. She has gone to her hotel – the Madagascar, off the Grands Boulevards."

"Then it is there that I shall look for the maid. No doubt she preceded her mistress to the hotel, or she will join her there very shortly."

"You would not make yourself known, of course? They might give you the slip. You have no authority to detain them, not in France."

"I should take my precautions, and I can always appeal to the police."

"Exactly. That would be your proper course. But you might lose valuable time, a great opportunity, and we wish to guard against that, so we shall associate one of our own people with you in your proceedings."

"Oh! Very well, if you wish. It will, no doubt, be best." The Italian readily assented, but a shrewd listener might have guessed from the tone of his voice that the proposal was not exactly pleasing to him.

"I will call in Block," said the Chief, and the second detective inspector appeared to take his instructions.

He was a stout, stumpy little man, with a barrel-like figure, greatly emphasized by the short frock coat he wore; he had smallish pig's eyes buried deep in a fat face, and his round, chubby cheeks hung low over his turned-down collar.

"This gentleman," went on the Chief, indicating Ripaldi, "is a member of the Roman police, and has been so obliging as to offer us his services. You will accompany him, in the first instance, to the Hôtel Madagascar. Put yourself in communication with Galipaud, who is there on duty."

"Would it not be sufficient if I made myself known to M. Galipaud?" suggested the Italian. "I have seen him here, I should recognize him –"

"That is not so certain; he may have changed his appearance. Besides, he does not know the latest developments, and might not be very cordial."

"You might write me a few lines to take to him."

"I think not. We prefer to send Block," replied the Chief, briefly and decidedly. He did not like this pertinacity, and looked at his colleagues as though he sought their concurrence in altering the arrangements for the Italian's mission. It might be wiser to detain him still.

"It was only to save trouble that I made the suggestion," hastily put in Ripaldi. "Naturally I am in your hands. And if I do not meet with the maid at the hotel, I may have to look further, in which case Monsieur – Block? Thank you – would no doubt render valuable assistance."

This speech restored confidence, and a few minutes later the two detectives, already excellent friends from the freemasonry of a common craft, left the station in a closed cab.

Chapter IX

"WHAT NEXT?" asked the Judge.

"That pestilent English officer, if you please, M. le Juge," said the detective. "That fire-eating, swashbuckling soldier, with his blustering barrack-room ways. I long to come to close quarters with him. He ridiculed me, taunted me, said I knew nothing – we will see, we will see."

"In fact, you wish to interrogate him yourself. Very well. Let us have him in."

When Sir Charles Collingham entered, he included the three officials in one cold, stiff bow, waited a moment, and then, finding he was not offered a chair, said with studied politeness:

"I presume I may sit down?"

"Pardon. Of course; pray be seated," said the Judge, hastily, and evidently a little ashamed of himself.

"Ah! Thanks. Do you object?" went on the General, taking out a silver cigarette-case. "May I offer one?" He handed round the box affably.

"We do not smoke on duty," answered the Chief, rudely. "Nor is smoking permitted in a court of justice."

"Come, come, I wish to show no disrespect. But I cannot recognize this as a court of justice, and I think, if you will forgive me, that I shall take three whiffs. It may help me keep my temper."

He was evidently making game of them. There was no symptom remaining of the recent effervescence when he was acting as the Countess's champion, and he was perfectly – nay, insolently calm and self-possessed.

"You call yourself General Collingham?" went on the Chief.

"I do not call myself. I am General Sir Charles Collingham, of the British Army."

"Retired?"

"No, I am still on the active list."

"These points will have to be verified."

"With all my heart. You have already sent to the British Embassy?"

"Yes, but no one has come," answered the detective, contemptuously.

"If you disbelieve me, why do you question me?"

"It is our duty to question you, and yours to answer. If not, we have means to make you. You are suspected, inculpated in a terrible crime, and your whole attitude is – is – objectionable – unworthy – disgr–"

"Gently, gently, my dear colleague," interposed the Judge. "If you will permit me, I will take up this. And you, M. le Général, I am sure you cannot wish to impede or obstruct us; we represent the law of this country."

"Have I done so, M. le Juge?" answered the General, with the utmost courtesy, as he threw away his half-burned cigarette.

"No, no. I do not imply that in the least. I only entreat you, as a good and gallant gentleman, to meet us in a proper spirit and give us your best help."

"Indeed, I am quite ready. If there has been any unpleasantness, it has surely not been of my making, but rather of that little man there." The General pointed to M. Floçon rather contemptuously, and nearly started a fresh disturbance.

"Well, well, let us say no more of that, and proceed to business. I understand," said the Judge, after fingering a few pages of the dispositions in front of him, "that you are a friend of the Contessa di Castagneto? Indeed, she has told us so herself."

"It was very good of her to call me her friend. I am proud to hear she so considers me."

"How long have you known her?"

"Four or five months. Since the beginning of the last winter season in Rome."

"Did you frequent her house?"

"If you mean, was I permitted to call on her on friendly terms, yes."

"Did you know all her friends?"

"How can I answer that? I know whom I met there from time to time."

"Exactly. Did you often meet among them a Signor – Quadling?"

"Quadling – Quadling? I cannot say that I have. The name is familiar somehow, but I cannot recall the man."

"Have you never heard of the Roman bankers, Correse & Quadling?"

"Ah, of course. Although I have had no dealing with them. Certainly I have never met Mr. Quadling."

"Not at the Countess's?"

"Never – of that I am quite sure."

"And yet we have had positive evidence that he was a constant visitor there."

"It is perfectly incomprehensible to me. Not only have I never met him, but I have never heard the Countess mention his name."

"It will surprise you, then, to be told that he called at her apartment in the Via Margutta on the very evening of her departure from Rome. Called, was admitted, was closeted with her for more than an hour."

"I am surprised, astounded. I called there myself about four in the afternoon to offer my services for the journey, and I too stayed till after five. I can hardly believe it."

"I have more surprises for you, General. What will you think when I tell you that this very Quadling – this friend, acquaintance, call him what you please, but at least intimate enough to pay her a visit on the eve of a long journey – was the man found murdered in the sleeping-car?"

"Can it be possible? Are you sure?" cried Sir Charles, almost starting from his chair. "And what do you deduce from all this? What do you imply? An accusation against that lady? Absurd!"

"I respect your chivalrous desire to stand up for a lady who calls you her friend, but we are officials first, and sentiment cannot be permitted to influence us. We have good reasons for suspecting that lady. I tell you that frankly, and trust to you as a soldier and man of honour not to abuse the confidence reposed in you."

"May I not know those reasons?"

"Because she was in the car – the only woman, you understand – between Laroche and Paris."

"Do you suspect a female hand, then?" asked the General, evidently much interested and impressed.

"That is so, although I am exceeding my duty in revealing this."

"And you are satisfied that this lady, a refined, delicate person in the best society, of the highest character – believe me, I know that to be the case – whom you yet suspect of an atrocious crime, was the only female in the car?"

"Obviously. Who else? What other woman could possibly have been in the car? No one got in at Laroche; the train never stopped till it reached Paris."

"On that last point at least you are quite mistaken, I assure you. Why not upon the other also?"

"The train stopped?" interjected the detective. "Why has no one told us that?"

"Possibly because you never asked. But it is nevertheless the fact. Verify it. Every one will tell you the same."

The detective himself hurried to the door and called in the porter. He was within his rights, of course, but the action showed distrust, at which the General only smiled, but he laughed outright when the still stupid and half-dazed porter, of course, corroborated the statement at once.

"At whose instance was the train pulled up?" asked the detective, and the Judge nodded his head approvingly.

To know that would fix fresh suspicion.

But the porter could not answer the question.

Someone had rung the alarm-bell – so at least the conductor had declared; otherwise they should not have stopped. Yet he, the porter, had not done so, nor did any passenger come forward to admit giving the signal. But there had been a halt. Yes, assuredly.

"This is a new light," the Judge confessed. "Do you draw any conclusion from it?" he went on to ask the General.

"That is surely your business. I have only elicited the fact to disprove your theory. But if you wish, I will tell you how it strikes me."

The Judge bowed assent.

"The bare fact that the train was halted would mean little. That would be the natural act of a timid or excitable person involved indirectly in such a catastrophe. But to disavow the act starts suspicion. The fair inference is that there was some reason, an unavowable reason, for halting the train."

"And that reason would be –"

"You must see it without my assistance, surely! Why, what else but to afford someone an opportunity to leave the car."

"But how could that be? You would have seen that person, some of you, especially at such a critical time. The aisle would be full of people, both exits were thus practically overlooked."

"My idea is – it is only an idea, understand – that the person had already left the car – that is to say, the interior of the car."

"Escaped how? Where? What do you mean?"

"Escaped through the open window of the compartment where you found the murdered man."

"You noticed the open window, then?" quickly asked the detective. "When was that?"

"Directly I entered the compartment at the first alarm. It occurred to me at once that someone might have gone through it."

"But no woman could have done it. To climb out of an express train going at top speed would be an impossible feat for a woman," said the detective, doggedly.

"Why, in God's name, do you still harp upon the woman? Why should it be a woman more than a man?"

"Because" – it was the Judge who spoke, but he paused a moment in deference to a gesture of protest from M. Floçon. The little detective was much concerned at the utter want of reticence displayed by his colleague.

"Because," went on the Judge with decision – "because this was found in the compartment;" and he held out the piece of lace and the scrap of beading for the General's inspection, adding quickly, "You have seen these, or one of them, or something like them before. I am sure of it; I call upon you; I demand – no, I appeal to your sense of honour, Sir Collingham. Tell me, please, exactly what you know."

Chapter X

THE GENERAL sat for a time staring hard at the bit of torn lace and the broken beads. Then he spoke out firmly:

"It is my duty to withhold nothing. It is not the lace. That I could not swear to; for me – and probably for most men – two pieces of lace are very much the same. But I think I have seen these beads, or something exactly like them, before."

"Where? When?"

"They formed part of the trimming of a mantle worn by the Contessa di Castagneto."

"Ah!" It was the same interjection uttered simultaneously by the three Frenchmen, but each had a very different note; in the Judge it was deep interest, in the detective triumph, in the Commissary indignation, as when he caught a criminal red-handed.

"Did she wear it on the journey?" continued the Judge.

"As to that I cannot say."

"Come, come, General, you were with her constantly; you must be able to tell us. We insist on being told." This fiercely, from the now jubilant M. Floçon.

"I repeat that I cannot say. To the best of my recollection, the Countess wore a long travelling cloak – an ulster, as we call them. The jacket with those bead ornaments may have been underneath. But if I have seen them – as I believe I have – it was not during this journey."

Here the Judge whispered to M. Floçon, "The searcher did not discover any second mantle."

"How do we know the woman examined thoroughly?" he replied. "Here, at least, is direct evidence as to the beads. At last the net is drawing round this fine Countess."

"Well, at any rate," said the detective aloud, returning to the General, "these beads were found in the compartment of the murdered man. I should like that explained, please."

"By me? How can I explain it? And the fact does not bear upon what we were considering, as to whether anyone had left the car."

"Why not?"

"The Countess, as we know, never left the car. As to her entering this particular compartment – at any previous time – it is highly improbable. Indeed, it is rather insulting her to suggest it."

"She and this Quadling were close friends."

"So you say. On what evidence I do not know, but I dispute it."

"Then how could the beads get there? They were her property, worn by her."

"Once, I admit, but not necessarily on this journey. Suppose she had given the mantle away – to her maid, for instance; I believe ladies often pass on their things to their maids."

"It is all pure presumption, a mere theory. This maid – she has not as yet been imported into the discussion."

"Then I would suggest that you do so without delay. She is to my mind a – well, rather a curious person."

"You know her – spoke to her?"

"I know her, in a way. I had seen her in the Via Margutta, and I nodded to her when she came first into the car."

"And on the journey – you spoke to her frequently?"

"I? Oh, dear, no, not at all. I noticed her, certainly; I could not help it, and perhaps I ought to tell her mistress. She seemed to make friends a little too readily with people."

"As for instance –?"

"With the porter to begin with. I saw them together at Laroche, in the buffet at the bar; and that Italian, the man who was in here before me; indeed, with the murdered man. She seemed to know them all."

"Do you imply that the maid might be of use in this inquiry?"

"Most assuredly I do. As I tell you, she was constantly in and out of the car, and more or less intimate with several of the passengers."

"Including her mistress, the Countess," put in M. Floçon.

The General laughed pleasantly.

"Most ladies are, I presume, on intimate terms with their maids. They say no man is a hero to his valet. It is the same, I suppose, with the other sex."

"So intimate," went on the little detective, with much malicious emphasis, "that now the maid has disappeared lest she might be asked inconvenient questions about her mistress."

"Disappeared? You are sure?"

"She cannot be found, that is all we know."

"It is as I thought, then. She it was who left the car!" cried Sir Charles, with so much vehemence that the officials were startled out of their dignified reserve, and shouted back almost in a breath: "Explain yourself. Quick, quick. What in God's name do you mean?"

"I had my suspicions from the first, and I will tell you why. At Laroche the car emptied, as you may have heard; everyone except the Countess, at least, went over to the restaurant for early coffee; I with the rest. I was one of the first to finish, and I strolled back to the platform to get a few whiffs of a cigarette. At that moment I saw, or thought I saw, the end of a skirt disappearing into the sleeping-car. I concluded it was this maid, Hortense, who was taking her mistress a cup of coffee. Then my brother came up, we exchanged a few words, and entered the car together."

"By the same door as that through which you had seen the skirt pass?"

"No, by the other. My brother went back to his berth, but I paused in the corridor to finish my cigarette after the train had gone on. By this time everyone but myself had returned to his berth, and I was on the point of lying down again for half an hour, when I distinctly heard the handle turned of the compartment I knew to be vacant all through the run."

"That was the one with berths 11 and 12?"

"Probably. It was next to the Countess. Not only was the handle turned, but the door partly opened –"

"It was not the porter?"

"Oh, no, he was in his seat – you know it, at the end of the car – sound asleep, snoring; I could hear him."

"Did anyone come out of the vacant compartment?"

"No; but I was almost certain, I believe I could swear that I saw the same skirt, just the hem of it, a black skirt, sway forward beyond the door, just for a second. Then all at once the door was closed again fast."

"What did you conclude from this? Or did you think nothing of it?"

"I thought very little. I supposed it was that the maid wished to be near her mistress as we were approaching Paris, and I had heard from the Countess that the porter had made many difficulties. But you see, after what has happened, that there was a reason for stopping the train."

"Quite so," M. Floçon readily admitted, with a scarcely concealed sneer.

He had quite made up his mind now that it was the Countess who had rung the alarm-bell, in order to allow of the escape of the maid, her confederate and accomplice.

"And you still have an impression that someone – presumably this woman – got off the car, somehow, during the stoppage?" he asked.

"I suggest it, certainly. Whether it was or could be so, I must leave to your superior judgment."

"What! A woman climb out like that? Bah! Tell that to some one else!"

"You have, of course, examined the exterior of the car, dear colleague?" now said the Judge.

"Assuredly, once, but I will do it again. Still, the outside is quite smooth, there is no foot-board. Only an acrobat could succeed in thus escaping, and then only at the peril of his life. But a woman – oh, no! It is too absurd."

"With help she might, I think, get up on to the roof," quickly remarked Sir Charles. "I have looked out of the window of my compartment. It would be nothing for a man, nor much for a woman if assisted."

"That we will see for ourselves," said the detective, ungraciously.

"The sooner the better," added the Judge, and the whole party rose from their chairs, intending to go straight to the car, when the policeman on guard appeared at the door, followed close by an English military officer in uniform, whom he was trying to keep back, but with no great success. It was Colonel Papillon of the Embassy.

"Halloa, Jack! You are a good chap," cried the General, quickly going forward to shake hands. "I was sure you would come."

"Come, sir! Of course I came. I was just going to an official function, as you see, but his Excellency insisted, my horse was at the door, and here I am."

All this was in English, but the attaché turned now to the officials, and, with many apologies for his intrusion, suggested that they should allow his friend, the General, to return with him to the Embassy when they had done with him.

"Of course we will answer for him. He shall remain at your disposal, and will appear whenever called upon." He returned to Sir Charles, asking, "You will promise that, sir?"

"Oh, willingly. I had always meant to stay on a bit in Paris. And really I should like to see the end of this. But my brother? He must get home for next Sunday's duty. He has nothing to tell, but he would come back to Paris at any time if his evidence was wanted."

The French Judge very obligingly agreed to all these proposals, and two more of the detained passengers, making four in all, now left the station.

Then the officials proceeded to the car, which still remained as the Chief Detective had left it.

Here they soon found how just were the General's previsions.

Chapter XI

THE THREE OFFICIALS went straight to where the still open window showed the particular spot to be examined. The exterior of the car was a little smirched and stained with the dust of the journey, lying thick in parts, and in others there were a few great splotches of mud plastered on.

The detective paused for a moment to get a general view, looking, in the light of the General's suggestion, for either hand or foot marks, anything like a trace of the passage of a feminine skirt, across the dusty surface.

But nothing was to be seen, nothing definite or conclusive at least. Only here and there a few lines and scratches that might be encouraging, but proved little.

Then the Commissary, drawing nearer, called attention to some suspicious spots sprinkled about the window, but above it towards the roof.

"What is it?" asked the detective, as his colleague with the point of his long fore-finger nail picked at the thin crust on the top of one of these spots, disclosing a dark, viscous core.

"I could not swear to it, but I believe it is blood."

"Blood! Good Heavens!" cried the detective, as he dragged his powerful magnifying glass out of his pocket and applied it to the spot. "Look, M. le Juge," he added, after a long and minute examination. "What say you?"

"It has that appearance. Only medical evidence can positively decide, but I believe it is blood."

"Now we are on the right track, I feel convinced. Someone fetch a ladder."

One of these curious French ladders, narrow at the top, splayed out at the base, was quickly leaned against the car, and the detective ran up, using his magnifier as he climbed.

"There is more here, much more, and something like – yes, beyond question it is – the print of two hands upon the roof. It was here she climbed."

"No doubt. I can see it now exactly. She would sit on the window ledge, the lower limbs inside the car here and held there. Then with her hands she would draw herself up to the roof," said the Judge.

"But what nerve! What strength of arm!"

"It was life and death. Within the car was more terrible danger. Fear will do much in such a case. We all know that. Well! What more?"

By this time the detective had stepped on to the roof of the car.

"More, more, much more! Footprints, as plain as a picture. A woman's feet. Wait, let me follow them to the end," said he, cautiously creeping forward to the end of the car.

A minute or two more, and he rejoined his colleagues on the ground level, and, rubbing his hands, declared joyously that it was all perfectly clear.

"Dangerous or not, difficult or not, she did it. I have traced her; have seen where she must have lain crouching ever so long, followed her all along the top of the car, to the end where she got down above the little platform exit. Beyond doubt she left the car when it stopped, and by arrangement with her confederate."

"The Countess?"

"Who else?"

"And at a point near Paris. The English General said the halt was within twenty minutes' run of the station."

"Then it is from that point we must commence our search for her. The Italian has gone on the wrong scent."

"Not necessarily. The maid, we may be sure, will try to communicate with her mistress."

"Still, it would be well to secure her before she can do that," said the Judge. "With all we know now, a sharp interrogation might extract some very damaging admissions from her," went on the detective, eagerly. "Who is to go? I have sent away both my assistants. Of course I can telephone for another man, or I might go myself."

"No, no, dear colleague, we cannot spare you just yet. Telephone by all means. I presume you would wish to be present at the rest of the interrogatories?"

"Certainly, you are right. We may elicit more about this maid. Let us call in the porter now. He is said to have had relations with her. Something more may be got out of him."

The more did not amount to much. Groote, the porter, came in, cringing and wretched, in the abject state of a man who has lately been drugged and is now slowly recovering. Although sharply questioned, he had nothing to add to his first story.

"Speak out," said the Judge, harshly. "Tell us everything plainly and promptly, or I shall send you straight to gaol. The order is already made out;" and as he spoke, he waved a flimsy bit of paper before him.

"I know nothing," the porter protested, piteously.

"That is false. We are fully informed and no fools. We are certain that no such catastrophe could have occurred without your knowledge or connivance."

"Indeed, gentlemen, indeed–"

"You were drinking with this maid at the buffet at Laroche. You had more drink with her, or from her hands, afterwards in the car."

"No, gentlemen, that is not so. I could not – she was not in the car."

"We know better. You cannot deceive us. You were her accomplice, and the accomplice of her mistress, also, I have no doubt."

"I declare solemnly that I am quite innocent of all this. I hardly remember what happened at Laroche or after. I do not deny the drink at the buffet. It was very nasty, I thought, and could not tell why, nor why I could not hold my head up when I got back to the car."

"You went off to sleep at once? Is that what you pretend?"

"It must have been so. Yes. Then I know nothing more, not till I was roused."

And beyond this, a tale to which he stuck with undeviating persistence, they could elicit nothing.

"He is either too clever for us or an absolute idiot and fool," said the Judge, wearily, at last, when Groote had gone out. "We had better commit him to Mazas and hold him there in solitary confinement under our hands. After a day or two of that he may be less difficult."

"It is quite clear he was drugged, that the maid put opium or laudanum into his drink at Laroche."

"And enough of it apparently, for he says he went off to sleep directly he returned to the car," the Judge remarked.

"He says so. But he must have had a second dose, or why was the vial found on the ground by his seat?" asked the Chief, thoughtfully, as much of himself as of the others.

"I cannot believe in a second dose. How was it administered – by whom? It was laudanum, and could only be given in a drink. He says he had no second drink. And by whom? The maid? He says he did not see the maid again."

"Pardon me, M. le Juge, but do you not give too much credibility to the porter? For me, his evidence is tainted, and I hardly believe a word of it. Did he not tell me at first he had not seen this maid after Amberieux at 8 P.M.? Now he admits that he was drinking with her at the buffet at Laroche. It is all a tissue of lies, his losing the pocket-book and his papers too. There is something to conceal. Even his sleepiness, his stupidity, are likely to have been assumed."

"I do not think he is acting; he has not the ability to deceive us like that."

"Well, then, what if the Countess took him the second drink?"

"Oh! Oh! That is the purest conjecture. There is nothing whatever to suggest or support that."

"Then how explain the finding of the vial near the porter's seat?"

"May it not have been dropped there on purpose?" put in the Commissary, with another flash of intelligence.

"On purpose?" queried the detective, crossly, foreseeing an answer that would not please him.

"On purpose to bring suspicion on the lady?"

"I don't see it in that light. That would imply that she was not in the plot, and plot there certainly was; everything points to it. The drugging, the open window, the maid's escape."

"A plot, no doubt, but organized by whom? These two women only? Could either of them have struck the fatal blow? Hardly. Women have the wit to conceive, but neither courage nor brute force to execute. There was a man in this, rest assured."

"Granted. But who? That fire-eating Sir Collingham?" quickly asked the detective, giving rein once more to his hatred.

"That is not a solution that commends itself to me, I must confess," declared the Judge. "The General's conduct has been blameworthy and injudicious, but he is not of the stuff that makes criminals."

"Who, then? The porter? No? The clergyman? No? The French gentlemen? Well, we have not examined them yet; but from what I saw at the first cursory glance, I am not disposed to suspect them."

"What of that Italian?" asked the Commissary.

"Are you sure of him? His looks did not please me greatly, and he was very eager to get away from here. What if he takes to his heels?"

"Block is with him," the Chief put in hastily, with the evident desire to stifle an unpleasant misgiving. "We have touch of him if we want him, as we may."

How much they might want him they only realized when they got further in their inquiry!

Chapter XII

ONLY THE TWO FRENCHMEN remained for examination. They had been left to the last by pure accident. The exigencies of the inquiry had led to the preference of others, but these two well-broken and submissive gentlemen made no visible protest. However much they may have chafed inwardly at the delay, they knew better than to object; any outburst of discontent would, they knew, recoil on themselves. Not only were they perfectly patient now when summoned before the officers of justice, they were most eager to give every assistance to the law, to go beyond the mere letter, and, if needs be, volunteer information.

The first called in was the elder, M. Anatole Lafolay, a true Parisian *bourgeois*, fat and comfortable, unctuous in speech, and exceedingly deferential.

The story he told was in its main outlines that which we already know, but he was further questioned, by the light of the latest facts and ideas as now elicited.

The line adroitly taken by the Judge was to get some evidence of collusion and combination among the passengers, especially with reference to two of them, the two women of the party. On this important point M. Lafolay had something to say.

Asked if he had seen or noticed the lady's maid on the journey, he answered "yes" very decisively and with a smack of the lips, as though the sight of this pretty and attractive person had given him considerable satisfaction.

"Did you speak to her?"

"Oh, no. I had no opportunity. Besides, she had her own friends – great friends, I fancy. I caught her more than once whispering in the corner of the car with one of them."

"And that was –?"

"I think the Italian gentleman; I am almost sure I recognized his clothes. I did not see his face, it was turned from me –towards hers, and very close, I may be permitted to say."

"And they were friendly?"

"More than friendly, I should say. Very intimate indeed. I should not have been surprised if – when I turned away as a matter of fact – if he did not touch, just touch, her red lips. It would have been excusable – forgive me, messieurs."

"Aha! They were so intimate as that? Indeed! And did she reserve her favours exclusively for him? Did no one else address her, pay her court on the quiet – you understand?"

"I saw her with the porter, I believe, at Laroche, but only then. No, the Italian was her chief companion."

"Did any one else notice the flirtation, do you think?"

"Possibly. There was no secrecy. It was very marked. We could all see."

"And her mistress too?"

"That I will not say. The lady I saw but little during the journey."

A few more questions, mainly personal, as to his address, business, probable presence in Paris for the next few weeks, and M. Lafolay was permitted to depart.

The examination of the younger Frenchman, a smart, alert young man, of pleasant, insinuating address, with a quick, inquisitive eye, followed the same lines, and was distinctly corroborative on all the points to which M. Lafolay spoke. But M. Jules Devaux had something startling to impart concerning the Countess.

When asked if he had seen her or spoken to her, he shook his head.

"No; she kept very much to herself," he said. "I saw her but little, hardly at all, except at Modane. She kept her own berth."

"Where she received her own friends?"

"Oh, beyond doubt. The Englishmen both visited her there, but not the Italian."

"The Italian? Are we to infer that she knew the Italian?"

"That is what I wish to convey. Not on the journey, though. Between Rome and Paris she did not seem to know him. It was afterwards; this morning, in fact, that I came to the conclusion that there was some secret understanding between them."

"Why do you say that, M. Devaux?" cried the detective, excitedly. "Let me urge you and implore you to speak out, and fully. This is of the utmost, of the very first, importance."

"Well, gentlemen, I will tell you. As you are well aware, on arrival at this station we were all ordered to leave the car, and marched to the waiting-room, out there. As a matter of course, the lady entered first, and she was seated when I went in. There was a strong light on her face."

"Was her veil down?"

"Not then. I saw her lower it later, and, as I think, for reasons I will presently put before you. Madame has a beautiful face, and I gazed at it with sympathy, grieving for her, in fact, in such a trying situation; when suddenly I saw a great and remarkable change come over it."

"Of what character?"

"It was a look of horror, disgust, surprise – a little perhaps of all three; I could not quite say which, it faded so quickly and was followed by a cold, deathlike pallor. Then almost immediately she lowered her veil."

"Could you form any explanation for what you saw in her face? What caused it?"

"Something unexpected, I believe, some shock, or the sight of something shocking. That was how it struck me, and so forcibly that I turned to look over my shoulder, expecting to find the reason there. And it was."

"That reason –?"

"Was the entrance of the Italian, who came just behind me. I am certain of this; he almost told me so himself, not in words, but the mistakable leer he gave her in reply. It was wicked, sardonic, devilish, and proved beyond doubt that there was some secret, some guilty secret perhaps, between them."

"And was that all?" cried both the Judge and M. Floçon in a breath, leaning forward in their eagerness to hear more.

"For the moment, yes. But I was made so interested, so suspicious by this, that I watched the Italian closely, awaiting, expecting further developments. They were long in coming; indeed, I am only at the end now."

"Explain, pray, as quickly as possible, and in your own words."

"It was like this, monsieur. When we were all seated, I looked round, and did not at first see our Italian. At last I discovered he had taken a back seat, through modesty perhaps, or to be out of observation – how was I to know? He sat in the shadow by a door, that, in fact, which leads into this room. He was thus in the background, rather out of the way, but I could see his eyes glittering in that far-off corner, and they were turned in our direction, always fixed upon the lady, you understand. She was next me, the whole time.

"Then, as you will remember, monsieur, you called us in one by one, and I, with M. Lafolay, was the first to appear before you. When I returned to the outer room, the Italian was still staring, but not so fixedly or continuously, at the lady. From time to time his eyes wandered towards a table near which he sat, and which was just in the gangway or passage by which people must pass into your presence.

"There was some reason for this, I felt sure, although I did not understand it immediately. Presently I got at the hidden meaning. There was a small piece of paper, rolled up or crumpled up into a ball, lying upon this table, and the Italian wished, nay, was desperately anxious, to call the lady's attention to it. If I had had any doubt of this, it was quite removed after the man had gone into the inner room. As he left us, he turned his head over his shoulder significantly and nodded very slightly, but still perceptibly, at the ball of paper.

"Well, gentlemen, I was now satisfied in my own mind that this was some artful attempt of his to communicate with the lady, and had she fallen in with it, I should have immediately informed you, the proper authorities. But whether from stupidity, dread, disinclination, a direct, definite refusal to have any dealings with this man, the lady would not – at any rate did not – pick up the ball, as she might have done easily when she in her turn passed the table on her way to your presence.

"I have no doubt it was thrown there for her, and probably you will agree with me. But it takes two to make a game of this sort, and the lady would not join. Neither on leaving the room nor on returning would she take up the missive."

"And what became of it, then?" asked the detective in breathless excitement. "I have it here." M. Devaux opened the palm of his hand and displayed the scrap of paper in the hollow rolled up into a small tight ball.

"When and how did you become possessed of it?"

"I got it only just now, when I was called in here. Before that I could not move. I was tied to my chair, practically, and ordered strictly not to move."

"Perfectly. Monsieur's conduct has been admirable. And now tell us – what does it contain? Have you looked at it?"

"By no means. It is just as I picked it up. Will you gentlemen take it, and if you think fit, tell me what is there? Some writing – a message of some sort, or I am greatly mistaken."

"Yes, here are words written in pencil," said the detective, unrolling the paper, which he handed on to the Judge, who read the contents aloud.

"Be careful. Say nothing. If you betray me, you will be lost too."

A long silence followed, broken first by the Judge, who said at last solemnly to Devaux:

"Monsieur, in the name of justice I beg to thank you most warmly. You have acted with admirable tact and judgment, and have rendered us invaluable assistance. Have you anything further to tell us?"

"No, gentlemen. That is all. And you – you have no more questions to ask? Then I presume I may withdraw?"

Beyond doubt it had been reserved for the last witness to produce facts that constituted the very essence of the inquiry.

Chapter XIII

THE EXAMINATION was now over, and, the dispositions having been drawn up and signed, the investigating officials remained for some time in conference.

"It lies with those three, of course – the two women and the Italian. They are jointly, conjointly concerned, although the exact degrees of guilt cannot quite be apportioned," said the detective.

"And all three are at large!" added the Judge.

"If you will issue warrants for arrest, M. le Juge, we can take them – two of them at any rate – when we choose."

"That should be at once," remarked the Commissary, eager, as usual, for decisive action.

"Very well. Let us proceed in that way. Prepare the warrants," said the Judge, turning to his clerk. "And you," he went on, addressing M. Floçon, "dear colleague, will you see to their execution? Madame is at the Hôtel Madagascar; that will be easy. The Italian Ripaldi we shall hear of through your inspector Block. As for the maid, Hortense Petitpré, we must search for her. That too, sir, you will of course undertake?"

"I will charge myself with it, certainly. My man should be here by now, and I will instruct him at once. Ask for him," said M. Floçon to the guard whom he called in.

"The inspector is there," said the guard, pointing to the outer room. "He has just returned."

"Returned? You mean arrived."

"No, monsieur, returned. It is Block, who left an hour or more ago."

"Block? Then something has happened – he has some special information, some great news! Shall we see him, M. le Juge?"

When Block appeared, it was evident that something had gone wrong with him. His face wore a look of hot, flurried excitement, and his manner was one of abject, cringing self-abasement.

"What is it?" asked the little Chief, sharply. "You are alone. Where is your man?"

"Alas, monsieur! How shall I tell you? He has gone – disappeared! I have lost him!"

"Impossible! You cannot mean it! Gone, now, just when we most want him? Never!"

"It is so, unhappily."

"Idiot! *Triple* idiot! You shall be dismissed, discharged from this hour. You are a disgrace to the force." M. Floçon raved furiously at his abashed subordinate, blaming him a little too harshly and unfairly, forgetting that until quite recently there had been no strong suspicion against the Italian. We are apt at times to expect others to be intuitively possessed of knowledge that has only come to us at a much later date.

"How was it? Explain. Of course you have been drinking. It is that, or your great gluttony. You were beguiled into some eating-house."

"Monsieur, you shall hear the exact truth. When we started more than an hour ago, our fiacre took the usual route, by the Quais and along the riverside. My gentleman made himself most pleasant."

"No doubt," growled the Chief.

"Offered me an excellent cigar, and talked – not about the affair, you understand – but of Paris, the theatres, the races, Longchamps, Auteuil, the grand restaurants. He knew everything, all Paris, like his pocket. I was much surprised, but he told me his business often brought him here. He had been employed to follow up several great Italian criminals, and had made a number of important arrests in Paris."

"Get on, get on! Come to the essential."

"Well, in the middle of the journey, when we were about the Pont Henri Quatre, he said, 'Figure to yourself, my friend, that it is now near noon, that nothing has passed my lips since before daylight at Laroche. What say you? Could you eat a mouthful, just a scrap on the thumb-nail? Could you?' "

"And you – greedy, gormandizing beast! You agreed?"

"My faith, monsieur, I too was hungry. It was my regular hour. Well – at any rate, for my sins I accepted. We entered the first restaurant, that of the 'Reunited Friends,' you know it, perhaps, monsieur? A good house, especially noted for tripe *à la mode de Caen*." In spite of his anguish, Block smacked his fat lips at the thought of this most succulent but very greasy dish.

"How often must I tell you to get on?"

"Forgive me, monsieur, but it is all part of my story. We had oysters, two dozen Marennes, and a glass or two of Chablis; then a good portion of tripe, and with them a bottle, only one, monsieur, of Pontet Canet; after that a beefsteak with potatoes and a little Burgundy, then a rum omelet."

"Great Heavens! You should be the fat man in a fair, not an agent of the Detective Bureau."

"It was all this that helped me to my destruction. He ate, this devilish Italian, like three, and I too, I was so hungry –forgive me, sir – I did my share. But by the time we reached the cheese, a fine, ripe Camembert, had our coffee, and one thimbleful of green Chartreuse, I was *plein jusqu'au bec*, gorged up to the beak."

"And what of your duty, your service, pray?"

"I did think of it, monsieur, but then, he, the Italian, was just the same as myself. He was a colleague. I had no fear of him, not till the very last, when he played me this evil turn. I suspected nothing when he brought out his pocketbook – it was stuffed full, monsieur; I saw that and my confidence increased – called for the reckoning, and paid with an Italian bank-note. The waiter looked doubtful at the foreign money, and went out to consult the manager. A minute after, my man got up, saying:

" 'There may be some trouble about changing that bank-note. Excuse me one moment, pray.' He went out, monsieur, and piff-paff, he was no more to be seen."

"Ah, *nigaud* (ass), you are too foolish to live! Why did you not follow him? Why let him out of your sight?"

"But, monsieur, I was not to know, was I? I was to accompany him, not to watch him. I have done wrong, I confess. But then, who was to tell he meant to run away?"

M. Floçon could not deny the justice of this defence. It was only now, at the eleventh hour, that the Italian had become inculpated, and the question of his possible anxiety to escape had never been considered.

"He was so artful," went on Block in further extenuation of his offence. "He left everything behind. His overcoat, stick, this book – his own private memorandum-book seemingly –"

"Book? Hand it me," said the Chief, and when it came into his hands he began to turn over the leaves hurriedly.

It was a small brass-bound note-book or diary, and was full of close writing in pencil.

"I do not understand, not more than a word here and there. It is no doubt Italian. Do you know that language, M. le Juge?"

"Not perfectly, but I can read it. Allow me."

He also turned over the pages, pausing to read a passage here and there, and nodding his head from time to time, evidently struck with the importance of the matter recorded.

Meanwhile, M. Floçon continued an angry conversation with his offending subordinate.

"You will have to find him, Block, and that speedily, within twenty-four hours – today, indeed – or I will break you like a stick, and send you into the gutter. Of course, such a consummate ass as you have proved yourself would not think of searching the restaurant or the immediate neighbourhood, or of making inquiries as to whether he had been seen, or as to which way he had gone?"

"Pardon me, monsieur is too hard on me. I have been unfortunate, a victim to circumstances, still I believe I know my duty. Yes, I made inquiries, and, what is more, I heard of him."

"Where? How?" asked the Chief, gruffly, but obviously much interested.

"He never spoke to the manager, but walked out and let the change go. It was a note for a hundred *lire*, a hundred francs, and the restaurant bill was no more than seventeen francs."

"Hah! That is greatly against him indeed."

"He was much pressed, in a great hurry. Directly he crossed the threshold he called the first cab and was driving away, but he was stopped –"

"The devil! Why did they not keep him, then?"

"Stopped, but only for a moment, and accosted by a woman."

"A woman?"

"Yes, monsieur. They exchanged but three words. He wished to pass on, to leave her, she would not consent, then they both got into the cab and were driven away together."

The officials were now listening with all ears.

"Tell me," said the Chief, "quick, this woman – what was she like? Did you get her description?"

"Tall, slight, well formed, dressed all in black. Her face – it was a policeman who saw her, and he said she was good-looking, dark, brunette, black hair."

"It is the maid herself!" cried the little Chief, springing up and slapping his thigh in exuberant glee. "The maid! The missing maid!"

Chapter XIV

THE JOY of the Chief of Detectives at having thus come, as he supposed, upon the track of the missing maid, Hortense Petitpré, was somewhat dashed by the doubts freely expressed by the Judge as to the result of any search. Since Block's return, M. Beaumont le Hardi had developed strong symptoms of discontent and disapproval at his colleague's proceedings.

"But if it was this Hortense Petitpré, how did she get there, by the bridge Henri Quatre, when we thought to find her somewhere down the line? It cannot be the same woman."

"I beg your pardon, gentlemen," interposed Block. "May I say one word? I believe I can supply some interesting information about Hortense Petitpré. I understand that someone like her was seen here in the station not more than an hour ago."

"*Peste*! Why were we not told this sooner?" cried the Chief, impetuously.

"Who saw her? Did he speak to her? Call him in; let us see how much he knows."

The man was summoned, one of the subordinate railway officials, who made a specific report.

Yes, he had seen a tall, slight, neat-looking woman, dressed entirely in black, who, according to her account, had arrived at 10.30 by the slow local train from Dijon.

"*Fichtre*!" said the Chief, angrily; "and this is the first we have heard of it."

"Monsieur was much occupied at the time, and, indeed, then we had not heard of your inquiry."

"I notified the station-master quite early, two or three hours since, about 9 A.M. This is most exasperating!"

"Instructions to look out for this woman have only just reached us, monsieur. There were certain formalities, I suppose."

For once the detective cursed in his heart the red-tape, roundabout ways of French officialism.

"Well, well! Tell me about her," he said, with a resignation he did not feel. "Who saw her?"

"I, monsieur. I spoke to her myself. She was on the outside of the station, alone, unprotected, in a state of agitation and alarm. I went up and offered my services. Then she told me she had come from Dijon, that friends who were to have met her had not appeared. I suggested that I should put her into a cab and send her to her destination. But she was afraid of losing her friends, and preferred to wait."

"A fine story! Did she appear to know what had happened? Had she heard of the murder?"

"Something, monsieur."

"Who could have told her? Did you?"

"No, not I. But she knew."

"Was not that in itself suspicious? The fact has not yet been made public."

"It was in the air, monsieur. There was a general impression that something had happened. That was to be seen on every face, in the whispered talk, the movement to and fro of the police and the guards."

"Did she speak of it, or refer to it?"

"Only to ask if the murderer was known; whether the passengers had been detained; whether there was any inquiry in progress; and then –"

"What then?"

"This gentleman," pointing to Block, "came out, accompanied by another. They passed pretty close to us, and I noticed that the lady slipped quickly on one side."

"She recognized her confederate, of course, but did not wish to be seen just then. Did he, the person with Block here, see her?"

"Hardly, I think; it was all so quick, and they were gone, in a minute, to the cab-stand."

"What did your woman do?"

"She seemed to have changed her mind all at once, and declared she would not wait for her friends. Now she was in quite a hurry to go."

"Of course! And left you like a fool planted there. I suppose she took a cab and followed the others, Block here and his companion."

"I believe she did. I saw her cab close behind theirs."

"It is too late to lament this now," said the Chief, after a short pause, looking at his colleagues. "At least it confirms our ideas, and brings us to certain definite conclusions. We must lay hands on these two. Their guilt is all but established. Their own acts condemn them. They must be arrested without a moment's delay."

"If you can find them!" suggested the Judge, with a very perceptible sneer.

"That we shall certainly do. Trust to Block, who is very nearly concerned. His future depends on his success. You quite understand that, my man?"

Block made a gesture half-deprecating, half-confident.

"I do not despair, gentlemen; and if I might make so bold, sir, I will ask you to assist? If you would give orders direct from the Prefecture to make the round of the cab-stands, to ask of all the agents in charge the information we need? Before night we shall have heard from the cabman who drove them what became of this couple, and so get our birds themselves, or a point of fresh departure."

"And you, Block, where shall you go?"

"Where I left him, or rather where he left me," replied the inspector, with an attempt at wit, which fell quite flat, being extinguished by a frigid look from the Judge.

"Go," said M. Floçon, briefly and severely, to his subordinate; "and remember that you have now to justify your retention on the force."

Then, turning to M. Beaumont le Hardi, the Chief went on pleasantly:

"Well, M. le Juge, it promises, I think; it is all fairly satisfactory, eh?"

"I am sorry I cannot agree with you," replied the Judge, harshly. "On the contrary, I consider that we – or more exactly you, for neither I nor M. Garraud accept any share in it – you have so far failed, and miserably."

"Your pardon, M. le Juge, you are too severe," protested M. Floçon, quite humbly.

"Well! Look at it from all points of view. What have we got? What have we gained? Nothing, or, if anything, it is of the smallest, and it is already jeopardized, if not absolutely lost."

"We have at least gained the positive assurance of the guilt of certain individuals."

"Whom you have allowed to slip through your fingers."

"Ah, not so, M. le Juge! We have one under surveillance. My man Galipaud is there at the hotel watching the Countess."

"Do not talk to me of your men, M. Floçon," angrily interposed the Judge. "One of them has given us a touch of his quality. Why should not the other be equally foolish? I quite expect to hear that the Countess also has gone, that would be the climax!"

"It shall not happen. I will take the warrant and arrest her now, at once, myself," cried M. Floçon.

"Well, that will be something, yet not much. Yes, she is only one, and not to my mind the most criminal. We do not know as yet the exact responsibility of each, the exact measure of their guilt; but I do not myself believe that the Countess was a prime mover, or, indeed, more than an accessory. She was drawn into it, perhaps involved, how or why we cannot know, but possibly by fortuitous circumstances that put an unavoidable pressure upon her; a consenting party, but under protest. That is my view of the lady."

M. Floçon shook his head. Prepossessions with him were tenacious, and he had made up his mind about the Countess's guilt.

"When you again interrogate her, M. le Juge, by the light of your present knowledge, I believe you will think otherwise. She will confess – you will make her, your skill is unrivalled – and you will then admit, M. le Juge, that I was right in my suspicions."

"Ah, well, produce her! We shall see," said the Judge, somewhat mollified by M. Floçon's fulsome flattery.

"I will bring her to your chamber of instruction within an hour, M. le Juge," said the detective, very confidently.

But he was doomed to disappointment in this as he was in other respects.

Chapter XV

LET US GO BACK a little in point of time, and follow the movements of Sir Charles Collingham.

It was barely 11 A.M. when he left the Lyons Station with his brother, the Reverend Silas, and the military attaché, Colonel Papillon. They paused for a moment outside the station while the baggage was being got together.

"See, Silas," said the General, pointing to the clock, "you will have plenty of time for the 11.50 train to Calais for London, but you must hurry up and drive straight across Paris to the Nord. I suppose he can go, Jack?"

"Certainly, as he has promised to return if called upon."

And Mr. Collingham promptly took advantage of the permission.

"But you, General, what are your plans?" went on the attaché.

"I shall go to the club first, get a room, dress, and all that. Then call at the Hôtel Madagascar. There is a lady there – one of our party, in fact – and I should like to ask after her. She may be glad of my services."

"English? Is there anything we can do for her?"

"Yes, she is an Englishwoman, but the widow of an Italian – the Contessa di Castagneto."

"Oh, but I know her!" said Papillon. "I remember her in Rome two or three years ago. A deuced pretty woman, very much admired, but she was in deep mourning then, and went out very little. I wished she had gone out more. There were lots of men ready to fall at her feet."

"You were in Rome, then, some time back? Did you ever come across a man there, Quadling, the banker?"

"Of course I did. Constantly. He was a good deal about – a rather free-living, self-indulgent sort of chap. And now you mention his name, I recollect they said he was much smitten by this particular lady, the Contessa di Castagneto."

"And did she encourage him?"

"Lord! How can I tell? Who shall say how a woman's fancy falls? It might have suited her to. They said she was not in very good circumstances, and he was thought to be a rich man. Of course we know better than that now."

"Why *now*?"

"Haven't you heard? It was in the *Figaro* yesterday, and in all the Paris papers. Quadling's bank has gone to smash; he has bolted with all the 'ready' he could lay hands upon."

"He didn't get far, then!" cried Sir Charles. "You look surprised, Jack. Didn't they tell you? This Quadling was the man murdered in the sleeping-car. It was no doubt for the money he carried with him."

"Was it Quadling? My word! What a terrible Nemesis. Well, *nil nisi bonum*, but I never thought much of the chap, and your friend the Countess has had an escape. But now, sir, I must be moving. My engagement is for twelve noon. If you want me, mind you send – 207 Rue Miromesnil, or to the Embassy; but let us arrange to meet this evening, eh? Dinner and a theatre – what do you say?"

Then Colonel Papillon rode off, and the General was driven to the Boulevard des Capucines, having much to occupy his thoughts by the way.

It did not greatly please him to have this story of the Countess's relations with Quadling, as first hinted at by the police, endorsed now by his friend Papillon. Clearly she had kept up her acquaintance, her intimacy to the very last: why otherwise should she have received him, alone, been closeted with him for an hour or more on the very eve of his flight? It was a clandestine acquaintance too, or seemed so, for Sir Charles, although a frequent visitor at her house, had never met Quadling there.

What did it all mean? And yet, what, after all, did it matter to him?

A good deal really more than he chose to admit to himself, even now, when closely questioning his secret heart. The fact was, the Countess had made a very strong impression on him from the first. He had admired her greatly during the past winter at Rome, but then it was only a passing fancy, as he thought – the pleasant platonic flirtation of a middle-aged man, who never expected to inspire or feel a great love. Only now, when he had shared a serious trouble with her, had passed through common difficulties and dangers, he was finding what accident may do – how it may fan a first liking into a stronger flame. It was absurd, of course. He was fifty-one, he had weathered many trifling affairs of the heart, and here he was, bowled over at last, and by a woman he was not certain was entitled to his respect.

What was he to do?

The answer came at once and unhesitatingly, as it would to any other honest, chivalrous gentleman.

"By George, I'll stick to her through thick and thin! I'll trust her whatever happens or has happened, come what may. Such a woman as that is above suspicion. She *must* be straight.

I should be a beast and a blackguard double distilled to think anything else. I am sure she can put all right with a word, can explain everything when she chooses. I will wait till she does."

Thus fortified and decided, Sir Charles took his way to the Hôtel Madagascar about noon. At the desk he inquired for the Countess, and begged that his card might be sent up to her. The man looked at it, then at the visitor, as he stood there waiting rather impatiently, then again at the card. At last he walked out and across the inner courtyard of the hotel to the office. Presently the manager came back, bowing low, and, holding the card in his hand, began a desultory conversation.

"Yes, yes," cried the General, angrily cutting short all references to the weather and the number of English visitors in Paris. "But be so good as to let Madame la Comtesse know that I have called."

"Ah, to be sure! I came to tell Monsieur le Général that madame will hardly be able to see him. She is indisposed, I believe. At any rate, she does not receive today."

"As to that, we shall see. I will take no answer except direct from her. Take or send up my card without further delay. I insist! Do you hear?" said the General, so fiercely that the manager turned tail and fled upstairs.

Perhaps he yielded his ground the more readily that he saw over the General's shoulder the figure of Galipaud the detective looming in the archway. It had been arranged that, as it was not advisable to have the inspector hanging about the courtyard of the hotel, the clerk or the manager should keep watch over the Countess and detain any visitors who might call upon her. Galipaud had taken post at a wine-shop over the way, and was to be summoned whenever his presence was thought necessary.

There he was now, standing just behind the General, and for the present unseen by him.

But then a telegraph messenger came in and up to the desk. He held the usual blue envelope in his hand, and called out the name on the address:

"Castagneto. Contessa Castagneto."

At sound of which the General turned sharply, to find Galipaud advancing and stretching out his hand to take the message.

"Pardon me," cried Sir Charles, promptly interposing and understanding the situation at a glance. "I am just going up to see that lady. Give me the telegram."

Galipaud would have disputed the point, when the General, who had already recognized him, said quietly:

"No, no, Inspector, you have no earthly right to it. I guess why you are here, but you are not entitled to interfere with private correspondence. Stand back;" and seeing the detective hesitate, he added peremptorily:

"Enough of this. I order you to get out of the way. And be quick about it!"

The manager now returned, and admitted that Madame la Comtesse would receive her visitor. A few seconds more, and the General was admitted into her presence.

"How truly kind of you to call!" she said at once, coming up to him with both hands outstretched and frank gladness in her eyes.

Yes, she was very attractive in her plain, dark travelling dress draping her tall, graceful figure; her beautiful, pale face was enhanced by the rich tones of her dark brown, wavy hair, while just a narrow band of white muslin at her wrists and neck set off the dazzling clearness of her skin.

"Of course I came. I thought you might want me, or might like to know the latest news," he answered, as he held her hands in his for a few seconds longer than was perhaps absolutely necessary.

"Oh, do tell me! Is there anything fresh?" There was a flash of crimson colour in her cheek, which faded almost instantly.

"This much. They have found out who the man was."

"Really? Positively? Whom do they say now?"

"Perhaps I had better not tell you. It may surprise you, shock you to hear. I think you knew him –"

"Nothing can well shock me now. I have had too many shocks already. Who do they think it is?"

"A Mr. Quadling, a banker, who is supposed to have absconded from Rome."

She received the news so impassively, with such strange self-possession, that for a moment he was disappointed in her. But then, quick to excuse, he suggested:

"You may have already heard?"

"Yes; the police people at the railway station told me they thought it was Mr. Quadling."

"But you knew him?"

"Certainly. They were my bankers, much to my sorrow. I shall lose heavily by their failure."

"That also has reached you, then?" interrupted the General, hastily and somewhat uneasily.

"To be sure. The man told me of it himself. Indeed, he came to me the very day I was leaving Rome, and made me an offer – a most obliging offer."

"To share his fallen fortunes?"

"Sir Charles Collingham! How can you? That creature!" The contempt in her tone was immeasurable.

"I had heard – well, someone said that –"

"Speak out, General; I shall not be offended. I know what you mean. It is perfectly true that the man once presumed to pester me with his attentions. But I would as soon have looked at a courier or a cook. And now –"

There was a pause. The General felt on delicate ground. He could ask no questions – anything more must come from the Countess herself.

"But let me tell you what his offer was. I don't know why I listened to it. I ought to have at once informed the police. I wish I had."

"It might have saved him from his fate."

"Every villain gets his deserts in the long run," she said, with bitter sententiousness. "And this Mr. Quadling is – but wait, you shall know him better. He came to me to propose – what do you think? That he – his bank, I mean – should secretly repay me the amount of my deposit, all the money I had in it. To join me in his fraud, in fact–"

"The scoundrel! Upon my word, he has been well served. And that was the last you saw of him?"

"I saw him on the journey, at Turin, at Modane, at – oh, Sir Charles, do not ask me any more about him!" she cried, with a sudden outburst, half-grief, half-dread. "I cannot tell you – I am obliged to – I – I –"

"Then do not say another word," he said, promptly.

"There are other things. But my lips are sealed – at least for the present. You do not – will not think any worse of me?"

She laid her hand gently on his arm, and his closed over it with such evident good-will that a blush crimsoned her cheek. It still hung there, and deepened when he said, warmly:

"As if anything could make me do that! Don't you know – you may not, but let me assure you, Countess – that nothing could happen to shake me in the high opinion I have of you. Come what may, I shall trust you, believe in you, think well of you – always."

"How sweet of you to say that! And now, of all times," she murmured quite softly, and looking up for the first time, shyly, to meet his eyes.

Her hand was still on his arm, covered by his, and she nestled so close to him that it was easy, natural, indeed, for him to slip his other arm around her waist and draw her to him.

"And now – of all times – may I say one word more?" he whispered in her ear. "Will you give me the right to shelter and protect you, to stand by you, share your troubles, or keep them from you –?"

"No, no, no, indeed, not now!" She looked up appealingly, the tears brimming up in her bright eyes. "I cannot, will not accept this sacrifice. You are only speaking out of your true-hearted chivalry. You must not join yourself to me, you must not involve yourself –"

He stopped her protests by the oldest and most effectual method known in such cases. That first sweet kiss sealed the compact so quickly entered into between them.

And after that she surrendered at discretion. There was no more hesitation or reluctance; she accepted his love as he had offered it, freely, with whole heart and soul, crept up under his sheltering wing like a storm-beaten dove reentering the nest, and there, cooing softly, "My knight – my own true knight and lord," yielded herself willingly and unquestioningly to his tender caresses.

Such moments snatched from the heart of pressing anxieties are made doubly sweet by their sharp contrast with a background of trouble.

Chapter XVI

THEY SAT THERE, these two, hand locked in hand, saying little, satisfied now to be with each other and their new-found love. The time flew by far too fast, till at last Sir Charles, with a half-laugh, suggested:

"Do you know, dearest Countess –"

She corrected him in a soft, low voice.

"My name is Sabine – Charles."

"Sabine, darling. It is very prosaic of me, perhaps, but do you know that I am nearly starved? I came on here at once. I have had no breakfast."

"Nor have I," she answered, smiling. "I was thinking of it when – when you appeared like a whirlwind, and since then, events have moved so fast."

"Are you sorry, Sabine? Would you rather go back to – to – before?" She made a pretty gesture of closing his traitor lips with her small hand.

"Not for worlds. But you soldiers – you are terrible men! Who can resist you?"

"Bah! It is you who are irresistible. But there, why not put on your jacket and let us go out to lunch somewhere – Durand's, Voisin's, the Café de le Paix? Which do you prefer?"

"I suppose they will not try to stop us?"

"Who should try?" he asked.

"The people of the hotel – the police – I cannot exactly say whom; but I dread something of the sort. I don't quite understand that manager. He has been up to see me several times, and he spoke rather oddly, rather rudely."

"Then he shall answer for it," snorted Sir Charles, hotly. "It is the fault of that brute of a detective, I suppose. Still they would hardly dare –"

"A detective? What? Here? Are you sure?"

"Perfectly sure. It is one of those from the Lyons Station. I knew him again directly, and he was inclined to be interfering. Why, I caught him trying – but that reminds me – I rescued this telegram from his clutches."

He took the little blue envelope from his breast pocket and handed it to her, kissing the tips of her fingers as she took it from him.

"Ah!" A sudden ejaculation of dismay escaped her, when, after rather carelessly tearing the message open, she had glanced at it.

"What is the matter?" he asked in eager solicitude. "May I not know?"

She made no offer to give him the telegram, and said in a faltering voice, and with much hesitation of manner, "I do not know. I hardly think – of course I do not like to withhold anything, not now. And yet, this is a business which concerns me only, I am afraid. I ought not to drag you into it."

"What concerns you is very much my business, too. I do not wish to force your confidence, still –"

She gave him the telegram quite obediently, with a little sigh of relief, glad to realize now, for the first time after many years, that there was someone to give her orders and take the burden of trouble off her shoulders.

He read it, but did not understand it in the least. It ran: "I must see you immediately, and beg you will come. You will find Hortense here. She is giving trouble. You only can deal with her. Do not delay. Come at once, or we must go to you. Ripaldi, Hôtel Ivoire, Rue Bellechasse."

"What does this mean? Who sends it? Who is Ripaldi?" asked Sir Charles, rather brusquely.

"He– he– oh, Charles, I shall have to go. Anything would be better than his coming here."

"Ripaldi? Haven't I heard the name? He was one of those in the sleeping-car, I think? The Chief of the Detective Police called it out once or twice. Am I not right? Please tell me – am I not right?"

"Yes, yes; this man was there with the rest of us. A dark man, who sat near the door –"

"Ah, to be sure. But what – what in Heaven's name has he to do with you? How does he dare to send you such an impudent message as this? Surely, Sabine, you will tell me? You will admit that I have a right to ask?"

"Yes, of course. I will tell you, Charles, everything; but not here – not now. It must be on the way. I have been very wrong, very foolish – but oh, come, come, do let us be going. I am so afraid he might –"

"Then I may go with you? You do not object to that?"

"I much prefer it – much. Do let us make haste!"

She snatched up her sealskin jacket, and held it to him prettily, that he might help her into it, which he did neatly and cleverly, smoothing her great puffed-out sleeves under each shoulder of the coat, still talking eagerly and taking no toll for his trouble as she stood patiently, passively before him.

"And this Hortense? It is your maid, is it not – the woman who had taken herself off? How comes it that she is with that Italian fellow? Upon my soul, I don't understand – not a little bit."

"I cannot explain that, either. It is most strange, most incomprehensible, but we shall soon know. Please, Charles, please do not get impatient."

They passed together down into the hotel courtyard and across it, under the archway which led past the clerk's desk into the street.

On seeing them, he came out hastily and placed himself in front, quite plainly barring their egress.

"Oh, madame, one moment," he said in a tone that was by no means conciliatory. "The manager wants to speak to you; he told me to tell you, and stop you if you went out."

"The manager can speak to madame when she returns," interposed the General angrily, answering for the Countess.

"I have had my orders, and I cannot allow her –"

"Stand aside, you scoundrel!" cried the General, blazing up; "or upon my soul I shall give you such a lesson you will be sorry you were ever born."

At this moment the manager himself appeared in reinforcement, and the clerk turned to him for protection and support.

"I was merely giving madame your message, M. Auguste, when this gentleman interposed, threatened me, maltreated me –"

"Oh, surely not; it is some mistake;" the manager spoke most suavely. "But certainly I did wish to speak to madame. I wished to ask her whether she was satisfied with her apartment. I find that the rooms she has generally occupied have fallen vacant, in the nick of time. Perhaps madame would like to look at them, and move?"

"Thank you, M. Auguste, you are very good; but at another time. I am very much pressed just now. When I return in an hour or two, not now."

The manager was profuse in his apologies, and made no further difficulty.

"Oh, as you please, madame. Perfectly. By and by, later, when you choose."

The fact was, the desired result had been obtained. For now, on the far side from where he had been watching, Galipaud appeared, no doubt in reply to some secret signal, and the detective with a short nod in acknowledgment had evidently removed his embargo.

A cab was called, and Sir Charles, having put the Countess in, was turning to give the driver his instructions, when a fresh complication arose.

Someone coming round the corner had caught a glimpse of the lady disappearing into the fiacre, and cried out from afar.

"Stay! Stop! I want to speak to that lady; detain her." It was the sharp voice of little M. Floçon, whom most of those present, certainly the Countess and Sir Charles, immediately recognized.

"No, no, no – don't let them keep me – I cannot wait now," she whispered in earnest, urgent appeal. It was not lost on her loyal and devoted friend.

"Go on!" he shouted to the cabman, with all the peremptory insistence of one trained to give words of command. "Forward! As fast as you can drive. I'll pay you double fare. Tell him where to go, Sabine. I'll follow – in less than no time."

The fiacre rattled off at top speed, and the General turned to confront M. Floçon.

The little detective was white to the lips with rage and disappointment; but he also was a man of promptitude, and before falling foul of this pestilent Englishman, who had again marred his plans, he shouted to Galipaud:

"Quick! After them! Follow her wherever she goes. Take this," – he thrust a paper into his subordinate's hand. "It is a warrant for her arrest. Seize her wherever you find her, and bring her to the Quai l'Horloge," the euphemistic title of the headquarters of the French police.

The pursuit was started at once, and then the Chief turned upon Sir Charles. "Now it is between us," he said, fiercely. "You must account to me for what you have done."

"Must I?" answered the General, mockingly and with a little laugh. "It is perfectly easy. Madame was in a hurry, so I helped her to get away. That was all."

"You have traversed and opposed the action of the law. You have impeded me, the Chief of the Detective Service, in the execution of my duty. It is not the first time, but now you must answer for it."

"Dear me!" said the General in the same flippant, irritating tone.

"You will have to accompany me now to the Prefecture."

"And if it does not suit me to go?"

"I will have you carried there, bound, tied hand and foot, by the police, like any common rapscallion taken in the act who resists the authority of an officer."

"Oho, you talk very big, sir. Perhaps you will be so obliging as to tell me what I have done."

"You have connived at the escape of a criminal from justice –"

"That lady? Psha!"

"She is charged with a heinous crime – that in which you yourself were implicated – the murder of that man on the train."

"Bah! You must be a stupid goose, to hint at such a thing! A lady of birth, breeding, the highest respectability – impossible!"

"All that has not prevented her from allying herself with base, common wretches. I do not say she struck the blow, but I believe she inspired, concerted, approved it, leaving her confederates to do the actual deed."

"Confederates?"

"The man Ripaldi, your Italian fellow traveller; her maid, Hortense Petitpré, who was missing this morning."

The General was fairly staggered at this unexpected blow. Half an hour ago he would have scouted the very thought, indignantly repelled the spoken words that even hinted a suspicion of Sabine Castagneto. But that telegram, signed Ripaldi, the introduction of the maid's name, and the suggestion that she was troublesome, the threat that if the Countess did not go, they would come to her, and her marked uneasiness thereat – all this implied plainly the existence of collusion, of some secret relations, some secret understanding between her and the others.

He could not entirely conceal the trouble that now overcame him; it certainly did not escape so shrewd an observer as M. Floçon, who promptly tried to turn it to good account.

"Come, M. le Général," he said, with much assumed *bonhomie*. "I can see how it is with you, and you have my sincere sympathy. We are all of us liable to be carried away, and there is much excuse for you in this. But now – believe me, I am justified in saying it – now I tell you that our case is strong against her, that it is not mere speculation, but supported by facts. Now surely you will come over to our side?"

"In what way?"

"Tell us frankly all you know– where that lady has gone, help us to lay our hands on her."

"Your own people will do that. I heard you order that man to follow her."

"Probably; still I would rather have the information from you. It would satisfy me of your good-will. I need not then proceed to extremities –"

"I certainly shall not give it you," said the General, hotly. "Anything I know about or have heard from the Contessa Castagneto is sacred; besides, I still believe in her – thoroughly. Nothing you have said can shake me."

"Then I must ask you to accompany me to the Prefecture. You will come, I trust, on my invitation." The Chief spoke quietly, but with considerable dignity, and he laid a slight stress upon the last word.

"Meaning that if I do not, you will have resort to something stronger?"

"That will be quite unnecessary, I am sure – at least I hope so. Still –"

"I will go where you like, only I will tell you nothing more, not a single word; and before I start, I must let my friends at the Embassy know where to find me."

"Oh, with all my heart," said the little detective, shrugging his shoulders. "We will call there on our way, and you can tell the porter. They will know where to find us."

Chapter XVII

SIR CHARLES COLLINGHAM and his escort, M. Floçon, entered a cab together and were driven first to the Faubourg St. Honoré. The General tried hard to maintain his nonchalance, but he was yet a little crestfallen at the turn things had taken, and M. Floçon, who, on the other hand, was elated and triumphant, saw it. But no words passed between them until they arrived at the portals of the British Embassy, and the General handed out his card to the magnificent porter who received them.

"Kindly let Colonel Papillon have that without delay." The General had written a few words: "I have got into fresh trouble. Come on to me at the Police Prefecture if you can spare the time."

"The Colonel is now in the Chancery: will not monsieur wait?" asked the porter, with superb civility.

But the detective would not suffer this, and interposed, answering abruptly for Sir Charles:

"No. It is impossible. We are going to the Quai l'Horloge. It is an urgent matter."

The porter knew what the Quai l'Horloge meant, and he guessed intuitively who was speaking. Every Frenchman can recognize a police officer, and has, as a rule, no great opinion of him.

"Very well!" now said the porter, curtly, as he banged the wicket-gate on the retreating cab, and he did not hurry himself in giving the card to Colonel Papillon.

"Does this mean that I am a prisoner?" asked Sir Charles, his gorge rising, as it did easily.

"It means, monsieur, that you are in the hands of justice until your recent conduct has been fully explained," said the detective, with the air of a despot.

"But I protest –"

"I wish to hear no further observations, monsieur. You may reserve them till you can give them to the right person."

The General's temper was sorely ruffled. He did not like it at all; yet what could he do? Prudence gained the day, and after a struggle he decided to submit, lest worse might befall him.

There was, in truth, worse to be encountered. It was very irksome to be in the power of this now domineering little man on his own ground, and eager to show his power. It was with a very bad grace that Sir Charles obeyed the curt orders he received, to leave the cab, to enter at a side door of the Prefecture, to follow this pompous conductor along the long vaulted passages of this rambling building, up many flights of stone stairs, to halt obediently at his command when at length they reached a closed door on an upper story.

"It is here!" said M. Floçon, as he turned the handle unceremoniously without knocking. "Enter."

A man was seated at a small desk in the centre of a big bare room, who rose at once at the sight of M. Floçon, and bowed deferentially without speaking.

"Baume," said the Chief, shortly, "I wish to leave this gentleman with you. Make him at home" – the words were spoken in manifest irony – "and when I call you, bring him at once to my cabinet. You, monsieur, you will oblige me by staying here."

Sir Charles nodded carelessly, took the first chair that offered, and sat down by the fire.

He was to all intents and purposes in custody, and he examined his gaoler at first wrathfully, then curiously, struck with his rather strange figure and appearance. Baume, as the Chief had called him, was a short, thick-set man with a great shock head sunk in low between a pair of enormous shoulders, betokening great physical strength; he stood on very thin but greatly twisted bow legs, and the quaintness of his figure was emphasized by the short black blouse or smock-frock he wore over his other clothes like a French artisan.

He was a man of few words, and those not the most polite in tone, for when the General began with a banal remark about the weather, M. Baume replied, shortly: "I wish to have no talk;" and when Sir Charles pulled out his cigarette-case, as he did almost automatically from time to time when in any situation of annoyance or perplexity, Baume raised his hand warningly and grunted: "Not allowed."

"Then I'll be hanged if I don't smoke in spite of every man jack of you!" cried the General, hotly, rising from his seat and speaking unconsciously in English.

"What's that?" asked Baume, gruffly. He was one of the detective staff, and was only doing his duty according to his lights, and he said so with such an injured air that the General was pacified, laughed, and relapsed into silence without lighting his cigarette.

The time ran on, from minutes into nearly an hour, a very trying wait for Sir Charles. There is always something irritating in doing antechamber work, in kicking one's heels in the waiting-room of any functionary or official, high or low, and the General found it hard to possess himself in patience, when he thought he was being thus ignominiously treated by a man like M. Floçon. All the time, too, he was worrying himself about the Countess, wondering first how she had fared; next, where she was just then; last of all, and longest, whether it was possible for her to be mixed up in anything compromising or criminal.

Suddenly an electric bell struck in the room. There was a table telephone at Baume's elbow; he took up the handle, put the tube to his mouth and ear, got his message answered, and then, rising, said abruptly to Sir Charles: "Come."

When the General was at last ushered into the presence of the Chief of the Detective Police, he found to his satisfaction that Colonel Papillon was also there, and at M. Floçon's side sat the instructing judge, M. Beaumont le Hardi, who, after waiting politely until the two Englishmen had exchanged greetings, was the first to speak, and in apology.

"You will, I trust, pardon us, M. le Général, for having detained you here and so long. But there were, as we thought, good and sufficient reasons. If those have now lost some of their cogency, we still stand by our action as having been justifiable in the execution of our duty. We are now willing to let you go free, because – because –"

"We have caught the person, the lady you helped to escape," blurted out the detective, unable to resist making the point.

"The Countess? Is she here, in custody? Never!"

"Undoubtedly she is in custody, and in very close custody too," went on M. Floçon, gleefully. "*Au secret*, if you know what that means – in a cell separate and apart, where no one is permitted to see or speak to her."

"Surely not that? Jack – Papillon – this must not be. I beg of you, implore, insist, that you will get his lordship to interpose."

"But, sir, how can I? You must not ask impossibilities. The Contessa Castagneto is really an Italian subject now."

"She is English by birth, and whether or no, she is a woman, a high-bred lady; and it is abominable, unheard-of, to subject her to such monstrous treatment," said the General.

"But these gentlemen declare that they are fully warranted, that she has put herself in the wrong – greatly, culpably in the wrong."

"I don't believe it!" cried the General, indignantly. "Not from these chaps, a pack of idiots, always on the wrong tack! I don't believe a word, not if they swear."

"But they have documentary evidence – papers of the most damaging kind against her."

"Where? How?"

"He – M. le Juge – has been showing me a note-book;" and the General's eyes, following Jack Papillon's, were directed to a small *carnet*, or memorandum-book, which the Judge, interpreting the glance, was tapping significantly with his finger.

Then the Judge said blandly, "It is easy to perceive that you protest, M. le Général, against that lady's arrest. Is it so? Well, we are not called upon to justify it to you, not in the very least. But we are dealing with a brave man, a gentleman, an officer of high rank and consideration, and you shall know things that we are not bound to tell, to you or to anyone."

"First," he continued, holding up the note-book, "do you know what this is? Have you ever seen it before?"

"I am dimly conscious of the fact, and yet I cannot say when or where."

"It is the property of one of your fellow travelers – an Italian called Ripaldi."

"Ripaldi?" said the General, remembering with some uneasiness that he had seen the name at the bottom of the Countess's telegram. "Ah! Now I understand."

"You had heard of it, then? In what connection?" asked the Judge, a little carelessly, but it was a suddenly planned pitfall.

"I now understand," replied the General, perfectly on his guard, "why the note-book was familiar to me. I had seen it in that man's hands in the waiting-room. He was writing in it."

"Indeed? A favourite occupation evidently. He was fond of confiding in that note-book, and committed to it much that he never expected would see the light – his movements, intentions, ideas, even his inmost thoughts. The book – which he no doubt lost inadvertently, is very incriminating to himself and his friends."

"What do you imply?" hastily inquired Sir Charles.

"Simply that it is on that which is written here that we base one part, perhaps the strongest, of our case against the Countess. It is strangely but convincingly corroborative of our suspicions against her."

"May I look at it for myself?" went on the General in a tone of contemptuous disbelief.

"It is in Italian. Perhaps you can read that language? If not, I have translated the most important passages," said the Judge, offering some other papers.

"Thank you; if you will permit me, I should prefer to look at the original;" and the General, without more ado, stretched out his hand and took the note-book.

What he read there, as he quickly scanned its pages, shall be told in the next chapter. It will be seen that there were things written that looked very damaging to his dear friend, Sabine Castagneto.

Chapter XVIII

RIPALDI'S DIARY – its ownership plainly shown by the record of his name in full, Natale Ripaldi, inside the cover – was a commonplace note-book bound in shabby drab cloth, its edges and corners strengthened with some sort of white metal. The pages were of coarse paper, lined blue and red, and they were dog-eared and smirched as though they had been constantly turned over and used.

The earlier entries were little more than a record of work to do or done.

"**Jan. 11.** To call at Café di Roma, 12.30. Beppo will meet me.

"**Jan. 13.** Traced M. L. Last employed as a model at S.'s studio, Palazzo B.

"**Jan. 15.** There is trouble brewing at the Circulo Bonafede; Louvaih, Malatesta, and the Englishman Sprot, have joined it. All are noted Anarchists.

"**Jan. 20.** Mem., pay Trattore. The Bestia will not wait. X. is also pressing, and Mariuccia. Situation tightens.

"**Jan. 23.** Ordered to watch Q. Could I work him? No. Strong doubts of his solvency.

"**Feb. 10**, 11, 12. After Q. No grounds yet.

"**Feb. 27.** Q. keeps up good appearance. Any mistake? Shall I try him? Sorely pressed. X. threatens me with Prefettura.

"**March 1.** Q. in difficulties. Out late every night. Is playing high; poor luck.

"**March 3.** Q. means mischief. Preparing for a start?

"**March 10.** Saw Q. about, here, there, everywhere."

Then followed a brief account of Quadling's movements on the day before his departure from Rome, very much as they have been described in a previous chapter. These were made mostly in the form of reflections, conjectures, hopes, and fears; hurry-scurry of pursuit had no doubt broken the immediate record of events, and these had been entered next day in the train.

"**March 17 (the day previous).** He has not shown up. I thought to see him at the buffet at Genoa. The conductor took him his coffee to the car. I hoped to have begun an acquaintance.

"**12.30.** Breakfasted at Turin. Q. did not come to table. Found him hanging about outside restaurant. Spoke; got short reply. Wishes to avoid observation, I suppose.

"But he speaks to others. He has claimed acquaintance with madame's lady's maid, and he wants to speak to the mistress. 'Tell her I must speak to her,' I heard him say, as I passed close to them. Then they separated hurriedly.

"At Modane he came to the Douane, and afterwards into the restaurant. He bowed across the table to the lady. She hardly recognized him, which is odd. Of course she must know him; then why –? There is something between them, and the maid is in it.

"What shall *I* do? I could spoil any game of theirs if I stepped in. What are they after? His money, no doubt.

"So am I; I have the best right to it, for I can do most for him. He is absolutely in my power, and he'll see that – he's no fool – directly he knows who I am, and why I'm here. It will be worth his while to buy me off, if I'm ready to sell myself, and my duty, and the Prefettura – and why shouldn't I? What better can I do? Shall I ever have such a chance again? Twenty, thirty, forty thousand lire, more, even, at one stroke; why, it's a fortune! I could go to the Republic, to America, North or South, send for Mariuccia – no, *cos petto!* I will continue free! I will spend the money on myself, as I alone will have earned it, and at such risk.

"I have worked it out thus:

"I will go to him at the very last, just before we are reaching Paris. Tell him, threaten him with arrest, then give him his chance of escape. No fear that he won't accept it; he *must*, whatever he may have settled with the others. *Altro!* I snap my fingers at them. He has most to fear from me."

The next entries were made after some interval, a long interval – no doubt, after the terrible deed had been done – and the words were traced with trembling fingers, so that the writing was most irregular and scarcely legible.

"Ugh! I am still trembling with horror and fear. I cannot get it out of my mind; I never shall. Why, what tempted me? How could I bring myself to do it?

"But for these two women – they are fiends, furies – it would never have been necessary. Now one of them has escaped, and the other – she is here, so cold-blooded, so self-possessed and quiet – who would have thought it of her? That she, a lady of rank and high breeding, gentle, delicate, tender-hearted. Tender? The fiend! Oh, shall I ever forget her?

"And now she has me in her power! But have I not her also? We are in the same boat – we must sink or swim, together. We are equally bound, I to her, she to me. What are we to do? How shall we meet inquiry? *Santissima Donna!* Why did I not risk it, and climb out like the maid? It was terrible for the moment, but the worst would have been over, and now –"

There was yet more, scribbled in the same faltering, agitated handwriting, and from the context the entries had been made in the waiting-room of the railroad station.

"I must attract her attention. She will not look my way. I want her to understand that I have something special to say to her, and that, as we are forbidden to speak, I am writing it herein – that she must contrive to take the book from me and read unobserved.

"*Cos petto!* She is stupid! Has fear dazed her entirely? No matter, I will set it all down."

Now followed what the police deemed such damaging evidence.

"Countess. Remember. Silence – absolute silence. Not a word as to who I am, or what is common knowledge to us both. It is done. That cannot be undone. Be brave, resolute; admit nothing. Stick to it that you know nothing, heard nothing. Deny that you knew *him*, or me. Swear you slept soundly the night through, make some excuse, say you were drugged, anything, only be on your guard, and say nothing about me. I warn you. Leave me alone. Or – but your interests are my interests; we must stand or fall together. Afterwards I will meet you – I *must* meet you somewhere. If we miss at the station front, write to me Poste Restante, Grand Hôtel, and give me an address. This is imperative. Once more, silence and discretion."

This ended the writing in the note-book, and the whole perusal occupied Sir Charles from fifteen to twenty minutes, during which the French officials watched his face closely, and his friend Colonel Papillon anxiously.

But the General's mask was impenetrable, and at the end of his reading he turned back to read and re-read many pages, holding the book to the light, and seeming to examine the contents very curiously.

"Well?" said the Judge at last, when he met the General's eye.

"Do you lay great store by this evidence?" asked the General in a calm, dispassionate voice.

"Is it not natural that we should? Is it not strongly, conclusively incriminating?"

"It would be so, of course, if it were to be depended upon. But as to that I have my doubts, and grave doubts."

"Bah!" interposed the detective; "that is mere conjecture, mere assertion. Why should not the book be believed? It is perfectly genuine –"

"Wait, sir," said the General, raising his hand. "Have you not noticed – surely it cannot have escaped so astute a police functionary – that the entries are not all in the same handwriting?"

"What! Oh, that is too absurd!" cried both the officials in a breath.

They saw at once that if this discovery were admitted to be an absolute fact, the whole drift of their conclusions must be changed.

"Examine the book for yourselves. To my mind it is perfectly clear and beyond all question," insisted Sir Charles. "I am quite positive that the last pages were written by a different hand from the first."

Chapter XIX

FOR SEVERAL MINUTES both the Judge and the detective pored over the note-book, examining page after page, shaking their heads, and declining to accept the evidence of their eyes.

"I cannot see it," said the Judge at last; adding reluctantly, "No doubt there is a difference, but it is to be explained."

"Quite so," put in M. Floçon. "When he wrote the early part, he was calm and collected; the last entries, so straggling, so ragged, and so badly written, were made when he was fresh from the crime, excited, upset, little master of himself. Naturally he would use a different hand."

"Or he would wish to disguise it. It was likely he would so wish," further remarked the Judge.

"You admit, then, that there is a difference?" argued the General, shrewdly. "But there is more than a disguise. The best disguise leaves certain unchangeable features. Some letters, capital Gs, Hs, and others, will betray themselves through the best disguise. I know what I am saying. I have studied the subject of handwriting; it interests me. These are the work of two different hands. Call in an expert; you will find I am right."

"Well, well," said the Judge, after a pause, "let us grant your position for the moment. What do you deduce? What do you infer therefrom?"

"Surely you can see what follows – what this leads us to?" said Sir Charles, rather disdainfully.

"I have formed an opinion – yes, but I should like to see if it coincides with yours. You think –"

"I know," corrected the General. "I know that, as two persons wrote in that book, either it is not Ripaldi's book, or the last of them was not Ripaldi. I saw the last writer at his work, saw him with my own eyes. Yet he did not write with Ripaldi's hand – this is incontestable, I am sure of it, I will swear it – ergo, he is not Ripaldi."

"But you should have known this at the time," interjected M. Floçon, fiercely. "Why did you not discover the change of identity? You should have seen that this was not Ripaldi."

"Pardon me. I did not know the man. I had not noticed him particularly on the journey. There was no reason why I should. I had no communication, no dealings, with any of my fellow passengers except my brother and the Countess."

"But some of the others would surely have remarked the change?" went on the Judge, greatly puzzled. "That alone seems enough to condemn your theory, M. le General."

"I take my stand on fact, not theory," stoutly maintained Sir Charles, "and I am satisfied I am right."

"But if that was not Ripaldi, who was it? Who would wish to masquerade in his dress and character, to make entries of that sort, as if under his hand?"

"Some one determined to divert suspicion from himself to others –"

"But stay – does he not plainly confess his own guilt?"

"What matter if he is not Ripaldi? Directly the inquiry was over, he could steal away and resume his own personality – that of a man supposed to be dead, and therefore safe from all interference and future pursuit."

"You mean – upon my word, I compliment you, M. le Général. It is really ingenious! Remarkable, indeed! Superb!" cried the Judge, and only professional jealousy prevented M. Floçon from conceding the same praise.

"But how– what– I do not understand," asked Colonel Papillon in amazement. His wits did not travel quite so fast as those of his companions.

"Simply this, my dear Jack," explained the General: "Ripaldi must have tried to blackmail Quadling, as he proposed, and Quadling turned the tables on him. They fought, no doubt, and Quadling killed him, possibly in self-defence. He would have said so, but in his peculiar position as an absconding defaulter he did not dare. That is how I read it, and I believe that now these gentlemen are disposed to agree with me."

"In theory, certainly," said the Judge, heartily. "But oh! For some more positive proof of this change of character! If we could only identify the corpse, prove clearly that it is not Quadling. And still more, if we had not let this so-called Ripaldi slip through our fingers! You will never find him, M. Floçon, never."

The detective hung his head in guilty admission of this reproach.

"We may help you in both these difficulties, gentlemen," said Sir Charles, pleasantly. "My friend here, Colonel Papillon, can speak as to the man Quadling. He knew him well in Rome, a year or two ago."

"Please wait one moment only;" the detective touched a bell, and briefly ordered two fiacres to the door at once.

"That is right, M. Floçon," said the Judge. "We will all go to the Morgue. The body is there by now. You will not refuse your assistance, monsieur?"

"One moment. As to the other matter, M. le General?" went on M. Floçon. "Can you help us to find this miscreant, whoever he may be?"

"Yes. The man who calls himself Ripaldi is to be found – or, at least, you would have found him an hour or so ago – at the Hotel Ivoire, Rue Bellechasse. But time has been lost, I fear."

"Nevertheless, we will send there."

"The woman Hortense was also with him when last I heard of them."

"How do you know?" began the detective, suspiciously.

"Psha!" interrupted the Judge; "that will keep. This is the time for action, and we owe too much to the General to distrust him now."

"Thank you; I am pleased to hear you say that," went on Sir Charles. "But if I have been of some service to you, perhaps you owe me a little in return. That poor lady! Think what she is suffering. Surely, to oblige me, you will now set her free?"

"Indeed, monsieur, I fear – I do not see how, consistently with my duty" protested the Judge.

"At least allow her to return to her hotel. She can remain there at your disposal. I will promise you that."

"How can you answer for her?"

"She will do what I ask, I think, if I may send her just two or three lines."

The Judge yielded, smiling at the General's urgency, and shrewdly guessing what it implied.

Then the three departures from the Prefecture took place within a short time of each other.

A posse of police went to arrest Ripaldi; the Countess returned to the Hôtel Madagascar; and the Judge's party started for the Morgue – only a short journey – where they were presently received with every mark of respect and consideration.

The keeper, or officer in charge, was summoned, and came out bareheaded to the fiacre, bowing low before his distinguished visitors.

"Good morning, La Pêche," said M. Floçon in a sharp voice. "We have come for an identification. The body from the Lyons Station – he of the murder in the sleeping-car – is it yet arrived?"

"But surely, at your service, Chief," replied the old man, obsequiously. "If the gentlemen will give themselves the trouble to enter the office, I will lead them behind, direct into the mortuary chamber. There are many people in yonder."

It was the usual crowd of sightseers passing slowly before the plate glass of this, the most terrible shop-front in the world, where the goods exposed, the merchandise, are hideous corpses laid out in rows upon the marble slabs, the battered, tattered remnants of outraged humanity, insulted by the most terrible indignities in death.

Who make up this curious throng, and what strange morbid motives drag them there? Those fat, comfortable-looking women, with their baskets on their arms; the decent workmen in dusty blouses, idling between the hours of work; the riffraff of the streets, male or female, in various stages of wretchedness and degradation? A few, no doubt, are impelled by motives we cannot challenge – they are torn and tortured by suspense, trembling lest they may recognize missing dear ones among the exposed; others stare carelessly at the day's 'take', wondering, perhaps, if they may come to the same fate; one or two are idle sightseers, not always French, for the Morgue is a favourite haunt with the irrepressible tourist doing Paris. Strangest of all, the murderer himself, the doer of the fell deed, comes here, to the very spot where his victim lies stark and reproachful, and stares at it spellbound, fascinated, filled more with remorse, perchance, than fear at the risk he runs. So common is this trait, that in mysterious murder cases the police of Paris keep a disguised officer among the crowd at the Morgue, and have thereby made many memorable arrests.

"This way, gentlemen, this way;" and the keeper of the Morgue led the party through one or two rooms into the inner and back recesses of the buildings. It was behind the scenes of the Morgue, and they were made free of its most gruesome secrets as they passed along.

The temperature had suddenly fallen far below freezing-point, and the icy cold chilled to the very marrow. Still worse was an all-pervading, acrid odour of artificially suspended animal decay. The cold-air process, that latest of scientific contrivances to arrest the waste of tissue, has now been applied at the Morgue to preserve and keep the bodies fresh, and allow them to be for a longer time exposed than when running water was the only aid. There are, moreover, many specially contrived refrigerating chests, in which those still unrecognized corpses are laid by for months, to be dragged out, if needs be, like carcasses of meat.

"What a loathsome place!" cried Sir Charles. "Hurry up, Jack! Let us get out of this, in Heaven's name!"

"Where's my man?" quickly asked Colonel Papillon in response to this appeal.

"There, the third from the left," whispered M. Floçon. "We hoped you would recognize the corpse at once."

"That? Impossible! You do not expect it, surely? Why, the face is too much mangled for anyone to say who it is."

"Are there no indications, no marks or signs, to say whether it is Quadling or not?" asked the Judge in a greatly disappointed tone.

"Absolutely nothing. And yet I am quite satisfied it is not him. For the simple reason that –"

"Yes, yes, go on."

"That Quadling in person is standing out there among the crowd."

Chapter XX

M. FLOÇON was the first to realize the full meaning of Colonel Papillon's surprising statement.

"Run, run, La Pêche! Have the outer doors closed; let no one leave the place."

"Draw back, gentlemen!" he went on, and he hustled his companions with frantic haste out at the back of the mortuary chamber. "Pray Heaven he has not seen us! He would know us, even if we do not him."

Then with no less haste he seized Colonel Papillon by the arm and hurried him by the back passages through the office into the outer, public chamber, where the astonished crowd stood, silent and perturbed, awaiting explanation of their detention.

"Quick, monsieur!" whispered the Chief; "point him out to me."

The request was not unnecessary, for when Colonel Papillon went forward, and, putting his hand on a man's shoulder, saying, "Mr. Quadling, I think," the police officer was scarcely able to restrain his surprise.

The person thus challenged was very unlike anyone he had seen before that day, Ripaldi most of all. The moustache was gone, the clothes were entirely changed; a pair of dark green spectacles helped the disguise. It was strange indeed that Papillon had known him; but at the moment of recognition Quadling had removed his glasses, no doubt that he might the better examine the object of his visit to the Morgue, that gruesome record of his own fell handiwork.

Naturally he drew back with well-feigned indignation, muttering half-unintelligible words in French, denying stoutly both in voice and gesture all acquaintance with the person who thus abruptly addressed him.

"This is not to be borne," he cried. "Who are you that dares –"

"Ta! Ta!" quietly put in M. Floçon; "we will discuss that fully, but not here. Come into the office; come, I say, or must we use force?"

There was no escaping now, and with a poor attempt at bravado the stranger was led away.

"Now, Colonel Papillon, look at him well. Do you know him? Are you satisfied it is –"

"Mr. Quadling, late banker, of Rome. I have not the slightest doubt of it. I recognize him beyond all question."

"That will do. Silence, sir!" This to Quadling. "No observations. I too can recognize you now as the person who called himself Ripaldi an hour or two ago. Denial is useless. Let him be searched; thoroughly, you understand, La Pêche? Call in your other men; he may resist."

They gave the wretched man but scant consideration, and in less than three minutes had visited every pocket, examined every secret receptacle, and practically turned him inside out.

After this there could no longer be any doubt of his identity, still less of his complicity in the crime.

First among the many damning evidences of his guilt was the missing pocket-book of the porter of the sleeping-car. Within was the train card and the passengers' tickets, all the papers which the man Groote had lost so unaccountably. They had, of course, been stolen from his person with the obvious intention of impeding the inquiry into the murder. Next, in another inner pocket was Quadling's own wallet, with his own visiting-cards, several letters addressed to him by name; above all, a thick sheaf of bank-notes of all nationalities – English, French, Italian, and amounting in total value to several thousands of pounds.

"Well, do you still deny? Bah! It is childish, useless, mere waste of breath. At last we have penetrated the mystery. You may as well confess. Whether or no, we have enough to convict you by independent testimony," said the Judge, severely. "Come, what have you to say?"

But Quadling, with pale, averted face, stood obstinately mute. He was in the toils, the net had closed round him, they should have no assistance from him.

"Come, speak out; it will be best. Remember, we have means to make you –"

"Will you interrogate him further, M. Beaumont le Hardi? Here, at once?"

"No, let him be removed to the Prefecture; it will be more convenient; to my private office."

Without more ado a fiacre was called, and the prisoner was taken off under escort, M. Floçon seated by his side, one policeman in front, another on the box, and lodged in a secret cell at the Quai l'Horloge.

"And you, gentlemen?" said the Judge to Sir Charles and Colonel Papillon. "I do not wish to detain you further, although there may be points you might help us to elucidate if I might venture to still trespass on your time?"

Sir Charles was eager to return to the Hôtel Madagascar, and yet he felt that he should best serve his dear Countess by seeing this to the end. So he readily assented to accompany the Judge, and Colonel Papillon, who was no less curious, agreed to go too.

"I sincerely trust," said the Judge on the way, "that our people have laid hands on that woman Petitpré. I believe that she holds the key to the situation, that when we hear her story we shall have a clear case against Quadling; and – who knows? – she may completely exonerate Madame la Comtesse."

During the events just recorded, which occupied a good hour, the police agents had time to go and come from the Rue Bellechasse. They did not return empty-handed, although at first it seemed as if they had made a fruitless journey. The Hôtel Ivoire was a very second-class place, a lodging-house, or hotel with furnished rooms let out by the week to lodgers with whom the proprietor had no very close acquaintance. His clerk did all the business, and this functionary produced the register, as he is bound by law, for the inspection of the police officers, but afforded little information as to the day's arrivals.

"Yes, a man calling himself Dufour had taken rooms about midday, one for himself, one for madame who was with him, also named Dufour – his sister, he said;" and he went on at the request of the police officers to describe them.

"Our birds," said the senior agent, briefly. "They are wanted. We belong to the detective police."

"All right." Such visits were not new to the clerk.

"But you will not find monsieur; he is out; there hangs his key. Madame? No, she is within. Yes, that is certain, for not long since she rang her bell. There, it goes again."

He looked up at the furiously oscillating bell, but made no move.

"Bah! They do not pay for service; let her come and say what she needs."

"Exactly; and we will bring her," said the officer, making for the stairs and the room indicated.

But on reaching the door, they found it locked. From within? Hardly, for as they stood there in doubt, a voice inside cried vehemently:

"Let me out! Help! Help! Send for the police. I have much to tell them. Quick! Let me out."

"We are here, my dear, just as you require us. But wait; step down, Gaston, and see if the clerk has a second key. If not, call in a locksmith – the nearest. A little patience only, my beauty. Do not fear."

The key was quickly produced, and an entrance effected.

A woman stood there in a defiant attitude, with arms akimbo; she, no doubt, of whom they were in search. A tall, rather masculine-looking creature, with a dark, handsome face, bold black eyes just now flashing fiercely, rage in every feature.

"Madame Dufour?" began the police officer.

"Dufour! Rot! My name is Hortense Petitpré; who are you? *La Rousse* (police)?"

"At your service. Have you anything to say to us? We have come on purpose to take you to the Prefecture quietly, if you will let us; or –"

"I will go quietly. I ask nothing better. I have to lay information against a miscreant – a murderer – the vile assassin who would have made me his accomplice – the banker, Quadling, of Rome!"

In the fiacre Hortense Petitpré talked on with such incessant abuse, virulent and violent, of Quadling, that her charges were neither precise nor intelligible.

It was not until she appeared before M. Beaumont le Hardi, and was handled with great dexterity by that practised examiner, that her story took definite form.

What she had to say will be best told in the clear, formal language of the official disposition.

The witness inculpated stated:

"She was named Aglaé Hortense Petitpré, thirty-four years of age, a Frenchwoman, born in Paris, Rue de Vincennes No. 374. Was engaged by the Contessa Castagneto, November 19, 189–, in Rome, as lady's maid, and there, at her mistress's domicile, became acquainted with the Sieur Francis Quadling, a banker of the Via Condotti, Rome.

"Quadling had pretensions to the hand of the Countess, and sought, by bribes and entreaties, to interest witness in his suit. Witness often spoke of him in complimentary terms to her mistress, who was not very favourably disposed towards him.

"One afternoon (two days before the murder) Quadling paid a lengthened visit to the Countess. Witness did not hear what occurred, but Quadling came out much distressed, and again urged her to speak to the Countess. He had heard of the approaching departure of the lady from Rome, but said nothing of his own intentions.

"Witness was much surprised to find him in the sleeping-car, but had no talk to him till the following morning, when he asked her to obtain an interview for him with the Countess, and promised a large reward. In making this offer he produced a wallet and exhibited a very large number of notes.

"Witness was unable to persuade the Countess, although she returned to the subject frequently. Witness so informed Quadling, who then spoke to the lady, but was coldly received.

"During the journey witness thought much over the situation. Admitted that the sight of Quadling's money had greatly disturbed her, but, although pressed, would not say when the first idea of robbing him took possession of her. (Note by Judge – that she had resolved to do so is, however, perfectly clear, and the conclusion is borne out by her acts. It was she who secured the Countess's medicine bottle; she, beyond doubt, who drugged the porter at Laroche. In no other way can her presence in the sleeping-car between Laroche and Paris be accounted for – presence which she does not deny.)

"Witness at last reluctantly confessed that she entered the compartment where the murder was committed, and at a critical moment. An affray was actually in progress between the Italian Ripaldi and the incriminated man Quadling, but the witness arrived as the last fatal blow was struck by the latter.

"She saw it struck, and saw the victim fall lifeless on the floor.

"Witness declared she was so terrified she could at first utter no cry, nor call for help, and before she could recover herself the murderer threatened her with the ensanguined knife. She threw herself on her knees, imploring pity, but the man Quadling told her that she was an eye-witness, and could take him to the guillotine – she also must die.

"Witness at last prevailed on him to spare her life, but only on condition that she would leave the car. He indicated the window as the only way of escape; but on this for a long time she refused to venture, declaring that it was only to exchange one form of death for another. Then, as Quadling again threatened to stab her, she was compelled to accept this last chance, never hoping to win out alive.

"With Quadling's assistance, however, she succeeded in climbing out through the window and in gaining the roof. He had told her to wait for the first occasion when the train slackened speed to leave it and shift for herself. With this intention he gave her a thousand francs, and bade her never show herself again.

"Witness descended from the train not far from the small station of Villeneuve on the line, and there took the local train for Paris. Landed at the Lyons Station, she heard of the inquiry in progress, and then, waiting outside, saw Quadling disguised as the Italian leave in company with another man. She followed and marked Quadling down, meaning to denounce him on the first opportunity. Quadling, however, on issuing from the restaurant, had accosted her, and at once offered her a further sum of five thousand francs as the price of silence, and she had gone with him to the Hôtel Ivoire, where she was to receive the sum. Quadling had paid it, but on one condition, that she would remain at the Hotel Ivoire until the following day. Apparently he had distrusted her, for he had contrived to lock her into her compartment. As she did not choose to be so imprisoned, she summoned assistance, and was at length released by the police."

This was the substance of Hortense Petitpré's deposition, and it was corroborated in many small details.

When she appeared before the Judge, with whom Sir Charles Collingham and Colonel Papillon were seated, the former at once pointed out that she was wearing a dark mantle trimmed with the same sort of passementerie as that picked up in the sleeping-car.

L'Envoi

QUADLING was in due course brought before the Court of Assize and tried for his life. There was no sort of doubt of his guilt, and the jury so found, but, having regard to certain extenuating circumstances, they recommended him to mercy. The chief of these was Quadling's positive assurance that he had been first attacked by Ripaldi; he declared that the Italian detective had in the first instance tried to come to terms with him, demanding 50,000 francs as his price for allowing him to go at large; that when Quadling distinctly refused to be black-mailed, Ripaldi struck at him with a knife, but that the blow failed to take effect.

Then Quadling closed with him and took the knife from him. It was a fierce encounter, and might have ended either way, but the unexpected entrance of the woman Petitpré took off Ripaldi's attention, and then he, Quadling, maddened and reckless, stabbed him to the heart.

It was not until after the deed was done that Quadling realized the full measure of his crime and its inevitable consequences. Then, in a daring effort to extricate himself, he intimidated the woman Petitpré, and forced her to escape through the sleeping-car window.

It was he who had rung the signal-bell to stop the train and give her a chance of leaving it. It was after the murder, too, that he conceived the idea of personating Ripaldi, and, having disfigured him beyond recognition, as he hoped, he had changed clothes and compartments.

On the strength of this confession Quadling escaped the guillotine, but he was transported to New Caledonia for life.

The money taken on him was forwarded to Rome, and was usefully employed in reducing his liabilities to the depositors in the bank.

The other word.

Sometime in June the following announcement appeared in all the Paris papers:

"Yesterday, at the British Embassy, General Sir Charles Collingham, K.C.B., was married to Sabine, Contessa di Castagneto, widow of the Italian Count of that name."

A Trap to Catch a Cracksman

E.W. Hornung

I WAS JUST putting out my light when the telephone rang a furious tocsin in the next room. I flounced out of bed more asleep than awake; in another minute I should have been past ringing up. It was one o'clock in the morning, and I had been dining with Swigger Morrison at his club.

"Hulloa!"

"That you, Bunny?"

"Yes – are you Raffles?"

"What's left of me! Bunny, I want you – quick."

And even over the wire his voice was faint with anxiety and apprehension.

"What on earth has happened?"

"Don't ask! You never know –"

"I'll come at once. Are you there, Raffles?"

"What's that?"

"Are you there, man?"

"Ye-e-es."

"At the Albany?"

"No, no; at Maguire's."

"You never said so. And where's Maguire?"

"In Half-moon Street."

"I know that. Is he there now?"

"No – not come in yet – and I'm caught."

"Caught!"

"In that trap he bragged about. It serves me right. I didn't believe in it. But I'm caught at last ... caught ... at last!"

"When he told us he set it every night! Oh, Raffles, what sort of a trap is it? What shall I do? What shall I bring?"

But his voice had grown fainter and wearier with every answer, and now there was no answer at all. Again and again I asked Raffles if he was there; the only sound to reach me in reply was the low metallic hum of the live wire between his ear and mine. And then, as I sat gazing distractedly at my four safe walls, with the receiver still pressed to my head, there came a single groan, followed by the dull and dreadful crash of a human body falling in a heap.

In utter panic I rushed back into my bedroom, and flung myself into the crumpled shirt and evening clothes that lay where I had cast them off. But I knew no more what I was doing than what to do next. I afterward found that I had taken out a fresh tie, and tied it rather better than usual; but I can remember thinking of nothing but Raffles in some diabolical man-trap, and of a grinning monster stealing in to strike him senseless with one murderous blow. I must have looked in the glass to array myself as I did; but the mind's eye was the seeing eye, and it was filled with this frightful vision of the notorious pugilist known to fame and infamy as Barney Maguire.

It was only the week before that Raffles and I had been introduced to him at the Imperial Boxing Club. Heavy-weight champion of the United States, the fellow was still drunk with his sanguinary triumphs on that side, and clamoring for fresh conquests on ours. But his reputation had crossed the Atlantic before Maguire himself; the grandiose hotels had closed their doors to him; and he had already taken and sumptuously furnished the house in Half-moon Street which does not re-let to this day. Raffles had made friends with the magnificent brute, while I took timid stock of his diamond studs, his jewelled watch-chain, his eighteen-carat bangle, and his six-inch lower jaw. I had shuddered to see Raffles admiring the gewgaws in his turn, in his own brazen fashion, with that air of the cool connoisseur which had its double meaning for me. I for my part would as lief have looked a tiger in the teeth. And when we finally went home with Maguire to see his other trophies, it seemed to me like entering the tiger's lair. But an astounding lair it proved, fitted throughout by one eminent firm, and ringing to the rafters with the last word on fantastic furniture.

The trophies were a still greater surprise. They opened my eyes to the rosier aspect of the noble art, as presently practised on the right side of the Atlantic. Among other offerings, we were permitted to handle the jewelled belt presented to the pugilist by the State of Nevada, a gold brick from the citizens of Sacramento, and a model of himself in solid silver from the Fisticuff Club in New York. I still remember waiting with bated breath for Raffles to ask Maguire if he were not afraid of burglars, and Maguire replying that he had a trap to catch the cleverest cracksman alive, but flatly refusing to tell us what it was. I could not at the moment conceive a more terrible trap than the heavyweight himself behind a curtain. Yet it was easy to see that Raffles had accepted the braggart's boast as a challenge. Nor did he deny it later when I taxed him with his mad resolve; he merely refused to allow me to implicate myself in its execution. Well, there was a spice of savage satisfaction in the thought that Raffles had been obliged to turn to me in the end. And, but for the dreadful thud which I had heard over the telephone, I might have extracted some genuine comfort from the unerring sagacity with which he had chosen his night.

Within the last twenty-four hours Barney Maguire had fought his first great battle on British soil. Obviously, he would no longer be the man that he had been in the strict training before the fight; never, as I gathered, was such a ruffian more off his guard, or less capable of protecting himself and his possessions, than in these first hours of relaxation and inevitable debauchery for which Raffles had waited with characteristic foresight. Nor was the terrible Barney likely to be more abstemious for signal punishment sustained in a far from bloodless victory. Then what could be the meaning of that sickening and most suggestive thud? Could it be the champion himself who had received the *coup de grâce* in his cups? Raffles was the very man to administer it – but he had not talked like that man through the telephone.

And yet – and yet – what else could have happened? I must have asked myself the question between each and all of the above reflections, made partly as I dressed and partly in the hansom on the way to Half-moon Street. It was as yet the only question in my mind. You must know what your emergency is before you can decide how to cope with it; and to this day I sometimes tremble to think of the rashly direct method by which I set about obtaining the requisite information. I drove every yard of the way to the pugilist's very door. You will remember that I had been dining with Swigger Morrison at his club.

Yet at the last I had a rough idea of what I meant to say when the door was opened. It seemed almost probable that the tragic end of our talk over the telephone had been caused by the sudden arrival and as sudden violence of Barney Maguire. In that case I was resolved to tell him that Raffles and I had made a bet about his burglar trap, and that I had come to see who had won. I might or might not confess that Raffles had rung me out of bed to this end. If, however, I was wrong about Maguire, and he had not come home at all, then my action would depend upon the menial who answered my reckless ring. But it should result in the rescue of Raffles by hook or crook.

I had the more time to come to some decision, since I rang and rang in vain. The hall, indeed, was in darkness; but when I peeped through the letterbox I could see a faint beam of light from the back room. That was the room in which Maguire kept his trophies and set his trap. All was quiet in the house: could they have haled the intruder to Vine Street in the short twenty minutes which it had taken me to dress and to drive to the spot? That was an awful thought; but even as I hoped against hope, and rang once more, speculation and suspense were cut short in the last fashion to be foreseen.

A brougham was coming sedately down the street from Piccadilly; to my horror, it stopped behind me as I peered once more through the letterbox, and out tumbled the dishevelled prizefighter and two companions. I was nicely caught in my turn. There was a lamppost right opposite the door, and I can still see the three of them regarding me in its light. The pugilist had been at least a fine figure of a bully and a braggart when I saw him before his fight; now he had a black eye and a bloated lip, hat on the back of his head, and made-up tie under one ear. His companions were his sallow little Yankee secretary, whose name I really forget, but whom I met with Maguire at the Boxing Club, and a very grand person in a second skin of shimmering sequins.

I can neither forget nor report the terms in which Barney Maguire asked me who I was and what I was doing there. Thanks, however, to Swigger Morrison's hospitality, I readily reminded him of our former meeting, and of more that I only recalled as the words were in my mouth.

"You'll remember Raffles," said I, "if you don't remember me. You showed us your trophies the other night, and asked us both to look you up at any hour of the day or night after the fight."

I was going on to add that I had expected to find Raffles there before me, to settle a wager that we had made about the man-trap. But the indiscretion was interrupted by Maguire himself, whose dreadful fist became a hand that gripped mine with brute fervor, while with the other he clouted me on the back.

"You don't say!" he cried. "I took you for some darned crook, but now I remember you perfectly. If you hadn't've spoke up slick I'd have bu'st your face in, sonny. I would, sure! Come right in, and have a drink to show there's – Jeehoshaphat!"

The secretary had turned the latch-key in the door, only to be hauled back by the collar as the door stood open, and the light from the inner room was seen streaming upon the banisters at the foot of the narrow stairs.

"A light in my den," said Maguire in a mighty whisper, "and the blamed door open, though the key's in my pocket and we left it locked! Talk about crooks, eh? Holy smoke, how I hope we've landed one alive! You ladies and gentlemen, lay round where you are, while I see."

And the hulking figure advanced on tiptoe, like a performing elephant, until just at the open door, when for a second we saw his left revolving like a piston and his head thrown back at its fighting angle. But in another second his fists were hands again, and Maguire was rubbing them together as he stood shaking with laughter in the light of the open door.

"Walk up!" he cried, as he beckoned to us three. "Walk up and see one o' their blamed British crooks laid as low as the blamed carpet, and nailed as tight!"

Imagine my feelings on the mat! The sallow secretary went first; the sequins glittered at his heels, and I must own that for one base moment I was on the brink of bolting through the street door. It had never been shut behind us. I shut it myself in the end. Yet it was small credit to me that I actually remained on the same side of the door as Raffles.

"Reel home-grown, low-down, unwashed Whitechapel!" I had heard Maguire remark within. "Blamed if our Bowery boys ain't cock-angels to scum like this. Ah, you biter, I wouldn't soil my knuckles on your ugly face; but if I had my thick boots on I'd dance the soul out of your carcass for two cents!"

After this it required less courage to join the others in the inner room; and for some moments even I failed to identify the truly repulsive object about which I found them grouped. There was no false hair upon the face, but it was as black as any sweep's. The clothes, on the other hand, were new to me, though older and more pestiferous in themselves than most worn by Raffles for professional purposes. And at first, as I say, I was far from sure whether it was Raffles at all; but I remembered the crash that cut short our talk over the telephone; and this inanimate heap of rags was lying directly underneath a wall instrument, with the receiver dangling over him.

"Think you know him?" asked the sallow secretary, as I stooped and peered with my heart in my boots.

"Good Lord, no! I only wanted to see if he was dead," I explained, having satisfied myself that it was really Raffles, and that Raffles was really insensible. "But what on earth has happened?" I asked in my turn.

"That's what I want to know," whined the person in sequins, who had contributed various ejaculations unworthy of report, and finally subsided behind an ostentatious fan.

"I should judge," observed the secretary, "that it's for Mr. Maguire to say, or not to say, just as he darn pleases."

But the celebrated Barney stood upon a Persian hearth-rug, beaming upon us all in a triumph too delicious for immediate translation into words. The room was furnished as a study, and most artistically furnished, if you consider outlandish shapes in fumed oak artistic. There was nothing of the traditional prize-fighter about Barney Maguire, except his vocabulary and his lower jaw. I had seen over his house already, and it was fitted and decorated throughout by a high-art firm which exhibits just such a room as that which was the scene of our tragedietta. The person in the sequins lay glistening like a landed salmon in a quaint chair of enormous nails and tapestry compact. The secretary leaned against an escritoire with huge hinges of beaten metal. The pugilist's own background presented an elaborate scheme of oak and tiles, with inglenooks green from the joiner, and a china cupboard with leaded panes behind his bullet head. And his bloodshot eyes rolled with rich delight from the decanter and glasses on the octagonal table to another decanter in the quaintest and craftiest of revolving spirit tables.

"Isn't it bully?" asked the prize-fighter, smiling on us each in turn, with his black and bloodshot eyes and his bloated lip. "To think that I've only to invent a trap to catch a crook, for a blamed crook to walk right into! You, Mr. Man," and he nodded his great head at me, "you'll recollect me telling you that I'd gotten one when you come in that night with the other sport? Say, pity he's not with you now; he was a good boy, and I liked him a lot; but he wanted to know too much, and I guess he'd got to want. But I'm liable to tell you now, or else bu'st. See that decanter on the table?"

"I was just looking at it," said the person in sequins. "You don't know what a turn I've had, or you'd offer me a little something."

"You shall have a little something in a minute," rejoined Maguire. "But if you take a little anything out of that decanter, you'll collapse like our friend upon the floor."

"Good heavens!" I cried out, with involuntary indignation, and his fell scheme broke upon me in a clap.

"Yes, *sir*!" said Maguire, fixing me with his bloodshot orbs. "My trap for crooks and cracksmen is a bottle of hocussed whiskey, and I guess that's it on the table, with the silver label around its neck. Now look at this other decanter, without any label at all; but for that they're the dead spit of each other. I'll put them side by side, so you can see. It isn't only the decanters, but the liquor looks the same in both, and tastes so you wouldn't know the difference till you woke up in your tracks. I got the poison from a blamed Indian away west, and it's ruther ticklish stuff. So I keep the label around the trap-bottle, and only leave it out nights. That's the idea, and that's all there is to it," added Maguire, putting the labelled decanter back in the stand. "But I figure it's enough for ninety-nine crooks out of a hundred, and nineteen out of twenty'll have their liquor before they go to work."

"I wouldn't figure on that," observed the secretary, with a downward glance as though at the prostrate Raffles. "Have you looked to see if the trophies are all safe?"

"Not yet," said Maguire, with a glance at the pseudo-antique cabinet in which he kept them. "Then you can save yourself the trouble," rejoined the secretary, as he dived under the octagonal table, and came up with a small black bag that I knew at a glance. It was the one that Raffles had used for heavy plunder ever since I had known him.

The bag was so heavy now that the secretary used both hands to get it on the table. In another moment he had taken out the jewelled belt presented to Maguire by the State of Nevada, the solid silver statuette of himself, and the gold brick from the citizens of Sacramento.

Either the sight of his treasures, so nearly lost, or the feeling that the thief had dared to tamper with them after all, suddenly infuriated Maguire to such an extent that he had bestowed a couple of brutal kicks upon the senseless form of Raffles before the secretary and I could interfere.

"Play light, Mr. Maguire!" cried the sallow secretary. "The man's drugged, as well as down."

"He'll be lucky if he ever gets up, blight and blister him!"

"I should judge it about time to telephone for the police."

"Not till I've done with him. Wait till he comes to! I guess I'll punch his face into a jam pudding! He shall wash down his teeth with his blood before the coppers come in for what's left!"

"You make me feel quite ill," complained the grand lady in the chair. "I wish you'd give me a little something, and not be more vulgar than you can 'elp."

"Help yourself," said Maguire, ungallantly, "and don't talk through your hat. Say, what's the matter with the 'phone?"

The secretary had picked up the dangling receiver.

"It looks to me," said he, "as though the crook had rung up somebody before he went off."

I turned and assisted the grand lady to the refreshment that she craved.

"Like his cheek!" Maguire thundered. "But who in blazes should he ring up?"

"It'll all come out," said the secretary. "They'll tell us at the central, and we shall find out fast enough."

"It don't matter now," said Maguire. "Let's have a drink and then rouse the devil up."

But now I was shaking in my shoes. I saw quite clearly what this meant. Even if I rescued Raffles for the time being, the police would promptly ascertain that it was I who had been rung up by the burglar, and the fact of my not having said a word about it would be directly damning to me, if in the end it did not incriminate us both. It made me quite faint to feel that we might escape the Scylla of our present peril and yet split on the Charybdis of circumstantial evidence. Yet I could see no middle course of conceivable safety, if I held my tongue another moment. So I spoke up desperately, with the rash resolution which was the novel feature of my whole conduct on this occasion. But any sheep would be resolute and rash after dining with Swigger Morrison at his club.

"I wonder if he rang me up?" I exclaimed, as if inspired.

"You, sonny?" echoed Maguire, decanter in hand. "What in hell could he know about you?"

"Or what could you know about him?" amended the secretary, fixing me with eyes like drills.

"Nothing," I admitted, regretting my temerity with all my heart. "But someone did ring me up about an hour ago. I thought it was Raffles. I told you I expected to find him here, if you remember."

"But I don't see what that's got to do with the crook," pursued the secretary, with his relentless eyes boring deeper and deeper into mine.

"No more do I," was my miserable reply. But there was a certain comfort in his words, and some simultaneous promise in the quantity of spirit which Maguire splashed into his glass.

"Were you cut off sudden?" asked the secretary, reaching for the decanter, as the three of us sat round the octagonal table.

"So suddenly," I replied, "that I never knew who it was who rang me up. No, thank you – not any for me."

"What!" cried Maguire, raising a depressed head suddenly. "You won't have a drink in my house? Take care, young man. That's not being a good boy!"

"But I've been dining out," I expostulated, "and had my whack. I really have."

Barney Maguire smote the table with terrific fist.

"Say, sonny, I like you a lot," said he. "But I shan't like you any if you're not a good boy!"

"Very well, very well," I said hurriedly. "One finger, if I must."

And the secretary helped me to not more than two.

"Why should it have been your friend Raffles?" he inquired, returning remorselessly to the charge, while Maguire roared "Drink up!" and then drooped once more.

"I was half asleep," I answered, "and he was the first person who occurred to me. We are both on the telephone, you see. And we had made a bet – "

The glass was at my lips, but I was able to set it down untouched. Maguire's huge jaw had dropped upon his spreading shirt-front, and beyond him I saw the person in sequins fast asleep in the artistic armchair.

"What bet?" asked a voice with a sudden start in it. The secretary was blinking as he drained his glass.

"About the very thing we've just had explained to us," said I, watching my man intently as I spoke. "I made sure it was a man-trap. Raffles thought it must be something else. We had a tremendous argument about it. Raffles said it wasn't a man-trap. I said it was. We had a bet about it in the end. I put my money on the man-trap. Raffles put his upon the other thing. And Raffles was right – it wasn't a man-trap. But it's every bit as good – every little bit – and the whole boiling of you are caught in it except me!"

I sank my voice with the last sentence, but I might just as well have raised it instead. I had said the same thing over and over again to see whether the wilful tautology would cause the secretary to open his eyes. It seemed to have had the very opposite effect. His head fell forward on the table, with never a quiver at the blow, never a twitch when I pillowed it upon one of his own sprawling arms. And there sat Maguire bolt upright, but for the jowl upon his shirt-front, while the sequins twinkled in a regular rise and fall upon the reclining form of the lady in the fanciful chair. All three were sound asleep, by what accident or by whose design I did not pause to inquire; it was enough to ascertain the fact beyond all chance of error.

I turned my attention to Raffles last of all. There was the other side of the medal. Raffles was still sleeping as sound as the enemy – or so I feared at first I shook him gently: he made no sign. I introduced vigor into the process: he muttered incoherently. I caught and twisted an unresisting wrist – and at that he yelped profanely. But it was many and many an anxious moment before his blinking eyes knew mine.

"Bunny!" he yawned, and nothing more until his position came back to him. "So you came to me," he went on, in a tone that thrilled me with its affectionate appreciation, "as I knew you would! Have they turned up yet? They will any minute, you know; there's not one to lose."

"No, they won't, old man!" I whispered. And he sat up and saw the comatose trio for himself.

Raffles seemed less amazed at the result than I had been as a puzzled witness of the process; on the other hand, I had never seen anything quite so exultant as the smile that broke through his blackened countenance like a light. It was all obviously no great surprise, and no puzzle at all, to Raffles.

"How much did they have, Bunny?" were his first whispered words.

"Maguire a good three fingers, and the others at least two."

"Then we needn't lower our voices, and we needn't walk on our toes. *Eheu!* I dreamed somebody was kicking me in the ribs, and I believe it must have been true."

He had risen with a hand to his side and a wry look on his sweep's face.

"You can guess which of them it was," said I. "The beast is jolly well served!"

And I shook my fist in the paralytic face of the most brutal bruiser of his time.

"He is safe till the forenoon, unless they bring a doctor to him," said Raffles. "I don't suppose we could rouse him now if we tried. How much of the fearsome stuff do you suppose I took? About a tablespoonful! I guessed what it was, and couldn't resist making sure; the minute I was satisfied, I changed the label and the position of the two decanters, little thinking I should stay to see the fun; but in another minute I could hardly keep my eyes open. I realized then that I was fairly poisoned with some subtle drug. If I left the house at all in that state, I must leave the spoil behind, or be found drunk in the gutter with my head on the swag itself. In any case I should have been picked up and run in, and that might have led to anything."

"So you rang me up!"

"It was my last brilliant inspiration – a sort of flash in the brain-pan before the end – and I remember very little about it. I was more asleep than awake at the time."

"You sounded like it, Raffles, now that one has the clue."

"I can't remember a word I said, or what was the end of it, Bunny."

"You fell in a heap before you came to the end."

"You didn't hear that through the telephone?"

"As though we had been in the same room: only I thought it was Maguire who had stolen a march on you and knocked you out."

I had never seen Raffles more interested and impressed; but at this point his smile altered, his eyes softened, and I found my hand in his.

"You thought that, and yet you came like a shot to do battle for my body with Barney Maguire! Jack-the-Giant-killer wasn't in it with you, Bunny!"

"It was no credit to me – it was rather the other thing," said I, remembering my rashness and my luck, and confessing both in a breath. "You know old Swigger Morrison?" I added in final explanation. "I had been dining with him at his club!"

Raffles shook his long old head. And the kindly light in his eyes was still my infinite reward.

"I don't care," said he, "how deeply you had been dining: *in vino veritas*, Bunny, and your pluck would always out! I have never doubted it, and I never shall. In fact, I rely on nothing else to get us out of this mess."

My face must have fallen, as my heart sank at these words. I had said to myself that we were out of the mess already – that we had merely to make a clean escape from the house – now the easiest thing in the world. But as I looked at Raffles, and as Raffles looked at me, on the threshold of the room where the three sleepers slept on without sound or movement, I grasped the real problem that lay before us. It was twofold; and the funny thing was that I had seen both horns of the dilemma for myself, before Raffles came to his senses. But with Raffles in his right mind, I had ceased to apply my own, or to carry my share of our common burden another inch. It had been an unconscious withdrawal on my part, an instinctive tribute to my leader; but, I was sufficiently ashamed of it as we stood and faced the problem in each other's eyes.

"If we simply cleared out," continued Raffles, "you would be incriminated in the first place as my accomplice, and once they had you they would have a compass with the needle pointing straight to me. They mustn't have either of us, Bunny, or they will get us both. And for my part they may as well!"

I echoed a sentiment that was generosity itself in Raffles, but in my case a mere truism.

"It's easy enough for me," he went on. "I am a common house-breaker, and I escape. They don't know me from Noah. But they do know you; and how do you come to let me escape? What has happened to you, Bunny? That's the crux. What could have happened after they all dropped off?" And for a minute Raffles frowned and smiled like a sensation novelist working out a plot; then the light broke, and transfigured him through his burnt cork. "I've got it, Bunny!" he exclaimed. "You took some of the stuff yourself, though of course not nearly so much as they did.

"Splendid!" I cried. "They really were pressing it upon me at the end, and I did say it must be very little."

"You dozed off in your turn, but you were naturally the first to come to yourself. I had flown; so had the gold brick, the jewelled belt, and the silver statuette. You tried to rouse the others. You couldn't succeed; nor would you if you did try. So what did you do? What's the only really innocent thing you could do in the circumstances?"

"Go for the police," I suggested dubiously, little relishing the prospect.

"There's a telephone installed for the purpose," said Raffles. "I should ring them up, if I were you. Try not to look blue about it, Bunny. They're quite the nicest fellows in the world, and what you have to tell them is a mere microbe to the camels I've made them swallow without a grain of salt. It's really the most convincing story one could conceive; but unfortunately there's another point which will take more explaining away."

And even Raffles looked grave enough as I nodded.

"You mean that they'll find out you rang me up?"

"They may," said Raffles. "I see that I managed to replace the receiver all right. But still – they may."

"I'm afraid they will," said I, uncomfortably. "I'm very much afraid I gave something of the kind away. You see, you had not replaced the receiver; it was dangling over you where you lay.

This very question came up, and the brutes themselves seemed so quick to see its possibilities that I thought best to take the bull by the horns and own that I had been rung up by somebody. To be absolutely honest, I even went so far as to say I thought it was Raffles!"

"You didn't, Bunny!"

"What could I say? I was obliged to think of somebody, and I saw they were not going to recognize you. So I put up a yarn about a wager we had made about this very trap of Maguire's. You see, Raffles, I've never properly told you how I got in, and there's no time now; but the first thing I had said was that I half expected to find you here before me. That was in case they spotted you at once. But it made all that part about the telephone fit in rather well."

"I should think it did, Bunny," murmured Raffles, in a tone that added sensibly to my reward. "I couldn't have done better myself, and you will forgive my saying that you have never in your life done half so well. Talk about that crack you gave me on the head! You have made it up to me a hundredfold by all you have done tonight. But the bother of it is that there's still so much to do, and to hit upon, and so precious little time for thought as well as action."

I took out my watch and showed it to Raffles without a word. It was three o'clock in the morning, and the latter end of March. In little more than an hour there would be dim daylight in the streets. Raffles roused himself from a reverie with sudden decision.

"There's only one thing for it, Bunny," said he. "We must trust each other and divide the labor. You ring up the police, and leave the rest to me."

"You haven't hit upon any reason for the sort of burglar they think you were, ringing up the kind of man they know I am?"

"Not yet, Bunny, but I shall. It may not be wanted for a day or so, and after all it isn't for you to give the explanation. It would be highly suspicious if you did."

"So it would," I agreed.

"Then will you trust me to hit on something – if possible before morning – in any case by the time it's wanted? I won't fail you, Bunny. You must see how I can never, never fail you after tonight!"

That settled it. I gripped his hand without another word, and remained on guard over the three sleepers while Raffles stole upstairs. I have since learned that there were servants at the top of the house, and in the basement a man, who actually heard some of our proceedings! But he was mercifully too accustomed to nocturnal orgies, and those of a far more uproarious character, to appear unless summoned to the scene. I believe he heard Raffles leave. But no secret was made of his exit: he let himself out and told me afterward that the first person he encountered in the street was the constable on the beat. Raffles wished him good-morning, as well he might; for he had been upstairs to wash his face and hands; and in the prize-fighter's great hat and fur coat he might have marched round Scotland Yard itself, in spite of his having the gold brick from Sacramento in one pocket, the silver statuette of Maguire in the other, and round his waist the jewelled belt presented to that worthy by the State of Nevada.

My immediate part was a little hard after the excitement of those small hours. I will only say that we had agreed that it would be wisest for me to lie like a log among the rest for half an hour, before staggering to my feet and rousing house and police; and that in that half-hour Barney Maguire crashed to the floor, without waking either himself or his companions, though not without bringing my beating heart into the very roof of my mouth.

It was daybreak when I gave the alarm with bell and telephone. In a few minutes we had the house congested with dishevelled domestics, irascible doctors, and arbitrary minions of the law.

If I told my story once, I told it a dozen times, and all on an empty stomach. But it was certainly a most plausible and consistent tale, even without that confirmation which none of the other victims was as yet sufficiently recovered to supply. And in the end I was permitted to retire from the scene until required to give further information, or to identify the prisoner whom the good police confidently expected to make before the day was out.

I drove straight to the flat. The porter flew to help me out of my hansom. His face alarmed me more than any I had left in Half-moon Street. It alone might have spelled my ruin.

"Your flat's been entered in the night, sir," he cried. "The thieves have taken everything they could lay hands on."

"Thieves in my flat!" I ejaculated aghast. There were one or two incriminating possessions up there, as well as at the Albany.

"The door's been forced with a jimmy," said the porter. "It was the milkman who found it out. There's a constable up there now."

A constable poking about in my flat of all others! I rushed upstairs without waiting for the lift. The invader was moistening his pencil between laborious notes in a fat pocketbook; he had penetrated no further than the forced door. I dashed past him in a fever. I kept my trophies in a wardrobe drawer specially fitted with a Bramah lock. The lock was broken – the drawer void.

"Something valuable, sir?" inquired the intrusive constable at my heels.

"Yes, indeed – some old family silver," I answered. It was quite true. But the family was not mine.

And not till then did the truth flash across my mind. Nothing else of value had been taken. But there was a meaningless litter in all the rooms. I turned to the porter, who had followed me up from the street; it was his wife who looked after the flat.

"Get rid of this idiot as quick as you can," I whispered. "I'm going straight to Scotland Yard myself. Let your wife tidy the place while I'm gone, and have the lock mended before she leaves. I'm going as I am, this minute!"

And go I did, in the first hansom I could find – but not straight to Scotland Yard. I stopped the cab in Piccadilly on the way.

Old Raffles opened his own door to me. I cannot remember finding him fresher, more immaculate, more delightful to behold in every way. Could I paint a picture of Raffles with something other than my pen, it would be as I saw him that bright March morning, at his open door in the Albany, a trim, slim figure in matutinal gray, cool and gay and breezy as incarnate spring.

"What on earth did you do it for?" I asked within.

"It was the only solution," he answered, handing me the cigarettes. "I saw it the moment I got outside."

"I don't see it yet."

"Why should a burglar call an innocent gentleman away from home?"

"That's what we couldn't make out."

"I tell you I got it directly I had left you. He called you away in order to burgle you too, of course!"

And Raffles stood smiling upon me in all his incomparable radiance and audacity.

"But why me?" I asked. "Why on earth should he burgle me?"

"My dear Bunny, we must leave something to the imagination of the police. But we will assist them to a fact or two in due season. It was the dead of night when Maguire first took us to his house; it was at the Imperial Boxing Club we met him; and you meet queer fish at the

Imperial Boxing Club. You may remember that he telephoned to his man to prepare supper for us, and that you and he discussed telephones and treasure as we marched through the midnight streets. He was certainly bucking about his trophies, and for the sake of the argument you will be good enough to admit that you probably bucked about yours. What happens? You are overheard; you are followed; you are worked into the same scheme, and robbed on the same night."

"And you really think this will meet the case?"

"I am quite certain of it, Bunny, so far as it rests with us to meet the case at all."

"Then give me another cigarette, my dear fellow, and let me push on to Scotland Yard."

Raffles held up both hands in admiring horror. "Scotland Yard!"

"To give a false description of what you took from that drawer in my wardrobe."

"A false description! Bunny, you have no more to learn from me. Time was when I wouldn't have let you go there without me to retrieve a lost umbrella – let alone a lost cause!"

And for once I was not sorry for Raffles to have the last unworthy word, as he stood once more at his outer door and gayly waved me down the stairs.

Three Words

Nathan Hystad

THE LIGHTS FLICKERED quickly down the hallway, making my vision swim. All signs over the past few weeks had pointed me to this moment. I nodded to Sarah who stood with her back to the door, salt gun raised. A strange odour cast out from the school's music room. The soundproofed door was black and didn't have one of those regular small windows with mesh inside like the other classrooms at this inner-city school.

On the count of three she moved and I whispered three words as I kicked at the door. It went flying in and was left hanging by the top hinge only. In that instant my body felt the weeks of sleep deprivation and mental exhaustion. I shook it off and raised my hand towards the blackness in the corner of the room.

It hovered there, crackling energy as it sucked the life out of the students hanging by their feet from the ceiling. The lights in the room had long ago blown out but Sarah and I had flipped our lenses over to *darkness*. I could see each of the kids wriggle and fight to stay alive but the demon just laughed at them. It hardly seemed to take us as a threat as we closed in on it, still sucking away. It was getting stronger every moment we let it linger and it knew it.

I lifted my arm and flicked the switch on my wrist. The pentagram projected against the ceiling and the demon faltered and fell to the ground. Dark mist poured off of it and back into the children's mouths as it flailed and screamed. Sarah tossed a blanket of chain mail doused in holy water and salt over the beast and the room shook when it convulsed in agony. The hall lights blew out as the energy demon shrieked and then lay still.

Some of the children groggily came to and Sarah and I rushed to get them down from their tethers. I hopped on a desk and cut at the ropes holding them. My knife slid quickly through the demon's twine and once again I was thankful for the Fellowship's hesitant gift to me. Abraham's knife, blessed by God, was enough to cut through most things I stood against.

Soon all seven kids were shakily thanking Sarah and me for saving them. I turned on my flashlight and set my knife down while Sarah smiled at me.

"Another textbook case, hey boss?" she gave me her patented sideways smirk. "See what I did there? Textbook... we're in a school..."

I groaned and quipped back, "That joke might just get you into detention." The flashlight blew up, and before we could turn the demon was on us.

"How did it get out of the net?" I yelled as I fumbled to grab my knife.

"I knew I should have tested it myself. They must have forgot to bless it... again!"

The kids all pushed back against the wall and screamed, reliving the horror the creature had bestowed upon them moments ago. Blackness surrounded me as it enveloped my essence, sucking the life from me. Panic shot from every pore of my body, but I felt the familiar handle of the knife in my grip as I shot my arm out. Mist poured from my mouth at the monster, but I severed it with the blade just as Sarah shot the thing in the side of its head, black ichor spraying me in the face. My life-mist shot back at me, and I hoped it hadn't kept any of it. Too much more of that and I would be dead sooner than I'd like.

The demon melted into the floor; all that was left were seven kids screaming, Sarah grimacing, and me wiping the ooze of a demon off my face. A pile of sulphur sat on the ground. She reached over and slipped her hand into mine, somehow making it all better.

* * *

"Good work, Mal." Bundross rarely said those words to me. I waited for the 'but'. "But, couldn't you have found this thing before it got to the kids?" There it was.

"I would have if the damn thing left a clue once in a while. I was lucky to have caught up to it at all. I don't know what's going on out there but these demons are getting much better at covering their tracks. Most of the time we don't know where they've been until we find a body."

Bundross took a long drink from his coffee cup and leaned back in his chair. "Mal, I know we don't always see eye to eye, but the Fellowship contacted me today." My heart sped up at the words and I looked to the side of the room, disappointed I hadn't noticed the scrying supplies sooner. Some used crystal balls, Bundross preferred a salad bowl with Holy water in it. To each their own.

"What did they want?" I asked, not sure I wanted to hear the answer. When the Fellowship stuck its nose into our business, it was always serious.

"Senator Marcus Morrison's daughter is missing." He paused to see my reaction I'm sure. I tried to keep my composure. I'd had a few run-ins with the Fellowship's top dog in the past, and if there was one thing I knew, Morrison had no love for me. He was a full-blown Warlock, but it seemed even he couldn't keep his daughter safe.

"And I suppose he wants this 'irresponsible, foolish braggart' to find her for him."

"He may think you go to extremes, and too often almost blow the Fellowship's cover, but you get the job done. And no, he doesn't want you to find her per se. It's the demon we need you to find, because wherever it is, she will be there."

"That's just semantics, sir. Well, I suppose I don't have a say. I'll get Sarah and we will be right on the case."

He paled and set his coffee cup down. I got a sinking feeling in my gut. "Mal, Sarah will not be able to join you on this one. I've given her another task; a shot at leading her own team. Out of state."

"What are you not telling me?"

"The demon is *Jelthesda*, Sarah's grandmother."

Well at least now I knew why my partner was sent out of town. Sarah was the one who caught Jelthesda and had her locked away for good. Wait, if she was out...

"But she's locked away. I saw her put in there myself. You know, that small black room with glowing Pentagrams and salted walls? The same type of room we have hundreds of demons stored away in."

Bundross leaned back and raised his hands to run across his balding head. "She's gone. Last night. Morrison's kid went missing an hour later – sulphur was found in the town car she'd been riding in."

Crap. Sarah's grandmother was a mean mama jama. A soul demon; one of the most subtle of their kind. With one touch, she could turn a soul over to the Devil, leaving the human body an empty husk with very little brain activity. Doctors often thought the victims are recipients of major head injuries since the demons left them with aneurism-type symptoms.

"I need to know the motivation. How did she break out and why go after Morrison's kid?"

"That's what we need you to find out. We can assume that she is using the girl as leverage against the head of the Fellowship. Go to the jail now and see if you can find anything, then head over to Morrison's office. The town car is there waiting for you to comb through it."

"Why me? Isn't there someone he trusts more that could do this?"

Bundross leaned forward and stared me in the eyes. "You're the best. Find her, bring the demon back to her cell, and you are free to leave the Fellowship's clutches. We will never demand anything from you again."

I left the room with thoughts of a cabin on a lake, a fire burning in the hearth and Sarah by my side. There was no time for that. I had a job to do.

* * *

The passageways under city hall were dimly lit as I made my way to the cells. I reached the end of the hall, which looked much like the rest of the walls. Only, there was a door here, it was just hidden. I knocked under the wall sconce, and a muffled voice asked a question. I answered the question and the wall slid open. Two huge guards stood with guns pointed at me.

"Easy fellas. It's me, Mal." I held my hand out and they took a DNA scan. The light flashed green and they stood to the side, letting me pass. You could never be too sure with shape-taking demons on the loose. It wouldn't be the first time one snuck in here to free one of their own.

Plasma lamps burned along the walls. There was no electricity down here because the Energy demons blew light bulbs up all the time. I passed by a few dark doorways and I peeked into the fourth down the hall. The neon pentagram lightly lit up the black demon I brought here just a couple days ago. I waved at it, and got a scream from inside in return. Demons don't really die as we know it. This one in particular was able to regenerate itself. It makes it really tough to rid the world of them. I knew I was safe here but it still caused me to jump back as it fought against its invisible restraints. Maybe I wasn't as safe as I thought – Jelthesda had broken out somehow.

I kept moving in the blue light until I ended up at the open door. I was told it was left as they'd found it. Or as close as they could with dumb guards trouncing around the jail-break site. The door was one-foot-thick, salt-lined, re-enforced platinum, which I was told no demon could get through. It appeared they were correct, because the door was just open, not beat down or blown up. Either she manipulated it from inside or someone had let her out.

The neon pentagrams were still on, glowing in all directions. There was a large one on the ceiling with a matching one under the glass floor. There was no way a demon should have been able to break the pull of the pentagram; they were embedded in glass and there was no way to break their power. It just didn't make sense. For her to leave the room, she must have had help.

I watched all the surveillance video, but I was no techie, and for all I knew it had been tampered with. It showed the door open, and the demon escape. Soul demons look just like humans, so out walked a beautiful woman, wearing nothing but long raven-black hair. Nothing was allowed in the rooms with the monsters, especially clothing. I felt embarrassed watching Sarah's grandmother walking around naked, and I started to turn away. Lucky I caught it before I did. There was a slight blur beside her. I rewound the video and saw the blur again. This time, it moved down the hall, paused, the door opened, then the blur followed behind Jelthesda.

Someone had broken her out and I was going to find out who.

* * *

Senator Marcus Morrison met me in the garage. He was a tall, imposing man. It was no doubt that he'd been voted in because of his powerful demeanour. I mean, who wouldn't want a beast of a man on their side in the government. He stood a head taller than me and his voice was deep.

"Mal. Thank you for helping me find Elizabeth. She means everything to me. When I find that demon bitch I will crush her."

I shook his hand and felt the brunt of his anger. I pulled it back and rubbed my knuckles as I thought about my next step. "Can I see the car please, sir?"

He led me to the town car and showed me the claw marks where his daughter had tried to stay in the car. The driver had been found drooling, and with minimal brain activity; classic soul demon stuff.

I assumed that Morrison's men had been through the car from top to bottom but I took a look around it anyway. After a half hour of nothing, I spotted something. I turned to see the Senator on his phone across the room. I whispered three words, my words; my secret words. The spot on the floor lit up, glowing softly and I took the tiny residue and swept it into a vial I'd been carrying in my pocket. This may be the proof I needed to incriminate but doubted that I'd get so lucky.

I quickly excused myself and wondered if Morrison had any idea what I'd just found back there. I doubted it.

* * *

If I were a soul-stealing demon bitch, where would I be? Believe me, I ask that question at least once a month; I needed some new material. Or maybe I just needed a new job.

So, what did I have so far? I had a blurry blob, helping Jelthesda escape the prison. I had a vial of magic residue from the back of a town car, and I had a missing twelve-year-old girl. I hated the Fellowship. I got caught up in some risky business years ago and they bailed me out. Let's just say my soul would be riding the lava sea in hell right now if they hadn't made the bargain. Now the bastards owned me, and this may have been my only way out. Except I have never trusted Morrison. Sure they helped stop the overflow of evil from Hell, but only when it was convenient for their own selfish ways.

I called in every favour I could over the next four hours and not one of them had seen hide nor hair of the raven-haired beauty. This wasn't uncommon. Even the narcs didn't want their soul handed over to the Devil so they would keep quiet, and I wasn't in the mood to force them to talk.

I sat in a shady neighborhood bar, and ordered a beer from the bottle. You can never tell what you are getting if you don't open it yourself. I knew something was missing but couldn't place my finger on it. If I didn't find Morrison's daughter in a few hours, statistics tell me she will either be dead or brain-dead. I didn't want to call Sarah but didn't think I had a choice. She may know where her grandmother might go.

I tried calling... no answer. I shot her a text... no reply. I had another beer, and still no answer. She always got back to me within fifteen minutes no matter what... and I mean no matter what. Panic pushed its way into my psyche, and I fought it off as I headed for the bathroom. I stepped over a drugged out slime-ball and locked the stall door behind me. After flushing the toilet I grabbed a vial from my coat pocket. When in need, you have to improvise. I'd never done a soul search in a toilet before but I thought it would probably work.

I dropped five drops in the water and said my words. I pictured Sarah and closed my eyes. My vision swam when I opened my eyes and the toilet water appeared to be spinning in the wrong direction. Then she appeared. Sarah's image showed up quite strongly and I knew she wasn't out of town. Then I saw the rope... she was tied to a pole in a dim room. The image moved slightly, and there was a smaller form beside her. Odds are it was Morrison's daughter.

My heart raced as I tried to figure it out. The image dimmed and I cursed at it, as I tried to pick out any distinguishable markings. And there it was, just before the toilet went back to normal; a box labeled 'Macleer's' behind them.

* * *

Macleer's was an old warehouse on Front Street. Sometimes luck plays a heavy role in what I do, and it just so happens that in my previous life, I worked a summer job for them. I was a pallet jack donkey, and I lasted a whole two months before they noticed I was horrible at the gig. I tried to pull it all together and figure out what was going on. I wasn't in the Fellowship's inner circle but I'd heard rumblings of a coup d'état over there. Sarah had her fingers on the pulse much better than I did, and from what she gathered, some of the Fellowship thought they were abusing their power by imprisoning the demons.

Race equality and all of that junk that makes headlines in this politically correct world we live in. Only thing was, this one wasn't making headlines because it all happened behind closed doors. What do you think would happen if the Earth's population actually knew they were constantly at battle with demons? Oh yeah, did I mention that werewolves were real too? How about succubae? They are the worst!

As I pulled up a block away from Macleer's, I wished I could call Sarah for backup. Too bad she was the one who needed rescuing. It all seemed so obvious, but at the time I was blinded by the idea of getting out of the Fellowship's clutches. No more back-alley sulphur quests, sniffing through fish market garbage looking for signs of a siren demon. You can guess what that one does.

I checked all of my supplies and was ready for whatever was waiting for me. I also had my words on the tip of my tongue, ready to exhaust them on my rivals. My three words that gave me most of my power. I loved those words, and knew I would have to give them up when I left the job. Maybe I could sneak away and keep them.

A clang a few feet away startled me and in my new-found panic, I saw a cat running away; its garbage can now rolling down the alley. The area was almost pitch black and I threw my goggles on to see if there was anything dangerous around. Nothing. I couldn't see any light from under the warehouse doors, but I found the handle and was almost surprised to find it unlocked.

Soul demons weren't overly strong by a seeker's standards, but they were often quite smart. They also gained brownie points for each soul they sent the big red guy's way, and I don't mean Santa Claus. I looked around for traps, but I doubted they could have foreseen me doing a toilet scrying session, and then knowing where Macleer's was. It was far-fetched to be honest.

I took out my sulphur reader and it was coming up with just trace amounts in the air. It appeared I might have been lucky again. I thought the vision I had was in the janitor's closet by the employee washrooms so I snuck along the wall to the back of the large open room. There it was, the room where Morrison's daughter and Sarah would be held. I pressed my ear against the door and thought I heard some heavy breathing, but no other noise. I tested the door handle and it was locked. Nothing a quick lock-pick in the dark couldn't solve. I tinkered with the door for what I thought was two minutes but judging by the sweat pouring off my face, was probably much longer. With a click, I opened the door slowly and quietly. My goggles were still on and I saw Sarah tied up near the back of the small room. Then where was Morrison's kid?

Something jumped in front of me and kicked me square in the chest. I flew back a yard or two and crashed to the floor. I hardly saw it but knew this was a damn, dirty ghoul. They'd do any task for a pound of human flesh; I just hoped the flesh wasn't off the girl... or me for that matter. It came at me, long arms swinging. I knew these things can't see in the dark, but they kind of have an extra-sensory thing going on like a bat. I ducked out of its way, and it stumbled but quickly turned around to face me. I grabbed a vial from my belt and threw the rock salt at it. The salt wasn't harmful but it would confuse its sensors for a moment. It clawed in front of itself blindly and I kicked the thing in the kneecap. It fell down hard and I followed it up with a swift kick to the face. The crunching sound told me it wouldn't be getting up for a while.

Sarah was fighting her bonds and her cries were muffled by a rag in her mouth. As I pulled the rag from her mouth, I saw her eyes rise to the ceiling. I spun but it was too late; Jelthesda's hand was on my face. I could feel the pull on my soul, and it was horrifying. The Devil was going to have to wait for this one. He could have it when I died, like the good old days.

I clutched her small wrist and tried to tear it away. Firm as hell. I felt my knife slip from my belt and hoped Sarah had something up her sleeve. The pain was excruciating and I fell to my knees. Just before I was about to black out, I saw him enter the room. Senator Marcus Morrison. He smiled as he watched my soul ripping from my body. I guess he forgot I still had my words.

"Telthaz, Finalta, Lumina!" I waved my hand at Jelthesda. She tore open, black ichor spraying all over Morrison's ridiculously expensive suit. He looked like he was about to vomit for a second but soon he was in front of me clutching my throat.

"I don't know how you do it, Mal. Always messing things up. I had a whole plan and everything. You were going to get framed for killing my daughter by letting out your partner's grandmother. I was going to bring back the demon and cry for the Fellowship's sympathy. All this equal rights, demons-have-feelings-too shit was going to be flushed down the toilet and we could keep on owning them. Stealing their ichor for power. Good thing I still have half of my plan to deal with." He licked his face, where the ichor had sprayed him. I swore he got a little bigger when he did it. My mouth hung open.

"Oh, I see you didn't know the little secret did you? Demon blood makes us stronger... much stronger. And the fools wanted to end my little farming project and stop holding them prisoner. I couldn't have that could I?"

"Why are you telling me this?" I felt his grip tighten on my throat. The powder I found in the back of the car was Warlock residue, and he would have the power to go invisible as well; the blurry figure in the video.

"Because you are going to be dead in a few minutes anyways."

"What about your daughter? Is she really dead?" I croaked.

"Her body is in your trunk as we speak. One of the casualties of war."

The man was sick and I had to think of a way to escape him and quick. I hoped my stalling him was enough for Sarah to do what I knew she was going to do.

Apparently it was. I saw the knife blade point towards me and the pain in my throat lessen as Morrison's face looked down. I guess Sarah had cut free from her bonds. Blood pooled out of the wound and Sarah backed away from behind him, blade in her hands.

"It wasn't supposed to happen like this. She told me I was invincible." He fell to the ground. I fell beside him, exhausted from the events, and my extreme use of my powers draining me completely.

Sarah was quickly at my side. "They tricked me... my grandmother said she was let go after cutting a deal with the Fellowship. She said she needed me. I couldn't ignore family. I'm such a fool."

I was about to black out so I had to say the other three words I'd been meaning to say. "I love you," followed by, "I'm sorry I killed your grandma."

* * *

The fire crackled lightly, warming the cabin on the cool autumn night. Sarah nestled in close as we lay naked under the wool blanket. It was itchy but I didn't mind at that moment. Morrison didn't die. Apparently all that demon blood he'd been consuming had made him part demon. The Fellowship had him locked away beside the rest of them, to forever spend his days basking in neon lights.

I hadn't quite escaped the Fellowship yet, but they put Bundross in charge for the time being, and he was someone I could actually get along with.

I saw a glow coming from the kitchen and turned to see blue light shining up to the ceiling from the sink.

"Speak of the Devil... or think of him," I whispered as I walked over to see what Bundross wanted.

His face looked up at me from the half full sink. There was some cutlery on the bottom soaking.

"You know Bundross, there is such thing as a cell phone. You know, that little computer thing we all carry around?"

"There's no time to argue. Three demons are wreaking havoc downtown. I need you two here now!" Bundross replied franticly.

I looked back and Sarah was already getting dressed. "Sure thing boss man. But you owe me another vacation day."

The vision blurred and just the water remained.

I was still in the business, and truth be told I was glad. And I still had my three words. Both sets of them.

The Marionettist

John A. Karr

Something old, something new, something borrowed, something blew.
The Old Bridal Rhyme, Debra Holland

SUMMERTIME, and the dyin's easy.

Late August. Late in the morning. For some – even the young – late in life.

Clouds crept like massive cancer cells through the skies of coastal North Carolina. Thunderstorms had opened up or threatened each afternoon since July, and the salty air hung hot and thick with the expectation of more violence.

The Wilmington Area Soccer League (WASL) had carved out fifty acres in New Hanover County. On it were over a dozen soccer fields, a stadium, a two-story management office and several maintenance sheds. The league welcomed all ages from five to eighteen.

On one of the rearmost fields, the Under Elevens (U-11) were locked in a 1-1 tie. The spectators – parents and siblings mostly – had set up chairs beneath a strip of thick sweet gums along the sidelines. The trees provided welcome relief from the sun, but today came with consequences far darker than any shade they provided. Had this been the fall or winter, concern or even alarm may have been raised at the site of the approaching airborne objects.

Lives may have been saved.

The game was tight. The parents had become emotionally invested in the contest during warm-ups. Some were boisterous, some were quiet and tense. All were focused on the game.

Above the trees, a small dot grew ever larger as it broke from the sun that rose over nearby Wrightsville Beach. It descended silently toward the last tree in the row sheltering the spectators. The dot grew into two objects, one above the other, connected by strands of black line.

Shouts of encouragement and disappointment carried along the sidelines in waves of verbal jousting. Bored siblings too young to be left at home played electronic devices, or meandered in and out of the shade. One such boy was Travis Suskind. A tiger butterfly gently summoned him from a daydream. It floated and flittered above the players and headed toward the trees on his side of the field. Travis stood, watched it circle twice as if swept up in a dust devil before vanishing in the green upper reaches. The boy crossed behind his shouting mother to investigate.

Movement caught his eye.

As he closed in on the tree, shredded particles of yellow with black stripes drifted down.

What would have ... a bird?

The boy's eyes grew wide.

Dangling a dozen feet from the ground was a three-foot puppet in a puffy black and white body suit, checkered, with matching pointy hat and exaggerated white cuffs at wrists and ankles.

The toy was in perpetual and surreal motion, arms moving in and out at various angles and legs pumping as if it rode a unicycle. The boy walked closer, staring, lips forming a half-smile. He could tell the puppet wasn't mechanical. The strings hanging from the arms of the flying machine above it made the puppet move, like Pinocchio, but this realization did nothing to dispel the fascination.

The eyelids of the little wooden man were closed at first, then snapped open beneath the brim of the peaked hat, giving the boy a start. Travis could not look away from the bright white ovals pitted with black circles. The head tilted, then righted as it appeared to discover the boy. This was repeated over and over to hypnotic effect.

Travis watched in awe and a little fear. One of the few adults to witness the attack, and live, later described the puppet as better suited to medieval England or France.

Travis froze as the small flying machine descended, propellers blurring, bringing the puppet down and toward him. The long legs in puffy pants continued to pump as if riding a unicycle, while the arms snaked out and back and the head tilted from side to side. Down it came, dancing in the air. It moved eerily, hypnotically.

By this time, other children had noticed.

Exclamations arose from the closest parents, in equal parts wonderment and alarm.

Four children and three adults reached the vicinity of the marionette as it moved before Travis. It reached out its long arms, one after the other, beckoning endlessly.

The ref checked his watch and blew the whistle to end the first half of the game.

Laughing, the sidelines children moved closer. Travis opened his arms, emulating the movements of the strange toy. Suddenly the puppet fell into his arms and the drone controller flew away.

A mother's shrill voice: "Travis Suskind! You get away –"

Her words and her son were obliterated when the marionette exploded.

Four children and three adults perished. Five more adults were injured. The trunk of the tree was gouged out to a depth roughly equal to that of a child's coffin.

* * *

The suit cop wore a serious face as he moved from one hospital bed to the next like a cheating husband shopping for a whore. He spoke softly but firmly, with what had to be practiced professionalism. He sounded like he gave just enough of a damn to earn his paycheck. But there was a ringing in the ear of his observer that could be altering audible perception.

He made notes in an electronic pad. A Wilmington Police badge hung in a clip at his breast pocket. He noticed her attention and approached, gaze flicking to the bandage around her head, then to her eyes.

"Ma'am, can you hear me?"

"There's ringing, but I hear you."

"Detective Ramos."

"Detective."

"And you are..."

Ramos would already have her information, but she played along. "Debra Holland of Wilmington, North Carolina."

"Mind a few questions?"

"It's after midnight, you know."

"I apologize. This is the first break I've had from the crime scene today."

"Yesterday, you mean."

He nodded and checked his watch. "Right. It's 12:03. Tomorrow."

She let his joke pass without comment. "I can give you nine minutes."

"12:12?" He paused with a quizzical expression on his face. "Doesn't Cinderella's carriage turn into a pumpkin at midnight? We're past that already."

"Sorry, can't hear you all of a sudden."

The detective raised a hand in capitulation. "Okay, okay. 12:12 deadline, then. What can you tell me about today's – *yesterday's* – tragedy?"

"Horrible! We were caught up in the game. Some kids were excited about something down on the sidelines. I stood up to see what was going on and the world exploded. Got a concussion and a bloody ear."

"Sorry for your injuries, ma'am. Do you recall –"

"Who would do such a thing? I mean, to kids? And adults, for that matter."

"Someone with a lot of hate. And from what we understand from other witnesses, a penchant for marionettes and flying drones."

"What leads do you have?"

"We're working on it."

"None, you mean!"

"That's why I'm here. Any idea what time the bomb went off?"

"After eleven." She produced a cell phone. A steady finger chose the photo app. "I snapped this picture of the field when my neighbor's son was picking up the ball for a throw-in. See the blur? That's when the explosion happened."

"Yes, ma'am. But the time –"

"There's a timestamp in the properties. See?" She expanded the zoom with her fingers.

"Eleven after ... eleven." He gently took the phone. "Mind if our experts take a look at this?"

"Okay, but it's just a blurred field and soccer kids."

Ramos texted the image to his own cell, checked for other pics before it and then handed it back.

"You need to catch this terrorist or whatever he is," Debra Holland said.

"Yes, ma'am. We'll bring him to justice. Don't hesitate to contact me if you recall something more." He checked his watch. "Came in under the deadline. Hope you feel better, Missus Holland."

"Miz. The coach – my husband – died last year. Never made it to the autumn season, really."

"Sorry, ma'am."

"Parkinson's disease and stress took him. Competitive soccer just wants winners. He tried to coach after his condition worsened but they didn't want a sickly man, even with injections every two hours for months on end. Then came the days when his freedom was taken away despite the shots. He just lay there, a prisoner in his own body."

"Try to rest, ma'am." The cop turned and started toward the next bed.

"Every couple hours. Don't be late. Remember – have to *remember*! – the time slots. Repeating pairs aid the memory. Repeating pairs. Repeating pairs. Don't be late or the coach turns to stone."

But Ramos didn't hear her. He spoke with the other two conscious victims and left after only a few more minutes. Soon afterward, a tall broad man carrying a bouquet of flowers entered the trauma unit. He had thinning hair and a blonde moustache. He looked around then fixed his gaze in her direction. He waited, as if seeing something in front of her bed, then took long strides toward her. He placed the flowers on the mobile table beside the bed.

"I don't know you," Debra Holland said.

"Care to answer some questions?" he said.

"You cops really should coordinate better," she said.

"I'm no cop," he replied, pulling one of the wheeled stools close and sitting.

"What, then?"

He shrugged. "Haunted citizen. Sometime reporter."

"Reporter? I just answered questions for the law. I'm done." She didn't care for the newcomer, or how he made a show of staring at her bed. Particularly the rails, which were lowered. "No hospital beds where you come from?"

"Handcuffs. I don't see any. Doesn't look like you confessed the murders to Ramos."

Holland blinked, but made a quick recovery. "I don't care for this line of discussion, Mister."

"Lars Kelsen."

"I didn't ask."

"A stranger points out you're a murderer and you're not curious for a name?"

"Do you always harass crime victims, Lars Kelsen?"

But the man didn't appear to hear her. Instead he stared alongside her bed. She glanced but didn't see anything noteworthy.

"Any idea why a boy's ghost would direct me to your area here?" he asked, coming out of it after a moment.

She reached for the nurse's call button. Kelsen did not appear concerned as she was about to press it. Her finger lingered, then moved away. A hint of a smile formed on her thin lips. "The bomb left me with a ringing head. Did you say 'ghost'?"

"Yes."

"Hallucinate much, Kelsen?"

"Apparently my Visitor was the first to reach your marionette bomb."

"Mine ...?"

"Apt word."

"You're insane!"

"Not enough to matter. Visitors usually arrive when justice fails, but this one's different. He's very new, for one, and happens to be a boy. Bad enough, but he appears *every hour*. Highly unusual."

"I'm sure it is."

"Every media outlet is covering the soccer field bombing. Names and photos have already been released. My Visitor is nine-year old Travis Suskind. And you ... you're Debra Holland. Except for the coaches and ref, you were the only adult at the field unrelated to any of the players."

Her tone sharpened. "Are you fond of puppets, Mr. Kelsen?"

"Can they fish? Normally it's just me and Hooper, but I suppose the dog might not mind one more."

They stared at one another.

"You're going to loose this contest," Holland declared.

Kelsen's brows raised. "Oh?"

"I can out-stare a dead man."

"A common trait of psychopaths."

"Make sure you tell the other victims here about your ... unique situation."

Kelsen's face darkened as he rose. "We all know that's not necessary."

She was silent.

Kelsen continued, almost casually. "It's too early to fear a lack of justice, yet Travis appears to me every hour. Obviously it's urgent, wouldn't you say?"

"I wouldn't begin to know."

"Sure you would. He's trying to prevent another attack. The media is reporting the bomb went off at 11:11. Interesting repetition. Had to be planned that way, wouldn't you say, Ms. Holland?"

"It's Miz Holland. My husband –"

"Yes, your husband who required his medications *every hour* at the end of his life."

"You read the article in the *Star News*, I assume."

"Coincidentally, Travis manifests every hour at repeating combinations. 3:33, 6:06, 10:10. You get the idea."

"Enough of this! I'm calling security."

"You could, but they know me pretty well." Kelsen stood, removed his flowers and placed them at the table of a true victim, sleeping with the aid of a morphine drip.

Holland tried again. "Maybe Detective Ramos would like to know you've been harassing of a victim lucky to be alive."

"Ask if he can scare up an explosives residue kit."

Debra Holland watched him leave with a much darker emotion than bemusement. She stood and found the hand sanitizer hanging on the wall. She rubbed it on her hands and forearms.

Why would Kelsen say all that, then leave? Crazy. Anyone who 'sees ghosts' had to be at least a little insane.

Or maybe he liked taking chances.

Or both.

* * *

It took three swipe attempts at the cell phone before he connected with the incoming call.

"Lars Kelsen."

The words came thin and with reverb, as if bouncing against cave walls. Once again, the image of young Travis stood before him, arms wide. Side view. Even if Kelsen attempted to circle around, his Visitor kept the same angle without discernable movement. It was art of the dead and Kelsen the lone patron. Gradually the sounds of clacking and clicking and conversation rose to the fore, while the Visitor faded.

"You were right," Ramos said. "It happened again already."

Kelsen swore.

"Is this like the Charlotte Bomber case you helped with?"

"Not really. He was more deliberate. Months between incidents." Kelsen glanced at the cell. The phone number was different from last time. Ramos was using a disposable. He didn't want to be linked to Kelsen in case things got ... ugly. "Where?"

"The management building of WASL Soccer."

"How?"

Ramos gave a quick info dump. 3:32 p.m. Monday. Two days after the bombing at the U-11 soccer field. Despite increased police presence, another marionette danced with the aid of a drone atop the roof of the private soccer league's headquarters. At the surrounding fields, kids were beginning to show up for practice. Inside, seated around a long table with a view of a broad window, the management of WASL was holding a meeting with several coaches.

3:33 p.m. A witness glimpsed a marionette dangling beneath a drone at the window. Seconds later, explosion.

Four adults murdered. Three more seriously injured.

Kelsen nodded though Ramos couldn't see him. "Where was Debra Holland?"

"Home. We had eyes on her place the whole time."

"She's doing it remotely. What about internet monitoring?"

"Not without a warrant."

"Can you get one now?"

"Judge says there's not enough probable against the widowed victim."

"Not good, then."

"No, it's not – hold on."

Warning chimes came through the phone. A dispatcher's modulated voice in the background. Dismayed voices responded. Ramos cursed.

"What?" Kelsen said, though he already had an idea.

"Third bombing, goddamn it! WASL again. Complex was closed to the public but cops fell this time. Fill you in later."

Kelsen looked at the cell for the time of day.

4:44.

* * *

The police needed a search warrant. Kelsen, not so much.

Except for waiting until most people would be asleep, he wasn't subtle about the entrance. There wasn't time. Like the San Bernardino terrorists, this one was hiding in plain sight. Kelsen parked his Wrangler a quarter mile away and walked; just another neighbor in cargo shorts and t-shirt. He had the address and Travis verified it for him by remaining just a few feet ahead.

Lights were on in the garage. Kelsen went up the side of the driveway and kicked in the side door. He figured if it exploded, at least the cops would have their probable cause. If he got shot, the place would also receive attention.

He took Debra Holland by surprise at a long wooden workbench. And again when she saw the .45 aimed at her chest. She didn't run.

"Sit," Kelsen said.

Instead she glanced at the bench.

"You're not fast enough," he assured her, raising the gun.

"I'm prepared for death, Kelsen, are you? There's enough here to –"

"Hooper will be well cared for."

"Aren't you curious as to how I made them?"

He shook his head. "I'm more interested in a world with one less terrorist."

She sat and pointed to her bandaged head. "Victim status goes a long way these days." She laughed. "My husband retired from the demolition business. His company even used drones to position explosives in the more dangerous nooks and crannies."

Kelsen spotted a roll of duct tape and tossed it into her lap. "Wrap it around your ankles, then put your forehead on the bench with your arms behind you."

He wrapped her wrists, then taped her to the chair.

Kelsen eyed the row of marionettes propped at the rear of the workbench. Seven of them. Each puppet meant more victims. There was no way the police were going to make an arrest in time. Keeping with Debra Holland's penchant for repetitive digits, there'd been three explosions within three days, with a rising casualty count. Included in that was Travis, who reminded him too much of Erik, had his son lived long enough.

The killer's eyes glowed from the florescent tube over the workbench. "Going to call the police now? Well?"

The marionettist laughed wildly and strained against her bindings.

Kelsen pulled out another chair and placed the marionette the bomber had just primed with blasting caps so it faced its creator.

"Hey!"

Kelsen's eyes held dark promise.

"What are you doing, fool? Call the police!"

Instead he eyed the laptop computer on the bench. The screen had darkened to half power. He slid a finger over the mouse window and the screen brightened to an image of a digital clock. A field beneath it was labeled "Go Time."

"It's one o'clock in the morning," Kelsen murmured. "Do you know where your child is?"

Debra Holland's eyes widened. "My husband died trying to coach those little bastards! They complained he was too weak and fired him!"

"Tell it to the ghost of Travis Suskind. He's standing beside you."

The bomber eyes shifted back and forth. "You're insane."

"I've been on enough of these meet and greets with murderers to know otherwise."

"You can't do this!"

"You can't blow people up either. Yet here we are."

"Call the goddamn police!"

Kelsen pressed a few keys and clicked the OK button.

The computer clock displayed 1:04.

Wide-eyed, the bomber strained against her bindings. Screams, pleas and curses followed Kelsen out of the garage. He hadn't taped her mouth but her vocals were muffled. Maybe it was just his impression, or maybe Travis had a ghostly hand in it. Either way, the neighbor's houses remained dark, the sidewalks empty.

With the .45 holstered at his waist and concealed by the t-shirt, Kelsen strode unhurriedly. He did not feel the sidewalk beneath his running shoes. The night air was warm and thick and the crickets and cicada vied for musical dominance.

The Wrangler was just another vehicle parked on the side of the road. Travis 'stood' on the passenger-side of the hood as Kelsen drove away. Air rushed through the open cab.

Kelsen drove out of the neighborhood and onto one of the four-lane feeder roads. A few miles away he pulled to a stop before a red traffic light. The night seemed to take a long pause. Even the vibration from the Wrangler's engine faded.

His Visitor abruptly vanished.

On the dashboard, the clock seemed frozen at 1:11.

It wasn't long before sirens wailed.

Mechanical Love

Kin S. Law

"TO BE HONEST, Mr. Ross, we're not sure exactly what we should charge," the prosecutor said over his sheaf of legal documents. His suit was clean and pressed, something only a civil servant would take time to do himself, but it was still the grey of deep water. The hearing room was the sort of impartial municipal blue that lent just the right aura of shark-filled waters. I could hear the cameras in the corners.

"Any chance you could hold onto that indecision? The stupid are cocksure while the intelligent are full of doubt," I said.

"Mr. Ross," the judge gave a warning.

"Let it be known consul has not advised Mr. Ross on proper court procedure," said my attorney. Venkman, his name was. Court-appointed, but seemed okay.

"Bertrand Russell," I said flatly.

"Excuse me?"

"Let's just move on."

"Mr. Ross, do you understand the potential charges that are being brought up against you?"

"Yes. I think they're ridiculous."

"I'm sorry, but they're not," Venkman attempted to console me. "The corporation's rights are very clear, and you certainly made it easy for them. Seriously, Isaac, did you have to give them so much to work with?"

"What about our rights? When did a person's rights to a fair trial get superseded by a faceless corporate entity?"

"Since you signed the agreement with the corporation," the prosecutor answered. "When you bought the unit. At the moment, we're considering violation of contract, piracy. Some kind of defamation tort, certainly, with how much media attention this case has gotten –"

"I bought her. Why can't I do what I like with her?" I was ignored.

"– homicide, of course, but we may consider dropping the charge to manslaughter."

"That's what this hearing is all about. Before we make this debacle any bigger, we want the story from your own lips," the judge said. Perfectly neutral.

"For the record, a court-appointed psychologist is present. Doctor Otomo?" Venkman paused.

"Present. Please begin."

"It's a long story," I tried. Not long, just... personal. Venkman was having none of it.

"If we can nip this thing in the bud, it's worth all of our time," Venkman pushed.

"Fine. I'll have to start from when I was a kid, though."

"We have agreed to take Mr. Isaac Ross' testimony in consideration of this unusual case," the prosecutor said. The judge didn't look too happy either.

"Okay," I began.

* * *

When I was two years old, the Krone Corporation had just gone public, and my father thought it would be a great idea to buy in on their stock. What better way to support his purchase than try out the latest product? At the time, Krone was already marketing a number of payment plans, consignments, and warranties, fancy ways of extracting money from hard-working people. I'm sorry, selling a luxury item.

To a toddler barely off the bottle, though, none of this mattered. What mattered was the sudden appearance of the beautiful young nanny in my nursery who didn't get mad when I peed on her, and was there for me twenty-four-seven, needing no rest, food, or time off. Please, don't say robot. That word means 'slave.'

That Model 4 caregiver from Krone was like Mother and Goddess rolled into one. One of my first memories is of hair softer than spun gold, of skin like milk and perfect sky-blue eyes. Of course she had been designed that way, with superhuman symmetry, perfect nanofiber skin, perfect everything. She fed me, and clothed me, and showed me how to use the toilet. She never complained, never recoiled at my young biological functions, and never, ever, not once scolded me. In the absence of my mother, Annie, as I called her, became my first true love.

As I grew taller and my needs expanded, Krone also grew as a company. Feminism had left fallow many roles the patriarchy had once relegated to women. I'm sure you recall the riots. Now those women were competing on equal terms with men, their biological handicaps addressed by medicine, advances in hydrophobic clothing, and acceptance that women did not have to be relegated to kitchens and secretarial work.

Krone grew rich on a demand for nannies that didn't want equal pay. Secretaries who were never late because their jealous boyfriends shredded all their clothes. Maids in insulting outfits, that cleaned when needed, whose hands got rid of smudges on contact, but could be stashed in a closet. Many of them could even hold an original conversation, but that feature was unpopular. There were shops on the street that let you spend time with one, alone. I had no idea what use that could be to an adult person, but my guess at the time was: perhaps, they needed a friend as much as I did. Anyway Krone grew rich on so-called 'stupid' AI: machines just smart enough to do the grunt work, not smart enough to overthrow their meatspace rulers.

This is my testimony; I think the prosecution will allow me the chance to incriminate myself.

Confessions.exe.

EVEN AT A young age I was adamant that Annie never be exchanged for any of her newer models, despite the growing need for an upgrade. Her sapphire pupils never wrinkled round the edges, her perfect skin never blemished, but she had been designed for a two-year old, not a first-grader. To learn how to walk me to school, or teach me arithmetic, or help tune my guitar, my father downloaded the company's updates directly into her drive. Contractually binding applications, that we paid for by the month. A two-second wait by the laptop, and suddenly Annie could sing and dance with the best of them. She could even scold me, and had the superhuman strength to shut me in my room when appropriate. She was my first governess, and at times I hated her for it.

Naturally, as I grew and had the farcical graduation that leads into middle school, I expected my Annie to grow with me. Years of wear and loving use said something different, but more importantly, Krone said something different. Their new models were smarter, more realistic, integrated with many of the devices already within our home. They could drive our cars, make breakfast wirelessly by speaking to our toasters, and even draw perfectly tempered baths without exposing themselves to harmful water. Of course, there were still updates available for Model 4's like Annie, but these were growing fewer and far between, more like quickly slapped together lip service than anything one could actually use. Like any technology, the passion was for the newest model, and the old was left on the wayside. When my Annie froze in the middle of teaching me the waltz, I knew- she was outdated. Krone had pulled her subscription updates, and all her fancy apps were useless.

Why didn't you outgrow her? One might ask. Just abandon her like any old toy or dead pet? No, not my Annie, never. During my high school years, I spent my weekends at the local tech shop, not to buy a motorcycle, or so I had money for dates. I did it for Annie. I could salvage what I wanted from my work, as easily as one might sneak a burger out to a friend at a restaurant.

Whenever I had some money saved, I went online and ordered the expensive one-time apps for Annie. Sometimes it took a whole month to pull together the funds. Sometimes I had to get several kinds of apps and customize it just so. Sometimes I would buy an app after months of saving only to realize most of the things I wanted Annie to do had quietly been disabled. Then the access app would flash me an advertisement for Krone's latest Model 7 that would do all those things right out of the box.

But it was worth it. All so Annie would lean over me in those clean, smooth fabrics and tuck me in like always, or read me stories, or sing in that dulcet voice that had never changed from my childhood. So many things do change, but I always had 'Over the Rainbow' sung by a tin woman.

Nostalgia.exe.

I NEVER MEANT for it to happen, but I suppose it was bound to. It was quite by accident you see, and even though this sort of thing is commonplace nowadays, I feel I have to have a matter of record. I was only trying to find her some better programming. I was about to graduate high school, and I would need some programs for my new lifestyle. Annie would need some new tricks to soothe me during those tough college exams, or help me figure out which classes I needed to take.

I had already discovered an underground network of people who hadn't been satisfied with their old tech, but did not want to give up their nostalgia. Their homebrew programs were sometimes buggy, but didn't ask me to pay for useless apps and advertisements. I found one taught Annie to play spades and console games, and even to develop into a more challenging player as she experienced these activities. All of it was, of course, third party. But now I needed things like career option analysis, researching different colleges, and a program to make her a good listener for getting over my failures. Things a mom would have done, that Father never did.

What? I violated Krone's copyright on the use of their proprietary software? Venkman and I looked it up before this hearing. Annie was more than eighteen years old, and any warranty or copyright had long since expired, or become public domain. It was established in Cal v. Poole that a personal android constitutes private property, and as long as it is not in competition with the company's product, mods are perfectly legal.

Are we contested about this? No? All right. Let's talk about the accident.

I still remember the day the biker clipped me on the campus, the way the hard asphalt slipped underneath and the scrape it left on the meat of my hand, just under the thumb. I never found out who it was. More importantly, the biker left me sprawled across the main thoroughfare of the college, just in front of Professor Gottfried's eight-cylinder, three-ton crossover SUV. The kind of car classified as a 'light truck.'

She ran over both my legs, crushing the ankles and smashed my shins to splinters.

The pain was, of course, excruciating, but more to the point, I was still conscious, and still very much aware of my fellow students screaming and pointing and telling everyone about all the blood spilling out of me. There was no shock, no relief from the agony, just the terrible broken feeling and the humiliation of lying in the street while an ambulance was called. Later, after the morphine and the surgery and the weeks of recovery, there would be more humiliation when the doctors told me I would not be able to live on my own, that while my bones knit back together I would need a live-in nurse to help with my day-to-day living.

"You should look into those new Krone nursing models," the doctor recommended. "I hear their short-term plans are very economical."

"I already have one," I remember saying.

The one thing Annie couldn't do was bathe an adult male. She was good with children, but a failsafe had been installed so people couldn't do... other things... to her. Kind of like a parental guidance chip. I do know Krone had long since stopped making updates compatible with my Annie. She was running OS-M03, while some of the top of the line models had left the numerical designation entirely, preferring a youth-friendly, slogan-apt totem animal instead. Things like T3DDY, or 0WL. PU55I.

I had to look for another option to help my personal hygiene. That was what I got it for, nothing else.

I'm sure you know where this is going, especially if you've read my file. I don't know who wrote the program, but the program's name was Bathtime.exe. It was supposed to help with my tender, healing legs and stop me from stretching or popping the stitches. All I had to do was load the program into Annie, give her the therapeutic, ultra-soft sponge and the gentle, lubricating, hypoallergenic bath soap.

FirstExperiences.exe.

I KNEW THERE were programmers out there who liked to troll, but not to this extent. I think in hindsight I am for ever grateful to them, for breaking down that last barrier between my Annie and me, cementing the connection that had been forged over years of tender care. Needless to say, the three months of healing were better than any honeymoon two flesh and blood people could ever have.

I came out of the therapy and the cast able to walk and hungry for more underground apps. I experimented on everything: D+D, NekoE 2.1, Bottlefeed 2. I bought a lot of lube. S&M 450 Beta was just becoming popular at the time, and I believe my user feedback became an integral part of the ubiquitous 780 Gamma everyone is using today. I know one of the things you, the prosecution, are hoping to get out of this case is the precedent to prosecute everyone using 780 Gamma. Don't deny it, not with those faces you've got on.

After a while, I settled on a series of vanilla programs, going for richness of detail rather than radical new experiences. Immersive scenarios you could act out in your own home, like cooking together, or having huge fights about nothing, or pretending to be out on a date. Seeing a movie and having Annie lean just slightly on my shoulder. Facial expressions you swore a real woman would never replicate.

Your Honor, this is relevant to my testimony. Please let me continue.

It was fun. Like her hair color and her clothes, I could now change her personality at a moment's notice. One night I could have a live-in girlfriend sweeter than any real woman. The next I could have an insatiable nymph in ripped stockings. And the next, a hellion who would make me coffee and push me to further my thesis. I hear real women are like this too, but I can't say for certain, having only known Annie's gentle touch. And Carol, of course. Limited data set.

That was right around when my father passed away.

Oedipus.exe.

I SUPPOSE with all those programs rattling around, I may have lost track of a few of them. Loaded things into her drive that I never bothered to erase. After a while I stopped running the explicit ones and just enjoyed Annie's company – whatever combination I had found worked with my busy lifestyle. I'm sure the forensics program divers will find exactly what went wrong, which app was actually responsible for Carol. Or they won't. I can't be sure, but it's important to mention. I don't think Annie did it, but in the interest of full disclosure...

Let's talk about her? All right.

Carol Darringer. She looked a lot like Annie the way I knew her originally. All blonde and blue-eyed. That drew me immediately, though I was very uncomfortable at first. But she was a programmer like me, just starting out. We had a lot to talk about – we had both read Sartre, and we loved Michel Gondry films. The one about the memories... we used to talk for hours at an all-night diner. She wanted to be a costume designer, making holographic dresses you had to code just right or some trending starlet would have a literal wardrobe malfunction.

When she asked me out, I was simply unprepared. I had never played the game, never accepted an invitation from a woman. But it was appealing, and Carol was pretty, and nice. We went to a movie festival. Then we went to a fashion show. I was fascinated by the programming potential. Then we went out just to be with each other. Coffee was an excuse.

I learned she had been married once before, very young. I met her after her group therapy session. That was how she came out to me about having been abused, and being naturally nervous about men. That was what drew her to me, she said, I seemed gentler and less experienced. Less likely to hurt her.

A week later I spent the night. At her place, naturally. The next month, I was at Carol's nearly every weekend.

EternalSunshine.exe.

I SUPPOSE it was only a matter of time before Carol found out about Annie.

I am still not sure which app made Annie ask me where I had been that weekend. There's a meal plan app and a scheduling app I put in during college, but I had mostly outgrown the need for it. Maybe I hadn't bothered to delete them – there isn't actually a screen on Annie's body to organize these things, and connecting her to one means shutting her down and rebooting her afterward. I was spending too much time with Carol to do a proper maintenance.

Excuses.exe.

ANYWAY, THE ODDNESS got worse. It got to the point where Annie would hobble out the front door after me with a sad puppy look to her android face. I had Carol over pretty often by then, and every time I would ask Annie to go into Father's room and not come out until I said so. Sometimes I would find Carol's things in odd places. A scarf she was missing for a week turned up neatly put away in my closet. Carol's lipstick in the side bathroom she never used. Things like that.

One evening, I woke to go to the bathroom and left Carol in bed. When I went back into the hall I nearly shat myself – there was a figure hovering outside the bathroom like a ghost.

"Jesus, Java and Jobs! Carol?" I whispered. No, it was Annie, padding around quietly on her perfectly sculpted legs. Her lips were a deep red, I remember. "Go back in Father's room, Annie."

"You have not given me new commands for a week," said Annie. "Is everything all right, Isaac?"

I paused. Hadn't I? Annie made my meals, she did my laundry and did things all over the house. Surely I had talked to her sometime that week? And what made her come out to ask? She should have stayed hidden, patiently sitting on Father's bed until I went to get her. Of course, I had loaded apps to make her more of a caregiver, but...

"I don't need anything, Annie," I said. "Go back in the room."

Annie went back in the room. But as she did, I could swear I heard her say in a soft voice, "Who is Carol?"

Who was Carol to me? I think I loved her. Probably. I could see us being together indefinitely, laughing at Gondry and designing runway shows together. Maybe not in the same way I loved Annie. People say love is never the same twice.

Can you love two people at the same time?

Can you love a person and Annie?

I found Carol the next morning in Father's room. When I walked in, she had Annie by the hand, prodding at her thumbs, at her fingers, pulling and pinching the skin. The material.

"Your maid, she's an older model, isn't she?" Carol said. "Why haven't I seen her before?"

"My father got her for me," I said. "She's very old. I guess I keep her here because I didn't know what you would think."

"What would I think?"

"Some people keep androids around for kinky things," I said. I paused. "I... was into that for awhile. But she got me through the accident, and she's been with me my whole life."

Carol paused, looking at me, then at Annie. She touched the plain housedress I had given Annie maybe two weeks ago – it was spotted slightly in one corner, from a cooking mess. I'd meant to get her another one.

"I think it's endearing," said Carol, and gave Annie a kiss on the cheek. Then she put Annie's hand back on her lap, gently, lovingly. After that I did not bother hiding Annie, and

Carol would say hello to her every time she came to the house. We did move her charging station into Father's room.

The weird things still happened, but now it was a little different. Carol's things would be neatly placed where she was likely to find them, like the couch or the nightstand. Carol also never mentioned when something was gone. Sometimes I would walk into a room and find Carol talking animatedly to Annie, or braiding her hair, or doing makeup over Annie's placid face. Annie, who sat being the best listener ever, not talking until Carol asked her a direct question, but ever ready with a helpful suggestion. My house felt warm and good.

BeKindRewind.exe.

CAROL DIED when I was out of the house. I know this doesn't help you rebuild the case, but that's the truth of it. I know the prosecutor is pushing for a homicide charge. He has a theory that I had somehow, for some reason programmed Annie to kill Carol Darringer. I know my account of events is unreliable, but if you want my true testimony, I don't have another version of events. This is what happened.

All I know is when I came into the house I was expecting my two favorite people in the world waiting for me. I was coming home elated. My thesis had been warmly accepted, and though I would not know if the professors would find merit with it, I was confident of my own work. I looked forward to sharing it with Carol, show her the applications of my theorems to her costume design. I had bought a bottle of champagne for us and a new book for Annie, which has now been entered as evidence. It was hard to fumble the keys, but in the end I managed to open the door.

Annie was standing there with the knife in her hand. Carol was on the ground. There wasn't a lot of blood, which threw me – I watch forensics dramas like everybody else. But there was a disturbance to the home. Things had been knocked askew, small things like our mail on the counter and the books on the coffee table. Nothing had been taken. But I knew someone else had been in there. The same way you know when somebody's been looking through your computer – files just a touch out of place on a desktop, or file open dates not quite right. Carol had gone to her last therapy meeting two weeks ago.

I know there won't be fingerprints on the knife, and probably not the surfaces – Annie's smudge-free hands. I know, probably, that the techs will have a problem pulling up her memory – I disabled the record function, a long time ago. Nobody needs to know about what the three of us did in private.

I called the ambulance as soon as I saw. Then I grabbed a handful of dishtowel and pressed it to Carol's wound. I still don't know why the police got there sooner than the paramedics, or why they pulled me off of Carol when I was screaming for them not to. I remember that, very clearly. Someone grabbing me, and my hands scrabbling to keep the pressure on. Then the hard kitchen counter, someone patting me down.

That's when I saw Annie had been standing over me with the knife the whole time. I had never given her an app to deal with an emergency. Certainly not a murder. I was only ever a pervert; I didn't plan on anything like this.

The rest you know. The police brought me in, and I spent a week while you people got your ducks in a row. Now I'm here.

You ask me if I think it was a murder? I do.

Do you have enough? All right. One final thing?

My name is Isaac A. Ross. I am of sound mind and under no duress. This testimony is my true and faithful account of the events that led up to the death of Carol Darringer.

That's my account, and I stand by it. I didn't kill Carol. Annie didn't kill Carol.

* * *

Later my testimony was played in court. Not in full, of course. Not that it mattered. There wasn't anything else I could do. I just hoped they would let Annie go... free? Without me, she had no instructions. Without Carol, she had nobody to love her.

I remembered Bertrand Russell again. "War does not determine who is right, only who is left." Maybe what these people needed from me was not my innocence. Maybe it was more comforting for them to put me away. But Annie would be left.

"...It is my opinion that the jury find Mr. Ross guilty of all charges," said the judge. "Would the prosecution like to add a final word?"

"No, Your Honor."

"Are you sure of it?"

"We are sure of it."

The Arrest of Arsène Lupin

Maurice Leblanc

IT WAS A strange ending to a voyage that had commenced in a most auspicious manner. The transatlantic steamship 'La Provence' was a swift and comfortable vessel, under the command of a most affable man. The passengers constituted a select and delightful society. The charm of new acquaintances and improvised amusements served to make the time pass agreeably. We enjoyed the pleasant sensation of being separated from the world, living, as it were, upon an unknown island, and consequently obliged to be sociable with each other.

Have you ever stopped to consider how much originality and spontaneity emanate from these various individuals who, on the preceding evening, did not even know each other, and who are now, for several days, condemned to lead a life of extreme intimacy, jointly defying the anger of the ocean, the terrible onslaught of the waves, the violence of the tempest and the agonizing monotony of the calm and sleepy water? Such a life becomes a sort of tragic existence, with its storms and its grandeurs, its monotony and its diversity; and that is why, perhaps, we embark upon that short voyage with mingled feelings of pleasure and fear.

But, during the past few years, a new sensation had been added to the life of the transatlantic traveler. The little floating island is now attached to the world from which it was once quite free. A bond united them, even in the very heart of the watery wastes of the Atlantic. That bond is the wireless telegraph, by means of which we receive news in the most mysterious manner. We know full well that the message is not transported by the medium of a hollow wire. No, the mystery is even more inexplicable, more romantic, and we must have recourse to the wings of the air in order to explain this new miracle. During the first day of the voyage, we felt that we were being followed, escorted, preceded even, by that distant voice, which, from time to time, whispered to one of us a few words from the receding world. Two friends spoke to me. Ten, twenty others sent gay or sombre words of parting to other passengers.

On the second day, at a distance of five hundred miles from the French coast, in the midst of a violent storm, we received the following message by means of the wireless telegraph:

> *Arsène Lupin is on your vessel, first cabin, blonde hair, wound right forearm, traveling alone under name of R–*

At that moment, a terrible flash of lightning rent the stormy skies. The electric waves were interrupted. The remainder of the dispatch never reached us. Of the name under which Arsène Lupin was concealing himself, we knew only the initial.

If the news had been of some other character, I have no doubt that the secret would have been carefully guarded by the telegraphic operator as well as by the officers of the vessel. But it was one of those events calculated to escape from the most rigorous discretion.

The same day, no one knew how, the incident became a matter of current gossip and every passenger was aware that the famous Arsène Lupin was hiding in our midst.

Arsène Lupin in our midst! The irresponsible burglar whose exploits had been narrated in all the newspapers during the past few months! The mysterious individual with whom Ganimard, our shrewdest detective, had been engaged in an implacable conflict amidst interesting and picturesque surroundings. Arsène Lupin, the eccentric gentleman who operates only in the chateaux and salons, and who, one night, entered the residence of Baron Schormann, but emerged empty-handed, leaving, however, his card on which he had scribbled these words: 'Arsène Lupin, gentleman-burglar, will return when the furniture is genuine.' Arsène Lupin, the man of a thousand disguises: in turn a chauffer, detective, bookmaker, Russian physician, Spanish bull-fighter, commercial traveler, robust youth, or decrepit old man.

Then consider this startling situation: Arsène Lupin was wandering about within the limited bounds of a transatlantic steamer; in that very small corner of the world, in that dining saloon, in that smoking room, in that music room! Arsène Lupin was, perhaps, this gentleman... or that one... my neighbour at the table... the sharer of my stateroom....

"And this condition of affairs will last for five days!" exclaimed Miss Nelly Underdown, next morning. "It is unbearable! I hope he will be arrested."

Then, addressing me, she added: "And you, Monsieur d'Andrézy, you are on intimate terms with the captain; surely you know something?"

I should have been delighted had I possessed any information that would interest Miss Nelly. She was one of those magnificent creatures who inevitably attract attention in every assembly. Wealth and beauty form an irresistible combination, and Nelly possessed both.

Educated in Paris under the care of a French mother, she was now going to visit her father, the millionaire Underdown of Chicago. She was accompanied by one of her friends, Lady Jerland.

At first, I had decided to open a flirtation with her; but, in the rapidly growing intimacy of the voyage, I was soon impressed by her charming manner and my feelings became too deep and reverential for a mere flirtation. Moreover, she accepted my attentions with a certain degree of favour. She condescended to laugh at my witticisms and display an interest in my stories. Yet I felt that I had a rival in the person of a young man with quiet and refined tastes; and it struck me, at times, that she preferred his taciturn humour to my Parisian frivolity. He formed one in the circle of admirers that surrounded Miss Nelly at the time she addressed to me the foregoing question. We were all comfortably seated in our deck-chairs. The storm of the preceding evening had cleared the sky. The weather was now delightful.

"I have no definite knowledge, mademoiselle," I replied, "but can not we, ourselves, investigate the mystery quite as well as the detective Ganimard, the personal enemy of Arsène Lupin?"

"Oh! Oh! You are progressing very fast, monsieur."

"Not at all, mademoiselle. In the first place, let me ask, do you find the problem a complicated one?"

"Very complicated."

"Have you forgotten the key we hold for the solution to the problem?"

"What key?"

"In the first place, Lupin calls himself Monsieur R–."

"Rather vague information," she replied.

"Secondly, he is traveling alone."

"Does that help you?" she asked.

"Thirdly, he is blonde."

"Well?"

"Then we have only to peruse the passenger-list, and proceed by process of elimination."

I had that list in my pocket. I took it out and glanced through it. Then I remarked: "I find that there are only thirteen men on the passenger-list whose names begin with the letter R."

"Only thirteen?"

"Yes, in the first cabin. And of those thirteen, I find that nine of them are accompanied by women, children or servants. That leaves only four who are traveling alone. First, the Marquis de Raverdan –"

"Secretary to the American Ambassador," interrupted Miss Nelly. "I know him."

"Major Rawson," I continued.

"He is my uncle," someone said.

"Mon. Rivolta."

"Here!" exclaimed an Italian, whose face was concealed beneath a heavy black beard.

Miss Nelly burst into laughter, and exclaimed: "That gentleman can scarcely be called a blonde."

"Very well, then," I said, "we are forced to the conclusion that the guilty party is the last one on the list."

"What is his name?"

"Mon. Rozaine. Does anyone know him?"

No one answered. But Miss Nelly turned to the taciturn young man, whose attentions to her had annoyed me, and said:

"Well, Monsieur Rozaine, why do you not answer?"

All eyes were now turned upon him. He was a blonde. I must confess that I myself felt a shock of surprise, and the profound silence that followed her question indicated that the others present also viewed the situation with a feeling of sudden alarm. However, the idea was an absurd one, because the gentleman in question presented an air of the most perfect innocence.

"Why do I not answer?" he said. "Because, considering my name, my position as a solitary traveller and the colour of my hair, I have already reached the same conclusion, and now think that I should be arrested."

He presented a strange appearance as he uttered these words. His thin lips were drawn closer than usual and his face was ghastly pale, whilst his eyes were streaked with blood. Of course, he was joking, yet his appearance and attitude impressed us strangely.

"But you have not the wound?" said Miss Nelly, naively.

"That is true," he replied, "I lack the wound."

Then he pulled up his sleeve, removing his cuff, and showed us his arm. But that action did not deceive me. He had shown us his left arm, and I was on the point of calling his attention to the fact, when another incident diverted our attention. Lady Jerland, Miss Nelly's friend, came running towards us in a state of great excitement, exclaiming:

"My jewels, my pearls! Someone has stolen them all!"

No, they were not all gone, as we soon found out. The thief had taken only part of them; a very curious thing. Of the diamond sunbursts, jewelled pendants, bracelets and necklaces, the thief had taken, not the largest but the finest and most valuable stones. The mountings were lying upon the table. I saw them there, despoiled of their jewels, like flowers from which the beautiful coloured petals had been ruthlessly plucked. And this theft must have been committed at the time Lady Jerland was taking her tea; in broad daylight, in a stateroom opening on a much frequented corridor; moreover, the thief had been obliged to force open the door of the stateroom, search for the jewel-case, which was hidden at the bottom of a hat-box, open it, select his booty and remove it from the mountings.

Of course, all the passengers instantly reached the same conclusion; it was the work of Arsène Lupin.

That day, at the dinner table, the seats to the right and left of Rozaine remained vacant; and, during the evening, it was rumoured that the captain had placed him under arrest, which information produced a feeling of safety and relief. We breathed once more. That evening, we resumed our games and dances. Miss Nelly, especially, displayed a spirit of thoughtless gayety which convinced me that if Rozaine's attentions had been agreeable to her in the beginning, she had already forgotten them. Her charm and good-humour completed my conquest. At midnight, under a bright moon, I declared my devotion with an ardour that did not seem to displease her.

But, next day, to our general amazement, Rozaine was at liberty. We learned that the evidence against him was not sufficient. He had produced documents that were perfectly regular, which showed that he was the son of a wealthy merchant of Bordeaux. Besides, his arms did not bear the slightest trace of a wound.

"Documents! Certificates of birth!" exclaimed the enemies of Rozaine, "Of course, Arsène Lupin will furnish you as many as you desire. And as to the wound, he never had it, or he has removed it."

Then it was proven that, at the time of the theft, Rozaine was promenading on the deck. To which fact, his enemies replied that a man like Arsène Lupin could commit a crime without being actually present. And then, apart from all other circumstances, there remained one point which even the most skeptical could not answer: Who except Rozaine, was travelling alone, was a blonde, and bore a name beginning with R? To whom did the telegram point, if it were not Rozaine?

And when Rozaine, a few minutes before breakfast, came boldly toward our group, Miss Nelly and Lady Jerland arose and walked away.

An hour later, a manuscript circular was passed from hand to hand amongst the sailors, the stewards, and the passengers of all classes. It announced that Mon. Louis Rozaine offered a reward of ten thousand francs for the discovery of Arsène Lupin or other person in possession of the stolen jewels.

"And if no one assists me, I will unmask the scoundrel myself," declared Rozaine.

Rozaine against Arsène Lupin, or rather, according to current opinion, Arsène Lupin himself against Arsène Lupin; the contest promised to be interesting.

Nothing developed during the next two days. We saw Rozaine wandering about, day and night, searching, questioning, investigating. The captain, also, displayed commendable activity. He caused the vessel to be searched from stern to stern; ransacked every stateroom under the plausible theory that the jewels might be concealed anywhere, except in the thief's own room.

"I suppose they will find out something soon," remarked Miss Nelly to me. "He may be a wizard, but he cannot make diamonds and pearls become invisible."

"Certainly not," I replied, "but he should examine the lining of our hats and vests and everything we carry with us."

Then, exhibiting my Kodak, a 9x12 with which I had been photographing her in various poses, I added: "In an apparatus no larger than that, a person could hide all of Lady Jerland's jewels. He could pretend to take pictures and no one would suspect the game."

"But I have heard it said that every thief leaves some clue behind him."

"That may be generally true," I replied, "but there is one exception: Arsène Lupin."

"Why?"

"Because he concentrates his thoughts not only on the theft, but on all the circumstances connected with it that could serve as a clue to his identity."

"A few days ago, you were more confident."

"Yes, but since I have seen him at work."

"And what do you think about it now?" she asked.

"Well, in my opinion, we are wasting our time."

And, as a matter of fact, the investigation had produced no result. But, in the meantime, the captain's watch had been stolen. He was furious. He quickened his efforts and watched Rozaine more closely than before. But, on the following day, the watch was found in the second officer's collar box.

This incident caused considerable astonishment, and displayed the humorous side of Arsène Lupin, burglar though he was, but dilettante as well. He combined business with pleasure. He reminded us of the author who almost died in a fit of laughter provoked by his own play. Certainly, he was an artist in his particular line of work, and whenever I saw Rozaine, gloomy and reserved, and thought of the double role that he was playing, I accorded him a certain measure of admiration.

On the following evening, the officer on deck duty heard groans emanating from the darkest corner of the ship. He approached and found a man lying there, his head enveloped in a thick grey scarf and his hands tied together with a heavy cord. It was Rozaine. He had been assaulted, thrown down and robbed. A card, pinned to his coat, bore these words: "Arsène Lupin accepts with pleasure the ten thousand francs offered by Mon. Rozaine." As a matter of fact, the stolen pocket-book contained twenty thousand francs.

Of course, some accused the unfortunate man of having simulated this attack on himself. But, apart from the fact that he could not have bound himself in that manner, it was established that the writing on the card was entirely different from that of Rozaine, but, on the contrary, resembled the handwriting of Arsène Lupin as it was reproduced in an old newspaper found on board.

Thus it appeared that Rozaine was not Arsène Lupin; but was Rozaine, the son of a Bordeaux merchant. And the presence of Arsène Lupin was once more affirmed, and that in a most alarming manner.

Such was the state of terror amongst the passengers that none would remain alone in a stateroom or wander singly in unfrequented parts of the vessel. We clung together as a matter of safety. And yet the most intimate acquaintances were estranged by a mutual feeling of distrust. Arsène Lupin was, now, anybody and everybody. Our excited imaginations attributed to him miraculous and unlimited power. We supposed him capable of assuming the most unexpected disguises; of being, by turns, the highly respectable Major Rawson or the noble Marquis de Raverdan, or even – for we no longer stopped with the accusing letter of R– or even such or such a person well known to all of us, and having wife, children and servants.

The first wireless dispatches from America brought no news; at least, the captain did not communicate any to us. The silence was not reassuring.

Our last day on the steamer seemed interminable. We lived in constant fear of some disaster. This time, it would not be a simple theft or a comparatively harmless assault; it would be a crime, a murder. No one imagined that Arsène Lupin would confine himself to those two trifling offenses. Absolute master of the ship, the authorities powerless, he could do whatever he pleased; our property and lives were at his mercy.

Yet those were delightful hours for me, since they secured to me the confidence of Miss Nelly. Deeply moved by those startling events and being of a highly nervous nature, she spontaneously sought at my side a protection and security that I was pleased to give her. Inwardly, I blessed Arsène Lupin. Had he not been the means of bringing me and Miss Nelly closer to each other? Thanks to him, I could now indulge in delicious dreams of love and happiness – dreams that, I felt, were not unwelcome to Miss Nelly. Her smiling eyes authorized me to make them; the softness of her voice bade me hope.

As we approached the American shore, the active search for the thief was apparently abandoned, and we were anxiously awaiting the supreme moment in which the mysterious enigma would be explained. Who was Arsène Lupin? Under what name, under what disguise was the famous Arsène Lupin concealing himself? And, at last, that supreme moment arrived. If I live one hundred years, I shall not forget the slightest details of it.

"How pale you are, Miss Nelly," I said to my companion, as she leaned upon my arm, almost fainting.

"And you!" she replied, "Ah! You are so changed."

"Just think! This is a most exciting moment, and I am delighted to spend it with you, Miss Nelly. I hope that your memory will sometimes revert –"

But she was not listening. She was nervous and excited. The gangway was placed in position, but, before we could use it, the uniformed customs officers came on board. Miss Nelly murmured:

"I shouldn't be surprised to hear that Arsène Lupin escaped from the vessel during the voyage."

"Perhaps he preferred death to dishonour, and plunged into the Atlantic rather than be arrested."

"Oh, do not laugh," she said.

Suddenly I started, and, in answer to her question, I said:

"Do you see that little old man standing at the bottom of the gangway?"

"With an umbrella and an olive-green coat?"

"It is Ganimard."

"Ganimard?"

"Yes, the celebrated detective who has sworn to capture Arsène Lupin. Ah! I can understand now why we did not receive any news from this side of the Atlantic. Ganimard was here! And he always keeps his business secret."

"Then you think he will arrest Arsène Lupin?"

"Who can tell? The unexpected always happens when Arsène Lupin is concerned in the affair."

"Oh!" she exclaimed, with that morbid curiosity peculiar to women, "I should like to see him arrested."

"You will have to be patient. No doubt, Arsène Lupin has already seen his enemy and will not be in a hurry to leave the steamer."

The passengers were now leaving the steamer. Leaning on his umbrella, with an air of careless indifference, Ganimard appeared to be paying no attention to the crowd that was hurrying down the gangway. The Marquis de Raverdan, Major Rawson, the Italian Rivolta, and many others had already left the vessel before Rozaine appeared. Poor Rozaine!

"Perhaps it is he, after all," said Miss Nelly to me. "What do you think?"

"I think it would be very interesting to have Ganimard and Rozaine in the same picture. You take the camera. I am loaded down."

I gave her the camera, but too late for her to use it. Rozaine was already passing the detective. An American officer, standing behind Ganimard, leaned forward and whispered in his ear. The French detective shrugged his shoulders and Rozaine passed on. Then, my God, who was Arsène Lupin?

"Yes," said Miss Nelly, aloud, "who can it be?"

Not more than twenty people now remained on board. She scrutinized them one by one, fearful that Arsène Lupin was not amongst them.

"We cannot wait much longer," I said to her.

She started toward the gangway. I followed. But we had not taken ten steps when Ganimard barred our passage.

"Well, what is it?" I exclaimed.

"One moment, monsieur. What's your hurry?"

"I am escorting mademoiselle."

"One moment," he repeated, in a tone of authority. Then, gazing into my eyes, he said: "Arsène Lupin, is it not?"

I laughed, and replied: "No, simply Bernard d'Andrézy."

"Bernard d'Andrézy died in Macedonia three years ago."

"If Bernard d'Andrézy were dead, I should not be here. But you are mistaken. Here are my papers."

"They are his; and I can tell you exactly how they came into your possession."

"You are a fool!" I exclaimed. "Arsène Lupin sailed under the name of R–"

"Yes, another of your tricks; a false scent that deceived them at Havre. You play a good game, my boy, but this time luck is against you."

I hesitated a moment. Then he hit me a sharp blow on the right arm, which caused me to utter a cry of pain. He had struck the wound, yet unhealed, referred to in the telegram.

I was obliged to surrender. There was no alternative. I turned to Miss Nelly, who had heard everything. Our eyes met; then she glanced at the Kodak I had placed in her hands, and made a gesture that conveyed to me the impression that she understood everything. Yes, there, between the narrow folds of black leather, in the hollow centre of the small object that I had taken the precaution to place in her hands before Ganimard arrested me, it was there I had deposited Rozaine's twenty thousand francs and Lady Jerland's pearls and diamonds.

Oh! I pledge my oath that, at that solemn moment, when I was in the grasp of Ganimard and his two assistants, I was perfectly indifferent to everything, to my arrest, the hostility of the people, everything except this one question: what will Miss Nelly do with the things I had confided to her?

In the absence of that material and conclusive proof, I had nothing to fear; but would Miss Nelly decide to furnish that proof? Would she betray me? Would she act the part of an enemy who cannot forgive, or that of a woman whose scorn is softened by feelings of indulgence and involuntary sympathy?

She passed in front of me. I said nothing, but bowed very low. Mingled with the other passengers, she advanced to the gangway with my Kodak in her hand. It occurred to me that she would not dare to expose me publicly, but she might do so when she reached a more private place. However, when she had passed only a few feet down the gangway, with a movement of simulated awkwardness, she let the camera fall into the water between the vessel and the pier. Then she walked down the gangway, and was quickly lost to sight in the crowd. She had passed out of my life forever.

For a moment, I stood motionless. Then, to Ganimard's great astonishment, I muttered: "What a pity that I am not an honest man!"

Such was the story of his arrest as narrated to me by Arsène Lupin himself. The various incidents, which I shall record in writing at a later day, have established between us certain ties... shall I say of friendship? Yes, I venture to believe that Arsène Lupin honours me with his friendship, and that it is through friendship that he occasionally calls on me, and brings, into the silence of my library, his youthful exuberance of spirits, the contagion of his enthusiasm, and the mirth of a man for whom destiny has naught but favours and smiles.

His portrait? How can I describe him? I have seen him twenty times and each time he was a different person; even he himself said to me on one occasion: "I no longer know who I am. I cannot recognize myself in the mirror." Certainly, he was a great actor, and possessed a marvellous faculty for disguising himself. Without the slightest effort, he could adopt the voice, gestures and mannerisms of another person.

"Why," said he, "why should I retain a definite form and feature? Why not avoid the danger of a personality that is ever the same? My actions will serve to identify me."

Then he added, with a touch of pride:

"So much the better if no one can ever say with absolute certainty: There is Arsène Lupin! The essential point is that the public may be able to refer to my work and say, without fear of mistake: Arsène Lupin did that!"

The Master of Mystery

Jack London

THERE WAS COMPLAINT in the village. The women chattered together with shrill, high-pitched voices. The men were glum and doubtful of aspect, and the very dogs wandered dubiously about, alarmed in vague ways by the unrest of the camp, and ready to take to the woods on the first outbreak of trouble. The air was filled with suspicion. No man was sure of his neighbor, and each was conscious that he stood in like unsureness with his fellows. Even the children were oppressed and solemn, and little Di Ya, the cause of it all, had been soundly thrashed, first by Hooniah, his mother, and then by his father, Bawn, and was now whimpering and looking pessimistically out upon the world from the shelter of the big overturned canoe on the beach.

And to make the matter worse, Scundoo, the shaman, was in disgrace, and his known magic could not be called upon to seek out the evil-doer. Forsooth, a month gone, he had promised a fair south wind so that the tribe might journey to the *potlatch* at Tonkin, where Taku Jim was giving away the savings of twenty years; and when the day came, lo, a grievous north wind blew, and of the first three canoes to venture forth, one was swamped in the big seas, and two were pounded to pieces on the rocks, and a child was drowned. He had pulled the string of the wrong bag, he explained – a mistake. But the people refused to listen; the offerings of meat and fish and fur ceased to come to his door; and he sulked within – so they thought, fasting in bitter penance; in reality, eating generously from his well-stored cache and meditating upon the fickleness of the mob.

The blankets of Hooniah were missing. They were good blankets, of most marvellous thickness and warmth, and her pride in them was greatened in that they had been come by so cheaply. Ty-Kwan, of the next village but one, was a fool to have so easily parted with them. But then, she did not know they were the blankets of the murdered Englishman, because of whose take-off the United States cutter nosed along the coast for a time, while its launches puffed and snorted among the secret inlets. And not knowing that Ty-Kwan had disposed of them in haste so that his own people might not have to render account to the Government, Hooniah's pride was unshaken. And because the women envied her, her pride was without end and boundless, till it filled the village and spilled over along the Alaskan shore from Dutch Harbor to St. Mary's. Her totem had become justly celebrated, and her name known on the lips of men wherever men fished and feasted, what of the blankets and their marvellous thickness and warmth. It was a most mysterious happening, the manner of their going.

"I but stretched them up in the sun by the side-wall of the house," Hooniah disclaimed for the thousandth time to her Thlinget sisters. "I but stretched them up and turned my back; for Di Ya, dough-thief and eater of raw flour that he is, with head into the big iron pot, overturned and stuck there, his legs waving like the branches of a forest tree in the wind. And I did but drag him out and twice knock his head against the door for riper understanding, and behold, the blankets were not!"

"The blankets were not!" the women repeated in awed whispers.

"A great loss," one added. A second, "Never were there such blankets." And a third, "We be sorry, Hooniah, for thy loss." Yet each woman of them was glad in her heart that the odious, dissension-breeding blankets were gone. "I but stretched them up in the sun," Hooniah began for the thousand and first time.

"Yea, yea," Bawn spoke up, wearied. "But there were no gossips in the village from other places. Wherefore it be plain that some of our own tribespeople have laid unlawful hand upon the blankets."

"How can that be, O Bawn?" the women chorussed indignantly. "Who should there be?"

"Then has there been witchcraft," Bawn continued stolidly enough, though he stole a sly glance at their faces.

"*Witchcraft!*" And at the dread word their voices hushed and each looked fearfully at each.

"Ay," Hooniah affirmed, the latent malignancy of her nature flashing into a moment's exultation. "And word has been sent to Klok-No-Ton, and strong paddles. Truly shall he be here with the afternoon tide."

The little groups broke up, and fear descended upon the village. Of all misfortune, witchcraft was the most appalling. With the intangible and unseen things only the shamans could cope, and neither man, woman, nor child could know, until the moment of ordeal, whether devils possessed their souls or not. And of all shamans, Klok-No-Ton, who dwelt in the next village, was the most terrible. None found more evil spirits than he, none visited his victims with more frightful tortures. Even had he found, once, a devil residing within the body of a three-months babe – a most obstinate devil which could only be driven out when the babe had lain for a week on thorns and briers. The body was thrown into the sea after that, but the waves tossed it back again and again as a curse upon the village, nor did it finally go away till two strong men were staked out at low tide and drowned.

And Hooniah had sent for this Klok-No-Ton. Better had it been if Scundoo, their own shaman, were undisgraced. For he had ever a gentler way, and he had been known to drive forth two devils from a man who afterward begat seven healthy children. But Klok-No-Ton! They shuddered with dire foreboding at thought of him, and each one felt himself the centre of accusing eyes, and looked accusingly upon his fellows – each one and all, save Sime, and Sime was a scoffer whose evil end was destined with a certitude his successes could not shake.

"Hoh! Hoh!" he laughed. "Devils and Klok-No-Ton! Than whom no greater devil can be found in Thlinket Land."

"Thou fool! Even now he cometh with witcheries and sorceries; so beware thy tongue, lest evil befall thee and thy days be short in the land!"

So spoke La-lah, otherwise the Cheater, and Sime laughed scornfully.

"I am Sime, unused to fear, unafraid of the dark. I am a strong man, as my father before me, and my head is clear. Nor you nor I have seen with our eyes the unseen evil things –"

"But Scundoo hath," La-lah made answer. "And likewise Klok-No-Ton. This we know."

"How dost thou know, son of a fool?" Sime thundered, the choleric blood darkening his thick bull neck.

"By the word of their mouths – even so."

Sime snorted. "A shaman is only a man. May not his words be crooked, even as thine and mine? Bah! Bah! And once more, bah! And this for thy shamans and thy shamans' devils! And this! And this!"

And snapping his fingers to right and left, Sime strode through the on-lookers, who made over-zealous and fearsome way for him.

"A good fisher and strong hunter, but an evil man," said one.

"Yet does he flourish," speculated another.

"Wherefore be thou evil and flourish," Sime retorted over his shoulder. "And were all evil, there would be no need for shamans. Bah! You children-afraid-of-the-dark!"

And when Klok-No-Ton arrived on the afternoon tide, Sime's defiant laugh was unabated; nor did he forbear to make a joke when the shaman tripped on the sand in the landing. Klok-No-Ton looked at him sourly, and without greeting stalked straight through their midst to the house of Scundoo.

Of the meeting with Scundoo none of the tribespeople might know, for they clustered reverently in the distance and spoke in whispers while the masters of mystery were together.

"Greeting, O Scundoo!" Klok-No-Ton rumbled, wavering perceptibly from doubt of his reception.

He was a giant in stature, and towered massively above little Scundoo, whose thin voice floated upward like the faint far rasping of a cricket.

"Greeting, Klok-No-Ton," he returned. "The day is fair with thy coming."

"Yet it would seem..." Klok-No-Ton hesitated.

"Yea, yea," the little shaman put in impatiently, "that I have fallen on ill days, else would I not stand in gratitude to you in that you do my work."

"It grieves me, friend Scundoo..."

"Nay, I am made glad, Klok-No-Ton."

"But will I give thee half of that which be given me."

"Not so, good Klok-No-Ton," murmured Scundoo, with a deprecatory wave of the hand. "It is I who am thy slave, and my days shall be filled with desire to befriend thee."

"As I —"

"As thou now befriendest me."

"That being so, it is then a bad business, these blankets of the woman Hooniah?"

The big shaman blundered tentatively in his quest, and Scundoo smiled a wan, gray smile, for he was used to reading men, and all men seemed very small to him.

"Ever hast thou dealt in strong medicine," he said. "Doubtless the evil-doer will be briefly known to thee."

"Ay, briefly known when I set eyes upon him." Again Klok-No-Ton hesitated. "Have there been gossips from other places?" he asked.

Scundoo shook his head. "Behold! Is this not a most excellent mucluc?"

He held up the foot-covering of sealskin and walrus hide, and his visitor examined it with secret interest.

"It did come to me by a close-driven bargain."

Klok-No-Ton nodded attentively.

"I got it from the man La-lah. He is a remarkable man, and often have I thought..."

"So?" Klok-No-Ton ventured impatiently.

"Often have I thought," Scundoo concluded, his voice falling as he came to a full pause. "It is a fair day, and thy medicine be strong, Klok-No-Ton."

Klok-No-Ton's face brightened. "Thou art a great man, Scundoo, a shaman of shamans. I go now. I shall remember thee always. And the man La-lah, as you say, is a remarkable man."

Scundoo smiled yet more wan and gray, closed the door on the heels of his departing visitor, and barred and double-barred it.

Sime was mending his canoe when Klok-No-Ton came down the beach, and he broke off from his work only long enough to ostentatiously load his rifle and place it near him.

The shaman noted the action and called out: "Let all the people come together on this spot! It is the word of Klok-No-Ton, devil-seeker and driver of devils!"

He had been minded to assemble them at Hooniah's house, but it was necessary that all should be present, and he was doubtful of Sime's obedience and did not wish trouble. Sime was a good man to let alone, his judgment ran, and withal, a bad one for the health of any shaman.

"Let the woman Hooniah be brought," Klok-No-Ton commanded, glaring ferociously about the circle and sending chills up and down the spines of those he looked upon.

Hooniah waddled forward, head bent and gaze averted.

"Where be thy blankets?"

"I but stretched them up in the sun, and behold, they were not!" she whined.

"So?"

"It was because of Di Ya."

"So?"

"Him have I beaten sore, and he shall yet be beaten, for that he brought trouble upon us who be poor people."

"The blankets!" Klok-No-Ton bellowed hoarsely, foreseeing her desire to lower the price to be paid. "The blankets, woman! Thy wealth is known."

"I but stretched them up in the sun," she sniffled, "and we be poor people and have nothing."

He stiffened suddenly, with a hideous distortion of the face, and Hooniah shrank back. But so swiftly did he spring forward, with in-turned eyeballs and loosened jaw, that she stumbled and fell down grovelling at his feet. He waved his arms about, wildly flagellating the air, his body writhing and twisting in torment. An epilepsy seemed to come upon him. A white froth flecked his lips, and his body was convulsed with shiverings and tremblings.

The women broke into a wailing chant, swaying backward and forward in abandonment, while one by one the men succumbed to the excitement till only Sime remained. He, perched upon his canoe, looked on in mockery; yet the ancestors whose seed he bore pressed heavily upon him, and he swore his strongest oaths that his courage might be cheered. Klok-No-Ton was horrible to behold. He had cast off his blanket and torn his clothes from him, so that he was quite naked, save for a girdle of eagle-claws about his thighs. Shrieking and yelling, his long black hair flying like a blot of night, he leaped frantically about the circle. A certain rude rhythm characterized his frenzy, and when all were under its sway, swinging their bodies in accord with his and venting their cries in unison, he sat bolt upright, with arm outstretched and long, talon-like finger extended. A low moaning, as of the dead, greeted this, and the people cowered with shaking knees as the dread finger passed them slowly by. For death went with it, and life remained with those who watched it go; and being rejected, they watched with eager intentness.

Finally, with a tremendous cry, the fateful finger rested upon La-lah. He shook like an aspen, seeing himself already dead, his household goods divided, and his widow married to his brother. He strove to speak, to deny, but his tongue clove to his mouth and his throat was sanded with an intolerable thirst. Klok-No-Ton seemed to half swoon away, now that his work was done; but he waited, with closed eyes, listening for the great blood-cry to go up – the great blood-cry, familiar to his ear from a thousand conjurations, when the tribespeople flung themselves like wolves upon the trembling victim. But only was there silence, then a low tittering, from nowhere in particular, which spread and spread until a vast laughter welled up to the sky.

"Wherefore?" he cried.

"Na! Na!" the people laughed. "Thy medicine be ill, O Klok-No-Ton!"

"It be known to all," La-lah stuttered. "For eight weary months have I been gone afar with the Siwash sealers, and but this day am I come back to find the blankets of Hooniah gone ere I came!"

"It be true!" they cried with one accord. "The blankets of Hooniah were gone ere he came!"

"And thou shalt be paid nothing for thy medicine which is of no avail," announced Hooniah, on her feet once more and smarting from a sense of ridiculousness.

But Klok-No-Ton saw only the face of Scundoo and its wan, gray smile, heard only the faint far cricket's rasping. "I got it from the man La-lah, and often have I thought," and, "It is a fair day and thy medicine be strong."

He brushed by Hooniah, and the circle instinctively gave way for him to pass. Sime flung a jeer from the top of the canoe, the women snickered in his face, cries of derision rose in his wake, but he took no notice, pressing onward to the house of Scundoo. He hammered on the door, beat it with his fists, and howled vile imprecations. Yet there was no response, save that in the lulls Scundoo's voice rose eerily in incantation. Klok-No-Ton raged about like a madman, but when he attempted to break in the door with a huge stone, murmurs arose from the men and women. And he, Klok-No-Ton, knew that he stood shorn of his strength and authority before an alien people. He saw a man stoop for a stone, and a second, and a bodily fear ran through him.

"Harm not Scundoo, who is a master!" a woman cried out.

"Better you return to your own village," a man advised menacingly.

Klok-No-Ton turned on his heel and went down among them to the beach, a bitter rage at his heart, and in his head a just apprehension for his defenceless back. But no stones were cast. The children swarmed mockingly about his feet, and the air was wild with laughter and derision, but that was all. Yet he did not breathe freely until the canoe was well out upon the water, when he rose up and laid a futile curse upon the village and its people, not forgetting to particularly specify Scundoo who had made a mock of him.

Ashore there was a clamor for Scundoo, and the whole population crowded his door, entreating and imploring in confused babel till he came forth and raised his hand.

"In that ye are my children I pardon freely," he said. "But never again. For the last time thy foolishness goes unpunished. That which ye wish shall be granted, and it be already known to me. This night, when the moon has gone behind the world to look upon the mighty dead, let all the people gather in the blackness before the house of Hooniah. Then shall the evil-doer stand forth and take his merited reward. I have spoken."

"It shall be death!" Bawn vociferated, "for that it hath brought worry upon us, and shame."

"So be it," Scundoo replied, and shut his door.

"Now shall all be made clear and plain, and content rest upon us once again," La-lah declaimed oracularly.

"Because of Scundoo, the little man," Sime sneered.

"Because of the medicine of Scundoo, the little man," La-lah corrected.

"Children of foolishness, these Thlinket people!" Sime smote his thigh a resounding blow. "It passeth understanding that grown women and strong men should get down in the dirt to dream-things and wonder tales."

"I am a travelled man," La-lah answered. "I have journeyed on the deep seas and seen signs and wonders, and I know that these things be so. I am La-lah —"

"The Cheater –"

"So called, but the Far-Journeyer right-named."

"I am not so great a traveler –" Sime began.

"Then hold thy tongue," Bawn cut in, and they separated in anger.

When the last silver moonlight had vanished beyond the world, Scundoo came among the people huddled about the house of Hooniah. He walked with a quick, alert step, and those who saw him in the light of Hooniah's slush-lamp noticed that he came empty-handed, without rattles, masks, or shaman's paraphernalia, save for a great sleepy raven carried under one arm.

"Is there wood gathered for a fire, so that all may see when the work be done?" he demanded.

"Yea," Bawn answered. "There be wood in plenty."

"Then let all listen, for my words be few. With me have I brought Jelchs, the Raven, diviner of mystery and seer of things. Him, in his blackness, shall I place under the big black pot of Hooniah, in the blackest corner of her house. The slush-lamp shall cease to burn, and all remain in outer darkness. It is very simple. One by one shall ye go into the house, lay hand upon the pot for the space of one long intake of the breath, and withdraw again. Doubtless Jelchs will make outcry when the hand of the evil-doer is nigh him. Or who knows but otherwise he may manifest his wisdom. Are ye ready?"

"We be ready," came the multi-voiced response.

"Then will I call the name aloud, each in his turn and hers, till all are called."

Thereat La-lah was first chosen, and he passed in at once. Every ear strained, and through the silence they could hear his footsteps creaking across the rickety floor. But that was all. Jelchs made no outcry, gave no sign. Bawn was next chosen, for it well might be that a man should steal his own blankets with intent to cast shame upon his neighbors. Hooniah followed, and other women and children, but without result.

"Sime!" Scundoo called out.

"Sime!" he repeated.

But Sime did not stir.

"Art thou afraid of the dark?" La-lah, his own integrity being proved, demanded fiercely.

Sime chuckled. "I laugh at it all, for it is a great foolishness. Yet will I go in, not in belief in wonders, but in token that I am unafraid."

And he passed in boldly, and came out still mocking.

"Some day shalt thou die with great suddenness," La-lah whispered, righteously indignant.

"I doubt not," the scoffer answered airily. "Few men of us die in our beds, what of the shamans and the deep sea."

When half the villagers had safely undergone the ordeal, the excitement, because of its repression, was painfully intense. When two-thirds had gone through, a young woman, close on her first child-bed, broke down and in nervous shrieks and laughter gave form to her terror.

Finally the turn came for the last of all to go in, and nothing had happened. And Di Ya was the last of all. It must surely be he. Hooniah let out a lament to the stars, while the rest drew back from the luckless lad. He was half-dead from fright, and his legs gave under him so that he staggered on the threshold and nearly fell. Scundoo shoved him inside and closed the door. A long time went by, during which could be heard only the boy's weeping. Then, very slowly, came the creak of his steps to the far corner, a pause, and the creaking of his return. The door opened and he came forth. Nothing had happened, and he was the last.

"Let the fire be lighted," Scundoo commanded.

The bright flames rushed upward, revealing faces yet marked with vanishing fear, but also clouded with doubt.

"Surely the thing has failed," Hooniah whispered hoarsely.

"Yea," Bawn answered complacently. "Scundoo groweth old, and we stand in need of a new shaman."

"Where now is the wisdom of Jelchs?" Sime snickered in La-lah's ear.

La-lah brushed his brow in a puzzled manner and said nothing.

Sime threw his chest out arrogantly and strutted up to the little shaman. "Hoh! Hoh! As I said, nothing has come of it!"

"So it would seem, so it would seem," Scundoo answered meekly. "And it would seem strange to those unskilled in the affairs of mystery."

"As thou?" Sime queried audaciously.

"Mayhap even as I." Scundoo spoke quite softly, his eyelids drooping, slowly drooping, down, down, till his eyes were all but hidden. "So I am minded of another test. Let every man, woman, and child, now and at once, hold their hands well up above their heads!"

So unexpected was the order, and so imperatively was it given, that it was obeyed without question. Every hand was in the air.

"Let each look on the other's hands, and let all look," Scundoo commanded, "so that –"

But a noise of laughter, which was more of wrath, drowned his voice. All eyes had come to rest upon Sime. Every hand but his was black with soot, and his was guiltless of the smirch of Hooniah's pot.

A stone hurtled through the air and struck him on the cheek.

"It is a lie!" he yelled. "A lie! I know naught of Hooniah's blankets!"

A second stone gashed his brow, a third whistled past his head, the great blood-cry went up, and everywhere were people groping on the ground for missiles. He staggered and half sank down.

"It was a joke! Only a joke!" he shrieked. "I but took them for a joke!"

"Where hast thou hidden them?" Scundoo's shrill, sharp voice cut through the tumult like a knife.

"In the large skin-bale in my house, the one slung by the ridge-pole," came the answer. "But it was a joke, I say, only –"

Scundoo nodded his head, and the air went thick with flying stones. Sime's wife was crying silently, her head upon her knees; but his little boy, with shrieks and laughter, was flinging stones with the rest.

Hooniah came waddling back with the precious blankets. Scundoo stopped her.

"We be poor people and have little," she whimpered. "So be not hard upon us, O Scundoo."

The people ceased from the quivering stone-pile they had builded, and looked on.

"Nay, it was never my way, good Hooniah," Scundoo made answer, reaching for the blankets. "In token that I am not hard, these only shall I take."

"Am I not wise, my children?" he demanded.

"Thou art indeed wise, O Scundoo!" they cried in one voice.

And he went away into the darkness, the blankets around him, and Jelchs nodding sleepily under his arm.

The Lenton Croft Robberies

Arthur Morrison

THOSE WHO RETAIN any memory of the great law cases of fifteen or twenty years back will remember, at least, the title of that extraordinary will case, 'Bartley v. Bartley and others,' which occupied the Probate Court for some weeks on end, and caused an amount of public interest rarely accorded to any but the cases considered in the other division of the same court. The case itself was noted for the large quantity of remarkable and unusual evidence presented by the plaintiff's side – evidence that took the other party completely by surprise, and overthrew their case like a house of cards. The affair will, perhaps, be more readily recalled as the occasion of the sudden rise to eminence in their profession of Messrs. Crellan, Hunt & Crellan, solicitors for the plaintiff – a result due entirely to the wonderful ability shown in this case of building up, apparently out of nothing, a smashing weight of irresistible evidence. That the firm has since maintained – indeed enhanced – the position it then won for itself need scarcely be said here; its name is familiar to everybody. But there are not many of the outside public who know that the credit of the whole performance was primarily due to a young clerk in the employ of Messrs. Crellan, who had been given charge of the seemingly desperate task of collecting evidence in the case.

This Mr. Martin Hewitt had, however, full credit and reward for his exploit from his firm and from their client, and more than one other firm of lawyers engaged in contentious work made good offers to entice Hewitt to change his employers. Instead of this, however, he determined to work independently for the future, having conceived the idea of making a regular business of doing, on behalf of such clients as might retain him, similar work to that he had just done with such conspicuous success for Messrs. Crellan, Hunt & Crellan. This was the beginning of the private detective business of Martin Hewitt, and his action at that time has been completely justified by the brilliant professional successes he has since achieved.

His business has always been conducted in the most private manner, and he has always declined the help of professional assistants, preferring to carry out himself such of the many investigations offered him as he could manage. He has always maintained that he has never lost by this policy, since the chance of his refusing a case begets competition for his services, and his fees rise by a natural process. At the same time, no man could know better how to employ casual assistance at the right time.

Some curiosity has been expressed as to Mr. Martin Hewitt's system, and, as he himself always consistently maintains that he has no system beyond a judicious use of ordinary faculties, I intend setting forth in detail a few of the more interesting of his cases in order that the public may judge for itself if I am right in estimating Mr. Hewitt's 'ordinary faculties' as faculties very extraordinary indeed. He is not a man who has made many friendships (this, probably, for professional reasons), notwithstanding his genial and companionable manners. I myself first made his acquaintance as a result of an accident resulting in a fire at the old house in which Hewitt's office was situated, and in an upper floor of which I occupied bachelor chambers. I was able to help in saving a quantity of extremely important papers relating to his business, and, while repairs were being made, allowed him to lock them in an old wall-safe in one of my rooms which the fire had scarcely damaged.

The acquaintance thus begun has lasted many years, and has become a rather close friendship. I have even accompanied Hewitt on some of his expeditions, and, in a humble way, helped him. Such of the cases, however, as I personally saw nothing of I have put into narrative form from the particulars given me.

"I consider you, Brett," he said, addressing me, "the most remarkable journalist alive. Not because you're particularly clever, you know, because, between ourselves, I hope you'll admit you're not; but because you have known something of me and my doings for some years, and have never yet been guilty of giving away any of my little business secrets you may have become acquainted with. I'm afraid you're not so enterprising a journalist as some, Brett. But now, since you ask, you shall write something – if you think it worth while."

This he said, as he said most things, with a cheery, chaffing good-nature that would have been, perhaps, surprising to a stranger who thought of him only as a grim and mysterious discoverer of secrets and crimes. Indeed, the man had always as little of the aspect of the conventional detective as may be imagined. Nobody could appear more cordial or less observant in manner, although there was to be seen a certain sharpness of the eye – which might, after all, only be the twinkle of good humour.

I *did* think it worth while to write something of Martin Hewitt's investigations, and a description of one of his adventures follows.

* * *

At the head of the first flight of a dingy staircase leading up from an ever-open portal in a street by the Strand stood a door, the dusty ground-glass upper panel of which carried in its center the single word 'Hewitt,' while at its right-hand lower corner, in smaller letters, 'Clerk's Office' appeared. On a morning when the clerks in the ground-floor offices had barely hung up their hats, a short, well-dressed young man, wearing spectacles, hastening to open the dusty door, ran into the arms of another man who suddenly issued from it.

"I beg pardon," the first said. "Is this Hewitt's Detective Agency Office?"

"Yes, I believe you will find it so," the other replied. He was a stoutish, clean-shaven man, of middle height, and of a cheerful, round countenance. "You'd better speak to the clerk."

In the little outer office the visitor was met by a sharp lad with inky fingers, who presented him with a pen and a printed slip. The printed slip having been filled with the visitor's name and present business, and conveyed through an inner door, the lad reappeared with an invitation to the private office. There, behind a writing-table, sat the stoutish man himself, who had only just advised an appeal to the clerk.

"Good morning, Mr. Lloyd – Mr. Vernon Lloyd," he said, affably, looking again at the slip. "You'll excuse my care to start even with my visitors – I must, you know. You come from Sir James Norris, I see."

"Yes; I am his secretary. I have only to ask you to go straight to Lenton Croft at once, if you can, on very important business. Sir James would have wired, but had not your precise address. Can you go by the next train? Eleven-thirty is the first available from Paddington."

"Quite possibly. Do you know any thing of the business?"

"It is a case of a robbery in the house, or, rather, I fancy, of several robberies. Jewelry has been stolen from rooms occupied by visitors to the Croft. The first case occurred some months ago – nearly a year ago, in fact. Last night there was another. But I think you had better get the details on the spot. Sir James has told me to telegraph if you are coming, so that he may meet you himself at the station; and I must hurry, as his drive to the station will be rather a long one. Then I take it you will go, Mr. Hewitt? Twyford is the station."

"Yes, I shall come, and by the 11.30. Are you going by that train yourself?"

"No, I have several things to attend to now I am in town. Good morning; I shall wire at once."

Mr. Martin Hewitt locked the drawer of his table and sent his clerk for a cab.

At Twyford Station Sir James Norris was waiting with a dog-cart. Sir James was a tall, florid man of fifty or thereabout, known away from home as something of a county historian, and nearer his own parts as a great supporter of the hunt, and a gentleman much troubled with poachers. As soon as he and Hewitt had found one another the baronet hurried the detective into his dog-cart. "We've something over seven miles to drive," he said, "and I can tell you all about this wretched business as we go. That is why I came for you myself, and alone."

Hewitt nodded.

"I have sent for you, as Lloyd probably told you, because of a robbery at my place last evening. It appears, as far as I can guess, to be one of three by the same hand, or by the same gang. Late yesterday afternoon –"

"Pardon me, Sir James," Hewitt interrupted, "but I think I must ask you to begin at the first robbery and tell me the whole tale in proper order. It makes things clearer, and sets them in their proper shape."

"Very well! Eleven months ago, or thereabout, I had rather a large party of visitors, and among them Colonel Heath and Mrs. Heath – the lady being a relative of my own late wife. Colonel Heath has not been long retired, you know – used to be political resident in an Indian native state. Mrs. Heath had rather a good stock of jewelry of one sort and another, about the most valuable piece being a bracelet set with a particularly fine pearl – quite an exceptional pearl, in fact – that had been one of a heap of presents from the maharajah of his state when Heath left India.

"It was a very noticeable bracelet, the gold setting being a mere feather-weight piece of native filigree work – almost too fragile to trust on the wrist – and the pearl being, as I have said, of a size and quality not often seen. Well, Heath and his wife arrived late one evening, and after lunch the following day, most of the men being off by themselves – shooting, I think – my daughter, my sister (who is very often down here), and Mrs. Heath took it into their heads to go walking – fern-hunting, and so on. My sister was rather long dressing, and, while they waited, my daughter went into Mrs. Heath's room, where Mrs. Heath turned over all her treasures to show her, as women do, you know. When my sister was at last ready, they came straight away, leaving the things littering about the room rather than stay longer to pack them up. The bracelet, with other things, was on the dressing-table then."

"One moment. As to the door?"

"They locked it. As they came away my daughter suggested turning the key, as we had one or two new servants about."

"And the window?"

"That they left open, as I was going to tell you. Well, they went on their walk and came back, with Lloyd (whom they had met somewhere) carrying their ferns for them. It was dusk and almost dinner-time. Mrs. Heath went straight to her room, and – the bracelet was gone."

"Was the room disturbed?"

"Not a bit. Everything was precisely where it had been left, except the bracelet. The door hadn't been tampered with, but of course the window was open, as I have told you."

"You called the police, of course?"

"Yes, and had a man from Scotland Yard down in the morning. He seemed a pretty smart fellow, and the first thing he noticed on the dressing-table, within an inch or two of where the bracelet had been, was a match, which had been lit and thrown down. Now nobody about the house had had occasion to use a match in that room that day, and, if they had, certainly wouldn't have thrown it on the cover of the dressing-table. So that, presuming the thief to have used that match, the robbery must have been committed when the room was getting dark – immediately before Mrs. Heath returned, in fact. The thief had evidently struck the match, passed it hurriedly over the various trinkets lying about, and taken the most valuable."

"Nothing else was even moved?"

"Nothing at all. Then the thief must have escaped by the window, although it was not quite clear how. The walking party approached the house with a full view of the window, but saw nothing, although the robbery must have been actually taking place a moment or two before they turned up.

"There was no water-pipe within any practicable distance of the window, but a ladder usually kept in the stable-yard was found lying along the edge of the lawn. The gardener explained, however, that he had put the ladder there after using it himself early in the afternoon."

"Of course it might easily have been used again after that and put back."

"Just what the Scotland Yard man said. He was pretty sharp, too, on the gardener, but very soon decided that he knew nothing of it. No stranger had been seen in the neighbourhood, nor had passed the lodge gates. Besides, as the detective said, it scarcely seemed the work of a stranger. A stranger could scarcely have known enough to go straight to the room where a lady – only arrived the day before – had left a valuable jewel, and away again without being seen. So all the people about the house were suspected in turn. The servants offered, in a body, to have their boxes searched, and this was done; everything was turned over, from the butler's to the new kitchen-maid's. I don't know that I should have had this carried quite so far if I had been the loser myself, but it was my guest, and I was in such a horrible position. Well, there's little more to be said about that, unfortunately. Nothing came of it all, and the thing's as great a mystery now as ever. I believe the Scotland Yard man got as far as suspecting *me* before he gave it up altogether, but give it up he did in the end. I think that's all I know about the first robbery. Is it clear?"

"Oh, yes; I shall probably want to ask a few questions when I have seen the place, but they can wait. What next?"

"Well," Sir James pursued, "the next was a very trumpery affair, that I should have forgotten all about, probably, if it hadn't been for one circumstance. Even now I hardly think it could have been the work of the same hand. Four months or thereabout after Mrs. Heath's disaster – in February of this year, in fact – Mrs. Armitage, a young widow, who had been a school-fellow of my daughter's, stayed with us for a week or so. The girls don't trouble about the London season, you know, and I have no town house, so they were glad to have their old friend here for a little in the dull time. Mrs. Armitage is a very active young lady, and was scarcely in the house half an hour before she arranged a drive in a pony-cart with Eva – my daughter – to look up old people in the village that she used to know before she was married. So they set off in the afternoon, and made such a round of it that they were late for dinner. Mrs. Armitage had a small plain gold brooch – not at all valuable, you know; two or three pounds, I suppose – which she used to pin up a cloak or anything of that sort. Before she went out she stuck this in the pin-cushion on her dressing-table, and left a ring – rather a good one, I believe – lying close by."

"This," asked Hewitt, "was not in the room that Mrs. Heath had occupied, I take it?"

"No; this was in another part of the building. Well, the brooch went – taken, evidently, by some one in a deuce of a hurry, for, when Mrs. Armitage got back to her room, there was the pin-cushion with a little tear in it, where the brooch had been simply snatched off. But the curious thing was that the ring – worth a dozen of the brooch – was left where it had been put. Mrs. Armitage didn't remember whether or not she had locked the door herself, although she found it locked when she returned; but my niece, who was indoors all the time, went and tried it once – because she remembered that a gas-fitter was at work on the landing near by – and found it safely locked. The gas-fitter, whom we didn't know at the time, but who since seems to be quite an honest fellow, was ready to swear that nobody but my niece had been to the door while he was in sight of it – which was almost all the time. As to the window, the sash-line had broken that very morning, and Mrs. Armitage had propped open the bottom half about eight or ten inches with a brush; and, when she returned, that brush, sash, and all were exactly as she had left them. Now I scarcely need tell *you* what an awkward job it must have been for anybody to get noiselessly in at that unsupported window; and how unlikely he would have been to replace it, with the brush, exactly as he found it."

"Just so. I suppose the brooch, was really gone? I mean, there was no chance of Mrs. Armitage having mislaid it?"

"Oh, none at all! There was a most careful search."

"Then, as to getting in at the window, would it have been easy?"

"Well, yes," Sir James replied; "yes, perhaps it would. It was a first-floor window, and it looks over the roof and skylight of the billiard-room. I built the billiard-room myself – built it out from a smoking-room just at this corner. It would be easy enough to get at the window from the billiard-room roof. But, then," he added, "that couldn't have been the way. Somebody or other was in the billiard-room the whole time, and nobody could have got over the roof (which is nearly all skylight) without being seen and heard. I was there myself for an hour or two, taking a little practice."

"Well, was anything done?"

"Strict inquiry was made among the servants, of course, but nothing came of it. It was such a small matter that Mrs. Armitage wouldn't hear of my calling in the police or anything of that sort, although I felt pretty certain that there must be a dishonest servant about somewhere. A servant might take a plain brooch, you know, who would feel afraid of a valuable ring, the loss of which would be made a greater matter of."

"Well, yes, perhaps so, in the case of an inexperienced thief, who also would be likely to snatch up whatever she took in a hurry. But I'm doubtful. What made you connect these two robberies together?"

"Nothing whatever – for some months. They seemed quite of a different sort. But scarcely more than a month ago I met Mrs. Armitage at Brighton, and we talked, among other things, of the previous robbery – that of Mrs. Heath's bracelet. I described the circumstances pretty minutely, and, when I mentioned the match found on the table, she said: 'How strange! Why, *my* thief left a match on the dressing-table when he took my poor little brooch!' "

Hewitt nodded. "Yes," he said. "A spent match, of course?"

"Yes, of course, a spent match. She noticed it lying close by the pin-cushion, but threw it away without mentioning the circumstance. Still, it seemed rather curious to me that a match should be lit and dropped, in each case, on the dressing-cover an inch from where the article was taken. I mentioned it to Lloyd when I got back, and he agreed that it seemed significant."

"Scarcely," said Hewitt, shaking his head. "Scarcely, so far, to be called significant, although worth following up. Everybody uses matches in the dark, you know."

"Well, at any rate, the coincidence appealed to me so far that it struck me it might be worth while to describe the brooch to the police in order that they could trace it if it had been pawned. They had tried that, of course, over the bracelet without any result, but I fancied the shot might be worth making, and might possibly lead us on the track of the more serious robbery."

"Quite so. It was the right thing to do. Well?"

"Well, they found it. A woman had pawned it in London – at a shop in Chelsea. But that was some time before, and the pawnbroker had clean forgotten all about the woman's appearance. The name and address she gave were false. So that was the end of that business."

"Had any of the servants left you between the time the brooch was lost and the date of the pawn ticket?"

"No."

"Were all your servants at home on the day the brooch was pawned?"

"Oh, yes! I made that inquiry myself."

"Very good! What next?"

"Yesterday – and this is what made me send for you. My late wife's sister came here last Tuesday, and we gave her the room from which Mrs. Heath lost her bracelet. She had with her a very old-fashioned brooch, containing a miniature of her father, and set in front with three very fine brilliants and a few smaller stones. Here we are, though, at the Croft. I'll tell you the rest indoors."

Hewitt laid his hand on the baronet's arm. "Don't pull up, Sir James," he said. "Drive a little farther. I should like to have a general idea of the whole case before we go in."

"Very good!" Sir James Norris straightened the horse's head again and went on. "Late yesterday afternoon, as my sister-in-law was changing her dress, she left her room for a moment to speak to my daughter in her room, almost adjoining. She was gone no more than three minutes, or five at most, but on her return the brooch, which had been left on the table, had gone. Now the window was shut fast, and had not been tampered with. Of course the door was open, but so was my daughter's, and anybody walking near must have been heard. But the strangest circumstance, and one that almost makes me wonder whether I have been awake today or not, was that there lay *a used match* on the very spot, as nearly as possible, where the brooch had been – and it was broad daylight!"

Hewitt rubbed his nose and looked thoughtfully before him. "Um – curious, certainly," he said, "Anything else?"

"Nothing more than you shall see for yourself. I have had the room locked and watched till you could examine it. My sister-in-law had heard of your name, and suggested that you should be called in; so, of course, I did exactly as she wanted. That she should have lost that brooch, of all things, in my house is most unfortunate; you see, there was some small difference about the thing between my late wife and her sister when their mother died and left it. It's almost worse than the Heaths' bracelet business, and altogether I'm not pleased with things, I can assure you. See what a position it is for me! Here are three ladies, in the space of one year, robbed one after another in this mysterious fashion in my house, and I can't find the thief! It's horrible! People will be afraid to come near the place. And I can do nothing!"

"Ah, well, we'll see. Perhaps we had better turn back now. By-the-by, were you thinking of having any alterations or additions made to your house?"

"No. What makes you ask?"

"I think you might at least consider the question of painting and decorating, Sir James – or, say, putting up another coach-house, or something. Because I should like to be (to the servants) the architect – or the builder, if you please – come to look around. You haven't told any of them about this business?"

"Not a word. Nobody knows but my relatives and Lloyd. I took every precaution myself, at once. As to your little disguise, be the architect by all means, and do as you please. If you can only find this thief and put an end to this horrible state of affairs, you'll do me the greatest service I've ever asked for – and as to your fee, I'll gladly make it whatever is usual, and three hundred in addition."

Martin Hewitt bowed. "You're very generous, Sir James, and you may be sure I'll do what I can. As a professional man, of course, a good fee always stimulates my interest, although this case of yours certainly seems interesting enough by itself."

"Most extraordinary! Don't you think so? Here are three persons, all ladies, all in my house, two even in the same room, each successively robbed of a piece of jewelry, each from a dressing-table, and a used match left behind in every case. All in the most difficult – one would say impossible – circumstances for a thief, and yet there is no clue!"

"Well, we won't say that just yet, Sir James; we must see. And we must guard against any undue predisposition to consider the robberies in a lump. Here we are at the lodge gate again. Is that your gardener – the man who left the ladder by the lawn on the first occasion you spoke of?"

Mr. Hewitt nodded in the direction of a man who was clipping a box border.

"Yes; will you ask him anything?"

"No, no; at any rate, not now. Remember the building alterations. I think, if there is no objection, I will look first at the room that the lady – Mrs. –" Hewitt looked up, inquiringly.

"My sister-in-law? Mrs. Cazenove. Oh, yes! You shall come to her room at once."

"Thank you. And I think Mrs. Cazenove had better be there."

They alighted, and a boy from the lodge led the horse and dog-cart away.

Mrs. Cazenove was a thin and faded, but quick and energetic, lady of middle age. She bent her head very slightly on learning Martin Hewitt's name, and said: "I must thank you, Mr. Hewitt, for your very prompt attention. I need scarcely say that any help you can afford in tracing the thief who has my property – whoever it may be – will make me most grateful. My room is quite ready for you to examine."

The room was on the second floor – the top floor at that part of the building. Some slight confusion of small articles of dress was observable in parts of the room.

"This, I take it," inquired Hewitt, "is exactly as it was at the time the brooch was missed?"

"Precisely," Mrs. Cazenove answered. "I have used another room, and put myself to some other inconveniences, to avoid any disturbance."

Hewitt stood before the dressing-table. "Then this is the used match," he observed, "exactly where it was found?"

"Yes."

"Where was the brooch?"

"I should say almost on the very same spot. Certainly no more than a very few inches away."

Hewitt examined the match closely. "It is burned very little," he remarked. "It would appear to have gone out at once. Could you hear it struck?"

"I heard nothing whatever; absolutely nothing."

"If you will step into Miss Norris' room now for a moment," Hewitt suggested, "we will try an experiment. Tell me if you hear matches struck, and how many. Where is the match-stand?"

The match-stand proved to be empty, but matches were found in Miss Norris' room, and the test was made. Each striking could be heard distinctly, even with one of the doors pushed to.

"Both your own door and Miss Norris' were open, I understand; the window shut and fastened inside as it is now, and nothing but the brooch was disturbed?"

"Yes, that was so."

"Thank you, Mrs. Cazenove. I don't think I need trouble you any further just at present. I think, Sir James," Hewitt added, turning to the baronet, who was standing by the door – "I think we will see the other room and take a walk outside the house, if you please. I suppose, by the by, that there is no getting at the matches left behind on the first and second occasions?"

"No," Sir James answered. "Certainly not here. The Scotland Yard man may have kept his."

The room that Mrs. Armitage had occupied presented no peculiar feature. A few feet below the window the roof of the billiard-room was visible, consisting largely of skylight. Hewitt glanced casually about the walls, ascertained that the furniture and hangings had not been materially changed since the second robbery, and expressed his desire to see the windows from the outside. Before leaving the room, however, he wished to know the names of any persons who were known to have been about the house on the occasions of all three robberies.

"Just carry your mind back, Sir James," he said. "Begin with yourself, for instance. Where were you at these times?"

"When Mrs. Heath lost her bracelet, I was in Tagley Wood all the afternoon. When Mrs. Armitage was robbed, I believe I was somewhere about the place most of the time she was out. Yesterday I was down at the farm." Sir James' face broadened. "I don't know whether you call those suspicious movements," he added, and laughed.

"Not at all; I only asked you so that, remembering your own movements, you might the better recall those of the rest of the household. Was anybody, to your knowledge – *anybody*, mind – in the house on all three occasions?"

"Well, you know, it's quite impossible to answer for all the servants. You'll only get that by direct questioning – I can't possibly remember things of that sort. As to the family and visitors – why, you don't suspect any of them, do you?"

"I don't suspect a soul, Sir James," Hewitt answered, beaming genially, "not a soul. You see, I can't suspect people till I know something about where they were. It's quite possible there will be independent evidence enough as it is, but you must help me if you can. The visitors, now. Was there any visitor here each time – or even on the first and last occasions only?"

"No, not one. And my own sister, perhaps you will be pleased to know, was only there at the time of the first robbery."

"Just so! And your daughter, as I have gathered, was clearly absent from the spot each time – indeed, was in company with the party robbed. Your niece, now?"

"Why hang it all, Mr. Hewitt, I can't talk of my niece as a suspected criminal! The poor girl's under my protection, and I really can't allow –"

Hewitt raised his hand, and shook his head deprecatingly.

"My dear sir, haven't I said that I don't suspect a soul? *Do* let me know how the people were distributed, as nearly as possible. Let me see. It was your, niece, I think, who found that Mrs. Armitage's door was locked – this door, in fact – on the day she lost her brooch?"

"Yes, it was."

"Just so – at the time when Mrs. Armitage herself had forgotten whether she locked it or not. And yesterday – was she out then?"

"No, I think not. Indeed, she goes out very little – her health is usually bad. She was indoors, too, at the time of the Heath robbery, since you ask. But come, now, I don't like this. It's ridiculous to suppose that *she* knows anything of it."

"I don't suppose it, as I have said. I am only asking for information. That is all your resident family, I take it, and you know nothing of anybody else's movements – except, perhaps, Mr. Lloyd's?"

"Lloyd? Well, you know yourself that he was out with the ladies when the first robbery took place. As to the others, I don't remember. Yesterday he was probably in his room, writing. I think that acquits *him*, eh?" Sir James looked quizzically into the broad face of the affable detective, who smiled and replied:

"Oh, of course nobody can be in two places at once, else what would become of the alibi as an institution? But, as I have said, I am only setting my facts in order. Now, you see, we get down to the servants – unless some stranger is the party wanted. Shall we go outside now?"

Lenton Croft was a large, desultory sort of house, nowhere more than three floors high, and mostly only two. It had been added to bit by bit, till it zigzagged about its site, as Sir James Norris expressed it, "like a game of dominoes." Hewitt scrutinized its external features carefully as they strolled around, and stopped some little while before the windows of the two bed-rooms he had just seen from the inside. Presently they approached the stables and coach-house, where a groom was washing the wheels of the dog-cart.

"Do you mind my smoking?" Hewitt asked Sir James. "Perhaps you will take a cigar yourself – they are not so bad, I think. I will ask your man for a light."

Sir James felt for his own match-box, but Hewitt had gone, and was lighting his cigar with a match from a box handed him by the groom. A smart little terrier was trotting about by the coach-house, and Hewitt stooped to rub its head. Then he made some observation about the dog, which enlisted the groom's interest, and was soon absorbed in a chat with the man. Sir James, waiting a little way off, tapped the stones rather impatiently with his foot, and presently moved away.

For full a quarter of an hour Hewitt chatted with the groom, and, when at last he came away and overtook Sir James, that gentleman was about re-entering the house.

"I beg your pardon, Sir James," Hewitt said, "for leaving you in that unceremonious fashion to talk to your groom, but a dog, Sir James – a good dog – will draw me anywhere."

"Oh!" replied Sir James, shortly.

"There is one other thing," Hewitt went on, disregarding the other's curtness, "that I should like to know: There are two windows directly below that of the room occupied yesterday by Mrs. Cazenove – one on each floor. What rooms do they light?"

"That on the ground floor is the morning-room; the other is Mr. Lloyd's – my secretary. A sort of study or sitting-room."

"Now you will see at once, Sir James," Hewitt pursued, with an affable determination to win the baronet back to good-humor – "you will see at once that, if a ladder had been used in Mrs. Heath's case, anybody looking from either of these rooms would have seen it."

"Of course! The Scotland Yard man questioned everybody as to that, but nobody seemed to have been in either of the rooms when the thing occurred; at any rate, nobody saw anything."

"Still, I think I should like to look out of those windows myself; it will, at least, give me an idea of what *was* in view and what was not, if anybody had been there."

Sir James Norris led the way to the morning-room. As they reached the door a young lady, carrying a book and walking very languidly, came out. Hewitt stepped aside to let her pass, and afterward said interrogatively: "Miss Norris, your daughter, Sir James?"

"No, my niece. Do you want to ask her anything? Dora, my dear," Sir James added, following her in the corridor, "this is Mr. Hewitt, who is investigating these wretched robberies for me. I think he would like to hear if you remember anything happening at any of the three times."

The lady bowed slightly, and said in a plaintive drawl: "I, uncle? Really, I don't remember anything; nothing at all."

"You found Mrs. Armitage's door locked, I believe," asked Hewitt, "when you tried it, on the afternoon when she lost her brooch?"

"Oh, yes; I believe it was locked. Yes, it was."

"Had the key been left in?"

"The key? Oh, no! I think not; no."

"Do you remember anything out of the common happening – anything whatever, no matter how trivial – on the day Mrs. Heath lost her bracelet?"

"No, really, I don't. I can't remember at all."

"Nor yesterday?"

"No, nothing. I don't remember anything."

"Thank you," said Hewitt, hastily; "thank you. Now the morning-room, Sir James."

In the morning-room Hewitt stayed but a few seconds, doing little more than casually glance out of the windows. In the room above he took a little longer time. It was a comfortable room, but with rather effeminate indications about its contents. Little pieces of draped silk-work hung about the furniture, and Japanese silk fans decorated the mantelpiece. Near the window was a cage containing a gray parrot, and the writing-table was decorated with two vases of flowers.

"Lloyd makes himself pretty comfortable, eh?" Sir James observed. "But it isn't likely anybody would be here while he was out, at the time that bracelet went."

"No," replied Hewitt, meditatively. "No, I suppose not."

He stared thoughtfully out of the window, and then, still deep in thought, rattled at the wires of the cage with a quill toothpick and played a moment with the parrot. Then, looking up at the window again, he said: "That is Mr. Lloyd, isn't it, coming back in a fly?"

"Yes, I think so. Is there anything else you would care to see here?"

"No, thank you," Hewitt replied; "I don't think there is."

They went down to the smoking-room, and Sir James went away to speak to his secretary. When he returned, Hewitt said quietly: "I think, Sir James – I *think* that I shall be able to give you your thief presently."

"What! Have you a clue? Who do you think? I began to believe you were hopelessly stumped."

"Well, yes. I have rather a good clue, although I can't tell you much about it just yet. But it is so good a clue that I should like to know now whether you are determined to prosecute when you have the criminal?"

"Why, bless me, of course," Sir James replied, with surprise. "It doesn't rest with me, you know – the property belongs to my friends. And even if they were disposed to let the thing slide, I shouldn't allow it – I couldn't, after they had been robbed in my house."

"Of course, of course! Then, if I can, I should like to send a message to Twyford by somebody perfectly trustworthy – not a servant. Could anybody go?"

"Well, there's Lloyd, although he's only just back from his journey. But, if it's important, he'll go."

"It is important. The fact is we must have a policeman or two here this evening, and I'd like Mr. Lloyd to fetch them without telling anybody else."

Sir James rang, and, in response to his message, Mr. Lloyd appeared. While Sir James gave his secretary his instructions, Hewitt strolled to the door of the smoking-room, and intercepted the latter as he came out.

"I'm sorry to give you this trouble, Mr. Lloyd," he said, "but I must stay here myself for a little, and somebody who can be trusted must go. Will you just bring back a police-constable with you? Or rather two – two would be better. That is all that is wanted. You won't let the servants know, will you? Of course there will be a female searcher at the Twyford police-station? Ah – of course. Well, you needn't bring her, you know. That sort of thing is done at the station." And, chatting thus confidentially, Martin Hewitt saw him off.

When Hewitt returned to the smoking-room, Sir James said, suddenly: "Why, bless my soul, Mr. Hewitt, we haven't fed you! I'm awfully sorry. We came in rather late for lunch, you know, and this business has bothered me so I clean forgot everything else. There's no dinner till seven, so you'd better let me give you something now. I'm really sorry. Come along."

"Thank you, Sir James," Hewitt replied; "I won't take much. A few biscuits, perhaps, or something of that sort. And, by the by, if you don't mind, I rather think I should like to take it alone. The fact is I want to go over this case thoroughly by myself. Can you put me in a room?"

"Any room you like. Where will you go? The dining-room's rather large, but there's my study, that's pretty snug, or –"

"Perhaps I can go into Mr. Lloyd's room for half an hour or so; I don't think he'll mind, and it's pretty comfortable."

"Certainly, if you'd like. I'll tell them to send you whatever they've got."

"Thank you very much. Perhaps they'll also send me a lump of sugar and a walnut; it's – it's a little fad of mine."

"A – what? A lump of sugar and a walnut?" Sir James stopped for a moment, with his hand on the bell-rope. "Oh, certainly, if you'd like it; certainly," he added, and stared after this detective with curious tastes as he left the room.

When the vehicle, bringing back the secretary and the policeman, drew up on the drive, Martin Hewitt left the room on the first floor and proceeded downstairs. On the landing he met Sir James Norris and Mrs. Cazenove, who stared with astonishment on perceiving that the detective carried in his hand the parrot-cage.

"I think our business is about brought to a head now," Hewitt remarked, on the stairs. "Here are the police officers from Twyford." The men were standing in the hall with Mr. Lloyd, who, on catching sight of the cage in Hewitt's hand, paled suddenly.

"This is the person who will be charged, I think," Hewitt pursued, addressing the officers, and indicating Lloyd with his finger.

"What, Lloyd?" gasped Sir James, aghast. "No – not Lloyd – nonsense!"

"He doesn't seem to think it nonsense himself, does he?" Hewitt placidly observed. Lloyd had sank on a chair, and, gray of face, was staring blindly at the man he had run against at the office door that morning. His lips moved in spasms, but there was no sound. The wilted flower fell from his button-hole to the floor, but he did not move.

"This is his accomplice," Hewitt went on, placing the parrot and cage on the hall table, "though I doubt whether there will be any use in charging *him*. Eh, Polly?"

The parrot put his head aside and chuckled. "Hullo, Polly!" it quietly gurgled. "Come along!"

Sir James Norris was hopelessly bewildered. "Lloyd – Lloyd," he said, under his breath. "Lloyd – and that!"

"This was his little messenger, his useful Mercury," Hewitt explained, tapping the cage complacently; "in fact, the actual lifter. Hold him up!"

The last remark referred to the wretched Lloyd, who had fallen forward with something between a sob and a loud sigh. The policemen took him by the arms and propped him in his chair.

* * *

"System?" said Hewitt, with a shrug of the shoulders, an hour or two after in Sir James' study. "I can't say I have a system. I call it nothing but common-sense and a sharp pair of eyes. Nobody using these could help taking the right road in this case. I began at the match, just as the Scotland Yard man did, but I had the advantage of taking a line through three cases. To begin with, it was plain that that match, being left there in daylight, in Mrs. Cazenove's room, could not have been used to light the table-top, in the full glare of the window; therefore it had been used for some other purpose – *what* purpose I could not, at the moment, guess. Habitual thieves, you know, often have curious superstitions, and some will never take anything without leaving something behind – a pebble or a piece of coal, or something like that – in the premises they have been robbing. It seemed at first extremely likely that this was a case of that kind. The match had clearly been *brought in* – because, when I asked for matches, there were none in the stand, not even an empty box, and the room had not been disturbed. Also the match probably had not been struck there, nothing having been heard, although, of course, a mistake in this matter was just possible. This match, then, it was fair to assume, had been lit somewhere else and blown out immediately – I remarked at the time that it was very little burned. Plainly it could not have been treated thus for nothing, and the only possible object would have been to prevent it igniting accidentally. Following on this, it became obvious that the match was used, for whatever purpose, not *as* a match, but merely as a convenient splinter of wood.

"So far so good. But on examining the match very closely I observed, as you can see for yourself, certain rather sharp indentations in the wood. They are very small, you see, and scarcely visible, except upon narrow inspection; but there they are, and their positions are regular. See, there are two on each side, each opposite the corresponding mark of the other pair. The match, in fact, would seem to have been gripped in some fairly sharp instrument, holding it at two points above and two below – an instrument, as it may at once strike you, not unlike the beak of a bird.

"Now here was an idea. What living creature but a bird could possibly have entered Mrs. Heath's window without a ladder – supposing no ladder to have been used – or could have got into Mrs. Armitage's window without lifting the sash higher than the eight or ten inches it was already open? Plainly, nothing. Further, it is significant that only *one* article was stolen at a time, although others were about. A human being could have carried any reasonable number, but a bird could only take one at a time. But why should a bird carry a match in its beak? Certainly it must have been trained to do that for a purpose, and a little consideration made that purpose pretty clear. A noisy, chattering bird would probably betray itself at once. Therefore it must be trained to keep quiet both while going for and coming away with its plunder. What readier or more probably effectual way than, while teaching it to carry without dropping, to teach it also to keep quiet while carrying? The one thing would practically cover the other.

"I thought at once, of course, of a jackdaw or a magpie – these birds' thievish reputations made the guess natural. But the marks on the match were much too wide apart to have been made by the beak of either. I conjectured, therefore, that it must be a raven. So that, when we arrived near the coach-house, I seized the opportunity of a little chat with your groom on the subject of dogs and pets in general, and ascertained that there was no tame raven in the place. I also, incidentally, by getting a light from the coach-house box of matches, ascertained that the match found was of the sort generally used about the establishment – the large, thick, red-topped English match. But I further found that Mr. Lloyd had a parrot which was a most intelligent pet, and had been trained into comparative quietness – for a parrot. Also, I learned that more than once the groom had met Mr. Lloyd carrying his parrot under his coat, it having, as its owner explained, learned the trick of opening its cage-door and escaping.

"I said nothing, of course, to you of all this, because I had as yet nothing but a train of argument and no results. I got to Lloyd's room as soon as possible. My chief object in going there was achieved when I played with the parrot, and induced it to bite a quill toothpick.

"When you left me in the smoking-room, I compared the quill and the match very carefully, and found that the marks corresponded exactly. After this I felt very little doubt indeed. The fact of Lloyd having met the ladies walking before dark on the day of the first robbery proved nothing, because, since it was clear that the match had *not* been used to procure a light, the robbery might as easily have taken place in daylight as not – must have so taken place, in fact, if my conjectures were right. That they were right I felt no doubt. There could be no other explanation.

"When Mrs. Heath left her window open and her door shut, anybody climbing upon the open sash of Lloyd's high window could have put the bird upon the sill above. The match placed in the bird's beak for the purpose I have indicated, and struck first, in case by accident it should ignite by rubbing against something and startle the bird – this match would, of course, be dropped just where the object to be removed was taken up; as you know, in every case the match was found almost upon the spot where the missing article had been left – scarcely a likely triple coincidence had the match been used by a human thief. This would have been done as soon after the ladies had left as possible, and there would then have been plenty of time for Lloyd to hurry out and meet them before dark – especially plenty of time to meet them *coming back*, as they must have been, since they were carrying their ferns. The match was an article well chosen for its purpose, as being a not altogether unlikely thing to find on a dressing-table, and, if noticed, likely to lead to the wrong conclusions adopted by the official detective.

"In Mrs. Armitage's case the taking of an inferior brooch and the leaving of a more valuable ring pointed clearly either to the operator being a fool or unable to distinguish values, and certainly, from other indications, the thief seemed no fool. The door was locked, and the gas-fitter, so to speak, on guard, and the window was only eight or ten inches open and propped with a brush. A human thief entering the window would have disturbed this arrangement, and would scarcely risk discovery by attempting to replace it, especially a thief in so great a hurry as to snatch the brooch up without unfastening the pin. The bird could pass through the opening as it was, and *would have* to tear the pin-cushion to pull the brooch off, probably holding the cushion down with its claw the while.

"Now in yesterday's case we had an alteration of conditions. The window was shut and fastened, but the door was open – but only left for a few minutes, during which time no sound was heard either of coming or going. Was it not possible, then, that the thief was *already* in the room, in hiding, while Mrs. Cazenove was there, and seized its first opportunity on her temporary absence? The room is full of draperies, hangings, and what not, allowing of plenty of concealment for a bird, and a bird could leave the place noiselessly and quickly. That the whole scheme was strange mattered not at all. Robberies presenting such unaccountable features must have been effected by strange means of one sort or another. There was no improbability. Consider how many hundreds of examples of infinitely higher degrees of bird-training are exhibited in the London streets every week for coppers.

"So that, on the whole, I felt pretty sure of my ground. But before taking any definite steps I resolved to see if Polly could not be persuaded to exhibit his accomplishments to an indulgent stranger. For that purpose I contrived to send Lloyd away again and have a quiet hour alone with his bird. A piece of sugar, as everybody knows, is a good parrot bribe; but a walnut, split in half, is a better – especially if the bird be used to it; so I got you to furnish me with both. Polly was shy at first, but I generally get along very well with pets, and a little perseverance soon led to a complete private performance for my benefit. Polly would take the match, mute as wax, jump on the table, pick up the brightest thing he could see, in a great hurry, leave the match behind, and scuttle away round the room; but at first wouldn't give up the plunder to *me*. It was enough. I also took the liberty, as you know, of a general look round, and discovered that little collection of Brummagem rings and trinkets that you have just seen – used in Polly's education, no doubt. When we sent Lloyd away, it struck me that he might as well be usefully employed as not, so I got him to fetch the police, deluding him a little, I fear, by talking about the servants and a female searcher. There will be no trouble about evidence; he'll confess. Of that I'm sure. I know the sort of man. But I doubt if you'll get Mrs. Cazenove's brooch back. You see, he has been to London today, and by this time the swag is probably broken up."

Sir James listened to Hewitt's explanation with many expressions of assent and some of surprise. When it was over, he smoked a few whiffs and then said: "But Mrs. Armitage's brooch was pawned, and by a woman."

"Exactly. I expect our friend Lloyd was rather disgusted at his small luck – probably gave the brooch to some female connection in London, and she realized on it. Such persons don't always trouble to give a correct address."

The two smoked in silence for a few minutes, and then Hewitt continued: "I don't expect our friend has had an easy job altogether with that bird. His successes at most have only been three, and I suspect he had many failures and not a few anxious moments that we know nothing of. I should judge as much merely from what the groom told me of frequently meeting Lloyd with his parrot. But the plan was not a bad one – not at all. Even if the bird had been caught in the act, it would only have been 'That mischievous parrot!' you see. And his master would only have been looking for him."

iMurder

Josh Pachter

THERE IT WAS in the iTunes App Store, the first entry beneath the heading 'Recommended For You.'

Actually, I'd never noticed a 'Recommended For You' tab in the App Store before, but I guess Apple's geniuses are always coming up with new stuff to keep their customers consuming.

In any event, there it was, iMurder, its icon a white skull and crossbones inside a black square with rounded corners, rated four stars and priced for a limited time only at 99¢.

"Tired of waiting around for an elderly relative to pass on," the App Store blurb wondered, "so you can collect your inheritance? Fed up with a nasty boss or difficult colleague at work? Jealous of that 'special friendship' your spouse seems to be developing with the next-door neighbor? iMurder can solve these and many other problems with the simple press of a button."

It had to be a hoax, I figured, some developer's idea of a joke that had somehow slipped through Apple's screening process. My curiosity awakened, though, I clicked on the link to the developer's website, *www.redrumi.com*, assuming I'd find a clever 404 message teasing me for being gullible enough to bother trying.

Instead, I was taken to a professionally designed home page, replete with orchestral background music, animated gifs, testimonials from satisfied users, and a link to information about an additional app from the same developer, iAlibi.

I went back to the App Store, typed in my iTunes password, and downloaded iMurder. At 99 cents, I figured, what did I have to lose?

* * *

For my first two years after grad school, I'd managed to cobble together a barely life-sustaining income as a 'Road Scholar,' driving from college to college in and around Cleveland, Ohio, and teaching one class here, two classes there as an adjunct instructor. Then I'd gotten a major break: a full professor at Cuyahoga Community College's Western Campus (not 10 miles from my fourth-floor one-bedroom apartment in Strongsville) had died – of a heart attack, in the middle of a class session, in front of 150 students – and I'd been brought in mid-semester and given a temporary full-time contract to take over his course load through the end of the term. (Turned out that three of his students had been secretly videotaping his lecture with their cell phones – and two of them actually *did* post their videos of his collapse and expiration on their Facebook pages.)

Anyway, my filling in for him made me the front runner to replace him permanently, and three months later I was in fact one of the two finalists for his position – but the search committee had ultimately decided on the other candidate, Andy Park, also a CCC adjunct but one with a couple years' seniority over me.

If only *Andy* would keel over and die, I knew, then the sweet taste of a full-time salary and a full benefits package that I'd so briefly enjoyed would be mine forever.

* * *

If this was fiction, a detective story I was writing for *Ellery Queen's Mystery Magazine* or some other periodical that pays authors by the word, I would now launch into a lengthy description of how I used the app – filled with lots of scene setting and descriptions of the furniture and littered with multitudes of unnecessary adjectives and adverbs. But in reality it all went very simply and smoothly.

I looked up Andy Park in the phone book. He was listed – both his phone number and his address. I got in my car and drove to his apartment. I climbed two flights of stairs and rang his doorbell. He was home.

When he opened the door and saw that it was me, a surprised and yet – unless this was perhaps my imagination – resigned expression came over his face.

"It's you," he said.

I nodded. "Yes," I said. "I want to show you something."

I pulled my iPhone from my pocket and launched the iMurder app. In the center of the screen that came up, the words 'Select Victim' appeared in an oblong drop-shadowed button. I touched the button, and the built-in camera's shutter window opened. I raised the phone and centered Andy in the frame and pushed the little camera icon at the bottom of the screen. The shutter irised closed, and the camera clicked.

A new screen showed Andy's frozen image with two buttons beneath it, one marked 'Cancel' and the other one 'Use.'

"I'm sorry, Andy," I said, and pressed the 'Use' button.

There was a pleasant chime, and Andy Park hit the ground like a lead weight dropped from a church steeple.

I leaned over him and felt his wrist for a pulse.

There wasn't one. He was dead.

Four stars, my eye, I thought. *This is* definitely *a five-star app!*

I swung Andy's apartment door shut and stood over him for a long moment, staring down at his body, visions of health insurance and new eyeglasses every 12 months and prescription drugs for a \$20 co-pay and tenure and, eventually, the opportunity to actually *retire*, dancing in my head.

And then, suddenly, a loud beeping erupted. It seemed to be coming from Andy's body. In a daze, I hunkered down beside him and patted him down. There was a telltale bulge in his left front pocket of his khakis, and I gingerly slipped my hand inside and retrieved his iPhone.

I touched the home button, and the screen illuminated.

Idiot, I thought, scarcely able to hear myself over the clamorous beeping that filled the air. *If you don't use a password, then any schmuck who stumbles across your phone can access your data.*

My head swimming, I slid to unlock, and the wallpaper photo of the Earth seen from space was replaced by a bright yellow screen with the logo "i911" in screaming red letters at the top.

As I stared at the screen, a pale-green text-message bubble popped into view: 'GPS coordinates identified. Officers have been dispatched. Anticipated time of arrival: two minutes. Please stand by.'

I blinked: once, twice, three times.

Finally rousing myself to action, I dropped Andy's iPhone onto his corpse, fished my own phone back out of the pocket where I'd stashed it and keyed in my password.

The iMurder icon was gone. I launched the App Store, and it wasn't there, either.

In the distance, I heard the wail of an approaching siren.

I swallowed, my mouth suddenly very dry, and searched on 'iAlibi.'

No result.

I switched over to Safari and went to *www.redrumi.com*.

'404,' the screen said. "We're sorry, but the website you requested is no longer available. Please check the URL and dial again."

Sighing, I returned to the App Store.

There was only one listing under my 'Recommended For You' tab: TimeStacker, which promised 'over 500 of the best ways to while away those long months and years behind bars.'

'A steal,' the blurb announced, 'at only $1.99. Available at this price for a limited time only!'

As the door burst open and two uniformed cops rushed into Andy's apartment, guns drawn, I typed in my iTunes password and bought the app.

Creature of the Thaumatrope

Tony Pi

THE CLOCKWORK THAUMATROPE rested on a small kidney-shaped table by the window in the office of Doctor Pierrick Harbin, gleaming golden in the afternoon sunlight except where blood had speckled it. Close by, the body of a scarred, swarthy man lay beside a fallen chair, face-up in a pool of dried blood.

"Here's my theory, Professor Voss." Inspector Georges Carmouche finished his examination of the corpse with his turquoise amphisbaena quizzing glass. I'd given him that very piece a few months ago as a belated gift to celebrate his promotion, proud as I was of my former protégé. "I believe Seznec was in this chair when Doctor Harbin stabbed him in the chest. No sign of the slightest resistance from the former boxer, which is truly odd considering Seznec's infamous short temper. There are seven other wounds, all made with the same letter opener."

As Chief Curator of Aigyptian Magic at *Le Musée d'Ys*, I'd somehow become entangled in a string of mystical mysteries, which made me the premier consultant for the city police when it came to all things occult. But it was through my role as a history consultant for Chimère Studios that I had become acquainted with the ingénue Laure Harbin.

Less than an hour ago, I'd been with Laure in the courtyard of my museum where I'd arranged for the Chimère crew to film a fairy chess scene for her next film, *Games of Air and Darkness*. That was where Carmouche had sent Sergeant Joncour to fetch us both, citing a deadly incident that involved Laure's father.

I'd taught Carmouche the skills of deduction he needed to become the youngest Inspector in Ys, but I wondered if Carmouche still leapt too soon to some conclusions.

"Are you sure Pierrick Harbin did this? Why would a respected alienist suddenly murder his patient?" I swept the lion's head handle of my walking stick in a wide arc to encompass the doctor's room, from the brass coat tree to the burr walnut desk. "See how tidy his office is? Harbin's books are flawlessly alphabetized, and every single item on his desk is perfectly aligned, down to the angles of his matched set of fountain pens."

"In the absence of other evidence, Pierrick Harbin remains our prime suspect," Carmouche argued.

I returned to the notebook on the doctor's desk. Black leather cover embossed with the image of a crescent moon, its brass sun-shaped lock had been left open. I turned to the last entry. "And yet this is a man who writes in a cryptic shorthand where every stroke is precise. Observation tells us that Doctor Harbin's a man well in control of himself and his environment. This killing, however, is doubtless the work of a savage."

"What of the witness? The doorman saw the doctor dash out, hiding his face with a hat. Not to mention the bloody shoeprint he left in the lift."

I sighed. "Damning to be sure, but we must examine all pieces of the puzzle lest we rush to a false accusation. Why didn't Seznec struggle, for example? The more we know, the more expediently we can figure out where Pierrick Harbin has gone." I made my way to the thaumatrope, leaned my walking stick against the windowsill and sat in the red leather chair that would have been opposite the patient. From here I could look down at Rue Morvarch, or turn my head to look at the door to the study. "Consider this thaumatrope."

The device in front of me consisted of an intricate box with two thin rods extending up to eye-level. Suspended between them, parallel to the table, was a white cardboard disk. Its top face held the image of a painted, grinning djinni.

"What is it?" Carmouche asked.

"Did you never play with a wonder-turner when you were young, my friend?"

He shook his head.

"It's a children's toy that works on the same principle as film." I opened the drawer in the table and found a dozen other similar disks bearing different images: an empty vase; a tightrope walker treading on air; and a pair of floating wings, to name a few. One in particular stood out, in that a child seemed to have drawn it. One side depicted a colourful leaping horse, while the flip side had a disembodied unicorn horn floating above a wooden fence.

I was about to demonstrate how the toy worked when the door to the waiting room opened. Laure Harbin slipped past the burly Sergeant Joncour, still dressed in her ethereal sylph costume from the film shoot.

She gasped when she saw the dead body.

Carmouche hastened between the young woman and the body on the floor, as though his outstretched arms sufficed in concealing the corpse. "Miss Harbin, you can't be in here."

Laure turned away. "You asked my help, Inspector." Her strawberry-blonde hair made for a startling yet pleasing contrast with her snowy white costume with fairy wings of lace and gossamer, a vision truly out of place at the scene of a bloody crime.

"But some things you don't need to see," Carmouche answered, concern in his voice.

It was I who had introduced Carmouche to Laure Harbin a few months ago, so that he could help her avert a blackmail scandal. He'd fallen in love with the fair woman, I suspect, as many men have. How could you not, as one of my colleagues had argued, once you'd seen her beauty grace the silver screen?

I stood, doffed my overcoat and draped it over Seznec's body. "Laure could help us solve this crime faster, Carmouche. She knows her father and his habits better than you or I."

"I just want us to find Papa," Laure said.

Reluctantly, Carmouche allowed it.

I sat back down and held up the disk with the unicorn horn. "Do you recognize this, Laure?"

Laure approached, but avoided looking towards the body. She took it from me with a look of recognition, then a quizzical frown. "That's one of the old wonder-turners Olivier made when we were children. My father taught us how they worked. It was so magical that we begged and begged for him to give us blanks to make our own. That was when my brother became serious about art, and I grew fascinated with film. I thought we'd lost them all, years ago. Why is it here?"

"I sent for Olivier as well, but he wasn't at his flat," Carmouche said.

"Olivier's preparing for a *vernissage* for the Salon des Arts Exhibition at his school, *L'Academie d'Ys*. Papa and I were supposed to attend the private viewing at five, together." Laure said. She turned the disk in her hand, again and again, as though remembering happier days.

I pulled out my pocket watch. Quarter past three. A *vernissage*, or varnishing day, afforded patrons of the arts to see the pieces before the official opening. I'd been to such private viewings before, as my son Ellery's a renowned artist back in Lyonesse.

I remembered when I first taught Ellery about thaumatropes when he was nine. My late wife and I had recognized his budding talent for art at that time and encouraged the boy however we could while we sought a proper school. The thaumatrope was part of that tutelage. I had shown him a bird flying free on one side of the cardboard disk, and a cage on the other, and when I twirled the strings El's eyes turned wide with wonder as the bird seemed to appear magically inside the cage. That was the kind of joy that parents cherished: watching their children discover new, fantastical truths about their world.

"Sergeant," Carmouche called out, "take my carriage to the academy and find Olivier Harbin."

Joncour nodded and departed.

I picked up the disk with the bodiless wings, which were beautifully painted by a skilled hand. On the other face was an eagle's head on a lion's body. "Did your brother make these others, too?"

"That does look like Olivier's style," Laure replied. "You're not suggesting that my brother's involved as well!"

"I make no such accusation, but we must see the whole picture. Just like this thaumatrope, we cannot envision the full griffin without its wings on the obverse face," I said, turning the disk to show Carmouche what I meant. "When the disk spins, our eyes will see the artwork on one side, then the other. If the rotation's fast enough, the separate images will linger in our minds and seemingly merge into one. It's called *persistence of vision*."

"Like how the frames of a film create the illusion of movement?"

"Exactly. You might be surprised to know that archaeologists have unearthed prehistoric wonder-turners. I've a couple of pieces at the museum related to ancient sphinx cults. This one here seems to be a homage to a griffin disk in the Criopolis collection." I indicated the golden thaumatrope. "Usually we'd tie strings to the holes on each side and twirl the disk to achieve the illusion, but Doctor Harbin has made a wind-up clockwork version to keep it turning. Most likely for the hypnotic effect, which is a common tool in therapy." I gave the disk currently in the machine a push, turning down the demonic djinni face to reveal the image on the obverse.

It was a bottle with stylized sigils encircling it.

In the legends, the djinn were creatures of smokeless fire, with the power to possess humans. A sorcerer with the proper spell could bind one to a lamp or bottle. The symbology implied an imprisoned spirit. Was the doctor trying to hypnotize Seznec, and how did it go wrong?

Carmouche scratched his head. "So it would be a bottled djinni? Tell me you have a theory, Professor."

"I'm afraid so." I mulled over a hypothesis that had come to the fore. "If I'm right, then Laure's brother is in mortal danger."

"You think my father's going to hurt Olivier?" Laure asked.

"I've only a hunch." I opened the window and called down. "Joncour!"

The sergeant was about to drive away in the alembic carriage when he heard my cry. He looked up. "Did I forget something, Professor?"

"Us. Wait there." I unhooked the djinni disk from the device. "Laure, the notebook. I tried deciphering the entries but could only ascertain the victim's name. The rest is in a strange shorthand."

Laure took the book, tucking the unicorn disk between its pages like a bookmark. "Papa uses a system he developed himself to keep his notes confidential, but I can read it."

Having no time to wait for the limbeck lift, we hurried out and took the stairs despite my limp. We piled into the horseless, with me taking the front seat next to Joncour while Laure and Carmouche rode awkwardly in the back. The wings on Laure's costume forced her to sit sideways, which meant she had to press her legs against the Inspector's. Carmouche turned red from ear to ear.

L'Academie d'Ys was halfway across the city, south of the Cemetery of the Drowned. As Joncour drove us through the streets with necessary but dizzying haste, I turned around to show them the djinni thaumatrope. "See the sigils drawn around the bottle? They're words of power copied from a grimoire, but only a couple still resemble the original. The rest are artist re-interpretations of the symbols that are so stylized that they've become powerless. Taking such liberties with magical symbology always leads to disaster."

Despite the bumpiness of the ride, Laure tried her best to decode the notes. "Monsieur Seznec wanted to be free of his growing urge to violence." She leafed through more of the notebook. "Papa's had many successes with thaumatropic hypnosis. The tightrope-walker disk to treat a fear of heights. A child's drawing of a unicorn to regress them in age. And the djinni to bottle up their inner demons."

We made a sharp turn and careened down Rue Velue. "I'm sure it worked, but not the way your father anticipated," I said. "Here's how I think it went wrong. The patient sits in front of the thaumatrope, and is hypnotized into bottling that anger. But these twisted magic sigils made that all too literal: their rage pours into the painted djinni bottle instead."

"But how does that lead to murder?" Carmouche asked.

"Recall the room. Where does the alienist sit?"

"On the other side of the thaumatrope. Oh." He took the disk from me and held it so that he would see what Doctor Harbin saw. "He'd see the djinni bottle upside down."

"Exactly. Upside down bottles pour what they contain out. Question is, was it only anger that poured into the doctor? No. I believe he somehow summoned a true and murderous djinni while treating Seznec."

Laure tried to hold in a sob, but couldn't.

Carmouche offered her his handkerchief. "We'll get him help. I promise." He turned to me. "Professor, why would Doctor Harbin – I mean this djinni – want to kill his son?"

"If he's possessed by a djinni, it stands to reason that the spirit might seek revenge against the man whose art was powerful enough to summon and imprison him in the bottle. The one man who could trap him again, and whose death would ensure his continued freedom."

"For once, I hope you're wrong," Carmouche said.

Joncour brought the carriage to a jarring halt in front of the academy.

Laure threw open the door and hopped out, leaving her father's notebook on the rear seat. She raced up the stone steps and through the great green doors.

"Joncour, stay with the Professor." Carmouche hurried after Laure.

I hated that he had left us behind, but I could never run that fast on account of my leg. I reached into the back for the notebook. "They might need us, Joncour. Let's go, but if you need to leave me behind, don't hesitate."

"*D'accord*, Professor."

My walking stick clacked against the marble floors of *L'Academie* as Joncour and I followed after the starlet and the Inspector. They were in sight and almost at the Salon des Arts when the doors to that exhibition hall burst open. Students and teachers flooded out in panic, shouting about a madman with a palmcannon. Carmouche grabbed Laure and shielded her from being knocked down. When they had all run past he drew his own firearm. "Don't follow!"

He cautiously stepped through the doorway and to the right, out of sight.

Laure called out. "Papa, please stop hurting people. This isn't you!"

Two more shots rang out within the Salon.

Joncour sprinted ahead and pulled Laure to safety to the side. He hid just beyond the threshold, peering into the room.

When I caught up, I could hear voices from within.

"Surrender, Doctor Harbin." It was Carmouche's voice, laced with pain.

"While I have the advantage?" replied a man's voice, low and as raspy as a crackling fire. "The man who had trapped me in those paints must die."

I peered in. The Salon des Arts was a grandiose chamber whose every wall was a partial mosaic of fresh works of student art. A grand chandelier of citrine foxfires-in-amber lit the room. Paintings on easels awaited varnishing throughout the room, at least those that hadn't been knocked to the floor during the commotion.

Doctor Harbin, a distinguished-looking man in a long gray overcoat and Homburg hat, hid behind the triton statue in the centre of the salon. His eyes seemed to glow with ruby flame.

To my right, Carmouche had hidden behind a grand portrait that he'd leaned against a ladder as impromptu cover. He'd been shot in his right shoulder.

Another man moaned in a corner on the far side of the salon, lying on the floor beneath a clutter of paintings and easels. Olivier?

Carmouche couldn't hit Doctor Harbin with his palmcannon while the madman hid behind the statue, but neither could Harbin fire a clean shot at either Carmouche or Olivier without abandoning his cover.

This stalemate couldn't last. Someone would surely die here unless I could find a sure way to stop the monster that Doctor Harbin had become. It pained me that Laure might lose her father, her brother, or Carmouche. But what could I do to stop this creature of the thaumatrope?

"We could try bottling it again," I decided. "This dark version of Pierrick Harbin exists now because he was hypnotized by the thaumatrope, allowing the djinn to possess him. Let's hope that means he's still highly suggestible. Where's the disk?"

"The one with the bottle? The Inspector still has it," Joncour said.

I cursed under my breath. Carmouche was too far away to toss me the thaumatrope.

But perhaps there was an alternative.

I flipped through the notebook in my hand and found the disk with the leaping unicorn still tucked within its pages. A symbol of childlike innocence. "He used this one to regress his patients in age. I'll have to try it. We've nothing else. I need string."

"Sergeant, the wings of my costume," Laure said. "Take lace from them."

While Joncour fumbled with the wings with his tubby fingers, I told Laure what else I needed. "Your father's still in there somewhere, Laure, despite his possession by the djinni. We'll try to reach the real Pierrick Harbin. Sing a song from your childhood, any song. We need your father to remember a happier past."

She nodded. After a moment's hesitation she began to sing aloud 'La Sirène qui Rire', a playful song about a laughing mermaid and her suitor.

I dared another look into the room. Harbin had turned his head in the direction of Laure's voice.

Needing both my hands to work the thaumatrope, I handed Joncour my walking stick, tied the strands of lace he had salvaged onto opposite sides of the disk, and set it a-spin. "If anything happens to me, Joncour, tell my son Ellery..."

Joncour clasped my shoulder. "Let me do it, sir."

"No. This solution's my thesis, and therefore it's mine to defend." My professorial bones wouldn't have it any other way.

With a deep breath, I stepped across the threshold into the Salon des Arts.

I was twenty yards away from the madman with glowing eyes, perhaps near enough to mesmerize him with the image on the thaumatrope spinning in my hands, perhaps not. Certainly I was standing well within range of his palmcannon, and a well-placed shot from the doctor might kill me. But Laure was relying on me to free her father from madness, so that we could save the two men in the room he'd already shot.

I had to trust in my gambit with the thaumatrope.

Doctor Harbin watched me from behind the marble triton statue in the heart of the room. I twirled the disk by its strings between my thumbs and forefingers. The painted cardboard flipped forwards and back, back and forth, so quickly that Harbin ought to see the two images on opposite sides merge into one like magic.

Behind me, hiding beyond the threshold, Laure sang the children's song, 'La Sirène qui Rire'. If my ploy with the wonder-turner failed, perhaps her voice would reach a part of her father that still valued the lives of others, and hold him from squeezing the trigger.

I limped into the salon towards the mad doctor. Though my heart raced, I kept the thaumatrope spinning. In a calm, monotone voice I addressed the doctor. "Pierrick Harbin, listen and watch. See this picture and think back. Remember your children. Remember Olivier, remember Laure. Look, and hear me."

Harbin was staring at the wonder-turner disk with an intensity that could almost set the cardboard on fire. The hand that held his weapon drooped.

"Don't risk your life for me, Professor. Get out!" Inspector Carmouche shouted from behind me.

I couldn't, not when the Inspector and Harbin's son were both hurt and trapped in the salon. The madman was still armed and thirsting for a kill.

Unfortunately, Carmouche's shout of caution drowned out Laure's song briefly, but it was enough to break the spell over her father.

Doctor Harbin blinked and aimed his palmcannon at me. But before he could fire it, Olivier joined his sister in song. They now sang 'La Sirène qui Rire' in round, lilting and playful in the overlap of lyrics. Though Olivier's voice was weak from his cannonshot wound, in joining Laure's *chanson* he doubled the power of the music over his father.

It was enough to disrupt the doctor's aim.

The lead shot flew past my ear. Despite myself I cringed, and one end of the thaumatrope slipped from between my fingers.

Doctor Harbin readied another shot. By my count he had a fifth and last bullet to his palmcannon, but even one could kill me all the same.

From his hiding spot Carmouche fired his own sidearm at Doctor Harbin, but his aim went wide. Instead, the lead shot embedded itself in a blue, impressionistic painting of a ballet dancer behind the madman.

The doctor dropped to one knee beside the statue's plinth, making himself a smaller target.

I was ready to grab the fallen end of the thaumatrope and try again, when someone snatched the disk out of my hand from behind.

Laure.

Laure sang again as she walked forward, spinning the thaumatrope she took from me. Her brother continued to sing in round, though his voice was growing weaker. Together they entranced Doctor Harbin once more with both music and toy.

I spoke in a low voice, choosing a cadence and lecturing voice that had proved effective in lulling my students to sleep.

"Go back in time, Pierrick. Watch Laure and Olivier discover the wonder-turner. How you smiled to see them make one themselves, this unicorn leaping free. You remember. You are there. You are calm."

Quiet, Doctor Harbin let the weapon in his hand droop as he continued to watch the thaumatrope spin.

"Your children laugh at the magic. You beam with pride." I moved nearer to the doctor, a few steps behind Laure. "Watch the wonder-turner. Listen to their song."

When Laure and I were mere steps away from him, she kept him focused on the spinning thaumatrope while I knelt and eased the palmcannon away from his hand.

"Watch. Listen. Bask in that moment."

I gestured for Joncour.

The sergeant hurried in, tossed me my walking stick, and stepped behind Doctor Harbin to restrain him. Though the doctor struggled, he was no match for the strapping young sergeant who forced him to the ground.

"Please don't hurt my father," Laure said as she dropped the thaumatrope. Torn at first between her raving father and her wounded brother, she made her choice and rushed to help Olivier.

I hobbled to Carmouche to tend to his shoulder. "We better get you and Olivier to the hospital."

"Thank you, Professor," said Carmouche. "Sorry about shouting out."

"It's forgotten. Can you stand?"

"Yes." He got to his feet and gazed at the raging Doctor Harbin, now cuffed and prone under the hefty weight of Sergeant Joncour. "Will that poor man ever recover?"

"In time. For now it's the sanatorium for him, for the safety of others and his own," I said. "But we know the cause and means of his possession, so there's hope. I'll help craft a proper thaumatrope bottle to trap the djinni, and find an alienist skilled enough to undo what Pierrick has done to himself. Until then, the Harbin children must remind their father of who he is, so that he will have the strength to oust the evil spirit inside him."

Carmouche nodded. "I've no doubt they will."

Even now, Laure and Olivier were still trying to reach their father with cries of *Papa*, as though the mere mention of a word could conjure back the true Pierrick Harbin.

But if any word could, perhaps it was that one.

The Murders in the Rue Morgue

Edgar Allan Poe

'*What song the Syrens sang, or what name Achilles assumed when he hid himself among women, although puzzling questions, are not beyond all conjecture.*'
Sir Thomas Browne

THE MENTAL features discoursed of as the analytical, are, in themselves, but little susceptible of analysis. We appreciate them only in their effects. We know of them, among other things, that they are always to their possessor, when inordinately possessed, a source of the liveliest enjoyment. As the strong man exults in his physical ability, delighting in such exercises as call his muscles into action, so glories the analyst in that moral activity which *disentangles*. He derives pleasure from even the most trivial occupations bringing his talent into play. He is fond of enigmas, of conundrums, of hieroglyphics; exhibiting in his solutions of each a degree of *acumen* which appears to the ordinary apprehension preternatural. His results, brought about by the very soul and essence of method, have, in truth, the whole air of intuition.

The faculty of re-solution is possibly much invigorated by mathematical study, and especially by that highest branch of it which, unjustly, and merely on account of its retrograde operations, has been called, as if *par excellence*, analysis. Yet to calculate is not in itself to analyse. A chess-player, for example, does the one without effort at the other. It follows that the game of chess, in its effects upon mental character, is greatly misunderstood. I am not now writing a treatise, but simply prefacing a somewhat peculiar narrative by observations very much at random; I will, therefore, take occasion to assert that the higher powers of the reflective intellect are more decidedly and more usefully tasked by the unostentatious game of draughts than by all the elaborate frivolity of chess. In this latter, where the pieces have different and *bizarre* motions, with various and variable values, what is only complex is mistaken (a not unusual error) for what is profound. The *attention* is here called powerfully into play. If it flag for an instant, an oversight is committed resulting in injury or defeat. The possible moves being not only manifold but involute, the chances of such oversights are multiplied; and in nine cases out of ten it is the more concentrative rather than the more acute player who conquers. In draughts, on the contrary, where the moves are *unique* and have but little variation, the probabilities of inadvertence are diminished, and the mere attention being left comparatively unemployed, what advantages are obtained by either party are obtained by superior *acumen*. To be less abstract – let us suppose a game of draughts where the pieces are reduced to four kings, and where, of course, no oversight is to be expected. It is obvious that here the victory can be decided (the players being at all equal) only by some *recherché* movement, the result of some strong exertion of the intellect. Deprived of ordinary resources, the analyst throws himself into the spirit of his opponent, identifies himself therewith, and not unfrequently sees thus, at a glance, the sole methods (sometime indeed absurdly simple ones) by which he may seduce into error or hurry into miscalculation.

Whist has long been noted for its influence upon what is termed the calculating power; and men of the highest order of intellect have been known to take an apparently unaccountable delight in it, while eschewing chess as frivolous. Beyond doubt there is nothing of a similar nature so greatly tasking the faculty of analysis. The best chess-player in Christendom *may* be little more than the best player of chess; but proficiency in whist implies capacity for success in all those more important undertakings where mind struggles with mind. When I say proficiency, I mean that perfection in the game which includes a comprehension of *all* the sources whence legitimate advantage may be derived. These are not only manifold but multiform, and lie frequently among recesses of thought altogether inaccessible to the ordinary understanding. To observe attentively is to remember distinctly; and, so far, the concentrative chess-player will do very well at whist; while the rules of Hoyle (themselves based upon the mere mechanism of the game) are sufficiently and generally comprehensible. Thus to have a retentive memory, and to proceed by 'the book,' are points commonly regarded as the sum total of good playing. But it is in matters beyond the limits of mere rule that the skill of the analyst is evinced. He makes, in silence, a host of observations and inferences. So, perhaps, do his companions; and the difference in the extent of the information obtained, lies not so much in the validity of the inference as in the quality of the observation. The necessary knowledge is that of *what* to observe. Our player confines himself not at all; nor, because the game is the object, does he reject deductions from things external to the game. He examines the countenance of his partner, comparing it carefully with that of each of his opponents. He considers the mode of assorting the cards in each hand; often counting trump by trump, and honor by honor, through the glances bestowed by their holders upon each. He notes every variation of face as the play progresses, gathering a fund of thought from the differences in the expression of certainty, of surprise, of triumph, or of chagrin. From the manner of gathering up a trick he judges whether the person taking it can make another in the suit. He recognises what is played through feint, by the air with which it is thrown upon the table. A casual or inadvertent word; the accidental dropping or turning of a card, with the accompanying anxiety or carelessness in regard to its concealment; the counting of the tricks, with the order of their arrangement; embarrassment, hesitation, eagerness or trepidation – all afford, to his apparently intuitive perception, indications of the true state of affairs. The first two or three rounds having been played, he is in full possession of the contents of each hand, and thenceforward puts down his cards with as absolute a precision of purpose as if the rest of the party had turned outward the faces of their own.

The analytical power should not be confounded with ample ingenuity; for while the analyst is necessarily ingenious, the ingenious man is often remarkably incapable of analysis. The constructive or combining power, by which ingenuity is usually manifested, and to which the phrenologists (I believe erroneously) have assigned a separate organ, supposing it a primitive faculty, has been so frequently seen in those whose intellect bordered otherwise upon idiocy, as to have attracted general observation among writers on morals. Between ingenuity and the analytic ability there exists a difference far greater, indeed, than that between the fancy and the imagination, but of a character very strictly analogous.

It will be found, in fact, that the ingenious are always fanciful, and the *truly* imaginative never otherwise than analytic.

The narrative which follows will appear to the reader somewhat in the light of a commentary upon the propositions just advanced.

Residing in Paris during the spring and part of the summer of 18–, I there became acquainted with a Monsieur C. Auguste Dupin. This young gentleman was of an excellent – indeed of an illustrious family, but, by a variety of untoward events, had been reduced to such poverty that the energy of his character succumbed beneath it, and he ceased to bestir himself in the world, or to care for the retrieval of his fortunes. By courtesy of his creditors, there still remained in his possession a small remnant of his patrimony; and, upon the income arising from this, he managed, by means of a rigorous economy, to procure the necessaries of life, without troubling himself about its superfluities. Books, indeed, were his sole luxuries, and in Paris these are easily obtained.

Our first meeting was at an obscure library in the Rue Montmartre, where the accident of our both being in search of the same very rare and very remarkable volume, brought us into closer communion. We saw each other again and again. I was deeply interested in the little family history which he detailed to me with all that candor which a Frenchman indulges whenever mere self is his theme. I was astonished, too, at the vast extent of his reading; and, above all, I felt my soul enkindled within me by the wild fervor, and the vivid freshness of his imagination. Seeking in Paris the objects I then sought, I felt that the society of such a man would be to me a treasure beyond price; and this feeling I frankly confided to him. It was at length arranged that we should live together during my stay in the city; and as my worldly circumstances were somewhat less embarrassed than his own, I was permitted to be at the expense of renting, and furnishing in a style which suited the rather fantastic gloom of our common temper, a time-eaten and grotesque mansion, long deserted through superstitions into which we did not inquire, and tottering to its fall in a retired and desolate portion of the Faubourg St. Germain.

Had the routine of our life at this place been known to the world, we should have been regarded as madmen – although, perhaps, as madmen of a harmless nature. Our seclusion was perfect. We admitted no visitors. Indeed the locality of our retirement had been carefully kept a secret from my own former associates; and it had been many years since Dupin had ceased to know or be known in Paris. We existed within ourselves alone.

It was a freak of fancy in my friend (for what else shall I call it?) to be enamored of the Night for her own sake; and into this *bizarrerie,* as into all his others, I quietly fell; giving myself up to his wild whims with a perfect *abandon*. The sable divinity would not herself dwell with us always; but we could counterfeit her presence. At the first dawn of the morning we closed all the messy shutters of our old building; lighting a couple of tapers which, strongly perfumed, threw out only the ghastliest and feeblest of rays. By the aid of these we then busied our souls in dreams – reading, writing, or conversing, until warned by the clock of the advent of the true Darkness. Then we sallied forth into the streets arm in arm, continuing the topics of the day, or roaming far and wide until a late hour, seeking, amid the wild lights and shadows of the populous city, that infinity of mental excitement which quiet observation can afford.

At such times I could not help remarking and admiring (although from his rich ideality I had been prepared to expect it) a peculiar analytic ability in Dupin. He seemed, too, to take an eager delight in its exercise – if not exactly in its display – and did not hesitate to confess the pleasure thus derived. He boasted to me, with a low chuckling laugh, that most men, in respect to himself, wore windows in their bosoms, and was wont to follow up such assertions by direct and very startling proofs of his intimate knowledge of my own. His manner at these moments was frigid and abstract; his eyes were vacant in expression; while his voice, usually a rich tenor, rose into a treble which would have sounded petulantly but for the deliberateness and entire distinctness of the enunciation. Observing him in these moods, I often dwelt meditatively upon the old philosophy of the Bi-Part Soul, and amused myself with the fancy of a double Dupin – the creative and the resolvent.

Let it not be supposed, from what I have just said, that I am detailing any mystery, or penning any romance. What I have described in the Frenchman, was merely the result of an excited, or perhaps of a diseased intelligence. But of the character of his remarks at the periods in question an example will best convey the idea.

We were strolling one night down a long dirty street in the vicinity of the Palais Royal. Being both, apparently, occupied with thought, neither of us had spoken a syllable for fifteen minutes at least. All at once Dupin broke forth with these words: "He is a very little fellow, that's true, and would do better for the Théâtre des Variétés."

"There can be no doubt of that," I replied unwittingly, and not at first observing (so much had I been absorbed in reflection) the extraordinary manner in which the speaker had chimed in with my meditations. In an instant afterward I recollected myself, and my astonishment was profound.

"Dupin," said I, gravely, "this is beyond my comprehension. I do not hesitate to say that I am amazed, and can scarcely credit my senses. How was it possible you should know I was thinking of –?" Here I paused, to ascertain beyond a doubt whether he really knew of whom I thought.

– "of Chantilly," said he, "why do you pause? You were remarking to yourself that his diminutive figure unfitted him for tragedy."

This was precisely what had formed the subject of my reflections. Chantilly was a quondam cobbler of the Rue St. Denis, who, becoming stage-mad, had attempted the rôle of Xerxes, in Crébillon's tragedy so called, and been notoriously Pasquinaded for his pains.

"Tell me, for Heaven's sake," I exclaimed, "the method – if method there is – by which you have been enabled to fathom my soul in this matter." In fact I was even more startled than I would have been willing to express.

"It was the fruiterer," replied my friend, "who brought you to the conclusion that the mender of soles was not of sufficient height for Xerxes *et id genus omne.*"

"The fruiterer! – you astonish me – I know no fruiterer whomsoever."

"The man who ran up against you as we entered the street – it may have been fifteen minutes ago."

I now remembered that, in fact, a fruiterer, carrying upon his head a large basket of apples, had nearly thrown me down, by accident, as we passed from the Rue C– into the thoroughfare where we stood; but what this had to do with Chantilly I could not possibly understand.

There was not a particle of *charlatanerie* about Dupin. "I will explain," he said, "and that you may comprehend all clearly, we will first retrace the course of your meditations, from the moment in which I spoke to you until that of the *rencontre* with the fruiterer in question. The larger links of the chain run thus – Chantilly, Orion, Dr. Nichols, Epicurus, Stereotomy, the street stones, the fruiterer."

There are few persons who have not, at some period of their lives, amused themselves in retracing the steps by which particular conclusions of their own minds have been attained. The occupation is often full of interest and he who attempts it for the first time is astonished by the apparently illimitable distance and incoherence between the starting-point and the goal. What, then, must have been my amazement when I heard the Frenchman speak what he had just spoken, and when I could not help acknowledging that he had spoken the truth. He continued:

"We had been talking of horses, if I remember aright, just before leaving the Rue C–. This was the last subject we discussed. As we crossed into this street, a fruiterer, with a large basket upon his head, brushing quickly past us, thrust you upon a pile of paving stones collected at a spot where the causeway is undergoing repair. You stepped upon one of the loose fragments, slipped, slightly strained your ankle, appeared vexed or sulky, muttered a few words, turned to look at the pile, and then proceeded in silence. I was not particularly attentive to what you did; but observation has become with me, of late, a species of necessity.

"You kept your eyes upon the ground – glancing, with a petulant expression, at the holes and ruts in the pavement, (so that I saw you were still thinking of the stones), until we reached the little alley called Lamartine, which has been paved, by way of experiment, with the overlapping and riveted blocks. Here your countenance brightened up, and, perceiving your lips move, I could not doubt that you murmured the word 'stereotomy,' a term very affectedly applied to this species of pavement. I knew that you could not say to yourself 'stereotomy' without being brought to think of atomies, and thus of the theories of Epicurus; and since, when we discussed this subject not very long ago, I mentioned to you how singularly, yet with how little notice, the vague guesses of that noble Greek had met with confirmation in the late nebular cosmogony, I felt that you could not avoid casting your eyes upward to the great *nebula* in Orion, and I certainly expected that you would do so. You did look up; and I was now assured that I had correctly followed your steps. But in that bitter *tirade* upon Chantilly, which appeared in yesterday's 'Musée,' the satirist, making some disgraceful allusions to the cobbler's change of name upon assuming the buskin, quoted a Latin line about which we have often conversed. I mean the line: *Perdidit antiquum litera sonum.*

"I had told you that this was in reference to Orion, formerly written Urion; and, from certain pungencies connected with this explanation, I was aware that you could not have forgotten it. It was clear, therefore, that you would not fail to combine the two ideas of Orion and Chantilly. That you did combine them I saw by the character of the smile which passed over your lips. You thought of the poor cobbler's immolation. So far, you had been stooping in your gait; but now I saw you draw yourself up to your full height. I was then sure that you reflected upon the diminutive figure of Chantilly. At this point I interrupted your meditations to remark that as, in fact, he was a very little fellow – that Chantilly – he would do better at the Théâtre des Variétés."

Not long after this, we were looking over an evening edition of the *Gazette des Tribunaux*, when the following paragraphs arrested our attention.

"*EXTRAORDINARY MURDERS. This morning, about three o'clock, the inhabitants of the Quartier St. Roch were aroused from sleep by a succession of terrific shrieks, issuing, apparently, from the fourth story of a house in the Rue Morgue, known to be in the sole occupancy of one Madame L'Espanaye, and her daughter Mademoiselle Camille L'Espanaye. After some delay, occasioned by a fruitless attempt to procure admission in the usual manner, the gateway was broken in with a crowbar, and eight or ten of the neighbors entered accompanied by two gendarmes. By this time the cries had ceased; but, as the party rushed up the first flight of stairs, two or more rough voices in angry contention were distinguished and seemed to proceed from the upper part of the house. As the second landing was* reached, these sounds, also, had ceased and everything remained perfectly quiet. The party spread themselves and hurried from room to room. Upon arriving at a large back chamber in the fourth story, (the door of which, being found locked, with the key inside, was forced open,) a spectacle presented itself which struck every one present not less with horror than with astonishment.

"The apartment was in the wildest disorder – the furniture broken and thrown about in all directions. There was only one bedstead; and from this the bed had been removed, and thrown into the middle of the floor. On a chair lay a razor, besmeared with blood. On the hearth were two or three long and thick tresses of grey human hair, also dabbled in blood, and seeming to have been pulled out by the roots. Upon the floor were found four Napoleons, an ear-ring of topaz, three large silver spoons, three smaller of métal d'Alger, and two bags, containing nearly four thousand francs in gold. The drawers of a bureau, which stood in one corner were open, and had been, apparently, rifled, although many articles still remained in them. A small iron safe was discovered under the bed (not under the bedstead). It was open, with the key still in the door. It had no contents beyond a few old letters, and other papers of little consequence.

"Of Madame L'Espanaye no traces were here seen; but an unusual quantity of soot being observed in the fire-place, a search was made in the chimney, and (horrible to relate!) the corpse of the daughter, head downward, was dragged therefrom; it having been thus forced up the narrow aperture for a considerable distance. The body was quite warm. Upon examining it, many excoriations were perceived, no doubt occasioned by the violence with which it had been thrust up and disengaged. Upon the face were many severe scratches, and, upon the throat, dark bruises, and deep indentations of finger nails, as if the deceased had been throttled to death.

"After a thorough investigation of every portion of the house, without farther discovery, the party made its way into a small paved yard in the rear of the building, where lay the corpse of the old lady, with her throat so entirely cut that, upon an attempt to raise her, the head fell off. The body, as well as the head, was fearfully mutilated – the former so much so as scarcely to retain any semblance of humanity.

"To this horrible mystery there is not as yet, we believe, the slightest clew."

The next day's paper had these additional particulars.

"The Tragedy in the Rue Morgue. Many individuals have been examined in relation to this most extraordinary and frightful affair. [The word 'affaire' has not yet, in France, that levity of import which it conveys with us,] "but nothing whatever has transpired to throw light upon it. We give below all the material testimony elicited.

"Pauline Dubourg, laundress, deposes that she has known both the deceased for three years, having washed for them during that period. The old lady and her daughter seemed on good terms – very affectionate towards each other. They were excellent pay. Could not speak in regard to their mode or means of living. Believed that Madame L. told fortunes for a living. Was reputed to have money put by. Never met any persons in the house when she called for the clothes or took them home. Was sure that they had no servant in employ. There appeared to be no furniture in any part of the building except in the fourth story.

"Pierre Moreau, tobacconist, deposes that he has been in the habit of selling small quantities of tobacco and snuff to Madame L'Espanaye for nearly four years. Was born in the neighborhood, and has always resided there. The deceased and her daughter had occupied the house in which the corpses were found, for more than six years. It was formerly occupied by a jeweller, who under-let the upper rooms to various persons. The house was the property of Madame L. She became dissatisfied with the abuse of the premises by her tenant, and moved into them herself, refusing to let any portion. The old lady was childish. Witness had seen the daughter some five or six times during the six years. The two lived an exceedingly retired life – were reputed to have money. Had heard it said among the neighbors that Madame L. told fortunes – did not believe it. Had never seen any person enter the door except the old lady and her daughter, a porter once or twice, and a physician some eight or ten times.

"Many other persons, neighbors, gave evidence to the same effect. No one was spoken of as frequenting the house. It was not known whether there were any living connexions of Madame L. and her daughter. The shutters of the front windows were seldom opened. Those in the rear were always closed, with the exception of the large back room, fourth story. The house was a good house – not very old.

"Isidore Muset, gendarme, deposes that he was called to the house about three o'clock in the morning, and found some twenty or thirty persons at the gateway, endeavoring to gain admittance. Forced it open, at length, with a bayonet – not with a crowbar. Had but little difficulty in getting it open, on account of its being a double or folding gate, and bolted neither at bottom nor top. The shrieks were continued until the gate was forced – and then suddenly ceased. They seemed to be screams of some person (or persons) in great agony – were loud and drawn out, not short and quick. Witness led the way up stairs. Upon reaching the first landing, heard two voices in loud and angry contention – the one a gruff voice, the other much shriller – a very strange voice. Could distinguish some words of the former, which was that of a Frenchman. Was positive that it was not a woman's voice. Could distinguish the words 'sacré' and 'diable.' The shrill voice was that of a foreigner. Could not be sure whether it was the voice of a man or of a woman. Could not make out what was said, but believed the language to be Spanish. The state of the room and of the bodies was described by this witness as we described them yesterday.

"Henri Duval, a neighbor, and by trade a silver-smith, deposes that he was one of the party who first entered the house. Corroborates the testimony of Musèt in general. As soon as they forced an entrance, they reclosed the door, to keep out the crowd, which collected very fast, notwithstanding the lateness of the hour. The shrill voice, this witness thinks, was that of an Italian. Was certain it was not French. Could not be sure that it was a man's voice. It might have been a woman's. Was not acquainted with the Italian language. Could not distinguish the words, but was convinced by the intonation that the speaker was an Italian. Knew Madame L. and her daughter. Had conversed with both frequently. Was sure that the shrill voice was not that of either of the deceased.

"– Odenheimer, restaurateur. This witness volunteered his testimony. Not speaking French, was examined through an interpreter. Is a native of Amsterdam. Was passing the house at the time of the shrieks. They lasted for several minutes – probably ten. They were long and loud – very awful and distressing. Was one of those who entered the building. Corroborated the previous evidence in every respect but one. Was sure that the shrill voice was that of a man – of a Frenchman. Could not distinguish the words uttered. They were loud and quick – unequal – spoken apparently in fear as well as in anger. The voice was harsh – not so much shrill as harsh. Could not call it a shrill voice. The gruff voice said repeatedly 'sacré,' 'diable,' and once 'mon Dieu.'

"Jules Mignaud, banker, of the firm of Mignaud et Fils, Rue Deloraine. Is the elder Mignaud. Madame L'Espanaye had some property. Had opened an account with his banking house in the spring of the year – (eight years previously). Made frequent deposits in small sums. Had checked for nothing until the third day before her death, when she took out in person the sum of 4000 francs. This sum was paid in gold, and a clerk went home with the money.

"Adolphe Le Bon, clerk to Mignaud et Fils, deposes that on the day in question, about noon, he accompanied Madame L'Espanaye to her residence with the 4000 francs, put up in two bags. Upon the door being opened, Mademoiselle L. appeared and took from his hands one of the bags, while the old lady relieved him of the other. He then bowed and departed. Did not see any person in the street at the time. It is a bye-street – very lonely.

"William Bird, tailor deposes that he was one of the party who entered the house. Is an Englishman. Has lived in Paris two years. Was one of the first to ascend the stairs. Heard the voices in contention. The gruff voice was that of a Frenchman. Could make out several words, but cannot now remember all. Heard distinctly 'sacré' and 'mon Dieu.' There was a sound at the moment as if of several persons struggling – a scraping and scuffling sound. The shrill voice was very loud – louder than the gruff one. Is sure that it was not the voice of an Englishman. Appeared to be that of a German. Might have been a woman's voice. Does not understand German.

"Four of the above-named witnesses, being recalled, deposed that the door of the chamber in which was found the body of Mademoiselle L. was locked on the inside when the party reached it. Every thing was perfectly silent – no groans or noises of any kind. Upon forcing the door no person was seen. The windows, both of the back and front room, were down and firmly fastened from within. A door between the two rooms was closed, but not locked. The door leading from the front room into the passage was locked, with the key on the inside. A small room in the front of the house, on the fourth story, at the head of the passage was open, the door being ajar. This room was crowded with old beds, boxes, and so forth. These were carefully removed and searched. There was not an inch of any portion of the house which was not carefully searched. Sweeps were sent up and down the chimneys. The house was a four story one, with garrets (mansardes.) A trap-door on the roof was nailed down very securely – did not appear to have been opened for years. The time elapsing between the hearing of the voices in contention and the breaking open of the room door, was variously stated by the witnesses. Some made it as short as three minutes – some as long as five. The door was opened with difficulty.

"Alfonzo Garcio, undertaker, deposes that he resides in the Rue Morgue. Is a native of Spain. Was one of the party who entered the house. Did not proceed up stairs. Is nervous, and was apprehensive of the consequences of agitation. Heard the voices in contention. The gruff voice was that of a Frenchman. Could not distinguish what was said. The shrill voice was that of an Englishman – is sure of this. Does not understand the English language, but judges by the intonation.

"Alberto Montani, confectioner, deposes that he was among the first to ascend the stairs. Heard the voices in question. The gruff voice was that of a Frenchman. Distinguished several words. The speaker appeared to be expostulating. Could not make out the words of the shrill voice. Spoke quick and unevenly. Thinks it the voice of a Russian. Corroborates the general testimony. Is an Italian. Never conversed with a native of Russia.

"Several witnesses, recalled, here testified that the chimneys of all the rooms on the fourth story were too narrow to admit the passage of a human being. By 'sweeps' were meant cylindrical sweeping brushes, such as are employed by those who clean chimneys. These brushes were passed up and down every flue in the house. There is no back passage by which any one could have descended while the party proceeded up stairs. The body of Mademoiselle L'Espanaye was so firmly wedged in the chimney that it could not be got down until four or five of the party united their strength.

"Paul Dumas, physician, deposes that he was called to view the bodies about day-break. They were both then lying on the sacking of the bedstead in the chamber where Mademoiselle L. was found. The corpse of the young lady was much bruised and excoriated. The fact that it had been thrust up the chimney would sufficiently account for these appearances. The throat was greatly chafed. There were several deep scratches just below the chin, together with a series of livid spots which were evidently the impression of fingers. The face was fearfully discolored, and the eye-balls protruded. The tongue had been partially bitten through. A large bruise was discovered upon the pit of the stomach, produced, apparently, by the pressure of a knee. In the opinion of M. Dumas, Mademoiselle L'Espanaye had been throttled to death by some person or persons unknown. The corpse of the mother was horribly mutilated. All the bones of the right leg and arm were more or less shattered. The left tibia much splintered, as well as all the ribs of the left side. Whole body dreadfully bruised and discolored. It was not possible to say how the injuries had been inflicted. A heavy club of wood, or a broad bar of iron – a chair – any large, heavy, and obtuse weapon would have produced such results, if wielded by the hands of a very powerful man. No woman could have inflicted the blows with any weapon. The head of the deceased, when seen by witness, was entirely separated from the body, and was also greatly shattered. The throat had evidently been cut with some very sharp instrument – probably with a razor.

"Alexandre Etienne, surgeon, was called with M. Dumas to view the bodies. Corroborated the testimony, and the opinions of M. Dumas.

"Nothing farther of importance was elicited, although several other persons were examined. A murder so mysterious, and so perplexing in all its particulars, was never before committed in Paris – if indeed a murder has been committed at all. The police are entirely at fault – an unusual occurrence in affairs of this nature. There is not, however, the shadow of a clew apparent."

The evening edition of the paper stated that the greatest excitement still continued in the Quartier St. Roch – that the premises in question had been carefully re-searched, and fresh examinations of witnesses instituted, but all to no purpose. A postscript, however, mentioned that Adolphe Le Bon had been arrested and imprisoned – although nothing appeared to criminate him, beyond the facts already detailed.

Dupin seemed singularly interested in the progress of this affair – at least so I judged from his manner, for he made no comments. It was only after the announcement that Le Bon had been imprisoned, that he asked me my opinion respecting the murders.

I could merely agree with all Paris in considering them an insoluble mystery. I saw no means by which it would be possible to trace the murderer.

"We must not judge of the means," said Dupin, "by this shell of an examination. The Parisian police, so much extolled for *acumen*, are cunning, but no more. There is no method in their proceedings, beyond the method of the moment. They make a vast parade of measures; but, not unfrequently, these are so ill adapted to the objects proposed, as to put us in mind of Monsieur Jourdain's calling for his *robe-de-chambre – pour mieux entendre la musique*. The results attained by them are not unfrequently surprising, but, for the most part, are brought about by simple diligence and activity. When these qualities are unavailing, their schemes fail. Vidocq, for example, was a good guesser and a persevering man. But, without educated thought, he erred continually by the very intensity of his investigations. He impaired his vision by holding the object too close. He might see, perhaps, one or two points with unusual clearness, but in so doing he, necessarily, lost sight of the matter as a whole. Thus there is such a thing as being too profound. Truth is not always in a well. In fact, as regards the more important knowledge, I do believe that she is invariably superficial. The depth lies in the valleys where we seek her, and not upon the mountain-tops where she is found. The modes and sources of this kind of error are well typified in the contemplation of the heavenly bodies. To look at a star by glances – to view it in a side-long way, by turning toward it the exterior portions of the *retina* (more susceptible of feeble impressions of light than the interior), is to behold the star distinctly – is to have the best appreciation of its luster – a lustre which grows dim just in proportion as we turn our vision *fully* upon it. A greater number of rays actually fall upon the eye in the latter case, but, in the former, there is the more refined capacity for comprehension. By undue profundity we perplex and enfeeble thought; and it is possible to make even Venus herself vanish from the firmament by a scrutiny too sustained, too concentrated, or too direct.

"As for these murders, let us enter into some examinations for ourselves, before we make up an opinion respecting them. An inquiry will afford us amusement," [I thought this an odd term, so applied, but said nothing] "and, besides, Le Bon once rendered me a service for which I am not ungrateful. We will go and see the premises with our own eyes. I know G–, the Prefect of Police, and shall have no difficulty in obtaining the necessary permission."

The permission was obtained, and we proceeded at once to the Rue Morgue. This is one of those miserable thoroughfares which intervene between the Rue Richelieu and the Rue St. Roch. It was late in the afternoon when we reached it; as this quarter is at a great distance from that in which we resided. The house was readily found; for there were still many persons gazing up at the closed shutters, with an objectless curiosity, from the opposite side of the way. It was an ordinary Parisian house, with a gateway, on one side of which was a glazed watch-box, with a sliding panel in the window, indicating a *loge de concierge*. Before going in we walked up the street, turned down an alley, and then, again turning, passed in the rear of the building – Dupin, meanwhile examining the whole neighborhood, as well as the house, with a minuteness of attention for which I could see no possible object.

Retracing our steps, we came again to the front of the dwelling, rang, and, having shown our credentials, were admitted by the agents in charge. We went up stairs – into the chamber where the body of Mademoiselle L'Espanaye had been found, and where both the deceased still lay. The disorders of the room had, as usual, been suffered to exist. I saw nothing beyond what had been stated in the *Gazette des Tribunaux*. Dupin scrutinized every thing – not excepting the bodies of the victims. We then went into the other rooms, and into the yard; a *gendarme* accompanying us throughout. The examination occupied us until dark, when we took our departure. On our way home my companion stepped in for a moment at the office of one of the daily papers.

I have said that the whims of my friend were manifold, and that *Je les ménageais*: – for this phrase there is no English equivalent. It was his humor, now, to decline all conversation on the subject of the murder, until about noon the next day. He then asked me, suddenly, if I had observed any thing *peculiar* at the scene of the atrocity.

There was something in his manner of emphasizing the word 'peculiar,' which caused me to shudder, without knowing why.

"No, nothing *peculiar*," I said; "nothing more, at least, than we both saw stated in the paper."

"*The Gazette*," he replied, "has not entered, I fear, into the unusual horror of the thing. But dismiss the idle opinions of this print. It appears to me that this mystery is considered insoluble, for the very reason which should cause it to be regarded as easy of solution – I mean for the *outré* character of its features. The police are confounded by the seeming absence of motive – not for the murder itself – but for the atrocity of the murder. They are puzzled, too, by the seeming impossibility of reconciling the voices heard in contention, with the facts that no one was discovered up stairs but the assassinated Mademoiselle L'Espanaye, and that there were no means of egress without the notice of the party ascending. The wild disorder of the room; the corpse thrust, with the head downward, up the chimney; the frightful mutilation of the body of the old lady; these considerations, with those just mentioned, and others which I need not mention, have sufficed to paralyze the powers, by putting completely at fault the boasted *acumen*, of the government agents. They have fallen into the gross but common error of confounding the unusual with the abstruse. But it is by these deviations from the plane of the ordinary, that reason feels its way, if at all, in its search for the true. In investigations such as we are now pursuing, it should not be so much asked 'what has occurred,' as 'what has occurred that has never occurred before.' In fact, the facility with which I shall arrive, or have arrived, at the solution of this mystery, is in the direct ratio of its apparent insolubility in the eyes of the police."

I stared at the speaker in mute astonishment.

"I am now awaiting," continued he, looking toward the door of our apartment – "I am now awaiting a person who, although perhaps not the perpetrator of these butcheries, must have been in some measure implicated in their perpetration. Of the worst portion of the crimes committed, it is probable that he is innocent. I hope that I am right in this supposition; for upon it I build my expectation of reading the entire riddle. I look for the man here – in this room – every moment. It is true that he may not arrive; but the probability is that he will. Should he come, it will be necessary to detain him. Here are pistols; and we both know how to use them when occasion demands their use."

I took the pistols, scarcely knowing what I did, or believing what I heard, while Dupin went on, very much as if in a soliloquy. I have already spoken of his abstract manner at such times. His discourse was addressed to myself; but his voice, although by no means loud, had that intonation which is commonly employed in speaking to some one at a great distance. His eyes, vacant in expression, regarded only the wall.

"That the voices heard in contention," he said, "by the party upon the stairs, were not the voices of the women themselves, was fully proved by the evidence. This relieves us of all doubt upon the question whether the old lady could have first destroyed the daughter and afterward have committed suicide. I speak of this point chiefly for the sake of method; for the strength of Madame L'Espanaye would have been utterly unequal to the task of thrusting her daughter's corpse up the chimney as it was found; and the nature of the wounds upon her own person entirely preclude the idea of self-destruction. Murder, then, has been committed by some third party; and the voices of this third party were those heard in contention. Let me now advert – not to the whole testimony respecting these voices – but to what was *peculiar* in that testimony. Did you observe any thing peculiar about it?"

I remarked that, while all the witnesses agreed in supposing the gruff voice to be that of a Frenchman, there was much disagreement in regard to the shrill, or, as one individual termed it, the harsh voice.

"That was the evidence itself," said Dupin, "but it was not the peculiarity of the evidence. You have observed nothing distinctive. Yet there *was* something to be observed. The witnesses, as you remark, agreed about the gruff voice; they were here unanimous. But in regard to the shrill voice, the peculiarity is – not that they disagreed – but that, while an Italian, an Englishman, a Spaniard, a Hollander, and a Frenchman attempted to describe it, each one spoke of it as that of *a foreigner*. Each is sure that it was not the voice of one of his own countrymen. Each likens it – not to the voice of an individual of any nation with whose language he is conversant – but the converse. The Frenchman supposes it the voice of a Spaniard, and 'might have distinguished some words *had he been acquainted with the Spanish*.' The Dutchman maintains it to have been that of a Frenchman; but we find it stated that '*not understanding French this witness was examined through an interpreter*.' The Englishman thinks it the voice of a German, and '*does not understand German*.' The Spaniard 'is sure' that it was that of an Englishman, but 'judges by the intonation' altogether, '*as he has no knowledge of the English*.' The Italian believes it the voice of a Russian, but '*has never conversed with a native of Russia*.' A second Frenchman differs, moreover, with the first, and is positive that the voice was that of an Italian; but, *not being cognizant of that tongue*, is, like the Spaniard, 'convinced by the intonation.' Now, how strangely unusual must that voice have really been, about which such testimony as this *could* have been elicited! – In whose *tones*, even, denizens of the five great divisions of Europe could recognise nothing familiar! You will say that it might have been the voice of an Asiatic – of an African. Neither Asiatics nor Africans abound in Paris; but, without denying the inference, I will now merely call your attention to three points. The voice is termed by one witness 'harsh rather than shrill.' It is represented by two others to have been 'quick and *unequal*.' No words – no sounds resembling words – were by any witness mentioned as distinguishable.

"I know not," continued Dupin, "what impression I may have made, so far, upon your own understanding; but I do not hesitate to say that legitimate deductions even from this portion of the testimony – the portion respecting the gruff and shrill voices – are in themselves sufficient to engender a suspicion which should give direction to all farther progress in the investigation of the mystery. I said 'legitimate deductions;' but my meaning is not thus fully expressed. I designed to imply that the deductions are the *sole* proper ones, and that the suspicion arises *inevitably* from them as the single result. What the suspicion is, however, I will not say just yet. I merely wish you to bear in mind that, with myself, it was sufficiently forcible to give a definite form – a certain tendency – to my inquiries in the chamber.

"Let us now transport ourselves, in fancy, to this chamber. What shall we first seek here? The means of egress employed by the murderers. It is not too much to say that neither of us believe in praeternatural events. Madame and Mademoiselle L'Espanaye were not destroyed by spirits. The doers of the deed were material, and escaped materially. Then how? Fortunately, there is but one mode of reasoning upon the point, and that mode *must* lead us to a definite decision. Let us examine, each by each, the possible means of egress. It is clear that the assassins were in the room where Mademoiselle L'Espanaye was found, or at least in the room adjoining, when the party ascended the stairs. It is then only from these two apartments that we have to seek issues. The police have laid bare the floors, the ceilings, and the masonry of the walls, in every direction. No *secret* issues could have escaped their vigilance. But, not trusting to *their* eyes, I examined with my own. There were, then, no secret issues. Both doors leading from the rooms into the passage were securely locked, with the keys inside. Let us turn to the chimneys. These, although of ordinary width for some eight or ten feet above the hearths, will not admit, throughout their extent, the body of a large cat. The impossibility of egress, by means already stated, being thus absolute, we are reduced to the windows. Through those of the front room no one could have escaped without notice from the crowd in the street. The murderers *must* have passed, then, through those of the back room. Now, brought to this conclusion in so unequivocal a manner as we are, it is not our part, as reasoners, to reject it on account of apparent impossibilities. It is only left for us to prove that these apparent 'impossibilities' are, in reality, not such.

"There are two windows in the chamber. One of them is unobstructed by furniture, and is wholly visible. The lower portion of the other is hidden from view by the head of the unwieldy bedstead which is thrust close up against it. The former was found securely fastened from within. It resisted the utmost force of those who endeavored to raise it. A large gimlet-hole had been pierced in its frame to the left, and a very stout nail was found fitted therein, nearly to the head. Upon examining the other window, a similar nail was seen similarly fitted in it; and a vigorous attempt to raise this sash, failed also. The police were now entirely satisfied that egress had not been in these directions. And, *therefore,* it was thought a matter of supererogation to withdraw the nails and open the windows.

"My own examination was somewhat more particular, and was so for the reason I have just given – because here it was, I knew, that all apparent impossibilities *must* be proved to be not such in reality.

"I proceeded to think thus – *a posteriori.* The murderers did escape from one of these windows. This being so, they could not have refastened the sashes from the inside, as they were found fastened; – the consideration which put a stop, through its obviousness, to the scrutiny of the police in this quarter. Yet the sashes *were* fastened. They *must,* then, have the power of fastening themselves. There was no escape from this conclusion. I stepped to the unobstructed casement, withdrew the nail with some difficulty and attempted to raise the sash. It resisted all my efforts, as I had anticipated. A concealed spring must, I now know, exist; and this corroboration of my idea convinced me that my premises at least, were correct, however mysterious still appeared the circumstances attending the nails. A careful search soon brought to light the hidden spring. I pressed it, and, satisfied with the discovery, forbore to upraise the sash.

"I now replaced the nail and regarded it attentively. A person passing out through this window might have reclosed it, and the spring would have caught – but the nail could not have been replaced. The conclusion was plain, and again narrowed in the field of my investigations. The assassins *must* have escaped through the other window. Supposing, then, the springs upon each sash to be the same, as was probable, there *must* be found a difference between the nails, or at least between the modes of their fixture. Getting upon the sacking of the bedstead, I looked over the head-board minutely at the second casement. Passing my hand down behind the board, I readily discovered and pressed the spring, which was, as I had supposed, identical in character with its neighbor. I now looked at the nail. It was as stout as the other, and apparently fitted in the same manner – driven in nearly up to the head.

"You will say that I was puzzled; but, if you think so, you must have misunderstood the nature of the inductions. To use a sporting phrase, I had not been once 'at fault.' The scent had never for an instant been lost. There was no flaw in any link of the chain. I had traced the secret to its ultimate result, – and that result was *the nail*. It had, I say, in every respect, the appearance of its fellow in the other window; but this fact was an absolute nullity (conclusive us it might seem to be) when compared with the consideration that here, at this point, terminated the clew. 'There *must* be something wrong,' I said, 'about the nail.' I touched it; and the head, with about a quarter of an inch of the shank, came off in my fingers. The rest of the shank was in the gimlet-hole where it had been broken off. The fracture was an old one (for its edges were incrusted with rust), and had apparently been accomplished by the blow of a hammer, which had partially imbedded, in the top of the bottom sash, the head portion of the nail. I now carefully replaced this head portion in the indentation whence I had taken it, and the resemblance to a perfect nail was complete – the fissure was invisible. Pressing the spring, I gently raised the sash for a few inches; the head went up with it, remaining firm in its bed. I closed the window, and the semblance of the whole nail was again perfect.

"The riddle, so far, was now unriddled. The assassin had escaped through the window which looked upon the bed. Dropping of its own accord upon his exit (or perhaps purposely closed), it had become fastened by the spring; and it was the retention of this spring which had been mistaken by the police for that of the nail, – farther inquiry being thus considered unnecessary.

"The next question is that of the mode of descent. Upon this point I had been satisfied in my walk with you around the building. About five feet and a half from the casement in question there runs a lightning-rod. From this rod it would have been impossible for any one to reach the window itself, to say nothing of entering it. I observed, however, that the shutters of the fourth story were of the peculiar kind called by Parisian carpenters *ferrades* – a kind rarely employed at the present day, but frequently seen upon very old mansions at Lyons and Bordeaux. They are in the form of an ordinary door, (a single, not a folding door) except that the lower half is latticed or worked in open trellis – thus affording an excellent hold for the hands. In the present instance these shutters are fully three feet and a half broad. When we saw them from the rear of the house, they were both about half open – that is to say, they stood off at right angles from the wall. It is probable that the police, as well as myself, examined the back of the tenement; but, if so, in looking at these *ferrades* in the line of their breadth (as they must have done), they did not perceive this great breadth itself, or, at all events, failed to take it into due consideration. In fact, having once satisfied themselves that no egress could have been made in this quarter, they would naturally bestow here a very cursory examination. It was clear to me, however, that the shutter belonging to the window at the head of the bed, would, if swung fully back to the wall, reach to within two feet of the lightning-rod. It was also evident that, by exertion of a very unusual degree of activity and courage, an entrance into the window, from the rod, might have been thus effected. – By reaching to the distance of two feet and a half (we now suppose the shutter open to its whole extent) a robber might have taken a firm grasp upon the trellis-work. Letting go, then, his hold upon the rod, placing his feet securely against the wall, and springing boldly from it, he might have swung the shutter so as to close it, and, if we imagine the window open at the time, might even have swung himself into the room.

"I wish you to bear especially in mind that I have spoken of a *very* unusual degree of activity as requisite to success in so hazardous and so difficult a feat. It is my design to show you, first, that the thing might possibly have been accomplished: – but, secondly and *chiefly*, I wish to impress upon your understanding the *very extraordinary* – the almost praeternatural character of that agility which could have accomplished it.

"You will say, no doubt, using the language of the law, that 'to make out my case,' I should rather undervalue, than insist upon a full estimation of the activity required in this matter. This may be the practice in law, but it is not the usage of reason. My ultimate object is only the truth. My immediate purpose is to lead you to place in juxtaposition, that *very unusual* activity of which I have just spoken with that *very peculiar* shrill (or harsh) and *unequal* voice, about whose nationality no two persons could be found to agree, and in whose utterance no syllabification could be detected."

At these words a vague and half-formed conception of the meaning of Dupin flitted over my mind. I seemed to be upon the verge of comprehension without power to comprehend – men, at times, find themselves upon the brink of remembrance without being able, in the end, to remember. My friend went on with his discourse.

"You will see," he said, "that I have shifted the question from the mode of egress to that of ingress. It was my design to convey the idea that both were effected in the same manner, at the same point. Let us now revert to the interior of the room. Let us survey the appearances here. The drawers of the bureau, it is said, had been rifled, although many articles of apparel still remained within them. The conclusion here is absurd. It is a mere guess – a very silly one – and no more. How are we to know that the articles found in the drawers were not all these drawers had originally contained? Madame L'Espanaye and her daughter lived an exceedingly retired life – saw no company – seldom went out – had little use for numerous changes of habiliment. Those found were at least of as good quality as any likely to be possessed by these ladies. If a thief had taken any, why did he not take the best – why did he not take all? In a word, why did he abandon four thousand francs in gold to encumber himself with a bundle of linen? The gold *was* abandoned. Nearly the whole sum mentioned by Monsieur Mignaud, the banker, was discovered, in bags, upon the floor. I wish you, therefore, to discard from your thoughts the blundering idea of *motive*, engendered in the brains of the police by that portion of the evidence which speaks of money delivered at the door of the house. Coincidences ten times as remarkable as this (the delivery of the money, and murder committed within three days upon the party receiving it), happen to all of us every hour of our lives, without attracting even momentary notice. Coincidences, in general, are great stumbling-blocks in the way of that class of thinkers who have been educated to know nothing of the theory of probabilities – that theory to which the most glorious objects of human research are indebted for the most glorious of illustration. In the present instance, had the gold been gone, the fact of its delivery three days before would have formed something more than a coincidence. It would have been corroborative of this idea of motive. But, under the real circumstances of the case, if we are to suppose gold the motive of this outrage, we must also imagine the perpetrator so vacillating an idiot as to have abandoned his gold and his motive together.

"Keeping now steadily in mind the points to which I have drawn your attention – that peculiar voice, that unusual agility, and that startling absence of motive in a murder so singularly atrocious as this – let us glance at the butchery itself. Here is a woman strangled to death by manual strength, and thrust up a chimney, head downward. Ordinary assassins employ no such modes of murder as this. Least of all, do they thus dispose of the murdered. In the manner of thrusting the corpse up the chimney, you will admit that there was something *excessively outré* – something altogether irreconcilable with our common notions of human action, even when we suppose the actors the most depraved of men. Think, too, how great must have been that strength which could have thrust the body up such an aperture so forcibly that the united vigor of several persons was found barely sufficient to drag it *down!*

"Turn, now, to other indications of the employment of a vigor most marvellous. On the hearth were thick tresses – very thick tresses – of grey human hair. These had been torn out by the roots. You are aware of the great force necessary in tearing thus from the head even twenty or thirty hairs together. You saw the locks in question as well as myself. Their roots (a hideous sight!) were clotted with fragments of the flesh of the scalp – sure token of the prodigious power which had been exerted in uprooting perhaps half a million of hairs at a time. The throat of the old lady was not merely cut, but the head absolutely severed from the body: the instrument was a mere razor. I wish you also to look at the *brutal* ferocity of these deeds. Of the bruises upon the body of Madame L'Espanaye I do not speak. Monsieur Dumas, and his worthy coadjutor Monsieur Etienne, have pronounced that they were inflicted by some obtuse instrument; and so far these gentlemen are very correct. The obtuse instrument was clearly the stone pavement in the yard, upon which the victim had fallen from the window which looked in upon the bed. This idea, however simple it may now seem, escaped the police for the same reason that the breadth of the shutters escaped them – because, by the affair of the nails, their perceptions had been hermetically sealed against the possibility of the windows having ever been opened at all.

"If now, in addition to all these things, you have properly reflected upon the odd disorder of the chamber, we have gone so far as to combine the ideas of an agility astounding, a strength superhuman, a ferocity brutal, a butchery without motive, a *grotesquerie* in horror absolutely alien from humanity, and a voice foreign in tone to the ears of men of many nations, and devoid of all distinct or intelligible syllabification. What result, then, has ensued? What impression have I made upon your fancy?"

I felt a creeping of the flesh as Dupin asked me the question. "A madman," I said, "has done this deed – some raving maniac, escaped from a neighboring *Maison de Santé.*"

"In some respects," he replied, "your idea is not irrelevant. But the voices of madmen, even in their wildest paroxysms, are never found to tally with that peculiar voice heard upon the stairs. Madmen are of some nation, and their language, however incoherent in its words, has always the coherence of syllabification. Besides, the hair of a madman is not such as I now hold in my hand. I disentangled this little tuft from the rigidly clutched fingers of Madame L'Espanaye. Tell me what you can make of it."

"Dupin!" I said, completely unnerved; "This hair is most unusual – this is no *human* hair."

"I have not asserted that it is," said he; "but, before we decide this point, I wish you to glance at the little sketch I have here traced upon this paper. It is a *fac-simile* drawing of what has been described in one portion of the testimony as 'dark bruises, and deep indentations of finger nails,' upon the throat of Mademoiselle L'Espanaye, and in another, (by Messrs. Dumas and Etienne,) as a 'series of livid spots, evidently the impression of fingers.'

"You will perceive," continued my friend, spreading out the paper upon the table before us, "that this drawing gives the idea of a firm and fixed hold. There is no *slipping* apparent. Each finger has retained – possibly until the death of the victim – the fearful grasp by which it originally imbedded itself. Attempt, now, to place all your fingers, at the same time, in the respective impressions as you see them."

I made the attempt in vain.

"We are possibly not giving this matter a fair trial," he said. "The paper is spread out upon a plane surface; but the human throat is cylindrical. Here is a billet of wood, the circumference of which is about that of the throat. Wrap the drawing around it, and try the experiment again."

I did so; but the difficulty was even more obvious than before. "This," I said, "is the mark of no human hand."

"Read now," replied Dupin, "this passage from Cuvier."

It was a minute anatomical and generally descriptive account of the large fulvous Ourang-Outang of the East Indian Islands. The gigantic stature, the prodigious strength and activity, the wild ferocity, and the imitative propensities of these mammalia are sufficiently well known to all. I understood the full horrors of the murder at once.

"The description of the digits," said I, as I made an end of reading, "is in exact accordance with this drawing. I see that no animal but an Ourang-Outang, of the species here mentioned, could have impressed the indentations as you have traced them. This tuft of tawny hair, too, is identical in character with that of the beast of Cuvier. But I cannot possibly comprehend the particulars of this frightful mystery. Besides, there were *two* voices heard in contention, and one of them was unquestionably the voice of a Frenchman."

"True; and you will remember an expression attributed almost unanimously, by the evidence, to this voice, – the expression, '*mon Dieu!*' This, under the circumstances, has been justly characterized by one of the witnesses (Montani, the confectioner,) as an expression of remonstrance or expostulation. Upon these two words, therefore, I have mainly built my hopes of a full solution of the riddle. A Frenchman was cognizant of the murder. It is possible – indeed it is far more than probable – that he was innocent of all participation in the bloody transactions which took place. The Ourang-Outang may have escaped from him. He may have traced it to the chamber; but, under the agitating circumstances which ensued, he could never have re-captured it. It is still at large. I will not pursue these guesses – for I have no right to call them more – since the shades of reflection upon which they are based are scarcely of sufficient depth to be appreciable by my own intellect, and since I could not pretend to make them intelligible to the understanding of another. We will call them guesses then, and speak of them as such. If the Frenchman in question is indeed, as I suppose, innocent of this atrocity, this advertisement which I left last night, upon our return home, at the office of *Le Monde,* (a paper devoted to the shipping interest, and much sought by sailors,) will bring him to our residence."

He handed me a paper, and I read thus:

CAUGHT – *In the Bois de Boulogne, early in the morning of the – inst., (the morning of the murder,) a very large, tawny Ourang-Outang of the Bornese species. The owner, (who is ascertained to be a sailor, belonging to a Maltese vessel,) may have the animal again, upon identifying it satisfactorily, and paying a few charges arising from its capture and keeping. Call at No. – , Rue – , Faubourg St. Germain – au troisième.*

"How was it possible," I asked, "that you should know the man to be a sailor, and belonging to a Maltese vessel?"

"I do *not* know it," said Dupin. "I am not *sure* of it. Here, however, is a small piece of ribbon, which from its form, and from its greasy appearance, has evidently been used in tying the hair in one of those long *queues* of which sailors are so fond. Moreover, this knot is one which few besides sailors can tie, and is peculiar to the Maltese. I picked the ribbon up at the foot of the lightning-rod. It could not have belonged to either of the deceased. Now if, after all, I am wrong in my induction from this ribbon, that the Frenchman was a sailor belonging to a Maltese vessel, still I can have done no harm in saying what I did in the advertisement. If I am in error, he will merely suppose that I have been misled by some circumstance into which he will not take the trouble to inquire. But if I am right, a great point is gained. Cognizant although innocent of the murder, the Frenchman will naturally hesitate about replying to the advertisement – about demanding the Ourang-Outang. He will reason thus: – 'I am innocent; I am poor; my Ourang-Outang is of great value – to one in my circumstances a fortune of itself – why should I lose it through idle apprehensions of danger? Here it is, within my grasp. It was found in the Bois de Boulogne – at a vast distance from the scene of that butchery. How can it ever be suspected that a brute beast should have done the deed? The police are at fault – they have failed to procure the slightest clew. Should they even trace the animal, it would be impossible to prove me cognizant of the murder, or to implicate me in guilt on account of that cognizance. Above all, I am known. The advertiser designates me as the possessor of the beast. I am not sure to what limit his knowledge may extend. Should I avoid claiming a property of so great value, which it is known that I possess, I will render the animal at least, liable to suspicion. It is not my policy to attract attention either to myself or to the beast. I will answer the advertisement, get the Ourang-Outang, and keep it close until this matter has blown over.' "

At this moment we heard a step upon the stairs.

"Be ready," said Dupin, "with your pistols, but neither use them nor show them until at a signal from myself."

The front door of the house had been left open, and the visitor had entered, without ringing, and advanced several steps upon the staircase. Now, however, he seemed to hesitate. Presently we heard him descending. Dupin was moving quickly to the door, when we again heard him coming up. He did not turn back a second time, but stepped up with decision, and rapped at the door of our chamber.

"Come in," said Dupin, in a cheerful and hearty tone.

A man entered. He was a sailor, evidently, – a tall, stout, and muscular-looking person, with a certain dare-devil expression of countenance, not altogether unprepossessing. His face, greatly sunburnt, was more than half hidden by whisker and *mustachio*. He had with him a huge oaken cudgel, but appeared to be otherwise unarmed. He bowed awkwardly, and bade us "good evening," in French accents, which, although somewhat Neufchatelish, were still sufficiently indicative of a Parisian origin.

"Sit down, my friend," said Dupin. "I suppose you have called about the Ourang-Outang. Upon my word, I almost envy you the possession of him; a remarkably fine, and no doubt a very valuable animal. How old do you suppose him to be?"

The sailor drew a long breath, with the air of a man relieved of some intolerable burden, and then replied, in an assured tone:

"I have no way of telling – but he can't be more than four or five years old. Have you got him here?"

"Oh no, we had no conveniences for keeping him here. He is at a livery stable in the Rue Dubourg, just by. You can get him in the morning. Of course you are prepared to identify the property?"

"To be sure I am, sir."

"I shall be sorry to part with him," said Dupin.

"I don't mean that you should be at all this trouble for nothing, sir," said the man. "Couldn't expect it. Am very willing to pay a reward for the finding of the animal – that is to say, any thing in reason."

"Well," replied my friend, "that is all very fair, to be sure. Let me think! – What should I have? Oh! I will tell you. My reward shall be this. You shall give me all the information in your power about these murders in the Rue Morgue."

Dupin said the last words in a very low tone, and very quietly. Just as quietly, too, he walked toward the door, locked it and put the key in his pocket. He then drew a pistol from his bosom and placed it, without the least flurry, upon the table.

The sailor's face flushed up as if he were struggling with suffocation. He started to his feet and grasped his cudgel, but the next moment he fell back into his seat, trembling violently, and with the countenance of death itself. He spoke not a word. I pitied him from the bottom of my heart.

"My friend," said Dupin, in a kind tone, "you are alarming yourself unnecessarily – you are indeed. We mean you no harm whatever. I pledge you the honor of a gentleman, and of a Frenchman, that we intend you no injury. I perfectly well know that you are innocent of the atrocities in the Rue Morgue. It will not do, however, to deny that you are in some measure implicated in them. From what I have already said, you must know that I have had means of information about this matter – means of which you could never have dreamed. Now the thing stands thus. You have done nothing which you could have avoided – nothing, certainly, which renders you culpable. You were not even guilty of robbery, when you might have robbed with impunity. You have nothing to conceal. You have no reason for concealment. On the other hand, you are bound by every principle of honor to confess all you know. An innocent man is now imprisoned, charged with that crime of which you can point out the perpetrator."

The sailor had recovered his presence of mind, in a great measure, while Dupin uttered these words; but his original boldness of bearing was all gone.

"So help me God," said he, after a brief pause, "I will tell you all I know about this affair; – but I do not expect you to believe one half I say – I would be a fool indeed if I did. Still, I am innocent, and I will make a clean breast if I die for it."

What he stated was, in substance, this. He had lately made a voyage to the Indian Archipelago. A party, of which he formed one, landed at Borneo, and passed into the interior on an excursion of pleasure. Himself and a companion had captured the Ourang-Outang. This companion dying, the animal fell into his own exclusive possession. After great trouble, occasioned by the intractable ferocity of his captive during the home voyage, he at length succeeded in lodging it safely at his own residence in Paris, where, not to attract toward himself the unpleasant curiosity of his neighbors, he kept it carefully secluded, until such time as it should recover from a wound in the foot, received from a splinter on board ship. His ultimate design was to sell it.

Returning home from some sailors' frolic the night, or rather in the morning of the murder, he found the beast occupying his own bed-room, into which it had broken from a closet adjoining, where it had been, as was thought, securely confined. Razor in hand, and fully lathered, it was sitting before a looking-glass, attempting the operation of shaving, in which it had no doubt previously watched its master through the key-hole of the closet. Terrified at the sight of so dangerous a weapon in the possession of an animal so ferocious, and so well able to use it, the man, for some moments, was at a loss what to do. He had been accustomed, however, to quiet the creature, even in its fiercest moods, by the use of a whip, and to this he now resorted. Upon sight of it, the Ourang-Outang sprang at once through the door of the chamber, down the stairs, and thence, through a window, unfortunately open, into the street.

The Frenchman followed in despair; the ape, razor still in hand, occasionally stopping to look back and gesticulate at its pursuer, until the latter had nearly come up with it. It then again made off. In this manner the chase continued for a long time. The streets were profoundly quiet, as it was nearly three o'clock in the morning. In passing down an alley in the rear of the Rue Morgue, the fugitive's attention was arrested by a light gleaming from the open window of Madame L'Espanaye's chamber, in the fourth story of her house. Rushing to the building, it perceived the lightning rod, clambered up with inconceivable agility, grasped the shutter, which was thrown fully back against the wall, and, by its means, swung itself directly upon the headboard of the bed. The whole feat did not occupy a minute. The shutter was kicked open again by the Ourang-Outang as it entered the room.

The sailor, in the meantime, was both rejoiced and perplexed. He had strong hopes of now recapturing the brute, as it could scarcely escape from the trap into which it had ventured, except by the rod, where it might be intercepted as it came down. On the other hand, there was much cause for anxiety as to what it might do in the house. This latter reflection urged the man still to follow the fugitive. A lightning rod is ascended without difficulty, especially by a sailor; but, when he had arrived as high as the window, which lay far to his left, his career was stopped; the most that he could accomplish was to reach over so as to obtain a glimpse of the interior of the room. At this glimpse he nearly fell from his hold through excess of horror. Now it was that those hideous shrieks arose upon the night, which had startled from slumber the inmates of the Rue Morgue. Madame L'Espanaye and her daughter, habited in their night clothes, had apparently been occupied in arranging some papers in the iron chest already mentioned, which had been wheeled into the middle of the room. It was open, and its contents lay beside it on the floor. The victims must have been sitting with their backs toward the window; and, from the time elapsing between the ingress of the beast and the screams, it seems probable that it was not immediately perceived. The flapping-to of the shutter would naturally have been attributed to the wind.

As the sailor looked in, the gigantic animal had seized Madame L'Espanaye by the hair, (which was loose, as she had been combing it,) and was flourishing the razor about her face, in imitation of the motions of a barber. The daughter lay prostrate and motionless; she had swooned. The screams and struggles of the old lady (during which the hair was torn from her head) had the effect of changing the probably pacific purposes of the Ourang-Outang into those of wrath. With one determined sweep of its muscular arm it nearly severed her head from her body. The sight of blood inflamed its anger into phrenzy. Gnashing its teeth, and flashing fire from its eyes, it flew upon the body of the girl, and imbedded its fearful talons in her throat, retaining its grasp until she expired. Its wandering and wild glances fell at this moment upon the head of the bed, over which the face of its master, rigid with horror, was just discernible. The fury of the beast, who no doubt bore still in mind the dreaded whip, was instantly converted into fear. Conscious of having deserved punishment, it seemed desirous of concealing its bloody deeds, and skipped about the chamber in an agony of nervous agitation; throwing down and breaking the furniture as it moved, and dragging the bed from the bedstead. In conclusion, it seized first the corpse of the daughter, and thrust it up the chimney, as it was found; then that of the old lady, which it immediately hurled through the window headlong.

As the ape approached the casement with its mutilated burden, the sailor shrank aghast to the rod, and, rather gliding than clambering down it, hurried at once home – dreading the consequences of the butchery, and gladly abandoning, in his terror, all solicitude about the fate of the Ourang-Outang. The words heard by the party upon the staircase were the Frenchman's exclamations of horror and affright, commingled with the fiendish jabberings of the brute.

I have scarcely anything to add. The Ourang-Outang must have escaped from the chamber, by the rod, just before the break of the door. It must have closed the window as it passed through it. It was subsequently caught by the owner himself, who obtained for it a very large sum at the *Jardin des Plantes*. Le Don was instantly released, upon our narration of the circumstances (with some comments from Dupin) at the bureau of the Prefect of Police. This functionary, however well disposed to my friend, could not altogether conceal his chagrin at the turn which affairs had taken, and was fain to indulge in a sarcasm or two, about the propriety of every person minding his own business.

"Let him talk," said Dupin, who had not thought it necessary to reply. "Let him discourse; it will ease his conscience, I am satisfied with having defeated him in his own castle. Nevertheless, that he failed in the solution of this mystery, is by no means that matter for wonder which he supposes it; for, in truth, our friend the Prefect is somewhat too cunning to be profound. In his wisdom is no stamen. It is all head and no body, like the pictures of the Goddess Laverna, – or, at best, all head and shoulders, like a codfish. But he is a good creature after all. I like him especially for one master stroke of cant, by which he has attained his reputation for ingenuity. I mean the way he has '*de nier ce qui est, et d'expliquer ce qui n'est pas.*' " (Rousseau – *Nouvelle Heloise*).

The Purloined Letter

Edgar Allan Poe

Nil sapientiae odiosius acumine nimio.
Seneca

AT PARIS, just after dark one gusty evening in the autumn of 18–, I was enjoying the twofold luxury of meditation and a meerschaum, in company with my friend C. Auguste Dupin, in his little back library, or book-closet, au troisiême, No. 33, Rue Dunôt, Faubourg St. Germain. For one hour at least we had maintained a profound silence; while each, to any casual observer, might have seemed intently and exclusively occupied with the curling eddies of smoke that oppressed the atmosphere of the chamber. For myself, however, I was mentally discussing certain topics which had formed matter for conversation between us at an earlier period of the evening; I mean the affair of the Rue Morgue, and the mystery attending the murder of Marie Rogêt. I looked upon it, therefore, as something of a coincidence, when the door of our apartment was thrown open and admitted our old acquaintance, Monsieur G–, the Prefect of the Parisian police.

We gave him a hearty welcome; for there was nearly half as much of the entertaining as of the contemptible about the man, and we had not seen him for several years. We had been sitting in the dark, and Dupin now arose for the purpose of lighting a lamp, but sat down again, without doing so, upon G.'s saying that he had called to consult us, or rather to ask the opinion of my friend, about some official business which had occasioned a great deal of trouble.

"If it is any point requiring reflection," observed Dupin, as he forebore to enkindle the wick, "we shall examine it to better purpose in the dark."

"That is another of your odd notions," said the Prefect, who had a fashion of calling every thing 'odd' that was beyond his comprehension, and thus lived amid an absolute legion of 'oddities'.

"Very true," said Dupin, as he supplied his visitor with a pipe, and rolled towards him a comfortable chair.

"And what is the difficulty now?" I asked. "Nothing more in the assassination way, I hope?"

"Oh no; nothing of that nature. The fact is, the business is very simple indeed, and I make no doubt that we can manage it sufficiently well ourselves; but then I thought Dupin would like to hear the details of it, because it is so excessively odd."

"Simple and odd," said Dupin.

"Why, yes; and not exactly that, either. The fact is, we have all been a good deal puzzled because the affair is so simple, and yet baffles us altogether."

"Perhaps it is the very simplicity of the thing which puts you at fault," said my friend.

"What nonsense you do talk!" replied the Prefect, laughing heartily.

"Perhaps the mystery is a little too plain," said Dupin.

"Oh, good heavens! who ever heard of such an idea?"

"A little too self-evident."

"Ha! Ha! Ha – Ha! Ha! Ha! – Ho! Ho! Ho!" roared our visitor, profoundly amused, "Oh, Dupin, you will be the death of me yet!"

"And what, after all, is the matter on hand?" I asked.

"Why, I will tell you," replied the Prefect, as he gave a long, steady and contemplative puff, and settled himself in his chair. "I will tell you in a few words; but, before I begin, let me caution you that this is an affair demanding the greatest secrecy, and that I should most probably lose the position I now hold, were it known that I confided it to anyone."

"Proceed," said I.

"Or not," said Dupin.

"Well, then; I have received personal information, from a very high quarter, that a certain document of the last importance, has been purloined from the royal apartments. The individual who purloined it is known; this beyond a doubt; he was seen to take it. It is known, also, that it still remains in his possession."

"How is this known?" asked Dupin.

"It is clearly inferred," replied the Prefect, "from the nature of the document, and from the non-appearance of certain results which would at once arise from its passing out of the robber's possession; that is to say, from his employing it as he must design in the end to employ it."

"Be a little more explicit," I said.

"Well, I may venture so far as to say that the paper gives its holder a certain power in a certain quarter where such power is immensely valuable." The Prefect was fond of the cant of diplomacy.

"Still I do not quite understand," said Dupin.

"No? Well; the disclosure of the document to a third person, who shall be nameless, would bring in question the honor of a personage of most exalted station; and this fact gives the holder of the document an ascendancy over the illustrious personage whose honor and peace are so jeopardized."

"But this ascendancy," I interposed, "would depend upon the robber's knowledge of the loser's knowledge of the robber. Who would dare – "

"The thief," said G., "is the Minister D–, who dares all things, those unbecoming as well as those becoming a man. The method of the theft was not less ingenious than bold. The document in question – a letter, to be frank – had been received by the personage robbed while alone in the royal boudoir. During its perusal she was suddenly interrupted by the entrance of the other exalted personage from whom especially it was her wish to conceal it. After a hurried and vain endeavor to thrust it in a drawer, she was forced to place it, open as it was, upon a table. The address, however, was uppermost, and, the contents thus unexposed, the letter escaped notice. At this juncture enters the Minister D– . His lynx eye immediately perceives the paper, recognises the handwriting of the address, observes the confusion of the personage addressed, and fathoms her secret. After some business transactions, hurried through in his ordinary manner, he produces a letter somewhat similar to the one in question, opens it, pretends to read it, and then places it in close juxtaposition to the other. Again he converses, for some fifteen minutes, upon the public affairs. At length, in taking leave, he takes also from the table the letter to which he had no claim. Its rightful owner saw, but, of course, dared not call attention to the act, in the presence of the third personage who stood at her elbow. The minister decamped; leaving his own letter – one of no importance – upon the table."

"Here, then," said Dupin to me, "you have precisely what you demand to make the ascendancy complete – the robber's knowledge of the loser's knowledge of the robber."

"Yes," replied the Prefect; "and the power thus attained has, for some months past, been wielded, for political purposes, to a very dangerous extent. The personage robbed is more thoroughly convinced, every day, of the necessity of reclaiming her letter. But this, of course, cannot be done openly. In fine, driven to despair, she has committed the matter to me."

"Than whom," said Dupin, amid a perfect whirlwind of smoke, "no more sagacious agent could, I suppose, be desired, or even imagined."

"You flatter me," replied the Prefect; "but it is possible that some such opinion may have been entertained."

"It is clear," said I, "as you observe, that the letter is still in possession of the minister; since it is this possession, and not any employment of the letter, which bestows the power. With the employment the power departs."

"True," said G.; "and upon this conviction I proceeded. My first care was to make thorough search of the minister's hotel; and here my chief embarrassment lay in the necessity of searching without his knowledge. Beyond all things, I have been warned of the danger which would result from giving him reason to suspect our design."

"But," said I, "you are quite au fait in these investigations. The Parisian police have done this thing often before."

"O yes; and for this reason I did not despair. The habits of the minister gave me, too, a great advantage. He is frequently absent from home all night. His servants are by no means numerous. They sleep at a distance from their master's apartment, and, being chiefly Neapolitans, are readily made drunk. I have keys, as you know, with which I can open any chamber or cabinet in Paris. For three months a night has not passed, during the greater part of which I have not been engaged, personally, in ransacking the D– Hotel. My honor is interested, and, to mention a great secret, the reward is enormous. So I did not abandon the search until I had become fully satisfied that the thief is a more astute man than myself. I fancy that I have investigated every nook and corner of the premises in which it is possible that the paper can be concealed."

"But is it not possible," I suggested, "that although the letter may be in possession of the minister, as it unquestionably is, he may have concealed it elsewhere than upon his own premises?"

"This is barely possible," said Dupin. "The present peculiar condition of affairs at court, and especially of those intrigues in which D– is known to be involved, would render the instant availability of the document – its susceptibility of being produced at a moment's notice – a point of nearly equal importance with its possession."

"Its susceptibility of being produced?" said I.

"That is to say, of being destroyed," said Dupin.

"True," I observed; "the paper is clearly then upon the premises. As for its being upon the person of the minister, we may consider that as out of the question."

"Entirely," said the Prefect. "He has been twice waylaid, as if by footpads, and his person rigorously searched under my own inspection."

"You might have spared yourself this trouble," said Dupin. "D–, I presume, is not altogether a fool, and, if not, must have anticipated these waylayings, as a matter of course."

"Not altogether a fool," said G., "but then he's a poet, which I take to be only one remove from a fool."

"True," said Dupin, after a long and thoughtful whiff from his meerschaum, "although I have been guilty of certain doggerel myself."

"Suppose you detail," said I, "the particulars of your search."

"Why the fact is, we took our time, and we searched everywhere. I have had long experience in these affairs. I took the entire building, room by room; devoting the nights of a whole week to each. We examined, first, the furniture of each apartment. We opened every possible drawer; and I presume you know that, to a properly trained police agent, such a thing as a secret drawer is impossible. Any man is a dolt who permits a 'secret' drawer to escape him in a search of this kind. The thing is so plain. There is a certain amount of bulk – of space – to be accounted for in every cabinet. Then we have accurate rules. The fiftieth part of a line could not escape us. After the cabinets we took the chairs. The cushions we probed with the fine long needles you have seen me employ. From the tables we removed the tops."

"Why so?"

"Sometimes the top of a table, or other similarly arranged piece of furniture, is removed by the person wishing to conceal an article; then the leg is excavated, the article deposited within the cavity, and the top replaced. The bottoms and tops of bedposts are employed in the same way."

"But could not the cavity be detected by sounding?" I asked.

"By no means, if, when the article is deposited, a sufficient wadding of cotton be placed around it. Besides, in our case, we were obliged to proceed without noise."

"But you could not have removed – you could not have taken to pieces all articles of furniture in which it would have been possible to make a deposit in the manner you mention. A letter may be compressed into a thin spiral roll, not differing much in shape or bulk from a large knitting-needle, and in this form it might be inserted into the rung of a chair, for example. You did not take to pieces all the chairs?"

"Certainly not; but we did better – we examined the rungs of every chair in the hotel, and, indeed the jointings of every description of furniture, by the aid of a most powerful microscope. Had there been any traces of recent disturbance we should not have failed to detect it instantly. A single grain of gimlet-dust, for example, would have been as obvious as an apple. Any disorder in the glueing – any unusual gaping in the joints – would have sufficed to ensure detection."

"I presume you looked to the mirrors, between the boards and the plates, and you probed the beds and the bed-clothes, as well as the curtains and carpets."

"That of course; and when we had absolutely completed every particle of the furniture in this way, then we examined the house itself. We divided its entire surface into compartments, which we numbered, so that none might be missed; then we scrutinized each individual square inch throughout the premises, including the two houses immediately adjoining, with the microscope, as before."

"The two houses adjoining!" I exclaimed; "You must have had a great deal of trouble."

"We had; but the reward offered is prodigious!"

"You include the grounds about the houses?"

"All the grounds are paved with brick. They gave us comparatively little trouble. We examined the moss between the bricks, and found it undisturbed."

"You looked among D–'s papers, of course, and into the books of the library?"

"Certainly; we opened every package and parcel; we not only opened every book, but we turned over every leaf in each volume, not contenting ourselves with a mere shake, according to the fashion of some of our police officers. We also measured the thickness of every book-cover, with the most accurate admeasurement, and applied to each the most jealous scrutiny of the microscope. Had any of the bindings been recently meddled with, it would have been utterly impossible that the fact should have escaped observation. Some five or six volumes, just from the hands of the binder, we carefully probed, longitudinally, with the needles."

"You explored the floors beneath the carpets?"

"Beyond doubt. We removed every carpet, and examined the boards with the microscope."

"And the paper on the walls?"

"Yes."

"You looked into the cellars?"

"We did."

"Then," I said, "you have been making a miscalculation, and the letter is not upon the premises, as you suppose."

"I fear you are right there," said the Prefect. "And now, Dupin, what would you advise me to do?"

"To make a thorough re-search of the premises."

"That is absolutely needless," replied G–. "I am not more sure that I breathe than I am that the letter is not at the Hotel."

"I have no better advice to give you," said Dupin. "You have, of course, an accurate description of the letter?"

"Oh yes!" – and here the Prefect, producing a memorandum-book proceeded to read aloud a minute account of the internal, and especially of the external appearance of the missing document. Soon after finishing the perusal of this description, he took his departure, more entirely depressed in spirits than I had ever known the good gentleman before. In about a month afterwards he paid us another visit, and found us occupied very nearly as before. He took a pipe and a chair and entered into some ordinary conversation. At length I said:

"Well, but G–, what of the purloined letter? I presume you have at last made up your mind that there is no such thing as overreaching the Minister?"

"Confound him, say I – yes; I made the re-examination, however, as Dupin suggested – but it was all labor lost, as I knew it would be."

"How much was the reward offered, did you say?" asked Dupin.

"Why, a very great deal – a very liberal reward – I don't like to say how much, precisely; but one thing I will say, that I wouldn't mind giving my individual check for fifty thousand francs to any one who could obtain me that letter. The fact is, it is becoming of more and more importance every day; and the reward has been lately doubled. If it were trebled, however, I could do no more than I have done."

"Why, yes," said Dupin, drawlingly, between the whiffs of his meerschaum, "I really – think, G–, you have not exerted yourself – to the utmost in this matter. You might – do a little more, I think, eh?"

"How? – In what way?"

"Why – puff, puff – you might – puff, puff – employ counsel in the matter, eh? – Puff, puff, puff. Do you remember the story they tell of Abernethy?"

"No; hang Abernethy!"

"To be sure! Hang him and welcome. But, once upon a time, a certain rich miser conceived the design of spunging upon this Abernethy for a medical opinion. Getting up, for this purpose, an ordinary conversation in a private company, he insinuated his case to the physician, as that of an imaginary individual.

" 'We will suppose,' said the miser, 'that his symptoms are such and such; now, doctor, what would you have directed him to take?'

" 'Take!' said Abernethy, 'why, take advice, to be sure.' "

"But," said the Prefect, a little discomposed, "I am perfectly willing to take advice, and to pay for it. I would really give fifty thousand francs to any one who would aid me in the matter."

"In that case," replied Dupin, opening a drawer, and producing a check-book, "you may as well fill me up a check for the amount mentioned. When you have signed it, I will hand you the letter."

I was astounded. The Prefect appeared absolutely thunder-stricken. For some minutes he remained speechless and motionless, looking incredulously at my friend with open mouth, and eyes that seemed starting from their sockets; then, apparently recovering himself in some measure, he seized a pen, and after several pauses and vacant stares, finally filled up and signed a check for fifty thousand francs, and handed it across the table to Dupin. The latter examined it carefully and deposited it in his pocket-book; then, unlocking an escritoire, took thence a letter and gave it to the Prefect. This functionary grasped it in a perfect agony of joy, opened it with a trembling hand, cast a rapid glance at its contents, and then, scrambling and struggling to the door, rushed at length unceremoniously from the room and from the house, without having uttered a syllable since Dupin had requested him to fill up the check.

When he had gone, my friend entered into some explanations.

"The Parisian police," he said, "are exceedingly able in their way. They are persevering, ingenious, cunning, and thoroughly versed in the knowledge which their duties seem chiefly to demand. Thus, when G– detailed to us his mode of searching the premises at the Hotel D–, I felt entire confidence in his having made a satisfactory investigation – so far as his labors extended."

"So far as his labors extended?" said I.

"Yes," said Dupin. "The measures adopted were not only the best of their kind, but carried out to absolute perfection. Had the letter been deposited within the range of their search, these fellows would, beyond a question, have found it."

I merely laughed – but he seemed quite serious in all that he said.

"The measures, then," he continued, "were good in their kind, and well executed; their defect lay in their being inapplicable to the case, and to the man. A certain set of highly ingenious resources are, with the Prefect, a sort of Procrustean bed, to which he forcibly adapts his designs. But he perpetually errs by being too deep or too shallow, for the matter in hand; and many a schoolboy is a better reasoner than he. I knew one about eight years of age, whose success at guessing in the game of 'even and odd' attracted universal admiration. This game is simple, and is played with marbles. One player holds in his hand a number of these toys, and demands of another whether that number is even or odd. If the guess is right, the guesser wins one; if wrong, he loses one. The boy to whom I allude won all the marbles of the school. Of course he had some principle of guessing; and this lay in mere observation and admeasurement of the astuteness of his opponents. For example, an arrant simpleton is his opponent, and, holding up his closed hand, asks, 'are they even or odd?' Our schoolboy replies, 'odd,' and loses; but upon the second trial he wins, for he then says to himself, 'the simpleton had them even upon the first trial, and his amount of cunning is just sufficient to make him have them odd upon the second; I will therefore guess odd;' – he guesses odd, and wins. Now, with a simpleton a degree above the first, he would have reasoned thus: 'This fellow finds that in the first instance I guessed odd, and, in the second, he will propose to himself, upon the first impulse, a simple variation from even to odd, as did the first simpleton; but then a second thought will suggest that this is too simple a variation, and finally he will decide upon putting it even as before. I will therefore guess even;' – he guesses even, and wins. Now this mode of reasoning in the schoolboy, whom his fellows termed 'lucky,' – what, in its last analysis, is it?"

"It is merely," I said, "an identification of the reasoner's intellect with that of his opponent."

"It is," said Dupin; "and, upon inquiring of the boy by what means he effected the thorough identification in which his success consisted, I received answer as follows: 'When I wish to find out how wise, or how stupid, or how good, or how wicked is any one, or what are his thoughts at the moment, I fashion the expression of my face, as accurately as possible, in accordance with the expression of his, and then wait to see what thoughts or sentiments arise in my mind or heart, as if to match or correspond with the expression.' This response of the schoolboy lies at the bottom of all the spurious profundity which has been attributed to Rochefoucault, to La Bougive, to Machiavelli, and to Campanella." **(footnote 1)**

"And the identification," I said, "of the reasoner's intellect with that of his opponent, depends, if I understand you aright, upon the accuracy with which the opponent's intellect is admeasured."

"For its practical value it depends upon this," replied Dupin; "and the Prefect and his cohort fail so frequently, first, by default of this identification, and, secondly, by ill-admeasurement, or rather through non-admeasurement, of the intellect with which they are engaged. They consider only their own ideas of ingenuity; and, in searching for anything hidden, advert only to the modes in which they would have hidden it. They are right in this much – that their own ingenuity is a faithful representative of that of the mass; but when the cunning of the individual felon is diverse in character from their own, the felon foils them, of course. This always happens when it is above their own, and very usually when it is below. They have no variation of principle in their investigations; at best, when urged by some unusual emergency – by some extraordinary reward – they extend or exaggerate their old modes of practice, without touching their principles. What, for example, in this case of D–, has been done to vary the principle of action? What is all this boring, and probing, and sounding, and scrutinizing with the microscope and dividing the surface of the building into registered square inches – what is it all but an exaggeration of the application of the one principle or set of principles of search, which are based upon the one set of notions regarding human ingenuity, to which the Prefect, in the long routine of his duty, has been accustomed? Do you not see he has taken it for granted that all men proceed to conceal a letter – not exactly in a gimlet hole bored in a chair-leg – but, at least, in some out-of-the-way hole or corner suggested by the same tenor of thought which would urge a man to secrete a letter in a gimlet-hole bored in a chair-leg? And do you not see also, that such recherchés nooks for concealment are adapted only for ordinary occasions, and would be adopted only by ordinary intellects; for, in all cases of concealment, a disposal of the article concealed – a disposal of it in this recherché manner – is, in the very first instance, presumable and presumed; and thus its discovery depends, not at all upon the acumen, but altogether upon the mere care, patience, and determination of the seekers; and where the case is of importance – or, what amounts to the same thing in the policial eyes, when the reward is of magnitude – the qualities in question have never been known to fail. You will now understand what I meant in suggesting that, had the purloined letter been hidden anywhere within the limits of the Prefect's examination – in other words, had the principle of its concealment been comprehended within the principles of the Prefect – its discovery would have been a matter altogether beyond question. This functionary, however, has been thoroughly mystified; and the remote source of his defeat lies in the supposition that the Minister is a fool, because he has acquired renown as a poet. All fools are poets; this the Prefect feels; and he is merely guilty of a *non distributio medii* in thence inferring that all poets are fools."

"But is this really the poet?" I asked. "There are two brothers, I know; and both have attained reputation in letters. The Minister I believe has written learnedly on the Differential Calculus. He is a mathematician, and no poet."

"You are mistaken; I know him well; he is both. As poet and mathematician, he would reason well; as mere mathematician, he could not have reasoned at all, and thus would have been at the mercy of the Prefect."

"You surprise me," I said, "by these opinions, which have been contradicted by the voice of the world. You do not mean to set at naught the well-digested idea of centuries. The mathematical reason has long been regarded as the reason par excellence."

" *'Il y a à parièr*,' " replied Dupin, quoting from Chamfort, " *'que toute idée publique, toute convention reçue est une sottise, car elle a convenue au plus grand nombre.'* The mathematicians, I grant you, have done their best to promulgate the popular error to which you allude, and which is none the less an error for its promulgation as truth. With an art worthy a better cause, for example, they have insinuated the term 'analysis' into application to algebra. The French are the originators of this particular deception; but if a term is of any importance – if words derive any value from applicability – then 'analysis' conveys 'algebra' about as much as, in Latin, *'ambitus'* implies 'ambition,' *'religio'* 'religion,' or *'homines honesti,'* a set of honorablemen."

"You have a quarrel on hand, I see," said I, "with some of the algebraists of Paris; but proceed."

"I dispute the availability, and thus the value, of that reason which is cultivated in any especial form other than the abstractly logical. I dispute, in particular, the reason educed by mathematical study. The mathematics are the science of form and quantity; mathematical reasoning is merely logic applied to observation upon form and quantity. The great error lies in supposing that even the truths of what is called pure algebra are abstract or general truths. And this error is so egregious that I am confounded at the universality with which it has been received. Mathematical axioms are not axioms of general truth. What is true of relation – of form and quantity – is often grossly false in regard to morals, for example. In this latter science it is very usually untrue that the aggregated parts are equal to the whole. In chemistry also the axiom fails. In the consideration of motive it fails; for two motives, each of a given value, have not, necessarily, a value when united, equal to the sum of their values apart. There are numerous other mathematical truths which are only truths within the limits of relation. But the mathematician argues, from his finite truths, through habit, as if they were of an absolutely general applicability – as the world indeed imagines them to be. Bryant, in his very learned 'Mythology,' mentions an analogous source of error, when he says that 'although the Pagan fables are not believed, yet we forget ourselves continually, and make inferences from them as existing realities.' With the algebraists, however, who are Pagans themselves, the 'Pagan fables' are believed, and the inferences are made, not so much through lapse of memory, as through an unaccountable addling of the brains. In short, I never yet encountered the mere mathematician who could be trusted out of equal roots, or one who did not clandestinely hold it as a point of his faith that x^2+px was absolutely and unconditionally equal to q. Say to one of these gentlemen, by way of experiment, if you please, that you believe occasions may occur where x^2+px is not altogether equal to q, and, having made him understand what you mean, get out of his reach as speedily as convenient, for, beyond doubt, he will endeavor to knock you down.

"I mean to say," continued Dupin, while I merely laughed at his last observations, "that if the Minister had been no more than a mathematician, the Prefect would have been under no necessity of giving me this check. I know him, however, as both mathematician and poet, and my measures were adapted to his capacity, with reference to the circumstances by which he was surrounded. I knew him as a courtier, too, and as a bold intriguant. Such a man, I considered, could not fail to be aware of the ordinary policial modes of action. He could not have failed to anticipate – and events have proved that he did not fail to anticipate – the waylayings to which he was subjected. He must have foreseen, I reflected, the secret investigations of his premises. His frequent absences from home at night, which were hailed by the Prefect as certain aids to his success, I regarded only as ruses, to afford opportunity for thorough search to the police, and thus the sooner to impress them with the conviction to which G–, in fact, did finally arrive – the conviction that the letter was not upon the premises. I felt, also, that the whole train of thought, which I was at some pains in detailing to you just now, concerning the invariable principle of policial action in searches for articles concealed – I felt that this whole train of thought would necessarily pass through the mind of the Minister. It would imperatively lead him to despise all the ordinary nooks of concealment. He could not, I reflected, be so weak as not to see that the most intricate and remote recess of his hotel would be as open as his commonest closets to the eyes, to the probes, to the gimlets, and to the microscopes of the Prefect. I saw, in fine, that he would be driven, as a matter of course, to simplicity, if not deliberately induced to it as a matter of choice. You will remember, perhaps, how desperately the Prefect laughed when I suggested, upon our first interview, that it was just possible this mystery troubled him so much on account of its being so very self-evident."

"Yes," said I, "I remember his merriment well. I really thought he would have fallen into convulsions."

"The material world," continued Dupin, "abounds with very strict analogies to the immaterial; and thus some color of truth has been given to the rhetorical dogma, that metaphor, or simile, may be made to strengthen an argument, as well as to embellish a description. The principle of the vis inertiæ, for example, seems to be identical in physics and metaphysics. It is not more true in the former, that a large body is with more difficulty set in motion than a smaller one, and that its subsequent momentum is commensurate with this difficulty, than it is, in the latter, that intellects of the vaster capacity, while more forcible, more constant, and more eventful in their movements than those of inferior grade, are yet the less readily moved, and more embarrassed and full of hesitation in the first few steps of their progress. Again: have you ever noticed which of the street signs, over the shop-doors, are the most attractive of attention?"

"I have never given the matter a thought," I said.

"There is a game of puzzles," he resumed, "which is played upon a map. One party playing requires another to find a given word – the name of town, river, state or empire – any word, in short, upon the motley and perplexed surface of the chart. A novice in the game generally seeks to embarrass his opponents by giving them the most minutely lettered names; but the adept selects such words as stretch, in large characters, from one end of the chart to the other. These, like the over-largely lettered signs and placards of the street, escape observation by dint of being excessively obvious; and here the physical oversight is precisely analogous with the moral inapprehension by which the intellect suffers to pass unnoticed those considerations which are too obtrusively and too palpably self-evident. But this is a point, it appears, somewhat above or beneath the understanding of the Prefect. He never once thought it probable, or possible, that the Minister had deposited the letter immediately beneath the nose of the whole world, by way of best preventing any portion of that world from perceiving it.

"But the more I reflected upon the daring, dashing, and discriminating ingenuity of D–; upon the fact that the document must always have been at hand, if he intended to use it to good purpose; and upon the decisive evidence, obtained by the Prefect, that it was not hidden within the limits of that dignitary's ordinary search – the more satisfied I became that, to conceal this letter, the Minister had resorted to the comprehensive and sagacious expedient of not attempting to conceal it at all.

"Full of these ideas, I prepared myself with a pair of green spectacles, and called one fine morning, quite by accident, at the Ministerial hotel. I found D– at home, yawning, lounging, and dawdling, as usual, and pretending to be in the last extremity of ennui. He is, perhaps, the most really energetic human being now alive – but that is only when nobody sees him.

"To be even with him, I complained of my weak eyes, and lamented the necessity of the spectacles, under cover of which I cautiously and thoroughly surveyed the whole apartment, while seemingly intent only upon the conversation of my host.

"I paid especial attention to a large writing-table near which he sat, and upon which lay confusedly, some miscellaneous letters and other papers, with one or two musical instruments and a few books. Here, however, after a long and very deliberate scrutiny, I saw nothing to excite particular suspicion.

"At length my eyes, in going the circuit of the room, fell upon a trumpery filigree card-rack of pasteboard, that hung dangling by a dirty blue ribbon, from a little brass knob just beneath the middle of the mantel-piece. In this rack, which had three or four compartments, were five or six visiting cards and a solitary letter. This last was much soiled and crumpled. It was torn nearly in two, across the middle – as if a design, in the first instance, to tear it entirely up as worthless, had been altered, or stayed, in the second. It had a large black seal, bearing the D– cipher very conspicuously, and was addressed, in a diminutive female hand, to D–, the minister, himself. It was thrust carelessly, and even, as it seemed, contemptuously, into one of the uppermost divisions of the rack.

"No sooner had I glanced at this letter, than I concluded it to be that of which I was in search. To be sure, it was, to all appearance, radically different from the one of which the Prefect had read us so minute a description. Here the seal was large and black, with the D– cipher; there it was small and red, with the ducal arms of the S– family. Here, the address, to the Minister, diminutive and feminine; there the superscription, to a certain royal personage, was markedly bold and decided; the size alone formed a point of correspondence. But, then, the radicalness of these differences, which was excessive; the dirt; the soiled and torn condition of the paper, so inconsistent with the true methodical habits of D–, and so suggestive of a design to delude the beholder into an idea of the worthlessness of the document; these things, together with the hyper-obtrusive situation of this document, full in the view of every visitor, and thus exactly in accordance with the conclusions to which I had previously arrived; these things, I say, were strongly corroborative of suspicion, in one who came with the intention to suspect.

"I protracted my visit as long as possible, and, while I maintained a most animated discussion with the Minister upon a topic which I knew well had never failed to interest and excite him, I kept my attention really riveted upon the letter. In this examination, I committed to memory its external appearance and arrangement in the rack; and also fell, at length, upon a discovery which set at rest whatever trivial doubt I might have entertained. In scrutinizing the edges of the paper, I observed them to be more chafed than seemed necessary. They presented the broken appearance which is manifested when a stiff paper, having been once folded and pressed with a folder, is refolded in a reversed direction, in the same creases or edges which had formed the original fold. This discovery was sufficient. It was clear to me that the letter had been turned, as a glove, inside out, re-directed, and re-sealed. I bade the Minister good morning, and took my departure at once, leaving a gold snuff-box upon the table.

"The next morning I called for the snuff-box, when we resumed, quite eagerly, the conversation of the preceding day. While thus engaged, however, a loud report, as if of a pistol, was heard immediately beneath the windows of the hotel, and was succeeded by a series of fearful screams, and the shoutings of a terrified mob. D– rushed to a casement, threw it open, and looked out. In the meantime, I stepped to the card-rack, took the letter, put it in my pocket, and replaced it by a facsimile, (so far as regards externals,) which I had carefully prepared at my lodgings – imitating the D– cipher, very readily, by means of a seal formed of bread.

"The disturbance in the street had been occasioned by the frantic behavior of a man with a musket. He had fired it among a crowd of women and children. It proved, however, to have been without ball, and the fellow was suffered to go his way as a lunatic or a drunkard. When he had gone, D– came from the window, whither I had followed him immediately upon securing the object in view. Soon afterwards I bade him farewell. The pretended lunatic was a man in my own pay."

"But what purpose had you," I asked, "in replacing the letter by a facsimile? Would it not have been better, at the first visit, to have seized it openly, and departed?"

"D–," replied Dupin, "is a desperate man, and a man of nerve. His hotel, too, is not without attendants devoted to his interests. Had I made the wild attempt you suggest, I might never have left the Ministerial presence alive. The good people of Paris might have heard of me no more. But I had an object apart from these considerations. You know my political prepossessions. In this matter, I act as a partisan of the lady concerned. For eighteen months the Minister has had her in his power. She has now him in hers – since, being unaware that the letter is not in his possession, he will proceed with his exactions as if it was. Thus will he inevitably commit himself, at once, to his political destruction. His downfall, too, will not be more precipitate than awkward. It is all very well to talk about the facilis descensus Averni; but in all kinds of climbing, as Catalani said of singing, it is far more easy to get up than to come down. In the present instance I have no sympathy – at least no pity – for him who descends. He is that monstrum horrendum, an unprincipled man of genius. I confess, however, that I should like very well to know the precise character of his thoughts, when, being defied by her whom the Prefect terms 'a certain personage' he is reduced to opening the letter which I left for him in the card-rack."

"How? Did you put anything particular in it?"

"Why – it did not seem altogether right to leave the interior blank – that would have been insulting. D–, at Vienna once, did me an evil turn, which I told him, quite good-humoredly, that I should remember. So, as I knew he would feel some curiosity in regard to the identity of the person who had outwitted him, I thought it a pity not to give him a clue. He is well acquainted with my MS., and I just copied into the middle of the blank sheet the words –

" '– Un dessein si funeste, S'il n'est digne d'Atrée, est digne de Thyeste. They are to be found in Crebillon's 'Atrée.' "

Footnote 1. In *Collected Works of Edgar Allan Poe*, ed. T.O. Mabbott (Harvard University Press, 1978), the scholar Mabbott notes that 'La Bougive' is 'undoubtedly a printer's error', and should read 'La Bruyère' (philosopher, 1645–96). He also states that the spelling of Rochefoucauld (writer, 1613–80) as 'Rochefoucault' is consistent with the sources Poe would have used.

The Whipping Boy

Conor Powers-Smith

USUALLY TYLER allowed himself twenty or thirty pages of reading before considering the day truly begun, but he'd managed barely three when Marta appeared in the library doorway and said, in the ringing voice she used in the house's larger spaces, "Someone at the door for you."

"Okay," he said. "Coming." He'd never been able to make his voice carry the way Marta could; it was either speak normally, or shout. He could almost see his words fade and vanish somewhere in the forty-odd feet between Marta and himself.

"Sandra Kay?" she said. "From Proxy?"

"I said I'm coming." But he wasn't. He was sitting motionless in his favorite armchair, not the one nearest the tall window in the south wall, nor the one nearest the fireplace in the east wall, but the only one close enough to both to receive their distinct variations of light and heat simultaneously. It was too far into spring to justify a fire, and Marta hadn't bothered to open the heavy velvet drapes, so it must've been no more than habit that had drawn him to the chair that day; which meant habit must be just as powerful in its own realm as were light and heat in theirs.

"Sandra Kay?" said Marta again. "From Proxy?"

Tyler marked his place and put the book aside, rose and started across the room. Marta turned to leave, and he said, or shouted, "Marta." She stopped, obviously against her inclination. When he was close enough to speak normally, he asked, "Where is everybody today?" His mother and Uncle Rob and Aunt Penny had been missing at breakfast.

"They're out." Marta was watching him with a quizzical, apprehensive expression, as if wondering not what he was thinking was going to do, but who he even was. She'd been the family's only full-time servant, cook and housekeeper and factotum all, since before he was born, and he'd seen that look of mingled curiosity and caution only for a brief period a few years before, after a drunken seventeen-year-old version of him had made a pass at her while she'd been spending her day off sunbathing by the pool.

"*Where* are they out?"

"I don't know," she said defensively. He must be making her nervous with his own anxiety. So it was his fault, which shouldn't have come as a surprise.

He left Marta there, and walked alone through the east wing, into the main part of the house. As soon as he entered the front hall, he was aware of being the subject of scrutiny. She was polite about it – she smiled while she scrutinized – but that didn't make it any more comfortable. She didn't look away, though there was plenty in the front hall to pretend interest in if she'd wanted to: two small paintings of ships at sea, and one large one, a portrait of his grandmother; several small abstract sculptures his mother had made, which Tyler had always assumed were very good; any number of little knickknacks on bookshelves and end tables, and of course the furniture itself was old and solid and highly polished. But Tyler had to do all the glancing-away necessary to prevent continuous eye contact.

"Mr. Stutz?" she said. "How are you? Sandra Kay, from Proxy." She looked about fifty, with straight, bottle-blonde hair framing a tan, once-pretty, still-pleasant face. "Thanks for meeting me. I hope I wasn't too pushy on the phone, but we really do need a decision today." Every time she stopped speaking, even for an instant, her wide, practiced smile reappeared, like water calming after a transient series of ripples. "I'm sure your lawyers told you the same thing?"

"They've been saying that since – They've been saying that the whole time. 'This is the last chance to do this or that. File this, file that. Decide.' "

She didn't point out what he already knew, that the delays caused by his wavering had cost his family quite a bit in added legal fees, court costs, and of course the exorbitant storage rates charged by her own company. She only smiled, and said, "I thought we could talk out in the garden. I saw it driving up. It looks beautiful. Have you walked around out there?"

"What do you mean? I've lived here my whole life."

"Right. I meant *do* you? Often?"

"Not really. But sure, whatever."

He followed her out through the portico, down the front steps, past a dark-blue sedan that must've been hers parked in the circular driveway, and across the gently sloping lawn toward the garden. It was what people called a beautiful day, the sky a shining blue, the few small clouds so brightly and purely white they seemed to be lit from within, the sun hanging fixed and patient, as if the passage of time were an optional feature of the scene, to be switched on or off at will. There was no breeze, and the sunlight was warm enough to be noticeable, but not so warm that the shade was markedly cooler. Birds chirped.

Sandra waited until they'd passed through the opening in the long row of red-speckled rose bushes which marked the perimeter of the garden, then said, "As soon as we have your go-ahead we can make the arrangements. The state's usually very quick when we get to this stage, so we can probably do the execution in less than a week."

"I think I've decided not to do it." Tyler sounded anything but decisive to himself.

"I see." Sandra wasn't looking at him, but at the beds of tulips, pink and white and yellow, lining both sides of the wide stone path. "These are gorgeous."

"Thanks," Tyler said, though he had nothing to do with the garden. His mother was inordinately proud of it, though all she did was tell the landscaping company what to put where.

"I guess you've talked to your lawyers?" said Sandra; then, when he didn't respond: "They'd know better than me, but I've seen a few of these. Driving under the influence, vehicular manslaughter. It'll probably work out to, what... seven years? Eight? More with leaving the scene."

"I didn't run. I'm the one who called nine-one-one."

"Oh. Well, more if there were priors." This he could hardly object to, since his license had been suspended twice before, once for a negligent operation pled down from DUI, once for a DUI they'd refused to budge on.

"Do you mind if I ask why?" she said. "Only, I hope it's not for financial reasons."

"It's not the money."

"Good, because you wouldn't be saving much at this point. Harvesting and storing your genetic material accounts for a significant portion of the final price, and the neural mapping's another big chunk."

"You'd think the thing itself would be the big-ticket item."

"The thing?"

"The thing. The clone."

"The *duplicate*." The correction was polite, but firm. "A clone's no more than an artificial twin. A duplicate's an exact copy: genetically indistinguishable, yes, but mentally and emotionally so too, since he or she shares the original's exact neural structure: personality, memories, everything. And he or she is a *person*, Mr. Stutz. You can't buy or sell a person."

"But you can execute them." The bitterness in his voice surprised him. "For something they didn't do."

"The question of guilt's a tricky one," she said, as professionally amiable as ever. "He or she – we'll just say *he*, for convenience – is identical to the original – the one who committed the act in question – the guilty one – in every way. Sort of like original sin. He *is* the original, and the original *is* him. In that light, how can one be guilty, and the other innocent?"

"Because one did it, and one didn't. One didn't even exist when it was done."

"One committed the act. But both are the person capable of committing it, and both are the person who did commit it. Both experienced everything leading up to it, and everything after it, and the act itself. Retroactively in one case, but no less intensely for that."

"If they're the same person, how can one have rights and the other not?"

"How do you mean? A duplicate has all the rights of any other individual."

"Rights? What, the right to be executed without trial?"

The tulips had given way to high, thick hydrangea bushes, their clusters of flowers hovering like pink and purple galaxies suspended in deep-green space. Sandra glanced back and forth as she said, "True, these cases don't go to trial. But that's incidental. The duplicate receives the same due process anyone else would, in the form of the plea agreement that precludes the trial."

"But he has no say in that. That's all done before he even exists. I mean that's what we're talking about, right?"

"The preliminaries are in place before we create the duplicate. But of course nothing's final until all the papers are signed. The execution can't go forward until we have the duplicate's consent."

"*Consent?*" He didn't sound bitter now, but incredulous, and close to despairing; he hadn't realized how much he'd been hoping to be convinced until Sandra's glib bombshell mooted the question, or seemed to. "Then why are we even talking about this? You can't make someone consent to his own execution."

"It's not a matter of *making* him do anything. I promise you, Mr. Stutz, there are ways."

They passed beneath the ivy-covered trellis archway leading into the inner garden. Here the path was bordered by high, thick bushes flowering yellow and orange, purple and blue. "You can't," Tyler said. "Even if you could, it's... slimy. Sending someone else to die so I can get out of jail?"

"Why slimy? Everyone's happy with the arrangement. The state gets quick closure without clogging up the courts or prisons. The DA gets a no-hassle conviction for the back of his baseball card. And the victim's family gets justice, and a lot more of it than they could otherwise hope for. The cliché's true, but it misses the point: 'It won't bring back their little girl.' But –"

"She wasn't a little girl. She was twenty-six, and her blood-alcohol was higher than mine, and she was in the middle of the street at three o'clock in the morning."

"Okay. Well, 'It won't bring back their daughter, sister, granddaughter. Mother?' " She didn't turn, so she couldn't have seen his short, tight nod, but she went on as if she had: "It won't bring her back, but that's not the point. Instead of picturing you in prison with your cable TV and all that, they get to watch you *die*. That may not be civilized, but it *is* satisfying. You can give them that."

They'd reached the heart of the garden, a wide circle of flowerbeds surrounding a three-tiered stone fountain. Water rose in a short, lazy spout from the fountain's highest level, and filled and flowed across the bowl below, spilling over the lip in what looked at first like a solid skirt, until the glinting sunlight picked it apart into separate slender threads. The lowest bowl was wide, and deep, and, except for the small furors where it received the water from above, still.

She followed the path, and he followed her, to the rim of the fountain. "Something else?" she asked.

"Yeah. I just can't do that to myself. Not myself, but someone exactly like me. It's just too easy to picture it happening to *me*, not a clone of me, *me*."

"You have to remember, it's not going to be pleasant either way. Eight years in prison is... about eighty anywhere else. And that's if you make it eight years."

"Why would anyone want to... hurt me in there?"

"I didn't mean that. I'm thinking of a former client, about your age, maybe a little younger. Got into a fight with his buddy one night, not long after last call. The kind of thing where you pick up a few picturesque bruises, a little shot of testosterone as a nightcap, and everybody's friends again in the morning. Or it would've been, if it hadn't spilled out onto the hotel balcony. This was spring break in Daytona. Nobody wanted it to happen, but nobody got to vote. In the end, one of the buddies was standing on the balcony, wondering what'd just happened, and the other was lying on the concrete three stories down with a broken back, paralyzed for life.

"The perpetrator – Buddy Number One – was all set to have a duplicate created. We weren't quite at this stage, but we were pretty far along in the process. But he backed out. Maybe he told himself he could beat it at trial, or that Buddy Number Two would suddenly decide to forgive and forget. I don't think the reality of what he was doing sank in until after the trial, at the sentencing. Seven years. He was crying when they took him away. Sobbing, I guess. He cried like he was innocent, which is the only way anyone ever does, or can. He cried like he hadn't had months to see it coming, hadn't had the chance to stop it with nothing more than a few hundred thousand dollars and his signature on a dotted line."

Her obvious scorn had a strange effect. Tyler's harried mind accepted the comfort of deriding one who was absent, though it was obvious that whatever Sandra thought or said about this particular rich young fool could be applied to the set in general, which certainly included Tyler himself. But even this implicit disdain fit snugly into a preexisting slot in his mind. He was used to viewing himself with disdain, and wasn't averse, under the proper circumstances, to having this opinion confirmed by others.

"It was maybe a month before he started calling," Sandra said. "Second thoughts. It was explained – many and many a time, by many and many a polite but firm representative of Proxy Solutions, LLC – that the time for second thoughts had come and gone. As had our involvement in his case. I talked to him once myself. For maybe the darkest half-hour of my life. I won't go into it – it'd feel like a violation, to repeat some of the things he told me – but I'll say this: some people do just fine in prison. And some people don't.

"Finally, maybe three months after the trial, the calls stopped. Less than a week later, he did it. He was working in the prison laundry, and he threw himself into one of the big industrial steam presses. You'd think that would kill a person instantly. But it took him three days to die. Third-degree burns all over his body, punctured lung, crushed spleen, kidneys, liver. Broken everything. Everything. There aren't enough painkillers on the planet. But finally he died, and everybody was very relieved."

She stared into the fountain for a few seconds, then said, "The really sad part is that it was all so unnecessary. I wish I'd had more experience at the time. I know I could've convinced him. Knowing what I know now, I would've approached it differently."

She fell silent again, staring into the fountain. Tyler was aware that she was ready to deliver her final pitch, aware, also, that she was waiting for a word of consent from him, a signal that he was willing to listen. All he said was, "Oh?" But that was enough.

"I would've addressed his real reason for backing out. He might've told himself he could beat it at trial, or that he couldn't stand to see his duplicate suffer, but those were just rationalizations. Deep down, *he* wanted to be the one to suffer. He didn't like himself much, Mr. Stutz. Hated himself, really. Whether he was justified in that opinion is... not my place to say. And it doesn't matter. I could've used that.

"A lot of people don't particularly care for themselves. But very few act on those feelings in a final way. An industrial steam press kind of way. Most are more circumspect. They find all sorts of ways to punish themselves. They cut themselves with razor blades or pull out their own hair, they go from one abusive relationship to the next, they drink or take drugs to excess, and then maybe up the stakes by getting behind the wheel. Gestures, mainly, cries for help, whatever you want to call it. No real harm meant, to themselves or anyone else. But of course accidents happen.

"Well, through the miracle of modern technology, we now have a method of self-destruction that puts all those nasty habits to shame. There are twelve seats in the execution chamber's observation gallery, and did you know, Mr. Stutz, that in these cases, a seat is reserved for the actual perpetrator? In fact the state usually *requires* him to be present as a condition of the plea agreement. They think it helps deter future incidents, but we know better, don't we, Mr. Stutz? Can you imagine a more satisfying act of self-destruction than watching your own execution?

"Apropos of all this, I've always thought the gurney they use for lethal injections looks very much like a cross. Like a crucifix, once the condemned is strapped in. Legs extended, arms outstretched. I definitely would've mentioned that to Buddy Number One."

"It's not standing up though, right?" he heard himself ask. "It's probably flat, like a table."

"The gurney? It depends on the state. In some, you're right, it's horizontal, like a table. In some it stands, and, really, I defy you not to see it as a cross. Then a crucifix. In this state... it stands."

She turned abruptly from the fountain, and said, "Shall we head back?"

She didn't bother to reiterate her arguments, or ask if he'd changed his mind. The whole way back through the garden, all she said was, "I have the papers in my car." All he gave in answer was a single grunted syllable, inarticulate and low but unequivocally affirmative.

He signed the papers standing in the driveway beside her car, not bothering to read them first. He squinted slightly in the sunlight, listened to the chirping of birds, and the low but rising rumble of engines.

When the Cadillac appeared from around a bend in the driveway, Sandra was already walking briskly toward it, her hands empty, the papers Tyler had just signed tucked safely away somewhere, beyond the possibility of reconsideration. Through the glare coming off the car's windshield, Tyler saw Uncle Rob behind the wheel, his mother in the front passenger seat, two figures in the back, one certainly Aunt Penny, the other probably one of his mother's friends they'd met somewhere and brought back for dinner.

The Cadillac had barely come to rest before Sandra called, in a peevish tone Tyler wouldn't have thought her capable of, "That was pretty goddamn close." He didn't know what she meant; the Cadillac hadn't come anywhere near hitting her, and Uncle Rob had parked it a good fifteen feet from her car.

He heard his mother's voice through the open passenger-side window, but couldn't make out the words. Sandra answered, "I said *about* eleven. I also said I'd *text* you when it was safe to come back."

One after another, the Cadillac's doors swung open, his mother emerging first. This time he caught what she said, which was: "But you did get it?"

"Not two minutes ago," Sandra said. "You could've ruined the whole thing. I *said* I'd text."

Tyler started toward them, but stopped short as his mother drifted a few feet from the Cadillac, far enough to reveal the figure standing behind her, who was staring at Tyler with hard disdain. Tyler stared back at himself, into eyes his own had met countless times in the mirror, now lent a hideous strangeness by their owner's impossible, undeniable independence.

His first thought was, *They let it wear my pants.* That was unmistakably his favorite pair of jeans. The shirt was his, too, a plain black polo disturbingly similar to the dark-blue one he currently wore. And that was one of his better pairs of sneakers; under those, he realized, the thing must be wearing his socks, and, under the jeans, his boxer shorts. Melodramatic as it might have been, he decided to have the clothes burned once they'd taken the thing away and dressed it in a prison jumpsuit, or whatever it would wear until the execution.

He'd just begun to wonder how that would work – whether Sandra would take the thing away with her, or Uncle Rob, or what – when a police cruiser rose slowly into view, slunk past the Cadillac, and came to rest on the far side of the drive, near Sandra's car. That answered that, though he still didn't know why they'd brought the thing back to the house at all. Was this part of Sandra's vague, vaunted method of securing consent? Had his mother and Uncle Rob and Aunt Penny spent all day pleading with the thing to lay down its life for the real Tyler? Was he now expected to do the same?

Apparently, thankfully, not. Among Sandra's admonitions was, "Why did you have to bring him back now? There's no reason for them to see each other. Don't you understand what a shock that is?"

"I'm not shocked," Tyler heard his other self say. Though they were only ten feet apart, he could barely understand the thing's words, so soft and weak was its voice.

"I didn't mean you," Sandra said. She hadn't looked back at Tyler since joining the group, and didn't now, only swept an arm out to indicate him.

"Then why don't you take it away?" the other him answered. Tyler thought he might have misheard, due to the softness of the thing's voice. The words made no sense in themselves.

"You wanted to come back," Sandra said. "You wanted to rub his face in it, just for your –"

"Enough, enough," the other Tyler interrupted. "Enough of this whole masquerade ball. You let it sleep in my bed, dress itself up in my clothes. You can keep those, by the way, or give them to charity, or burn them. You make the poor stupid thing think it's me, and then you –"

"We don't *make* him think anything. We *let* him."

"*Okay.* Congratulations. You want to lecture me on the etiquette of this, maybe you should –"

"We only do what's necessary to secure consent. We're not cruel. Seeing him executed isn't enough? You had to rub it in his face, too? In your own face?" Sandra turned, and started toward her car, leaving the other Tyler to glare silently at her back. She nodded at the two uniformed cops who were by now standing beside the cruiser, the back passenger-side door of which gaped ominously open.

Despite an obvious effort, Sandra's eyes met Tyler's for an instant. He couldn't begin to decipher her expression. Then she was past. A moment later, a door slapped shut, an engine came to life, and a car began its slow escape.

Tyler didn't turn to watch Sandra leave, nor to look at the cops, not even as they grasped his arms and drew him, slowly, patiently, irresistibly, toward the cruiser. He watched Uncle Rob and Aunt Penny and his mother climb the front steps, cross the portico, and disappear into the house, all without looking at him. When they were gone, he watched himself, the original Tyler, the one who'd actually committed the crimes for which he'd just signed his life away. That Tyler stood staring back with disdain and satisfaction. And something else: anticipation.

The Invisible Ray

Arthur B. Reeve

"I WON'T DENY that I had some expectations from the old man myself."

Kennedy's client was speaking in a low, full chested, vibrating voice, with some emotion, so low that I had entered the room without being aware that any one was there until it was too late to retreat.

"As his physician for over twelve years," the man pursued, "I certainly had been led to hope to be remembered in his will. But, Professor Kennedy, I can't put it too strongly when I say that there is no selfish motive in my coming to you about the case. There is something wrong – depend on that."

Craig had glanced up at me and, as I hesitated, I could see in an instant that the speaker was a practitioner of a type that is rapidly passing away, the old-fashioned family doctor.

"Dr. Burnham, I should like to have you know Mr. Jameson," introduced Craig. "You can talk as freely before him as you have to me alone. We always work together."

I shook hands with the visitor.

"The doctor has succeeded in interesting me greatly in a case which has some unique features," Kennedy explained. "It has to do with Stephen Haswell, the eccentric old millionaire of Brooklyn. Have you ever heard of him?"

"Yes, indeed," I replied, recalling an occasional article which had appeared in the newspapers regarding a dusty and dirty old house in that part of the Heights in Brooklyn whence all that is fashionable had not yet taken flight, a house of mystery, yet not more mysterious than its owner in his secretive comings and goings in the affairs of men of a generation beyond his time. Further than the facts that he was reputed to be very wealthy and led, in the heart of a great city, what was as nearly like the life of a hermit as possible, I knew little or nothing. "What has he been doing now?" I asked.

"About a week ago," repeated the doctor, in answer to a nod of encouragement from Kennedy, "I was summoned in the middle of the night to attend Mr. Haswell, who, as I have been telling Professor Kennedy, had been a patient of mine for over twelve years. He had been suddenly stricken with total blindness. Since then he appears to be failing fast, that is, he appeared so the last time I saw him, a few days ago, after I had been superseded by a younger man. It is a curious case and I have thought about it a great deal. But I didn't like to speak to the authorities; there wasn't enough to warrant that, and I should have been laughed out of court for my pains. The more I have thought about it, however, the more I have felt it my duty to say something to somebody, and so, having heard of Professor Kennedy, I decided to consult him. The fact of the matter is, I very much fear that there are circumstances which will bear sharp looking into, perhaps a scheme to get control of the old man's fortune."

The doctor paused, and Craig inclined his head, as much as to signify his appreciation of the delicate position in which Burnham stood in the case. Before the doctor could proceed further, Kennedy handed me a letter which had been lying before him on the table. It had evidently been torn into small pieces and then carefully pasted together.

The superscription gave a small town in Ohio and a date about a fortnight previous.

> *Dear Father* [it read]: *I hope you will pardon me for writing, but I cannot let the occasion of your seventy-fifth birthday pass without a word of affection and congratulation. I am alive and well. Time has dealt leniently with me in that respect, if not in money matters. I do not say this in the hope of reconciling you to me. I know that is impossible after all these cruel years. But I do wish that I could see you again. Remember, I am your only child and even if you still think I have been a foolish one, please let me come to see you once before it is too late. We are constantly travelling from place to place, but shall be here for a few days.*
> *Your loving daughter,*
> *GRACE HASWELL MARTIN.*

"Some fourteen or fifteen years ago," explained the doctor as I looked up from reading the note, "Mr. Haswell's only daughter eloped with an artist named Martin. He had been engaged to paint a portrait of the late Mrs. Haswell from a photograph. It was the first time that Grace Haswell had ever been able to find expression for the artistic yearning which had always been repressed by the cold, practical sense of her father. She remembered her mother perfectly since the sad bereavement of her girlhood and naturally she watched and helped the artist eagerly. The result was a portrait which might well have been painted from the subject herself rather than from a cold photograph.

"Haswell saw the growing intimacy of his daughter and the artist. His bent of mind was solely toward money and material things, and he at once conceived a bitter and unreasoning hatred for Martin, who, he believed, had 'schemed' to capture his daughter and an easy living. Art was as foreign to his nature as possible. Nevertheless they went ahead and married, and, well, it resulted in the old man disinheriting the girl. The young couple disappeared bravely to make their way by their chosen profession and, as far as I know, have never been heard from since until now. Haswell made a new will, and I have always understood that practically all of his fortune is to be devoted to founding the technology department in a projected university of Brooklyn."

"You have never seen this Mrs. Martin or her husband?" asked Kennedy.

"No, never. But in some way she must have learned that I had some influence with her father, for she wrote to me not long ago, enclosing a note for him and asking me to intercede for her. I did so. I took the letter to him as diplomatically as I could. The old man flew into a towering rage, refused even to look at the letter, tore it up into bits, and ordered me never to mention the subject to him again. That is her note, which I saved. However, it is the sequel about which I wish your help."

The physician folded up the patched letter carefully before he continued. "Mr. Haswell, as you perhaps know, has for many years been a prominent figure in various curious speculations, or rather in loaning money to many curious speculators. It is not necessary to go into the different schemes which he has helped to finance. Even though most of them have been unknown to the public they have certainly given him such a reputation that he is much sought after by inventors.

"Not long ago Haswell became interested in the work of an obscure chemist over in Brooklyn, Morgan Prescott. Prescott claims, as I understand, to be able to transmute copper into gold. Whatever you think of it offhand, you should visit his laboratory yourselves, gentlemen.

I am told it is wonderful, though I have never seen it and can't explain it. I have met Prescott several times while he was trying to persuade Mr. Haswell to back him in his scheme, but he was never disposed to talk to me, for I had no money to invest. So far as I know about it the thing sounds scientific and plausible enough. I leave you to judge of that. It is only an incident in my story and I will pass over it quickly. Prescott, then, believes that the elements are merely progressive variations of an original substance or base called 'protyle,' from which everything is derived. But this fellow Prescott goes much further than any of the former theorists. He does not stop with matter. He believes that he has the secret of life also, that he can make the transition from the inorganic to the organic, from inert matter to living protoplasm, and thence from living protoplasm to mind and what we call soul, whatever that may be."

"And here is where the weird and uncanny part of it comes in," commented Craig, turning from the doctor to me to call my attention particularly to what was about to follow.

"Having arrived at the point where he asserts that he can create and destroy matter, life, and mind," continued the doctor, as if himself fascinated by the idea," Prescott very naturally does not have to go far before he also claims a control over telepathy and even a communication with the dead. He even calls the messages which he receives by a word which he has coined himself, 'telepagrams.' Thus he says he has unified the physical, the physiological, and the psychical – a system of absolute scientific monism."

The doctor paused again, then resumed. "One afternoon, about a week ago, apparently, as far as I am able to piece together the story, Prescott was demonstrating his marvellous discovery of the unity of nature. Suddenly he faced Mr. Haswell.

" 'Shall I tell you a fact, sir, about yourself?' he asked quickly. 'The truth as I see it by means of my wonderful invention? If it is the truth, will you believe in me? Will you put money into my invention? Will you share in becoming fabulously rich?'

"Haswell made some noncommittal answer. But Prescott seemed to look into the machine through a very thick plate-glass window, with Haswell placed directly before it. He gave a cry. 'Mr. Haswell,' he exclaimed, 'I regret to tell you what I see. You have disinherited your daughter; she has passed out of your life and at the present moment you do not know where she is.'

" 'That's true,' replied the old man bitterly, 'and more than that I don't care. Is that all you see? That's nothing new.'

" 'No, unfortunately, that is not all I see. Can you bear something further? I think you ought to know it. I have here a most mysterious telepagram.'

" 'Yes. What is it? Is she dead?'

" 'No, it is not about her. It is about yourself. Tonight at midnight or perhaps a little later,' repeated Prescott solemnly, 'you will lose your sight as a punishment for your action.'

" 'Pouf!' exclaimed the old man in a dudgeon, 'if that is all your invention can tell me, goodbye. You told me you were able to make gold. Instead, you make foolish prophecies. I'll put no money into such tomfoolery. I'm a practical man,' and with that he stamped out of the laboratory.

"Well, that night, about one o'clock, in the silence of the lonely old house, the aged caretaker, Jane, whom he had hired after he banished his daughter from his life, heard a wild shout of 'Help! Help!' Haswell, alone in his room on the second floor, was groping about in the dark.

" 'Jane,' he ordered, 'a light – a light.'

" 'I have lighted the gas, Mr. Haswell,' she cried.

"A groan followed. He had himself found a match, had struck it, had even burnt his fingers with it, yet he saw nothing.

"The blow had fallen. At almost the very hour which Prescott, by means of his weird telepagram had predicted, old Haswell was stricken.

I'm blind,' he gasped. 'Send for Dr. Burnham.'

"I went to him immediately when the maid roused me, but there was nothing I could do except prescribe perfect rest for his eyes and keeping in a dark room in the hope that his sight might be restored as suddenly and miraculously as it had been taken away.

"The next morning, with his own hand, trembling and scrawling in his blindness, he wrote the following on a piece of paper:

"*Mrs. GRACE MARTIN.*
Information wanted about the present whereabouts of Mrs. Grace Martin, formerly Grace Haswell of Brooklyn.
STEPHEN HASWELL, Pierrepont St., Brooklyn.

"This advertisement he caused to be placed in all the New York papers and to be wired to the leading Western papers. Haswell himself was a changed man after his experience. He spoke bitterly of Prescott, yet his attitude toward his daughter was completely reversed. Whether he admitted to himself a belief in the prediction of the inventor, I do not know. Certainly he scouted such an idea in telling me about it.

"A day or two after the advertisements appeared a telegram came to the old man from a little town in Indiana. It read simply: 'Dear Father: Am starting for Brooklyn today. Grace.'

"The upshot was that Grace Haswell, or rather Grace Martin, appeared the next day, forgave and was forgiven with much weeping, although the old man still refused resolutely to be reconciled with and receive her husband. Mrs. Martin started in to clean up the old house. A vacuum cleaner sucked a ton or two of dust from it. Everything was changed. Jane grumbled a great deal, but there was no doubt a great improvement. Meals were served regularly. The old man was taken care of as never before. Nothing was too good for him. Everywhere the touch of a woman was evident in the house. The change was complete. It even extended to me. Some friend had told her of an eye and ear specialist, a Dr. Scott, who was engaged. Since then, I understand, a new will has been made, much to the chagrin of the trustees of the projected school. Of course I am cut out of the new will, and that with the knowledge at least of the woman who once appealed to me, but it does not influence me in coming to you."

"But what has happened since to arouse suspicion?" asked Kennedy, watching the doctor furtively.

"Why, the fact is that, in spite of all this added care, the old man is failing more rapidly than ever. He never goes out except attended and not much even then. The other day I happened to meet Jane on the street. The faithful old soul poured forth a long story about his growing dependence on others and ended by mentioning a curious red discoloration that seems to have broken out over his face and hands. More from the way she said it than from what she said I gained the impression that something was going on which should be looked into.

"Then you perhaps think that Prescott and Mrs. Martin are in some way connected in this case?" I hazarded.

I had scarcely framed the question before he replied in an emphatic negative. "On the contrary, it seems to me that if they know each other at all it is with hostility. With the exception of the first stroke of blindness" here he lowered his voice earnestly "practically every misfortune that has overtaken Mr. Haswell has been since the advent of this new Dr. Scott. Mind, I do not wish even to breathe that Mrs. Martin has done anything except what a daughter should do. I think she has shown herself a model of forgiveness and devotion. Nevertheless the turn of events under the new treatment has been so strange that almost it makes one believe that there might be something occult about it – or wrong with the new doctor."

"Would it be possible, do you think, for us to see Mr. Haswell?" asked Kennedy, when Dr. Burnham had come to a full stop after pouring forth his suspicions. "I should like to see this Dr. Scott. But first I should like to get into the old house without exciting hostility."

The doctor was thoughtful. "You'll have to arrange that yourself," he answered. "Can't you think up a scheme? For instance, go to him with a proposal like the old schemes he used to finance. He is very much interested in electrical inventions. He made his money by speculation in telegraphs and telephones in the early days when they were more or less dreams. I should think a wireless system of television might at least interest him and furnish an excuse for getting in, although I am told his daughter discourages all tangible investment in the schemes that used to interest his active mind."

"An excellent idea," exclaimed Kennedy. "It is worth trying anyway. It is still early. Suppose we ride over to Brooklyn with you. You can direct us to the house and we'll try to see him."

It was still light when we mounted the high steps of the house of mystery across the bridge. Mrs. Martin, who met us in the parlour, proved to be a stunning looking woman with brown hair and beautiful dark eyes. As far as we could see the old house plainly showed the change. The furniture and ornaments were of a period long past, but everything was scrupulously neat. Hanging over the old marble mantel was a painting which quite evidently was that of the long since deceased Mrs. Haswell, the mother of Grace. In spite of the hideous style of dress of the period after the war, she had evidently been a very beautiful woman with large masses of light chestnut hair and blue eyes which the painter had succeeded in catching with almost life-likeness for a portrait.

It took only a few minutes for Kennedy, in his most engaging and plausible manner, to state the hypothetical reason of our call. Though it was perfectly self-evident from the start that Mrs. Martin would throw cold water on anything requiring an outlay of money Craig accomplished his full purpose of securing an interview with Mr. Haswell. The invalid lay propped up in bed, and as we entered he heard us and turned his sightless eyes in our direction almost as if he saw.

Kennedy had hardly begun to repeat and elaborate the story which he had already told regarding his mythical friend who had at last a commercial wireless 'televue,' as he called it on the spur of the moment, when Jane, the aged caretaker, announced Dr. Scott. The new doctor was a youthfully dressed man, clean-shaven, but with an undefinable air of being much older than his smooth face led one to suppose. As he had a large practice, he said, he would beg our pardon for interrupting but would not take long.

It needed no great powers of observation to see that the old man placed great reliance on his new doctor and that the visit partook of a social as well as a professional nature. Although they talked low we could catch now and then a word or phrase. Dr. Scott bent down and examined the eyes of his patient casually. It was difficult to believe that they saw nothing, so bright was the blue of the iris.

"Perfect rest for the present," the doctor directed, talking more to Mrs. Martin than to the old man. "Perfect rest, and then when his health is good, we shall see what can be done with that cataract."

He was about to leave, when the old man reached up and restrained him, taking hold of the doctor's wrist tightly, as if to pull him nearer in order to whisper to him without being overheard. Kennedy was sitting in a chair near the head of the bed, some feet away, as the doctor leaned down. Haswell, still holding his wrist, pulled him closer. I could not hear what was said, though somehow I had an impression that they were talking about Prescott, for it would not have been at all strange if the old man had been greatly impressed by the alchemist.

Kennedy, I noticed, had pulled an old envelope from his pocket and was apparently engaged in jotting down some notes, glancing now and then from his writing to the doctor and then to Mr. Haswell.

The doctor stood erect in a few moments and rubbed his wrist thoughtfully with the other hand, as if it hurt. At the same time he smiled on Mrs. Martin. "Your father has a good deal of strength yet, Mrs. Martin," he remarked. "He has a wonderful constitution. I feel sure that we can pull him out of this and that he has many, many years to live."

Mr. Haswell, who caught the words eagerly, brightened visibly, and the doctor passed out. Kennedy resumed his description of the supposed wireless picture apparatus which was to revolutionise the newspaper, the theatre, and daily life in general. The old man did not seem enthusiastic and turned to his daughter with some remark.

"Just at present," commented the daughter, with an air of finality, "the only thing my father is much interested in is a way in which to recover his sight without an operation. He has just had a rather unpleasant experience with one inventor. I think it will be some time before he cares to embark in any other such schemes."

Kennedy and I excused ourselves with appropriate remarks of disappointment. From his preoccupied manner it was impossible for me to guess whether Craig had accomplished his purpose or not.

"Let us drop in on Dr. Burnham since we are over here," he said when we had reached the street. "I have some questions to ask him."

The former physician of Mr. Haswell lived not very far from the house we had just left. He appeared a little surprised to see us so soon, but very interested in what had taken place.

"Who is this Dr. Scott?" asked Craig when we were seated in the comfortable leather chairs of the old-fashioned consulting-room.

"Really, I know no more about him than you do," replied Burnham. I thought I detected a little of professional jealousy in his tone, though he went on frankly enough, "I have made inquiries and I can find out nothing except that he is supposed to be a graduate of some Western medical school and came to this city only a short time ago. He has hired a small office in a new building devoted entirely to doctors and they tell me that he is an eye and ear specialist, though I cannot see that he has any practice. Beyond that I know nothing about him."

"Your friend Prescott interests me, too," remarked Kennedy, changing the subject quickly.

"Oh, he is no friend of mine," returned the doctor, fumbling in a drawer of his desk. "But I think I have one of his cards here which he gave me when we were introduced some time ago at Mr. Haswell's. I should think it would be worth while to see him. Although he has no use for me because I have neither money nor influence, still you might take this card. Tell him you are from the university, that I have interested you in him, that you know a trustee with money to invest – anything you like that is plausible. When are you going to see him?"

"The first thing in the morning," replied Kennedy. "After I have seen him I shall drop in for another chat with you. Will you be here?"

The doctor promised, and we took our departure.

Prescott's laboratory, which we found the next day from the address on the card, proved to be situated in one of the streets near the waterfront under the bridge approach, where the factories and warehouses clustered thickly. It was with a great deal of anticipation of seeing something happen that we threaded our way through the maze of streets with the cobweb structure of the bridge carrying its endless succession of cars arching high over our heads. We had nearly reached the place when Kennedy paused and pulled out two pairs of glasses, those huge round tortoiseshell affairs.

"You needn't mind these, Walter," he explained. "They are only plain glass, that is, not ground. You can see through them as well as through air. We must be careful not to excite suspicion. Perhaps a disguise might have been better, but I think this will do. There they add at least a decade to your age. If you could see yourself you wouldn't speak to your reflection. You look as scholarly as a Chinese mandarin. Remember, let me do the talking and do just as I do."

We had now entered the shop, stumbled up the dark stairs, and presented Dr. Burnham's card with a word of explanation along the lines which he had suggested. Prescott, surrounded by his retorts, crucibles, burettes, and condensers, received us much more graciously than I had had any reason to anticipate. He was a man in the late forties, his face covered with a thick beard, and his eyes, which seemed a little weak, were helped out with glasses almost as scholarly as ours.

I could not help thinking that we three bespectacled figures lacked only the flowing robes to be taken for a group of medieval alchemists set down a few centuries out of our time in the murky light of Prescott's sanctum. Yet, though he accepted us at our face value, and began to talk of his strange discoveries there was none of the old familiar prating about matrix and flux, elixir, magisterium, magnum opus, the mastery and the quintessence, those alternate names for the philosopher's stone which Paracelsus, Simon Forman, Jerome Cardan, and the other medieval worthies indulged in. This experience at least was as up-to-date as the Curies, Becquerel, Ramsay, and the rest.

"Transmutation," remarked Prescott, "was, as you know, finally declared to be a scientific absurdity in the eighteenth century. But I may say that it is no longer so regarded. I do not ask you to believe anything until you have seen; all I ask is that you maintain the same open mind which the most progressive scientists of today exhibit in regard to the subject."

Kennedy had seated himself some distance from a curious piece or rather collection of apparatus over which Prescott was working. It consisted of numerous coils and tubes.

"It may seem strange to you, gentlemen," Prescott proceeded, "that a man who is able to produce gold from, say, copper should be seeking capital from other people. My best answer to that old objection is that I am not seeking capital, as such. The situation with me is simply this. Twice I have applied to the patent office for a patent on my invention. They not only refuse to grant it, but they refuse to consider the application or even to give me a chance to demonstrate my process to them. On the other hand, suppose I try this thing secretly. How can I prevent any one from learning my trade secret, leaving me, and making gold on his own account? Men will desert as fast as I educate them. Think of the economic result of that; it would turn the world topsy-turvy. I am looking for some one who can be trusted to the last limit to join with me, furnish the influence and standing while I furnish the brains and the invention. Either we must get the government interested and sell the invention to it, or we must get government protection and special legislation. I am not seeking capital; I am seeking protection. First let me show you something."

He turned a switch, and a part of the collection of apparatus began to vibrate.

"You are undoubtedly acquainted with the modern theories of matter," he began, plunging into the explanation of his process. "Starting with the atom, we believe no longer that it is indivisible. Atoms are composed of thousands of ions, as they are called, – really little electric charges. Again, you know that we have found that all the elements fall into groups. Each group has certain related atomic weights and properties which can be and have been predicted in advance of the discovery of missing elements in the group. I started with the reasonable assumption that the atom of one element in a group could be modified so as to become the atom of another element in the group, that one group could perhaps be transformed into another, and so on, if only I knew the force that would change the number or modify the vibrations of these ions composing the various atoms.

"Now for years I have been seeking that force or combination of forces that would enable me to produce this change in the elements – raising or lowering them in the scale, so to speak. I have found it. I am not going to tell you or any other man whom you may interest the secret of how it is done until I find some one I can trust as I trust myself. But I am none the less willing that you should see the results. If they are not convincing, then nothing can be."

He appeared to be debating whether to explain further, and finally resumed: "Matter thus being in reality a manifestation of force or ether in motion, it is necessary to change and control that force and motion. This assemblage of machines here is for that purpose. Now a few words as to my theory."

He took a pencil and struck a sharp blow on the table. "There you have a single blow," he said, "just one isolated noise. Now if I strike this tuning fork you have a vibrating note. In other words, a succession of blows or wave vibrations of a certain kind affects the ear and we call it sound, just as a succession of other wave vibrations affects the retina and we have sight. If a moving picture moves slower than a certain number of pictures a minute you see the separate pictures; faster it is one moving picture.

"Now as we increase the rapidity of wave vibration and decrease the wave length we pass from sound waves to heat waves or what are known as the infra-red waves, those which lie below the red in the spectrum of light. Next we come to light, which is composed of the seven colours as you know from seeing them resolved in a prism. After that are what are known as the ultra-violet rays, which lie beyond the violet of white light. We also have electric waves, the waves of the alternating current, and shorter still we find the Hertzian waves, which are used in wireless. We have only begun to know of X-rays and the alpha, beta, and gamma rays from them, of radium, radioactivity, and finally of this new force which I have discovered and call 'protodyne,' the original force.

"In short, we find in the universe Matter, Force, and Ether. Matter is simply ether in motion, is composed of corpuscles, electrically charged ions, or electrons, moving units of negative electricity about one one-thousandth part of the hydrogen atom. Matter is made up of electricity and nothing but electricity. Let us see what that leads to. You are acquainted with Mendeleeff's periodic table?"

He drew forth a huge chart on which all the eighty or so elements were arranged in eight groups or octaves and twelve series. Selecting one, he placed his finger on the letters 'Au,' under which was written the number, 197.2. I wondered what the mystic letters and figures meant.

"That," he explained, "is the scientific name for the element gold and the figure is its atomic weight. You will see," he added, pointing down the second vertical column on the chart, "that gold belongs to the hydrogen group – hydrogen, lithium, sodium, potassium, copper, rubidium, silver, caesium, then two blank spaces for elements yet to be discovered to science, then gold, and finally another unknown element."

Running his finger along the eleventh, horizontal series, he continued: "The gold series – not the group – reads gold, mercury, thallium, lead, bismuth, and other elements known only to myself. For the known elements, however, these groups and series are now perfectly recognised by all scientists; they are determined by the fixed weight of the atom, and there is a close approximation to regularity.

"This twelfth series is interesting. So far only radium, thorium, and uranium are generally known. We know that the radioactive elements are constantly breaking down, and one often hears uranium, for instance, called the 'parent' of radium. Radium also gives off an emanation, and among its products is helium, quite another element. Thus the transmutation of matter is well known within certain bounds to all scientists today like yourself, Professor Kennedy. It has even been rumoured but never proved that copper has been transformed into lithium – both members of the hydrogen-gold group, you will observe. Copper to lithium is going backward, so to speak. It has remained for me to devise this protodyne apparatus by which I can reverse that process of decay and go forward in the table, so to put it – can change lithium into copper and copper into gold. I can create and destroy matter by protodyne."

He had been fingering a switch as he spoke. Now he turned it on triumphantly. A curious snapping and crackling noise followed, becoming more rapid, and as it mounted in intensity I could smell a pungent odour of ozone which told of an electric discharge. On went the machine until we could feel heat radiating from it. Then came a piercing burst of greenish-blue light from a long tube which looked like a curious mercury vapour lamp.

After a few minutes of this Prescott took a small crucible of black lead. "Now we are ready to try it," he cried in great excitement. "Here I have a crucible containing some copper. Any substance in the group would do, even hydrogen if there was any way I could handle the gas. I place it in the machine – so. Now if you could watch inside you would see it change; it is now rubidium, now silver, now caesium. Now it is a hitherto unknown element which I have named after myself, presium, now a second unknown element, cottium – ah! – there we have gold."

He drew forth the crucible, and there glowed in it a little bead or globule of molten gold.

"I could have taken lead or mercury and by varying the process done the same thing with the gold series as well as the gold group," he said, regarding the globule with obvious pride. "And I can put this gold back and bring it out copper or hydrogen, or better yet, can advance it instead of cause it to decay, and can get a radioactive element which I have named morganium – after my first name, Morgan Prescott. Morganium is a radioactive element next in the series to radium and much more active. Come closer and examine the gold."

Kennedy shook his head as if perfectly satisfied to accept the result. As for me I knew not what to think. It was all so plausible and there was the bead of gold, too, that I turned to Craig for enlightenment. Was he convinced? His face was inscrutable.

But as I looked I could see that Kennedy had been holding concealed in the palm of his hand a bit of what might be a mineral. From my position I could see the bit of mineral glowing, but Prescott could not.

"Might I ask," interrupted Kennedy, "what that curious greenish or bluish light from the tube is composed of?"

Prescott eyed him keenly for an instant through his thick glasses. Craig had shifted his gaze from the bit of mineral in his own hand, but was not looking at the light. He seemed to be indifferently contemplating Prescott's hand as it rested on the switch.

"That, sir," replied Prescott slowly, "is an emanation due to this new force, protodyne, which I use. It is a manifestation of energy, sir, that may run changes not only through the whole gamut of the elements, but is capable of transforming the ether itself into matter, matter into life, and life into mind. It is the outward sign of the unity of nature, the –"

"The means by which you secure the curious telepagrams I have heard of?" inquired Kennedy eagerly.

Prescott looked at him sharply, and for a moment I thought his face seemed to change from a livid white to an apoplectic red, although it may have been only the play of the weird light. When he spoke it was with no show of even suppressed surprise.

"Yes," he answered calmly. "I see that you have heard something of them. I had a curious case a few days ago. I had hoped to interest a certain capitalist of high standing in this city. I had showed him just what I have showed you, and I think he was impressed by it. Then I thought to clinch the matter by a telepagram, but for some reason or other I failed to consult the forces I control as to the wisdom of doing so. Had I, I should have known better. But I went ahead in self-confidence and enthusiasm. I told him of a long banished daughter with whom, in his heart, he was really wishing to become reconciled but was too proud to say the word. He resented it. He started to stamp out of this room, but not before I had another telepagram which told of – a misfortune that was soon to overtake the old man himself. If he had given me a chance I might have saved him, at least have flashed a telepagram to that daughter myself, but he gave me no chance. He was gone.

"I do not know precisely what happened after that, but in some way this man found his daughter, and today she is living with him. As for my hopes of getting assistance from him, I lost them from the moment when I made my initial mistake of telling him something distasteful. The daughter hates me and I hate her. I have learned that she never ceases advising the old man against all schemes for investment except those bearing moderate interest and readily realised on. Dr. Burnham – I see you know him – has been superseded by another doctor, I believe. Well, well, I am through with that incident. I must get assistance from other sources. The old man, I think, would have tricked me out of the fruits of my discovery anyhow. Perhaps I am fortunate. Who knows?"

A knock at the door cut him short. Prescott opened it, and a messenger boy stood there. "Is Professor Kennedy here?" he inquired.

Craig motioned to the boy, signed for the message, and tore it open. "It is from Dr. Burnham," he exclaimed, handing the message to me.

"Mr. Haswell is dead," I read. "Looks to me like asphyxiation by gas or some other poison. Come immediately to his house. Burnham."

"You will pardon me," broke in Craig to Prescott, who was regarding us without the slightest trace of emotion, "but Mr. Haswell, the old man to whom I know you referred, is dead, and Dr. Burnham wishes to see me immediately. It was only yesterday that I saw Mr. Haswell and he seemed in pretty good health and spirits. Prescott, though there was no love lost between you and the old man, I would esteem it a great favour if you would accompany me to the house. You need not take any responsibility unless you desire."

His words were courteous enough, but Craig spoke in a tone of quiet authority which Prescott found it impossible to deny. Kennedy had already started to telephone to his own laboratory, describing a certain suitcase to one of his students and giving his directions. It was only a moment later that we were panting up the sloping street that led from the river front. In the excitement I scarcely noticed where we were going until we hurried up the steps to the Haswell house.

The aged caretaker met us at the door. She was in tears. Upstairs in the front room where we had first met the old man we found Dr. Burnham working frantically over him.

It took only a minute to learn what had happened. The faithful Jane had noticed an odour of gas in the hall, had traced it to Mr. Haswell's room, had found him unconscious, and instinctively, forgetting the new Dr. Scott, had rushed forth for Dr. Burnham. Near the bed stood Grace Martin, pale but anxiously watching the efforts of the doctor to resuscitate the blue-faced man who was stretched cold and motionless on the bed.

Dr. Burnham paused in his efforts as we entered. "He is dead, all right," he whispered, aside. "I have tried everything I know to bring him back, but he is beyond help."

There was still a sickening odour of illuminating gas in the room, although the windows were now all open.

Kennedy, with provoking calmness in the excitement, turned from and ignored Dr. Burnham.

"Have you summoned Dr. Scott?" he asked Mrs. Martin.

"No," she replied, surprised. "Should I have done so?"

"Yes. Send James immediately. Mr. Prescott, will you kindly be seated for a few moments."

Taking off his coat, Kennedy advanced to the bed where the emaciated figure lay, cold and motionless. Craig knelt down at Mr. Haswell's head and took the inert arms, raising them up until they were extended straight. Then he brought them down, folded upward at the elbow at the side. Again and again he tried this Sylvester method of inducing respiration, but with no more result than Dr. Burnham had secured. He turned the body over on its face and tried the new Schaefer method. There seemed to be not a spark of life left.

"Dr. Scott is out," reported the maid breathlessly, "but they are trying to locate him from his office, and if they do they will send him around immediately."

A ring at the doorbell caused us to think that he had been found, but it proved to be the student to whom Kennedy had telephoned at his own laboratory. He was carrying a heavy suitcase and a small tank.

Kennedy opened the suitcase hastily and disclosed a little motor, some long tubes of rubber fitting into a small rubber cap, forceps, and other paraphernalia. The student quickly attached one tube to the little tank, while Kennedy grasped the tongue of the dead man with the forceps, pulled it up off the soft palate, and fitted the rubber cap snugly over his mouth and nose.

"This is the Draeger pulmotor," he explained as he worked, "devised to resuscitate persons who have died of electric shock, but actually found to be of more value in cases of asphyxiation. Start the motor."

The pulmotor began to pump. One could see the dead man's chest rise as it was inflated with oxygen forced by the accordion bellows from the tank through one of the tubes into the lungs. Then it fell as the oxygen and the poisonous gas were slowly sucked out through the other tube. Again and again the process was repeated, about ten times a minute.

Dr. Burnham looked on in undisguised amazement. He had long since given up all hope. The man was dead, medically dead, as dead as ever was any gas victim at this stage on whom all the usual methods of resuscitation had been tried and had failed.

Still, minute after minute, Kennedy worked faithfully on, trying to discover some spark of life and to fan it into flame. At last, after what seemed to be a half-hour of unremitting effort, when the oxygen had long since been exhausted and only fresh air was being pumped into the lungs and out of them, there was a first faint glimmer of life in the heart and a touch of colour in the cheeks. Haswell was coming to. Another half-hour found him muttering and rambling weakly.

"The letter – the letter," he moaned, rolling his glazed eyes about. "Where is the letter? Send for Grace."

The moan was so audible that it was startling. It was like a voice from the grave. What did it all mean? Mrs. Martin was at his side in a moment.

"Father, father, – here I am – Grace. What do you want?"

The old man moved restlessly, feverishly, and pressed his trembling hand to his forehead as if trying to collect his thoughts. He was weak, but it was evident that he had been saved.

The pulmotor had been stopped. Craig threw the cap to his student to be packed up, and as he did so he remarked quietly, "I could wish that Dr. Scott had been found. There are some matters here that might interest him."

He paused and looked slowly from the rescued man lying dazed on the bed toward Mrs. Martin. It was quite apparent even to me that she did not share the desire to see Dr. Scott, at least not just then. She was flushed and trembling with emotion. Crossing the room hurriedly she flung open the door into the hall.

"I am sure," she cried, controlling herself with difficulty and catching at a straw, as it were, "that you gentlemen, even if you have saved my father, are no friends of either his or mine. You have merely come here in response to Dr. Burnham, and he came because Jane lost her head in the excitement and forgot that Dr. Scott is now our physician."

"But Dr. Scott could not have been found in time, madame," interposed Dr. Burnham with evident triumph.

She ignored the remark and continued to hold the door open.

"Now leave us," she implored, "you, Dr. Burnham, you, Mr. Prescott, you, Professor Kennedy, and your friend Mr. Jameson, whoever you may be."

She was now cold and calm. In the bewildering change of events we had forgotten the wan figure on the bed still gasping for the breath of life. I could not help wondering at the woman's apparent lack of gratitude, and a thought flashed over my mind. Had the affair come to a contest between various parties fighting by fair means or foul for the old man's money – Scott and Mrs. Martin perhaps – against Prescott and Dr. Burnham? No one moved. We seemed to be waiting on Kennedy. Prescott and Mrs. Martin were now glaring at each other implacably.

The old man moved restlessly on the bed, and over my shoulder I could hear him gasp faintly, "Where's Grace? Send for Grace."

Mrs. Martin paid no attention, seemed not to hear, but stood facing us imperiously as if waiting for us to obey her orders and leave the house. Burnham moved toward the door, but Prescott stood his ground with a peculiar air of defiance. Then he took my arm and started rather precipitately, I thought, to leave.

"Come, come," said somebody behind us, "enough of the dramatics."

It was Kennedy, who had been bending down, listening to the muttering of the old man.

"Look at those eyes of Mr. Haswell," he said. "What colour are they?"

We looked. They were blue.

"Down in the parlour," continued Kennedy leisurely, "you will find a portrait of the long deceased Mrs. Haswell. If you will examine that painting you will see that her eyes are also a peculiarly limpid blue. No couple with blue eyes ever had a black-eyed child. At least, if this is such a case, the Carnegie Institution investigators would be glad to hear of it, for it is contrary to all that they have discovered on the subject after years of study of eugenics. Dark-eyed couples may have light-eyed children, but the reverse, never. What do you say to that, madame?"

"You lie," screamed the woman, rushing frantically past us. "I am his daughter. No interlopers shall separate us. Father!"

The old man moved feebly away from her.

"Send for Dr. Scott again," she demanded. "See if he cannot be found. He must be found. You are all enemies, villains."

She addressed Kennedy, but included the whole room in her denunciation.

"Not all," broke in Kennedy remorselessly. "Yes, madame, send for Dr. Scott. Why is he not here?"

Prescott, with one hand on my arm and the other on Dr. Burnham's, was moving toward the door.

"One moment, Prescott," interrupted Kennedy, detaining him with a look. "There was something I was about to say when Dr. Burnham's urgent message prevented it. I did not take the trouble even to find out how you obtained that little globule of molten gold from the crucible of alleged copper. There are so many tricks by which the gold could have been 'salted' and brought forth at the right moment that it was hardly worth while. Besides, I had satisfied myself that my first suspicions were correct. See that?"

He held out the little piece of mineral I had already seen in his hand in the alchemist's laboratory.

"That is a piece of willemite. It has the property of glowing or fluorescing under a certain kind of rays which are themselves invisible to the human eye. Prescott, your story of the transmutation of elements is very clever, but not more clever than your real story. Let us piece it together. I had already heard from Dr. Burnham how Mr. Haswell was induced by his desire for gain to visit you and how you had most mysteriously predicted his blindness. Now, there is no such thing as telepathy, at least in this case. How then was I to explain it? What could cause such a catastrophe naturally? Why, only those rays invisible to the human eye, but which make this piece of willemite glow – the ultra-violet rays."

Kennedy was speaking rapidly and was careful not to pause long enough to give Prescott an opportunity to interrupt him.

"These ultra-violet rays," he continued, "are always present in an electric arc light though not to a great degree unless the carbons have metal cores. They extend for two octaves above the violet of the spectrum and are too short to affect the eye as light, although they affect photographic plates. They are the friend of man when he uses them in moderation as Finsen did in the famous blue light treatment. But they tolerate no familiarity. To let them – particularly the shorter of the rays – enter the eye is to invite trouble. There is no warning sense of discomfort, but from six to eighteen hours after exposure to them the victim experiences violent pains in the eyes and headache. Sight may be seriously impaired, and it may take years to recover. Often prolonged exposure results in blindness, though a moderate exposure acts like a tonic. The rays may be compared in this double effect to drugs, such as strychnine. Too much of them may be destructive even to life itself."

Prescott had now paused and was regarding Kennedy contemptuously. Kennedy paid no attention, but continued: "Perhaps these mysterious rays may shed some light on our minds, however. Now, for one thing, ultra-violet light passes readily through quartz, but is cut off by ordinary glass, especially if it is coated with chromium. Old Mr. Haswell did not wear glasses. Therefore he was subject to the rays – the more so as he is a blond, and I think it has been demonstrated by investigators that blonds are more affected by them than are brunettes.

"You have, as a part of your machine, a peculiarly shaped quartz mercury vapour lamp, and the mercury vapour lamp of a design such as that I saw has been invented for the especial purpose of producing ultra-violet rays in large quantity. There are also in your machine induction coils for the purpose of making an impressive noise, and a small electric furnace to heat the salted gold. I don't know what other ingenious fakes you have added.

The visible bluish light from the tube is designed, I suppose, to hoodwink the credulous, but the dangerous thing about it is the invisible ray that accompanies that light. Mr. Haswell sat under those invisible rays, Prescott, never knowing how deadly they might be to him, an old man.

"You knew that they would not take effect for hours, and hence you ventured the prediction that he would be stricken at about midnight. Even if it was partial or temporary, still you would be safe in your prophecy. You succeeded better than you hoped in that part of your scheme. You had already prepared the way by means of a letter sent to Mr. Haswell through Dr. Burnham. But Mr. Haswell's credulity and fear worked the wrong way. Instead of appealing to you he hated you. In his predicament he thought only of his banished daughter and turned instinctively to her for help. That made necessary a quick change of plans."

Prescott, far from losing his nerve, turned on us bitterly. "I knew you two were spies the moment I saw you," he shouted. "It seemed as if in some way I knew you for what you were, as if I knew you had seen Mr. Haswell before you came to me. You, too, would have robbed an inventor as I am sure he would. But have a care, both of you. You may be punished also by blindness for your duplicity. Who knows?"

A shudder passed over me at the horrible thought contained in his mocking laugh. Were we doomed to blindness, too? I looked at the sightless man on the bed in alarm.

"I knew that you would know us," retorted Kennedy calmly. "Therefore we came provided with spectacles of Euphos glass, precisely like those you wear. No, Prescott, we are safe, though perhaps we may have some burns like those red blotches on Mr. Haswell, light burns."

Prescott had fallen back a step and Mrs. Martin was making an effort to appear stately and end the interview.

"No," continued Craig, suddenly wheeling, and startling us by the abruptness of his next exposure, "it is you and your wife here – Mrs. Prescott, not Mrs. Martin – who must have a care. Stop glaring at each other. It is no use playing at enemies longer and trying to get rid of us. You overdo it. The game is up."

Prescott made a rush at Kennedy, who seized him by the wrist and held him tightly in a grasp of steel that caused the veins on the back of his hands to stand out like whipcords.

"This is a deep-laid plot," he went on calmly, still holding Prescott, while I backed up against the door and cut off his wife; "but it is not so difficult to see it after all. Your part was to destroy the eyesight of the old man, to make it necessary for him to call on his daughter. Your wife's part was to play the role of Mrs. Martin, whom he had not seen for years and could not see now. She was to persuade him, with her filial affection, to make her the beneficiary of his will, to see that his money was kept readily convertible into cash.

"Then, when the old man was at last out of the way, you two could decamp with what you could realise before the real daughter, cut off somewhere across the continent, could hear of the death of her father. It was an excellent scheme. But Haswell's plain, material newspaper advertisement was not so effective for your purposes, Prescott, as the more artistic 'telepagram,' as you call it. Although you two got in first in answering the advertisement, it finally reached the right person after all. You didn't get away quickly enough.

"You were not expecting that the real daughter would see it and turn up so soon. But she has. She lives in California. Mr. Haswell in his delirium has just told of receiving a telegram which I suppose you, Mrs. Prescott, read, destroyed, and acted upon. It hurried your plans, but you were equal to the emergency. Besides, possession is nine points in the law. You tried the gas, making it look like a suicide. Jane, in her excitement, spoiled that, and Dr. Burnham, knowing where I was, as it happened, was able to summon me immediately. Circumstances have been against you from the first, Prescott."

Craig was slowly twisting up the hand of the inventor, which he still held. With his other hand he pulled a paper from his pocket. It was the old envelope on which he had written upon the occasion of our first visit to Mr. Haswell when we had been so unceremoniously interrupted by the visit of Dr. Scott.

"I sat here yesterday by this bed," continued Craig, motioning toward the chair he had occupied, as I remembered. "Mr. Haswell was telling Dr. Scott something in an undertone. I could not hear it. But the old man grasped the doctor by the wrist to pull him closer to whisper to him. The doctor's hand was toward me and I noticed the peculiar markings of the veins.

"You perhaps are not acquainted with the fact, but the markings of the veins in the back of the hand are peculiar to each individual – as infallible, indestructible, and ineffaceable as finger prints or the shape of the ear. It is a system invented and developed by Professor Tamassia of the University of Padua, Italy. A superficial observer would say that all vein patterns were essentially similar, and many have said so, but Tamassia has found each to be characteristic and all subject to almost incredible diversities. There are six general classes in this case before us, two large veins crossed by a few secondary veins forming a V with its base near the wrist.

"Already my suspicions had been aroused. I sketched the arrangement of the veins standing out on that hand. I noted the same thing just now on the hand that manipulated the fake apparatus in the laboratory. Despite the difference in make-up Scott and Prescott are the same.

"The invisible rays of the ultra-violet light may have blinded Mr. Haswell, even to the recognition of his own daughter, but you can rest assured, Prescott, that the very cleverness of your scheme will penetrate the eyes of the blindfolded goddess of justice. Burnham, if you will have the kindness to summon the police, I will take all the responsibility for the arrest of these people."

The Man Wore Motley

Stephen D. Rogers

I BLAMED Henderson for what happened.

I had to blame someone and I picked him.

Henderson had planned the liquor store job. Henderson had promised to look after my kid brother. Henderson had survived.

After pulling on the body armor, I checked the straps before slipping into my windbreaker. I raised my arms, held them in front of me, swung them to the sides. Satisfied with my range of motion, I checked myself in the mirror bolted to the wall.

Older than I used to be.

Henderson survived and my kid brother didn't. I'd waited seven years to redress the balance, and now the pieces were finally in place.

As I heard the toilet flush behind me, I collected the maps, blueprints, and timetables from the faded tan bedspread and slid them into the bottom of the duffle bag.

Zipped the duffel bag shut.

The bathroom door opened, the cheap plywood quivering under the strain.

Henderson emerged wiping his hands on a towel that he tossed onto the night table. Everything with him was disposable. "We ready to go?"

Nodding, I lifted the duffel bag and shook three times to distribute the weight evenly. "Unless you want to change first."

"Better to be called garish than 'the accused.' "

Henderson wore a bright neon Hawaiian shirt that overhung orange pants striped with green. He always dressed like a clown on these jobs, believing the wild clothing made it harder for witnesses to correctly describe his physical attributes.

Maybe he was right, but this time the costume wouldn't be enough. "Let's go."

Henderson grabbed my arm. "You sure about your information?"

"I'm sure."

Henderson released me. "In that case, we'll never have to step foot in places like this again."

I examined the room with a critical eye.

Water stains dotted the ceiling. Darkened one wall. Maybe were responsible for the discolored patches in the carpeting, but then that could have been anything, even blood.

I'd killed time in worse places. Heck, I'd lived in worse places. So had Henderson.

I nodded towards the exit. "After you."

Henderson left the room. I waited ten seconds before following, as two men leaving a hotel room together might be memorable. Too easy to find on the surveillance recordings.

Of course it didn't matter, but I couldn't let Henderson know that. He had to think this was business as usual, that the plan we'd rehearsed was the true one, that everybody was coming out of this alive.

I stepped into the hall and pulled the door tight. Tested the knob to make sure the lock had engaged. Otherwise, memorable.

Henderson punched through the door at the end of the hall.

The long stretch of carpeting I tread was no better than that in the room. Two of the bulbs were burned out or missing. Someone had torn a ragged strip from the wallpaper.

No, Henderson would never again spend time here.

We'd approach the bank from the east, driving the car we'd leave running outside the bank to confuse the authorities. Dave and Luchesi would approach from the west, parking out back and down the street.

I'd wondered about pairing Dave with Luchesi, but Dave said he'd be cool. Too late to change the plan now.

By the time I stepped outside the motel, Henderson had started the engine and popped the trunk.

I placed the duffle bag inside and slammed the trunk shut.

He gave me a sharp look as I slid next to him. "You trying to break the hinges or what?"

The car was stolen and about to be abandoned. "They'll live."

Henderson grunted before taking us out of the parking lot and into the flow.

I checked the time. "Apparently you've never had one open on you. I was transporting a body down Route 3 when I saw the trunk in my rearview mirror."

"Ouch."

"Between my speed and the crosswind coming off the ocean, I watched his baseball cap fly out of the trunk and tumble through the guardrail as I grabbed the breakdown lane."

"You probably slammed the trunk too hard."

Ignoring the criticism, I pressed on. "I got out and made sure the latch caught. I could see that cap about a hundred feet up the highway, but over the rise I could see a statie coming, and I didn't much fancy answering a trooper's questions with a body in the trunk."

"You leave the cap?"

"If it's not still there, it was probably picked up by some guy on an inmate work crew."

"I don't know what's worse, being in prison, or getting a taste of being out and then having to go back." Henderson paused. "I did an overnight once. That was enough for me."

"More than enough for anybody."

"I know guys who get out and can't wait to get back in. Guys like that make me nervous." Henderson pulled to the side of the road and shifted into park but kept the engine running. "Are you sure you're not waiting to lose?"

"I'm determined to win. More determined than you can imagine." Let him make of that what he would. "Why are we stopped?"

"I want to make sure. You haven't worked in a long time."

"Been lining up the perfect job. I must have traipsed through half the banks in Massachusetts finding just the right location. I'm no more interested in getting caught than you are. One last big score."

Henderson shifted into drive but kept his foot on the brake. "We're professionals."

"That's for sure. Other than us it's all cowboys and gangsters. Everybody high or desperate to get that way."

"Desperados." Henderson let up on the brake, and we were finally moving again. "Prisons are full of them."

"So what's up with Luchesi?"

Henderson nodded. "He's all right. Just does enough to take the edge off. The important thing is he scares people. When Luchesi's got my back, I know I don't have to worry about heroes."

"I wasn't doubting your choice of partners."

"Sounded for a minute like you were." Henderson gave me a look. "What about Dave?"

"Best driver I know. Can't be touched if there's snow on the ground."

"You see snow on the ground?"

"I'm just saying."

Henderson sniffed. "Let me tell you about Luchesi. We did an armored car one time. The job went smoothly enough until our driver decided to double-cross us by driving off with the money."

"You don't need to worry about Dave. All he wants to do is drive." I didn't dare say more.

"Luchesi, he blew out both of the driver's kneecaps. Then he waited until we finished dividing the driver's share before he put three in the brain pan."

"Wasn't it hard to count with the driver screaming the whole time?"

Henderson shrugged. "Afterwards, Luchesi torched the guy's car, burned down his house, and crippled his wife."

"Your friend doesn't mess around."

"He's like a teenager with an unlimited texting plan. He loves to send messages."

"I'll remember that." I pulled a small bottle of water from my windbreaker and let some moisture trickle down the back of my throat. Pulling off a job within a job could leave one a little dry.

"Got another one of those?"

I handed him the bottle. "Help yourself."

Henderson finished the water and tossed me the empty with a grin. "Thanks."

Let him laugh while he could. I'd be the one laughing long after he stopped. Long after he screamed himself hoarse.

Seven years I'd imagined this day.

As Henderson parallel parked in front of the bank, I called Dave. We were on schedule, and they were in position. "We enter in fifteen seconds."

Henderson and I left the car and met at the open trunk.

There was no sign we'd been made. Nobody sitting in parked cars. Nobody standing at windows. Nobody watching from up on a roof.

I unzipped the duffel and withdrew two masks. Henderson was Bozo the Clown. I wasn't.

We donned our masks and now I didn't need to worry so much about facial expressions giving me away.

As I pulled the duffle from the trunk, I glanced up and down the street again. "Let's go."

Henderson closed the trunk and chirped the doors locked.

We marched up the short walk to the front door of the bank.

Henderson had been right when he said I hadn't done this for a while. My brother's death had hollowed me, creating a space that filled with anguish. Anguish made way for rage. Rage made way for the plan.

The lobby opened up in front us. Tellers were to the right. Straight ahead, vault in the back. To the left of that, the passageway that led to the back offices.

After dropping the duffle just inside the door, I showed the guard my gun and pocketed his.

A high school graduate, he'd still been deciding how to respond to the sight of Luchesi herding the back office employees into the lobby. The kid had probably received the bulk of his training in customer service.

Luchesi motioned the customers to him. That was enough; they moved. There was something about Luchesi that made the werewolf mask superfluous.

Henderson passed us and walked towards the tellers. "This is a robbery. Nobody do anything stupid and nobody gets hurt. That means no alarms, no cell phones, no questions."

As Henderson waved the tellers to head for the lobby, he reminded them to stay away from the alarms. "Stay calm. Give me your drawer keys. Nobody's going to get hurt."

I counted three customers, ten staff, and the guard. Nobody appeared interested in becoming a dead hero, and Luchesi seemed more than capable of making sure that didn't change.

We'd achieved control.

I told the guard to lock the front door. After confirming he'd done as I instructed, I pulled the sign from the duffle bag and stuck it to the window. "Join the others."

Henderson continued talking as he went behind the counter. "Examine your neighbors. Is there anybody not here who should be? Maybe in the bathroom, an attic, some closet? Tell us now or they die."

Nobody volunteered any information.

"No? Okay then. Everybody sit where you are with legs crossed. Put your hands high in the air. If you can't sit with crossed legs, sit with them in front of you. Everybody does what we ask, nobody gets hurt."

Popcorn in reverse as the customers and employees dropped to the ground at their own speeds. I tensed as I watched for anybody taking advantage of the commotion to reach for a weapon or phone. Popcorn as hands went up.

Henderson might have been talking but they all faced Luchesi. After all, he was the immediate threat. He scared even me.

Putting Luchesi out of my mind, I placed the duffel bag on the table. Next to the wooden block with the date sat a cactus plant.

Someone more superstitious than me might have seen the cactus as a sign that my new life in Mexico was within reach. Since I'd experienced no premonitions that my brother wouldn't return from Henderson's job, I didn't much believe in signs. I didn't much believe in anything.

Except plans. We'd leave here in the car Dave was driving. We'd switch vehicles at the mall. Before we reached the highway, we'd split and switch cars yet again before I started the long drive south.

I took two empty backpacks out of the duffel and left them at a teller window for Henderson. Then I approached the manager and motioned her to stand. Even without my research, I could pick her out. She dressed just a bit better than the other employees, her dark jacket tailored to fit her thick frame.

"Susan, we want to be out of here as quickly as possible. So do you. Your cooperation determines how smoothly this goes. Do you understand?"

"Yes."

Whether or not she'd been robbed before, Susan seemed composed enough to follow orders. "You and I are going into the vault. You're going to unlock the cash boxes, and then we're out of your hair."

Susan nodded. "I understand."

I looked away from her to assess the situation.

Luchesi owned the crowd. Henderson hadn't reported any problems emptying the teller drawers into the backpacks. Dave's silence indicated no complications were developing out back.

The plan was unfolding nicely.

"Let's go." I waved Susan to proceed me.

She took a look back at the rest of the group, and something in her manner made me think she was sharing good thoughts with a special someone.

"Don't worry. Cooperate and you'll be fine."

Susan unlocked the heavy steel gate and led me into the open vault.

On the left were the customer safety deposit boxes, a wall of silver bricks that couldn't be opened without special keys or too much time. On the right were the cash and coin boxes.

The vault. I'd achieved the most crucial territory and the central objective of the plan. Of both plans.

"Stick to the cash and travelers checks. I'm not interested in lugging around five hundred pounds of pennies so we're not going to waste time opening them up. Understand?"

Susan nodded.

I dropped the duffle bag to the floor and unzipped the bag with one hand so that I could keep my gun on her. "Just a reminder: don't set off any alarms."

Susan unlocked the first box and opened the door. Unlocked the second. "What if the police arrive before you leave?"

"They won't, not unless someone makes a mistake." With my left hand, I pulled out each of the remaining empty backpacks and tossed them onto the floor.

The bank manager continued unlocking and opening. "If the police arrive before you leave, I'm offering myself as a hostage. Let the others go."

"That's very noble, Susan, but unnecessary. We'll be long gone before the police show up." I kicked the bags across the floor. "No dye packs. No marked bills. No tracking devices."

"If I do as you ask, you'll let them go?" She seemed prepared to stop work until I answered.

"Don't worry. I have no intention of using anyone here as a bargaining chip." Which was not the same as not intending to make someone hostage.

"I'm going to believe you." Susan transferred stacks of money to the backpacks, careful to follow my directions, moving quickly but not so quickly that she made mistakes.

"You're doing great. I'll be back in a second. Just remember the rules."

I stepped out of the vault.

Luchesi watched the front door as he nonchalantly managed the crowd. Henderson remained out of sight behind the counter emptying the foot drawers.

The last seven years went away as I raised my gun.

I shot Luchesi in the back of the head and then before he fell I shot the guard twice. Above the screams, I yelled, "Guard had a gun. The guard had a gun."

Henderson rose with weapon drawn, popped up like the clown he was.

I shouted above the din, "Everybody relax! The guard made a mistake. That's all. It's over and we're on track again. Silence!"

The screams settled down to mutters and sobs.

I nodded at Henderson. "You all set over there?"

"Near enough."

"I'll watch them. You take over in the vault." I'd killed the guard. That made me the more threatening figure. As if anybody had anything to fear from someone wearing a Hawaiian shirt.

Henderson placed the filled backpacks on the counter and huffed through the Bozo mask as he moved towards me. "What happened?"

"I stepped out to make sure everything was under control and saw the guard draw a second piece. I shot him but not before he fired."

Henderson glanced around the room. "Could have been worse."

So much for the Henderson's loyalty to his partner. "Send out the manager with what she's bagged and finish the job yourself. She's a nervous wreck, and we don't have time for her to fumble."

Henderson stepped closer. "We're still a go."

"Nothing's changed except the size of our shares."

"Wounded he would have slowed us down. Better dead than in prison." Henderson continued into the vault.

I glanced at the nearest surveillance camera. The recordings would show that I was the one who shot Luchesi, but by then the truth wouldn't matter. My only concern at the moment was that Henderson believed the story I'd spun. If he guessed what really happened, the wrong person might leave this bank alive.

I took a quick breath. "Everybody be calm. Please return to your positions in the center of the lobby, sitting with legs crossed or in front of you, arms raised. The guard made a mistake but it's over. Before you know it, we'll be gone."

Each person tried to stay within bounds but as far away from the guard and Luchesi as possible. Luchesi. Dave would be glad to hear I'd killed the man who killed his father.

Somebody developed hiccups. One of the women from the back offices. So much for fear being a way to stop them.

Susan emerged from the vault carrying two backpacks.

"Drop them over there and join the others. Sit with your legs crossed or straight out in front of you, arms in the air."

Susan sat on the edge of the group nearest me, far from the nervous wreck I'd described to Henderson.

I told everybody to remain in place. "You might think you can make it, but nobody outruns a bullet."

Henderson, neither, but dying would be too easy for him. That's why I'd spent seven years perfecting this plan.

Not seeing anyone working up the nerve to become a hero, I backed towards the vault. "We'll be out of here shortly. Everybody's going to be fine."

Most only had eyes for the dead Luchesi.

From the doorway to the vault, I watched Henderson crouch to load the last of the money into a backpack.

"You know, Henderson, the whole time we were discussing this job, we never talked about Kenny."

Henderson didn't even look up. "That was a bad break."

A bad break, he said. A bad break?

I almost shot him right there and then. Fortunately, I remembered how close to success I was.

A bad break.

Kenny suffered a bad break the time he fell from the oak tree in the back yard. He was once grounded for two months after breaking Mom's favorite lamp. His heart was broken when Ashley Wade went to the prom with someone else.

Being shot to death during the robbery Henderson planned was a hell of a lot worse than a bad break.

"It's your fault my brother's dead."

"Mine?" Henderson finally paused to meet my eyes. "I don't think so. But does now really seem like the time to discuss this?"

"Now is late enough."

"I don't believe– Listen, what happened was your fault. You're the one who forced him on me, told me he was good with a gun. Then, when I actually needed him, he froze." Henderson returned to filling the backpack with stacks of money. "You're the one who killed him."

"No Henderson. You killed him."

I tugged and I swung and I pushed the vault door shut.

Cutting off Henderson's shout.

Spun the dial.

Cutting off his last chance of escape.

Returned to the lobby where nobody appeared to have moved and told them not to rescue my partner.

Cutting off his air.

"When the police arrive, warn them that the bank robber stuck in the vault is armed, dangerous, and none too pleased."

I gathered the filled backpacks, picturing Henderson in orange prison jumpsuits, wondering if he'd find them garish enough. Henderson took part in an armed robbery where two people were killed. He'd go down for murder.

Henderson was going to be stuck behind bars until the day he died.

"I'd like to thank each one of you for your cooperation. I'd also like to offer my condolences to those of you who were close to the security guard. I, too, know the pain of loss. That in fact is why I'm here today."

Bells rang in the distance. Sirens.

I headed for the rear door and freedom.

My kid brother was at long last avenged. For the love of my brother I'd done this. For the love of my brother I was leaving everything behind to start the life he wanted to live.

If not for his dream of moving south of the border, he probably never would have allowed me to convince him to join Henderson's crew in the first place.

"Adios, bro." Those were the last words I said to him. "Adios." I paused before exiting the bank and imagined Henderson scraping at the inside of the vault. Imagined him scraping at the inside of a prison cell. Smiled.

Pushing through the bank's rear door, I walked into the sunshine.

I blamed Henderson for what happened.

I had to blame someone. I picked him.

The House

Steve Shrott

I HEARD SOUNDS outside in the backyard, grabbed a flashlight and flew out the door. I hadn't even bothered to put on shoes.

I crept into each corner of the yard, but saw nothing, except maybe a small rabbit rush off when the light hit his eyes. I had a lingering thought that someone had been there, but maybe it's just as you get older you get more suspicious of things. I went back inside the house, my wife's worried eyes looking up for answers. But I had none to give her.

Charlotte and I had lived in the house on Genesee Street for eight years when the trouble started.

We had taken the kids for a weekend up to Mission lake, a sort of mini family vacation. When we returned home, the lock had been broken and some of our possessions stolen. The weird thing was what the thieves had taken – wedding pictures, a Father's Day mug that Michael had made me at school, and a plaque that Susie had given us that said 'World's Greatest Parents.'

I didn't understand it. To anyone else these items were worthless. To my wife Charlotte and I, not having them broke our hearts.

The police investigated, but found no fingerprints, and even suggested that one of our children had been involved. I have to admit I did get angry at the cop when he said it. But I asked my kids later if they knew anything. Of course, they said no.

Our family tried to get back to normal, but this made all of us feel violated.

The next evening, we all sat on our seven-year-old couch and watched TV, a usual Friday night. If anyone had peeked through the window, they would have assumed we were relaxed and happy. We were, however, four anxious and frightened people.

Charlotte turned to me. "Did you hear something?'

I took in a long breath of air. "Charlotte, we have to relax. Yes, something happened, but we can't get all bent out of shape with every sound we hear."

She kissed my cheek and smiled. "You're right honey."

But I saw through the smile. She was still haunted by the intrusion into our house.

Everything was fine for a few days, but then on Tuesday evening, in the middle of watching our favorite show, *The Millers*, our TV went off.

I picked up the remote, and repeatedly pushed the on/off button. Nothing happened. I checked the back of the TV, the wires. Everything seemed fine as far as I could tell.

A crazy thought hit me. I went outside to the backyard, and opened up the TV box. I shone the flashlight on it.

There was a thin green wire and a thin red one. Both had been cut. Someone had been there.

I called the police again. An officer came out, examined the box, and agreed that it had been tampered with. But, as before, there were no fingerprints. He couldn't say for sure there was a connection between this, and the robbery, but thought it might be a possibility. At the moment, however, he had nothing to go on.

I called the repairman, and tried to console my wife and kids.

That night I couldn't sleep. I began wondering if any of our recent issues could be related to the last column I wrote for *The Covington Times*.

I had come down pretty hard on the liberal candidate, Ross Harley. It was all factual information, but perhaps it upset certain loyal constituents, and they took it out on me, the messenger. Of course, I had no real proof of this.

The next day I went to my gym to try and relax. After hitting the weights, I headed to the sauna. Things always seemed better after a sweat.

The sauna room at Fitness One was small, but that was okay since not too many people used it. When I entered, I saw two guys I'd known forever – Milt Rosenberg and Saul Averback. They both sat on the bench, towels draped over them. Perspiration dotted their foreheads as if the sun was right in the room. I took a seat next to them.

Milt, although seventy or so, still had most of his thick black hair. He had worked as a lawyer most of his life, but had retired recently, saying it's time he had a little fun. Saul, a pale and mostly bald man, worked in real estate. At sixty-two, he was still a go-getter. Although I'd heard from other friends that he wasn't making so many deals these days.

Milt wiped his forehead. "Any clue who did this stuff, Tim?"

"No idea."

Saul wiped his forehead with a bit of towel. "Do you think someone's out to get you?"

"The only thing I could think of is that someone on Ross Harley's team might be upset about my article."

Milt nodded. "The new Liberal. You did say some pretty harsh stuff."

I shrugged. "He's making promises he can't keep. I did my research. There's not enough money in the town budget to put up a new theatre."

Saul leaned close to me. "Tim, that sounds dangerous, antagonizing a man like him. He has connections."

That's when it hit me that maybe I did have to be more careful. Not just with what I wrote, but with my family too. I went home and brought everyone into the living room.

"Look guys, I'm sure everything is going to be fine. But I want you all to keep an extra-special watch on each other. I don't know what's going on lately. Or what's going to happen next, so we have to be vigilant."

Susie looked up with her big blue eyes and asked what "vig-i-lant" meant.

I smiled and said, "Careful, Susie, it just means, be careful."

For the next few days, things seemed to go back to normal. But then, on Friday, after supper, I heard sounds on the roof. I rushed outside and looked at the front of the house. I saw nothing. I went around to the backyard and shone the flashlight all over. At first everything looked okay. Then I noticed about twenty tiles from the roof had been torn off, and tossed onto the ground.

I felt the air move, then saw a figure running. I didn't have a clue who it was, but I chased after him. He ran to the next side street, Wallaby. I followed – at least for a while until my fifty-year old energy gave out. I stood catching my breath as he continued to run.

I was lucky about one thing. They had recently installed streetlights on Wallaby. Although, I couldn't see the face, I knew who it was.

When my son was younger, the boy next door had been his best buddy. Other kids would call him a "spaz" 'cause he ran like a horse galloping. That's how I knew the runner was Andrew Neilson.

Was he the one behind everything?

And if so, why?

There was one possibility that clicked for me. Charlotte and I had had problems with the Neilson Family.

Last year, Andrew's brother, Harry was going to university. The Neilsons claimed we were making too much noise, and he couldn't study. He failed and they blamed us. We had a huge yelling match, and never talked after that.

I had to talk to them about Andrew. They always spoke their mind, so I wasn't surprised when their door opened and Frank Neilson scowled at me and said, "What do you want?"

I decided to be equally blunt. "I just saw Andrew in my backyard. He tore tiles off my roof."

"How do you know it was him?"

"I just know." I didn't want to get him more upset by mentioning Andrew's running style. "I need to speak to him."

Roger Neilson stared at me daggers. "I don't think so."

"If you don't want me going to the cops, you better let me. I think a police record might hinder Andrew from getting into Stanford. I know he applied."

Roger Neilson looked like he was going to tackle me. I was saved by his wife Marissa, who was obviously listening. She pulled him aside and whispered into his ear. Frank pursed his lips as if wanting to yell, but took a breath then nodded. Marissa called upstairs to their son.

Andrew came running down the stairs, his face all puffed out and red. His pupils, like always, were extra large. It was no secret he did a lot of grass. I stared at him as if I were a police detective dealing with a murderer. "Why were you in my backyard, Andrew?"

"I wasn't."

"Uh huh."

Marissa leaned toward him. "Were you there, Andrew?"

He said, no. But his inflection went up instead of down, like a five year old saying that he didn't spill the juice on the floor even though his hands were still wet.

"Mr. Mathews saw you, Andrew. He recognized you."

Andrew flushed.

Roger spread his hands. "Tell him the truth. Be a man for once."

Andrew's eyes looked down at his shoes. "Okay I was there. The guy said I just had to do a couple of things and he'd give me money."

I shook my head. "So you took the tiles off."

Andrew nodded.

"Did you cut my TV wires too?"

He nodded again.

Frank looked at his son as if he were Attila the Hun. "It was for drug money, wasn't it? For stinking drugs."

Andrew didn't say anything.

I tried to keep the focus on my issue. "Who was the man, Andrew?"

"I don't know. He called me, said it was just a prank."

"A prank?"

"Yeah, he said you'd find it funny."

I didn't believe anyone would find cutting wires funny. "Some things were stolen too, Andrew."

"I didn't have nothing to do with that, I swear." His scared-straight face indicated to me that he was probably telling the truth.

"Where'd you meet this man?"

"I never did. My friend Randy said he got money off him for doing stuff, and he asked if I wanted to make some cash too. He said he'd give the guy my number. Then he called me."

"Can you tell me where this Randy lives?"

"No. He'll crush me if I tell."

His father glared at him. "Give it to him."

Andrew, his face scrunched up, began breathing like an asthmatic. Then he wrote down the number on a piece of paper, his hand seeming to have an almost parkinsonian twitch.

I left and went home.

I felt a little better that night, knowing I was making strides toward figuring out what was going on. But in the morning, I saw that the pink door of my garage had been covered in purple paint. Stuck to the garage door was a note. "Keep your opinions about Ross Harley to yourself or you'll regret it."

So I was right. It was related to my article. I called the police who said they'd contact Harley.

I hopped into my car and drove to the office. It was a tough day and with the crazy stuff I was dealing with at home; I really needed to go to the gym.

I lay back, enjoying the soothing heat of the sauna, as I talked to my two old friends. Milt shook his head. "So you think this kid Randy is the key?"

"I don't know. Maybe he likes Harley. Or maybe one of Harley's associates paid him to do this stuff."

Saul turned to me. "You know, Harley used to be a police officer. So I have my doubts that this investigation is going to go too far. I'm a little concerned, Tim. The election is still a few months away and who knows what can happen in that time. Look..." He tapped me on the shoulder. "...Gina and I have a guest room. If you wanted to..."

"No, no. That's very kind of you. But actually, I've been thinking about moving to that new subdivision. I'm not sure yet, but if you can maybe get me some details, I'd appreciate it."

"No problem."

The next night I visited Randy's house. There was a tall boy with red hair inside the garage. He seemed to be repairing a flat on his bike. I assumed that was him. I walked over. "You Randy?"

He looked at me with frightened eyes, and began heading toward his house. Andrew must have said that I was coming to see him.

"Randy, you're not in trouble. I just want information."

He stopped, turned around.

"Did someone on the Harley campaign tell you to do stuff to me?"

He shrugged. "Don't know. This guy just phoned and asked if I wanted to make some money."

"You painted my garage door purple and left the note, didn't you?"

He paused a little too long.

"I see the purple paint in your garage."

He looked back at the tins of paint, then at me. "Yes I did it. I'm sorry. It's just I needed the money. I also took some of your things. I have them in the garage."

He reached back to a box and handed them to me. I could see that the wedding album and everything else was in there too. I felt my whole body relax even though I still didn't know who was behind all this. "I assume you did all this for drug money."

He shook his head. "No, I just got accepted into Queens College for engineering and my mom says I'm gonna have to pay for it myself. She doesn't have the money. I have a day job at the hardware store, and a night thing at the movie theatre, but no way am I going to make enough."

I actually felt sorry for him. At least he was trying to do something with his life.

"You gonna tell the police on me?"

I thought about it for a moment. "No, just don't do this stuff anymore, eh?"

He nodded. "I'm sorry Mr. Mathews."

I turned around to go home, then turned back. "Look, Randy, if you wanted to paint the garage back to pink, I'd pay you. Maybe I could find a few other things for you to do too."

He gave me a big smile. "That be great, Mr. Mathews. Thank you."

When I got home, I was hoping to make Charlotte happy by showing her that all our mementos were back. But her eyes were moist. She wiped them as she told me a rock had been thrown in the house, breaking a window.

That hit me hard. I knew it wasn't Randy or Andrew. But who? Things were getting dangerous. If a rock had hit someone, who knows what could have happened.

Just as I was trying to get over this horrible news, the police called and said, just as Saul had predicted, that they hadn't turned up nothing. Perhaps Harley still did have strong connections on the force.

In that moment, I made a decision. "Honey, I've asked Saul to check out some houses in the new development. We're going to move."

"What?"

"We have to protect the kids."

She didn't ask any questions, just nodded and hugged me.

"I'll let Saul know that we're serious when I see him at the club tomorrow."

I went outside to check the house. It had been my new daily job to make sure everything was okay.

I looked at the front. It seemed fine.

I looked over at the Neilsons' house and saw several cars. Two couples went inside carrying gift wrapped boxes. Some kind of party that, of course, we weren't invited to. I heard loud music playing. I should have complained about the noise they made, just to get even. But I didn't.

A few moments later, I heard people talking and it seemed to be coming from my back yard. I raced around and saw a man and woman standing in front of our eaves trough. The man was tapping it. He smiled at me showing a lot of gold fillings.

"What are you doing?"

"Just seeing if it's secure. Ours is always getting loose."

His older, blonde-haired wife patted the man on his shoulder. "George is a bit finicky about things. He wants to make sure that everything is perfect if we're going to buy the house."

I stared at her, trying to understand. "Buy the house?"

"It's kind of perfect for us. Not too big, seems like a good neighborhood. I know we've been dragging our feet for a few weeks. But I promise it won't be too much longer."

"A few weeks?"

The lady smiled. "Yes, I told you, George wants to make sure everything is perfect before he goes forward."

That's when it hit me. I knew who had been behind everything.

The next day, when I went to the sauna it was one man short.

Milt shook his head. "So Saul is in jail?"

"Yeah, business was so slow he resorted to hiring kids to do things to various houses so they'd move out."

Milt spread his hands. "What about the note from Harley?"

"Apparently, Saul was worried I was getting too close to the real answer, so he had Randy put the note on the garage door."

"So you're not moving?"

I shook my head. "Why would I leave? This house has everything I want. It's not too big, has a good neighborhood and the eaves trough is pretty solid."

Catzized

Annette Siketa

IN THE END, and in spite of the hi-tech security system, the theft of the Catzize, a flawless almond shaped emerald, was ridiculously simple – a crowded jewellers, a fire alarm, and a predictable panic. By the next morning however, events had taken an even more dramatic turn, which the cleaner, Florrie Brown, discovered when she arrived at the jewellers for work.

"Oh, Ada," she blurted, rushing into the home of her long time friend, Ada Harris, "you'll never guess what's happened now."

Ada peered owlishly over her spectacles. "Why do people always say that when they know full well the person won't?"

Florrie ignored the rebuke and gushed, "Miss Pritchard the store manager. She's dead, electrocuted in her bath last night."

"For goodness sake slow down. Make yourself some tea then tell me all."

Suitably refreshed, Florrie began her tale. "Miss Pritchard was driven home by her boyfriend after the robbery. He then went off to get some Chinese take away, and when he returned, he found her in the bath, hair fried and very dead."

"And how was she electrocuted?"

"Apparently, there is a shelf directly above the bath, and somehow she knocked a radio into the water."

"Who is in charge of the investigation?"

Florrie was justifiably confused. "The robbery or the death?"

"Oh, definitely the death."

Florrie produced a business card and read aloud, "Detective Inspector John Simmonds."

Mrs. Harris smiled. She had a 'nose' for sniffing out trouble, and had it not been for her recent intervention, the Inspector would not have caught a psychopathic killer.

"Tell me what you know about the robbery, Florrie."

"It was lunchtime and the shop was full. Everything seemed normal, and then at about 12.30, the fire alarm went off. Everyone was momentarily stunned as there was no obvious smell of smoke, but when water started pouring out of the sprinklers, Miss Pritchard began throwing items into the safe and ordering everyone out."

"Who was the last to leave?"

Florrie thought for a moment. "Well, as the door was locked when the fire brigade arrived, presumably it was Miss Pritchard."

"And the Catzize?"

"In the panic and confusion, nobody noticed until later that it was missing from its display pad."

"Were there any other alarms?"

Florrie leaned forward and spoke in a whisper. "Well, that's the strange part. The security system did not activate. I know there was a silent alarm; being the cleaner I was warned about it. It was connected directly to the police station, and I overheard someone say it didn't go off."

"I don't suppose you know anything about the boyfriend."

"His name is Christopher Meekin and he has something to do with electronics, but he's already been cleared. He was visiting a client when the robbery took place, and luckily for him, was snapped by a speed camera while on the way to buying the take away."

Mrs. Harris was impressed. "How on earth do you know all that?"

"Because the police were still ferreting around the shop this morning when I arrived. Meekin's boss came in and grumbled to the Inspector about the forthcoming fine. You see, Meekin was driving a company car, not his own."

Ada slowly nodded her head, and the following morning, renewed her acquaintance with Inspector Simmonds. "Your information is correct," he said with a note of wariness. "What's your interest?"

"Oh, just curiosity," she said airily. "Would it be possible to view Miss Pritchard's house?" Mrs. Harris smiled engagingly as she added, "I'd also like to talk to the boyfriend."

Had it not been for their recent collaboration, Inspector Simmonds would have refused both requests. As it was, he had a grudging respect for the 'old bat', so gave her a set of keys.

"I'm interviewing Meekin at 4 this afternoon," he added. "I don't know how receptive he'll be to your presence, and if he insists on your leaving, then you must." He paused and then added, "What are you looking for? And don't tell me it's just curiosity because I don't believe you."

"I don't know," she said thoughtfully. "The whole thing is just a little too neat."

* * *

Melissa Pritchard, or so it appeared, had expensive tastes. Her house was exquisitely appointed, dominated by Royal Albert's 'Country Roses' pottery. The décor was repeated in the bathroom, and as Florrie had stated, there was a shelf with towels just above the bath. The toilet was in the corner to the left of the bath, with the power point about twelve inches above the cistern.

Mrs. Harris scrutinised every detail. "And this is exactly how it was?" she said to P.C. Mary Osborne, who had volunteered to drive her to the house.

"I presume so."

"You didn't attend?"

"No, I was busy with the robbery. Hello Ezzie." A magnificent Persian cat, its manner and movement conveying self-importance, had strolled into the bathroom. Mary murmured softly as she stroked its imperious head.

"Ezzie?" queried Ada.

"Short for Esmeralda, and I bet she wants feeding." Mary smiled sheepishly. "To be honest, that's why I offered to bring you. You see, I knew Melissa. We belonged to the same cat society. We weren't close friends," she quickly added, seeing Ada's look of surprise, "but as a fellow cat lover, it would be criminal to let anything bad happen to such a beautiful animal before alternate arrangements can be made."

"Very commendable," said Ada, whose love of cats only extended to the porcelain variety. "Were there any signs of a struggle or anything unusual?" she asked as the Persian continued to purr.

"No," said Mary, brushing hair off her uniform. "Just a towel and a mouse."

Mrs. Harris blinked. "Did you say a mouse?"

"Yes. My theory is that it suddenly appeared, perhaps it was running around the rim of the bath, and after such a hectic and stressful day, Melissa simply panicked, somehow knocking both the mouse and the radio into the water." Mary paused reflectively. "She probably screamed. It's surprising that the boyfriend didn't hear anything."

"He wasn't here at the time," said Ada, now inspecting the wall above the cistern.

"So he says," said Mary dubiously.

Mrs. Harris looked at her enquiringly. "Why do you say that?"

Mary shrugged. "Call it coppers instinct. Just because a traffic camera snapped the car, doesn't mean Meekin was driving it. The robbery and Melissa's death, and him with perfect alibis for both. It's too coincidental for my liking."

There was a short pause and then Mrs.s Harris said, "Given the circumstances, that cat is not a very good mouser. By the way, who's looking after it?"

"Me I suppose. I'll contact the... Ezzie, get down!" The cat had jumped onto the bath and then onto the shelf. It looked at Mary defiantly for a moment, and then leapt to the floor and disappeared beyond the door.

* * *

Christopher Meekin nursed a cup of plastic tea as Inspector Simmonds began his questioning. "Do you prefer Christopher or Chris?" Meekin shrugged indifferently. "Very well, Chris. This interview is informal. The coroner requires a full report, so I need to ask a few general questions. Firstly, how long had you known Melissa Pritchard?"

"About a year."

"How did you meet?"

"At a sandwich shop near the jewellers. At first, it was the usual nods and greetings, but after a while, we started talking and I invited her out for a drink."

"And you liked her?"

Meekin shrugged again. "Yeah, sure, she was a nice lady."

Inspector Simmonds cleared his throat. He was not fond of asking deeply personal questions. "Was it an intimate relationship?"

Meekin's face flushed with anger. "None of your damned business. My private life is my own affair."

Inspector Simmonds sighed heavily. "Nevertheless, I need an answer."

Meekin hesitated and Mrs.s Harris, who had been sitting quietly and unobtrusively, leaned forward slightly. His answer was of great interest to her.

"Well," he said presently, "Bill Clinton said it wasn't sex, so I suppose the answer is 'no'."

"I see," said the Inspector, his face inscrutable. "Do you know if Melissa had any enemies or was in any kind of trouble?"

"I believe she was struggling with her mortgage, but then, who isn't nowadays?"

"How do you know this?"

"Just conversation. It came up once or twice."

"What happened when you drove her home after the robbery?"

"She was badly shaken as you might expect, so she called me and asked me to drive her home. I could see at once that she was in no fit state to do anything. In fact, when her mobile phone rang, she dropped it."

"Somebody rang her? Do you know who it was?"

"A friend I suppose, because she told them what had happened and that I was driving her home." Meekin buried his face in his hands. "If only she hadn't sent me out for that damned Chinese. If I'd been there, I could have performed CPR and perhaps saved her life."

Under the table, Inspector Simmonds felt a tap on his shoe. "This lady is helping us with our investigation. You do not have to answer her questions, and nothing will be inferred if you do not. However, your co-operation would be greatly appreciated."

As Meekin wiped his eyes and nodded in ascent, Ada smiled in understanding. "Mr. Meekin, have you ever served in the armed forces?"

Christopher Meekin was clearly taken aback. "What? Um... no."

"Can you tell me about your profession?"

"I'm a business solutions consultant."

Ada gave an embarrassed cough. "Forgive me, Mr. Meekin, but most people of my age don't understand modern jargon. What exactly is a business solutions consultant?"

"I assist companies to determine what computer software they require. For example, a tracking system for a haulage company. If the software doesn't exist, I help our developers invent it. It's a very tailor-made environment."

"Marvellous," said Ada flatteringly. " I can barely work the remote for my television. How long did it take you to learn it?"

"I studied computer programming at university. It was progressive, as is the computer industry, so arguably I'm still learning."

"And how long have you been in your present position?"

"About 18 months."

"Did you ever discuss your work with Melissa?"

"Of course."

"So, presumably you spent much time in her home."

"Well, I know where everything is if that's what you mean."

"Her cat...oh what is its name? It's clear slipped my mind."

Meekin frowned thoughtfully. "Missy or Mitzy, something like that."

"Ah, yes. Well, I met Missy earlier today, and as I commented to someone at the time, considering what was found in the bath, she's not a very good mouser."

Meekin looked at Ada as though she was from another planet. "Found in the bath? What are you talking about?"

"You found Melissa so surely you must have seen it."

"See what?" he retorted, his voice rising. "I checked her pulse and then rang for an ambulance. All I saw was the radio and the cat."

Mrs. Harris's blue eyes twinkled as she said, "It's not important. Thank you for answering my questions. Inspector?"

Fifteen minutes later, Meekin exited the police station. Ada sat back in her chair and slowly chewed her thumbnail. It was a habit she had developed over the years whenever she was deep in thought.

"What was all that guff about the army and his job?" asked a bewildered Inspector Simmonds.

"Nothing, it was to put him at ease. Have you opened the safe yet?"

"No, we're waiting for a representative from the parent company." He looked at her shrewdly. "Do you suspect there's somebody in it?"

Ada ignored the question. "Inspector, I strongly urge you to put a tail on Meekin, at least for the next 24 hours. So far, he's behaved perfectly normally, but there's something I'm not entirely convinced of. Also, do not open the safe. Everything hinges on what's inside, but we need time."

"To do what?" When Ada told him, the veteran police officer was incredulous. "You want me to waste valuable time and resources to perform an autopsy...on a mouse?"

"I know it's strange, but I must know whether it was dead before it hit the water."

"Strange? It's ludicrous. Why is it so important?"

"To catch a killer of course."

Inspector Simmonds stared at her open-mouthed. "Who was murdered?"

"Melissa Pritchard. I know the 'who', and I've a pretty good idea as to the 'why', but what I don't know is the 'how', and that mouse is the key."

Inspector Simmonds sighed resignedly. Once before he'd trusted Ada's intuition, and she'd been right. "All right, but if there's any repercussions, you can answer to the Chief Constable personally."

The following afternoon, at the Inspector's invitation, Ada read two reports. The first was the autopsy on the mouse, the second was an account of Meekin's movements since leaving the station. She now knew everything. The only problem now was how to prove it.

* * *

Mrs. Harris, Inspector Simmonds, Christopher Meekin and Mary Osborne, sat in Melissa Pritchard's ostentatious living room. They had been settled for some time, with only a gentle hissing noise from the gas fire invading the stilted silence.

"Mrs. Harris," said the Inspector quietly, "what are we waiting for?"

"The murderer... and here she is." The cat had strolled into the room and jumped into Mary's lap.

Inspector Simmonds and Christopher Meekin exchanged speechless glances, whereas Mary Osborne, her hands caressing the cat, did not react at all.

"Of course," Ada went on, "she had help. In order for the subterfuge to work, the mouse had to be dead. A live one simply wouldn't stay put, and the autopsy showed that it's neck was broken beforehand, probably in a trap. It was placed under the towels. The cat acted instinctively, and as it tried to get at the mouse, pushed the radio into the water. Tell me, Mary, when did Melissa first approach you about the robbery?"

The Inspector stared in disbelief. "Mrs. Harris, are you suggesting that P.C. Osborne was complicit in the robbery and the death?"

"She's the only one who could have done both."

Mary Osborne spoke in a dreamy, remote voice. "Have you ever watched a cat? They are the most perfect creatures in the world. Nothing interferes with their natural order. Melissa was manipulative and ugly. She wanted the emerald and I wanted Ezzie."

"I don't understand any of this," the Inspector admitted.

"Take a good look around, Inspector," said Mrs. Harris. "Melissa was living beyond her means. As Mr. Meekin told us, she was having financial problems, and when she learnt that the Catzize was to be displayed in the shop, she saw its theft as the solution. As store manager, she would have full knowledge of the security arrangements, but she had two problems. Firstly, how to set off the computer controlled fire alarm, and secondly, how to circumvent the silent alarm connected to the police station. As to the first problem, she enticed Mr. Meekin into divulging sufficient computer information for the purpose. Secondly, she developed a friendship with Mary, probably through the cat society, and persuaded her to block the silent alarm at precisely 12.30."

"So, what went wrong?"

"Melissa did not do her homework properly. Yes she knew how to set off the fire alarm, but she did not know how to stop the sprinkler. Realising that she'd lost the opportunity of a lifetime, to borrow from Mr. Meekin, she was in no fit state to do anything. Then, when he was driving her home, Mary phoned her on her mobile. Melissa blurted everything out and Mary told her to get rid of him, hence the take away.

"But what Mary didn't know, was that in the panic and confusion in the shop, Melissa had not snatched the emerald. Conversely, what Melissa did not know, was that Mary had decided to kill her. Using her knowledge of police forensics, she carefully crafted the cat and mouse plan, knowing it would be virtually impossible to determine whether Melissa's death was an accident, or when the supposed loss of the stone was discovered, a suicide borne from remorse.

"When Mr. Meekin left to get the Chinese, Mary slipped inside and under the pretext of running a soothing bath, placed the already dead mouse on the shelf. The cat, as Mary well knew, would act instinctively. I don't suppose it mattered that Melissa didn't have the stone, Mary simply wanted rid of her to get the cat. It would be an understatement to say that Mr. Meekin was most fortunate to be snapped by that camera, otherwise he would have extreme difficulty proving his innocence."

Christopher Meekin asked the obvious question. "What happened to the stone?"

Mrs. Harris chuckled as she said, "It never left the shop. When the plan went awry, like the cat, Melissa acted instinctively. She put the stone in the safe and then locked the front door behind her. Think about it. Who would stop to lock a supposedly burning building?"

"And what put you onto Mary?" asked the Inspector.

"Familiarity. Unlike dogs, cats are renowned for their disobedience, but even the most arrogant cat will respond to a familiar voice. Mr. Meekin didn't remember its name because it had no importance."

The following afternoon, Inspector Simmons said, "The emerald has been recovered and Mary has made a full confession. I can't believe someone would commit murder just for a cat."

"Not just for a cat," said Ada sombrely, "for the love of a cat. You know, that emerald was well-named."

"How so?"

"Because rather than capitalizing on its wealth, both Melissa and Mary were hypnotised by a Catzeye."

Ghosts, Bigfoot, and Free Lunches

Dan Stout

DETECTIVE RONSON slid his hat back, disturbing the thin stubble he called a head of hair. He'd spent all day standing in the middle of an impossible homicide investigation, the coroner was still trying to tag all the pieces of the body, and from the sounds over his shoulder, the media was knocking on the apartment door. It was days like today that made him hate his job.

"Keep the press out, Jesenko," he growled, loud enough to be heard without turning around. A moment later perfume clouded the air next to him, and he realized he should've growled even louder. He turned to see who was invading his crime scene.

It was a woman – a square jawed redhead who barely came up to his chest. She was on the younger side of middle age, and reminded Ronson of the nuns who used to whack his hands with a ruler when he got math problems wrong.

"Molly Pinkerton," she said, without extending a hand. "You Ronson?"

Ronson grunted, glaring over her shoulder at his man at the door. Jesenko shrugged and held up a sheet of paper. Ronson recognized the mayoral seal at the top of the letterhead, and rolled his eyes. He really hated his job.

The woman craned her head around, taking in everything but the big detective. She said, "I got a call from –"

Ronson broke in. "The Mayor." He jerked a thumb at Jesenko. "I saw your hall pass. I like that you've got a detective's name, Pinkerton, but you can go home."

Pinkerton's eyebrows rose, creasing the freckles sprinkled liberally across her forehead.

"I'm here to – "

"Yeah, I know," Ronson interrupted again. "The Mayor called asking you to assist us in our investigation. That's nice. Thanks to you and His Honor. But we don't need assistance. And you should clear out. This is no game for a bureaucrat, or accountant, or whatever it is you do."

"Hotel Detective," she said.

Ronson needed a moment to let that sink in.

"Tell me you're kidding," he said.

"Not a lot of career choices with a name like 'Pinkerton'." She smiled, and Ronson was surprised to see braces ringing her teeth. They glinted silver, matching the lapel pin on her suit coat. Then the smile was gone and she was looking him right in the eyes.

"And I'm here as a favor to the mayor, not you. I'd really rather be back at The Aphrodite working my own beat, instead of finding a killer who isn't my problem. So why don't you give me the lowdown and I can get out of here all the faster, okay?" She turned away from him, eyeing the damage in the apartment and the hustle of the crime scene team.

Ronson considered having her thrown out, then summoned a mental image of the mayoral seal and thought better of it. He breathed out, his anger whistling softly as it passed through the gap in his front teeth. He surveyed the crime scene one more time, making him feel like a gambler desperately re-ordering the cards in a crap poker hand.

"Alright... this whole thing is lifted out of cheap paperback," he said. "Penthouse apartment, twenty stories straight down from the windows. Doors locked from the inside, and no access to other units, either through maintenance entrances or window ledges. One victim, killed in the bedroom: the apartment's sole resident, Samuel Milligan. Corporate kingpin, fitness nut, and close personal friend of the mayor. But you probably know all that, don't you?"

Pinkerton nodded once, and Ronson went on.

"Whoever done for this guy was a monster. The body's a total mess. Trust me, you don't want to see it." Ronson didn't have much desire to see it again, either. Milligan's throat had been torn out, parts of him scattered around the bedroom, and his blood splattered the walls like bath water shaken from a dog's coat.

"It doesn't even look like the place had been tossed for cash, just torn to pieces for the hell of it." He kicked a shattered table leg to the side. Broken furniture was strewn over the floor, vases full of flowers had fallen from the end tables and bookshelves, scattering colorful petals across the mayhem. Even the goldfish bowl was smashed; when Ronson had arrived at the scene he'd been shocked to find the tiny fish twitching slightly in the scant handful of water still at the bottom of the shattered bowl.

He turned back to face Molly. "Now I'm stuck here while some overpaid custodian plays detective. That sum it up nicely for you?"

Ronson finished with a well-practiced sneer, which amazingly seemed to have no effect on her. Truth was, Ronson didn't think she was a custodian. She held herself well, and probably did a good job cleaning drunks out of the lobby, but right now she was mostly a pain in his rear and he wanted her gone.

But the insult hadn't had any more impact than his sneer. Instead, she surveyed the crime scene, strolling to the bedroom to glance at the devastated body, then returned to the living room. She ran a finger across the bookshelf while she skimmed the titles, and nudged the flower petals on the carpet with the pointed toe of her shoe.

Ronson almost grinned. Good luck getting this hand to turn out decent, lady.

He decided to change tactics. "Look," he said, "it may not be safe here. The perp might still be in the building."

For the second time since she'd walked in, Pinkerton smiled.

"Might be," she said.

"Yeah, might be. We had a squad car patrolling the area when the call came in about the noise –"

"Let me guess. That was about 6:15 am?"

Ronson grunted.

"And you've been here all day and into the night?"

This time he didn't even bother to grunt, just watched her with narrowed eyes. Pinkerton turned and walked into the kitchen.

Ronson stuck a well-chewed pencil nib in his mouth and wished for the thousandth time that it tasted like menthol. He tried to return to his notepad, but gave it up for a lost cause. He walked to the window and pulled back the fine fabric of the curtain. Night was falling. The city sky never had stars, but the streetlights were beginning to flicker to life. Only the moon was bright enough to cut through the city's ambient light, and that would be rising soon enough.

Maybe it was the thought of the moon or the onset of darkness that made him call out over his shoulder, "You work at The Aphrodite, huh? That's the haunted hotel."

He'd heard of it. Half the force wouldn't walk into it for love nor money. It was a scam operation, running on urban legends and gullible tourists. They probably liked that superstitious cops didn't come poking around.

From the other room, Pinkerton responded. "Do you believe that, Detective?"

He strangled a laugh and let the curtain fall across the night sky.

"No such thing as ghosts, bigfoot, or free lunches." Ronson's version of a smile staggered across his face, less polished and much less used than his sneer. "My Grandma taught me that."

"Smart woman."

"She was."

Pinkerton re-emerged from the kitchen, holding a Tupperware container filled with water, a lone goldfish swimming laps in it. She shrugged. "I mean, two out of three ain't bad."

Before he could respond she held the Tupperware container and its occupant up at eye level. She looked at the fish, then at the detective.

"This fish isn't in its bowl."

"No," said Ronson, looking back at his notepad.

"So when you arrived it was...." She cocked an eyebrow.

Ronson jerked his chin at the damp section of carpet. "There."

"And it's in here now." She tapped the Tupperware container.

The big detective was silent.

Pinkerton stared at the spot where he'd recovered the fish, her free hand idly adjusting her lapel pin. "You saved it. Big heart for a cop."

Ronson rolled his eyes again. A man had been slaughtered in the next room, his throat torn out, and the mayor had sent him a hotel detective with a membership in the Humane Society. He turned his back on Pinkerton just as she spoke up.

"There's no botany books on the shelves." She said it loud, like it was a bombshell revelation.

Ronson couldn't help himself. He turned back and stared. "What?"

"Flowers all over the place, but no technical books. And the flowers aren't professionally arranged. Looks like the victim picked wildflowers as he found them, just based on whether he thought they were pretty. Probably while he was jogging in the park."

Ronson's brow creased. "You saw the track shoes by the door," he said.

She nodded, "Mud covering on the toes, tracks showing lots of wear."

He respected the observation. It was the same way that he had pegged the victim as a fitness nut. Milligan had liked to run, and he didn't stick to the sidewalks.

"This guy," she said, setting the goldfish down on one of the few intact end tables, "used to sit right there." She pointed to a space on one of the bookshelves, directly above the broken remnants of its last bowl. "But there're water stains on the shelf above his previous home."

Ronson followed the movement of her finger, and sure enough, there was a higher water stain. He followed its trail downward, and saw what he was looking for.

"It was another flower vase," he said, "it's there on the floor." It had been a white vase; its shards now lay among delicate red teardrop-shaped petals, shed by the flower during its fall. He looked up. "Just like all the other broken vases in this place. You have a point here, Pinkman?"

Pinkerton ignored him. She tapped the edge of the bowl and watched the goldfish respond. "Do you recognize that flower, Detective?"

"Jesus," Ronson sighed, wincing unconsciously at the ruler rap he would have gotten from the nuns for that one. "Lady, I have no idea."

"Neither did your victim. Remember the lack of botany books." Pinkerton fiddled with the pin on her lapel, straightening it then changing her mind and taking it off. "That is *Pontus moerisanius*, better known as wolf's-tears."

"Okay?"

"Wolf's-tears is one of the less common causes of lycanthropy." Pinkerton's lapel pin was extremely long. She used it to clean the dirt out from beneath one thumbnail. "But it gets the job done."

"Lycanth–"

"Werewolves."

"I know what it means," lied Ronson. "What I don't know is just what the hell you're talking about."

"That wolf's-tears flower was amateurishly picked and placed in a vase right there." She pointed again, this time with the pin. "The poorly trimmed stem sagged down, and the flowers dipped into the goldfish bowl below."

"Can't say as I blame him," she said. "All his life, food comes from the same direction: up above. When this red flower shows up, why wouldn't he take a bite? He probably figured..." She tsk'd. "Well, you know what they say about free lunches."

Ronson stared at her, the beginnings of a right proper headache setting in. The administration had never sent a lunatic to interfere with a case before.

"Your men showed up at 6:15 this morning, Detective. Right after sunrise. Just in time for the monster which spent the night locked in this apartment with the late Mr. Milligan to try to go back to his bowl." She looked at the goldfish, then at her wristwatch. "You've been here all day and into the night. It's a full moon again tonight, Detective, and I think you're right... your perp might still be in the building after all."

Ronson wondered whether he'd have to restrain this woman when sudden movement caught his eye. The Tupperware bowl started to shake back and forth, water sloshing over the side. The goldfish seemed to take up more of the container, and Ronson found it harder and harder to track its outline. Almost like it was shifting, changing in some way. He looked away from the fish and back up at Pinkerton.

She still gripped the lapel pin, which shone silver in the luxurious light of Sam Milligan's penthouse. Her eyes were on the fish, and her mouth was pulled into a frown. When she spoke it was in a quiet voice, not meant for Ronson's ears.

"Sorry, little guy," she said, and stabbed the pin into the water.

The fish – or thing – made a noise that to Ronson's ears sounded like a gurgled howl. The water swirled pale red, then went still.

Pinkerton stared at him. "You're welcome," she said.

Ronson turned around and found a chair to slump into. He truly hated his job.

Blood and Silver Beneath the Many Moons

Brian Trent

THREE MORNING MOONS were up and a fourth was rising when Inspector Caridwen finally admitted that she was lost. Her police cruiser had been navigating these winding country roads for an hour, and the snow was coming down harder now.
She was looking for a hill.

One problem was that these hinterlands beyond the old colony were nothing but hills, with roads that ran like narrow capillaries between them. Caridwen's deep-set eyes stared out from her bristly face, worriedly considering the clouds.

Another problem, she thought anxiously, was that she wasn't sure she wanted to find the hill.

The inspector grunted nervously and parked her cruiser in the middle of the road. She steadied her nerves, opened the door, and breathed deeply of the chilly, pine-scented air.

The scent of blood-tang struck her snout at once. Caridwen leapt from her car, aghast at the pungency. Snow began to speckle the exposed fur of her wrists, face and neck.

Despite wearing her crisp police uniform, the inspector dropped to all fours and loped up the nearest hill for a better view of the area. The blood-tang was radiating off a higher altitude, and as she crested the hill she stopped fast, grunting with new fear.

The scent of death had summoned every boar in the immediate region. They swarmed the base of a large hill that rose like a white tower to the sky, pacing and grunting unhappily at the murder of one of their own.

* * *

The boars in these parts were larger and thicker than most, even when standing on two legs. Caridwen felt a pang of shame that she had bought into the stories that the rural boars had reverted to being quadrupeds. Her shame burned brighter when she realized that it was she herself who had made a beastly lope, and she quickly shook snow from her hooves and uniform, and walked down to where they had gathered.

"We warned you inspector!" roared a male with jutting tusks, stomping around on his skinny legs in frustration and anguish. "How many more murders will it take before you listen to us!"

And another boar added, "This is the work of monsters! Only real monsters could commit this blasphemy!" Caridwen recognized this voice, and she half-turned to see craggy old Darkmane, the ancient peddler who sold her charms, oils, and talismans across six counties. Darkmane's shriveled white eyes – nearly the same hue as her winter fur – widened in a protestation of sincerity.

Caridwen craned her neck to view the icy hill and the blue sky that crowned it, the triple moons like pale jewels perched over the crest. She rounded the crowd and began the strenuous, near-vertical ascent. The stench of blood reached her nostrils far before reaching the summit, and she thought: *This is going to be a bad one, Caridwen. Worse than the others.*

Sheriff Garn met Caridwen at the ledge and extended a hoof, pulling her up the last meter of the climb. His calm brown eyes, set in a face of wiry hair, fixed her with a sensitive, overwrought stare. Caridwen remembered that once, during their academy days, he had loved her.

"Caridwen," Garn began, but she gently brushed past him and took in her first view of the three bodies.

"Apis protect us," she whispered. Garn bowed his head.

* * *

It wasn't enough to say the cubs had been murdered. Caridwen's procedural mind galloped to keep ahead of her prickling revulsion and horror. She remembered the photos loaned to her – photos of grinning, striped piglets standing arm-in-arm for the camera – and she tried reconciling those snapshots with these pink slabs of mutilated meat. The killer had shorn the striped fur from their bodies, leaving them smooth, naked and terrible. The fleshy carcasses leaked blood from dozens of stab wounds; the hilltop snow was stained red beneath them. A coroner squatted by the carnage, scratching at his tusks as he made final measurements on the slain with his wooden instruments.

Behind her, Garn said quietly, "As best we can tell, the killer brought them alive and bound to the hilltop. Look here. Metal twine was used to restrain their arms and legs."

"They were alive when he skinned them?" Caridwen asked dully.

Sheriff Garn swallowed hard. He glanced to the coroner. "Yes, Caridwen. I mean, Inspector. There are violent signs of struggle against their bonds that suggests they were... um... alive when..."

"When the killer went to work on them?"

Her old academy friend gave a quick, hasty nod.

"No one heard the screams?"

The coroner said, "They were muzzled." He turned aside, rolling up his equipment bag. "There are clear signs of it on their snouts."

Muzzled? Caridwen and Garn regarded each other for a long while, ignoring the cloying stench of viscera.

"Who found the bodies?" she asked finally.

He shook his notepad in his cloven grip. "Local seamstress named Gullinbursti. She stumbled upon them in her sleep."

Caridwen's ears bristled with interest. "In her sleep? You mean she's a sleeprunner?"

"Bad case of it her entire life. She gets up in the middle of the night and goes galloping on all fours. Terribly embarrassing. Her husband usually bolts the doors shut at night, but last night he forgot and she got out."

"Does she go somewhere in particular when this happens?"

"Sleeprunners tend to be led by their snouts. That usually means they wake up nosing through a neighbor's garbage, or covered in dirt from a midnight burrowing for fragrant roots and tubers. But Gullinbursti didn't do that. When her husband woke and saw she was missing, he tracked her across the snow to this hilltop. He found her up here, awake and panic-stricken, amid the bodies. The scent of blood must have led her here."

Caridwen sighed. "Do I need to ask the obvious?"

"She didn't kill them." The sheriff's snout quivered. "She's just a sleeprunner who stumbled onto a crime scene. Her squeals of anguish damn near woke the entire valley."

Caridwen put a hand on his shoulder. She had meant it as a comforting gesture, but the longing in his eyes – a haunted, festering desire that had not faded one bit from their academy days – immediately told her she had made a mistake. He was a nice boar, professional and trustworthy, but they had been in different emotional places back then and after one drunken mating on the evening of their graduation, he had described a life path that repelled her. Garn wanted a family, his own litter. Caridwen panicked at the suggestion. It had been more than jitters; she'd felt an almost mindless phobia at the thought of her own litter of piglets in a crib, mewling and calling for her. Caridwen told herself it was probably common for a career woman to avoid being tied down by family, but she was secretly ashamed of her reaction and she thereafter broke off contact with Garn.

Besides, she loved being on the force. Loved working a case.

Caridwen squatted beside the corpses and ran her hoof through the gore-clotted fur. Each pale breast sported a gaping red fissure, ribs splayed like crooked teeth.

"We have the bastard's boot-prints," Garn said, pointing to the dimpled pattern in the snow. "The killer approached the hill from the southwest."

The inspector scratched beneath her chin. "No," she said after a moment. "There's more than one set of prints here." She grimaced, baring her teeth. "I'd say three sets of footprints. One killer for each cub. A team did this, Garn."

The sheriff looked thunderstruck. It had been a long morning for him; he never did have the nerves or stomach for this work. He rubbed his neck, absently ruffling the fur so that it stood out in messy spikes. Above, four out of five moons had congregated, strung along the sky in a line of sallow, judgmental eyes. By their pale luminosity, something gleamed amid the hilltop snow.

Caridwen's first thought was that she was seeing a chunk of ice crystals, or perhaps a fragment from the cubs' bygone clothes. She squatted and pinched it from the snow.

Garn frowned. "What is that?"

"A shard of metal. Do we know if the cubs – ow!" She cursed and flung the metallic fragment from her hoof.

"What happened?"

"It burned me!" She gaped at the gray flesh beneath her fur sizzling and puckering. Small tendrils of smoke curled from the surrounding follicles.

Garn stared. "Acid?"

"No," she said thoughtfully, rubbing the wound. "Silver."

* * *

If the moons had been silent witnesses, the gathering clouds now wept for the slain, a mix of snow and winter rain. The piglets were gingerly placed onto stretchers and carried downhill. Inspector Caridwen readjusted her cap around her furry ears and began the descent towards the village. The crowd squealed their grief once more and slowly, reluctantly, began a miserable, wet dispersal.

Standing alone on the gravel path, the village mayor awaited them.

He was a gray boar, stout and standing tall, wearing spectacles and dressed in classic old colony fatigues. He fidgeted with a top hat and his ears were flat back with displeasure.

"I'm drafting a village curfew," he said as they reached him. "No one out after sundown until the perpetrator is caught. When the perpetrator is caught." He peered at them over the rim of his spectacles. "Walk with me, officers."

Together they strode into the village center, a cobblestone oval of benches and flowerbox planters. A jagged monument stood in the center like an upturned black fang, protected by an iron fence woven with frozen white flowers.

Garn pointed to the odd black monument. "This village was founded in 296! Can that be right?" He indicated the bronze placard nailed to the monument.

"It's right and we're proud of it," the mayor said crisply, one of his ears stirring. "Selene Falls was established around one of the very first landing sites."

Caridwen nodded towards the surrounding buildings. "That explains these homes. I've never seen such tall, distinctive mansions. Their wooden exteriors are just an outer plating, isn't that right? The frames beneath are actual colony ship modules, disassembled upon landing, to build this village."

The mayor smiled. He had small, worn teeth.

"I would be delighted to discuss our village's past, but at the moment I am more concerned about its present. Do you have a suspect?"

"We're following a number of leads," she said, rubbing her hoof where the silver had burned her.

The mayor maintained his dignified strut, sleet dancing off his top hat, as he crossed to the largest of the mansions. They reached the mansion awning, shielded temporarily from the storm. Caridwen thought he was going to invite them in, but he stood there, ears fully upright now.

The mayor raised an eyebrow. "My office is at your disposal. Inspector, I understand you'll be requiring a place to stay for a few days."

Garn began to say something, but Caridwen rapidly cut him off: "I noticed an inn and tavern on my way into town. That'll do nicely."

The mayor keyed into his door and bid them a good evening. The door made a metallic groan as it opened, and Caridwen caught a glimpse of an unusual foyer, ornate and angular, with strange metal furnishings along the walls and ceiling. An elderly boar in a shawl descended a grand staircase and took his hat from him. Then the door groaned shut and Caridwen and Garn were alone in the storm.

Garn gave a surprised cough. "What the hell kind of door was that?"

"It's a converted shuttle hatch," Caridwen said thoughtfully.

"A what?"

"It's not important, Garn. What is important is that the hilltop where the bodies were found has been used for murder before."

"How can you know that?"

She wanted to yell: *Because I used my nose. I could smell the coppery stink of old blood beneath the snow.* But she could see he was upset. She had known that eventually she'd run into him again. She wished it hadn't been on a case as macabre as this.

"Let's talk at the tavern," she said, turning her collar up against the storm. "But I think it's clear those bodies were never meant to be found. The hilltop is some awful sacrificial spot. The sleeprunner happened to blunder up there that night, and the killers beat a hasty retreat."

They walked briskly across the town square. The moons were milky splotches in the winter sky, turning Selene Falls' ancient inn and tavern, and the rocky hill it sat against, into a vision both luminous and dark.

* * *

The inn's connecting tavern wasn't so rustic as it was a smoky, corrugated den with musty shadows nestling in the metallic rafters and crossbeams. Odd banners hung from wall posts like in ancient paintings of medieval haunts and castles; Caridwen noted the folksy heraldry of lions rampant, wolves, and fleur-de-lis. The bar was a rectangle of scarred, lacerated wood in the center of the room, surrounded by islands of tables in which grim-faced boars drank from cheap mugs.

The sleet washed over the windows, creating a melting gloom that stretched shadows and deepened the pitting in the wood.

Lovely, Caridwen mused.

The owner was a lank, loose-jointed boar with sunken eyes and thin bristles. He looked like something diseased and Caridwen felt an instinctive revulsion. He also seemed stoned, dreamily rubbing the counter with a sodden rag, barely looking at anyone around him.

Garn grabbed two beers and chose a table by the window.

"We're on duty," she cautioned.

"We're fitting in," he replied, and clinked his mug against hers. He swallowed a hefty sip, wiped the foam from his snout, and said, "Why the hilltop? If the killers wanted privacy, they could have found a cave or deep ravine or dense thicket. Why drag the piglets up the crest and murder them there?"

"Because last night all five moons were out. The killers were committing deliberate, calculated blasphemy."

He blinked his small brown eyes. "A moon-hating cult?"

She produced a plastic evidence bag and placed it on the table. The silver shard glowed by the tavern's lamplight.

"Silver," Garn grumbled. "Where the hell did it come from?"

She pushed aside her beer. "How well do you know your history? Three hundred years ago, the first ships settled here and opened up mines to produce coinage and trade goods."

"But no one uses silver for money, Caridwen! It's the most toxic thing on the planet!" He swished his beer and then grinned boyishly. "A person could say that about money, itself. Or love."

"Garn..."

"Are you honestly saying you've never thought about us? Not once, since that night after the academy?"

Caridwen sighed. "We were going in two different directions. It wasn't personal."

He considered this. "It felt very personal, Caridwen." He swished his mug again and took a long gulp.

He was still guzzling from the mug when the window cracked.

Garn's mug seemed to fall apart in his hands; the bottom of it exploded into a frothy soup of beer. At the same time his head snapped to the right and he fell sideways out of his chair into a spreading pool of blood.

Caridwen dove from her booth as the window cracked twice more; the bullets stitching glossy holes in the glass.

She drew her police-issue pistol and darted for the doorway, casting a quick and anguished glance to the sheriff. He was down, headshot, but blinking languidly as if he couldn't believe it. Most of the customers had fled to the other end of the bar away from the firing zone, but two patrons were rushing to provide Garn assistance, moons bless them!

Crouching low, Caridwen kicked open the tavern door. Two reports instantly sounded from the square, rising above the rattling sleet. A coat-rack in the corner shuddered and danced from each impact.

Inspector Caridwen studied the courtyard for signs of the sniper. The town monument? Could that be where the bastard was hiding? Or was he further off, in the blackened perimeter of the square where any vacant window or awning could hold danger?

Caridwen glanced again to Garn. Her horror crawled up her throat.

The two tavern patrons were not tending to her old friend. They had held him down, and sawed his head off with a shiny hacksaw. Now they held it aloft in sick triumph, spinal column dangling like a red weed from the neck.

Caridwen's anguish nearly overrode her senses; for a moment she felt the full heat of her boarblood pound in her head until she literally saw red. Only her academy training spared her from a full-on frenzy. She carefully aimed and shot the nearest patron through the chest. The second one, holding Sheriff Garn's decapitated head, rushed her and swung a heavy cleaver at her neck. She ducked, smelled the metal as it sailed an inch over her ears –

SILVER! IT WAS SILVER LIKE THE FRAGMENT IN THE GRASS!

– and shot him twice, once in the gut and then in the throat. He squealed wretchedly and dropped Garn's head; it hit the floor with a wet splat, the spinal column curled out like a tail. The patron sank to his knees, making wet choking sounds, and died.

Caridwen quickly scanned the tavern. Only the skinny bartender was left, clutching his dirty cloth.

"Hooves!" she demanded. "Let me see your hooves, facing out! Now!"

He obeyed in a dazed fashion of compliance. She wondered if he was high on wispweed.

She said, "Who's out there?"

"I... I don't know," he mumbled as if in a daze and then added, as if it might help, "I've just been born."

"What?!"

Again, her training saved her. She had been alternating her view from the bartender to the front door, a scope of ninety degrees. Her ears, attuned to the rhythm of sleet, heard the splashing of an interloper. Caridwen stepped aside as gunfire erupted into the tavern.

She hopped the bar counter and delivered an unforgiving swat of her pistol to the bartender's head. "Get down!"

The sickly-looking boar moaned and reached for his head. Caridwen struck him again and he stopped moving. But beneath his fur, at a seam in his fur-line where he'd been pawing, something shone by lamplight. A vertical row of metal teeth, like surgical staples, but upon closer inspection...

Caridwen felt her stomach knot.

It was a zipper!

Still holding the pistol, she jerked at it, peeled off the mask – he was wearing a full headmask! It came off like an orange peel.

"No!" she screamed. She fell backwards, crawling desperately away from the hairless, pink monstrosity underneath.

Human.

The old stories, the superstitious folktales, came flooding back to her. How a shuttle of wereboars had fled a far-away world in which shapeshifters were the persecuted minority.

How they had entered a deep-freeze sleep for the journey. How they found this world of many moons. Moons out all the time, day or night.

But according to the story, no human had come with them. Those ancestral monsters were left behind on their human-dominated world! So how the hell could humans be here now, masked and among us?

Caridwen scurried for the back door. As she drew near the window the glass exploded around her: a shotgun blast. She emptied her clip in the direction of the shot and changed course, towards the wine cellar door.

She grabbed the handle and drew it open on a rocky corridor with work-lights strung from the ceiling. A toxic odor hit her at once.

Silver.

She was going into a silver mine.

* * *

The sinister alloy choked her nostrils. She felt her fur tingling down to the roots, a body-wide crawling sensation as if under siege by stinging insects. She heard footsteps in the corridor ahead. Hushed voices, overlapping tongues. Edgy, eager, terrible.

They knew she was here. Word had gone out among their secret hive. They were coming for her.

Caridwen fought the knotting of her stomach and aimed her pistol into the dark ahead of her. She waited, arms outstretched and drew a bead just below the furthest work-light.

That's when she saw her arms begin to change.

The unreality swept through her, outsurging the pain crackling along her nerves. Her bristly fur was withdrawing into her pores. Her joints twisted and popped. Caridwen dropped her pistol in a sudden, spastic convulsion.

"No!" she cried, and thought: *The mines! Deep into the mines, the moonlight can't reach! She was cut off from their loving influence...*

And on the heels of that realization was an even deeper, unutterable terror.

If the moonlight is responsible for us being boars, she thought, then deep down we must all be...

* * *

Her new body, they told her, was nothing to be ashamed of.

She should be proud of her furless limbs, her flat face, her new smell. She was human now. Had always been human, deep down. In the mineshaft where she regained consciousness, she found herself surrounded by fellow humans. Some of them even shaved their heads, in ritualistic defiance against the return of the boar.

"But I'm not a boar," the woman said. She blinked and looked at a badge that said INSPECTOR CARIDWEN. "And I don't remember being an inspector..."

"Because that was another life, and now you'll need to convince others you are the inspector they know," the mayor said. He held his boar mask in one arm like a trophy; his human face was sharp and fierce, suggestive of righteous ambition. "Ordinarily we'd just give you a new identity and vocation. But we need more of us on the police force. More people to shed the beast and shape the society that is coming."

He handed her a syringe with jade fluid inside. She considered it with a dreamy, slow-blinking gaze.

"It suppresses the change," he explained. "Even when you're out there in the moonlight, which is all the time on this cursed planet. You'll have to wear a mask. You'll convince others you still are Inspector Caridwen, while we organize. While we prepare for the coming days."

She looked at him with moist, blue eyes. "I'm scared."

"That's because you've just been born," he touched her shoulder. "You were a monster before, Caridwen. Welcome back to the human family."

Murder on the Cogsworthy Express

Cameron Trost

"THIS TRAIN is so delightfully smooth," the young man with a colonial accent and a sunny face remarked as he awkwardly dipped Lady Varnstapple. "It's like clockwork. Or is it my dancing that gives that impression?"

The heiress of the inestimable Varnstapple Metals and Minerals fortune might have offered the poor lad a polite giggle if she had suspected he was trying to be clever, but she knew full well that he had no idea just how significant his remark had been. She decided to simultaneously inform and mock him, even though both would likely go unappreciated by his feeble mind.

"It is not your dancing, but the train itself. However, the Cogsworthy Express doesn't run *like* clockwork. It *is* clockwork."

The look of confusion on his face confirmed her suspicions.

He dipped her again, almost in time with the exotic music being played by a gypsy quintet at the far end of the carriage.

He laughed and winked at her before saying, "My dear girl, trains run on steam. They are fuelled by coal. There is no such thing as a clockwork train."

"Did nobody tell you before you boarded this train just how special it is? Why did you choose to travel on the Cogsworthy for its maiden voyage?"

He bit his lip, realising that he had displayed his ignorance yet again. It was a good job he was dashingly handsome and that his father owned an immense patch of colonial desert, which contained enormous deposits of dozens of types of invaluable minerals. These two qualities made up for his dire lack of intellect, wit, and charm – and the fact that he danced like a deaf and crippled war veteran.

"I'm not sure," he admitted. "I'm not really interested in trains, you see. My father sent me here to meet people."

Lady Varnstapple suppressed a smirk. It was all too clear. The clumsy colonial boy's father had undoubtedly sent him on the voyage in the hope that he would meet a sophisticated young heiress like her.

"Allow me to enlighten you," she said, unable to recall his name. He had introduced himself before asking her to dance, and she was sure her father knew his father, but she was terrible with names. "The Cogsworthy Express is the world's first clockwork train. That is why it's so smooth and almost completely silent. That is also why it never runs late. Every turn of every cog in its mechanism is timed to ensure that it arrives at its destination not a second too early or late."

"How remarkable! Now that I think of it, the only sound I heard before the wheels started turning when we left New Tunston Station was a faint ticking, and there wasn't even a hint of smoke in the air."

"That's right," Lady Varnstapple encouraged him in a patronising tone. "There is no need for coal at all. The train's mechanism is wound up at each station by workers and timed perfectly so that the wheels come to a halt at the next stop."

The music ceased and the couple stopped dancing. The young man hesitated to unclasp his left hand from his partner's tender right hand, and to remove his right hand from her corseted waist.

Twenty other passengers also stopped and took glasses of champagne and amuse-bouches from the waiters in attendance while the gypsy band drank absinthe and got ready to play their next piece.

"Who is that man staring at you?" the colonial lad whispered.

Lady Varnstapple turned her swanlike neck slowly and with such poise that the intricate clockwork earrings she wore barely even moved. Her glance was intended to be casual, but when she saw who it was, she couldn't help but allow a flicker of shock to give herself away.

The man's nostrils flared and his immaculate handlebar moustache twitched angrily.

"Excuse me. I'm quite weary from all this dancing and talk of engineering. I must retire to my compartment for the night," she explained.

"Are you..."

"Really," she insisted. "I need some rest. It was a pleasure dancing with you," she lied. "Thank you."

Lady Varnstapple made her way through the crowd and out of the compartment, leaving the colonial lad confused and disappointed.

He turned to look back to where the man who had caused the young heiress such distress was standing, but he was no longer there.

* * *

The gypsy band was playing a final number and three energetic couples were still dancing, determined to outdo each other for the remaining onlookers, when Lady Varnstapple's companion, a plain-looking and diligent country girl, came bursting into the carriage in a most unseemly fashion.

The expression of utter distress on her rustic face immediately placed her beyond reproach, and before she had even opened her mouth, all present knew that something terrible had happened.

Her jaw dropped and began to tremble. She obviously wanted to speak but was unable to articulate a single word.

Instead, she screamed.

The gypsies froze, their instruments suddenly silenced.

The dancers became statues.

For a terrible moment after the scream, only the ticking of the train's clockwork and the muffled clacking of wheels on the tracks could be heard.

"Good grief, girl! What is it? Waiter, get her a glass of gin! Hop to it smartly now!"

It was Sir Grant Pithleswhistle who had spoken with the assurance of a man who was used to being obeyed and the confidence of one who never questioned his own judgement.

"It's Lady Varnstapple," the girl sobbed.

"Yes?" Lady Powellswright prompted in a drunken slur. She had been dancing with her equally inebriated husband in a very intimate fashion. They had both been planning on retreating to their luxury compartment shortly.

"Lady Varnstapple," the distraught girl repeated.

"Yes? She's not... is she?"

All the poor girl could manage was a nod, and it looked as though she was about to collapse when a middle-aged man who had been sitting by the door, sipping cognac and observing the other passengers, jumped to his feet and took her by the waist.

"Good move, my man!" Sir Grant Pithleswhistle exclaimed.

The waiter arrived a moment later with a glass of gin and helped the devastated girl raise it to her trembling lips.

"Which compartment?" the man supporting her asked softly. He was dressed entirely in black, from his pointed boots to the kerchief around his neck. A silver pocket watch chain attached to his waistcoat and the silver and amethyst rings on his fingers were the only items he wore that stood out against his dark attire. His beard and moustache were grey and his head was shaven.

"She's in compartment two," she whispered.

The man disappeared through the door from which Lady Varnstapple's companion had appeared and hurried along the corridor until he reached the compartment. It was the only one with the door hanging open.

He stopped at the doorway and looked inside.

The heiress was lying on her bed, still dressed in her evening gown and jewellery. At first glance, one could have been excused for thinking that she was merely sleeping, but no lady of her standing would have been so remiss as to lie down in all her finery.

He looked around the compartment and was immediately convinced that there was no indication of theft. The lady's affairs seemed to be in order and numerous items of great value could be seen on her dresser. Yet the feeling that there had been foul play couldn't be shaken off.

"What has happened?" a firm voice demanded as half a dozen people came rushing along the corridor. "Ladies and gentlemen, please stand clear!"

They stopped.

"Who are you?" the man demanded. He wore the uniform of the railway company.

"My name is Eardley Holborn. I am a clockwork artist at the Urseau Institute of Mechanical Theatrics."

The man was taken aback for an instant, but he quickly resumed his authoritarian attitude.

"Well, that sounds very impressive, Mr. Holbon. However, I'll handle things from here."

Mr. Holborn ignored him.

"We need a doctor."

"Of course, we do. Doctor! Do we have a doctor on board?"

There was no reply.

Mr. Holborn stepped into the compartment and knelt down beside the bed.

"You can't do that! Get out!"

But Mr. Holborn wasn't listening. He placed his fingers the lady's neck to check her pulse.

She was cold.

"We're too late," he said.

"This is no good. This is terrible. On our maiden voyage too."

"You monster! All you can think about is the reputation of the company! This young woman has lost her life. Get out!"

"You can't tell..."

"Get out," Mr. Holborn whispered with the quiet menace of a venomous snake. "Go and bring the maid to me."

The man backed out of the compartment, then shouted at the other passengers who were crowded in the corridor to fetch the girl.

She appeared fourteen seconds later by Mr. Holborn's reckoning. The waiter and Sir Grant were in attendance.

"I know this must be a horrible shock to you, but we need to know exactly what happened to your lady. Can you answer some questions?"

She nodded.

"Please, think carefully about what you tell me."

"I will."

"How did you find your lady?"

"I came back from supper, expecting that she would still be dancing. When I opened the door, I saw her on the bed. She never lies down in her evening clothes, so I knew something was wrong."

"Was the door unlocked?"

"No, it was locked. I didn't even bother to knock since I didn't think she was there. I just unlocked the door."

"It's not murder then," Sir Grant said with a sigh. "That, at least, is a relief."

Mr. Holborn stroked his beard. He couldn't quite put his finger on it, but he wasn't so sure. A spritely young heiress suddenly dies. It wasn't unheard of, but he wasn't prepared to accept that there was no sign of mischief just yet.

He walked across to the window and confirmed that it was locked from the inside.

"A locked compartment on a moving train," Sir Grant observed.

"Does anybody else have a key?" Mr. Holborn asked.

"No, sir. I have the only key."

"This is a truly puzzling affair."

"Had Lady Varnstapple been ill recently?" Sir Grant asked.

"No, not at all, Sir Grant."

"It is highly irregular that a young woman in the prime of life should just drop dead, don't you agree, sir?"

"I agree, but what other possibility is there. She was alone in a locked compartment and there is no visible sign of foul play."

Mr. Holborn studied the body again. There was no blood. No bruising marked her neck. There were no signs of struggle at all.

"Perhaps she was poisoned and retired to her compartment early because she wasn't feeling well."

"That is a possibility," Sir Grant admitted. "But we don't know when she retired for the night or when she died, do we?"

"We need to gather all the passengers who were present at the dance together. Waiter, can you organise that with the concierge? I can't stand the fellow and don't want to talk to him."

The waiter nodded.

"Oh, and one other thing," he said aloud before leaning over and whispering in the waiter's ear.

"I'll try," the waiter said, and then hurried back along the corridor.

"Ladies and gentleman, would you be so kind as to make your way back to the dance carriage? We would like to speak to everybody who spoke to or even saw Lady Varnstapple this evening."

* * *

More than thirty passengers were gathered in the carriage along with the wait staff and gypsy musicians. Everybody was looking around nervously, wondering whether a murderer was amongst them.

The waiter hurried over to Mr. Holborn and whispered in his ear. The latter smiled to himself.

"My name is Eardley Holborn. I think that you are all aware by now that the young Lady Varnstapple was found dead in her compartment just moments ago."

The crowd murmured.

"I would like to ascertain her movements prior to turning in for the night. Who spoke to her?"

The young man from the colonies came forward. "My name is Harold Spirespeare. I danced with Lady Varnstapple until about ten o'clock. She went back to her compartment because a strange man was staring at her."

The carriage was filled with dozens of whispering voices.

"Who is this man? Is he here?"

"I haven't been able to find him. He disappeared."

"You're quite sure about this, Harold. It wouldn't do to make up tales."

"I saw him. He was staring at her angrily. He had dark hair and a thick, curled moustache."

Everybody looked around and the men all inspected each other. There were three men with dark hair and moustaches that matched Harold's description, but the man he had seen wasn't one of them.

"Did you get a good look at this man, Harold?"

"Not really. Just a glance and then he was gone."

Mr. Holborn suspected a disguise. At the theatre, actors completely changed their appearance in a matter of seconds. The man who had scared the heiress was certainly amongst the passengers. There was no way he could have left the speeding train.

"Did anybody else see Lady Varnstapple leave?"

"I did," a woman timidly admitted. "I remember thinking it was quite early, and she seemed to be in such a hurry to leave."

"Harold said it was around ten o'clock. Is that right?"

"Not around. It was ten on the dot."

Mr. Holborn pulled his pocket watch out and flipped it open. His watch always kept perfect time. It was seven minutes to eleven. Lady Varnstapple's companion had entered the carriage in a state of dismay precisely nine minutes earlier. That meant that Lady Varnstapple had died between ten and ten forty-four. That was a narrow window.

"Had she drunk anything while you were dancing, Harold?"

"Not a drop."

"You're sure?"

"Yes, I am. She didn't drink. She told me she never did."

Mr. Holborn surveyed the crowd. He had a question to ask. It was the most important question of all. He knew of a couple of ways Lady Varnstapple could have been murdered despite the fact that she had been locked securely in her compartment. Murder may have seemed impossible to everybody else, but his knowledge of clockwork mechanics told him otherwise. What he needed to know was whether there was a motive and whether a talent capable of committing the crime was present in that carriage.

"Does anybody present know why somebody might want Lady Varnstapple dead?"

The question was met with silence. The ticking of the clockwork train and the clacking of its wheels was all that could be heard.

Then, her companion spoke.

"I do, sir."

"Yes?"

"She refused an offer of marriage. Her suitor was furious."

Mr. Holborn's gaze swept across the carriage.

"Is he here?"

"No, but Harold's description fits him."

"What is his name?"

"Sir Jarvis Lexingthorpe," she said.

Mr. Holborn grinned. He had his man.

"You've heard that name before?" Sir Grant asked him.

"I have indeed. We've met before. He is a master of miniature clockwork mechanics. As much as I admire his talents, I never took a liking to the chap. That said, I'd have never picked him as a murderer."

"Remove your disguise and step forward!" Sir Grant ordered.

Nobody moved.

"That won't be necessary, Sir Grant." It was the concierge. He had just entered the carriage accompanied by two other railwaymen.

"You've found them?" Mr. Holborn asked.

"Yes, in the compartment of Professor Xander Humbercombe."

The crowd gasped and four men promptly grabbed the elderly professor. He offered no resistance.

"A master of disguise!" Sir Grant exclaimed.

"Indeed," Mr. Holborn agreed, shaking his head.

The railwaymen strode over and took the murderer into custody.

"How?" the passengers echoed.

"Clockwork brilliance," Mr. Holbron remarked.

The concierge handed him a pair of earrings.

"Earrings?" somebody asked.

"Yes, these are exquisite yet perfectly normal earrings. They were found in the rubbish bin in Professor Humbercombe's compartment."

He turned to the murderer.

"That was your only mistake. You should have thrown them out the window."

"Not quite his only mistake," the concierge interjected. "We also found a considerable quantity of dark hair clippings in the bin and his shaving brush and razor were still wet."

"Well, well," Mr. Holborn added.

"I don't understand!" a woman complained.

"Let me explain. The modus operandi was ingenious. The way I approached the puzzle was to ask myself how a woman locked safely in her compartment could be killed. The only possibility that occurred to me was that some kind of timed device had been used."

The crowd, including Sir Jarvis, listened intently. He made no attempt to break free.

"There were no signs of violence evident on the body of poor Lady Varnstapple, so I wondered whether she had been poisoned. I suspected that the earrings she had worn tonight were the key to her murder because they appeared to be the only means by which a lethal dose of poison could be delivered by a clockwork device."

The passengers gasped.

"I checked behind the lobes of her ears and found two pinpricks just below where each earring passed through. That explains why Sir Jarvis glared at her at ten o'clock. The earrings must have been timed to activate shortly after that time. He knew that she would react to his presence by retiring to her compartment and, as a result, there would be no witnesses to her death."

"How incredibly monstrous!" one man proclaimed. "You evil creature, Sir Jarvis!"

"Only a master of clockwork could have manufactured such hideous contraptions. Sir Jarvis is such a man. He must have made the imitation earrings and found a propitious moment to swap them for the real ones. Closer inspection will reveal that the earrings have tiny clockwork mechanisms inside that enable them to automatically wind up after a predetermined interval of time. I expect that tiny darts then flick out and inject the poison."

"It's the work of the devil himself!" a woman screamed at Sir Jarvis before fainting into her husband's arms.

"The work of a clever mind and a dark, jealous heart," Mr. Holborn declared, looking Sir Jarvis straight in the eye. "He will be brought to justice and will surely die under the clockwork cutter."

He checked his pocket watch.

"Ladies and gentlemen, the train will arrive at Cogsworthy Station in precisely three hours, twenty-four minutes, and seventeen seconds. Rest assured the police will be waiting for this fiend."

The Stolen White Elephant

Mark Twain

Left out of A Tramp Abroad, *because it was feared that some of the particulars had been exaggerated, and that others were not true. Before these suspicions had been proven groundless, the book had gone to press.*
M.T.

I

THE FOLLOWING CURIOUS HISTORY was related to me by a chance railway acquaintance. He was a gentleman more than seventy years of age, and his thoroughly good and gentle face and earnest and sincere manner imprinted the unmistakable stamp of truth upon every statement which fell from his lips. He said:

You know in what reverence the royal white elephant of Siam is held by the people of that country. You know it is sacred to kings, only kings may possess it, and that it is, indeed, in a measure even superior to kings, since it receives not merely honor but worship. Very well; five years ago, when the troubles concerning the frontier line arose between Great Britain and Siam, it was presently manifest that Siam had been in the wrong. Therefore every reparation was quickly made, and the British representative stated that he was satisfied and the past should be forgotten. This greatly relieved the King of Siam, and partly as a token of gratitude, but partly also, perhaps, to wipe out any little remaining vestige of unpleasantness which England might feel toward him, he wished to send the Queen a present – the sole sure way of propitiating an enemy, according to Oriental ideas. This present ought not only to be a royal one, but transcendently royal. Wherefore, what offering could be so meet as that of a white elephant? My position in the Indian civil service was such that I was deemed peculiarly worthy of the honor of conveying the present to her Majesty. A ship was fitted out for me and my servants and the officers and attendants of the elephant, and in due time I arrived in New York harbor and placed my royal charge in admirable quarters in Jersey City. It was necessary to remain awhile in order to recruit the animal's health before resuming the voyage.

All went well during a fortnight – then my calamities began. The white elephant was stolen! I was called up at dead of night and informed of this fearful misfortune. For some moments I was beside myself with terror and anxiety; I was helpless. Then I grew calmer and collected my faculties. I soon saw my course – for, indeed, there was but the one course for an intelligent man to pursue. Late as it was, I flew to New York and got a policeman to conduct me to the headquarters of the detective force. Fortunately I arrived in time, though the chief of the force, the celebrated Inspector Blunt, was just on the point of leaving for his home. He was a man of middle size and compact frame, and when he was thinking deeply he had a way of knitting his brows and tapping his forehead reflectively with his finger, which impressed you at once with the conviction that you stood in the presence of a person of no common order. The very sight of him gave me confidence and made me hopeful. I stated my errand. It did not flurry him in the least; it had no more visible effect upon his iron self-possession than if I had told him somebody had stolen my dog. He motioned me to a seat, and said, calmly:

"Allow me to think a moment, please."

So saying, he sat down at his office table and leaned his head upon his hand. Several clerks were at work at the other end of the room; the scratching of their pens was all the sound I heard during the next six or seven minutes. Meantime the inspector sat there, buried in thought. Finally he raised his head, and there was that in the firm lines of his face which showed me that his brain had done its work and his plan was made. Said he – and his voice was low and impressive:

"This is no ordinary case. Every step must be warily taken; each step must be made sure before the next is ventured. And secrecy must be observed – secrecy profound and absolute. Speak to no one about the matter, not even the reporters. I will take care of them; I will see that they get only what it may suit my ends to let them know." He touched a bell; a youth appeared. "Alaric, tell the reporters to remain for the present." The boy retired. "Now let us proceed to business – and systematically. Nothing can be accomplished in this trade of mine without strict and minute method."

He took a pen and some paper. "Now – name of the elephant?"

"Hassan Ben Ali Ben Selim Abdallah Mohammed Mois Alhammal Jamsetjejeebhoy Dhuleep Sultan Ebu Bhudpoor."

"Very well. Given name?"

"Jumbo."

"Very well. Place of birth?"

"The capital city of Siam."

"Parents living?"

"No – dead."

"Had they any other issue besides this one?"

"None. He was an only child."

"Very well. These matters are sufficient under that head. Now please describe the elephant, and leave out no particular, however insignificant – that is, insignificant from your point of view. To men in my profession there are no insignificant particulars; they do not exist."

I described, he wrote. When I was done, he said:

"Now listen. If I have made any mistakes, correct me."

He read as follows:

"Height, 19 feet; length from apex of forehead to insertion of tail, 26 feet; length of trunk, 16 feet; length of tail, 6 feet; total length, including trunk, and tail, 48 feet; length of tusks, $9\frac{1}{2}$ feet; ears keeping with these dimensions; footprint resembles the mark left when one up-ends a barrel in the snow; color of the elephant, a dull white; has a hole the size of a plate in each ear for the insertion of jewelry and possesses the habit in a remarkable degree of squirting water upon spectators and of maltreating with his trunk not only such persons as he is acquainted with, but even entire strangers; limps slightly with his right hind leg, and has a small scar in his left armpit caused by a former boil; had on, when stolen, a castle containing seats for fifteen persons, and a gold-cloth saddle-blanket the size of an ordinary carpet."

There were no mistakes. The inspector touched the bell, handed the description to Alaric, and said:

"Have fifty thousand copies of this printed at once and mailed to every detective office and pawnbroker's shop on the continent." Alaric retired. "There – so far, so good. Next, I must have a photograph of the property."

I gave him one. He examined it critically, and said:

"It must do, since we can do no better; but he has his trunk curled up and tucked into his mouth. That is unfortunate, and is calculated to mislead, for of course he does not usually have it in that position." He touched his bell.

"Alaric, have fifty thousand copies of this photograph made the first thing in the morning, and mail them with the descriptive circulars."

Alaric retired to execute his orders. The inspector said:

"It will be necessary to offer a reward, of course. Now as to the amount?"

"What sum would you suggest?"

"To begin with, I should say – well, twenty-five thousand dollars. It is an intricate and difficult business; there are a thousand avenues of escape and opportunities of concealment. These thieves have friends and pals everywhere –"

"Bless me, do you know who they are?"

The wary face, practised in concealing the thoughts and feelings within, gave me no token, nor yet the replying words, so quietly uttered:

"Never mind about that. I may, and I may not. We generally gather a pretty shrewd inkling of who our man is by the manner of his work and the size of the game he goes after. We are not dealing with a pickpocket or a hall thief now, make up your mind to that. This property was not 'lifted' by a novice. But, as I was saying, considering the amount of travel which will have to be done, and the diligence with which the thieves will cover up their traces as they move along, twenty-five thousand may be too small a sum to offer, yet I think it worthwhile to start with that."

So we determined upon that figure as a beginning. Then this man, whom nothing escaped which could by any possibility be made to serve as a clue, said:

"There are cases in detective history to show that criminals have been detected through peculiarities, in their appetites. Now, what does this elephant eat, and how much?"

"Well, as to what he eats – he will eat anything. He will eat a man, he will eat a Bible – he will eat anything between a man and a Bible."

"Good very good, indeed, but too general. Details are necessary – details are the only valuable things in our trade. Very well – as to men. At one meal – or, if you prefer, during one day – how many men will he eat, if fresh?"

"He would not care whether they were fresh or not; at a single meal he would eat five ordinary men."

"Very good; five men; we will put that down. What nationalities would he prefer?"

"He is indifferent about nationalities. He prefers acquaintances, but is not prejudiced against strangers."

"Very good. Now, as to Bibles. How many Bibles would he eat at a meal?"

"He would eat an entire edition."

"It is hardly succinct enough. Do you mean the ordinary octavo, or the family illustrated?"

"I think he would be indifferent to illustrations, that is, I think he would not value illustrations above simple letterpress."

"No, you do not get my idea. I refer to bulk. The ordinary octavo Bible weighs about two pounds and a half, while the great quarto with the illustrations weighs ten or twelve. How many Dore Bibles would he eat at a meal?"

"If you knew this elephant, you could not ask. He would take what they had."

"Well, put it in dollars and cents, then. We must get at it somehow. The Dore costs a hundred dollars a copy, Russia leather, beveled."

"He would require about fifty thousand dollars worth – say an edition of five hundred copies."

"Now that is more exact. I will put that down. Very well; he likes men and Bibles; so far, so good. What else will he eat? I want particulars."

"He will leave Bibles to eat bricks, he will leave bricks to eat bottles, he will leave bottles to eat clothing, he will leave clothing to eat cats, he will leave cats to eat oysters, he will leave oysters to eat ham, he will leave ham to eat sugar, he will leave sugar to eat pie, he will leave pie to eat potatoes, he will leave potatoes to eat bran; he will leave bran to eat hay, he will leave hay to eat oats, he will leave oats to eat rice, for he was mainly raised on it. There is nothing whatever that he will not eat but European butter, and he would eat that if he could taste it."

"Very good. General quantity at a meal – say about –"

"Well, anywhere from a quarter to half a ton."

"And he drinks –"

"Everything that is fluid. Milk, water, whisky, molasses, castor oil, camphene, carbolic acid – it is no use to go into particulars; whatever fluid occurs to you set it down. He will drink anything that is fluid, except European coffee."

"Very good. As to quantity?"

"Put it down five to fifteen barrels – his thirst varies; his other appetites do not."

"These things are unusual. They ought to furnish quite good clues toward tracing him."

He touched the bell.

"Alaric; summon Captain Burns."

Burns appeared. Inspector Blunt unfolded the whole matter to him, detail by detail. Then he said in the clear, decisive tones of a man whose plans are clearly defined in his head and who is accustomed to command:

"Captain Burns, detail Detectives Jones, Davis, Halsey, Bates, and Hackett to shadow the elephant."

"Yes, sir."

"Detail Detectives Moses, Dakin, Murphy, Rogers, Tupper, Higgins, and Bartholomew to shadow the thieves."

"Yes, sir."

"Place a strong guard – A guard of thirty picked men, with a relief of thirty – over the place from whence the elephant was stolen, to keep strict watch there night and day, and allow none to approach – except reporters – without written authority from me."

"Yes, sir."

"Place detectives in plain clothes in the railway; steamship, and ferry depots, and upon all roadways leading out of Jersey City, with orders to search all suspicious persons."

"Yes, sir."

"Furnish all these men with photograph and accompanying description of the elephant, and instruct them to search all trains and outgoing ferryboats and other vessels."

"Yes, sir."

"If the elephant should be found, let him be seized, and the information forwarded to me by telegraph."

"Yes, sir."

"Let me be informed at once if any clues should be found – footprints of the animal, or anything of that kind."

"Yes, sir."

"Get an order commanding the harbor police to patrol the frontages vigilantly."

"Yes, sir."

"Despatch detectives in plain clothes over all the railways, north as far as Canada, west as far as Ohio, south as far as Washington."

"Yes, sir."

"Place experts in all the telegraph offices to listen to all messages; and let them require that all cipher despatches be interpreted to them."

"Yes, sir."

"Let all these things be done with the utmost's secrecy – mind, the most impenetrable secrecy."

"Yes, sir."

"Report to me promptly at the usual hour."

"Yes, Sir."

"Go!"

"Yes, sir."

He was gone.

Inspector Blunt was silent and thoughtful a moment, while the fire in his eye cooled down and faded out. Then he turned to me and said in a placid voice:

"I am not given to boasting, it is not my habit; but – we shall find the elephant."

I shook him warmly by the hand and thanked him; and I *felt* my thanks, too. The more I had seen of the man the more I liked him and the more I admired him and marveled over the mysterious wonders of his profession. Then we parted for the night, and I went home with a far happier heart than I had carried with me to his office.

II

NEXT MORNING it was all in the newspapers, in the minutest detail. It even had additions – consisting of Detective This, Detective That, and Detective The Other's 'Theory' as to how the robbery was done, who the robbers were, and whither they had flown with their booty. There were eleven of these theories, and they covered all the possibilities; and this single fact shows what independent thinkers detectives are. No two theories were alike, or even much resembled each other, save in one striking particular, and in that one all the other eleven theories were absolutely agreed. That was, that although the rear of my building was torn out and the only door remained locked, the elephant had not been removed through the rent, but by some other (undiscovered) outlet. All agreed that the robbers had made that rent only to mislead the detectives. That never would have occurred to me or to any other layman, perhaps, but it had not deceived the detectives for a moment. Thus, what I had supposed was the only thing that had no mystery about it was in fact the very thing I had gone furthest astray in. The eleven theories all named the supposed robbers, but no two named the same robbers; the total number of suspected persons was thirty-seven. The various newspaper accounts all closed with the most important opinion of all – that of Chief Inspector Blunt. A portion of this statement read as follows:

The chief knows who the two principals are, namely, 'Brick' Duffy and 'Red' McFadden. Ten days before the robbery was achieved he was already aware that it was to be attempted, and had quietly proceeded to shadow these two noted villains; but unfortunately on the night in question their track was lost, and before it could be found again the bird was flown – that is, the elephant. Duffy and McFadden are the boldest scoundrels in the profession; the chief has reasons for believing that they are the men who stole the stove out of the detective headquarters on a bitter night last winter – in consequence of which the chief and every detective present were in the hands of the physicians before morning, some with frozen feet, others with frozen fingers, ears, and other members.

When I read the first half of that I was more astonished than ever at the wonderful sagacity of this strange man. He not only saw everything in the present with a clear eye, but even the future could not be hidden from him. I was soon at his office, and said I could not help wishing he had had those men arrested, and so prevented the trouble and loss; but his reply was simple and unanswerable:

"It is not our province to prevent crime, but to punish it. We cannot punish it until it is committed."

I remarked that the secrecy with which we had begun had been marred by the newspapers; not only all our facts but all our plans and purposes had been revealed; even all the suspected persons had been named; these would doubtless disguise themselves now, or go into hiding.

"Let them. They will find that when I am ready for them my hand will descend upon them, in their secret places, as unerringly as the hand of fate. As to the newspapers, we must keep in with them. Fame, reputation, constant public mention – these are the detective's bread and butter. He must publish his facts, else he will be supposed to have none; he must publish his theory, for nothing is so strange or striking as a detective's theory, or brings him so much wondering respect; we must publish our plans, for these the journals insist upon having, and we could not deny them without offending. We must constantly show the public what we are doing, or they will believe we are doing nothing. It is much pleasanter to have a newspaper say, 'Inspector Blunt's ingenious and extraordinary theory is as follows,' than to have it say some harsh thing, or, worse still, some sarcastic one."

"I see the force of what you say. But I noticed that in one part of your remarks in the papers this morning you refused to reveal your opinion upon a certain minor point."

"Yes, we always do that; it has a good effect. Besides, I had not formed any opinion on that point, anyway."

I deposited a considerable sum of money with the inspector, to meet current expenses, and sat down to wait for news. We were expecting the telegrams to begin to arrive at any moment now. Meantime I reread the newspapers and also our descriptive circular, and observed that our twenty-five thousand dollars reward seemed to be offered only to detectives. I said I thought it ought to be offered to anybody who would catch the elephant. The inspector said:

"It is the detectives who will find the elephant; hence the reward will go to the right place. If other people found the animal, it would only be by watching the detectives and taking advantage of clues and indications stolen from them, and that would entitle the detectives to the reward, after all. The proper office of a reward is to stimulate the men who deliver up their time and their trained sagacities to this sort of work, and not to confer benefits upon chance citizens who stumble upon a capture without having earned the benefits by their own merits and labors."

This was reasonable enough, certainly. Now the telegraphic machine in the corner began to click, and the following despatch was the result:

FLOWER STATION, N.Y., 7.30 A.M. Have got a clue. Found a succession of deep tracks across a farm near here. Followed them two miles east without result; think elephant went west. Shall now shadow him in that direction. DARLEY, Detective.

"Darley's one of the best men on the force," said the inspector. "We shall hear from him again before long."

Telegram No. 2 came:

BARKER'S, N.J., 7.40 A.M. Just arrived. Glass factory broken open here during night, and eight hundred bottles taken. Only water in large quantity near here is five miles distant. Shall strike for there. Elephant will be thirsty. Bottles were empty. BAKER, Detective.

"That promises well, too," said the inspector.

"I told you the creature's appetites would not be bad clues."

Telegram No. 3:

TAYLORVILLE, L.I. 8.15 A.M. A haystack near here disappeared during night. Probably eaten. Have got a clue, and am off. HUBBARD, Detective.

"How he does move around!" said the inspector "I knew we had a difficult job on hand, but we shall catch him yet."

FLOWER STATION, N.Y., 9 A.M. Shadowed the tracks three miles westward. Large, deep, and ragged. Have just met a farmer who says they are not elephant tracks. Says they are holes where he dug up saplings for shade-trees when ground was frozen last winter. Give me orders how to proceed. DARLEY, Detective.

"Aha! a confederate of the thieves! The thing, grows warm," said the inspector.

He dictated the following telegram to Darley:

Arrest the man and force him to name his pals. Continue to follow the tracks to the Pacific, if necessary. Chief BLUNT.

Next telegram:

CONEY POINT, PA., 8.45 A.M. Gas office broken open here during night and three months' unpaid gas bills taken. Have got a clue and am away. MURPHY, Detective.

"Heavens!" said the inspector; "would he eat gas bills?"

"Through ignorance – yes; but they cannot support life. At least, unassisted."

Now came this exciting telegram:

IRONVILLE, N.Y., 9.30 A.M. Just arrived. This village in consternation. Elephant passed through here at five this morning. Some say he went east, some say west, some north, some south – but all say they did not wait to notice, particularly. He killed a horse; have secured a piece of it for a clue. Killed it with his trunk; from style of blow, think he struck it left-handed. From position in which horse lies, think elephant traveled northward along line of Berkley Railway. Has four and a half hours' start, but I move on his track at once. HAWES, Detective.

I uttered exclamations of joy. The inspector was as self-contained as a graven image. He calmly touched his bell.

"Alaric, send Captain Burns here."

Burns appeared.

"How many men are ready for instant orders?"

"Ninety-six, sir."

"Send them north at once. Let them concentrate along the line of the Berkley road north of Ironville."

"Yes, sir."

"Let them conduct their movements with the utmost secrecy. As fast as others are at liberty, hold them for orders."

"Yes, sir."

"Go!"

"Yes, sir."

Presently came another telegram:

SAGE CORNERS, N.Y., 10.30. Just arrived. Elephant passed through here at 8.15. All escaped from the town but a policeman. Apparently elephant did not strike at policeman, but at the lamp-post. Got both. I have secured a portion of the policeman as clue. STUMM, Detective.

"So the elephant has turned westward," said the inspector. "However, he will not escape, for my men are scattered all over that region." The next telegram said:

GLOVER'S, 11.15 Just arrived. Village deserted, except sick and aged. Elephant passed through three-quarters of an hour ago. The anti-temperance mass-meeting was in session; he put his trunk in at a window and washed it out with water from cistern. Some swallowed it – since dead; several drowned. Detectives Cross and O'Shaughnessy were passing through town, but going south – so missed elephant. Whole region for many miles around in terror – people flying from their homes. Wherever they turn they meet elephant, and many are killed. BRANT, Detective.

I could have shed tears, this havoc so distressed me. But the inspector only said:

"You see – we are closing in on him. He feels our presence; he has turned eastward again." Yet further troublous news was in store for us. The telegraph brought this:

HOGANSPORT, 12.19. Just arrived. Elephant passed through half an hour ago, creating wildest fright and excitement. Elephant raged around streets; two plumbers going by, killed one – other escaped. Regret general. O'FLAHERTY, Detective.

"Now he is right in the midst of my men," said the inspector. "Nothing can save him."

A succession of telegrams came from detectives who were scattered through New Jersey and Pennsylvania, and who were following clues consisting of ravaged barns, factories, and Sunday-school libraries, with high hopes hopes amounting to certainties, indeed. The inspector said:

"I wish I could communicate with them and order them north, but that is impossible. A detective only visits a telegraph office to send his report; then he is off again, and you don't know where to put your hand on him."

Now came this despatch:

> BRIDGEPORT, CT., 12.15. Barnum offers rate of $4,000 a year for exclusive privilege of using elephant as traveling advertising medium from now till detectives find him. Wants to paste circus-posters on him. Desires immediate answer. BOGGS, Detective.

"That is perfectly absurd!" I exclaimed.

"Of course it is," said the inspector. "Evidently Mr. Barnum, who thinks he is so sharp, does not know me – but I know him."

Then he dictated this answer to the despatch:

> Mr. Barnum's offer declined. Make it $7,000 or nothing. Chief BLUNT.

"There. We shall not have to wait long for an answer. Mr. Barnum is not at home; he is in the telegraph office – it is his way when he has business on hand. Inside of three –"

> Done. – P.T. BARNUM.

So interrupted the clicking telegraphic instrument. Before I could make a comment upon this extraordinary episode, the following despatch carried my thoughts into another and very distressing channel:

> BOLIVIA, N.Y., 12.50. Elephant arrived here from the south and passed through toward the forest at 11.50, dispersing a funeral on the way, and diminishing the mourners by two. Citizens fired some small cannon-balls into him, and then fled. Detective Burke and I arrived ten minutes later, from the north, but mistook some excavations for footprints, and so lost a good deal of time; but at last we struck the right trail and followed it to the woods. We then got down on our hands and knees and continued to keep a sharp eye on the track, and so shadowed it into the brush. Burke was in advance. Unfortunately the animal had stopped to rest; therefore, Burke having his head down, intent upon the track, butted up against the elephant's hind legs before he was aware of his vicinity. Burke instantly arose to his feet, seized the tail, and exclaimed joyfully, "I claim the re–" but got no further, for a single blow of the huge trunk laid the brave fellow's fragments low in death. I fled rearward, and the elephant turned and shadowed me to the edge of the wood, making tremendous speed, and I should inevitably have been lost, but that the remains of the funeral providentially intervened again and diverted his attention. I have just learned that nothing of that funeral is now left; but this is no loss, for there

is abundance of material for another. Meantime, the elephant has disappeared again. MULROONEY, Detective.

We heard no news except from the diligent and confident detectives scattered about New Jersey, Pennsylvania, Delaware, and Virginia – who were all following fresh and encouraging clues – until shortly after 2 P.M., when this telegram came:

BAXTER CENTER, 2.15. Elephant been here, plastered over with circus-bills, and he broke up a revival, striking down and damaging many who were on the point of entering upon a better life. Citizens penned him up and established a guard. When Detective Brown and I arrived, some time after, we entered enclosure and proceeded to identify elephant by photograph and description. All marks tallied exactly except one, which we could not see – the boil-scar under armpit. To make sure, Brown crept under to look, and was immediately brained – that is, head crushed and destroyed, though nothing issued from debris. All fled, so did elephant, striking right and left with much effect. Has escaped, but left bold blood-track from cannon-wounds. Rediscovery certain. He broke southward, through a dense forest. BRENT, Detective.

That was the last telegram. At nightfall a fog shut down which was so dense that objects but three feet away could not be discerned. This lasted all night. The ferry-boats and even the omnibuses had to stop running.

III

NEXT MORNING the papers were as full of detective theories as before; they had all our tragic facts in detail also, and a great many more which they had received from their telegraphic correspondents. Column after column was occupied, a third of its way down, with glaring head-lines, which it made my heart sick to read. Their general tone was like this:

THE WHITE ELEPHANT AT LARGE! HE MOVES UPON HIS FATAL MARCH! WHOLE VILLAGES DESERTED BY THEIR FRIGHT-STRICKEN OCCUPANTS! PALE TERROR GOES BEFORE HIM, DEATH AND DEVASTATION FOLLOW AFTER! AFTER THESE, THE DETECTIVES! BARNS DESTROYED, FACTORIES GUTTED, HARVESTS DEVOURED, PUBLIC ASSEMBLAGES DISPERSED, ACCOMPANIED BY SCENES OF CARNAGE IMPOSSIBLE TO DESCRIBE! THEORIES OF THIRTY-FOUR OF THE MOST DISTINGUISHED DETECTIVES ON THE FORCE! THEORY OF CHIEF BLUNT!

"There!" said Inspector Blunt, almost betrayed into excitement, "This is magnificent! This is the greatest windfall that any detective organization ever had. The fame of it will travel to the ends of the earth, and endure to the end of time, and my name with it."

But there was no joy for me. I felt as if I had committed all those red crimes, and that the elephant was only my irresponsible agent. And how the list had grown! In one place he had 'interfered with an election and killed five repeaters.' He had followed this act with the destruction of two pool fellows, named O'Donohue and McFlannigan, who had 'found a refuge in the home of the oppressed of all lands only the day before, and were in the act of exercising for the first time the noble right of American citizens at the polls, when stricken down by the relentless hand of the Scourge of Siam.' In another, he had 'found a crazy sensation-preacher preparing his next season's heroic attacks on the dance, the theater, and other things which can't strike back, and had stepped on him.' And in still another place he had 'killed a lightning-rod agent.' And so the list went on, growing redder and redder, and more and more heartbreaking. Sixty persons had been killed, and two hundred and forty wounded. All the accounts bore just testimony to the activity and devotion of the detectives, and all closed with the remark that 'three hundred thousand citizens and four detectives saw the dread creature, and two of the latter he destroyed.'

I dreaded to hear the telegraphic instrument begin to click again. By and by the messages began to pour in, but I was happily disappointed in their nature. It was soon apparent that all trace of the elephant was lost. The fog had enabled him to search out a good hiding-place unobserved. Telegrams from the most absurdly distant points reported that a dim vast mass had been glimpsed there through the fog at such and such an hour, and was 'undoubtedly the elephant.' This dim vast mass had been glimpsed in New Haven, in New Jersey, in Pennsylvania, in interior New York, in Brooklyn, and even in the city of New York itself! But in all cases the dim vast mass had vanished quickly and left no trace. Every detective of the large force scattered over this huge extent of country sent his hourly report, and each and every one of them had a clue, and was shadowing something, and was hot upon the heels of it.

But the day passed without other result.

The next day the same.

The next just the same.

The newspaper reports began to grow monotonous with facts that amounted to nothing, clues which led to nothing, and theories which had nearly exhausted the elements which surprise and delight and dazzle.

By advice of the inspector I doubled the reward.

Four more dull days followed. Then came a bitter blow to the poor, hard-working detectives – the journalists declined to print their theories, and coldly said, "Give us a rest."

Two weeks after the elephant's disappearance I raised the reward to seventy-five thousand dollars by the inspector's advice. It was a great sum, but I felt that I would rather sacrifice my whole private fortune than lose my credit with my government. Now that the detectives were in adversity, the newspapers turned upon them, and began to fling the most stinging sarcasms at them. This gave the minstrels an idea, and they dressed themselves as detectives and hunted the elephant on the stage in the most extravagant way. The caricaturists made pictures of detectives scanning the country with spy-glasses, while the elephant, at their backs, stole apples out of their pockets. And they made all sorts of ridiculous pictures of the detective badge – you have seen that badge printed in gold on the back of detective novels no doubt, it is a wide-staring eye, with the legend, 'WE NEVER SLEEP.' When detectives called for a drink, the would-be facetious barkeeper resurrected an obsolete form of expression and said, "Will you have an eye-opener?" All the air was thick with sarcasms.

But there was one man who moved calm, untouched, unaffected, through it all. It was that heart of oak, the chief inspector. His brave eye never drooped, his serene confidence never wavered. He always said:

"Let them rail on; he laughs best who laughs last."

My admiration for the man grew into a species of worship. I was at his side always. His office had become an unpleasant place to me, and now became daily more and more so. Yet if he could endure it I meant to do so also – at least, as long as I could. So I came regularly, and stayed – the only outsider who seemed to be capable of it. Everybody wondered how I could; and often it seemed to me that I must desert, but at such times I looked into that calm and apparently unconscious face, and held my ground.

About three weeks after the elephant's disappearance I was about to say, one morning, that I should have to strike my colors and retire, when the great detective arrested the thought by proposing one more superb and masterly move.

This was to compromise with the robbers. The fertility of this man's invention exceeded anything I have ever seen, and I have had a wide intercourse with the world's finest minds. He said he was confident he could compromise for one hundred thousand dollars and recover the elephant. I said I believed I could scrape the amount together, but what would become of the poor detectives who had worked so faithfully? He said:

"In compromises they always get half."

This removed my only objection. So the inspector wrote two notes, in this form:

> DEAR MADAM, – *Your husband can make a large sum of money (and be entirely protected from the law) by making an immediate appointment with me. Chief BLUNT.*

He sent one of these by his confidential messenger to the 'reputed wife' of Brick Duffy, and the other to the reputed wife of Red McFadden.

Within the hour these offensive answers came:

> YE OWLD FOOL: *brick McDuffys bin ded 2 yere. BRIDGET MAHONEY.*

> CHIEF BAT, – *Red McFadden is hung and in heving 18 month. Any Ass but a detective know that. MARY O'HOOLIGAN.*

"I had long suspected these facts," said the inspector; "this testimony proves the unerring accuracy of my instinct."

The moment one resource failed him he was ready with another. He immediately wrote an advertisement for the morning papers, and I kept a copy of it:

> A. – *xwblv.242 N. Tjnd – fz328wmlg. Ozpo, – ; 2m! ogw. Mum*

He said that if the thief was alive this would bring him to the usual rendezvous. He further explained that the usual rendezvous was a place where all business affairs between detectives and criminals were conducted. This meeting would take place at twelve the next night.

We could do nothing till then, and I lost no time in getting out of the office, and was grateful indeed for the privilege.

At eleven the next night I brought one hundred thousand dollars in bank notes and put them into the chief's hands, and shortly afterward he took his leave, with the brave old undimmed confidence in his eye. An almost intolerable hour dragged to a close; then I heard his welcome tread, and rose gasping and tottered to meet him. How his fine eyes flamed with triumph! He said:

"We've compromised! The jokers will sing a different tune tomorrow! Follow me!"

He took a lighted candle and strode down into the vast vaulted basement where sixty detectives always slept, and where a score were now playing cards to while the time. I followed close after him. He walked swiftly down to the dim remote end of the place, and just as I succumbed to the pangs of suffocation and was swooning away he stumbled and fell over the outlying members of a mighty object, and I heard him exclaim as he went down:

"Our noble profession is vindicated. Here is your elephant!"

I was carried to the office above and restored with carbolic acid. The whole detective force swarmed in, and such another season of triumphant rejoicing ensued as I had never witnessed before. The reporters were called, baskets of champagne were opened, toasts were drunk, the handshakings and congratulations were continuous and enthusiastic. Naturally the chief was the hero of the hour, and his happiness was so complete and had been so patiently and worthily and bravely won that it made me happy to see it, though I stood there a homeless beggar, my priceless charge dead, and my position in my country's service lost to me through what would always seem my fatally careless execution of a great trust. Many an eloquent eye testified its deep admiration for the chief, and many a detective's voice murmured, "Look at him – just the king of the profession; only give him a clue, it's all he wants, and there ain't anything hid that he can't find." The dividing of the fifty thousand dollars made great pleasure; when it was finished the chief made a little speech while he put his share in his pocket, in which he said, "Enjoy it, boys, for you've earned it; and, more than that, you've earned for the detective profession undying fame."

A telegram arrived, which read:

MONROE, MICH., 10 P.M. First time I've struck a telegraph office in over three weeks. Have followed those footprints, horseback, through the woods, a thousand miles to here, and they get stronger and bigger and fresher every day. Don't worry – inside of another week I'll have the elephant. This is dead sure. DARLEY, Detective.

The chief ordered three cheers for "Darley, one of the finest minds on the force," and then commanded that he be telegraphed to come home and receive his share of the reward.

So ended that marvelous episode of the stolen elephant. The newspapers were pleasant with praises once more, the next day, with one contemptible exception. This sheet said, "Great is the detective! He may be a little slow in finding a little thing like a mislaid elephant he may hunt him all day and sleep with his rotting carcass all night for three weeks, but he will find him at last if he can get the man who mislaid him to show him the place!"

Poor Hassan was lost to me forever. The cannonshots had wounded him fatally, he had crept to that unfriendly place in the fog, and there, surrounded by his enemies and in constant danger of detection, he had wasted away with hunger and suffering till death gave him peace.

The compromise cost me one hundred thousand dollars; my detective expenses were forty-two thousand dollars more; I never applied for a place again under my government; I am a ruined man and a wanderer in the earth, but my admiration for that man, whom I believe to be the greatest detective the world has ever produced, remains undimmed to this day, and will so remain unto the end.

Sentimental Simpson

Edgar Wallace

ACCORDING TO certain signs, the Amateur Detective thought his French window had been forced by a left-handed man who wore square-toed boots, the muddy print of the latter against the enamel of the door seemed to prove this beyond doubt. The direction of the knife-cuts in the putty about the window-glass supported the left-handed view.

Another point:

Only a left-handed man would have thought of sawing through the left fold of the shutter.

The occupier of Wisteria Lodge explained all this to the real detective, who sat stolidly on the other side of the table in the occupier's dining-room at three o'clock in the morning, listening to the interesting hypothesis.

"I think if you look for a left-handed man with square-toed boots – or they may be shoes," said the householder quietly, even gently, "you will discover the robber."

"Ah," said the real detective, and swallowed his whisky deliberately.

"The curious thing about the burglary is this," the sufferer went on, "that although my cash-box was opened and contained over £400, the money was untouched. The little tray on top had not been even lifted out. My dear wife kept a lock of hair of her pet pom 'Chu Chin' – the poor little dear was poisoned last year by those horrible people at 'The Limes.' I'm sure they did it –"

"What about this lock of hair?" asked the detective, suddenly interested.

"It was damp, quite damp," explained the householder. "Now, as I say, my theory is that the man wore square-toed boots and a mackintosh. He was undoubtedly left-handed."

"I see," said the real detective.

Then he went forth and took Sentimental Simpson out of his bed, not because he wore square-toed shoes (nor was he left-handed), but because there were certain telltale indications which pointed unmistakably to one man.

Mr. Simpson came blinking into the passage holding a paraffin lamp in his hand. He wore a shirt and an appearance of profound surprise.

"Hullo, Mr. Button," he said. "Lor' bless me, you gave me quite a start. I went to bed early tonight with the toothache, an' when I heard you knock I says to myself –"

"Get your trousers on," said Detective-Sergeant Button.

Simpson hesitated for just a fraction of a second and then retired to his sleeping apartment. Mr. Button bent his head and listened attentively for the sound of a stealthily opened window.

But Simpson did not run.

"And your coat and boots," said Button testily. "I'm surprised at you, Simpson – you never gave me this trouble before."

Simpson accepted the reproach with amazement.

"You don't mean to tell me that you want me?" he said incredulously, and added that if heaven in its anger deprived him of his life at that very moment, and on the spot, which he indicated with a grimy forefinger, he had been in bed since a quarter to ten.

"Don't let us have an argument," pleaded Mr. Button, and accompanied his guest to the police station.

On the day of the trial, whilst he was waiting in the corridor to go up the flight of stairs that leads to the dock, Simpson saw his captor.

"Mr. Button," he said, "I hope there is no ill-feeling between you and me?"

"None whatever, Simpson."

"I don't think you are going to get a conviction," said Simpson thoughtfully. He was a round-faced, small-eyed man with a gentle voice, and when he looked thoughtful his eyes had the appearance of having retreated a little farther into his head. "I bear no ill-will to you, Mr. Button – you've got your business and I've got mine. But who was the 'snout'?"

Mr. Button shook his head. Anyway, the informer is a sacred being, and in this case there was, unfortunately, no informer. Therefore, there was a double reason for his reticence.

"Now what is the good of being unreasonable?" he said reprovingly. "You ought to know better than to ask me a question like that."

"But what made you think it was me?' persisted Simpson, and the sergeant looked at him.

"Who got upset over a lock of hair?" he asked significantly, and the eyes of his prisoner grew moist.

"Hair was always a weakness of mine," he said, with a catch in his voice. "A relic of what you might call a loved one... somebody who has passed, Mr. Button, to... to the great beyond (if you'll forgive the expression). It sort of brings a... well, we've all got our feelings."

"We have," admitted Button kindly; "and talking about feelings, Simpson, what are my feelings going to be if I get a ticking off from the judge for bringing you up without sufficient evidence? I don't think you'll escape, mind you, but you know what juries are! Now, what about making a nice little statement, Simpson? Just own up that you 'broke and entered' and I'll go into the box and say a good word for you. You don't want to make me look silly, do you?"

"I don't," confessed Simpson; "at the same time, I don't want to make myself look silly by owning up to a crime which, in a manner of speaking, is abhorrent to my nature."

"You read too many books," said his captor unpleasantly; "that is where you get all those crack-jaw words from. Think of what my poor wife will say if I get it in the neck from the judge... it'll break her heart..."

"Don't," gulped Mr. Simpson. "Don't do it... I can't stand it, Mr. Button."

What he might have done had the conversation been protracted is a matter for speculation. At that instant the warders haled him up the steps that lead to the dock.

And such was the weakness of the evidence against him that the jury found him Not Guilty without leaving the box.

"I cannot congratulate the police on the conduct of this case," said the judge severely, and Simpson, looking upon the crestfallen face of Sergeant Button, thought of Mrs. Button's broken heart, and had to be assisted from the dock.

So Mr. Simpson went back to his little room in Castel Street. He had an uncomfortable feeling that he had failed a friend in the hour of his need, and he strove vainly to banish from his mind the thought of the shattered harmony of Detective Button's household.

It drew him just a little farther from contact with the world in which he lived, for he was not a popular partner and had few friends. One by one they had fallen away in consequence of his degrading weakness. Lew Saffron, who had openly and publicly stated at the 'Nine

Crowns' that Simpson was the greatest artist that had ever smashed a safe, and had as publicly challenged the American push to better Mr. Simpson's work in connection with the unauthorized opening of Epstein's Jewelry Emporium, even Lew eventually dropped him after a disastrous partnership.

"It would have been a success and we'd have got away with the finest parcel of stones that ever was taken in one haul," he said, relative to a certain Hatton Garden job which he had worked with Simpson; "but what happened? He got the safe open and I was downstairs, watching the street for the copper, expecting him to come down with the stuff. I waited for ten minutes and then went up, and what did I see? This blank, blank Simpson sitting on the blank, blank floor, and crying his blank, blank eyes out over some old love-letters that Van Voss kept in his safe! Letters from a blank, blank typist that Van Voss had been in love with. He said they touched him to the core. He wanted to go and kill Van Voss, and by the time I'd got him quiet the street was full of bulls... we got away over the roof... no more Simpson for me, thank you!"

Mr. Simpson sighed as he realized his lonely state. Nevertheless his afternoon was not unprofitably spent, for there were six more chapters of Christy's Old Organ to be read before, red-eyed, he returned the book to the free library which he patronized.

He had an appointment that evening with Charles Valentino, the keeper of a bar at Kennington and a man of some standing in the world-beneath-the-world.

He was a tall man with a drooping moustache (though his appearance is of no importance), and he was fattish of figure, heavy and deliberate of speech. He greeted Mr. Simpson reproachfully and in his heaviest manner.

"What's this I hear about the job you did, Simpson? I couldn't believe my eyes when I read it in the newspaper. Got acquitted, too! You ought to have had ten years!"

Mr. Simpson looked uncomfortable.

"Left four hundred and thirty pounds in treasury notes in a box that you had opened, that wasn't even locked? What's the matter with you, Simpson?"

Charles Valentino's tone was one of amazement, incredulity, and admonishment.

"I can't help it, Mr. Valentino." Tears were in Sentimental Simpson's eyes. "When I saw that lock of 'air on the tray and I thought perhaps that it was a lock of the 'air of his mother, treasured, so to speak –"

Here Mr. Simpson's voice failed him, and he had to swallow before he continued:

"It's me weakness, Mr. Valentino; I just couldn't go any farther."

Mr. Valentino puffed thoughtfully at his cigar.

"You owe me seventy pounds; I suppose you know that?" he asked unpleasantly. "Seventy pounds is seventy pounds."

Simpson nodded.

"It cost me thirty pounds for a mouthpiece," Valentino continued, and by 'mouthpiece' he referred to the advocate who had pleaded Simpson's cause: "twenty-five pounds for that new lot of tools I got you, when you came out of 'stir' last May; ten pounds I lent you to do that Manchester job, which you never paid me back – the so-called jewelry you brought down was all Birmingham stuff, nine carat, and not worth the freight charges – and here you had a chance of getting real money... well, I'm surprised at you, that's all I can say, Simpson."

Simpson shook his head unhappily.

Mr. Valentino, thinking that perhaps he had gone as far as was necessary, beckoned the Italian waiter (the conference took place at a little brasserie in Soho) and invited his companion.

"What will you have, Simpson?"

"Gin," said the wretched Simpson.

"Gin goes with tears." Mr. Valentino was firm. "Have a more manly drink, Simpson."

"Beer," corrected Simpson despondently.

"Now I'll tell you what it is," said Mr. Valentino when their needs had been satisfied. "Things can't go on as they are going. I am a commercial man, and I've got to make money. I don't mind taking a risk when there's loot at the end of it, but I tell you, Simpson, straight, that I am going to chuck it up unless some of yon hooks pay more attention to business. "Why," went on Mr. Valentino indignantly, "in the old days I never had this kind of trouble with you boys! Willie Topple never gave me, what I might term, a moment's uneasiness."

It was always serious when Mr. Valentino dragged Willie Topple from his grave in Exeter Gaol and set him up as a model of industry, and Sentimental Simpson moved uncomfortably in his velvet chair.

"Willie was always on the spot, and if he did a job, there was the stuff all nicely packed up," said Mr. Valentino reminiscently. "He'd just step into the saloon bar, order a drink, and shove the stuff across the counter. 'You might keep this box of chocolates for me, Mr. Valentino,' that's what he'd say, and there it was, every article wrapped in tissue paper. I used to compare them with the list published in the Hue and Cry, and never once did Willie deliver short."

He sighed.

"Times have changed," he said bitterly. "Some of you boys have got so careless that me heart's in me mouth every time a 'split' strolls into the bar. And what do I get out of it? Why, Willie Topple drew seventeen hundred pounds commission from me in one year – you owe me seventy!"

"I admit it is a risk being a fence " began Mr. Simpson.

"A what?" said the other sharply. "What was that word you used, Simpson?"

Mr. Simpson was silent.

"Never use that expression to me. A fence! Do you mean the receiver of stolen property? I mind things for people. I take a few articles, so to speak, in pawn for my customers. I'm surprised at you, Simpson."

He did not wait for Mr. Simpson to express his contrition, but bending forward over the table, lowered his voice until it was little more than a rumble of subterranean sound.

"There's a place in Park Crescent, No. 176," he said deliberately. "That's the very job for you, Simpson. Next Sunday night is the best time, because there will only be the kid in the house. There's lashings of jewelry, pearl necklaces, diamond plaques, and the father and mother are away at Brighton. They are going to a wedding. I have had a 'nose' in the house, a window-cleaner, and says all the stuff is kept in a little safe under the mother's bed. The best time is after eleven. They go to bed early... and a pantry window that you can reach from the back of the house, only a wall to climb, and that's in a mews. Now, what do you say, Simpson?"

Mr. Simpson scratched his chin.

"I'll have a look round," he said cautiously. "I don't take much notice of these window-cleaners. One put me on to the job at Purley –"

"Let bygones be bygones," said Mr. Valentino. "I know all about that Purley business. You'd have made a profit if your dam' curiosity hadn't made you stop to read the funeral cards in the cook's bedroom. And after we'd got the cook called away to the north so that you should have no trouble and an empty house to work in! The question is, will you do this, or shall I put Harry Welting on to it? He is not as good a man as you, I admit, Simpson, though he hasn't your failings."

"I'll do it," said Mr. Simpson, and the other nodded approvingly.

"If a fiver is any good to you...?" he said.

"It will be a lot of good to me," said Mr. Simpson fervently, and the money was passed.

It was midnight on the 26th June, and it was raining – according to Mr. Simpson's extravagant description – cats and dogs, when he turned into Park Mews, a deserted and gloomy thoroughfare devoted to the storage of mechanical vehicles. He had marked the little gate in the wall by daylight. The wall itself was eight feet in height and surmounted by spikes. Mr. Simpson favored walls so guarded. The spikes, if they were not too old, served to attach the light rope he carried. In two minutes he was over the wall and was working scientifically at the pantry window. Ten minutes afterwards he was hanging up his wet mackintosh in the hall. He paused only to slip back the bolts in the door, unfasten the chain, and turn the key softly, before he mounted the thickly carpeted stairs.

The house was in darkness. Only the slow tick of the hall-clock broke the complete stillness, and Mr. Simpson walked up the stairs, keeping time to the clock, so that any accidental creak he might make might be confounded by a listener with the rhythmic noise of the timepiece.

The first bedroom which he entered was without occupant. He gathered from the richness and disposition of the furniture, and the handsomeness of the appointments, that this was the room occupied by the father and mother now participating in the Brighton festivities.

He made a thorough and professional examination of the dressing-table, found and pocketed a small diamond brooch of no enormous value, choked for a second at the silver-framed picture of a little girl that stood upon the dressing- table, but crushed down his emotions ruthlessly.

The second bedroom was less ornate, and like the other, untenanted. Here he drew blank. It was evidently a room reserved for visitors; the dressing- table was empty as also was the wardrobe. Then he remembered and went back to the room he had searched and flashed his lamp under the bed. There was no sign of a safe. It may be in the third room, thought Mr. Simpson, and turned the handle of the door softly. He knew, the moment he stepped inside, that the big four-poster bed he could dimly see was occupied. He could hear the regular breathing of the sleeper and for a second hesitated, then stepping forward carefully, he moved to the side of the bed, listening again.

Yes, the breathing was regular. He dare not put his lamp upon the sleeper. This must be the child's room, he guessed, and contented himself with stooping and showing a beam of light beneath the bed. He gasped. There was the 'safe'. A squat, steel box. He put out the light and laid the torch gently upon the floor, then groping beneath the bed, he gripped the box and slid it toward him. It was very heavy, but not too heavy to carry.

Drawing the treasure clear of the bed, he slipped his torch in his pocket and lifted the box. If it had been the safe he had expected, his success would have been impossible of achievement. As it was, the weight of this repository taxed his strength. Presently he had it well gripped and began a slow retreat. He was half-way across the room when there was a click, and instantly the room was flooded with light. In his natural agitation the box slipped from his fingers; he made a wild grab to recover his hold, and did succeed in putting it down without noise, but no more. And then he turned, open-mouthed, to the child who was watching him curiously from the bed.

Never in his life had Sentimental Simpson seen a child so fairylike, so ethereal in her loveliness. A mass of golden hair was tied back by a blue ribbon, and the big eyes that were fixed on him showed neither fear nor alarm. She sat up in bed, her thin white hands clasping the knees doubled beneath the coverlet, an interested and not unamused spectator of Mr. Simpson's embarrassment.

"Good evening, Mr. Burglar," she said softly, and smiled.

Simpson swallowed something.

"Good evening, miss," he said huskily. "I hope I haven't come into the wrong house. A friend of mine told me to call and get a box he had forgotten –"

"You're a burglar," she said, nodding wisely; "of course you're a burglar. I am awfully glad to see you. I have always wanted to meet a burglar."

Mr. Simpson, a prey to various emotions, could think of no suitable reply. He looked down at the box and he looked at the child, and then he blinked furiously.

"Come and sit here," she pointed to a chair by the side of the bed.

The dazed burglar obeyed.

"How long have you been a burglar?" she demanded.

"Oh, quite a long time, miss," said Mr. Simpson weakly.

She shook her head reproachfully.

"You should not have said that – you should have said that this was your first crime," she said. "When you were a little boy, were you a burglar?"

"No, miss," said the miserable Simpson.

"Didn't your mother ever tell you that you mustn't be a burglar?" asked the child, and Simpson broke down.

"My poor old mother!" he sobbed.

It is true to say that in her lifetime the late Mrs. Simpson had evoked no extravagant expressions of affection from her children, who had been rescued from her tender care at an early age, and had been educated at the rate-payers' expense at the local workhouse. But the word 'mother' always affected Mr. Simpson that way.

"Poor man," said the child tenderly. She reached out her hand and laid it upon Mr. Simpson's bowed head. "Do your little children know that you are a burglar?" she asked.

"No, miss," sobbed Simpson.

He had no little children. He had never been married, but any reference to his children always brought a lump into his throat. By spiritual adoption he had secured quite a large family. Sometimes, in periods of temporary retirement from the activities and competition of life, he had brooded in his cell, his head in his hands, on how his darling little Doris would miss her daddy, and had in consequence enjoyed the most exquisite of mental tortures.

"Are you a burglar because you are hungry?"

Mr. Simpson nodded. He could not trust himself to speak.

"You should say – 'I'm starving, miss!' " she said gently. "Are you starving?"

Mr. Simpson nodded again.

"Poor burglar!"

Again her hand caressed his head, and now he could not restrain himself any more. He fell on his knees by the side of the bed and, burying his head in his arms, his shoulders heaved.

He heard her slip out of bed on the other side and the shuffle of her slippered feet as she crossed the room.

"I am going to get you some food, Mr. Burglar," she said softly.

All Mr. Simpson's ill-spent life passed before his anguished eyes as he waited. He would reform, he swore. He would live an honest life. The influence of this sweet, innocent child should bear its fruit. Dear little soul, he thought, as he mopped his tear-stained face, she was down there in that dark, cold kitchen, getting him food. How brave she was! It was a long time before she came back bearing a tray that was all too heavy for her frail figure to support. He took it from her hands reverently and laid it on the table.

She was wearing a blue silk kimono that emphasized the purity of her delicate skin. He could only look at her in awe and wonder.

"You must eat, Mr. Burglar," she said gently.

"I couldn't eat a mouthful, miss," he protested tearfully. "What you said to me has so upset me, miss, that if I eat a crumb, it will choke me."

He did not mention, perhaps he had forgotten, that an hour previous he had supped to repletion. She seemed to understand, and sat down on the edge of the bed, her grave eyes watching him.

"You must tell me about yourself," she said. "I should like to know about you, so that I can pray for you, Mr. Burglar."

"Don't, miss!" blubbered Mr. Simpson.

"Don't do it! I can't stand it! I have been a terrible man. I used to be a lob-crawler once. You don't know what a lob-crawler is? I used to pinch tills. And then I used to do ladder work. You know, miss, I put ladders up against the windows whilst the family was in the dining-room and got away with the stuff. And then I did that job at Hoxton, the fur burglary. There was a lot about it in the papers – me and a fellow named Moses. He was a Hebrew gentleman," he added unnecessarily.

The girl nodded.

"But I am going to give it up, though, miss," said Simpson huskily. "I am going to chuck Valentino, and if I owe him seventy pounds, why, I'll pay him out of the money I earn honestly."

"Who is Valentino?"

"He's a fence, miss; you wouldn't know what a fence is. He keeps the 'Bottle and Glass' public-house down Atherby Road, Kennington."

"Poor man," she said, shaking her head. "Poor burglar, I am so sorry for you."

Mr. Simpson choked. "I think I'll go, miss, if you don't mind." She nodded and held out her hand.

He took it in his and kissed it. He had seen such things done in the pictures. Yet it was with a lightened heart, and with a knowledge of a great burden of crime and sin rolled away from his conscience that he walked down the stairs, his head erect, charged with a high purpose. He opened the door and walked out, literally and figuratively into the arms of Inspector John Coleman, X. Division; Sergeant Arthur John Welby of X. Division; and Detective Sergeant Charles John Smith, also of X. Division.

"Bless my heart and soul," said the Inspector, "if it isn't Simpson!"

Mr. Simpson said nothing for a moment, then:

"I have been visiting a friend."

"And now you are coming to stay with us. What a week-end you are having!" said Sergeant Smith.

At four o'clock in the morning, Mr. Simpson stirred uneasily on his wooden bed. A voice had disturbed him; it was a loud and an aggressive voice, and it came from the corridor outside his cell. He heard the click and clash of a turning lock.

"So far as I am concerned," said the voice, "I am a perfectly innocent man, and if any person has made a statement derogatory to my good name I will have the law on him, if there is a law."

"Oh, there's a law all right," said the voice of Detective Smith. "In you go, Valentino," and then the door was slammed.

Mr. Simpson sat up and took notice.

Valentino!

The next morning, when he was conducted by the assistant gaoler to perform his ablutions, he caught a glimpse of that respectable licensed victualler. It was the merest glimpse, for the grating in the cell-door is not a large one, but he heard Mr. Valentino's exclamation of annoyance, and when he returned, that worthy man hissed at him:

"So you're the nose, are you, Simpson, you dirty dog!"

"Don't say it, Mr. Valentino," said Simpson brokenly, for it hurt him that any man should think him guilty of so despicable an action.

That their crime was associated was proved when they stepped into the dock together, with policemen between them, the constabulary having been inserted for the sake of peace and quietness. Yet, despite his position, Mr. Simpson was by no means depressed. His heart sang a song of joy at his reformation. Perhaps he would see the girl, that angel child, again; that was all he hoped.

Looking round the court eagerly, a wave of joy swept through his being, for he had seen her. That was enough. He would serve whatever sentence was passed, and tears of happiness fell from his eyes and splashed on the steel rail of the dock. The assistant gaoler thoughtfully wiped them off. Rust spots are very difficult to eradicate, unless they are dealt with immediately.

And then to his delight she came forward. A sweet figure of childhood, she seemed, as she stood in the witness stand. Her eyes rested on him for a second and she smiled...

"If you want to cry, cry on the floor!" hissed the assistant gaoler, and rubbed the rail savagely with his handkerchief.

A lawyer rose in the body of the court.

"Your name is Marie Wilson?" he said.

"Yes, sir," she replied in a voice of such pure harmony that a thrill ran through Simpson's system.

"You are professionally known as "Baby Bellingham?"

"Yes, sir," said the child.

"And you are at present engaged at the Hilarity Theatre in a play called *The Child and the Burglar*?"

"Yes, sir," she answered, with a proud glance at the dazzled Simpson.

"And I thinly I am stating the fact," said the lawyer, "that your experience last night was practically a repetition of the action of your play?"

"Yes, sir," said the child, "except that he wouldn't say his lines. I did try hard to make him."

The magistrate was looking at a paper on his desk.

"I see there is a report of this occurrence in this morning's newspaper," he said, and read the headline: "CHILD ACTRESS REDUCES HARDENED BURGLAR TO TEARS BY HER ARTISTRY".

Miss Wilson nodded gravely.

"After I had gone downstairs to get him his supper and had rung up the police on the telephone," she said, "I also rang up my press agent. My papa says that I must always ring up my press agent. Papa says that two lines on the news page is worth two columns amongst the advertisements. Papa says –"

It was ten months after this when Mr. Simpson and Mr. Valentino met. They were loading coke into a large cart drawn by a famous old blind horse which is the pride of Dartmoor Gaol. The warder in charge of the party was at sufficient distance away to allow a free interchange of courtesies.

"And when I get out," said Mr. Valentino, tremulous with wrath, "I am going to make Kennington too hot to hold you, Simpson. A chicken-hearted fellow like you oughtn't to be in the business. To think that a respectable tradesman should be herded with common felons because a babbling, bat-eyed hook gets sloppy over a kid and gives away his friends – an actress too... stringing you along, you poor turnip! Doin' her play with you as the 'ero! My God, you're a disgrace to the profession!"

But Simpson was standing erect, leaning on his shovel and staring across the yard.

In the angle of two high walls was a mound of loose earth which had been brought in to treat the governor's garden, and on the face of the dun-colored heap were vivid green shoots tipped with blue; they had come, it seemed, in a night, for this was the month of early spring.

"Bluebells!" quavered Mr. Simpson. His lip trembled and he wiped his eyes with the cuff of his yellow coat.

Bluebells always made Mr. Simpson cry.

Sir Gilbert Murrell's Picture

Victor L. Whitechurch

THE AFFAIR of the goods truck on the Didcot and Newbury branch of the Great Western Railway was of singular interest, and found a prominent place in Thorpe Hazell's notebook. It was owing partly to chance, and partly to Hazell's sagacity, that the main incidents in the story were discovered, but he always declared that the chief interest to his mind was the unique method by which a very daring plan was carried out.

He was staying with a friend at Newbury at the time, and had taken his camera down with him, for he was a bit of an amateur photographer as well as book-lover, though his photos generally consisted of trains and engines. He had just come in from a morning's ramble with his camera slung over his shoulder, and was preparing to partake of two plasmon biscuits, when his friend met him in the hail.

"I say, Hazell," he began, "you're just the fellow they want here."

"What's up?" asked Hazell, taking off his camera and commencing some 'exercises'.

"I've just been down to the station. I know the stationmaster very well, and he tells me an awfully queer thing happened on the line last night."

"Where?"

"On the Didcot branch. It's a single line, you know, running through the Berkshire Downs to Didcot."

Hazell smiled, and went on whirling his arms round his head.

"Kind of you to give me the information," he said, "but I happen to know the line. But what's occurred?"

"Well, it appears a goods train left Didcot last night bound through to Winchester, and that one of the waggons never arrived here at Newbury."

"Not very much in that," replied Hazell, still at his 'exercises', "unless the waggon in question was behind the brake and the couplings snapped, in which case the next train along might have run into it."

"Oh, no. The waggon was in the middle of the train."

"Probably left in a siding by mistake," replied Hazell.

"But the station-master says that all the stations along the line have been wired to, and that it isn't at any of them."

"Very likely it never left Didcot."

"He declares there is no doubt about that."

"Well, you begin to interest me," replied Hazell, stopping his whirligigs and beginning to eat his plasmon. "There may be something in it, though very often a waggon is mislaid. But I'll go down to the station."

"I'll go with you, Hazell, and introduce you to the stationmaster. He has heard of your reputation."

Ten minutes later they were in the stationmaster's office, Hazell having re-slung his camera.

"Very glad to meet you," said that functionary, "for this affair promises to be mysterious. *I* can't make it out at all."

"Do you know what the truck contained?"

"That's just where the bother comes in, sir. It was valuable property. There's a loan exhibition of pictures at Winchester next week, and this waggon was bringing down some of them from Leamington. They belong to Sir Gilbert Murrell – three of them, I believe – large pictures, and each in a separate packing-case."

"H'm – this sounds very funny. Are you sure the truck was on the train?"

"Simpson, the brakesman, is here now, and I'll send for him. Then you can hear the story in his own words."

So the goods guard appeared on the scene. Hazell looked at him narrowly, but there was nothing suspicious in his honest face.

"I know the waggon was on the train when we left Didcot," he said in answer to inquiries, "and I noticed it at Upton, the next station, where we took a couple off. It was the fifth or sixth in front of my brake. I'm quite certain of that. We stopped at Compton to take up a cattle truck, but I didn't get out there. Then we ran right through to Newbury, without stopping at the other stations, and then I discovered that the waggon was not on the train. I thought very likely it might have been left at Upton or Compton by mistake, but I was wrong, for they say it isn't there. That's all I know about it, sir. A rum go, ain't it?"

"Extraordinary!" exclaimed Hazell. "You must have made a mistake."

"No, sir, I'm sure I haven't."

"Did the driver of the train notice anything?"

"No, sir."

"Well, but the thing's impossible," said Hazell. "A loaded waggon couldn't have been spirited away. What time was it when you left Didcot?"

"About eight o'clock, sir."

"Ah – quite dark. You noticed nothing along the line?"

"Nothing, sir."

"You were in your brake all the time, I suppose?"

"Yes, sir – while we were running."

At this moment there came a knock at the stationmaster's door and a porter entered.

"There's a passenger train just in from the Didcot branch," said the man, "and the driver reports that he saw a truck loaded with packing-cases in Churn siding."

"Well, I'm blowed!" exclaimed the brakesman. "Why, we ran through Churn without a stop – trains never do stop there except in camp time."

"Where is Churn?" asked Hazell, for once at a loss.

"It's merely a platform and a siding close to the camping ground between Upton and Compton," replied the stationmaster, "for the convenience of troops only, and very rarely used except in the summer, when soldiers are encamped there." *

[* The incident here recorded occurred before June, 1905, in which month Churn was dignified with a place in Bradshaw as a 'station' at which trains stop by signal. – V.L.W.]

"I should very much like to see the place, and as soon as possible," said Hazell.

"So you shall," replied the stationmaster. "A train will soon start on the branch. Inspector Hill shall go with you, and instruction shall be given to the driver to stop there, while a return train can pick you both up."

In less than an hour Hazell and Inspector Hill alighted at Churn. It is a lonely enough place, situated in a vast flat basin of the Downs, scarcely relieved by a single tree, and far from all human habitation with the exception of a lonely shepherd's cottage some half a mile away.

The 'station' itself is only a single platform, with a shelter and a solitary siding, terminating in what is known in railway language as a 'dead end' – that is, in this case, wooden buffers to stop any trucks. This siding runs off from the single line of rail at points from the Didcot direction of the line.

And in this siding was the lost truck, right against the 'dead end', filled with three packing-cases, and labeled 'Leamington to Winchester, via Newbury'. There could be no doubt about it at all. But how it had got there from the middle of a train running through without a stop was a mystery even to the acute mind of Thorpe Hazell.

"Well," said the inspector when they had gazed long enough at the truck; "we'd better have a look at the points. Come along."

There is not even a signal-box at this primitive station. The points are actuated by two levers in a ground frame, standing close by the side of the line, one lever unlocking and the other shifting the same points.

"How about these points?" said Hazell as they drew near. "You only use them so occasionally, that I suppose they are kept out of action?"

"Certainly," replied the inspector, "a block of wood is bolted down between the end of the point rail and the main rail, fixed as a wedge – ah! There it is, you see, quite untouched; and the levers themselves are locked – here's the keyhole in the ground frame. This is the strangest thing I've ever come across, Mr. Hazell."

Thorpe Hazell stood looking at the points and levers sorely puzzled. They must have been worked to get that truck in the siding, he knew well. But how?

Suddenly his face lit up. Oil evidently had been used to loosen the nut of the bolt that fixed the wedge of wood. Then his eyes fell on the handle of one of the two levers, and a slight exclamation of joy escaped him.

"Look," said the inspector at that moment, "it's impossible to pull them off," and he stretched out his hand towards a lever. To his astonishment Hazell seized him by the collar and dragged him back before he could touch it.

"I beg your pardon," he exclaimed, "hope I've not hurt you, but I want to photograph those levers first, if you don't mind."

The inspector watched him rather sullenly as he fixed his camera on a folding tripod stand he had with him, only a few inches from the handle of one of the levers, and took two very careful photographs of it.

"Can't see the use of that, sir," growled the inspector. But Hazell vouchsafed no reply.

"Let him find it out for himself," he thought.

Then he said aloud:

"I fancy they must have had that block out, inspector – and it's evident the points must have been set to get the truck where it is. How it was done is a problem, but if the doer of it was anything of a regular criminal, I think we might find *him*."

"How?" asked the puzzled inspector.

"Ah," was the response, "I'd rather not say at present. Now, I should very much like to know whether those pictures are intact?"

"We shall soon find that out," replied the inspector, "for we'll take the truck back with us." And he commenced undoing the bolt with a spanner, after which he unlocked the levers.

"H'm – they work pretty freely," he remarked as he pulled one.

"Quite so," said Hazell, "they've been oiled recently."

There was an hour or so before the return train would pass, and Hazell occupied it by walking to the shepherd's cottage.

"I am hungry," he explained to the woman there, "and hunger is Nature's dictate for food. Can you oblige me with a couple of onions and a broomstick?"

And she talks today of the strange man who "kept a swingin' o' that there broomstick round 'is 'ead and then eat them onions as solemn as a judge."

The first thing Hazell did on returning to Newbury was to develop his photographs. The plates were dry enough by the evening for him to print one or two photos on gaslight-paper and to enclose the clearest of them with a letter to a Scotland Yard official whom he knew, stating that he would call for an answer, as he intended returning to town in a couple of days. The following evening he received a note from the stationmaster, which read:

> *Dear Sir, I promised to let you know if the pictures in the cases on that truck were in any way tampered with. I have just received a report from Winchester by which I understand that they have been unpacked and carefully examined by the Committee of the Loan Exhibition. The Committee are perfectly satisfied that they have not been damaged or interfered with in any way, and that they have been received just as they left the owner's hands.*
>
> *We are still at a loss to account for the running of the waggon on to Churn siding or for the object in doing so. An official has been down from Paddington, and, at his request, we are not making the affair public – the goods having arrived in safety. I am sure you will observe confidence in this matter.*

"More mysterious than ever," said Hazell to himself. "I can't understand it at all."

The next day he called at Scotland Yard and saw the official.

"I've had no difficulty with your little matter, you'll be glad to hear," he said. "We looked up our records and very soon spotted your man."

"Who is he?"

"His real name is Edgar Jeffreys, but we know him under several aliases. He's served four sentences for burglary and robbery – the latter, a daring theft from a train, so he's in your line, Mr. Hazell. What's he been up to, and how did you get that print?"

"Well," replied Hazell, "I don't quite know yet what he's been doing. But I should like to be able to find him if anything turns up. Never mind how I got the print – the affair is quite a private one at present, and nothing may come of it."

The official wrote an address on a bit of paper and handed it to Hazell.

"He's living there just now, under the name of Allen. We keep such men in sight, and I'll let you know if he moves."

When Hazell opened his paper the following morning he gave a cry of joy. And no wonder, for this is what he saw:

MYSTERY OF A PICTURE
SIR GILBERT MURRELL AND THE WINCHESTER LOAN EXHIBITION
AN EXTRAORDINARY CHARGE

The Committee of the Loan Exhibition of Pictures to be opened next week at Winchester are in a state of very natural excitement brought about by a strange charge that has been made against them by Sir Gilbert Murrell.

Sir Gilbert, who lives at Leamington, is the owner of several very valuable pictures, among them being the celebrated 'Holy Family' by Velasquez. This picture, with two others, was dispatched by him from Leamington to be exhibited at Winchester, and yesterday he journeyed to that city in order to make himself satisfied with the hanging arrangements, as he had particularly stipulated that 'The Holy Family' was to be placed in a prominent position.

The picture in question was standing on the floor of the gallery, leaning against a pillar, when Sir Gilbert arrived with some representatives of the Committee.

Nothing occurred till he happened to walk behind the canvas, when he astounded those present by saying that the picture was not his at all, declaring that a copy had been substituted, and stating that he was absolutely certain on account of certain private marks of his at the back of the canvas which were quite indecipherable, and which were now missing. He admitted that the painting itself in every way resembled his picture, and that it was the cleverest forgery he had ever seen; but a very painful scene took place, the hanging committee stating that the picture had been received by them from the railway company just as it stood.

At present the whole affair is a mystery, but Sir Gilbert insisted most emphatically to our correspondent, who was able to see him, that the picture was certainly not his, and said that as the original is extremely valuable he intends holding the Committee responsible for the substitution which, he declares, has taken place.

It was evident to Hazell that the papers had not, as yet, got hold of the mysterious incident at Churn. As a matter of fact, the railway company had kept that affair strictly to themselves, and the loan committee knew nothing of what had happened on the line.

But Hazell saw that inquiries would be made, and determined to probe the mystery without delay. He saw at once that if there was any truth in Sir Gilbert's story the substitution had taken place in that lonely siding at Churn. He was staying at his London flat, and five minutes after he had read the paragraph had called a hansom and was being hurried off to a friend of his who was well known in art circles as a critic and art historian.

"I can tell you exactly what you want to know," said he, "for I've only just been looking it up, so as to have an article in the evening papers on it. There was a famous copy of the picture of Velasquez, said to have been painted by a pupil of his, and for some years there was quite a controversy among the respective owners as to which was the genuine one – just as there is today about a Madonna belonging to a gentleman at St. Moritz, but which a Vienna gallery also claims to possess.

"However, in the case of 'The Holy Family', the dispute was ultimately settled once and for all years ago, and undoubtedly Sir Gilbert Murrell held the genuine picture.

What became of the copy no one knows. For twenty years all trace of it has been lost. There – that's all I can tell you. I shall pad it out a bit in my article, and I must get to work on it at once. Good-bye!"

"One moment – where was the copy last seen?"

"Oh! The old Earl of Ringmere had it last, but when he knew it to be a forgery he is said to have sold it for a mere song, all interest in it being lost, you see."

"Let me see, he's a very old man, isn't he?"

"Yes – nearly eighty – a perfect enthusiast on pictures still, though."

"Only *said* to have sold it," muttered Hazell to himself, as he left the house; "that's very vague – and there's no knowing what these enthusiasts will do when they're really bent on a thing. Sometimes they lose all sense of honesty. I've known fellows actually rob a friend's collection of stamps or butterflies. What if there's something in it? By George, what an awful scandal there would be! It seems to me that if such a scandal were prevented I'd be thanked all round. Anyhow, I'll have a shot at it on spec. And I must find out how that truck was run off the line."

When once Hazell was on the track of a railway mystery he never let a moment slip by. In an hour's time, he was at the address given him at Scotland Yard. On his way there he took a card from his case, a blank one, and wrote on it, 'From the Earl of Ringmere'. This he put into an envelope.

"It's a bold stroke," he said to himself, "but, if there's anything in it, it's worth trying."

So he asked for Allen. The woman who opened the door looked at him suspiciously, and said she didn't think Mr. Allen was in.

"Give him this envelope," replied Hazell. In a couple of minutes she returned, and asked him to follow her.

A short, wiry-looking man, with sharp, evil-looking eyes, stood in the room waiting for him and looking at him suspiciously.

"Well," he snapped, "what is it – what do you want?"

"I come on behalf of the Earl of Ringmere. You will know that when I mention Churn," replied Hazell, playing his trump card boldly.

"Well," went on the man, "what about that?"

Hazell wheeled round, locked the door suddenly, put the key in his pocket, and then faced his man. The latter darted forward, but Hazell had a revolver pointing at him in a twinkling.

"You – detective!"

"No, I'm not – I told you I came on behalf of the Earl – that looks like hunting up matters for his sake, doesn't it?"

"What does the old fool mean?" asked Jeffreys.

"Oh! I see you know all about it. Now listen to me quietly, and you may come to a little reason. You changed that picture at Churn the other night."

"You seem to know a lot about it," sneered the other, but less defiantly.

"Well, I do – but not quite all. You were foolish to leave your traces on that lever, eh?"

"How did I do that?" exclaimed the man, giving himself away.

"You'd been dabbling about with oil, you see, and you left your thumb-print on the handle. I photographed it, and they recognised it at Scotland Yard. Quite simple."

Jeffreys swore beneath his breath.

"I wish you'd tell me what you mean," he said.

"Certainly. I expect you've been well paid for this little job."

"If I have, I'm not going to take any risks. I told the old man so. He's worse than I am – he put me up to getting the picture. Let him take his chance when it comes out – I suppose he wants to keep his name out of it, that's why you're here."

"You're not quite right. Now just listen to me. You're a villain, and you deserve to suffer; but I'm acting in a purely private capacity, and I fancy if I can get the original picture back to its owner that it will be better for all parties to hush this affair up. Has the old Earl got it?"

"No, not yet," admitted the other, "he was too artful. But he knows where it is, and so do I."

"Ah – now you're talking sense! Look here! You make a clean breast of it, and I'll take it down on paper. You shall swear to the truth of your statement before a commissioner for oaths – he need not see the actual confession. I shall hold this in case it is necessary; but if you help me to get the picture back to Sir Gilbert, I don't think it will be."

After a little more conversation, Jeffreys explained. Before he did so, however, Hazell had taken a bottle of milk and a hunch of wholemeal bread from his pocket, and calmly proceeded to perform 'exercises' and then to eat his 'lunch', while Jeffreys told the following story:

"It was the old Earl who did it. How he got hold of me doesn't matter – perhaps I got hold of him – maybe I put him up to it – but that's not the question. He'd kept that forged picture of his in a lumber room for years, but he always had his eye on the genuine one. He paid a long price for the forgery, and he got to think that he ought to have the original. But there, he's mad on pictures.

"Well, as I say, he kept the forgery out of sight and let folks think he'd sold it, but all the time he was in hopes of getting it changed somehow for the original.

s"One pal was with me – in the siding, ready to clap on the side brake when the truck was running in. I was to work the points, and my other pal, who had the most awkward job of all, was on the goods train – under a tarpaulin in a truck. He had two lengths of very stout rope with a hook at each end of them.

"When the train left Upton, he started his job. Goods trains travel very slowly, and there was plenty of time. Counting from the back brake van, the truck we wanted to run off was No. 5. First he hooked No. 4 truck to No. 6 – fixing the hook at the side of the end of both trucks, and having the slack in his hand, coiled up.

"Then when the train ran down a bit of a decline he uncoupled No. 5 from No. 4 – standing on No. 5 to do it. That was easy enough, for he'd taken a coupling staff with him; then he paid out the slack till it was tight. Next he hooked his second rope from No. 5 to No. 6, uncoupled No. 5 from No. 6, and paid out the slack of the second rope.

"Now you can see what happened. The last few trucks of the train were being drawn by a long rope reaching from No. 4 to No. 6, and leaving a space inbetween. In the middle of this space No. 5 ran, drawn by a short rope from No. 6. My pal stood on No. 6, with a sharp knife in his hand.

"The rest was easy. I held the lever, close by the side of the line – coming forward to it as soon as the engine passed. The instant the space appeared after No. 6 I pulled it over, and No. 5 took the siding points, while my pal cut the rope at the same moment.

"Directly the truck had run by and off I reversed the lever so that the rest of the train following took the main line. There is a decline before Compton, and the last four trucks came running down to the main body of the train, while my pal hauled in the slack and finally coupled No. 4 to No. 6 when they came together. He jumped from the train as it ran very slowly into Compton. That's how it was done."

Hazell's eyes sparkled.

"It's the cleverest thing I've heard of on the line," he said.

"Think so? Well, it wanted some handling. The next thing was to unscrew the packing-case, take the picture out of the frame, and put the forgery we'd brought with us in its place. That took us some time, but there was no fear of interruption in that lonely part. Then I took the picture off, rolling it up first, and hid it. The old Earl insisted on this. I was to tell him where it was, and he was going to wait for a few weeks and then get it himself."

"Where did you hide it?"

"You're sure you're going to hush this up?"

"You'd have been in charge long ago if I were not."

"Well, there's a path from Churn to East Ilsley across the downs, and on the right-hand of that path is an old sheep well – quite dry. It's down there. You can easily find the string if you look for it – fixed near the top."

Hazell took down the man's confession, which was duly attested. His conscience told him that perhaps he ought to have taken stronger measures.

"I told you I was merely a private individual," said Hazell to Sir Gilbert Murrell. "I have acted in a purely private capacity in bringing you your picture."

Sir Gilbert looked from the canvas to the calm face of Hazell.

"Who are you, sir?" he asked.

"Well, I rather aspire to be a book-collector; you may have read my little monogram on 'Jacobean Bindings?'"

"No," said Sir Gilbert, "I have not had that pleasure. But I must inquire further into this. How did you get this picture? Where was it – who –"

"Sir Gilbert," broke in Hazell, "I could tell you the whole truth, of course. I am not in any way to blame myself. By chance, as much as anything else, I discovered how your picture had been stolen, and where it was."

"But I want to know all about it. I shall prosecute – I –"

"I think not. Now, do you remember where the forged picture was seen last?"

"Yes; the Earl of Ringmere had it – he sold it."

"Did he?"

"Eh?"

"What if he kept it all this time?" said Hazell, with a peculiar look.

There was a long silence.

"Good heavens!" exclaimed Sir Gilbert at length. "You don't mean *that*. Why, he has one foot in the grave – a very old man – I was dining with him only a fortnight ago."

"Ah! Well, I think you are content now, Sir Gilbert?"

"It is terrible – terrible! I have the picture back, but I wouldn't have the scandal known for worlds."

"It never need be," replied Hazell. "You will make it all right with the Winchester people?"

"Yes – yes – even if I have to admit I was mistaken, and let the forgery stay through the exhibition."

"I think that would be the best way," replied Hazell, who never regretted his action.

"Of course, Jeffreys ought to have been punished," he said to himself; "but it was a clever idea – a clever idea!"

"May I offer you some lunch?" asked Sir Gilbert.

"Thank you; but I am a vegetarian, and –"

"I think my cook could arrange something – let me ring."

"It is very good of you, but I ordered a dish of lentils and a salad at the station restaurant. But if you will allow me just to go through my physical training ante luncheon exercises here, it would save me the trouble of a more or less public display at the station."

"Certainly," replied the rather bewildered Baronet; whereupon Hazell threw off his coat and commenced whirling his arms like a windmill.

"Digestion should be considered *before* a meal," he explained.

Chains of Command

Sylvia Spruck Wrigley and Ruth Nestvold

VIOLET PATEL had been an officer on the *FedCom Reliant* for three years, seven months, two days and eighteen hours, and she still didn't understand how quantum entanglement worked. She sighed in frustration, barely seeing the stars glittering above the encased deck as their ship sped through endless night. After confirming that the gauges were green, she checked the chemical containers to ensure they were intact and the ingredients in the form necessary, then sat by the radar screen, monitoring movement. Once the tingling electric smell disappeared, she thumbed the switch to signal a successful transition. With that, her shift was over.

She took the gleaming steps upstairs to her cabin. *Above deck*, she reminded herself, *not upstairs*. Would she ever get it right? The twisted mix of high tech and archaic jargon was like a rite of passage that Violet was failing. Squeaking mast-joints seemed to underscore her dark thoughts. *Reliant* was a battered old cargo ship ferrying space junk to the colonies, a creaky monster that still used hydrogen systems, only still in use because of its huge payload storage. The hypersail was ungainly and the reflectors needed constant polishing.

The top deck rumbled with a sound like an imminent earthquake – the shadow flaps lowering as they approached the outer atmosphere of GJ3379458b, where they would drop the payload into orbit around the terraformed world before turning around and heading back to Las Velas.

When she joined the Corps, she'd envisioned herself on a Cosmiclipper, zipping across the outer boundaries in a small ship capable of impossible speeds. Or serving with the ASF, exploring asteroid belts on mining expeditions. Of course, she'd also imagined that once on a FedCom ship, the science – and directions – would become second nature. It was in her blood, after all – as her mother repeatedly reminded her.

"Midshipman Patel!"

She turned to see a group led by First Officer Tierney. She snapped to attention. "Sir?"

"Check the status of the aft pods to port, batteries charged and nav systems online. Captain Hobbs is doing an inspection at three bells."

Violet paused, glancing left and right. A brief hesitation, but it was enough.

Sub-Lieutenant Gomez sniggered. "That way." He pointed over Violet's shoulder.

"Yes, sir!" She saluted and strode away with her back ramrod straight, trying to ignore the chuckles behind her.

Three years, seven months, two days and eighteen hours on this ship, and she still had to think about which side was port. And they knew it.

* * *

She vented with Dixie in the mess that evening. "I don't see why we can't we just use normal terms. For'ard, stern, aft, starboard, fathom, sail." Violet tapped her fingers on the stainless steel table with each word.

"You'll get used to it eventually." Dixie reached into her pouch and sprinkled salt from Baidu on her food. "Want some?"

Vi stabbed at the tough nutrapastie, shaking her head. She'd learned by now that seasoning didn't help. "I wonder if I'm cut out for space life."

Dixie laughed. "Too late now! Hey, are you going to eat that?"

"No." She shoved her plate across the table, her appetite gone. "Sometimes I wish I could get out, go home, and start over."

"Come on, Vi. Last week Captain Hobbs commended you for your understanding of pressure and lift. You're our go-to girl for points of procedure. You know the Operational Data Manual like no one else."

"That's because I have to study twice as hard to grasp it at all."

Dixie crunched on Violet's nutrapastie. "No, it's because you care about getting it right," she said around her mouthful. "The Corps is full of dimwits, and you aren't one of them." She finished off the second plate and leaned back. "I'm on nav tonight. See you at cards later?"

Vi shook her head. "I've got the night watch. I need to get some sleep before."

"Breakfast then." They rose and hugged before picking up their trays. "Stop beating yourself up, Vi."

* * *

If only it were that easy.

After a short nap, Violet relieved Schandin, the new guy on the ship, just before the bells buzzed for shift change. Night watch wasn't much work, just keeping an eye on the instruments in case of a system failure, but it screwed with her sleep patterns.

Schandin swiped his ID to check out but didn't leave. He pointed at the stars surrounding the deck. "Gorgeous. You're lucky to be assigned to this ship. When we get to Las Velas, I'm going to be locked in a synth station for the rest of my seven years."

"You aren't staying with us?" She scanned the instrument displays before glancing up. Diamond lights hung low in the sky, looking close enough to reach out and touch.

" 'Fraid not," he said. "I don't come from a good family like you. I'm lucky Captain Hobbs lets me do watch now and again."

"Lucky, huh? Here I am stuck on this old freighter."

"Stuck?"

"Yeah. I don't know if I'm cut out for this. But the only legit early exit is a medical release. I could maybe jump ship at some throwback colony and hide out until they stopped searching – and ruin my sister's career. I'm not the type for that kind of high drama."

Schandin chuckled. "At least your connections got you here, cruising the skies on a piece of living history."

Violet circled the deck and checked the controls in the engine room. Funny how differently they viewed the old freighter. "Well, you can't rack up many medals for making deliveries. No one shakes your hand or plans a parade. In my family that's what counts. But here I am, stuck on this clunker."

"Hey, I'd be happy to trade," Schandin said, grinning.

After he left, Vi gazed back out at the stars, wondering if there really were any way to get out of the Corps. Her dreams of amazing her superiors with innate talent inherited from a long line of Space Corps commanders had faded within months of joining the *Reliant*. The captain was encouraging, but she knew the truth: she was a disgrace to her family.

She'd just finished testing the recorder when she heard a scraping noise and then a clank behind her. She whirled around to see a dark silhouette limping towards the rigging, one leg dragging behind. Dark, greasy hair fell into his face, touching the collar of his ragged shirt.

A chill slithered up her spine. "Hey," she said, her voice a half-whisper. She cleared her throat and tried again. "Halt! Who goes there?"

The figure turned, and one luminous, yellow eye fixed on her. The other was covered with a patch. Heavy chains hung from his arms. He gave a low moan, a sound full of pain and sorrow.

Violet froze.

One pale finger pointed at her from a ripped sleeve. Starlight glinted on the tarnished brass buttons of an ancient FedCom uniform. She retreated, her back pressing against the smooth steel engine room door. Slowly he dropped his arm, the chains rattling like bangles. Then he continued his slow scrape-drag towards the back of the ship. *Aft.* As he disappeared into the dark shadows, she thought she heard him whisper her name.

She drew a deep breath and wiped her sweaty palms on her uniform. Heart pounding, she ran for the switches to light up the far deck. No one was there. She checked the instruments for any anomalous readings. Nothing. It was impossible to board the ship in transit. Whatever she'd seen, it had to be crew.

By the time her shift was over, she'd come to the conclusion that it was a prank – Gomez or maybe even Tierney. Perhaps they'd been watching from the shadows, hoping to see her panic. They'd succeeded in scaring her, but she was damned if she'd let them know.

As soon as she was off-duty, she went to the comms room to check the logs. If she could trace the movements, she might be able to narrow down which berth the jerk had come from. Captain Hobbs walked out as she arrived, giving her a brief nod. She looked away, not wanting to make a report until she could prove who was out there. But there was no unexpected activity in the sensory report, only Violet on her watch. She could see exactly where she'd turned from the recorder and retreated towards the engine room. The data was crystal clear: no other crew member playing a prank on her, no one but herself, running foolishly around the deck.

She put the reader down carefully, hoping she wasn't going stir crazy.

* * *

Violet had been on the *Reliant* for three years, seven months, fourteen days and five hours when she saw the figure in the tattered FedCom uniform again. She'd been fearing the vision, constantly imagining movement in the shadows. She hadn't told anyone what she'd seen, not even Dixie. What rational person admitted to seeing things that weren't there?

There was a soft metallic clang and a wisp of movement. She turned to see the yellow eye in the dim light. The figure lurched forward, but Violet crossed her arms and stood her ground. She had to find out what was behind this.

"Violet Patel." The deep voice sounded like gravel and dust. Chained hands reached towards her, and the thought of ice-cold, rotting fingers on her skin broke her resolve. As she ran for the panel in the stairwell to raise the alarm, she heard the words, "I choose you." Then the howling klaxon drowned out all sound.

When she turned, nothing was there.

It took mere minutes before the first sleepy crew members were by her side, but it was enough time for her to recover her wits. She couldn't tell them tales of ghosts and zombies.

She pointed to the spot where the vision had appeared in the shadows. "I saw someone there. But I'm the only one who is supposed to be on deck during my watch."

Gomez sneered. "You woke us up for something you imagined you saw out of the corner of your eye?"

"Regulations require me to report any movement immediately if it cannot be clarified, and that's what I did," Violet said, taking refuge in policy.

Captain Hobbs arrived, his hair mussed as if he'd just gotten out of bed. Which he probably had.

He told her to go over the details again. "I stopped at the comms room on the way here," he said. "The logs show no motion other than your patrol."

A chill ran down her spine, and she pulled her jacket tighter. "I swear I saw something, sir."

His expression was stern, but he didn't rebuke her. "If you believe you saw something, it is your duty to report it, of course. But you are finishing a run of night watches. I suspect exhaustion is the culprit. Ordinary-Midshipman Patel, you are dismissed. Get some sleep. Report for orders at four bells."

Vi returned to her cabin, embarrassed. She shouldn't have sounded the alarm. Now she was the laughing-stock of the ship.

There was tapping on her hatch, and Dixie poked her head through. "Are you okay? What happened?"

"There was something out there, I swear it." She scooted over on her bunk to make room. "What did you see?"

"A man, a stranger, tall, long hair, dragging a leg behind, with a patch on one eye. Spooky."

Dixie leaned forward, her eyes wide. "Did you see what he was wearing?"

"An old FedCom uniform."

"That sounds like the ghost of Captain Adams!"

Violet just stared at her friend blankly.

"If you hung out in the main hall more, you would have heard of him," Dixie said, laughing. "Captain Adams is one of the legends of this ship, and Tierney tells the greatest stories about him. In the morning we have to tell her!"

"Okay, sure." Right now she just wanted to get some sleep.

Dixie got up and started climbing the narrow ladder. Before she reached the hatch, she turned again. "I can't believe you saw Captain Adams!"

* * *

Vi was dreading mess the next day, knowing everyone would be out to get her for waking them in the middle of the night. As she loaded her tray with scramble, someone jostled her arm, spilling it over the counter. Gomez joined her when she headed for the tables. "Regulations require me to report every movement, sir," he said in a high-pitched voice. "Even if it is a figment of my imagination."

Dixie came to her rescue. "Just wait 'til you hear Vi's story, glamhead." She guided Violet to the table where Tierney sat. "Too bad Violet hasn't heard your ghost stories before or she would have known what she saw last night," Dixie said to the First Officer. "Tell her about Captain Adams."

Tierney gazed at them as they sat down opposite. "You think she saw our ghost?"

"From the way she described him, yeah."

"If it's true, that's quite an honor, Patel."

"Could someone just tell me what this is all about?" Violet asked.

Tierney pushed aside her empty tray and leaned back in her chair, coffee in hand and a smile on her lips. "Captain Adams was an early captain of the *Reliant*, back during the Libran wars, before the Settling. Then the unthinkable happened – mutiny." On the last word, she raised her voice with dramatic flair. The mess grew quieter and eyes turned her way. "Spooked by deep space, the crew members thought Adams had pushed too far. They were afraid of being lost in the outer reaches, without hydrogen, out of reach of hyperspace eddies, the ship drifting forever." Tierney paused for effect, and Vi noticed crew members gathering around their table, the trays in their hands forgotten. "The officers conspired together and incited the crew against the captain. Together, they broke into his cabin and dragged him to the outer deck." Her voice dropped to a near-whisper. "The same deck where Patel was alone last night. Adams agreed to step down if they would accept his choice as acting captain, someone he trusted to get them back to civilization. The officers refused. They chained him to the deck. Then they turned the *Reliant* around."

By now nearly every face was turned towards Tierney.

After another dramatic pause, the First Officer continued. "The crew steered the *Reliant* off course, straight into deep space. Luckily, the Space Corps sent out a rescue ship as soon as *Reliant's* signal was lost. They found the ship in time, and the mutineers were arrested, but it was too late for Captain Adams. They found his rotting corpse on the deck, maggots everywhere."

She glanced around at her audience. "Since that day, the *Reliant* has its very own ghost. Captain Adams appears every few decades to choose a new captain, the most trustworthy and competent soul." Tierney smiled. "Even the brass believe it. So, Patel, now you know why your vision was an honor. Did Adams say anything to you?"

"Like 'You should be captain of this ship, Midshipman Patel'?" Dixie added with a laugh.

Violet shook her head, as much from the strange story as anything else. For some reason, she didn't want to tell them about the words, *I choose you*. It would sound like bragging. "No, he didn't say anything like that."

"Too bad," Dixie said. "I wonder who he *will* choose." She looked around at the crew members who had been listening to Tierney's story, her gaze fixing on Gomez. "I guess we all better be particularly nice to our fellow mates, or Adams is sure to pass us by."

* * *

Vi had been on the *FedCom Reliant* for six years, two months, eleven days, and four hours the next time the klaxon sounded on the deck. She was at the front decks, tightening the turnbuckles. After the siren shrieked, she was the first to arrive in the engine room, where she found Kayne frantically jabbing a mop at the corner of the satfinder.

"What's wrong?" she shouted over the alarm.

The other woman shuddered. "A big, black bug with lots of legs! It ran right across the input speakers while I was getting the meta data."

Violet bit her lip to keep from laughing. Cockroaches, the bane of big old ships like the Reliant, with plenty of dark corners. She grabbed disinfectant from the storage cupboard. "It must have come from the tagalong when we picked up supplies at Geuse. It's not the first time."

She entered the code to silence the klaxon and sent a message to the hygiene team, just as Captain Hobbs came on deck, followed by half-a-dozen other crew members.

"Stowaway," she said with a grin.

"Was it Adams again?"

Kayne flushed. "No, sir. Vermin. I shouldn't have hit the alarm, but I was rattled."

"We've already disinfected the area, sir," Vi said, coming to the other woman's aid. "Cockroaches and ghosts alike should be done for. In case they aren't, I notified hygiene."

Hernandez and Gog appeared on deck with electro-traps to look for signs of any more stowaways, and the rest of them left the deck.

"Too bad it wasn't Adams," Captain Hobbs said beside her. "I've always liked the idea of him still on board, protecting his ship from incompetents."

Violet chuckled. Over the years, she'd become fond of the ancient freighter. Its quirks and history gave it character. But she was surprised to learn Hobbs was a closet romantic.

"I dream about him sometimes, watching over the ship," she admitted.

* * *

When they docked at Las Velas, Vi used her seniority – almost her full seven years now – to get shore leave as soon as they arrived. She commandeered a prime spot at the bar in the Sail and Sparrow and handed over her card. "A tall, ice-cold gandt. And keep it topped until I can't find the glass."

The barmaid chuckled and brought her first drink.

Violet had just begun to relax when she heard a loud voice behind her.

"Hey, Patel!"

Violet turned to see Gomez approaching, followed by several companions. "We served together on the *Reliant*," he said to his friends. "You still on that old heap, Patel?"

She nodded.

"Why am I not surprised!" Gomez laughed. "You were never cut out for space life, were you?"

Without waiting for an answer, he and his friends headed for a table by the window.

She downed her drink and walked out into the muggy Velas night. *Not cut out for space life, huh?* That from the idiot who damaged the props because he hadn't checked the min pressure needed for full speed. She should have told his friends that, should have said *something*.

As she stormed to the dock, she saw Captain Hobbs coming down the galley. She walked straight up to him. "I want to transfer. I've spent my entire career on the *Reliant*. I need some experience on another ship."

The captain clapped her on the back. "Excellent news! So you're sticking with the Corps? I was worried you'd finish your seven years and walk away."

Vi took a deep breath. It hadn't occurred to her that asking for a transfer would imply she wanted to stay.

"The Corps needs more people like you," Hobbs continued. "Focused and thorough. I always thought you didn't rate yourself highly enough, letting those flyboys put you down. But they're just out for the thrill, no good on a big ship, let alone a piece of history like the *Reliant*. She needs loving care and attention to detail, not being pressed to prove how fast she can go."

She felt herself blushing at the praise. "She's a good ship, sir."

Hobbs smiled. "That she is. Would you like some help with the paperwork for your transfer?"

Violet nodded. Had she just decided her future in a fit of pique? Well, it wasn't forever; she could extend for a year or two and then move on. It wasn't like she had any better ideas.

The captain clapped her on the shoulder again. "Come find me at three bells tomorrow and we'll look into it."

After he strode off into the city, Vi spent a sleepless night wondering what she had done.

* * *

Violet Patel had been on the *FedCom Solidarity* for eight years, six months, fifteen days and ten hours, when the moment she'd been waiting for finally arrived: she received official notice that she was now considered eligible for command of her own ship.

The years since she left the *Reliant* hadn't been as bad as she'd feared. The legend of Captain Adams comforted her as she struggled to adapt to other ships and crew. And then came her assignment to the *Solidarity*, another ancient ship with a reputation for stability rather than speed. Vi's first reaction had been dismay, but it turned out to be the perfect match for her talents and disposition, her patience and attention to detail. She learned to love the intricacies of the ship. The crew had a reputation for being defiant and difficult, but Violet became a mediator between high command and those who felt abandoned on an old clunker. She'd felt that way herself once, after all. Most officers assigned to the outer reaches immediately begged for transfer to another ship. Vi remained and quickly rose through the ranks to Lieutenant Commander.

On their next stop at Las Velas, she said her goodbyes and reported to Admiral Yamoto for her first assignment as captain.

Yamoto swiped through her records on the reader hovering above his desk. "Good reports here, Commander Patel: reliable, trustworthy, knows her ships inside and out. Special commendations from your time on the *Solidarity*. With these references, you could choose any open command you wanted." He looked across the desk at her. "Why are you requesting a command in my division? Here we have mostly cargo ships, not exactly vehicles for fame and adventure."

She found herself strangely nervous, despite nearly two decades experience in the Corps. "I'd prefer command of a freighter, sir. Slow and steady, like me. I'm not cut out for a battleship or a Cosmiclipper." She took a deep breath. "I would be honored to take command of a cargo ship like the FedCom Reliant, where I spent most of my first seven years."

The Admiral shot her a look of surprise. "Solid thinking, Commander Patel. As it happens, Captain Hobbs retired several years ago, and the current captain... well, I suspect she would be happy for a change of scenery. I think your request can be arranged."

* * *

After nineteen years, four months, and two weeks of active service, Violet Patel boarded the *Reliant* again, this time as her new captain. She toured the ship, smiling at the clunky-looking solar array and the mast-joints that still creaked. She tightened a turnbuckle on the front decks and passed through the engine room, checking the temperatures and pressure. The *Reliant* was in fine shape.

Vi could feel her smile growing wider as she made her way to the captain's quarters for the first time and tossed her trunk on the bed. She ran her fingers along the polished steel walls, finding it hard to believe she was now in charge of the beautiful old freighter.

She didn't feel like unpacking yet, so she shoved her trunk into the hold. It wouldn't go in all the way. Frowning, she tugged it clear to see why. At the back was an old wooden crate draped with cloth. Vi dragged the box out into the center of the room, curious. Shoving the cloth aside, she lifted the creaking lid and peered inside.

On top was a ragged uniform with big brass buttons and a slightly moth-eaten pair of dark pants. Underneath she found a heavy chain, a lanky black wig, and a luminous golden orb with an elastic strap. She pulled out a crumbling scrap of paper, almost as old as the ship itself. She could barely make out the words in the faded scrawl: *Captain Adams*.

Cheating the Gallows

Israel Zangwill

Curious Couple

THEY SAY THAT a union of opposites makes the happiest marriage, and perhaps it is on the same principle that men who chum are always so oddly assorted. You shall find a man of letters sharing diggings with an auctioneer and a medical student pigging with a stockbroker's clerk. Perhaps each thus escapes the temptation to talk 'shop' in his hours of leisure while he supplements his own experiences of life by his companion's.

There could not be an odder couple than Tom Peters and Everard G. Roxdal – the contrast began with their names, and ran through the entire chapter. They had a bedroom and a sitting-room in common, but it would not be easy to find what else. To his landlady, worthy Mrs. Seacon, Tom Peters' profession was a little vague, but everybody knew that Roxdal was the manager of the City and Suburban Bank, and it puzzled her to think why a bank manager should live with such a seedy-looking person, who smoked clay pipes and sipped whiskey and water all the evening when he was at home. For Roxdal was as spruce and erect as his fellow-lodger was round-shouldered and shabby; he never smoked and he confined himself to a small glass of claret at dinner.

It is possible to live with a man and see very little of him. Where each of the partners lives his own life in his own way, with his own circle of friends and external amusements, days may go by without the men having five minutes together. Perhaps this explains why these partnerships jog along so much more peaceably than marriages, where the chain is drawn so much tighter, and galls the partners rather than links them. Diverse, however, as were the hours and habits of the chums, they often breakfasted together, and they agreed in one thing – they never stayed out at night. For the rest Peters sought his diversions in the company of journalists and frequented debating rooms, where he propounded the most iconoclastic views; while Roxdal had highly respectable houses open to him in the suburbs and was, in fact, engaged to be married to Clara Newell, the charming daughter of a retired corn merchant, a widower with no other child.

Clara naturally took up a good deal of Roxdal's time, and he often dressed to go to the play with her, while Peters stayed at home in a faded dressing-gown and loose slippers. Mrs. Seacon liked to see gentlemen about the house in evening dress, and made comparisons not favourable to Peters. And this in spite of the fact that he gave her infinitely less trouble than the younger man.

It was Peters who first took the apartments, and it was characteristic of his easy-going temperament that he was so openly and naively delighted with the view of the Thames obtainable from the bedroom window that Mrs. Seacon was emboldened to ask twenty-five per cent more than she had intended. She soon returned to her normal terms, however, when his friend Roxdal called the next day to inspect the rooms and overwhelmed her with a demonstration of their numerous shortcomings. He pointed out that their being on the ground floor was not an advantage, but a disadvantage, since they were nearer the noises of the street – in fact, the house being a corner one, the noises of two streets.

Roxdal continued to exhibit the same finicking temperament in the petty details of the ménage. His shirt fronts were never sufficiently starched, nor his boots sufficiently polished. Tom Peters, having no regard for rigid linen, was always good-tempered and satisfied, and never acquired the respect of his landlady. He wore blue check shirts and loose ties even on Sundays. It is true he did not go to church, but slept on till Roxdal returned from morning service, and even then it was difficult to get him out of bed, or to make him hurry up his toilette operations. Often the mid-day meal would be smoking on the table while Peters would smoke in the bed, and Roxdal, with his head thrust through the folding doors that separated the bedroom from the sitting-room, would be adjuring the sluggard to arise and shake off his slumbers and threatening to sit down without him, lest the dinner be spoilt. In revenge, Tom was usually up first on week-days, sometimes at such un-earthly hours that Polly had not yet removed the boots from outside the bedroom door, and would bawl down to the kitchen for his shaving water. For Tom, lazy and indolent as he was, shaved with the unfailing regularity of a man to whom shaving has become an instinct. If he had not kept fairly regular hours, Mrs. Seacon would have set him down as an actor, so clean-shaven was he. Roxdal did not shave. He wore a full beard and, being a fine figure of a man to boot, no uneasy investor could look upon him without being re-assured as to the stability of the bank he managed so successfully. And thus the two men lived in an economical comradeship, all the firmer, perhaps, for their mutual incongruities.

A Woman's Instinct

IT WAS ON a Sunday afternoon in the middle of October, ten days after Roxdal had settled in his new rooms, that Clara Newell paid her first visit to him there. She enjoyed a good deal of liberty, and did not mind accepting his invitation to tea. The corn merchant, himself indifferently educated, had an exaggerated sense of the value of culture, and so Clara, who had artistic tastes without much actual talent, had gone in for painting and might be seen, in pretty toilettes, copying pictures in the Museum. At one time it looked as if she might be reduced to working seriously at her art, for Satan, who finds mischief still for idle hands to do, had persuaded her father to embark the fruits of years of toil in bubble companies. However, things turned out not so bad as they might have been, a little was saved from the wreck, and the appearance of a suitor, in the person of Everard G. Roxdal, ensured her a future of competence, if not of the luxury she had been entitled to expect. She had a good deal of affection for Everard, who was unmistakably a clever man, as well as a good-looking one. The prospect seemed fair and cloudless. Nothing presaged the terrible storm that was about to break over these two lives. Nothing had ever for a moment come to vex their mutual contentment till this Sunday afternoon. The October sky, blue and sunny, with an Indian summer sultriness, seemed an exact image of her life, with its aftermath of a happiness that had once seemed blighted.

Everard had always been so attentive, so solicitous, that she was as much surprised as chagrined to find that he had apparently forgotten the appointment. Hearing her astonished interrogation of Polly in the passage, Tom shambled from the sitting-room in his loose slippers and his blue check shirt, with his eternal clay pipe in his mouth, and informed her that Roxdal had gone out suddenly earlier in the afternoon.

"G-g-one out," stammered poor Clara; all confused. "But he asked me to come to tea."

"Oh, you're Miss Newell, I suppose," said Tom.

"Yes, I am Miss Newell."

"He has told me a great deal about you, but I wasn't able honestly to congratulate him on his choice till now."

Clara blushed uneasily under the compliment, and under the ardour of his admiring gaze. Instinctively she distrusted the man. The very first tones of his deep bass voice gave her a peculiar shudder. And then his impoliteness in smoking that vile clay was so gratuitous.

"Oh, then you must be Mr. Peters," she said in return. "He has often spoken to me of you."

"Ah!" said Tom, laughingly, "I suppose he's told you all my vices. That accounts for your not being surprised at my Sunday attire."

She smiled a little, showing a row of pearly teeth. "Everard ascribes to you all the virtues," she said.

"Now that's what I call a friend!" he cried, ecstatically. "But won't you come in? He must be back in a moment. He surely would not break an appointment with you." The admiration latent in the accentuation of the last pronoun was almost offensive.

She shook her head. She had a just grievance against Everard, and would punish him by going away indignantly.

"Do let me give you a cup of tea," Tom pleaded. "You must be awfully thirsty this sultry weather. There! I will make a bargain with you! If you will come in now, I promise to clear out the moment Everard returns and not spoil your tête-à-tête." But Clara was obstinate; she did not at all relish this man's society, and besides, she was not going to throw away her grievance against Everard. "I know Everard will slang me dreadfully when he comes in if I let you go," Tom urged. "Tell me at least where he can find you."

"I am going to take the 'bus at Charing Cross, and I'm going straight home," Clara announced determinedly. She put up her parasol in a pet, and went up the street into the Strand. A cold shadow seemed to have fallen over all things. But just as she was getting into the 'bus, a hansom dashed down Trafalgar Square, and a well-known voice hailed her. The hansom stopped, and Everard got out and held out his hand.

"I'm so glad you're a bit late," he said. "I was called out unexpectedly, and have been trying to rush back in time. You wouldn't have found me if you had been punctual. But I thought," he added, laughing, "I could rely on you as a woman."

"I was punctual," Clara said angrily. "I was not getting out of this 'bus, as you seem to imagine, but into it, and was going home."

"My darling!" he cried remorsefully. "A thousand apologies." The regret on his handsome face soothed her. He took the rose he was wearing in the button-hole of his fashionably-cut coat and gave it to her.

"Why were you so cruel?" he murmured, as she nestled against him in the hansom. "Think of my despair if I had come home to hear you had come and gone. Why didn't you wait a moment?"

A shudder traversed her frame. "Not with that man, Peters!" she murmured.

"Not with that man, Peters!" he echoed sharply. "What is the matter with Peters?"

"I don't know," she said. "I don't like him."

"Clara," he said, half-sternly, half-cajolingly, "I thought you were above these feminine weaknesses; you are punctual, strive also to be reasonable. Tom is my best friend.

From boyhood we have been always together. There is nothing Tom would not do for me, or I for Tom. You must like him, Clara; you must, if only for my sake."

"I'll try," Clara promised, and then he kissed her in gratitude and broad daylight.

"You'll be very nice to him at tea, won't you?" he said anxiously. "I shouldn't like you two to be bad friends."

"I don't want to be bad friends," Clara protested; "only the moment I saw him a strange repulsion and mistrust came over me."

"You are quite wrong about him – quite wrong," he assured her earnestly. "When you know him better, you'll find him the best of fellows. Oh, I know," he said suddenly, "I suppose he was very untidy, and you women go so much by appearances!"

"Not at all," Clara retorted. " 'Tis you men who go by appearances."

"Yes, you do. That's why you care for me," he said, smiling.

She assured him it wasn't, and she didn't care for him so much as he plumed himself, but he smiled on. His smile died away, however, when he entered his rooms and found Tom nowhere.

"I daresay you've made him run about hunting for me," he grumbled.

"Perhaps he knew I'd come back, and went away to leave us together," she answered. "He said he would when you came."

"And yet you say you don't like him!"

She smiled reassuringly. Inwardly, however, she felt pleased at the man's absence.

Polly Receives a Proposal

IF CLARA NEWELL could have seen Tom Peters carrying on with Polly in the passage, she might have felt justified in her prejudice against him. It must be confessed, though, that Everard also carried on with Polly. Alas! It is to be feared that men are much of a muchness where women are concerned; shabby men and smart men, bank managers and journalists, bachelors and semi-detached bachelors. Perhaps it was a mistake after all to say the chums had nothing patently in common. Everard, I am afraid, kissed Polly rather more often than Clara, and although it was because he respected her less, the reason would perhaps not have been sufficiently consoling to his affianced wife. For Polly was pretty, especially on alternate Sunday afternoons, and when at ten PM she returned from her outings, she was generally met in the passage by one or other of the men. Polly liked to receive the homage of real gentlemen, and set her white cap at all indifferently. Thus, just before Clara knocked on that memorable Sunday afternoon, Polly, being confined to the house by the unwritten code regulating the lives of servants, was amusing herself by flirting with Peters.

"You are fond of me a little bit," the graceless Tom whispered, "aren't you?"

"You know I am, sir," Polly replied.

"You don't care for anyone else in the house?"

"Oh no, sir, and never let anyone kiss me but you. I wonder how it is, sir?" Polly replied ingenuously.

"Give me another," Tom answered.

She gave him another, and tripped to the door to answer Clara's knock.

And that very evening, when Clara was gone and Tom still out, Polly turned without the faintest atom of scrupulosity, or even jealousy, to the more fascinating Roxdal, and accepted his amorous advances. If it would seem at first sight that Everard had less excuse for such frivolity than his friend, perhaps the seriousness he showed in this interview may throw a different light upon the complex character of the man.

"You're quite sure you don't care for anyone but me?" he asked earnestly.

"Of course not, sir!" Polly replied indignantly. "How could I?"

"But you care for that soldier I saw you out with last Sunday?"

"Oh no, sir, he's only my young man," she said apologetically.

"Would you give him up?" he hissed suddenly.

Polly's pretty face took a look of terror. "I couldn't, sir! He'd kill me. He's such a jealous brute, you've no idea."

"Yes, but suppose I took you away from here?" he whispered eagerly. "Somewhere where he couldn't find you – South America, Africa, somewhere thousands of miles across the seas."

"Oh, sir, you frighten me!" whispered Polly, cowering before his ardent eyes, which shone in the dimly-lit passage.

"Would you come with me?" he hissed. She did not answer; she shook herself free and ran into the kitchen, trembling with a vague fear.

The Crash

ONE MORNING, earlier than his earliest hour of demanding his shaving water, Tom rang the bell violently and asked the alarmed Polly what had become of Mr. Roxdal.

"How should I know, sir?" she gasped. "Ain't he been in, sir?"

"Apparently not," Tom answered anxiously. "He never remains out. We have been here three weeks now, and I can't recall a single night he hasn't been home before twelve. I can't make it out." All enquiries proved futile.

Mrs. Seacon reminded him of the thick fog that had come on suddenly the night before.

"What fog?" asked Tom.

"Lord! Didn't you notice it, sir?"

"No, I came in early, smoked, read, and went to bed about eleven. I never thought of looking out of the window."

"It began about ten," said Mrs. Seacon, "and got thicker and thicker. I couldn't see the lights of the river from my bedroom. The poor gentleman has been and gone and walked into the water." She began to whimper.

"Nonsense, nonsense," said Tom, though his expression belied his words. "At the worst I should think he couldn't find his way home, and couldn't get a cab, so put up for the night at some hotel. I daresay it will be all right." He began to whistle as if in restored cheerfulness. At eight o'clock there came a letter for Roxdal, marked immediate, but as he did not turn up for breakfast, Tom went round personally to the City and Suburban Bank. He waited half-an-hour there, but the manager did not make his appearance. Then he left the letter with the cashier and went away with anxious countenance.

That afternoon it was all over London that the manager of the City and Suburban had disappeared, and that many thousand pounds of gold and notes had disappeared with him.

Scotland Yard opened the letter marked immediate, and noted that there had been a delay in its delivery, for the address had been obscure, and an official alteration had been made. It was written in a feminine hand and said: "On second thoughts I cannot accompany you. Do not try to see me again. Forget me. I shall never forget you." There was no signature.

Clara Newell, distracted, disclaimed all knowledge of this letter. Polly deposed that the fugitive had proposed flight to her, and the routes to Africa and South America were especially watched. Some months passed without result. Tom Peters went about overwhelmed with grief and astonishment. The police took possession of all the missing man's effects. Gradually the hue and cry dwindled, died.

Faith and Unfaith

"AT LAST WE meet!" cried Tom Peters, while his face lit up in joy. "How are you, dear Miss Newell?" Clara greeted him coldly. Her face had an abiding pallor now. Her lover's flight and shame had prostrated her for weeks. Her soul was the arena of contending instincts. Alone of all the world she still believed in Everard's innocence, felt that there was something more than met the eye, divined some devilish mystery behind it all.

And yet that damning letter from the anonymous lady shook her sadly. Then, too, there was the deposition of Polly. When she heard Peters' voice accosting her all her old repugnance resurged. It flashed upon her that this man – Roxdal's boon companion – must know far more than he had told to the police. She remembered how Everard had spoken of him, with what affection and confidence! Was it likely he was utterly ignorant of Everard's movements? Mastering her repugnance, she held out her hand. It might be well to keep in touch with him; he was possibly the clue to the mystery. She noticed he was dressed a shade more trimly, and was smoking a meerschaum. He walked along at her side, making no offer to put his pipe out.

"You have not heard from Everard?" he asked. She flushed. "Do you think I'm an accessory after the fact?" she cried.

"No, no," he said soothingly. "Pardon me, I was thinking he might have written – giving no exact address, of course. Men do sometimes dare to write thus to women. But, of course, he knows you too well – you would have put the police on his track."

"Certainly," she exclaimed, indignantly. "Even if he is innocent he must face the charge."

"Do you still entertain the possibility of his innocence?"

"I do," she said boldly, and looked him full in the face. His eyelids drooped with a quiver. "Don't you?"

"I have hoped against hope," he replied, in a voice faltering with emotion. "Poor old Everard! But I am afraid there is no room for doubt. Oh, this wicked curse of money – tempting the noblest and the best of us."

The weeks rolled on. Gradually she found herself seeing more and more of Tom Peters, and gradually, strange to say, he grew less repulsive. From the talks they had together, she began to see that there was really no reason to put faith in Everard; his criminality, his faithlessness, were too flagrant. Gradually she grew ashamed of her early mistrust of Peters; remorse bred esteem, and esteem ultimately ripened into feelings so warm, that when Tom gave freer vent to the love that had been visible to Clara from the first, she did not repulse him.

It is only in books that love lives forever. Clara, so her father thought, showed herself a sensible girl in plucking out an unworthy affection and casting it from her heart. He invited the new lover to his house, and took to him at once. Roxdal's somewhat supercilious manner had always jarred upon the unsophisticated corn merchant. With Tom the old man got on much better. While evidently quite as well-informed and cultured as his whilom friend, Tom knew how to impart his superior knowledge with the accent on the knowledge rather than on the superiority, while he had the air of gaining much information in return. Those who are most conscious of defects of early education are most resentful of other people sharing their consciousness. Moreover, Tom's bonhomie was far more to the old fellow's liking than the studied politeness of his predecessor, so that on the whole Tom made more of a conquest of the father than of the daughter. Nevertheless, Clara was by no means unresponsive to Tom's affection and when, after one of his visits to the house, the old man kissed her fondly and spoke of the happy turn things had taken and how, for the second time in their lives, things had mended when they seemed at their blackest, her heart swelled with a gush of gratitude and joy and tenderness, and she fell sobbing into her father's arms.

Tom calculated that he made a clear five hundred a year by occasional journalism, besides possessing some profitable investments which he had inherited from his mother, so that there was no reason for delaying the marriage. It was fixed for May Day, and the honeymoon was to be spent in Italy.

The Dream and the Awakening

BUT CLARA was not destined to happiness. From the moment she had promised herself to her first love's friend, old memories began to rise up and reproach her. Strange thoughts stirred in the depths of her soul, and in the silent watches of the night she seemed to hear Everard's accents, charged with grief and upbraiding. Her uneasiness increased as her wedding-day drew near. One night, after a pleasant afternoon spent in being rowed by Tom among the upper reaches of the Thames, she retired to rest full of vague forebodings. And she dreamt a terrible dream. The dripping form of Everard stood by her bedside, staring at her with ghastly eyes. Had he been drowned on the passage to his land of exile? Frozen with horror, she put the question.

"I have never left England!" the vision answered.

Her tongue clove to the roof of her mouth.

"Never left England?" she repeated, in tones which did not seem to be hers.

The wraith's stony eyes stared on, but there was silence.

"Where have you been then?" she asked in her dream.

"Very near you," came the answer.

"There has been foul play then!" she shrieked.

The phantom shook its head in doleful assent.

"I knew it!" she shrieked. "Tom Peters – Tom Peters has done away with you. Is it not he? Speak!"

"Yes, it is he – Tom Peters – whom I loved more than all the world." Even in the terrible oppression of the dream she could not resist saying, woman-like:

"Did I not warn you against him?"

The phantom stared on silently and made no reply.

"But what was his motive?" she asked at length.

"Love of gold – and you. And you are giving yourself to him," it said sternly.

"No, no, Everard! I will not! I will not! I swear it! Forgive me!" The spirit shook its head sceptically.

"You love him. Women are false – as false as men."

She strove to protest again, but her tongue refused its office.

"If you marry him, I shall always be with you! Beware!" The dripping figure vanished as suddenly as it came, and Clara awoke in a cold perspiration. Oh, it was horrible!

The man she had learnt to love, the murderer of the man she had learnt to forget! How her original prejudice had been justified! Distracted, shaken to her depths, she would not take counsel even of her father, but informed the police of her suspicions. A raid was made on Tom's rooms, and lo! The stolen notes were discovered in a huge bundle. It was found that he had several banking accounts, with a large, recently-paid amount in each bank. Tom was arrested. Attention was now concentrated on the corpses washed up by the river. It was not long before the body of Roxdal came to shore, the face distorted almost beyond recognition by long immersion, but the clothes patently his, and a pocket-book in the breast-pocket removing the last doubt.

Mrs. Seacon and Polly and Clara Newell all identified the body. Both juries returned a verdict of murder against Tom Peters, the recital of Clara's dream producing a unique impression in the court and throughout the country. The theory of the prosecution was that Roxdal had brought home the money, whether to fly alone or to divide it, or whether even for some innocent purpose, as Clara believed, was immaterial. That Peters determined to have it all, that he had gone out for a walk with the deceased, and, taking advantage of the fog, had pushed him into the river, and that he was further impelled to the crime by love for Clara Newell, as was evident from his subsequent relations with her. The judge put on the black cap. Tom Peters was duly hung by the neck till he was dead.

Brief Resume of the Culprit's Confession

WHEN YOU ALL read this I shall be dead and laughing at you. I have been hung for my own murder. I am Everard G. Roxdal. I am also Tom Peters. We two were one. When I was a young man my moustache and beard wouldn't come. I bought false ones to improve my appearance. One day, after I had become manager of the City and Suburban Bank, I took off my beard and moustache at home, and then the thought crossed my mind that nobody would know me without them. I was another man. Instantly it flashed upon me that if I ran away from the Bank, that other man could be left in London, while the police were scouring the world for a non-existent fugitive.

But this was only the crude germ of the idea. Slowly I matured my plan. The man who was going to be left in London must be known to a circle of acquaintance beforehand. It would be easy enough to masquerade in the evenings in my beardless condition, with other disguises of dress and voice. But this was not brilliant enough. I conceived the idea of living with him. It was Box and Cox reversed. We shared rooms at Mrs. Seacon's. It was a great strain, but it was only for a few weeks. I had trick clothes in my bedroom like those of quick-change artistes; in a moment I could pass from Roxdal to Peters and from Peters to Roxdal. Polly had to clean two pairs of boots a morning, cook two dinners, etc., etc. She and Mrs. Seacon saw one or the other of us every moment; it never dawned upon them they never saw us both together. At meals I would not be interrupted, ate off two plates, and conversed with my friend in loud tones. At other times we dined at different hours. On Sundays he was supposed to be asleep when I was in church. There is no landlady in the world to whom the idea would have occurred that one man was troubling himself to be two (and to pay for two, including washing). I worked up the idea of Roxdal's flight, asked Polly to go with me, manufactured that feminine letter that arrived on the morning of my disappearance. As Tom Peters I mixed with a journalistic set. I had another room where I kept the gold and notes till I mistakenly thought the thing had blown over.

Unfortunately, returning from here on the night of my disappearance, with Roxdal's clothes in a bundle I intended to drop into the river, it was stolen from me in the fog, and the man into whose possession it ultimately came appears to have committed suicide. What, perhaps, ruined me was my desire to keep Clara's love, and to transfer it to the survivor. Everard told her I was the best of fellows. Once married to her, I would not have had much fear. Even if she had discovered the trick, a wife cannot give evidence against her husband, and often does not want to. I made none of the usual slips, but no man can guard against a girl's nightmare after a day up the river and a supper at the Star and Garter. I might have told the judge he was an ass, but then I should have had penal servitude for bank robbery, and that is worse than death. The only thing that puzzles me, though, is whether the law has committed murder or I suicide.

Biographies & Sources

Ernest Bramah

The Coin of Dionysius

(Originally Published in *Max Carrados*, Metheun & Co., 1914)

Owing to his reclusive nature, little is known about Ernest Bramah's (1868–1942) background. The English writer began his adult life as a farmer, but gave it up after three years, pursuing instead a writing career at a London newspaper. 'The Coin of Dionysius' is the first story to feature the blind detective Max Carrados, who deftly solves cases using his heightened skills of perception. Like Bramah, Carrados avidly collects and studies coins, with the coin descriptions being both remarkably precise and witty. The Max Carrados stories existed alongside the Sherlock Holmes tales in *The Strand*, and enjoyed equal success at the time.

Tara Campbell

The Cost of Security

(First Publication)

Tara Campbell [www.taracampbell.com] is a Washington, D.C.-based writer of crossover sci-fi. With a BA in English and an MA in German, she has a demonstrated aversion to money and power. Originally from Anchorage, Alaska, she has also lived in Oregon, Ohio, New York, Germany and Austria. She's an assistant fiction editor with *Barrelhouse*, and volunteers with children's literacy organization 826DC. Tara writes book reviews and a monthly column for the *Washington Independent Review of Books*. Other publication credits include stories in *Barrelhouse, Punchnel's, Toasted Cake Podcast, Luna Station Quarterly, SciFi Romance Quarterly, Masters Review* and *Queen Mob's Teahouse*.

G.K. Chesterton

The Blue Cross

(Originally Published under the title 'Valentin Follows a Curious Trail', in the *Saturday Evening Post*, Philadelphia, 1910. Retitled as 'The Blue Cross' in *The Story-Teller*, London, 1910.)

Gilbert Keith Chesterton (1874–1936) is best known for his creation of the worldly priest-detective Father Brown. The Edwardian writer's literary output was immense: around 200 short stories, nearly 100 novels and about 4000 essays, as well as weekly columns for multiple newspapers. Chesterton was a valued literary critic, and his own authoritative works included biographies of Charles Dickens and Thomas Aquinas, and the theological book *The Everlasting Man*. Chesterton also debated with such notable figures as George Bernard Shaw and Bertrand Russell. His detective stories were essentially moral; Father Brown is an empathetic force for good, battling crime while defending the vulnerable.

Wilkie Collins

Brother Griffith's Story of the Biter Bit

(Originally Published in *The Atlantic Monthly*, 1858)

Wilkie Collins (1824–89) was born in London's Marylebone and he lived there almost consistently for 65 years. Writing over 30 major books, 100 articles, short stories and essays and a dozen or more plays, he is best known for *The Moonstone*, often credited as the first detective story, and *The Woman in White*. He was good friends with Charles Dickens, with whom he collaborated, as well as took inspiration from, to help write novels like *The Lighthouse* and *The Frozen Deep*. Finally becoming internationally reputable in the 1860s, Collins truly showed himself as the master of his craft as he wrote many profitable novels in less than a decade and earned himself the title of a successful English novelist, playwright and author of short stories.

Richard Harding Davis

In the Fog

(Originally Published by R.H. Russell, 1901)

Born in Philadelphia, Pennsylvania, Richard Harding Davis (1864–1916) was an American journalist, playwright and author. His mother was the successful novelist Rebecca Harding Davis and his father was a newspaper editor. Davis published his first collection of short stories while at university, going on to become a prominent journalist. He acted as a war correspondent during the Spanish-American War of 1898, the Second Boer War, and the First World War, and wrote unflinchingly on delicate issues like execution. Davis travelled widely and gained a reputation as an intrepid adventurer, producing a number of thriller spy novels.

Charles Dickens

Hunted Down

(Originally Published in the *New York Ledger*, 1859)

The iconic and much-loved Charles Dickens (1812–70) was born in Portsmouth, England, though he spent much of his life in Kent and London. At the age of 12 Charles was forced into working in a factory for a couple of months to support his family. He never forgot his harrowing experience there, and his novels always reflected the plight of the working class. A prolific writer, Dickens kept up a career in journalism as well as writing short stories and novels, with much of his work being serialized before being published as books. He gave a view of contemporary England with a strong sense of realism, yet incorporated the occasional ghost and horror elements. He continued to work hard until his death, leaving *The Mystery of Edwin Drood* unfinished.

Jennifer Dornan-Fish

Skitter and Click

(First Publication)

Jennifer Dornan-Fish has a Ph.D. in anthropology and is a professor by day, writer by night. She has also been a private investigator, K9 Wilderness Search and Rescue unit, dog walker, ditch digger, photographer, social justice activist, and video game writer. Her short fiction has appeared in *Daily Science Fiction*, *Interzone*, and elsewhere. A dual Irish/American citizen, she has also lived in Senegal, Belize, the UK, and Micronesia. She now lives in the Bay Area with her husband and son. You can follow her writing at dornan-fish.com.

James Dorr

Paperboxing Art

(Originally Published in *New Mystery*, 1997)

Indiana (USA) writer James Dorr's *The Tears of Isis* was a 2014 Bram Stoker Award® nominee for Superior Achievement in a Fiction Collection. Other books include *Strange*

Mistresses: Tales of Wonder and Romance, Darker Loves: Takes of Mystery and Regret, and his all-poetry *Vamps (A Retrospective).* Currently in press is a novel-in-stories, *Tombs: A Chronicle of Latter-day Times of Earth.* An Active Member of HWA and SFWA with nearly 400 individual appearances from *Alfred Hitchcock's Mystery Magazine* to *Xenophilia,* Dorr invites readers to visit his blog at jamesdorrwriter.wordpress.com.

Arthur Conan Doyle

The Red-Headed League
(Originally Published in *The Strand*, 1891)
The Adventure of the Speckled Band
(Originally Published in *The Strand*, 1892)
Arthur Conan Doyle (1859–1930) was born in Edinburgh, Scotland. As a medical student he was so impressed by his professor's powers of deduction that he was inspired to create the illustrious and much-loved figure Sherlock Holmes. Holmes is known for his keen power of observation and logical reasoning, which often astounds his companion Dr. Watson. However, Doyle became increasingly interested in spiritualism, leaving him keen to explore more fantastical elements in his stories. Whatever the subject, Doyle's vibrant and remarkable characters have breathed life into all of his stories, engaging readers throughout the decades.

Marcelle Dubé

Home Run
(First Publication)
Marcelle Dubé writes mystery, science fiction and fantasy fiction. Her short stories have appeared in magazines and award-winning anthologies. Her novels include the *Mendenhall Mystery* series (some of her short stories, including 'Home Run', are also set in the world of Mendenhall Chief of Police Kate Williams). Her latest standalone novel is *Ghosts of Morocco*, a 'women's thriller' set in Morocco and the Yukon. Marcelle grew up near Montreal in Canada and after trying out a number of different provinces (not to mention Belgium), she settled in the Yukon, where people outnumber carnivores, but not by much. Visit her at: www.marcellemdube.com.

Martin Edwards

Foreword: Crime & Mystery Short Stories
Martin Edwards is the author of 18 novels, including the Lake District Mysteries, and the Harry Devlin series. His groundbreaking genre study *The Golden Age of Murder* has won the Edgar, Agatha, and H.R.F. Keating awards. He has edited 28 crime anthologies, has won the CWA Short Story Dagger and the CWA Margery Allingham Prize, and is series consultant for the British Library's Crime Classics. In 2015, he was elected eighth President of the Detection Club, an office previously held by G.K. Chesterton, Agatha Christie, and Dorothy L. Sayers.

R. Austin Freeman

The Aluminium Dagger
(Originally Published in *Pearson's Magazine*, 1909)
London-born Richard Austin Freeman (1862 –1943) was at the forefront of Edwardian detective fiction, along with his contemporary G.K. Chesterton. Freeman trained as a

physician, working as a colonial surgeon in West Africa until illness sent him back to England. He continued to practise medicine, producing in his spare time a crime series centred on the character Dr Thorndyke. An early forensic scientist, Thorndyke uses a precise scientific approach to analyse data in his laboratory. Freeman is credited as being the first to develop the inverted detective story, where the focus rests not on the culprit – who can be known from the start – but on the process of solving the case.

H.L. Fullerton
Suggestive Thoughts
(First Publication)
H.L. Fullerton lives in the State of New York; writes fiction – mostly speculative, occasionally about murderers; uses words instead of emoticons; likes semi-colons and the occasional interrobang; might be in trouble with prepositions; loves lists and bullet points; believes apostrophes are commas gone wild; saves dangling participles; binge-reads while watching television; is sometimes published in anthologies like *Writers of the Future, Vol. 32*, *Mysterion*, and the *Triangulation* series (including *Last Contact*, *Lost Voices* and *Beneath the Surface*) and hopes to sell enough stories to support a growing tsundoku habit.

Jacques Futrelle
The Problem of Cell 13
(Originally Published in the *Boston American*, 1905)
The American writer Jacques Futrelle (1875–1912) was born in Georgia, and famously died onboard the *Titanic* aged 37, after having seen his wife safely onto a lifeboat. Futrelle paved a career in journalism from the age of 18, and went on to write fiction and drama. In 1895, he married the writer L. May Peel and took a job working for the *New York Herald*. Augustus S.F.X Van Dusen, the amateur detective dubbed 'The Thinking Machine', appears in over 40 of Futrelle's stories. 'The Problem of Cell 13' was the first to feature this character, who uses logic to solve seemingly impossible cases.

Jennifer Gifford
I Am Nightmare
(First Publication)
Jennifer Gifford has always had a fascination with the dark and humorous side of fiction. She hates creepy old dolls, spiders, and garden gnomes, but loves lighthouses and abandoned buildings. She has been published on *Danse Macabre* and Mysteryauthors.com, as well as in *M-Brane's Science Fiction Magazine*. Her latest work can be found at *Dunesteef Audio Fiction* and *Breath & Shadow Magazine*. Jennifer is currently a senior editor at *Bete Noire Magazine* and has been nominated for the L. Ron Hubbard Writers of the Future Award four times. Her latest novel, *Superior Lies*, is now available from Ashmoor Creek Press.

Anna Katharine Green
A Mysterious Case
(Originally Published in *The Old Stone House and Other Stories*, G.P. Putnam's Sons, 1891)
Mother of detective fiction Anna Katharine Green (1846–1935) was born in Brooklyn, New York. A poet even at a young age, she later turned her hand to detective novels, perhaps partly inspired by stories from her lawyer father. She enjoyed immediate success with *The Leavenworth Case*, the first outing for the amiable but eccentric Inspector Ebenezer Gryce.

Having found a successful formula, but always coming up with original and intriguing plots, Green went on to write around 30 novels as well as several short stories. She created interesting detective heroes and established several conventions of the genre, her name becoming synonymous with popular, original and well-written detective fiction.

Arthur Griffiths

The Rome Express

(Originally Published by John Milne, 1896)

Major Arthur Griffiths (1838–1908), believed to have also written under the pseudonym 'Alfred Alymer', was born in India. His career spanned the English military and civil services, including work as deputy governor of Chatham, Milbank and Wormwood Scrubbs prisons. His thorough knowledge of police methods and experience working as a prison inspector fed through to his detective fiction and established him as an authority on prison systems. Griffiths was also regarded as an eminent crime historian, with *Mysteries of Police and Crime* (1898) considered a valuable source of information on Victorian murders, including the Jack the Ripper case.

E.W. Hornung

A Trap to Catch a Cracksman

(Originally Published in *A Thief in the Night*, Chatto & Windus, 1905)

Ernest William Hornung (1866–1921) was born in Middlesborough, England. As a young adult he spent time in Australia, a setting which would inspire his later novels, before eventually settling in London. His marriage to Constance Doyle led to him becoming the brother-in-law of Arthur Conan Doyle. Echoing his brother-in-law's gift for characterization, Hornung's most famous character creation, Raffles the 'gentleman thief', has often been considered the criminal parallel to Conan Doyle's Sherlock. Hornung wrote several stories in his series based around the illicit exploits of the memorable Raffles and his companion 'Bunny', which would go on to inspire stage and screen adaptations.

Nathan Hystad

Three Words

(First Publication)

Nathan Hystad is an author from outside of Edmonton, Alberta, Canada. He lives there with his wife, dog, and piles of books. When he isn't working on a novel, he's writing short fiction, where he explores many themes and genres. One moment he may be haunted by a ghost, and the next aliens may be forcing him to dig up their ancestral bones. Follow along his twelve-part science fiction serial at www.kraxon.com with a new episode each month of 2016. He also runs Woodbridge Press, a new genre press with exciting projects on the go.

John A. Karr

The Marionettist

(First Publication)

John A. Karr is an IT worker who tries to exercise both the imagination and physical manifestation on a daily basis. Empty-nested, he and his wife recently relocated to Wilmington, North Carolina to live near the mighty Atlantic Ocean. He is the author of a handful of novels, a couple of novellas and a growing list of short stories. His novel

Ghostly Summons features the same protagonist as the tale in this collection. He is currently working on a science fiction novel that involves terraforming Mars. See more at www.johnakarr.com.

Kin S. Law
Mechanical Love
(First Publication)
Kin S. Law is a child of two worlds, a New Yorker of Hong Kong descent. He has lived in London, adores France, but is only meh about underpants. He is the author of the *Lands Beyond* steampunk series, starting with *Future That Never Was*, which began as self-pub but will be relaunched soon. Kin also has Opinions about Things but mostly likes good books, anime, and science fiction that will never be brought back from the dead, blast those ineffable vulpine executives. Browncoats forever. Remember, to geek is to love.

Maurice Leblanc
The Arrest of Arsène Lupin
(Originally Published in *Je sais tout*, 1905)
Born in Rouen, France, Maurice Leblanc (1864–1941) dropped his law studies in favour of a literary career, publishing his first novel, *Une Femme*, in 1887. His fame is largely due to his Arsène Lupin series of stories. 'The Arrest of Arsène Lupin' was the first story to feature the roguish gentleman criminal, appearing in 1905 as a commissioned piece for a new journal. The character was an instant success, and the thief-turned-detective went on to appear in over 60 of Leblanc's works. Some of the Lupin tales even feature a parodied Sherlock Holmes, with Lupin invariably outwitting his English rival.

Jack London
The Master of Mystery
(Originally Published in *Out West*, 1902)
Jack London (1876–1916) was born as John Griffith Chaney in San Francisco, California. As a young man he went to work in the Klondike during the Gold Rush, which became the setting for two of his best-known novels, *White Fang* and *The Call of the Wild*. However it is his short stories that have often received wider critical acclaim. Coming from a working-class background, London was a keen social activist and wrote several stories and articles from a socialist standpoint. It is thought that he is one of the first fiction authors to have enjoyed prosperity and worldwide fame from his writings alone.

Arthur Morrison
The Lenton Croft Robberies
(Originally Published in *The Strand*, 1894)
Arthur Morrison (1863–1945) was born in the East End of London. He later became a writer for *The Globe* newspaper and showed a keen interest in relating the real and bleak plight of those living in London slums. When Arthur Conan Doyle killed off Sherlock Holmes in 1893, a vacuum opened up for detective heroes. In the wake Morrison created Martin Hewitt, publishing stories about him in *The Strand Magazine*, which had also first published Sherlock Holmes. Though a man with genius deductive skill, Morrison's Hewitt character was the polar opposite to Holmes: genial and helpful to the police. He was perhaps the most popular and successful of these new investigator fiction heroes.

Ruth Nestvold

Chains of Command

(First Publication)

Ruth Nestvold has published widely in science fiction and fantasy, her fiction appearing in such markets as *Asimov's*, *F&SF*, *Baen's Universe*, *Strange Horizons*, *Realms of Fantasy*, and Gardner Dozois' *The Year's Best Science Fiction*. Her work has been nominated for the Nebula, Tiptree, and Sturgeon Awards. In 2007, the Italian translation of her novella 'Looking Through Lace' won the 'Premio Italia' award for best international work. Her novel *Yseult* appeared in German translation as *Flamme und Harfe* with Random House Germany and has since been translated into Dutch and Italian. She maintains a website at www.ruthnestvold.com and blogs at ruthnestvold.wordpress.com.

Josh Pachter

iMurder

(Copyright © 2011 by Josh Pachter. Originally Published in *Ellery Queen's Mystery Magazine*. Reprinted by permission of the author.)

American author Josh Pachter has published more than 70 short stories in *Ellery Queen's Mystery Magazine*, *Alfred Hitchcock's Mystery Magazine* and many other periodicals and anthologies in the US and internationally. *The Tree of Life*, a collection of 10 of his short stories set in the island emirate of Bahrain, was published by Wildside Press in 2015, and is also available as an e-book titled *The Mahboob Chaudri Mystery MEGAPACK*. In his day job, he is the Assistant Dean for Communication Studies and Theater at Northern Virginia Community College's Loudoun Campus in Sterling, Virginia.

Tony Pi

Creature of the Thaumatrope

(First Publication)

Tony Pi writes fantastical mysteries in addition to his other works in fantasy and science fiction, such as 'Dynamics of A Hanging' (reprinted in *The Improbable Adventures of Sherlock Holmes*) and 'Come-From-Aways' (reprinted in *The Time Traveler's Almanac* and *Casserole Diplomacy and Other Stories*). He was a finalist for the John W. Campbell Award for Best New Writer in 2009. Some of his inspirations are Arthur Conan Doyle, Agatha Christie, and Isaac Asimov. Further adventures of Professor Voss appear in *Beneath Ceaseless Skies*, *Abyss and Apex*, and the anthologies *Clockwork Canada* and *Ages of Wonder*.

Edgar Allan Poe

The Murders in the Rue Morgue

(Originally Published in *Graham's Magazine*, 1841)

The Purloined Letter

(Originally Published in *The Gift for 1845*, Carey & Hart, 1844)

The versatile writer Edgar Allan Poe (1809–49) was born in Boston, Massachusetts. He is extremely well known as an influential author, poet, editor and literary critic that wrote during the American Romantic Movement. Poe is generally considered the inventor of the detective fiction genre, and his works are famously filled with terror, mystery, death and hauntings. Some of his better-known works include his poems 'The Raven' and 'Annabel Lee', and the short stories 'The Tell Tale Heart' and 'The Fall of the House of Usher'.

The dark, mystifying characters of his tales have captured the public's imagination and reflect the struggling, poverty-stricken lifestyle he lived his whole life.

Conor Powers-Smith
The Whipping Boy
(Originally Published on the *Daily Science Fiction* website, 2014)
Conor Powers-Smith grew up in New Jersey and Ireland. He currently lives on Cape Cod, in Massachusetts, where he works as a reporter. His stories have appeared in *AE*, *Analog*, *Daily Science Fiction*, *Nature*, and other magazines, as well as several anthologies, including the Flame Tree *Science Fiction Short Stories* collection. He enjoys the psychological and crime fiction of James M. Cain, Patricia Highsmith, and Richard Wright, as well as the classic noir of Dashiell Hammett and Raymond Chandler, though he considers John Swartzwelder's character Frank Burly the most entertaining detective in fiction.

Arthur B. Reeve
The Invisible Ray
(Originally Published in *The Poisoned Pen: The Further Adventures of Craig Kennedy*, Grosset and Dunlap, 1911)
Arthur Benjamin Reeve (1880–1936) was born in New York, graduating from Princeton and going on to study law. However he ended up working as an editor and journalist, writing about several famous crime cases, before gaining wide popularity for his stories about fictional detective Professor Craig Kennedy, the first of which were published in *Cosmopolitan* magazine. Kennedy shares many similarities with both Conan Doyle's Holmes and Freeman's Dr. Thorndyke, as he solves crimes with science, logic and a knowledge of technology, as well as having a companion in several stories who chronicles his work, very similarly to Watson.

Stephen D. Rogers
The Man Wore Motley
(First Publication)
Stephen D. Rogers lives in Buzzards Bay, Massachusetts. Over 900 of his shorter pieces have been selected to appear in a wide variety of magazines and anthologies, mystery and non-mystery alike. He is the author of the collections *Shot to Death* and *Three-Minute Mysteries*, and one-fifth of the writing team behind the trivia book *A Miscellany of Murder*. While he reads across the genres, he has a special spot in his heart for crime fiction.

Steve Shrott
The House
(First Publication)
Steve Shrott writes in a variety of genres from his home in Toronto, Canada. His mystery short stories have been published in numerous print magazines and ezines. His work has appeared in 12 anthologies – four from Sisters-in-Crime. He has had two humorous mystery novels published, *Audition For Death* and *Dead Men Don't Get Married*, as well as a book on how to write humor. Steve's comedy material has been used by well-known performers of stage and screen. Some of his jokes are in The Smithsonian Institute.

Annette Siketa

Catzized

(First Publication)

In 2008, a routine eye operation tragically rendered Annette Siketa blind, changing her life dramatically. It was her penchant for creating imaginative stories for her grandson that 'saved' her, though at the time she knew nothing about professional writing. She persevered, learned the craft, and has now written a variety of award-winning short stories and novels, including the children's adventure/mystery *The Ghosts of Camals College*. The sleuthing granny Ada Harris featured in Catzized also appears in the novel *Murder by the Sea* (available from Smashwords). Annette's latest novel, *The Sisterhood – Curse of Abbot Hewitt*, will soon be released by Sinister Grin Press.

Dan Stout

Ghosts, Bigfoot, and Free Lunches

(First Publication)

Dan Stout lives in Columbus, Ohio, where he writes about half-truths and double-crosses. His fiction draws on his travels throughout Europe, Asia, and the Pacific Rim as well as a convoluted employment history spanning everything from subpoena server to assistant well driller. Dan's stories have appeared in publications such as *The Saturday Evening Post, Nature, Plan B Magazine,* and *Mad Scientist Journal.* Dan can be found on Facebook or on the web at DanStout.com.

Brian Trent

Blood and Silver Beneath the Many Moons

(First Publication)

Brian Trent's dark fantasy and science-fiction work appears in a wide array of publications including *Analog, Fantasy & Science Fiction, Cosmos, Daily Science Fiction, Nature, Apex, Galaxy's Edge, Pseudopod, Escape Pod,* and numerous year's best anthologies. His story 'Shortcuts' appears in Flame Tree Publishing's *Science Fiction Short Stories*. His literary influences are varied, and his interests include technology, classical history, and sociology – particularly the interplay between all three. Trent lives in New England, where he is a novelist, poet, and screenwriter. He can be found online at www.briantrent.com.

Cameron Trost

Murder on the Cogsworthy Express

(First Publication)

Cameron Trost is a writer of strange, mysterious, and creepy tales about people just like you. His short stories have been published in dozens of magazines and anthologies, and many of them can be found in his collection, *Hoffman's Creeper and Other Disturbing Tales*. He lives in the subtropical city of Brisbane, Australia. He is the vice-president and Queensland community leader of the Australian Horror Writers' Association, and an Australian Shadows Award-winning editor. Rainforests, thunderstorms, and whisky are a few of his favourite things. Visit Cameron at www.trostlibrary.blogspot.com.

Mark Twain

The Stolen White Elephant

(Originally Published by James R. Osgood, 1882)

Mark Twain (1835–1910) was born Samuel Langhorne Clemens in Florida, Missouri. Twain's name is synonymous with his American classics *The Adventures of Tom Sawyer* and its sequel, *Adventures of Huckleberry Finn*. Twain was born shortly after an appearance by Halley's Comet, and he predicted that he would 'go out with it', too. As chance would have it, he died the day after the comet returned in 1910. Twain was a very influential author whose works are timeless pieces that are still being taught today in classrooms to students of all ages.

Edgar Wallace
Sentimental Simpson
(Originally Published in *The Cat Burglar and Other Stories*, George Newnes Ltd., 1929)
Edgar Wallace (1875–1932) was born illegitimately to an actress, and adopted by a London fishmonger and his wife. On leaving school at the age of 12, he took up many jobs, including selling newspapers. This foreshadowed his later career as a war correspondent for such periodicals as the *Daily Mail* after he had enrolled in the army. He later turned to writing stories inspired by his time in Africa, and was incredibly prolific over a large number of genres and formats. Wallace is credited as being one of the first writers of detective fiction whose protagonists were policemen as opposed to amateur sleuths.

Victor L. Whitechurch
Sir Gilbert Murrell's Picture
(Originally Published in *Thrilling Stories of the Railway*, Pearson, 1912)
Victor Lorenzo Whitechurch (1868–1933) was a clergyman, educated at Chichester Theological College in England. He was also a fiction writer, best known for characters such as the vegetarian, fitness fanatic and detective Thorpe Hazell; and spy Ivan Koravitch. Whitechurch wrote several stories inspired by his clerical vocation, however he was also a railway enthusiast, as evidenced by his many railway mysteries featuring the detective Godfrey Page, and later better developed with his Thorpe Hazell stories.

Sylvia Spruck Wrigley
Chains of Command
(First Publication)
Sylvia Spruck Wrigley was born in Germany and spent her childhood in Los Angeles. She now lives in Andalucia where she writes about plane crashes and faeries, which have more in common than most people might imagine. Her fiction was nominated for a Nebula in 2014 and her short stories have been translated into over a dozen languages. Her first novella, 'Domnall and the Borrowed Child', was published in 2015 by Tor.com and is available now at all good bookstores. You can find out more about her at www.intrigue.co.uk.

Israel Zangwill
Cheating the Gallows
(Originally Published in *The Idler*, 1893)
Israel Zangwill (1864–1926) was born in London to a family of Jewish immigrants. He became famous for his political activism, championing the Jewish cause and writing about the Jewish East End of London. Zangwill's play *The Melting Pot* gave rise to the popular term 'melting pot' to describe the American absorption of immigrants. His novel *The Big Bow Mystery* is renowned for being one of the earliest locked room mysteries, which also lays out all the evidence for the reader but uses misdirection to keep it from being easily solved.

GOTHIC FANTASY

For our books, calendars, blog
and latest special offers please see:
flametreepublishing.com